Praise for *A Sport of Nature*

'Gordimer writes ... with a relish that is sometimes wicked and an authority that seems absolute.'

—*The New Yorker*

'There is an emotional tension in the prose that is cumulative and subtle. The novel gathers force like a slow-moving avalanche of words, breaking from time to time into italicized passages close to prose poems. With Hillela, Nadine Gordimer continues to bear testimony that writing can matter as much as skin and hair.'

—*Washington Post Book World*

'*A Sport of Nature* is a valiant, beautifully rendered attempt to do justice, its heart unbowed by the enormity of its burden.'

—*The Boston Globe*

'What is riveting in this novel is the people themselves, the moments, the situations. The triumph of *A Sport of Nature* is not so much Hillela's triumph as the exquisite accuracy with which Gordimer has, once again, exposed the complicated nervous system of her country.'

—Lynn Freed, *San Francisco Chronicle*

'Fine, incisive ... Wraps moral and political struggle in elegantly spun incident and luminous prose. ... Gordimer distills political events into personal pain, and the pain depicted here ... resonates.'

— *Kirkus Reviews*

'Achieves a remarkable imaginative integration of private and public experience. ... A brilliant, engrossing novel'

—*Library Journal*

NOVELS

The Lying Days / A World of Strangers / Occasion for Loving
The Late Bourgeois World / A Guest of Honour
The Conservationist / Burger's Daughter / July's People /
My Son's Story / None to Accompany Me
The House Gun / The Pickup / Get a Life /
No Time Like the Present

STORY COLLECTIONS

The Soft Voice of the Serpent / Six Feet of the Country
Friday's Footprint / Not for Publication
Livingstone's Companions
A Soldier's Embrace / Something Out There
Jump / Loot / Beethoven Was One-Sixteenth Black
Life Times: Stories 1952–2007

ESSAYS

The Black Interpreters / On the Mines (*with David Goldblatt*)
Lifetimes under Apartheid (*with David Goldblatt*)
The Essential Gesture – Writing, Politics and Places
(*edited by Stephen Clingman*)
Writing and Being
Living in Hope and History: Notes from Our Century
Telling Times: Writing and Living, 1954–2008

EDITOR, CONTRIBUTOR
Telling Tales

A SPORT OF NATURE

NADINE GORDIMER's many novels include *The Conservationist*, joint winner of the Booker Prize, *Get A Life*, *Burger's Daughter*, *July's People*, *My Son's Story*, *The Pickup* and, most recently, *No Time Like the Present*. Her collections of short stories include *The Soft Voice of the Serpent*, *Something Out There*, *Jump*, *Loot* and, most recently, *Beethoven Was One-Sixteenth Black*. She has also collected and edited *Telling Tales*, a story anthology published in fourteen languages whose royalties go to HIV/AIDS organisations. In 2010 her nonfiction writings were collected in *Telling Times* and a substantial selection of her stories was published in *Life Times*. Nadine Gordimer was awarded the Nobel Prize for Literature in 1991. She lives in South Africa.

A SPORT OF NATURE

Nadine Gordimer

B L O O M S B U R Y
LONDON · NEW DELHI · NEW YORK · SYDNEY

First published in Great Britain by Penguin Books 1988
This paperback edition published 2013

Bloomsbury Publishing Plc
50 Bedford Square
London WC1B 3DP

www.bloomsbury.com

Bloomsbury Publishing, London, New York, New Delhi and Sydney

A CIP catalogue record for this book is available from the British Library

ISBN 978 1 4088 4048 1

10 9 8 7 6 5 4 3 2 1

Typeset by MPS Limited
Printed and bound in Great Britain by CPI (UK) Ltd, Croydon CR0 4YY

For Oriane and Hugo

Lusus naturae—Sport of nature.
A plant, animal, etc., which exhibits abnormal variation or a departure from the parent stock or type ... a spontaneous mutation; a new variety produced in this way.

—Oxford English Dictionary

A Suncrush for My Sweetheart

Somewhere along the journey the girl shed one name and emerged under the other. As she chewed gum and let slide by the conveyer belt of balancing rocks, the wayside halts where black children waved, the grazing buck sloping away to the horizon in a blast of fear set in motion by the passing train, she threw Kim up to the rack with her school panama and took on Hillela. The brown stockings collapsed down her legs, making fine hairs prickle pleasurably. She would dig sandals and a dress out of her suitcase and change without concern for the presence of other women in the compartment. She was going, each time, to her aunt, one of her mother's sisters, in whose home she was given every advantage. She was coming from the Rhodesian girls' school to which, she would say when asked why she didn't go to school in South Africa, she was sent because her father had grown up in Salisbury. She was not the only child whose parents were divorced or parted or whatever it was they were. But she was the only Hillela among Susans and Clares and Fionas. What sort of a name was that? Didn't know, couldn't tell them. What she did tell them, without a moment's hesitation, was that anyway she was always called by her second name, Kim. As the years passed, not even her teachers called her anything but Kim. No-one remarked when she went with the other Kims, Susans, Clares and Fionas to the Anglican Church on Sundays, although in her school record 'religious faith' was filled in as Jewish.

Olga met her at the station. Later, it was at the airport; Olga must have told her father it was ridiculous to subject her to that two-day hot and tedious train trip. Or maybe Olga paid for the air-ticket; she was generous: she would say, never to the child herself but to company while she ruffled the child's fringe or put an arm round her—Oh this's the little daughter I didn't have.—

The room was made ready with a rose in the summer holidays and in winter freesias or jonquils that smelled like Olga's embrace, towels thick as sheepskin coats, and a fluted dish of her favourite Liquorice All-Sorts. There were some things that were hers: holiday clothes left behind each time when she went back to school, books, trinkets fallen out of favour. Her absence was more permanent than her presence. There was always the sign of some other occupancy of the room. Olga stored out-of-season clothes in the cupboards; other guests who slept in the pretty bed forgot things; books that Olga didn't want on display downstairs but didn't want to throw away made a jumble-sale assortment on the bookshelf. One holiday, a photograph of the girl's mother in a Victorian plush-and-silver frame stood beside the Liquorice All-Sorts. The face was composed in a way the girl had never seen: hair scrolled like a parchment roll from either temple and again from the forehead, lips a lovely shape shiny as liquid tar. The shape was not disturbed by a smile. The eyes were the only feature that matched any recognizable living reality; they were the eyes of a woman seeing herself in a mirror.

Her mother ended at the shoulders. They were squared in a jacket with shoulder-tabs and revers.

—Was she in the army?—

Olga was watching the girl the way she watched people she brought together in careful selection for the harmony and interest of her dinner parties, and she laughed as at the reward of some original remark outside the usual pleasantries. —Ruthie in the army! That's what we wore, in the Forties. The last word in fashion. You had to look glamorous in something that suggested a uniform. That jacket was dark red—I remember it as if it were in front of me. And see the ear-rings. She *would* have her ears pierced. We thought it was old-fashioned or common: grandmothers had floppy lobes with holes in them, and young Afrikaans girls from the *plaas* wore those thin gold circles. But Ruth paid Martha to do hers. That was our old nannie; when we were quite grown up she still used to come to help with the washing. Ruth sat down to the table one lunch-time with cotton threads hanging through little crusts of blood on her ears. Ugh. We squealed and made a fuss, of course ... she must have been fourteen.—

They looked at the photograph politely, together. (It was about this time that Olga would take her eldest son, Clive, and Hillela to art exhibitions.) Hillela did not come out with anything else unexpected.

—It's for you to take back to school. Isn't that an enchanting frame I found—

It was standing there in its place on the bedside-table after the girl left, and was there when she came back each time for other holidays. Her mother was not dead. She lived in Mozambique and never visited. The child had asked questions once or twice, when she was young enough to believe adults gave you answers worth hearing, and had been given an oblique reply. Her father said her mother had 'made another life'. Olga, deciding when the child was 'old enough to know the truth', told her her father had forbidden her mother to have any contact with her. Her mother lived with 'another man'.

The man to whom he was an other, then, must be her father; yet she called her father 'Len' as someone might for whom *he* was another man.

Len was a rep. A title of profession to her, like doctor or professor, although she found she had to explain to other girls this meant he represented firms that sold hotel lines. And what were 'lines'? Really—was there anything those kids did know? *Lines.* Different kinds of things that hotels and restaurants need. Bread-cutters, food-warmers, slicers, trays, fish-fryers, even plastic flowers, mirrors, pictures for decoration. There had been a time, she must have been very small, when she had played and slept and eaten beside him in his big car with all the boxes of samples, catalogues and order-books piled up in the back. He had made her a nest in there, on rugs stained with cold drinks and icecream she spilt. —A Suncrush for my sweetheart.— She sat on bar-stools in country hotels. He bought her sweet orange-coloured drinks. He washed her panties in the hotel basins while she fell asleep watching him.

—I remember those dorps, with Len.—

—Oh you can't! Really, Hilly? But you were only three or four.— Olga rearranged her social commitments in order to spend time with her sons and adoptive daughter during the holidays. On summer mornings she oiled herself, spreading her toes to get at the interstices and twisting her neck, over which a string of pearls bobbled, while the four youngsters played waterpolo in the pool. When they came out to dry off and her attention slid from her *Vogue* or Hebrew grammar, there were those interludes of shared physical well-being that melt the inhibitions between generations.

—He used to talk to people in a language I didn't know. And there was the boy who carried the boxes in and out, I didn't understand what he was saying, either. Of course Len was speaking Afrikaans, and the native boy whatever his language was. So English was ours. Len's and mine. I'm sure I thought only we could talk it. And the wife of one of the hotel owners once gave me an Alice band for my hair, it had Minnie Mouse on it.—

—When was that?— Mark looked at his cousin and saw a stranger in their midst, now and then, sometimes with a resentful curiosity, sometimes with envy of experiences not shared.

—Oh, when I was little.—

Olga impressed the discipline of her smile on her second son. —I *said*. Three or four, that's all.—

—And she used to travel about with Uncle Len?—

—For a short while. It was before he went back to Rhodesia.—

4

Brian stretched out his small hand and clasped Hillela's ankle, claiming her. His face appealed to his mother. She acknowledged him with a chummy tilt of the head.

Jethro came across the lawn that day carrying a tray of fruit juice and hot scones. His waiter's flat feet and the rubber soles of his blancoed tackies on the dense clipped grass gave him an endearing bouncing gait. The girl broke the water, having won by the length of an outstretched hand a race against the boys. It seemed she emerged for him. Jethro's home was in Rhodesia and every time she returned from school she had the aura of an emissary. —They teaching you so nice to swim there.— He put down the tray and stood shaking his head and smiling at the dripping, heaving girl.

Through water-matted lashes she saw the face magnified like some dark friendly creature bumped against in the deep. —I'm in the first team. (Blew her nose in her fingers, and Olga's forehead flickered a frown.) We beat Marandellas and Gwelo last term.—

—And Bulawayo? You not going to Bulawayo?—

—No, I still haven't been to Bulawayo.—

Olga kissed a damp cheek as she handed her a glass of juice. —Why don't you pretend you've been to Bulawayo, darling, for heaven's sake. It means so much to him. He thinks of you children as his own.—

Olga took Hillela with her to the hairdresser as if she were a sister—one could hardly say that Olga, who was the one with strong family feeling, had sisters: Ruth in Lourenço Marques somewhere, Pauline someone she had grown away from, their interests so divergent. At eight or nine the salon—as it was referred to by the man who did Olga's hair—with its chemical garden-sweetness and buzz of warm air from the dryers, fuzz of sheddings on the floor, made the child drowse off as a little animal curls up, recognizing a kind of safety. All was comfortably ritualistic, pampered, sheltered in the ideal of femininity constructed by the women entrapped there. Olga gave her money to go out and buy sweets; she tripped back quietly happy in anticipation of the soothing, sucking comfort to come as she lolled, humming or whispering to herself in the company of ladies deaf within their second, steel crania.

Fashions changed; she was older. Olga's hair, pulled with a crochet hook through holes in a rubber cap, was being tinted in streaks while her nails were steeping in tepid oil. Olga was still learning Hebrew (made fun of her attempt to speak it on her visits to Israel) but instead of her grammar was now reading a manual about isometric exercises a friend had brought from New York. Every now and then her concentration and the pressure of her elbows against the steel tube frame of the chair she occupied, the empty shape of her shantung trousers as she pulled in abdominal muscles stiffly as a bolt drawn, showed she was putting theory into practice.

It was the time when beautiful girls, by definition, had hair as long and straight as possible. When Olga and her sisters were adolescent, on the contrary, curls had been necessary, and they had suffered the processes that produced them. Hillela had curly hair like her father, but of course she would want to look like everybody else; boys instinctively are attracted to what they don't even know is the fashionable style of beauty. Olga was paying for Hillela's hair to be heated and ironed straight.

Hillela no longer falls asleep at the hairdresser's.

A jaw with a well-turned angle on either side, a slightly prognathous mouth and the full lips that cover with a tender twitch the uneven front tooth; it has defied an orthodontist who made conform perfectly the smiles of Clive and Mark. The cheekbones lift against the eyes at the outer corners, underlining them, aslant. All right so far. But it's difficult to meet the eyes. They are darkness; there is a film to it like the film of colours that swims on a puddle of dark oil she has seen spilled on the earth at a

6

garage. They react under their own regard as pupils do under an oculist's light; but doubly: the change observed is also experienced as a change of focus. Nothing can be more exact than an image perceived by itself.

The face is small and thin for the depth from the cup at the base of the collar-bones to the wide-set breasts. In the trance of women gazing at themselves in the mirrors they face, she is seeing herself. The mirror ends her there.

On Saturday afternoons when there were no sports meetings the *songololo* made its way to one of the parks in the city of Salisbury. In traditional school terminology imported from Europe the procession of girls was known as a crocodile, but the boys of their counterpart school dubbed them collectively by the African name for the large earthworm in its shiny hoops of articulated mail that is part of the infant vocabulary of every white child in Southern Africa, even if it never learns another word of an African language. The boys' image was based on accurate observation. The brown stockings the girls wore gave their troop the innumerable brown legs on which the *songololo* makes its undulating way round obstacles. So it was the girls flowed round people on the pavements, and over pedestrian crossings. In the park the image broke up joyfully (the littlest girls), cautiously (the solemn, hand-holding ten-year-olds), slyly (the adolescents skilled in undetectable insubordination). The first stage on the escape route was the public lavatories. *Miss Hurst, we have to go.* The teacher who accompanied the *songololo* sat on a bench and read, looking up now and then to enjoy the luxury of huge shade under a *mnondo* tree that came down over her like a Victorian glass bell. She was the only one who saw the gigantesque beauty of the park, in one season its storm-clouds of mauve jacaranda, in another the violent flamboyants flashing bloodily under the sun, or the tulip-trees and bauhinias that in their time shimmered, their supporting skeletons of trunk and branches entirely swarmed

7

over, become shapes composed of petals alive with bees as a corpse come alive with maggots. The adolescents were excited by the humus smells, the dripping scents of unfolding, spore-bearing, dying vegetation in clumps and groves of palms, man-high ferns and stifling creepers where the sun had no power of entry and leaves transformed themselves into the pale sticky cobra-heads of some sort of lily. The darkness sent the girls off giggling urgently to that other dankness, of *Whites Only, Ladies, Men,* housed separately from *Nannies*—for the black nursemaids sent to air white infants in the park. When the girls at last came out of *Ladies* the boys from the counterpart school were already emerged from *Men,* and pretending not to be waiting for them. Disappearing into the fecundity of municipal jungles, there the girls wore the boys' cheesecutters, wrestled in amorous quarrelsomeness, smoked, throwing the forbidden cigarette pack in forbidden pollution into the gloomy, overhung ponds, swatted mosquitoes on one another as an excuse for fondling, and—one or two who were known to be 'experienced'—managed to find a spidery hideout to *vry*. Like *songololo*, a Zulu word foreign to English-speakers, this Afrikaans one was used by every English-speaking adolescent. To *vry* was to excite each other further; sexually, with kisses and limited intimacies. There were indiscretions less private than *vrying*. Dares, too, provided heightened excitement. Hillela once led a move to tuck the school dress up into pants and wade in a green bog of water-plants and slime. The boys were challenged to follow. Their narrow grey trousers wouldn't roll up beyond mid-calf; somehow, one of them was overcome by boys and girls as the vigorous big ants on the ground on which he fell would overcome a beetle or moth, and his trousers were taken off him. He was pulled slithering to join Hillela and his distress caused his flesh to rise. The other boys, and some of the girls, almost forgot the danger of shrieking with laughter. They pelted uprooted lily pads on the poor blind thing Hillela saw standing firm under baggy school underpants.

She came out of the water at once, pulled down her dress, dragged stockings over her dirty wet legs, and burst from the thicket, not caring if her bedraggled state were noticed. She did not speak to her friends for the rest of the afternoon, but apparently had ready, loyal to her peers, her answer to Miss Hurst's question about her wet stockings. She had slipped and fallen; very well, then, she had permission to take off her stockings. Just this once.

Just this once. By such narrow margins the group of girls who had grown from juniors to seniors together kept the status of trust that was traded in return for their taking over irksome small responsibilities from the teaching staff. A clique of senior prefects had discovered how to open, without breaking, the glass box that held the key to the dormitories' fire escape; they slipped out regularly at night to go to parties. A foolproof line of supply and use of *dagga* was established; brought in by and bought off one of the black kitchen workers, it was smoked in the lab, where there were stronger odours to disguise its fragrance. The group shepherded little ones to Sunday school in town and took turns to disappear (someone had to represent the senior presence to the bible-class instructor) and meet boyfriends at a vacant lot. They were educating themselves for their world in Southern Africa in the way the school helplessly abetted, teaching them at morning prayers to love thy neighbour as thyself before they sat down for the day in classrooms where only white children were admitted.

Now and then one of these school-worldly girls went too far; for example, the one who went for a ride on a motorbike down Jameson Avenue during her turn to slip away from Sunday-school duty. She was seen by a parent as he came out of a Greek shop with cigarettes and the Sunday paper; seen in her school uniform with her spread thighs 'clinging to the back of a boy'. The headmistress floundered embarrassedly through all the moral props; feminine modesty, the honour of the school, bad example to the innocent Sunday-school charges, and then, in a complicity both she and the girl understood perfectly, let her off just this once (with the punishment that would satisfy everyone: docking of half-term holiday) because the transgression was one accepted within their recognized code of virtues and concomitant vices.

Among the privileges granted to the senior girls was permission to go in mufti, in groups of not less than four but unaccompanied by a teacher, to a Saturday-afternoon cinema. The housemistress had to be told the title of the film to be seen; it was supposed to be an educational film, but there was not much choice in the few cinemas of Salisbury in the late Fifties. The housemistress had to approve Elvis Presley and James Dean. At the cinema the schoolgirls met a wider circle of boys than that of their counterpart school. Although Hillela's hair, once out of the care of her aunt's hairdresser, sprang elastically back to ripples again, she was as sought-after in the popcorn-smelling dark as anyone else. The cinemas were always full on Saturdays, right up to the back rows, which blacks and coloureds were allowed to occupy. There was the day she was struggling back through the crowded foyer at intermission with five icecream cones for her friends, and the tall boy with the sallow face and strange blond hair asked so nicely if he could help her. When they reached the row where her friends were sitting, he handed over the cones and disappeared to wherever his seat was. But she knew he had been looking at her, before, a number of times, while she had played her part: of not being aware of him. Then he began to smile at her when he saw her queueing for tickets, and she even waved casually back. Arriving for a James Dean she was to see for the second or third time, she said, Where're you sitting? preparatory to asking if he wouldn't like to sit with 'us'.

He had promised to keep a seat for a friend; wouldn't she come along with them, instead? His friend did not arrive, or did not exist. He did not shift his leg towards hers or take her hand. Now and then both had the same reaction to the film and instinctively would turn to smile at one another in the dark. The look of him, that had attracted her attention for some weeks, took on a strong bodily presence beside her. She did not expect this one to touch her, was not offended that he didn't. When the lights went up she was glad to see his face. She liked particularly his eyes, a greeny-grey with hair-thin splinters of yellow sunburst in the iris, whose charm was that they seemed too luminous for his sallow skin and tarnished curly hair—like lights left burning in a room in daylight. His name was Don; he was an apprentice electrician. It was considered a catch to have a boy who was no longer at school; a grown-up. He spoke with an unfamiliar accent—Afrikaans, perhaps, but different from the *Boere* accent from South Africa that was made fun of at school. He explained that his family came from the Cape; they had lived in Salisbury only for the last five years. He had passed his matric in Salisbury; they discussed the subjects he had taken, and those she was studying for a more junior exam, now. He said he really wanted to be a lawyer; he was going to start studying by correspondence; but that wasn't what he wanted, he wanted to go to a real university.

A lawyer? —One of my aunts is married to a lawyer. Not the aunt I stay with in the holidays—the other one.—

He nodded, looking first at her, then away from what he read there. —You'll go to university, then.—

She did not seem to like being reminded of what lay beyond school. —Don't know.—

—Well, maybe you'll get a job.—

—Maybe.—

—My sisters want to be models and that. But girls like you … you can be anything.—

She had the instinct to console without thinking for what. —Oh I'm not rich. My father's a rep, and he's married again.—

—But your aunt?—

Out of her mouth came the words she had heard many times: —I'm like the daughter she didn't have.—

It was taken for granted that you brought any new conquest into the Saturday group. But this one was very quiet among them; and she wanted to hear him talk. He had told her he played the guitar. She wanted him to play for her, but how could he keep a guitar at his feet in a cinema? They laughed; but halfway through the film they were seeing that day, she put her mouth very near his ear and whispered— Can't I come to your place and hear you play?— The girls were used to covering up for one another, if someone had something better to do than sit in the cinema. He was silent; then he whispered, Come. They crouched out along the row.

The walk was long; she thought it would have made more sense to take the bus. He talked less and less, and every now and then touched at the ear as if her breath had burnt it. Soon she saw they were in a coloured township and he didn't need to say what he couldn't bring himself to. They came to a small house natty with careful paint and souvenirs—a mailbox in the form of a miniature windmill, a brass bell with imitation pine-cone strikers. There were signs on the doors along the passage: CHARLENE'S PAD, KEEP OUT SLEEPERS AT WORK. In a room with three neat beds Don shared with smaller brothers, he made solemn preparations with the guitar while Hillela sat on a bed and read over a framed illuminated text of that poem she had had to learn at primary school: '... If you can talk with crowds and keep your virtue, / Or walk with Kings—nor lose the common touch; / If neither foes nor loving friends can hurt you; / If all men count with you, but none too much; / If you can fill the unforgiving minute, / With sixty seconds' worth of distance run, / Yours is the Earth and everything that's in it, / And—which is more—you'll be a Man, my son!' It hung where Don would be able to see it when he lay in his bed. He sat there with one foot on a fruit-box to support the leg on which the guitar rested. She grew excited at the surprise of how well he played—a different kind of excitement from that roused by the park. —But you should be in a band! If I closed my eyes,

I'd swear there was a record on!— Under his achievement and her admiration he expanded into ease and hospitality. He fetched two bottles of Pepsi and the end of a banana loaf from the kitchen— My mom bakes on weekends, when she's home from work—and cut the piece share-and-share-alike. They were alone in the house. He took her into the family sittingroom, folded back the plastic sheet that covered the sofa so that she could have the best seat, and showed her how he had taught himself to accompany a Cliff Richard recording. She couldn't tell the difference between the two performers. In the patronage that is the untalented's surrogate achievement, she had the wonderful idea that he should get together a band and play for the end-of-term dance. Why not? He went solemn at the responsibility; and then something in him lifted, the light eyes pale-bright, the lips and teeth fresh and sweet in that twilit face.

But she herself was no longer at the school at the end of term. She went only once again to the house with the windmill mailbox. A little girl with woolly pigtails was told—Charlene, don't stare.— A middle-aged woman with Don's eyes brought milky cups of tea and called Hillela 'miss'. —My mom's shy with people.— He said it as if she were not there; and the woman addressed Hillela in the third person: —Wouldn't the young lady like a cold drink instead?—

The following week she was sent for by the headmistress. Len was sitting in one of the two chairs that were always placed, slightly turned towards one another, in front of the desk at which the headmistress sat. So someone had died; not long before, a girl had been summoned like this to the presence of a parent, and learned of a death in the family. Hillela stared at Len. Olga? Her other aunt, Pauline? The woman—somewhere—who was her mother? A cousin? She woke up, and went over mechanically and kissed him; he kept his face stiff, as if he had something to confess that might spill.

The headmistress began in her classroom story-telling voice. Hillela had been seen with a coloured boy. While she was enjoying on trust the privilege of going to the cinema with her classmates, she had used the opportunity to meet a coloured boy. —A pupil at a school like this one. From her kind of home. The Jewish people have so much self-respect—I've always admired them for that. Mr Capran, if I knew how Hillela could do what she has done, I could help her. But I cannot comprehend it.— This was not a matter of just this once. It could not be. It was not something that happened within the scope of peccadilloes recognized at a broadminded school for girls of a high moral standard. Len took Hillela away with him. All he said was (with her beside him in the car again)—I don't understand, either.—

She felt now the fear she had not felt in the headmistress's study. She hid in the image of Len's little sweetheart. —I didn't know he was coloured.—

With a father's shyness, Len was listening for more to come.

—We all meet boys in town.— She was about to add, even when we're supposed to be in Sunday school with the little kids. But the habit of loyalty to those who at least had been her kind, even if she couldn't claim them any longer, stopped her mouth. She did not know whether her father knew she had been to the boy's home. She didn't know whether to explain about the banana loaf, a little sister who stared, the mother who called her 'miss'. An opposing feeling was distilled from her indecision. She resented the advances of that boy, that face, those unnatural eyes that shouldn't have belonged to one of his kind at all, like that hair, the almost real blond hair. The thought of him was repugnant to her.

Hillela stayed in Salisbury for a few days that time with Len and his wife, Billie, in their flat. He had married the restaurant hostess of an hotel—inevitable, Olga remarked, as a second choice for a lonely man in his job. What other type did he have the chance to meet? Len had brought Billie down to Johannesburg once; Hillela

14

heard talk that she was found to be a good-hearted creature, much more sensible than she appeared, and perfectly all right for Hillela's father. To Hillela she looked, in the tight skirt that held her legs close together as she hurried smiling between tables, like a mermaid wriggling along on its fancy tail. Olga smelled lovely when you were near her, but the whole flat and even the car smelled of Billie's perfume, as smoke impregnates all surfaces.

Billie was exactly the same at home as in the hotel restaurant where Len treated his daughter to a meal. It was part of her professional friendliness, jokiness, to be familiar without ever prying; she no more allowed herself to mention the reason for the girl's absence from school than she would have let a regular arriving to dine with his family know that she remembered seating him at a table for two with his mistress the week before. But on the subject of herself she was without inhibitions. At home she kept up a patter account of near-disasters between the kitchens and restaurant—'I almost wet myself' was her summing-up of laughter or anxiety—and expressed exasperation with those bloody stupid *munts* of waiters indiscriminately as she showed affection for 'my Jewboy'—kissing Len in passing, on ear or bald patch. Neither did she care for physical privacy; 'Come in, luv'—while the schoolgirl made to back out of the bathroom door opened by mistake. A rosy body under water had the same graceful white circlets round the waist as round the neck, like the pretty markings on some animal. The poll of fine hair dipped blonde, the same as the hair of her head, but growing out brown, was an adornment between the legs. Gold ear-rings, ankle chain and rings sent schools of fingerling reflections wriggling up the sides of the bathtub. —I could stay in for hours—I don't blame Cleopatra, do you, fancy bathing yourself in milk ... but I don't care for the bubble stuff, Len buys it ... dries out your skin, you know, you shouldn't use it, specially in this place ... my skin was so soft, at home, that rainy old climate. My sisters and me, we used to put all sorts of things in the water, anything we read about in beauty magazines. Oh I remember the mess—boiled nettles, oatmeal, I don't know what—a proper porridge, it turned out. But we had a lot of fun. That's the only thing I miss about England—me sisters, two of them's still only teenagers, you know—your age. It's a pity they aren't nearer—(a gift she would have offered.)

The girl sat on the lavatory seat, as one of them might have done. —What are they called?—

—Oh there's Doreen, she comes after Shirley, there's only eleven months between them (my pa was a lively old devil). People think they're twins, but they're very different personalities, very different ...—

—Still at school?— In the cloudy blur of the bathroom, the taboo subject lost its embarrassing reference as the woman's body lost any embarrassment of exposure.

—Doreen couldn't take it. She's doing hairdressing. Shirley's the ambitious one. She's Scorpio. She'll go for an advertising job, you need A-levels to get a foot in there. Or maybe a travel agency. Oh she's always moaning how lucky her old sister is, living out here. But they're both full of fun. A pity you don't have any sisters ... and it's a bit late for Len and me to make one for you!—

They laughed together; like the sisters. —Oh have a baby, Billie, it doesn't matter; have a baby. Even if it's a boy—

—Will you come and mind it for me? Change its smelly napkins? Oooh, I'm not sure I like the idea, don't talk me into it— In her bedroom Billie offered the loan of anything 'you have a yen for' in her wardrobe; like the cardboard doll on which Hillela had tabbed paper dresses when she was a small child, she held up against herself successive images of Billie, in her splendid female confidence either never naked or never dressed, advancing down the aisles of the restaurant.

Len must have cancelled his usual long-distance sales trip that kept him away from home up in Northern Rhodesia, Lusaka and the Copper Belt, from Tuesdays to Fridays. Bewilderment took the form of tact in what was—Hillela had caught the resonance of Olga's tone in bland remarks—'a simple soul'; he seemed to have fallen back on regarding the girl's presence as if it were that of a normal half-term break. He did a little business round about, and kept Hillela with him. She smoked a cigarette from the pack in the glove-box and he made no remark. When she had put out the stub he turned his head away from the road, without looking at her. —*My little sweetheart.*— Both knew, not seeing each other, that both smiled. Balancing rocks were passing; he did not see them, either, the routes he took were worn to grooves that rose over his head and enclosed him. The moments balanced, for her, rock by rock.

—Hillela, the best thing'll be to go back, now, you know that.—

He felt her attention all down the side of his body.

—Not to the school. Of course, you can't ... that's over. Back to Johannesburg. It's decided that's the best thing. Olga knows the good schools, somewhere you'll like. I've discussed it all with Olga.—

The rocks, passing, passing, were still balanced. They leaned out far, they held, sometimes on a single precarious point of contact, in tension against the pull of the earth that wanted to bring them crashing down.

—It wouldn't be fair to Billie. She's on her feet for long hours and she's very tired when she gets home—you know that. And with me out of town all week. The flat is small ... it really would be too much for her if we found a bigger place. Billie's young, and she's right ... she can't be expected to take on ...—

He slowed to turn a corner. His face came round full upon her. —The two of us.—

*

17

Arthur, Olga's husband, acknowledged her presence while taking off his glasses and cleaning the inner corners of his eyes between thumb and forefinger; when he replaced the glasses she was a closed subject. The elder cousins had the reined air of being under constraint not to question her about what had happened. The innocents, the servant Jethro and little Brian, surrounded her with pleasure at her unexpected arrival. In the kitchen, grinning and chewing the Italian salami left on plates cleared from the diningroom: —Is very, very good you come to us in Jo'burg now.— Moving back and forth about his mother like a cat turning against table legs: —Is Hillela staying for always? In school-time, too? Is she going to boarding-school, is she going to be home every afternoon with Clive and Mark and me?—

Olga had a series of bright and authoritative prepared statements. —She's going to live in Johannesburg. We don't know yet if she'll board.—

The rose was in its vase and the guest sweet-dish filled. Olga came in and closed the door behind her. She was the one who had explained menstruation as natural and sexual intercourse as beautiful, when the right time had come for information about these. Olga was the one who had paid for her teeth to be brought into conformation, bought her clothes chosen in good taste, and cared for her hair and skin so that she should grow up pleasing in the way Olga herself was and knew to be valued.

Olga's lips pressed together until the flesh whitened to a cleft on either side of her nose and she began to cry. She became even more distressed when she saw the girl was afraid of this amazing evidence of disorder in an adult who knew how to arrange everything comfortably and safely. She drew Hillela to sit down beside her on that bed with its little heart-shaped cushions, quilted satin coverlet and posy-printed muslin skirts, and gripped her hands.

—I wish I knew what I did wrong—what I didn't do for you, darling Hilly. But I never understood Ruthie—I adored her but I couldn't ... I just never ... And now I've let my sister down again, I know it. It's not your fault, I don't blame you for anything, please believe that, *I blame myself*, you are like my own child, but sometimes you can't do the right thing even for your own—you see that with lots of parents. There must be something I should have done, something I didn't understand. But I just have to face the fact that maybe we're not right for you ... You know your Aunt Pauline and I don't have much to do with each other—not because we don't love each other, we do, we do!—and anyway we both still love our sister whatever anyone says about her—but maybe, well, we agree perhaps you'll fit in better with Pauline's family. Pauline doesn't like Arthur, or our kind of friends or this house—you must have sensed it, even in the few times the whole family has been brought together. She thinks (a cough of laughter among the tears)—she says what you need is 'a breath of air', the kind we don't breathe here. So you see how it is. Maybe you'll have more to occupy your interests. Keep your mind busy. Pauline leads a more varied life—oh yes, I'm the first to admit it. My temperament is different. In that way, she and Ruthie were alike—adventurous. But of course with Pauline, I mean Pauline's serious-minded ... Anyway—it's out of the question you should be in the care of someone like Billie.—

Adults go on talking, all through childhood the monologue never stops.

When she who people say was once Hillela thinks of that time—and no-one who knew her then knows whether she ever does—that is all she retains of it. The tantrum that blew up inside her so bewilderingly that morning has long since been transformed, as electricity goes through pylons from voltage to voltage astride space and in time, and merged as the energy of other passions. Only those who never grow up take childhood events unchanged and definitive, through their lives. It is only in the memory of someone who claims to be her Aunt Olga that the actual tantrum exists, in static anecdotal repetition, in its form of a mysterious defence of *Billie*, Billie of all people!—poor Len's tarty second wife.

Don't Lean Your Smelly Arm
Over My Face

Clumsy with emotion, wrenching her hands out of Olga's, the girl knocked against the bookshelf and sent down one of a pair of charming 18th-century Imari cats Olga had thought to put in the room during the last school holidays because the girl was fond of cats: The little porcelain animal fell on the long-haired carpeting that was soft under bare feet in a bedroom, but the up-raised paw and one end of the gilded bow on the collar broke.

Olga agitated defensively, as if the destruction lying there were not a loss but an accusation made by Olga against herself. —It doesn't matter. Oh I didn't mean to upset you ... and over Billie ... Doesn't matter. It can be put together again. Oh darling, I'm so sorry! Please!—

—You don't have to watch out for any treasures here, anyway.— Pauline trod on silverfish that ran from the pages of stacked journals she moved to make room for the girl's clothes in a cupboard.

—It's going to be repaired.—

But Pauline intended to start the girl off the way she should go on; it didn't help anybody to be protected from the facts. —Things like that can't be put together again. Oh yes, you can glue them, they look the same as before, to you and me; but their value for people like Olga is gone. They can't take pleasure in anything that hasn't got a market value. If they can't look at it and think: I could get so-and-so for that if I wanted to sell it.—

—So now Olga won't be able to sell it?—

21

—You don't have to worry your young head over that. Olga doesn't need to sell anything; it's just that she needs to own things whose price is set down in catalogues.—

Pauline and Joe's house was not nearly so beautiful as Olga's, and fewer services were provided. As if still at boarding-school, Hillela had to make her own bed in the room she shared with her cousin Carole; there was no Jethro in white suit serving at table, and no cook in the kitchen. Bettie, the maid-of-all-work, was helped by members of the family, the swimming pool was old and pasted your flesh with wet leaves. Alpheus—son of the weekly washerwoman—lived in what had been the second garage (Pauline's old car stood in the yard) and doubled as gardener at weekends: Joe was giving him a chance as a clerk in his law office and Pauline was paying for him to take correspondence courses.

But in the shared bedroom a kind of comfort the girl had not known before built up. Categories kept separate by the institutional order of boarding-school and the aesthetic order of the room with the fresh flower were casually trampled down. Clothes, schoolbooks, hairbrushes, magazines, face creams, Coke bottles, deodorants, posters, tampons, oranges and chocolate bars, records and tennis rackets—all were woven into an adolescents' nest nobody disturbed. Pauline respected its privacy but assumed participation in the adult world. Before Olga's dinner parties the children were given their meal in another room; Carole had been accustomed, since she had wandered in sucking her bottle, to dipping in and out of conversations among her parents' friends in gatherings that cropped up at meals, in the livingroom or on the verandah. There was nothing to giggle over hotly in secret, in this house, because sexual matters were discussed openly as authority was criticised.

Pauline and Joe had been able to avoid segregated education for their son Alexander by sending him to a school for all races, over the border in an independent neighbouring black state.

But there was some reluctance, even at the expense of this advantage, to part with both their children. The other was the younger, and a girl—they decided to keep her under the parental eye at home, although to spare her, at least, the education primed with doctrinal discrimination at South African government schools. Olga (even in her sister Pauline's house nobody denied the generosity of Olga when it came to family obligations) must have been paying the fees for Hillela at the expensive private school at which she had joined her cousin. From there one day Carole came home in tears because at the school refectory where black waiters served lunch to the schoolgirls, one had said to a black man, Don't lean your smelly arm over my face.

Pauline made Carole repeat the remark.

Don't lean your smelly arm over my face.

Pauline was staring at her husband to impress upon him every syllable.

—That's what we pay through the nose for. Serves us right. Let's take them out of that place *now* and put them in a government school. Take them away at once.—

Joe's small features were made smaller and closer by the surrounding fat of his face. His dainty mouth always moved a moment, sensitively, before he spoke. —Where to? There's nowhere to go from anything that happens here.— He put on his glasses and gently studied the two girls, his daughter and his wife's niece, while Pauline's voice flew about the room.

—Exactly! Idiots we've been. No possibility to buy your way out of what this country is. So why pay? Racism is free. Send them to a government school, let them face it as it's written in your glorious rule of law, canonized by the church, a kaffir is a kaffir, God Save White South Africa—anything, anything but the filth of ladylike, keep-your-little-finger-curled prejudice—

It was the first time the niece saw the full splendour of this aunt. Pauline's eyes rounded up attention; her long, rough-towelled hair, prematurely and naturally marked with elegant strokes of grey while Olga's blond streaks required artifice, seemed to come alive, stirring and standing out as physical characteristics create the illusion of doing in people possessed by strong emotion. The maid Bettie, bringing in a parcel that had been delivered, changed expression as if she had put her head through a door into the tension of air before thunder.

Joe heard Pauline out. —No, we won't concede, we'll confront. We'll explain to Miss Gidding what we expect of the school; what we mean by table manners.— (He caught Hillela's eye to bring a smile from her.)

Again the two chairs turned to one another facing the desk in a headmistress's study.

Pauline's rising inflections, the text of which her daughter and niece could supply like words that go along with a tune, came through the walls to the anteroom where they waited, but no doubt it was the cross-examination technique of inaudible Joe that must have convinced the headmistress of need for the course she took. Hillela had not witnessed the incident at school, she had been eating at another table, but she was a member of the family and was called with Carole into the presence: parents, headmistress behind the desk. The headmistress wished to apologize for the offence given by the behaviour of one of their fellow pupils. Lack of politeness to the staff, whether black or white, was not tolerated at the school. The girl in question would be informed, and so would her parents. But it was to be understood by Carole and Hillela that the matter was not to be spread about as a subject for school gossip. Humiliating a fellow pupil would be a repetition of the original offence. —We want to guide, not accuse.—

Joe took them all off for an icecream before he returned to his office. Pauline was elated and sceptical, every now and then drawing a deep breath through narrowed nostrils, her black eyes moving as if to pick out faces in an invisible audience. —'The parents are such important people'—

—She did not say important, she did not say that—

—All right, that's what she meant—'she is quite sure such behaviour wasn't learnt at home'. Well, then, must have been learnt at school, mmh? You heard me put that to her. How absolutely ridiculous, anyway, that schoolgirls shouldn't wait on themselves. But no, the procedures of the Northern Suburbs dinner table are those into which young ladies are to be inducted—she didn't like it at all when I told her that, did she?— And the reaction of that Calder child comes from the attitudes that secretly go with those procedures: she said what she did *innocently*. In case you're ever tempted, girls, that's what's called gracious living.—

Hillela and Joe laughed but Carole's pallor as she withdrew into herself made her freckles stand out all over her face like a rash. In the car, she was suddenly weeping as she did when she reported: Don't lean your smelly arm over my face.

—Good god, what is it now?— Pauline accused Joe.

—It's all right for you. Now she won't speak to me again.—

At Olga's house, arguments, confessions or chastisings never took place in front of others, but Pauline didn't believe in confining weak moments and dark thoughts behind bedroom doors. —Now listen, Carole. And you too, Hillela. When you do what's right, here, you nearly always have to give up something. Something easy and nice. You have to accept that you won't be popular— with some people. But are they really the kind of people you want as friends? And there are a great many other people with whom you'll be popular just because they appreciate what you've done.—

—Where? I don't know where they are. You, and daddy—your friends. It's all fine for Sasha, over there up on a nice green hill in Swaziland. It's easy for him to be what you want.—

—Bettie. Alpheus. The waiters at the school—yes, maybe they'll never know you're the one who did it, but they'll appreciate

25

the change when they're not treated like dirt by little schoolgirls any longer.—

—At school they'll all just say I got Annette Calder into trouble over a kitchen boy. She won't speak to Hillela, either, now.—

Hillela did not know for whom, her cousin or Pauline, she spoke up. —I'm not keen on Annette, anyway, she's the one who had the idea all the boys must wear suits to the end of term dance. And when we had to draw a self-portrait in the style of a famous painting, she drew herself as the Virgin Mary, blue veil and all.—

Joe settled the back of his neck, appreciatively.

—Hillela's kicked out of that Rhodesian place (Carole stopped, to look for her way of escape if the others were to close in on her) and at this place, now, people won't speak to her because we stick up for Africans all the time.—

Joe drove with drooping head, as, in the political trial in which he was appearing for the Defence, he listened to State evidence. —Let us drop it, now, Pauline.—

—No, no. I don't want Hillela to be confused in any way about this. What Hillela did in Rhodesia wasn't wrong—nothing to be guilty about, nothing—but it didn't mean anything. She was pleasing herself, showing off a bit and taking a silly risk. When one's very young one gets a kick out of just being defiant. But that's anti-social, that's all. It's quite different from what we've all decided and done today. If the girls are made to suffer in some small way at school now, it's *for something*, it's principled. I don't have any time for rebels without a cause.—

But there was no consequence at the school. If the Calder girl and her parents were summoned to the headmistress's study, the girl herself was so well-brought-up that she had already the confidence of her kind to avoid any challenge of it. Nothing short of a revolution, the possibility of which was inconceivable to such confidence, could really harm it. So why bother to defend oneself? She and her accuser, Carole, took the opportunity to pretend the words had never been said or heard. Carole, as she moved up into senior positions in the school, became influential in the debating society and was able to introduce such subjects as 'Should there be censorship?' to girls whose parents read detective stories and best-selling sex novels while in her home banned books about South African life and laws were passed around and discussed. She even managed to have approved for debate 'Should there be different standards of education for black and white children?' though most of the girls had not heard that 'Bantu Education' had been introduced in the country, and there was a better attendance for 'Should we have sex education at school?' A self-service canteen had replaced the black waiters, for reasons of economy. Carole and Hillela, at Pauline's suggestion, arranged to have black children invited to a special performance of the school's production of *Peter Pan*; still schoolgirls themselves, Carole and Hillela were so advantaged (as Pauline reminded them) by their educational opportunities at school and by home background that they were able to help coach black students who came in from the townships to the centre run by Pauline's supplementary education committee, KNOW. The two girls were kept occupied on Saturday mornings in a red-brick church that once must have been in the veld outside the black miners' compounds but was by then hemmed in by workshops and industrial yards. Its ivy hung ragged from its porch and in the bushes that had been a garden were trampled places where, Pauline told, homeless black people slept. Their rags and their excreta made it necessary to watch where you set your feet; but the black boys and girls who came up singing in harmony—now mellow, now cricket-shrill—between the broken ornamental bricks of the path gave off the hopefulness of sweet soap and freshly-ironed clothes. It was in return for their lessons that they sang, and whenever they sang those whose enviable knowledge subdued the children into shy incomprehension in class became the uncomprehending ones: Mrs Pauline and

27

her colleagues, and the two white schoolgirls, smiling, appreciative. Pauline asked what the songs meant and wrote it down for quotation in the committee's letter of appeal for funds. (—Look at this tip left under the plate.— She waved before her family Olga's response: a cheque for ten pounds.) Hillela was heard singing the songs in the shower. Recalled—by this sign of musicality he had not had the chance to develop in himself—from absorption in documents of the treason trial whose level of reality made all other aspects of the present become like a past for him, Joe bought her a guitar.

—Where on earth'd you find time to look for that?—

He answered Pauline gravely as if under oath. —In Pretoria. During the lunch adjournment. In a music shop.—

—And now?— Pauline's smile quizzed gestural asides; she was the one who had to complete these for their initiators. Hillela and her uncle came together and hugged—people who have fallen in love for a moment; but it was Pauline who arranged for Hillela to have lessons with the folk-guitarist son of one of Pauline's friends. Hillela was soon accomplished enough to play and sing in a language she understood, performing Joan Baez songs at protest meetings to which Joe and Pauline gave their support: against the pass laws, apartheid in the universities, removals of black populations under the Group Areas Act. Carole, like her cousin, was under age to be a signatory to petitions but could take a turn at manning tables where they were set out. The two adolescents were absorbed into activities in which a social conscience had the chance to develop naturally as would a dress-sense under Olga's care.

Family likeness was to be recognized in Pauline, for one who had once been the daughter Olga never had. A girl younger than Hillela was brought to the house by Joe; but a schoolgirl with the composure of someone much older. On her the drab of school uniform was not a shared identity but a convention worn like a raincoat thrown over the shoulders. She turned the attention of a clear smile when spoken to yet, as an adult gets out of the way polite acknowledgement of the presence of children, firmly returned the concentration of her grey eyes to Joe, who read through documents those eyes were following from familiarity with the contents. Pauline spread cream cheese, strewed a pollen of paprika, shaved cucumber into transparent lenses and opened a tin of olives. She sniffed at her hands and washed them in the sink before carrying into the livingroom the mosaic of snacks worthy of her sister Olga. The girl drank fruit juice and ate steadily without a break in the span of the room's preoccupation, while Pauline hovered with small services in the graceful alertness of a cocktail party hostess.

—D'you know who that was?— Pauline came into the bedroom where Carole and Hillela had holed up.

—Daddy said. Rose somebody. I see she goes to Eastridge High. Horrible school.—

Pauline's vivid expression waited for its import to be comprehended. —That's Rosa Burger. Both her parents are in prison.—

Theirs was one of the trials in which Joe was part of the legal defence team. The red-haired handsome woman with the strut of high insteps who had accompanied the Burger girl was also one of the accused, though out on bail, like the old black gentleman who came to stay in Pauline and Joe's house for a few weeks. There were discussions about this, at table, before it happened; the old man had some illness or other and dreaded, Joe said, the strain of travelling from Soweto to the court in Pretoria every day. Hotels did not admit black people. Sasha's room was made ready for the guest; then Pauline decided it was too hot, the afternoon sun beat through the curtains, and Carole and Hillela were moved out of their room, for him.

There was a rose in a vase on the bedside table. Although Alpheus occupied the converted garage, no black person had ever

29

slept in the house before. The old gentleman really was that—a distinguished political leader and also a hereditary chief who was to be addressed by his African title specifically because the government had deposed him. The ease of the house tightened while he was there. Other people who came to stay were left to fit in with the ways of the household, but there was uncertainty about what would make this guest feel at home. When he was heard hawking in the bathroom the girls shared with him, they looked at each other and suppressed laughter and any remark to members of the family. Joe put out whisky but the old gentleman didn't take alcohol; Pauline got Bettie to squeeze orange juice; it was too acid for him. He drank hot water; so a flask was always to be ready, beside the rose. He had a magnificent head, Pauline explained; he ought to be painted, for posterity. She phoned her sister Olga, patron of the arts (let her move on from the 18th to the 20th century for once) who could tell one of her artist friends of the opportunity for sittings with someone a little different from the wives of Chairmen of Boards, someone whose life would go down in history. —My poor sister—her first reaction is always to be afraid of *trouble!* Would it be all right? Not cause any *trouble?* I think she was nervous her famous friend would land in jail for so much as committing the shape of Chief's nose to paper.—

The old man put his hand to his nostrils as one dismayedly adjusts a tie before being photographed.

—More likely her famous friend would be nervous of getting no more contracts for murals in government buildings, after such a commission.— Joe made one of his corrections.

It was not a painter but a sculptor who came. The old black man had agreed to a portrait—Oh I have been photographed I don't know how many times—as courteously as he accepted every other necessity of being in strange hands. Pauline and Joe's open-plan house had no doors except those of the kitchen, bedrooms and bathrooms; everyone went to and fro, some considerately lowering

30

the volume of voice of activity, past the chosen sunlit corner where the old man sat, one polished shoe slightly extended, the other drawn slightly back so that knee and stout Zulu thigh were at an angle of painfully-maintained relaxation and confidence. The sculptor built up thick clay scales, mealy and dun; the old man's own great head shone, cast in black flesh and polished with light, the broad shining nostrils wide in dignity, the cross-hatched texture of the big mouth held firm under majestic down-scrolls of moustache, the small fine ears etched against the heavy skull. He felt the presence of the schoolgirl watching; the eyelids came to life and drooped slightly over black eyes ringed with milky grey, as if they had looked at white people so long they had begun to reflect their pallor.

The two guests in the house—the permanent one and the temporary one—met face to face again. She was in her skimpy cotton pyjamas, running barefoot at dawn to the bathroom, he was coming from there, the big slow black man, knotted calves bare, feet pushed into unlaced shoes, wearing an old army surplus greatcoat over his nakedness. Against the indignity, for him, the child and the old man passed each other without a sign. It is not possible he could have lived long enough to have reason to remember; but she might have kept somewhere the impression of the grey lint in the khaki furze of the coat and the grey lint in the furze of the noble trophy, his head.

The trial went on so long it became part of the normal background to the life of adults, Pauline and Joe, while from month to month nothing is constant for adolescents, looking in the mirror to see the bridge of a nose rising (Carole's), the two halves of a behind rounding (Hillela's) and changing a gait, the very act of walking, into some kind of message for the world. In the newspapers were photographs of blacks burning their passes, raising fists and thumbs, staring elated defiance. Then there were the photographs that, like memory, hold a moment clear out of what goes by in such blaring, buffeting, earthquake anger and flooding fear that the senses lose it, like blood lost, in an after-shudder that empties all being. Close black dots of newsprint cohered into the shout as it left an open mouth and the death-kick of bullets that flung bodies into a last gesture at life.

Newspapers are horror happening to other people. Hillela was invited by her Aunt Olga to the special dinner connected with Passover (Olga liked to keep up these beautiful old Jewish traditions which the girl, named in honour of her Zionist great-grandfather, would certainly never be given any sense of in Pauline's house); the talk round the unleavened bread and bitter herbs of deliverance was of Canada, America or England. Olga and Arthur thought of leaving the country. Pauline and Joe cancelled their annual family holiday so that they could donate a substantial sum to funds for victims: maintenance for the dependants of political prisoners and money for needs that could not be publicly earmarked, that they did not want to be told about by those who received it, or to mention in their frank information confided to their children on the question of priorities at such a time: Yet the children must realize—people were living 'Underground', which meant they were fugitive, spending a night or a week here or there, always in fear of arrest for themselves and bringing danger of arrest to those who hid them.

There was some sort of argument on the telephone between Pauline and Olga, also not fully explained, but as a result of which Hillela, alone, went on holiday after all—with Olga, Arthur and their sons. Joe annoyed Pauline by refusing to see the holiday in context. —Plettenberg Bay's beautiful. You'll have a wonderful time. The beaches are so long you feel you can walk round Africa. And you'll go to the Tsitsikamma Forest—

Pauline, cutting sweet peppers for a stew and crunching slices as she worked, could not be silenced entirely. —Olga suddenly wakes up to the fact: she has 'as much right over you' as I have,

I've no right to deprive you of a holiday. For reasons of my own. That was her phrase exactly: 'for reasons of your own'. That's all Sharpeville and sixty-nine dead meant to her. She is *also* Ruthie's sister, etcetera. She has you to dinner a few times a year ... but suddenly she's Ruthie's sister, she feels responsible— Pauline turned her anger into a grin and popped a wheel of pepper into the girl's mouth.

Joe put a hand on Hillela's head in absolution. —Really beautiful. Hillela ought to see it.—

The day Hillela returned from the holiday a woman was sitting with Pauline under the dangling swags of orange bignonia creeper that made private one end of the verandah. The old dog came up barking blindly behind his cataracts, then recognized Hillela's smell under new clothes and swung about panting joyfully while Pauline jumped up and stopped her where she had approached, hugging her, admiring—Olga, eh? Everything she chooses to wear is always exquisite—her voice whipping around them distractedly, a lasso rising and falling.

—Shall I bring out some tea when I've dumped my things?—

—No, no. I won't be long: As soon as I'm free ... I'll come and hear all about ...— Behind her, Hillela saw crossed legs, the stylized secondary female characteristic of curved insteps in high-heeled shoes, the red hair of the woman who had come that time with the Burger girl, Rosa.

Everyone else was out; Carole must have had a friend sleeping over, there were short pyjamas that didn't belong under the pillow on the second bed. The kitchen was empty; Bettie in her yard room. Beginning to move again along the familiar tracks of life in this house, Hillela went into the dining area of the living-room to see if there was any fruit in the big Swazi bowl kept there. The voices on the verandah just beneath the windows did not interest her much. Pauline's less arresting than usual, evading rather than demanding attention: —The woman who works

33

for me sleeps in; her friends come and go through the yard all the time ... she has to have a private life of her own. There's someone Joe's given a job to—we've converted the second garage for him. So even if I had some sort of out-house ... it's just not possible ... even if I got a promise from Bettie and that young chap not to say anything ... how would I know that their friends ... We're right on the street, it's not a big property. There's nowhere anyone like that would be safe.—

—It wouldn't be for long. Haven't you somewhere in the house; anything.—

—If it were somebody I knew. I'd feel the obligation, never mind the consequences, I assure you. But what you tell me— it's just a name. And you don't know the person, either, I mean, through no fault of yours it might just be a plant ... a trap.—

—These 'strangers' are more than friends. There are times when personal feelings don't come into it. Now ... well, people are expected to put their actions where their mouths have been.—

At supper Sasha was there but Carole had gone with a youth camp project to build a clinic for blacks in the Transkei.

—Tell us about Olga's house—is it lovely? Up on the hills or near the beach? Oh of course it must be lovely! What heaven, just to run out of bed straight onto the beach, and on that side of the headland, completely private, right away from the crowds. And did you eat lots of gorgeous crayfish—oh crayfish straight out of the sea, with lemon and butter ... Pure ozone going down. No wonder you look so well, Olga's transformed you as only Olga can. Even waterskiing lessons! She just has a gift for giving pleasure, a special sort of generosity of her own.— Pauline herself seized upon a generosity and sisterly pride as if something sadly discovered to have been packed away in herself. Her interest in Olga's beach house, in the outings and beach parties (—And they liked your guitar-playing in the moonlight, eh?—) worked up intoxicatingly in her, that glance of hers that always seemed to create its own public found an agitating response invisible to others at table. —So you didn't only see the dolphins, you actually swam among them? Those wonderful creatures. Joe, what about that record? Wasn't there once a record of dolphins singing or talking? Made under the sea? Cousteau or somebody. It would be a nice present for Hillela to give Olga, to thank her, I must see if I can get it— She began to eat stolidly, eyes down on the plate like a child who has been forced to do so. The withdrawal of animation left a vacuum from which no-one could escape. Another voice came out of her, for Joe alone. —And there's your work to think of. That's what I should have said. That's the point. If we—all right, I, but it's the same thing, no-one would separate the culpability, would they—if we were to get involved in this kind of thing ... It'd only have to come out once, and your credibility—

He closed his eyes momentarily and opened them again.

—I mean professional integrity would be finished. For good. And what you can do in court is of far more importance—

He moved his head, prompting correction.

—No, well, I'm not making any excuses. We know nothing is more important than what people like that have done ... but your work's absolutely necessary, too, in the same context. One has to be sensible. I should have made that point. She should go to others for this kind of thing. I should have told her. Not lawyers' houses. I should have said, if you were to be accused of being involved in any way other than professionally, you'd never be able to take on such cases again ... would you? They ought to understand they also need people like you.—

—You acted correctly. That's the end of it.—

The boy and girl saw Pauline's hands falter on knife and fork. She put them down and her hands sought each other, each stiff finger pushed through the interstices between those of the other hand. —'People are expected to put their actions where their

35

mouths have been.' You can imagine how the word will get around. She's the kind who'll see to that.—

Joe dismissed this with a twist of lip and tongue to dislodge a tomato pip from a tooth.

Pauline drew her hair back tightly held on her crown a moment, exposing her nakedness, the temples that were always covered, then dropped the thick hair again. —Dolphins, Hillela. I love those stories about how they save drowning people and push sinking fishing-boats to shore. I wish they were true.—

Whatever the reason, the parents must have gone out later that night. They couldn't have been there? Sasha and his cousin helped Bettie wash up and gossiped in the kitchen. Bettie's nails, outgrown the patches of magenta varnish in the middle, flashed through the dirty water. —Did Miss Olga take her girl with her or her boy?—

—Jethro and Emily came. At least, they followed by train.—

—Lucky, lucky. I want to go to the sea. Sasha, why don't you take me sometimes?—

—Come on, Bettie ... when we go on holiday you go on your own holiday, you don't have to do the same old housework in a different place.—

Bettie's laughter jiggled her like a puppet. —I want to swim and get a tan same like Hillela.— They all laughed—she flung her arm, wet hand extended, round Hillela and Hillela's head rested a moment under her cocked one, cradled against her mauvish-black, damp neck.

Sasha had his mother's insistence on facing the facts. —You wouldn't be allowed on the beach. Isn't that true, Hillela?—

—Well, Jethro's afraid of the sea anyway, but Emily used to go down early in the morning, when nobody was there.—

—They lucky, like I say. Miss Olga gave them a fridge for their rooms. Emily's pay is very high, very high. I wish I could be working for Miss Olga!—

—Better than your pay?—

—*Better* than my pay, Sasha? More than ninety pounds a month.—

—My parents wouldn't take you to a place where you couldn't even walk on the beach.—

Bettie wiped the sink with the absent vigour of a task performed through a lifetime. —I'm not thinking about walking, I'm thinking about money, what I must pay my mother for looking after my children, what I must pay for schoolbooks, for uniform, for church—

—We're not rich people like Olga.—

Bettie laughed. —Maybe you not rich, I don't know.—

—You know how hard my mother works to help—black people, I mean. And she doesn't get paid.—

—Yes, she works hard. I work hard and I'm thinking about money. Money is the thing that helps me. Are you going to lock up, lovey?—

She took out of the oven a pot containing her man's supper and a jug with the remains of the dinner coffee and went off across the yard to her room.

The two young people played the records they liked as loudly as they wished. They sat on the floor in the livingroom under rocking waves of the rhythm to which their pleasurable responses were adjusted by repeated surrender to it, as each generation finds a tidal rhythm for its blood in a different musical mode. Hillela gazed at her feet, transformed by the sun and sea into two slick and lizard-like creatures, thin brown skin sliding satiny over the tendons when she moved her toes. Her attention drew the boy's.

—What was all that about?— A tip of the head towards the dining-table.

She took a moment to make sure he was not referring to Bettie. —Someone was here when I came home today.—

—Someone we know?—

37

—Not you. You weren't here when she came before. Quite long ago. Before the Chief stayed.—

—But you don't know who?— After a moment he began again. —Were you there?—

—I was unpacking my things. They were on the verandah.— She bent her head and began stroking over her feet and ankles. —I heard them talking when I went to fetch a banana—

—And?—

—I was thinking about something else.—

—A-ha, some chap you got keen on at Plett, mmh?— She mimicked Bettie. —Maybe, I don't know.—

He rolled onto his stomach and began playing with her toes to help her remember. —But you understand what they were talking about, now.—

—Well, I remember some things.—

—Such as?— He scratched suddenly down the sole of her foot and her toes curled back over his hand in reflex.

—Oh you know.—

—Me? How could I?—

—You heard what Pauline said, at dinner.—

—Yes. It's about someone on the run from the police, isn't it.— He traced down her toes with his forefinger. —Look how clean the sea has made your nails. You've got a funny-looking little toe, here.—

—Pauline told me that toe was broken when I was two years old, in Lourenço Marques with my mother.—

—Do you remember?—

—I was too small.—

—Not your mother either? What's she like?—

—No. —I suppose like Olga and Pauline—

He laughed. —Olga-and-Pauline, how's it possible to imagine such a creature!—

—She's a sister.—

—Well, yes. I don't remember her, either.—

—Sasha, would you say I look Portuguese?—

—How does Portuguese look? Like a market gardener?—

—My short nose and these (touching cheekbones), my eyes and this kind of hair that isn't brown or black; the way it grows from my forehead—look.—

He took her head in his hands and jerked it this way and that.

—Yes, you look Portuguese—no, more like an Eskimo, that's it, or a Shangaan or a Lapp or a—

—I don't look like you, any of you, do I.—

—But why Portuguese?—

—She had a Portuguese lover.—

—But you were already born, two years old, you ass.—

—She could've been there before.—

—Did they ever say anything?—

—They only tell us what they think we ought to know.—

—And your father?—

—They wouldn't tell Len, would they?—

Sasha still had her head between his hands. —So you're not my cousin after all.—

—Of course we are. You dope. She's still Pauline's sister.—

He let go her head and rolled back on the floor. Slowly he began to play with her toes again. He spoke as if they had not been alone together all evening, and now were. —Maybe I'll also be on the run. As soon as I leave school next year, I could be called up in the ballot for the army.—

—You'll have to go.—

He rested his cheek on her feet. She put out a hand and stroked his hair, practising caresses newly learned. He moved in refusal, rubbing soft unshaven stubble against her insteps: —No.—

—Yes, you'll have to go.—

—I don't understand them. They send me to school with black kids, and then they tell me it can't be helped: the law says I've got to go into the army and learn to kill blacks. That's what the army's really going to be for, soon. They talk all the time about unjust laws. He's up there in court defending blacks. And I'll have to fight them one day. You're bloody lucky you're a girl, Hillela.—

She drew away her feet and swivelling slowly round, lay down, her chin to his forehead, his forehead to her chin, close. Sasha, Carole and Hillela sometimes tussled all three together in half-aggressive, giggling play that broke up the familiar perspective from which human beings usually confront one another. She righted herself, eye to eye, mouth to mouth. The knowledge that they were cousins came up into their eyes, between them; she, his cousin, kissed him first, and slowly the knowledge disappeared in rills of feeling. It washed away as the light empty shells at the Bay were turned over and over by films of water and drawn away under the surf. He touched her breasts a little; he had noticed, living with her as a sister, that her breasts were deep and large under the token family modesty of flimsy pyjama top or bath towel tucked round under the arms. She slid the delicious shock of her strange sisterly hand down under his belt; her fingertips nibbled softly at him and, busy at her real mouth, he longed to be swallowed by her—it—the pure sensation she had become to him: for them to be not cousin, brother, sister, but the mysterious state incarnate in her. After a while they were Sasha and Hillela again; or almost. Light under the bedroom door showed Hillela was still up, preparing her books for the new term, when the parents came home; locked in the bathroom, Sasha had buried, with pants thrust to the bottom of the linen basket, his sweet wet relief from the manhood of guns and warring. Tenderness was forgotten: like any other misdeed undetected by adults.

Forgotten and repeated, as anything that manages to escape judgment may be repeated when the unsought opportunity makes space for it again.

Go-Go Dancer

Olga gave her a cheque (—Now that you're grown up I don't know what you'd really like—) and a package wrapped in Japanese rice paper with a real peony, under the ribbon, duplicating its peony motifs. The black students at the Saturday school (Pauline would have made the suggestion) gave her a pink-and-gold pop-up birthday card taped to a cigarette box covered with tinfoil. She was seventeen. Inside the Japanese paper package was the pair of Imari cats. Inside the cigarette box was an Ndebele bead necklace. Pauline picked up first one porcelain cat, then the other, and smiled, running her finger where she had found the cracks. The repairs were detectable as a fine line of gold.

—Real gold?—

—Oh yes, Hillela. But they've lost their value for a collection. Just a souvenir.—

Carole yearned for these porcelain cats. Hillela generously presented her with the undamaged one. Pauline was amused to see the pair parted, one with a space carefully cleared for it on Carole's bedside table, the other among shells and mascots and packets of chewing gum on the window-sill above Hillela's bed. —Now you've reduced their value still further. Don't tell Olga, for god's sake. You'll never make an art collector.—

When the two girls were alone Carole made an offer. —I don't mind swapping for the mended one.—

—No. I'd give them both to you, if I could.—

The Ndebele necklace fastened with a loop over a button, and the thread broke the second or third time Hillela wore it; the beads frayed off and in time rolled away into cracks in a drawer.

The wink of their glint under dust and fluff caught her eye: she had missed many Saturdays at the classes in the old church; without making any decision, it was understood that Carole alone would be accompanying her mother each week. Hillela and her new friend Mandy von Herz lied about where they were going or had been, even if the destination were innocent as a walk to the corner shop. They disappeared, even in company, into a privacy of glances, whispers, gazes past adults to whom they were either talking or appeared to be listening; an impatience sparked silently from them. Perhaps Mandy knew about Sasha; such secrets are binding as vows, affirm a buried solidarity even among crowds. Without mixing much with other girls, the pair were immensely popular at school, admired by those who could not keep up with their nerve. Hillela, an old lag, introduced to selected boarders the technique learned in Rhodesia for getting in and out of school at night. When discovered, they were too grateful for the freedom they had had, to mention her name.

GO-GO DANCERS LIVEN SATURDAY STREETS: a Sunday paper publishes a photograph of two young girls, flying legs and hair, dancing in a shop window. So this is what Hillela is doing with her Saturday mornings, now.

But Pauline must have decided, with the wise counsel of Joe, to take it tolerantly, carefully, considering the girl's background. —What on earth is go-go dancing, darling? And whose idea was the shop window?—
—It's a boutique run by some friends of Mandy. They're paying us ten rands each.—
There would be no second time for the proud young wage-earners of the new currency just introduced; as Pauline said, how lucky they were to get off even once without trouble at the school; and this issue wasn't really one on which she could have tackled

42

the headmistress as she had over the waiter. (The headmistress must have been grateful that the girls' names were not published; there was no summons to her study.) Carole was the only member of the family who allowed herself to be openly upset by the incident. —You should see Hillela and Mandy dancing! You don't know! They're wonderful! You should just see them!— But one thing Pauline and Joe never feared was that Carole would be influenced by her cousin; like her brother Sasha, Carole was too well-adjusted for that.

Pauline was frank with Hillela, always frank: one of the problems with Hillela was that she never seemed able to explain what made her do what she did? Having got away with dancing in a shop window in a bikini with a bit of fringe bobbing on her backside, one Friday she did not come home from school and had not appeared by eleven o'clock at night. Carole confided later that she herself had 'got hell' from her parents for not reporting earlier she had no idea where Hillela was. Pauline thought Hillela, as the elder of the two, must be allowed the self-respect of more freedom than Carole. The girls had heard it many times: I don't want to behave towards you the way Olga and Ruthie and I were treated when we were young, I'd rather take risks with you than do what our parents did to Ruthie.

But now a kind of dread came into the house; Carole could not explain what it was: —As if we'd done something awful—to you, or more that you were telling something awful to us ... I don't know ... — Pauline telephoned the von Herz girl's home. Her parents had been to the police and hospitals, already assuming disaster. They were not surprised to hear that Mandy's new best friend was also missing. —I have never liked this friendship.— The mother was frank, too.

—Anti-semitic cow. I could hear it.— A moment's distraction flared in Pauline. But the convention of action set by the other family provided an acceptable channel for the dread. The feeling it was something about which nothing could be done was contained. Carole went along with Pauline and Joe to a police station. All the time Hillela's particulars were being given to a young Afrikaner policeman Carole was watching a white girl, a girl Hillela's age, with Hillela's little face, and big breasts shaking as she cried, a girl with blood dried dark like sap from a cut next to a swollen eye, being pawed helplessly, to comfort her, by restless and wary friends in the motorbike set. The light in that place where neither Carole nor her cousin had ever been was so strong that the shadows at midnight were the shadows of day. Bootfalls and clangings echoed from somewhere; shouts in languages Carole and Hillela heard spoken by the black waiters and cleaners at school, Bettie, Alpheus, Alpheus's mother, and did not understand. —The policeman asked all sorts of mad things. Did you take drugs. Did you go to discos in Hillbrow. Did you have any 'previous convictions'—and all in the most terrible *japie* English, just repeating what he's been taught to say, like a little kid who can't even read yet.—

Two other policemen were swinging their legs where they sat on a table and a third flirted in Afrikaans, over the phone. How tall was Hillela Capran? What did she weigh? Any distinguishing marks? Pauline, her hair bristling with the static of anxiety, would not give Joe a chance to answer any questions, but had to turn to Carole for these bodily statistics that obsess adolescent girls, always weighing and measuring themselves. Pauline had brought an identifying photograph, yes; one of the three of them—her children and their cousin—with Carole and Sasha cut away.

Did Hillela ever realize that no door was locked in the house that night? The front and back doors, the sliding glass ones that led to the verandah where Pauline had refused what was asked of her by the woman with red hair—all were open, the way a window is left wide in the hope of enticing back a strayed cat.

44

In the morning the whole house was swept full of night air, the leaf-smell of dawn. Carole explained how she had tried to stay awake that night but must have slept: she opened her eyes and saw the second bed still neat and empty. Bettie was crying, the flanges of her black nose lined with rosy wet. While drinking coffee standing up in the kitchen, Pauline and Joe, with Carole listening, discussed whether or not to telephone Olga. —Oh my god—Olga ... What suggestions could she have. She didn't have enough understanding to take her after that Rhodesian business, so how could she have any idea at all of how to deal with this?— Yet Pauline came back from the duty call somehow relieved, though scornful. —I told you. D'you know what she said? First she didn't know what to say ... then she came up with the bright idea Hillela might have gone to Mozambique.— Joe seemed actually to be considering the supposition, so Pauline exposed it in all its uselessness. —She hasn't had a word from her mother since she was old enough to read, we haven't even an address any more, so the notion she would run away to Ruthie ... really. Olga reads too many romantic novels from her ladies' book club.—

—Olga'd like to go and look for Ruthie, herself, maybe ... so it's a perfectly reasonable idea for her to have.—

—Well, I happen to love Ruthie, too, but I'm capable of being a bit more intelligently objective than my sister Olga—

—She reproached you?—

—Not that ... unless you read her silences. She didn't dare. But what does it matter now. Doesn't help us.—

—Carole. D'you think there's any chance Hillela might have had a notion to go to Lourenço Marques?— Joe gestured lightness; it would not be such a serious matter if her cousin had. —D'you ever get the impression she longs for her mother, or at least for some idea of her? Or might go for the adventure of it? Take the von Herz girl along?—

Well, Hillela would know how Carole had to answer her father's weighing-up of circumstantial evidence. It was only surprising when Hillela did ask her young cousin: —How?—

—I said you wouldn't go to Len or to your mother. It wouldn't be anything we would think of. So then they went on and on, whether you were unhappy, whether you didn't love us—all that stuff, I nearly passed out with embarrassment.—

But Joe was accustomed to persisting logically towards the uncovering of motivation. —If she were to be unhappy, to whom would she go?—

Carole didn't tell Hillela what she had said then: —Sasha. I think. If he were around.—

—Sasha? Really? Not you!—

—Why Sasha!—

They still suspected Carole of covering up for her cousin.

—She would. I don't know … because he's older … but he's not here. So she couldn't have.—

They did something Carole would never have thought they would do. Pauline telephoned Swaziland—to the school. Sasha was out on a cross-country run but he was allowed to telephone home when he returned half-an-hour later. Hillela? He had not heard from her. They did not write to each other—Pauline knew very well Hillela never wrote, even when she was away at Plett with Olga, she didn't write.

Had she ever spoken to him of any friends she didn't want the family to know about?—it was natural for young people, part of growing up, beginning to be independent of their parents, to have little secrets. But it would be necessary for him to betray a confidence in an emergency like this, to prevent possible harm coming to his cousin.

Pauline came from the telephone with the dread settled upon her again. —No idea where she could be. He got quite cross when I said, if she should phone him or turn up there … There's

46

an inter-school match today, he'll be away playing soccer at Manzini.—

Pauline went to take her Saturday-morning coaching classes as usual. She did not know what else to do? She would not help Hillela by letting down black children who travelled all the way from Soweto in their eagerness for education. Carole stayed with Joe, at home, to be there for Hillela if she came.

In the afternoon there was the slam of a car door and footsteps running up the drive; all three in the livingroom stood up ceremoniously to receive Hillela restored to them—but Sasha, Sasha was in the doorway. Sasha walked into the familiar house empty of the presence of Hillela. An amazing rage broke over them. He smashed their sensible calm like a bottle flung against a wall, and his words were the jagged pieces held before the faces of his mother, his father, Carole. —What've you done?—

He stood in the doorway apart from them, turned to Pauline. He was unshaven, a grown man, and his nose was running, a little boy's. —You bitch. What've you done? You think everything you do is the only thing. Only you know what to think, how to live. Everybody's got to be like you. Something's right because it fits in with you. If it doesn't it's stupid, it's shit. Not everybody's going to be exactly like you and dad. You *understand* what everybody needs, you never ask them. You know what blacks ought to have and you know what Hillela needs, you're so sure it's not Olga, it's not her father, it's *you* ... You send me to school with blacks because that's normal, that's the way it ought to be here but isn't, it *isn't*, and *you* don't have to go into the army afterwards and kill them, only I, I have to do that, I have to do what's wrong, not you. You take Hillela in, that's the *right thing,* and now, if she's dead ... (Carole wept with shock to see her brother weep.) ... If you've killed her then she's done what's wrong, you've got nothing to do with it, she doesn't *fit in* ... And if I get blown up or shot defending this bloody country where do I fit in? You despise Olga

47

for wanting to run away to Canada, but you don't have to go into the army, I do, *I do.* You don't know what happened to Hillela, no, because you're careful not to let anything happen to you—

Pauline stood still, breathing deeper and deeper, her intimacy with her son making certain the sense under the ridiculous tirade would find the vital places, known only to him and her, to wound her.

And because of Hillela, then, Joe did something inconceivable for him: he called his son a bastard. The hollow house filled with anger and pain that would never have been let loose, things were said that should never, would never be said by people like them.

Pauline tugged out one by one the crude homemade shafts that pierced her, shameless, as if exposing before her husband and almost-grown children the privacy of the body where he had begotten them and from which she had ejected them into the world. Her hair was a great wick by which she might catch alight. —Yes cheap, stupid, shit, this place, and you've been sent away so's you don't have to dirty yourself with it while you're growing up. You haven't had to listen to it from your friends at school, the way the girls have to. You haven't got to teach Alpheus to spell while he dreams about being a lawyer, the way your father has to—you know only blacks who're your equals, getting the same education you're getting. You're too high and mighty to make any compromises because you don't have to, you're a spoilt brat. There're all kinds of ways of making a spoilt brat, I see that, and—you're right— this is *my* way. I've had my way and I've done it. You're my way. We can't all live at Waterford Kamhlaba School, you know. There's the world out there— There's this place. And Joe and I have to decide every day of our lives how to live here, *whites only*, no choice about that, no phalanstery without passes and black locations, white this and black that, beach houses for Olga and the kids I teach living fourteen people in two rooms in Soweto!—

—And Alpheus in the garage.—

—Where shall I put him? *Your* room? Would you like that? Do I run an orphanage here? —What do you know about the decisions your father has to make, taking cases *pro deo* when he could be making money as a divorce lawyer for whites with wives who must have enough alimony to have their faces lifted. We do know what's cheap, what's stupid, what's *shit*. Yes. We've spent our lives finding out how to live in the midst of it, part of it, and ... and behave as decently as one can ... until it's changed. I do think I know what's right, even if I don't always manage to do it. And, my Christ, the last thing I want is for you to have to be exactly like me, like us. That's what I've been preparing you for since you were two bricks and a tickey ... for change. But you have to think for it, work for it; and every day of the week do what you're not sure of, or despise yourself for ... it's not a clean process ... getting out of the shit ... it's not going to be for you, either, don't think it can be, you're old enough to realize.—

—You don't have to tell me. My name's the one in the ballot. I'm going to have to go to the army.—

—Am I responsible for that?—

—Yes, because you don't have to go.—

—Stop talking nonsense, Sasha.—

—No, Joe, if that's true, then our life has been useless. Yours and mine.—

—You, you, your life. Who gives a fuck for you fishing for a pat on the back. I'm not listening, do you hear, I'm not listening—

Pauline lifted her long, blunt-nailed hand, to raise against her son or to protect herself, silver bangles from which the chasing had long worn off sliding down towards her elbow: the gesture was not concluded. There was an intrusion. The telephone rang. Hillela was speaking from a police station in Durban. She was fine. Mandy von Herz was fine. They had been recognized by the police on the North Beach. The police were being really nice, they

49

allowed her to phone. Joe spoke to the sergeant and arranged for the girls to be put on the train that evening.

—And him?— Hoarse Pauline presented Joe with the presence of Sasha, swollen-lipped, before them. Her voice was slurred as if she were stunned by drink. —Does the school know you're here?—

He did not answer.

His mother lifted her big head again. —And what are we going to do about that? He could be expelled. —Where do they think you are?—

—Manzini.—

—So. Joe—you decide with him how to get out of this mess. A prefect simply runs away when he's sent to a soccer match. What school can overlook that? What d'you suggest we do now? Simply walks out and hitches a lift home without a word to anyone, like any dropout, any delinquent—

Joe kept the professional manner he had adopted over the other matter, with the Durban police. —I'll phone, I'll explain.—

Pauline's great head and red-scratched cheeks faced everyone, the inhabited helmet and mask of authority. —What'll you explain?—

—He was under stress. A family matter.—

Hillela's nose is peeling and there is a bracelet made of turban shells on her right wrist. When she sees her cousin Sasha, home, reading the Sunday paper, she puts a hand over her opened mouth. —Was it your half-term—

They all hear Sasha. —No. A couple of us seniors got a chance of a lift, so they gave us a weekend.—

The house needs to recuperate from the dread Hillela left behind her, and from the emotions Sasha let loose. Pauline has made a lamb curry with accompanying chapatis, yoghurt-and-cucumber salad, bananas with coconut, and peach chutney—the young people's favourite lunch. Joe asks what the swimming was like. Oh wonderful, though not as good as Plett. —The water was so warm we all went in on Friday night—about two in the morning!—

—Who'd you meet up with?— Carole slips into innocent schoolgirl gossip.

—No-one in particular. Mandy knows some chaps from Michael-house, it turned out it was their half-term, and they knew someone I met at Plett.—

—Who's that?—

Sasha swallows a large mouthful and turns on his sister. —Nosey.—

Hillela is smiling at Sasha, but he doesn't look at her face. She glances down at her arm as if something, a touch of light, has directed attention there. She rolls the shell bracelet off over her fist. —I brought this for you, Carole. Sasha—I would've got you something if I'd known you'd be here—

The Shadow of a Palm Tree

There was a time and place for Hillela to give account of herself.

Olga's Rover kept by Jethro shiny as the taps in her bathroom stood outside the gate. Olga sat in Pauline's worn livingroom with Pauline, waiting. Olga got up and hugged her; —Hillela, oh Hillela.— She was sweaty from the day at school and did not know when it would be all right to break the sweet-smelling embrace. —You want to tidy up a bit?— Olga lifted the hair at the back of the girl's head, gauging it needed an expert cut.

—There's a chicken sandwich in the kitchen, darling. Leftovers from the grand lunch I gave Olga.—

—It was a perfectly good lunch, believe me. I usually have an apple and a bit of cheese.—

—Yes, one can see that by the shape you keep. But I can't be bothered. There are too many other things to do. I'm hungry; I eat bread and peanut butter to fuel myself; I spread around the arse ...—

She came back barefoot, her face washed, hair pushed behind her ears.

—Your sandwich.—

She turned and fetched it from the kitchen.

Olga kept smiling at her, frowning and smiling at once, as people do in order not to make fools of themselves in some way. Olga would leave it to Pauline: Pauline accepted with the gesture of inevitability. —It's all been passed off just as if you've been—I don't know, spending the weekend with a friend, as if it were any other time you or Carole ... ? But the fact is, my dear little Hillela, you gave us all a terrible twenty-four hours. Not only us, your immediate family here where you belong, but also Olga ... Olga was running around hospitals and police stations, just like us.—

Olga's smile broke. —We don't want to reproach you, darling. We only want to know why. Why you could just go off like that.—

—You know how much freedom I give you and Carole and Sasha. If you had an invitation, if you planned to go to Durban, you could so easily have asked me ...—

Pauline told Joe, Olga told Arthur: the girl answered unnaturally openly: —On Friday after tennis we were hot, and we began talking about the sea. So we thought, why not go?—

—Without money, without a change of clothes?—

The girl reassured Olga. They had their gym shorts, pullovers and swimming costumes in their attaché cases; Mandy had money. They had no trouble getting lifts. First a man and his wife going to their farm near Harrismith, and then they waited about half-an-hour at the roadside before a van driver stopped, he was on his way back to Cato Manor because his boss let him keep the van over the weekend, but he specially went right into Durban, for them.

—Isn't Cato Manor a black location?—

Pauline broke in across her sister. —Prejudice is one thing, Hillela, and you know in this house I take full responsibility for bringing you up without any colour-feeling, any colour-consciousness. But you must realize that there are risks one doesn't take. Just as I often tell you children one shouldn't leave money lying around where it can be a temptation to poor people ... Young girls just do not take lifts from men—men of any colour.—

Olga had her hand at her own throat. —We're so afraid for you, Hillela.—

Mandy von Herz was removed from the school by her parents, since she refused to remain there under a ban on associating with Hillela Capran. Mr von Herz came to see Joe—he did not think such matters should be discussed with women—because he believed Hillela's family should know that Mandy had been afraid to take a lift with the black man, and the black man himself had been afraid to pick up two white girls, but it was Hillela who had flagged him down and Hillela who had persuaded him. He was an elderly black man, apparently, and had some respect for his position as well as theirs, thank God.

—Sanctimonious creep!— Pauline was only sorry she hadn't been allowed to get at von Herz and tell him what she thought of him. Of course, his way of dealing with his daughter was to take the easy way out, and blame someone else's child.

Pauline herself never explained why she brought in Olga to deal with Hillela that time. Perhaps there had been the suggestion, since Olga was always saying she, too, was responsible for Ruthie's child, that she might try her hand again. Olga could take her away, to a new environment; Pauline had heard Arthur was thinking of emigrating to Canada.

Maybe the girl would be happier there.

—Why?—Joe disliked unqualified statements. There was nothing to substantiate that the girl was unhappy, anyway.

—Maybe even Olga would be different, there.—

But that was no reason. Pauline could offer no reason except the one unexpressed because he knew it well enough: Hillela didn't resist, it was simply that she seemed not to notice all that Pauline and Joe had to offer that was worthwhile. It had been a misconception to think she had to be rescued from among Olga's objets d'art, Olga's Japanese screens placed before the waste ground of torn plastic and human excreta, Olga's Carpeaux *Reclining Nude* (even if its provenance was merely 'attributed to') in place of surplus blacks, not fit for any labour force, sleeping under bushes. To resist Pauline would at least have meant to have belonged with Olga; why didn't Hillela understand that was the choice? The only choice. Pauline was moved by her ignorance, innocence one must call it, at that age. She could not be abandoned. Pauline said it as if a note from the school had just informed her of the child's undetected astigmatism or dyslexia: —She's a-moral. I mean, in the sense of the morality of this country.—

Pauline had won the battle with her son; she had no need to think about it. But from the jagged glass of his attack needle-splinters were travelling unfelt through her, maiming the exercise of certain powers in her as a limb is maimed by the lodging of a minute foreign body in the bloodstream, and forcing her to use substitutes, as the body adapts another of its parts to take over the function of the nerve-damaged one. She no longer surged forward to provide what would keep the girl's mind healthily engaged with the realities of the country, but apparently was trying to circle round what might occupy that mind itself, what needed to be dealt with and got out of the way.

She would never come empty-handed. She did not bring fancy clothes and chocolates as Olga did, but the shared instinct remained, vestigial, from the neighbourly conventions of her discarded Jewish childhood. She wandered into the girls' room when her own daughter was not there. —Look what I found. Ruthie's things. We each had boxes like this one, but mine was yellow. They were supposed to be for sewing, although we never did any ...—

When Ruthie finally went away, her sisters came in and packed up her possessions as if she were dead. Len had wanted them given to charity. Pauline and Olga took some souvenirs of the life Ruthie had abandoned; might she not come back for them some day?

Their sister was not dead; here was her daughter; maybe she had come for them.

The box was padded and covered with water-marked taffeta that buzzed under the girl's drawn fingernail like breath over a paper-covered comb. There were spill-stains and a seal—red nail-varnish dried stony. Pauline sat on the bed beside Hillela, a fellow schoolgirl, while they picked about together in the box. Pauline explained tarnished metal wings and crowns from the war. —Insignia. Our boyfriends sent them, we had pins attached at the back so we could wear them as brooches. We were so ignorant and silly. And so far from the war. No air raids, no blackout. No rationing. No brothers. There's something about a colonial society that trivialises. Often I think: the fact that civilians here missed out the war has got something to do with whites feeling they can avoid the reality of the other experience, too. Even though that's all round them. Being black, living as blacks have to—it's a misfortune that happens to somebody else ... oh what's this? Old bus tickets ... we used to live in Mountain View, one time.—

There was an autograph book with gilded edges: —'Speech is silver, Silence is golden'—that was contributed by a teacher, for sure, and what about this one, 'When in this book you look, and on this page you frown, think of the friend who spoilt it, by writing upside-down'. We kids didn't think anything could be wittier.—

A small box within the box held a doll's comb and hair-rollers. —Oh for her Shirley Temple doll, I remember, she wouldn't let me touch its hair—

Hillela found a photograph.

Pauline looked from the photograph to her, from her to the photograph.

—That's you, Hillela, that's you.—

A little girl whose stomach pushes up her dress stands in a public playground before a seesaw and swings. The shadow of palm fronds lies on the ground. Her long hair is rumpled into a topknot and sand shows in matt swathes clinging to her stumpy, baby legs.

—Where was I?—

56

—Oh at the sea.—

—Is it Lourenço Marques?— Hillela was looking for landmarks in a tourist's amateur focus where towers tilt and historic features are cut off.

Olga explained sexual intercourse when the time came for that; now it was Pauline's turn to find her appropriate moment.

—Yes. Yes. It must have been Lourenço Marques.—

Pauline had evidence other than the shadow of a palm tree. —My sister went on a holiday with you to Lourenço Marques when you were two, and it's not quite the way they've told you ... if they've told you anything. She's quite unlike me in most ways, but I understand her. You see, she had been handed over from our father to Len, there were his mother and aunts watching her waist to see if she was going to be pregnant, as she should be, in the first year. They were an orthodox Jewish family—oh it's only thanks to Ruthie, whose name poor old Len never speaks, that he's been freed to marry his little Cockney waitress! There were the family dinners on Friday nights, the cake sales for Zionist funds, and especially the same old parties—weddings, barmitzvahs; those tribal Jews don't know what it is to enjoy themselves spontaneously. Ruthie drank whisky and other nice young Jewish wives didn't, Ruthie danced as if she were not married, with the prospective husbands of other girls. She went on holiday to Lourenço Marques and she fell in love, yes—but it was with what she suddenly imagined real life to be. She fell in love with that wailing *fado*, she wanted passion and tragedy, not domesticity. Passion and tragedy were not where she would have looked for them, here—they were around her, but in the lives of blacks, and she was somehow never able to be aware of anything outside her own skin (that's her charm, in a way), let alone skin of another colour. So she took the kitsch as real. She fell in love with the sleazy dockside nightclubs, the sexuality and humidity, the freedom of prostitutes. That's what she kept going back for. To wash

57

off the Calvinism and koshering of this place. The way people go to a spa to ease their joints. That's really what she went for, and then there was the young man in the white suit who could hardly speak English and danced with her all night. It all took place in half-darkness (you can't imagine how dingy and sordid those places were), she never saw it clearly, she never wanted to come back into the daylight. I know Ruthie. Poor thing, she was all our colonial bourgeois illusions rolled into one; she thought that was Europe. Latin. She thought it was European culture. And she hated South Africa—but she thought what was wrong with this country was that it didn't have *that*—

Hillela heard someone else's story through with polite attention. Towards the end she picked up the photograph again; she had the self-absorption of someone trying to get into a garment too small for her. —I loved swinging, and a seesaw with a wooden head at either end, I don't think they were horses' heads, something like a bull's, they bumped me up and down.—

Pauline was almost delicate in the old suggestion: —D'you think you really remember? You were not quite two. Other playgrounds, perhaps.— She shared with Olga and other adults the idea that life begins, for children, at a period set existentially by adults.

—With Len, on the road. He used to stop in little dorps and take me into school playgrounds wherever there were swings.—

And then the girl held out the photograph of herself, which she seemed to have succeeded in inhabiting. —Would you like to have it?—

Pauline had decided what was needed was to fill up the vacuum of the past so that the young life could take root in the grit of the present. She should have said: Now, why don't you want the photograph? But a sliver of glass paralyzed the nerve. What took over its function was something she despised: a pretence at being pleased, moved etc. —I'd love to. Oh thank you.—

Hillela was looking at her with something—love?—that was natural, she was not like Sasha, not a child who judged—something not exactly compassion, more open and invading than that. With *knowing.* Pauline tried to remember what. She tried to arrange the knowing logically, to apply to the confidences about Ruthie, her sister, the girl's mother, shared for the first time on an adult level. But she had the strange feeling it was something it couldn't be, impossible—what she knew about herself: her refusal to hide a man on the run.

And then, that day, Hillela kissed her on the cheek.

What is to be done with these things? They can't be thrown away. Just as it is necessary to keep the broken and repaired porcelain cat Olga gave her to ask forgiveness for something—Pauline's offering cannot be refused, either. Autograph book, toy hair-rollers, tokens from boys away in a war—the box goes into a cupboard that can be reached only by standing on a chair, where old tennis rackets and compendia of games are stored. There is a writing-case of grey leather stamped with a picture of the Sphinx Pauline found, as well. Carole likes to write letters. Emptied of junk, it shall be for her. Inside, two porcupine quills, a broken ear-ring; the case is very nicely made, Carole will love it, there are loops for pens and an inner compartment—a few papers still in there.

Letters. Ruthie's letters she had not wanted; she left behind her what she did not want to be (so Pauline had explained) and what was not wanted by its owner surely does not belong to anybody? The letters are not in envelopes and not tied together by ribbons the way such things are described in the love stories lent by girls at school. As they are turned over the ends and beginnings of lines, divided by folds, are deciphered automatically as signposts presenting themselves in passing.

Don't worry if
terribly for you

because I'll never, never
their idea of what
but that's not how I want
tongue in your ear, in your

Go away somewhere in the house to read. The cat passes through the house sometimes like that; a secret in its mouth, avoiding all contact. The letters are in English ... how could they be understood if they had been in Portuguese? They aren't letters, no, but drafts, the page numbers changed, lines crossed out and rewritten or restored—exactly like the drafts made for weekly school essays. *I wake up in the morning and I don't open my eyes because then I'll see where I am, that you're not here, that it's him lying there.* The last phrase scratched over and a full-stop stabbed over the comma after 'here'. *What's the good of living like this, always with your thoughts somewhere else. It's a waste, a waste. I go about like a zombie, a robot (you understand what that is? A dead person walking, or a traffic light where you cross the street, you go when it's green, you stop when it's red). My body somewhere else, also. I can't tell you how I long for you. I put my hands where you do and pretend it's you.*

A rippling sensation up the back makes the shoulders hunch. The hand that wrote the words was like this one—the one that holds the paper: the same.

When I got out of the bath this morning I saw myself in the mirror and thought of you looking at me and you won't believe me but my nipples came out and got hard. I watched in the glass.

The same, the same. As a deep breath taken fills the lungs, so the hands open as if to do things they did not know they could, the whole body centres on itself in a magical power. It sings in the head, the sense of the body.

They say this or that is 'only physical' but when you see something ugly and horrible like L's grandmother, can't eat, smells, can't see (she doesn't recognize anybody but he drags me along to show her the baby) you know that a body is what you are left with when you get old, so why

60

should you ignore (crossed out) *take no notice of it when you are young and it is marvellous, marvellous. If only they knew how marvellous. Maravilhoso. Is that right, my darling darling, how's my progress? I've bought a dictionary. I know you don't like to hear about anything that happened to me before you—real Latin jealousy, I laugh to tease you, but really it's so sweet to me to have a man inside me who possesses a woman completely, nothing to do with being introduced: this is my wife. And this is my child, this is my dog.*

Singing in the head, and the flush that comes before tears, but in another part of the body, and another kind of wetness.

I look at the others—my poor sisters, the one with that circumcised ox Arthur who will soon be rich enough, that's for sure, to climb on top of her in a bed that used to belong to the Empress Josephine or someone, and the other one with her musty 'professional man' she shares the serious things in life with, even if the 'only physical' can't be too great with a good soul like that. And she's such a magnificent girl—I wish you'd meet her. No I don't! What I wish is she had a man like you to bring her to life. What's the use of trying to change other people's lives if you don't get a chance to live the only one you're going to have. We didn't ask to be born here. Nobody's going to give it back to you, nobody's going to thank you. I know, through you, I can be sure of what I feel and that's the only thing you can be sure of (written above: 'that matters'). *I've had a husband, I've given birth. So what does it mean? These things were done to me. But with you I do things. I'm all over my body, I'm there wherever you touch me, and I'm there wherever I touch you. My tongue in your ear, in your armpit fur and your sweet backside. Oh my god Vasco, Vasco, my Vasco, the taste of you!*

The same, the same. All sensations alive in the body, breasts, lips of the mouth and the vagina, thorax, thighs, charged, the antenna of every invisible hair stretching out. A thirst of the skin.

When I come back here you are still in my mouth. Like what? I read somewhere it's supposed to be the taste of bitter almonds. Not true, not for yours, anyway. I wish I could describe it. Like strawberries, like lemon rind. I always did eat the rind of the slice of lemon people put in drinks. I'm crazy today, don't listen to me. It was so sad not to know all these wonderful things for 24 years. My sister was talking today about fellow man. I don't know what she's going on about. There's only one other person, and if you don't find him ... nothing else. It is so sad to be alone in your body. Do you understand what I write, my love? I can't help writing to you, anyway. I never used to write letters, even during the war, my boyfriends used to send reams and I'd hardly write back. Honestly. I didn't know letters could be like this. When you read, do you understand enough? Enough to love me. Do I make you grow big for me. Do I

The draft is unfinished. But there is an avowal written large and dug deep across the page: RUTH. Ruthie. Ruth; mother. Sweating and trembling with Ruthie's desire; Ruthie has become mother.

The letter is being torn into small pieces, torn again through the syllables when an intact word stares up. On the way to bury the fragments in the yard bin outside the kitchen: there stands, in the path, the girl Alpheus has living with him in the garage. The girl's stomach lifts her dress as the babyish potbelly of the child did in the photograph. The girl is pregnant; tries to efface herself from the notice of the white people in the house, and so, cornered, murmurs to the white girl her own age, Good afternoon, madam. The bits of paper cannot be put into the bin under anyone's eyes. The fragments are taken to school and buried in the communal trash there, with the banana-skins and half-eaten sandwiches of tea-break.

It must have done some good. To bring the past into the open— in particular the past she didn't have in memory, only heard obliquely referred to by others—would draw the girl herself more into the open? At least, Pauline thought it might have done. She had suggested to Joe that through Portuguese legal colleagues in Mozambique they might try again to make contact with Ruthie; middle-aged, like the rest of them by now, though who could imagine Ruthie fortyish!

Joe could. —A woman alone, no profession, drifting. It's downhill.—

—But she's not alone.—

—A woman who had a lover years ago. D'you think that type of thing lasts? Fourteen years hanging around nightclubs and bars. Poor Ruth. What was it he was supposed to be? Disc jockey? Professional dancing partner?—

But Joe had things to think of other than writing to ask colleagues to investigate a family matter, the whereabouts of a woman last known to have been cohabiting with a Portuguese citizen of no fixed employment. If Ruthie came to mind it was incongruously as one of the sentimental Latin love songs to which she once danced all night would have sounded against the singing of political prisoners caged in the Black Maria between prison and court.

The adolescent children continued to live a normal life—if, Pauline objected, one could regard as normal any life in the context of what was happening. Joe did not agree wholly with Pauline, in practice—though of course he did in principle—that they were old enough to pitch the tenor of their young lives entirely to the defiant cries and dirges of the time and place in which they were growing up. The atmosphere at home was enough to counteract that of the school where—yes, he knew, he knew—at prayers every morning Hillela and Carole had to offer thanks for the infinite mercy of a God in whose name other children were given an inferior education, were banished with their mothers to barren reserves, and deprived of fathers forced to become migratory labourers in order that the children might not starve. That was what was happening in the Transkei, where the family had had such wonderful camping holidays, where they had bought delicious oysters for nothing—in the new currency, the equivalent of twenty-five cents a dozen!—from the Mpondo women who gathered them off the rocks. Carole, although only ten at the time of a great bus boycott, had been old enough to understand the issue through the cloud of sunset dust in which thousands of black people tramped at the roadside; for many weeks, when her mother had fetched her from school in the afternoons, they had not driven home to milk and biscuits but taken the road to Alexandra Township and picked up as many of those people as the car would hold. Carole sat on the knees of washerwomen and office cleaners, to make room; there was a rotting-cheese smell of dirty socks; she had been afraid when the police made her mother stop, asked for the passes of the black people, and told her she would be fined for overloading her car. Hillela was not living with the family then. She had been taken in later. The year before Sharpeville; so this epoch in Hillela's history was dated, in Pauline's house, by the public one, as at school human history was dated by the advent of Christianity, B.C. or A.D. By the time Hillela was living there, Pauline used to come home from regular visits to someone in prison (could it have been the red-haired woman?) and tell of the cockiness and courage of this person who must have been a friend—Carole knew her, Carole iced a cake Bettie baked for her, but the prison matron wouldn't allow the prisoner to receive it; Pauline brought it home again and the girls ate it.

Hillela, too, had driven with Pauline on an issue that could be understood through participation. Pauline canvassed in a campaign for a 'No' vote in the referendum for white people to decide whether the country should leave the British Commonwealth and declare itself a republic with a whites-only government. Hillela had not been frightened when men or women who came to the door were rude to Pauline: and she and Pauline laughed and didn't care, drove on comradely to the next street.

This seventeenth year—Hillela's—Joe was sometimes away in country districts defending chiefs who were deposed by the government for resisting laws which forced their people to reduce their herds and give up grazing rights, huddle out of the way of whites. When he was home she or Carole would be sent to carry a cup of tea into his small study where he once looked up—a smile for Hillela—and told her he was 'trying to find a legal needle in a haystack of bad laws—grounds to defend people who have no rights to defend, anymore'. At Olga's Friday night *seder* there was in the background a radio report of the hut-burnings and murders between chiefs who, Joe told in the other house, opposed the government and those who were bribed to support it. Arthur did not submit to Olga's objection that the temporal babble of the radio had no place in the timeless state of grace invoked at a Friday night ceremonial dinner. —A bunch of savages. What do they understand about culling, over-grazing. What's the point of throwing out money trying to teach them something. Let them go ahead and kill each other, that's all they know.—

There were no challenges over such statements in this house; Olga's George IV table was a peat-coloured pool reflecting the flowers of the centre piece, the tiny silver nest of sugared almonds before each place, the agreeable controlled faces of Olga's kind of people. Olga always took the option of compassionate distress, never choosing sides; her fears for herself were the basis of her abhorrence of violence. —My cook's afraid to go home there. It's too awful.—

Pauline and Carole were often out at protest meetings when Hillela came home from wherever it was she had been 'with her friends'—the explanation Pauline accepted, so long as Hillela phoned to say if she wanted to spend the night with one of the friends, and left the telephone number where she could be reached; a reasonable enough rule. Hillela helped Carole paint banners, NO TO A RACIST REPUBLIC; at school the headmistress announced a special church service and election of a student committee to plan a celebration for the public holiday on which the republic was to be declared. Once Hillela was going into a coffee bar when she saw a straggle of people coming down the centre of the city street, white people gathering flanks of accompanying black bystanders as they hampered traffic, NO TO A RACIST REPUBLIC: she handed her guitar to one of her friends and watched the group as if it were a wedding procession. Suddenly she ran forward, waving wildly, grasped Carole's hand; smiling, half-hopped-and-skipped, keeping up with her cousin and aunt for a few paces. Then she fell back. Pauline's grand head, made out among many, was disappearing round the corner.

In the coffee bar Hillela was greeted: Are you nuts? Where'd you go off to like that? She and her friends took turns to play the guitar and they sang 'House of the Rising Sun' and a new hit from America, 'We Shall Overcome'. The Greek proprietor did not mind these gatherings in Nick's Café, renamed, to keep up with somebody's times, somewhere, Arrivederci Roma; the impromptu music attracted custom. But when the kids started sharing round among themselves a home-rolled cigarette he recognized the scent of the stuff and lost his temper, chasing them out. At the same time—it must have been—a street or two away the police were breaking up an illegal procession. Pauline and Carole (she was under age, she would have had to appear *in camera*) were lucky not to have been among those arrested and charged under the Riotous Assemblies Act. Of which Pauline was perfectly aware, Joe warned.

Pauline's eyes were searching her invisible audience, her judges. —You must take some risks.—

—Not this particular one. With a child who's a minor. It isn't worth it.—

Mandy von Herz's removal to another school and the parental ban on her association with her friend Hillela made no difference, for a few months: they continued to spend most of their time together. The friendship ended of itself. Hillela's friend left school and took courses in beauty culture and modelling; she was a very pretty girl, her parents approved of her planning a future through the marketable assets of her face and body, so long as this was done in good taste. She went to country club dances with young men in velvet butterfly ties and white dinner jackets, instead of roaming away from the white suburbs. Hillela had moved on with friends-of-friends out of the group Mandy von Herz abandoned; she played her guitar on Sunday nights in a disused warehouse taken over by young people in the decaying end of town and, crammed into the cars of people she didn't know, went to parties that came about in Fordsburg and Pageview, areas Pauline had never taken her to because the people who lived there were not white and had no vote to canvass. She brought to Pauline and Joe's house one day someone introduced as Gert. Joe asked for the surname and Hillela turned to its owner. Prinslop, he said. Not coloured, but an Afrikaans boy: he seemed unable to put a sentence together—whether in his own language or English—in the company of Pauline, Joe, Carole, and Sasha back for the holidays, but he was offered supper. Pauline and Joe encouraged the young people to bring home their friends; the only way to know with whom they were mixing. Perhaps the boy was overwhelmed by the fluency of this highly articulate and talkative family. He looked like any bullet-headed blue-eyed son of a railway worker from Brixton or miner from a Reef dorp, the half-educated whites who were also the master race.

Hillela took Sasha along to the warehouse with Gert Prinsloo an evening soon after.

Indians and coloureds among the white boys and girls there are no shock to him; he doesn't go to a segregated school as his sister and cousin do. But Gert Prinsloo; the black boys at school call that kind 'the *Boere*': in a year or two he'll be a foreman yelling at black workers or a security policeman interrogating political prisoners.

Hillela has come to look for Sasha, missing in the herd-laughter of young males with newly-broken uncontrolled voices. —D'you want to go home?— She picks up her guitar; she is going to stay, anyway.

—What does that chap do? He looks like a cop.—

She gestures: he's just one of the people who turn up here. —I think works in a shop that sells tape-recorders and things. Radios. Or repairs them. But what he really does is play weird instruments—the homemade ones Africans play. It's fantastic, wait till you hear.—

She sits down on the floor beside Sasha, cross-legged, the guitar on her lap. She slips her hand over his forearm and opens her palm against his; their fingers interlace and close. As she has gestured: here, he and Hillela are just people who have turned up among others, known only by first names, there is no familial identity.

After a lot of noisy confusion, records set playing and taken off, girls shrilling and boys braying, this Gert Prinsloo settles himself in a space with two oxhide drums, a wooden xylophone and the little instrument of which out-of-tune reproductions are sold in every tourist shop. (Sasha has an *mbira* on the wall of his cubicle in Swaziland.) The son of the *Boere* has begun to drum. The girls and boys begin to clap and sway and stamp. They, crowd round him so that, from the sitting level, the player cannot be seen any more. But Hillela has pressed Sasha's hand down on the boards to show he and she will not get up. She is smiling, with her body sway- ing from the waist (like a snake rising from the charmer's basket, he was to remember, or like one of those nature films shown at school, where the expansion of a flower from its calyx is speeded up). This happens to the sound of Gert Prinsloo's drumming that makes of the walls of that place one huge distended eardrum, and to the flying notes, hollow and gentle, that he hammers out all over from the anvil of the wooden xylophone; but the rain-drop music of the *mbira* is lost in the beat of the crowd's blood, they overwhelm it with their own noise.

He comes over sniffing gutturally and making awkward genteel gestures to wipe the sweat off the back of his neck. His mouth is pegged down in bashful happiness.

—Where'd you learn?—

He laughs and hunches. —No, well, I just picked it up. First from listening, you know, watching. Then having a go myself. I'd always played guitar and that.—

But where? Someone must have taught you the music—it's not written down, is it? It's traditional African stuff.—

He moves his hands about, begins to speak and stops; he is embarrassed by and will only embarrass by what he has to tell. —We had a fish and chips shop. My mother, after my pa passed away. One of the boys that worked in the kitchen, he used to play these things. I got my guitar when I was about fourteen, and we both used to play it. He first taught me guitar.—

—He sings in their languages, too. Come on Gert, one of their songs. Come on. Please.—

It is always difficult for anyone to refuse Hillela; even people who don't have, like Pauline and Olga and the family, a duty towards her. She butts the boy with her guitar. He takes it with lowered head but when he begins to sing, in the black man's voice and cadence, in the black man's language—as white people hear work-gangs sing in the street, only their song making them present among the whites driving by—his inarticulacy, his fumbling self is broken away. That he is singing against the sobbing beat of a pop singer does not matter; a song that is not his own sings through him.

Hillela asks him to tell what he's singing about; producing him for Sasha; she knows the sort of thing Sasha likes to know.

At once there is difficulty, again, finding words. —Not really a song. Not really. It's like, you know, it's a native boy who's come here to town to work. He's singing, saying, we come to Jo'burg because we hoping we get something nice, but now we don't get it. That's all it's about.—

When the joint comes round Sasha feels her—Hillela—look to him before she takes a draw. But she needn't have worried, the weed has been smoked traditionally, long before white kids discovered it, by the local people in the country where he goes to school; he hasn't ever brought any home only because he doesn't want to be the one to be blamed for corrupting the two girls. And Hillela doesn't drink; he sees that.

Hillela was all right that night;—a member of the family, after all, was keeping an eye on her. Sasha had his mother's car to take her home in. First they delivered a lot of other people to various parts of town. It was late. Pauline was away at the All In African Conference in Maritzburg. Joe and Carole were so deep in the hibernation of the small hours that the house seemed empty; without Pauline all the watchtowers of the spirit were unattended, its drawbridges down. Anything could be let in, nothing would be recorded. Hillela fell asleep in Sasha's bed, this bed which his cousin and sister used to raid, beating him with pillows. There had been a coup; he had usurped and was on guard in place of his mother. He kept himself awake and measured the passing of darkness by the soft sensation of the girl's breath spreading on his neck and then drawing back like breath clouding and disappearing on a window pane. When he gauged he must, he separated her warmth from his own, so that once again she became herself, he became himself.

Carole did not know that her cousin was home from a party, had come into their bedroom and slid into her own bed.

Sasha switched on the witness of his lamp and searched his sheets for frail dark question-mark hairs that Bettie, who insisted on making his bed as a holiday treat for him, would recognize as not his brassy-blond sheddings. He did not want to be reminded—to have to remember in the morning.

Opportunities

Hillela could have been like anybody else. She had the opportunity. The same opportunity as Carole and Sasha. Or Olga's spoilt children—if that had been what she preferred. She was a white child, with choices; that was the irony of it. Young blacks had no choice, only necessity and plenty of ignorance about how to deal with that, in addition. Alpheus was so ambitious, so eager to better himself, become a lawyer, and now he had to saddle himself with a girl and baby on the way.—The trouble is we're much too timid in these matters. Scared of appearing to boss them around—but, in the end, it's not a kindness or a respect. When I saw the girl was living there, I should have told Alpheus straight out that he must take her to a birth control clinic. I should've taken her myself.—

Joe always listened to Pauline patiently. —Oh come on.—

—Well, damn it all, I'm paying for his courses, maybe I should use that to stop him making things impossible for himself. Nineteen years old. A baby, and next year another baby, how will he support them on a clerk's salary? We undertook to subsidise his studies, not a family.—

—Oh ma, it'll be lovely to have a little baby— Carole had pleaded happily, like that, for a puppy or a kitten.

—Oh *lovely*. A squalling infant while he's supposed to be studying for exams. I fixed up the garage so's he wouldn't have to live in a crowded location room, so's he'd have the kind of working conditions you kids have.—

—Bettie says, God has sent a child, what can you do.— Hillela quoted, and she and Carole laughed.

—She knows damn well. I had her fitted with a loop years ago. Alpheus's poor mother, doing four washes a week—

—And breaking the washing machine once a month.— Joe settled back into his soft chin philosophically.

—Rebecca's beaming all over, ma, she says her son is going to have a clever son like himself.—

—Poor old Rebecca! Where's he going to find to live?— Pauline's defiant eyes, questioning—them all: the room, the walls, and beyond. Philosophers like her husband had no answers, they knew only how to accept problems. Carole was a good enough little girl without the originality to swerve aside and seek answers to her mother's questioning, which she followed as naturalists say a duckling follows the first pair of feet it sees when it hatches. And Hillela—when did that intelligent girl (more intelligent than her own daughter, Pauline confessed confidentially to Joe; an intelligence more like Pauline's own than that Carole had inherited) when did the girl receive questions, or the possibility of answers, as *addressed to her?* —A whole family pushed into a garage in the yard. We can't have them here living under conditions as bad as those in a location. That wasn't the intention. Alpheus knows it. Rebecca knows it.—

If Sasha had been there he might have answered Pauline.

When Sasha was home Joe had to think of conversation that would start up their father-and-son relationship again; the battery went flat in the long partings, he himself away where the clamorous struggle between power and powerlessness was reduced to a sleepy hum and rustle of courtrooms through whose high windows light slanted as in a church, the boy away at that school for the future which had to be hidden in a little green African kingdom belonging to the 19th century. Joe had come out of his working cubbyhole on a Sunday morning. They were stretched on the grass drinking beer together. Joe mentioned young Alpheus had moved a girl into the garage and got her pregnant—Pauline felt she ought to have done something about it.

Sasha rolled right over before he spoke. —Emasculate him?—

A response lifted clean out of some five-finger-exercise liberation theology picked up from black boys at the school. It was easy for a youngster like Joe's to see things that priggishly hysterical way. Joe patiently ignored, patiently explained. —He's had a poor schooling and it's a hell of a struggle for him to keep up with the courses he's doing. She's absolutely right, the last thing he needs is a wife and kid as well. If he were a white boy, we'd all be calling it hopelessly irresponsible, and that's what it is. Towards his mother, to us, as well as himself. But what can one do.—

This question was not a question, was the summation of more than the small nuisance of Alpheus. Adults, who always knew what the children should do, at this time were withdrawn, in the presence of the children, into a state of waiting to be told or given a sign. For themselves. In various countries and eras children understand marriage as what it is for their parents in that place and period. Living with Pauline and Joe, the children saw that the meaning of marriage was that Pauline and Joe expected this sign from one another. The volume of the cheerful, restless house was turned down (as Pauline would sometimes stride into the girls' room, pulling a mock-agonized face, and turn down the volume of their record-player). The rooms strewn with evidence of everyone's activities were under dustsheets of adult preoccupation. The newspapers Pauline and Joe read and had always let pile up beside sofa and chairs, where they served in place of Olga's coffee tables, gave information but no guidance. Carole lifted her head like a young buck alert to something—what, it does not yet know—the mature animals have noticed, and Hillela went on with her translation of *Tartarin de Tarascon* while Pauline read out aloud to Joe: —'I don't want to be equal with Europeans. I want them to call us baas. I wish I can live till we rule, I will do the same to them: I will send the police to demand passes from whites. Their wives are going to wash the clothes for our wives.

We don't want to mix with whites, we left the African National Congress because we saw Europeans among us. We are fighting for the full rights of Africans. We do not fight to dance and sit with Europeans.'—

—The government bans a non-racial movement like the ANC, it gets black racists as primitive as its white ones. It bans again; and an even worse reaction will come. Are you surprised?—

When Pauline left the drawbridge down and the watchtowers unguarded she had been at a conference where blacks sat with whites. Only as an observer—she had got in with the help of black friends—the Chief had been a guest in her house. The civil rights organization to which she belonged was one of those that had decided not to take part; they said the All-In African Conference was a front, dominated by communists who had indoctrinated and infiltrated the African National Congress and its allies.

There were chants and freedom songs one didn't need to know the language to respond to with an almost physical expansion of being; after having been shut away, so white, so long. For herself, she came back home with 'Nelson Mandela's words in my ears, something you can't stop hearing'. Carole and Hillela saw her unblinking hunter's eyes stilled and magnified with real tears when she played the tape she had run while the man spoke for the first time in nine years (he had just been released from bans) to the assembly of all colours, to the government, and to the whole country. He knew what he could do. He called for a national convention. —Explain to the girls what that is, Joe.— And Joe explained that a national convention would be that meeting to culminate all meetings, one where white leaders from up there in the House of Parliament in Cape Town (on holiday one year, Olga had pointed out to Hillela and her sons the beautiful white building among oak trees) and black leaders emerged from prison, Underground and exile would decide in a proper and constitutional manner upon the dismantling of apartheid. Sasha, Carole

74

and Hillela had been taken to see a court in session, once. While Joe explained, they would be visualizing something rather like that, the solemnity at mahogany tables, the carafes of water, the security men standing round the walls to keep intruders from shouting *we do not fight to dance and sit with Europeans.*

Mandela's voice said that should the government fail to summon a national convention before declaring a republic, all sections of the population would be called on to stage a stay-at-home, a general strike, for three days. This would be a protest against the establishment of that republic based completely on white domination over a non-white majority, and also a last attempt to persuade the government to heed blacks' legitimate claims. The last day of the strike would coincide with the day on which the government intended to proclaim the republic. Pauline read out something again: Nelson Mandela's statement to the press that these demonstrations would not be anti-white, and would be peaceful.

Round about the Easter holidays—must have been; Sasha was home—a heavy brown paper parcel arrived at the house. Joe saw it first. —What's this?—

—Leave it to me.— Pauline slit the wrapping with a bread-knife, taking care not to penetrate the contents. Inside were piles of leaflets with the terminology that brought comfort, a confir-mation of what that house was, as the art dealers' catalogues, giving evidence of the survival of rare and beautiful objects, did in Olga's house. *All freedom-loving South Africans are called upon to make the next six weeks a time of active protest, demonstration and organization against a Verwoerd republic.* Carole went round the neighbourhood stuffing the leaflets into people's mailboxes and racing embarrassedly away while their dogs barked to get at her; Pauline kept a pile in her car from which she stuck sheets under the windscreen-wipers of other cars all over town, wherever she happened to park. Joe could not make any unprofessional outward show of partisanship but even Sasha put up a leaflet on the door of his room. It was discussed at table that blacks were stock-piling mealie-meal, sugar, and cheap tinned fish, in some rumour or premonition of being starved into submission while the police would hold the townships under siege.

Sasha was in a phase of anxious concern for physical fitness; he and Hillela played squash at a health club, that month before the stay-at-home. So it was known where Hillela was passing her time. Sasha and Hillela also went very often to the cinema together on those Highveld autumn afternoons when there is no wind, no cloud to move across the sun, summer growth has ceased but no leaf falls: the day stands still. A crime to be inside a dark stale cinema on such an afternoon, Pauline would have said. There were few other people; expanses of empty seats separated dim figures. Sasha's forearm stayed aligned, rigid and tight, against Hillela's along the single armrest between them. They saw any film, many films; neither ever told Carole, Pauline or Joe about these films.

Sasha did not accompany his cousin again to her warehouse haunt; no-one was surprised that that sort of thing did not have much appeal for him. He played chess with his father, instead. One evening Joe got up in the middle of the game the moment Pauline came home. In Joe's pale face expression was buried in complicated folds; even urgency did not show.

—You'd better get rid of those leaflets.—

—I don't think there are more than a dozen or so left ... why? What's happened?—

—Get rid of them now, tonight. It's what might happen. There are raids all over the place. Four whites have been detained in Pretoria. Liberal Party people. They're watching everybody.—

—Are we going to burn them?—

Pauline didn't answer Carole; her big head was lowered, not seeing her invisible audience, now.

—Put them down the lavatory, do whatever you like. Only get rid of them. And Pauline, we'd better go through other papers arid stuff we may have. If they come, there isn't anything they won't manage to find incriminating, at the moment. And don't use our dustbin. They grub everywhere.—

Joe took two cartons of papers away in his car before he and Pauline went to bed. But nobody noticed that Sasha had not taken the leaflet off his door. *All freedom-loving South Africans are called upon to make the next six weeks a time of active protest.* Only Hillela. —What about that?— She was passing him in the passage.

—What about it?—

It was not for her to say. She was accustomed to different practices in the different houses where she was taken in as one of the family.

He did not like to linger with Hillela just outside his bedroom door. He went inside and closed it.

On the Highveld in May the sun is still bright—always bright, up there, while the air enters the nose with a whiff of winter's freezing ether; something to be remembered in tropical parts of Africa, where much of the time it gives great heat but no light, buried in soggy cloud. May was the month when Olga changed her wardrobe. When Hillela used to come back from Rhodesia to spend the holidays with her, she would help Olga carry silky dresses and delicate-coloured sandals to the store-cupboards, and bring back from them garments of suède and angora against which she would pass her cheek. Olga still regarded it as her pleasure and her duty to fit out the girl at the same time as she shopped, each change of season, for new fashions for herself. An arrangement had been made for Hillela to come shopping with her, but she telephoned to postpone their date. —People say there's some trouble in town. We'll put it off until things settle down again.—

It was the appointed day for the beginning of the stay-at-home. As young freedom-loving South Africans Carole and Hillela had been kept home from school.

—Olga planned to take you shopping this afternoon? Today?—
Pauline smiled, shook her head, shook her head, over her sister.
—Hundreds of people are being arrested, but of course they're black, and so far as they're concerned, she only knows her treasure Jethro and her treasure the cook and her treasure the gardener. Meetings are prohibited. You can be detained without trial. The place is swarming with police. And Olga's shopping trip is postponed.—

Hillela went to the city, anyway—with Carole and Pauline, to see how effective or not the strike was. Joe had told Alpheus not to come to the office but the black servants went about their work and moved as usual along their own backyard network, placing ten-cent bets with the Fah-Fee runner and borrowing a cup of sugar or an onion in the exchange of plenty from white kitchens. The garbage had not been collected but rot doesn't begin to smell in one day. All the white suburbs were quiet.

So was the city; but it was a different kind of quiet. There was only the static cackling gibberish from radio communication in passing police cars. Without its volume of blacks the city had gone mute. Without its blacks it was a place of buildings. —Like Sunday.— Carole was right; on Sundays the blacks were in their ghettos, that was where they were supposed to be, then, but this was a Monday, and they had not come back. The rhythm of life of this city, that had its black morning spate and black afternoon ebb, was withheld. The half-empty streets waited for a drama that was still to be written. For the present, there was an aspect strange as natural disaster, about which there is never anyone to question: the few blacks in straggling queues at the bus-stations, in the streets, looked the woman and two girls in the eye without a flicker of any acknowledgement. Why they had come to work, whether these white people approved them as the good kind of black or thought them traitors to their cause—that was not whites' business.

Pauline drove out in the direction of Soweto but could not risk getting too near, with the girls in the car. There were police patrol cars everywhere. From the vantage point where Pauline, Carole and Hillela stopped, the distant cubes of Soweto houses were miles of tombstones in a vast graveyard; yet all the life that was gone from the city was down there; if you had been able to get near enough.

Alpheus and his girl were walking out of the yard gate as Pauline and the girls arrived home. He opened the gate for the car, and Pauline paused as it passed him. —The stay-at-home seems to be fairly successful. We've just been into town.—

Alpheus and his girl were dressed to stroll out on a public holiday. He had a way of standing quietly as if waiting to be dismissed. He smiled. —Thank you.—

In the yard, Pauline sat a moment with her hands on the steering-wheel. —What does he thank for? The information? He's always like that. If every black were like him, nothing would ever change. If Joe hadn't told him to, he wouldn't even have supported the strike. Maybe it's a mistake to have removed him from the condition of his own people. I don't know, anymore.—

Carole and Hillela also stayed at home when the school held its prayers and celebrations for the Republic. On the day, Pauline and Joe kept open house for friends as depressed and confused as themselves; when Hillela left to go and lunch at Olga's (a compensation offered for the postponed shopping trip) they were arguing over Mandela's reasons for calling off the stay-at-home on its second day—as for the national convention, no-one had ever expected for a moment the government would consider that.

—This is the lovely young daughter I didn't have.—

It was too chilly to swim, but in Olga's pavilion beside the pool Jethro carried round a whole poached salmon—the stately pink corpse laid out with the cook's radish roses and swags of

79

golden mayonnaise—and Hillela was allowed a glass of the French champagne served in honour of some guests, in the way of Arthur's business, from another country. The lady was settled in her chair like a beautifully-marked butterfly—amber hair and the deep blue oval of a sapphire on each earlobe, pale fingers banded with gold and diamonds and tipped with red nails. She made soft noises of approval over Hillela. Jethro paused in his procession to beam on the girl, while everyone except Arthur smiled at them both. —Miss Hilly, you been there to my country again? You staying all the time here in Jo'burg now, you don't like go there sometime see you daddy?—

Olga charmed, speaking to him in the third person. —Next time Jethro goes home, he's going to take Miss Hilly with him, isn't that right?— And Jethro bowed his way round, laughing.

—He thinks of the children in this house as his own.—

—How wonderful. You can't get anybody loyal like that, not in Europe, not at any price.—

Olga took care not to neglect her young niece in the presence of distinguished company. She turned aside from talk of the villa in Italy, belonging to these guests, which she and Arthur were being pressed to visit, and had a confidential moment with Hillela. —How is Pauline ... I worry about Pauline. What is the point of all the things she gets herself involved in. That bus boycott—they had to pay in the end, surely. The Republic—it's been declared ... And she neglects herself. She used to be so striking-looking. If you live here you must abide by the law of the country.—

Olga and Arthur believed you must abide by the law of the country but were once again making contingency plans not to go on living there.

—There's a delightful place on the market, not far from ours. I think the position's even better than ours. Why don't you buy a little pied-à-terre in Italy? It'd be lovely to have you as neighbours now and then—

—The way things are going, it might have to be more than that!— Olga laughed when she said it, and the butterfly lady did not pause to take in the inference: —Though I can understand, if I lived in this beautiful country, with those wonderful vineyard estates at the Cape, and those marvellous beaches, so clean—not like Europe—uncrowded, I wouldn't see much reason to go anywhere else—

Arthur broke in when he saw an advantage in doing so. —We've got a place at the Cape. Nice place right on the best beach in the country. You can come out and spend as long as you like there, any time.—

—I still think we should take up Michael's offer to look round for us in Italy.—

Arthur had a way of blinking, refusing to acknowledge the regard of others, conversely, as Pauline always felt that regard, sought it. His head hung forward from his thick shoulders while he chewed—like an ox, yes.

Hillela had her first driving lesson on the day a republic was declared; the day on which one drives for the first time is like that on which one first found one's balance on a bicycle—something never forgotten. Her cousin Clive had just passed his driving test. Stopping, starting, giggling at herself, with Clive sitting beside her she went up and down Olga's long drive the whole afternoon, pausing only when admiring Jethro came over the lawn with the cream scones and tea, and finally ending her first journey only when Olga called out that drinks were being served, and the car must be 'put to bed'. Very carefully Hillela drove it successfully into its bay beside Arthur's two other cars.

Clive presented his pupil, an arm across her shoulders the way he would walk off a sports field with a fellow player. —You should just see how quickly Hillela caught on. She can even declutch properly, already.— By some quirk of heredity, he had Pauline's black, demanding eyes, and the red, live mouth of the handsome male. No-one took a photograph. But Olga kept the image of the pair, the children belonging to her sister Ruthie and herself, so full of their little achievements, so happy, so innocent in their burgeoning, although she could never place the day, the year when it was imprinted.

Olga drove her niece back to Pauline's house. She embraced her and held her hands before letting her leave the car. She seemed saddened by something she could never say—all children who are sent to boarding-school know this mood in adults, who have exiled them.

—I'll see you next Monday, then, Olga. And thanks for a lovely day.—

Olga took comfort and forgiveness. —Oh yes, darling. And I know exactly what we're going to buy. Monday—if everything's all right. But I'm sure this whole business is over now.—

Nelson Mandela went Underground after the All-In African Conference Pauline had attended in Maritzburg. When he surfaced he was tried and imprisoned; and when he was taken from prison and tried once again, this time for treason, and sentenced to life imprisonment, no-one was allowed to record the speech he made from the dock; so the schoolgirl Hillela, present when her aunt played a tape-recording of his speech made at Maritzburg, was one of the few people to hear the sound of Mandela's voice for many years, and perhaps to remember it. She had the opportunity to do so, anyway.

Through the high hum of the blood in adolescence, that distances the voices of adults, the tense discussions between Pauline and Joe continued as if taking place somewhere else and from time to time breaking in with a name or phrase overheard. It was cold; the snug of a sweater round the neck; a fire at night; it must have been June. Mandela was the name. From that Underground where he had gone he sent portents and messages like those the Latin writers Hillela was having to construe for the winter exams said came from the flight of birds or from sibyls speaking through the mouths of caves. Pauline supported Mandela's call for an international economic boycott of South Africa. 'Supported', when obtruding from adult conversation at Olga's, applied to whether or not a divorced wife received alimony from an ex-husband, or whether a relative was adequately provided for by her family. (For example Len—his daughter understood from oblique references—did not 'support' her.) 'Supported', in Pauline and Joe's dialogue which plunged into tunnels of silence or absent attention to other things but never ceased, perhaps not even in dreams, meant that one or both of them thought they had found some sort of sign. Not the sure and certain instruction they had been waiting for, but something to which one could attach oneself, and feel the tug of history. Pauline supported economic boycott as a way out: for the thousands of blacks imprisoned and banned as, it seemed, the dismal only result of the politics of protest; for the whites, her friends, braver than herself, who were also banned or imprisoned as part of the same tactical failure Mandela admitted. And for herself, companion of the blacks' route, with nowhere to go now that marches were banned, fearful of and not free to enter (a family, a husband's surer contribution within legal opposition to consider) the unimaginable darkness of the Underground— for her, rescue from being stranded, from ending up white as her sister Olga was white.

There was the unaccountable doubt of Joe to set Pauline's hands raking up through the electric crackle of her hair.

—But what are you talking about? Who will suffer? People who work in towns and have shoes on their feet and drink bottled beer and spray their armpits with deodorants? Or the ones on the farms and in the 'homelands' who live on dry mealie-meal? How much more can they suffer than they do already? What will boycotts deprive them of they don't already lack? What've *we* got we couldn't do without if it means bringing down this government—if we *really* mean we're ready to sacrifice these wonderful privileges everyone's afraid we'll miss so much—

—And what do those rural people use to buy that bit of mealie-meal? Money sent home by the labourers in the mines and the factories, the construction workers. And if—if—what an hypothesis that is, when has economic boycott ever been fully imposed—and if American and European investment were to dry up, what would happen to those mines, factories, building projects? What happens to the men they employed, the men who sent back the money for mealie-meal?—

—You sound like a member of the Chamber of Commerce. I can't believe it. As if you were trying to explain economics to a five-year-old. For Christ' sake! I *know* the consequences as well as you do. They've made the calculation because there's nothing else left to do—except kill. Don't you see? They've made the decision—one generation more to suffer, but if it's going to be worse than it's ever been, it'll be for something.—

—Pauline ... you can't even pass a starving cat in the street.—

—I'll leam. I'll learn.—

—No, my girl. Against your own good sense and reason, you actually imagine it quite differently. You dream the American bankers will all band together in the name of FREE-DOM for South African blacks and the boys in Pretoria will take down the flag and tear up the statute book.—

Pauline's hair fell across her cheeks, flew back. —Hah, you're the one who doesn't face facts. Everything's going to come right through the loopholes you manage to find in disgusting laws. The government stops up one mouse-hole, you find another. You work yourself to death, but what's changed? What will you be at our Nuremberg?— In her face was the cruel pleasure, already distressing her while indulged, of turning her fears for Joe into hurt inflicted on him. —The one who tried to serve justice

84

through the rule of law, or the one who betrayed justice by trying to serve it through the rule of unjust laws?——

Yet soon the controller of the four winds in that house was back in self-conflict again, a state felt by others in the house as a change in atmospheric pressure, in diet, rather than understood. The Swazi fruit bowl was often empty; Bettie borrowed the girls' pocket-money to buy soap flakes on Rebecca's 'day' because she had told Pauline 'two time', without result, that the supply had run out. Another sign had come from the Underground. It was a spear; the shape of the object itself, its clear and familiar associations (the dates of Kaffir Wars to be memorised, the mascot shields and assegais sold along Len's roads in Rhodesia) pierced the half-attention with which the new phase of the Pauline-Joe dialogue was registered by the children. *Umkhonto we Sizwe:* translated for whites as 'The Spear of the Nation'; the voice from nowhere and everywhere—Mandela's—announced it.

—Why should whites be told they can join Umkhonto when we couldn't be members of the ANC? I mean, if there's been a change of policy, why doesn't it apply to ANC as well?——

Joe had a special, almost sorrowful tone for use in court when it was necessary to suggest to an evasive witness that he was in fact well aware of circumstances of which he claimed ignorance. —But, Pauline, isn't it just exactly in order that no-one will be able to say there's been a change of policy. Controlled, symbolic violence—that's the business of Umkhonto. ANC doesn't change; it retains its principles—

—Yes, yes, non-violence, that's all the difference is. He was talking about its stand against violence—

—Wait a minute. If it were to retain its non-violent principles but yield another, it would be impossible to deny officially that it had not changed *at all*, impossible to refute the charge that Umkhonto or the Spear of the Nation or whatever you like to call it is proof that the ANC has abandoned non-violent tactics.

ANC hasn't changed, can't, won't change; not at this stage. ANC is what it always was, the classic non-violent, non-racial liberation movement. Its claim for support from the West depends on its clean record—victim of but not prepetrator of violence. Credibility with black Africa and black Americans depends on its clean record—a revolutionary movement by blacks for blacks. These two principles are the moral basis. If you accept the need for violence, you lose credibility with the West from which, though god knows why, help is still expected to come. If you let in whites, you lose credibility with the blacks outside—and some inside, as we know.——

The exchange is suspended by the disruption of the end of a meal, the need for sleep (the fire crumbling down; Carole and Hillela sauntering off to bed) or the time come for a return to Joe's office. But the preoccupation continues, present as the creak of floorboards in the night, and sounds now from here, now from there, in the house and from the garden where, on Saturdays, Alpheus earns his lodging by the token of weeding the grass or burning leaves.

If Olga had seen Pauline during that winter she would have noticed with concern the skin, darkened like bruised rose petals, and the minute cysts, grains of waste her body was not eliminating, under Pauline's eyes; the impatient flick of the lids with which she monitored thoughts she did not want to have.

—So we are invited to join in the dirty work.——

—No. On the contrary. It's a recognition that you don't have to be black to have the revolutionary temperament.——

—That's fine. But *blacks* who don't have the revolutionary temperament may still say 'I support the ANC but I won't join a violent movement'—and keep their self-respect.——

When friends were present, voices rose and clashed. Lying on her bed in the room filled with all the sentimental sexual totems of young girls who go to good schools, Hillela heard the drum-roll and piercing notes of adult ritual, produced by a preoccupation and passion remote from the yearnings, wild anticipations and dreads that do not come from outside but grow like the bones and flesh, the tree of self.

—What about '60, that leaflet the communists put out? The police were picking them up from gutters everywhere ... The Party called upon communists, then, to work with the Congress Alliance. They'd found a way to get round the national versus socialist revolution wrangle. For whites, South Africa is an advanced capitalist state in the last stage of imperialism; but for blacks, it is still a colony. So a traditional national movement like the ANC has a 'progressive function' that a workers' party can support. Well, now they've got where they wanted to be; the government's done it for them. Protest politics has come to a dead end. The time's come when blacks must think about revolutionary tactics. Whites are invited to join Umkhonto, and who's going to join?—the CP whites, those in the Congress of Democrats, and those Underground. ANC's become a front organization, a national monument, and the white communists are entrenched in its avatar, Umkhonto. So they'll make sure the national black revolution is a red one.—

—Oh my god, here's another who sees a red under every bed.—

—We all made a mistake, not joining the Congress of Democrats.—

—But why?—

—We should have got in there and kept it what it was supposed to be, kept the communists out of control.—

—And what would you have made of it? Another dead end?—

—Oh Joe, I know you think we're all dodos—

—No, no, I know *I* am. My wings are atrophied; I don't expect anything, of myself—

Their laughter prodded him; they were drinking wine as part of their ceremonial palaver.

87

—But we do! *I* do!— Pauline's fierce cry. —I wish I'd joined COD when I nearly did, after Maritzburg. Then I'd be in it up to the neck now.—

—You'd be prepared to see things blown up?—

—Things, yes. Buildings. Their white House blown up, there in van Riebeeck's garden; that would shift their backsides if nothing else will.—

—And people?—

—Controlled violence against symbolic targets doesn't take life.—

—Oh no? Some old nightwatchman who gets in the way? Passersby? There's no such thing as completely controlled violence.—

—Oh I don't know ... Of course you're right. I just don't know.—

—It's necessary to demystify, always demystify. Controlled violence is a sanitized term for killing. Killing anyone who gets in the way of your symbolic target. Including your own people, if a bomb blows up in their own hands. Yourself. Killing is killing. Violence is pain and death.—

—The police have been handing those out to blacks, year after year.—

—Yes. Let the blood be on the government's hands.—

Killing is killing. Violence is pain and death. Torn streamers from the fabric of adult life, drifting across the imaginary scenes and dialogues in the busy consciousness of a seventeen-year-old girl match nothing there. To kill or not to kill: her urgent choices are not these, could not even conceive of these. Indecision is between which group of friends she should choose to 'go with' more steadily than the other; whether to enjoy being swayed by some dominating personality in the one, or to enjoy being herself the boldest, the brightest, the most magnetic, in the other. She would be smouldering over some piece of injustice meted out to her at school and seeing herself—where?—anywhere she has never been, some apartment in a city never seen, Los Angeles or Paris, as comfortable as Olga's house but of course not at all like Olga's, or Pauline's or anybody's, with good-time friends (but not like the friends she makes do with now) or just one person, a man older than herself who adores her and makes love to her and takes her all over the world. Or perhaps with a boy her age whom she has not yet met, but who would have a certain family likeness without being in any way connected with, not even speaking the same language as any family she knew—a boy with whom she would play the guitar and grow vegetables, make love and have babies the way ordinary people (even Alpheus and his girl) did.

Violence is pain and death. That was an after-world that might not exist at all, like heaven or hell, for her—a girl who did not have the Jewish faith under which one school had listed her, nor the Christian faith in the promises and threats of morning prayers at the next school; at most, something like old age, in which no seventeen-year-old can believe for herself. They—the voices elsewhere in the house—had thoughts that did hot reach her; and she had some—and some experiences relived and pondered not more than the thickness of a room's wall away from, but unknown to them: inconceivable. The girl must have known that: they never made the emotional show Olga did, but she knew she was their own child to them, just as their son was.

It is unlikely that Hillela will have remembered at any time the exaggerated emotions and highly-coloured scroll of unrolled life that absorbed her totally when she was seventeen. It is the torn streamers that were to come back to her: *killing is killing, violence is pain and death.*

Sasha worked in a bottle store that winter's school holidays and his cousin and her current band of friends came in one lunch-time to buy beer and a yellow concoction they had a craze for, called—the sort of useless detail that is all that remains of a period—Neptune's Nectar, made of cane spirit and synthetic passion-fruit flavouring. Sasha, stacking wine bottles, lifted his head from behind boxes only to meet Hillela's eyes (she gave him an imitation of himself for Carole's sisterly amusement, later) and then disappeared as if he had not seen the band. For her it was the old game of shop, from the occasions when all the cousins played together. The band surrounded him. It was his turn as shopkeeper; but Sasha refused to serve them. —You're under age.—

Sasha changed so much each time he was away at school; once it was his voice, now it was his jaw which, anticipating the man's face it would one day support, had set out the structure of a squared chin dented where the two halves of his face had joined in Pauline's womb. It always took a few days for Hillela to forget what he had looked like the last time he was home; to find him again.

—Oh don't be wet.— She balanced between irritation and wariness, and he knew it, knew Hillela. By claiming family influence over him, she would gain prestige if he gave in, but if he refused, she would on the contrary be associated with his 'wetness'.

—Go and ask one of the others.— He indicated, eyes on his uninterrupted activity, two men attending to customers along the aisles of bottles glaucous as cabochon rubies and emeralds.

—The hell with it, let's push off.—

—There's another place right on the corner.—

Hillela stood willing him to turn round and do her bidding. Two girls and a boy began pulling bottles at random out of cases and clinking them onto shelves all around Sasha, pushing and laughing. —Let's give him a hand, man.— —Slow's a funeral.—

Hillela looked at them as if she had just walked into the shop and had had her attention to her own errand momentarily distracted by an incident taking place there. The cashier's head was turned; the pudgy ears of the man behind the counter responded with shopkeepers' alertness, specific to petty theft as a hunting dog's to gunshot. They were Hillela's friends; Sasha could have turned, now, and cried out—*Hillela ... !* To save his pocket-money job, schoolboy well-fed by Pauline and Bettie, being educated for higher occupations at a school open to all races? (There were things Sasha was cursed, from the beginning, to know beyond his years.) Or to give her 'friends' the satisfaction of confirming that he didn't have his share of their mindless boldness, happily, swaggeringly defying harmless conventions of behaviour while remaining perfectly safe within the terrible conventions of this country. *Hillela!* He didn't cry. She didn't hear.

Hillela walked out of the shop. The manager came down the aisle, his male breasts spread by shoulders drawn back authoritatively. —These are your friends? I don't want them here.—

—Calm down, old man. We don't want to be here either, old man.— They talked all over him agilely. Looked for Hillela, but she was gone; out they sauntered.

Only when they had left did Sasha commit his kind of disloyalty to her, that she would never know. —I don't know any of them. They walked in and started.—

That evening brother, sister and cousin gathered in the girls' room; Hillela was at home, for once. Carole was grateful and shyly expressed her pleasure in whatever small ways she could when Hillela stayed in; they did not listen to, but she played again and again a record singing about love in a hoarse, laryngitic style that had become her unconfessed mating call. Carole was working in the library of a newspaper; Hillela was a temporary hand in a depot for a photographic laboratory. Like rookies in an army, these recruits to the world of daily bread-winning compared and gossiped about their holiday jobs. —I'd rather dig ditches. Anything's better than selling people stuff for more money than you've paid for it.— The great-grandson of a Lithuanian pedlar was generations away from his progenitor's necessity; and he was also Pauline's son. —What about writing out dockets for little rolls of film all day long—'Why aren't they ready?', 'This print's got a scratch', "There's something wrong with the colours'.— —Well at least developing film is a service, it's *doing* something for the money— —But Hilly's not the one who does it, is she? She's just in between.— —Most of the people in the big cities are just that. Taking money, handing over something they know nothing about. I'd rather dig ditches.—

The record had come to an end and Carole glided to place the arm at the start again without the other two noticing. Hillela addressed her male cousin's lowered eyes and the mouth that adults interpreted as sulky but was an expression of need for answers they could not give him. —Most people know nothing about anything they do. About why they do anything. It's just because they feel like it ... it's fun. Doesn't mean anything. They just go ahead.—

If that might have signalled the surfacing of what had happened at the bottle store in her lunch hour, a confession or a defiance, how could one tell, with Hillela—incidents of that magnitude in the adolescent world which would have caused a family rumpus at Olga's, where political passions were the politics of family relationships, at Pauline's could not expect to attract any attention. Certainly not in comparison with what was about to happen in her house that night. Before Sasha could respond—if he would have responded at all—Bettie came in (Bettie never knocked on the children's doors, even though they were grown up, now). —There's someone who wants Miss Pauline. I told him she's out but he says no, then he wants someone else to come.—

—Who is it? Man or woman?—

—A boy. (Bettie's way of indicating a black man.) I think I see him sometime here before ... He won't say the name.— She was used to Pauline's semi-clandestine black visitors; pulled a you-know-the-kind face: these people always got money out of Pauline, while she had to work for hers.

Sasha followed her, but came back at once. —He says he knows you, Carole. I've never seen the guy.—

He sat at the kitchen table with his elbow resting on it and the chair turned away, legs stretched and spread, smiling, a man in the self-confidence of his rotundity and charm. It was as if the three young people were arriving before him by appointment, for an interview. He leaned forward and held out a hand. —Carole, how's it? Your mummy not here? You remember me, mmh?—

Carole's voice rose to cover embarrassment at Bettie's confining a friend of the family to the kitchen. —Oh yes! But come inside!—

—Donsi. Donsi Masuku. And I've seen your sister, too. So this's the young man of the family—

In the livingroom he made himself comfortable. —When do you think she'll come, your mother? Okay, whenever it is, that's all right— I'll wait. What's your name? Sasha. Sa-sha. That's a Russian name, ay? Sasha, can you get me a beer—why don't we have a beer together? What kind of records have you got—I heard some music going ... You got any Duke? How I love that man. I used to play trumpet, I used to play drums, one time ... I was even with a group. Did you ever hear of the Extra Strongs—the name comes from those peppermint sweets, you know them, XXX Mints. Yes. That was our group. We took part in the Big Band shows, Soweto, Cape Town, Durban. We cut a disc. Old seventy-eight. One day if I find it, I'll bring it to play for you, Carole, you'll see. But nowadays I haven't got the wind (slapping his belly) or it's got stuck there inside (making them laugh at him). Haven't got the time, maybe haven't got the heart for it ... Now—come on, Donsi, what's the matter with you, man! Must never lose the heart, you know that—I'm telling you, kids, never lose the heart, because if you lose that ... they've got you!—

Pauline and Joe walked in on him dancing with Carole and Hillela. Pauline's eyes had a moment of stillness, hesitation, when she saw who he was: one of those whose followers said things, now, she had read out aloud. *I want them to call us baas. Their wives are going to wash the clothes for our wives. I don't want to be equal with Europeans. We left the African National Congress because we saw Europeans among us.* But the innocent bodily warmth, the faint odour of black beneficed the house, absolved whiteness; she came forward in irresistible pleasure of release. Joe offered more beer and then excused himself; he had work to finish. —You legal men do your best for us, we know.— Joe smiled his creased smile. The compliment tossed at him was a convention of guestly graciousness, total insincerity innocent of critical innuendo: the delightful man knew Joe was aware he was an initiator of a move that blacks should not take bail and should refuse defence in the white man's courts against the white man's laws. —Lovely kids you've got. They've been giving me a good time. Really nice. And she can play the guitar—this one!—

—I'm so glad they looked after you. How *are* you, Donsi? Good god, you come out of detention looking as if you've been on holiday—I saw your name listed in the paper and I was so pleased ... but I didn't know where you'd be—somebody told me your wife and the children had gone to her mother somewhere in Natal.—

—Yes, mealie-pap, mealie-pap, nothing but mealie-pap, you put on weight, they fatten you up for the kill.—

—Well, you were never exactly dainty.—

—But it was muscle, you know? I've always been keen on body-building ... but in there, man! Look—can I talk to you now?— He leaned in a swift sketch of urgency and confidentiality, then looked up beaming dismissal at the three young people. —Bye-bye girls, and thanks, hey. Bye, Sasha.—

As they left the room sharing the mood of his good nature he was already speaking at a different pitch, his chair pulled close to

Pauline. —Bongi and our kids are there in the car. Outside your house.—

In the passage, Carole stopped. —All this time, in the car! Ma'll be furious with me. Why didn't he *say* ...— Her brother, at once irritated by his sister's subservience to their mother, left them, and her cousin soothed her by closing their bedroom door on the adults and making her giggle: —Can you just imagine Pauline sitting for an hour in a dark car while Joe was inside dancing?—

They read in bed. Then Pauline was there, as a window flies open in a storm. —Now listen—you are not to mention this to anyone. D'you understand? *Anyone* at all. Give me the extra blankets out of your cupboard. You don't need two pillows, Carole ... They're going to sleep here for a couple of hours and then they'll be gone. If ever anyone mentions his name, you've never heard of him, all right?—

The wind of pursuit, of exposure, the wind snuffed by police dogs entered the frail shelter of personal talismans, blew on the Imari cats and the records of love songs. In the night, there was the refugee wail of a baby; very early, the unmistakable sounds of Pauline, her pace, her pattern of movements producing clinks and clatters in the kitchen, accompanying dreams with the sound-track of consciousness. Carole probably woke as well, but did not speak. Before she sank back to sleep again, or perhaps in the precious shallows before it was time to emerge for school, Hillela heard with the obscure anguish of the subconscious, Donsi Masuku's laugh. Happy dangerous laugh, affirmation that, like the baby's cry of protest, could prick the ears of straining dogs and vibrate the antennae of police cars.

Sasha had slept in the livingroom. The wife had neatly made up again Sasha's bed after she and her husband had occupied it. There were still-warm places on the rug where the black children had been bedded down. One of them must have been a boy; a small toy car with one wheel missing was left where it had rolled. Sasha did not hoard souvenirs, posters and photographs the way the girls did. When he was away at school, there was nothing of him in his room at home that could not as well have belonged to the household in common: books, chess set, squash racket. He rescued the little car from some other small boy's childhood, and kept it on his desk.

The house had the air of having been suddenly quit. Joe always left early; Pauline was not there. The night visitors were gone; Carole went into the yard to feed the cat: —Their car's still here.— A horn of hair stood up on her brother's unbrushed head. She twirled it, he batted at her hand. —You look like a unicorn. No, a cross rhino.— —Leave me.— But the girls' teasing attention was a kind of homage. His cousin came to the breakfast table in pyjamas. Her softness rose and fell here and there against the pink cotton knit, thinned by many launderings, as she helped herself to jam or juice. She spoke with her mouth full, smiling and gesturing, instinctively choosing her moment. —You should have seen him yesterday, when a couple of us went to say hello— he stuck up his neck behind a pile of boxes just like an ostrich, you know that snooty look they have, looking down at you.—

While the family were eating the early supper Bettie had cooked, they heard a familiar car rattle into the yard; Pauline's imminent presence was, as always, like the turn of a tide. Expressions changed. Then she was among them, her hair smelling of dust, a streak of red from inner corner to pupil in one of her great eyes. No-one asked where she had been. —What has Bettie given you? Chicken and rice *and* potatoes— nice and starchy. Oh, I bought a box of avocados on the road—Carole, let's have a salad—there's a dear.— Sasha was suddenly smiling at his mother in amazement, amusement, in love; another benediction on the house. He left the table and came back with a glass of wine for her. —I don't know if it's all right. There's a bottle open in the fridge.—

Someone must have come to fetch the car Masuku left behind. Next evening Carole remarked that it was gone, to Sasha and Hillela, who seemed to have forgotten it was ever there.

Pauline kept the mood, like a heightened colour rising to the cheeks, of having allowed herself to act purely on the impulse of her nature, which was simply to give. Principles, political allegiances with their attendant reservations were the rational and intellectual restraints laid upon this instinct; she revered them, and so the mood alternated with a kind of nervous shame. She had commandeered all the money in the house that night—her own, Sasha's first week's pay, even got Joe to drive to his office at midnight to fetch whatever might be in the petty cash kept there—to give to the family in flight. The spectacle of the woman with her open-mouthed sleeping baby on her back, trooping into the kitchen, the two other children dressed for the journey to exile in white knee-socks, as if for the only occasions the young woman had to go by, roused in Pauline some sort of atavistic consciousness of like journeys she herself with her children could have been propelled on—the panic of pogroms, the screech of cattle trains leaving a last station, the crawl of the homeless along the roads of war. Alone in the kitchen at five in the morning, she cooked food for the family to take along; she prepared a suitcase of medicaments and clothes. Without comment, at her request, Joe helped Donsi Masuku siphon petrol from his car to fill the tank of hers.

Bettie had found cupboards left in disorder, the kitchen raided. Pretending not to know, she demanded where the big plastic container was. And the flask to keep the breakfast coffee hot?

To the young people, Pauline added an awkward rider to her warning. —*Nothing*—to anyone. Is that clear? Not to any of my friends, either.—

This time Pauline had not refused succour; and the man who sought it was not one of those whom she 'supported'. She had known this Donsi as a young black party-goer at white houses.

Everybody knew him, then; a messenger in some editorial office who tagged along with those favoured invited guests, black journalists, for the free drinks, and paid for his presence by his ability to enjoy himself and generate in his hosts the pleasure of getting on well with blacks. He was (to the perception of whites, anyway) too much of a fat and happy light-weight to be of use in the political struggle, which in those circles meant the African National Congress. His name began to come up as a regional leader of those who left the Congress because they did not want to mix with whites until, they said, white power was broken; it was only later it was noticed he wasn't at parties any longer. His people did not want to dance or sit with whites. But she had found him dancing with her daughter and niece; and she had risked arrest by driving him and his family to a place near the border where someone was waiting to smuggle them across. Donsi Masuku had learnt from a relative in the political branch of the police (there were family connections who betrayed, there were family connections who saved) that he was about to be rearrested and charged, this time in a major trial for treason. What she had done was not something she could explain to friends with whom she supported the African National Congress, and who (no doubt) had heard of her failure to give asylum in a context she might be expected to. Joe had witnessed; but Joe would not confront her with the paradox. Joe could not, because he himself never would share her fierce faction partisanship or her ferocious doubts: Joe (as she taunted him) defended all who needed defence against a common evil.

As one who has strayed feels a rush of strong and relieved attachment to a permanent liaison, Pauline wanted to be continually among these friends, now. She did not ask Joe to calculate the risk she had taken as opposed to those she had refused; but he volunteered nothing to reassure her that the police might not discover the number of the car that assisted a black man to leave the country illegally. She knew from his silence that the risk existed. The company of friends was something she needed to wrap around herself against dread. Although it was school holidays and she and Joe made it a rule to be at home when their son was, she accepted the chance to go away with friends for a weekend; Carole did not work on Saturdays and would come along, but the other two had the obligation of their jobs to fulfill. It distressed Pauline that Sasha disliked his holiday occupation so much; that she had been too preoccupied to help him find something interesting. She confided him to the care of adaptable Hillela.—Take Sasha along when you and your friends go out. Don't let him know I asked you.—

The house to themselves. Children with the house to themselves. When they were still children, what wild release that signalled; romping from room to room, all lights burning, bedtime banished, the thrills of outlawry within the safety of home: Bettie's protests to scatter them, shrieking, only to recommence the game of freedom, because her authority was no more founded than the game.

On Friday night after Pauline, Joe and Carole had left, Bettie cooked the meal of chops and chips (Sasha's favourite long ago) for which Pauline had left instructions. Hillela sat on the floor untidily as a rag doll propped there, telephoning, all animation gathered into her chance to talk without interruption from others wanting to use the phone. She was making arrangements to go out; Sasha knew. He went away to some other part of the house so as not to listen to another's conversation. But she did not go out.

Sasha?

He heard her looking for him.

Sasha? Sasha?

She was in the garden, now. He went to his mother's room, which overlooked the direction of the voice. From the silent observation of the room that held the humming continuum of

Pauline and Joe's lives, he saw her shadow sloping away from her. He waited to hear her call again.

—Sasha?—

The cat came running, as it would to anything that sounded like a summons to food or fondling. Their shadows joined where she stooped to chide and croon to it for being so stupid. He opened the closed window that marked absence and jumped. Out of the stiff cold oleander bushes whose dead leaves smoothed past his legs like blunt knives, his shadow joined hers and the cat's. For a while the angled, elongated mobile that was the three shadows jazzed, darted, and leant towards and away from the tilted phantom of the house, all cast over the dead lawn by the light of stars in a spill of cracked ice across the sky. The cat's eyes, as she drew the pair into one of her zany night ecstasies, were moons, rather than the new sliver lifted too high and far in the black clarity of space. Their round phosphorescent gold, the flash of translucence as she pranced in profile, were the moons of summer, the nights of the smell of burning flesh from suburban braaivleis. Then she was gone.

Sasha had on his sweater but like most young males who live in a climate of long summers and never accept the brief reality of winter, he wore about the house, in all seasons, the same shorts and rubber-thonged sandals. The cold steeped his legs palpably as water; Hillela puffed out a breath to see it hang in air. They went through the gate, each with arms crossed, hugging self, and began to walk; to walk the streets of the suburb as people are brought out by a summer night. Block after block; they passed through the planes, bared horizontals and verticals stripped by winter; only among the pavement jacarandas, that do not shed their leaves till spring, each streetlight swam, a luminous fish in a cave of green hollowed out of the night. Although when the three young people were together, or with friends, the adolescent fidgety abhorrence of silence, the need to talk because one is alive, possessed them, the two did not talk much. Hillela hummed one of her guitar tunes now and then. When they did exchange a remark, a phrase or a laugh shattered the clear cold like a stone thrown. At times there was the feeling, in the rhythm of their progress, that they might be making for somewhere, but neither said, nor asked of the other, where; at others (when a corner was reached), that they were looking for a destination. There was none; or none other. They arrived back at the gate. All the lights were burning in the house, except in Pauline and Joe's bedroom, where a window stood open. Bettie had not locked up, knowing there was no-one to reproach her neglect. The house was one of those legendary ships that sail on, fully rigged, without a living soul aboard.

They stamped in, Hillela putting her hands, warm from her pockets, over red-cold ears. Now she would go to the telephone, now she would put on lipstick, fluff her hair with her fingers and leave him there ... Now he waited for her to come and call goodbye. She appeared with a pair of his soccer socks on over her jeans, threw a second pair for him to catch. —Don't worry, I haven't been rummaging into any of your things. They weren't put in your room yet, they were among stuff Rebecca's washed.—

The house to themselves. Even the children had slipped away for ever in the adult silences of a night walk. He offered: —D'you want a fire?—

—Too much fag to go out for wood.—

—I feel like a drink.—

—Okay, I'll make tea. Coffee?—

—I mean a drink. What about you?—

But without waiting for her to say, he went to take a bottle of wine and forgot the glasses. She brought the first thing she saw in the kitchen, two cocoa mugs. —Hillela!—

—It'll taste the same.—

He went for glasses. Smiling, she watched him open the bottle. —You're supposed to wipe the rim.—

—Why, it's not dirty.—

—I don't know. They always do at Olga's. And Arthur sniffs it first.—

—And what's that in aid of.—

—To see if it's corked.—

He filled the glasses. —The education you're getting—what a great start in life.—

Hillela took his sharpness kindly, with enjoyment. Her cheekbones, dusky-red with cold, lifted under her strange shining eyes, whose iris, he had examined and explained to her, had no grain to differentiate it from the dark pupil. —At least I'm learning to drive.—

—But you ought to get your learner's licence, you know. I suppose you're driving around illegally all over the place.—

—In what?—

—Your friends let you, I'm sure.—

Hillela was always in command of the subject; changed it at will. —Teach me to play chess.—

He looked at her. —Now?—

—Yes.—

He drank, drew a note sounded from the glass with thumb and forefinger, didn't look at her.

—What for?—

—To play, of course. Oh you think I'm too stupid.—

At once his face was sullen with anxiety.—You are not stupid, Hillela.— He moved his head as if tethered somewhere; and broke loose. —You are the most intelligent person in this house.—

She laughed, made an exaggerated movement pretending to spill her wine. —There's no-one here except you!—

—And it's true.—

—Then only you think so.— At once she turned away quickly from what she had said. —Come on. We've got all night.—

They took the bottle and went into Joe's study, intending to fetch the beautiful chess set that was kept on a filing cabinet, but instead of returning to the livingroom settled themselves there, with the radiator turned on and the wine at hand, in that single room in the house that was never for general use, where Bettie was not even allowed to dust because of the importance and confidentiality of the papers and documents filed and piled within it. They lifted the legs of the burdened desk and pulled from beneath it the sheepskin foot-rug, to sit on; they dumped the papers from a stool to make of it a low table between them. Given in, Sasha was explaining to her. —It's too abstract for you. You'll learn, all right. But you'll only want to play when there's nothing else to do. And that's not what chess is. How shall I say—you'll always be wanting to do something else.—

She was setting up the men, an Africanised set made of malachite in Rhodesia (maybe even exported by her father, who at one time had dealt in curios). —I don't want to do something else.—

In the small hours, the child abandoned in the dark and cold came back to possess a body again for a moment. Sasha woke to some awful interruption; he had the sensation of terrible discovery and disbelief he had had when, for a period when he was already around eight years old, he would find he had wet the bed. But it was a regular slamming, and not a physical sensation, that had wakened him; his bed was dry, he was not alone, there was the wonderful heavy warmth of breasts against him, and the passing time that brought him to consciousness was measured by the gentle clock of another's breathing. Hillela was there. There was nobody else. He got up and went, knowing his way in the dark in this empty house, to that bedroom where the window had been left open and was banging to and fro in the wind.

Her charges had cooked breakfast for themselves when Bettie pushed the kitchen door open with the armful of pots and dishes brought back from her man's dinner the night before. She was satisfied rather than pleased. —You old enough now not to make such a mess!— She washed up for them, her reproaches affectionate, a routine assertion of her field of efficiency. Although Hillela was like a daughter in the house, she did not have quite the proxy authority to give Bettie the day off. Sasha told her she needn't bother, he and Hillela would find their own food. —And tonight? For dinner?— —It's Saturday. We'll be out. Saturday night, Bettie.— She swept eggshells into the bin, laughing. —Him? When do you ever go out dancing? Hillela, she'll be having a good time, but you ... Sasha ... You afraid of the girls, I'm sure.— Not a man, to her, yet the white man in the house, for that weekend: —Please, Sasha, go and see what's wrong in Alpheus's place. There's no light, the water's not hot, nothing. She can't warm the food for the baby.—

—Probably a fuse blown, that's all. I think there's a box of wires in the broom cupboard. You know, on that small shelf. Alpheus can replace it himself.—

—No, no, you must go. If he messes something up, who is it going to be in trouble? Me, that's the one.—

—You're a terrible nag. Why can't you trust Alpheus?—

—Because Alpheus he'll sit there with candles and he won't ask! Won't say nothing! I'm the one, for everybody. Must speak for everybody.—

Sasha was throwing corks and broken kitchen utensils out of a drawer, looking for the fuse wire.

—Oh you are good to me. Thanks, eh. Thanks, Mouser.— To be called by that name was to meet with blankness someone who makes the claim in the street: Don't you know me? It was himself, *Mouser*, one of the many pet names of childhood that evolve far from their origin, in the manner of Cockney rhyming slang. It might have had something to do with big ears, with a liking for getting into small closed places, with pinching cheese, or the cat-like patience and curiosity of a solemn small boy. Even his mother, who had so many such names to express her delight in him then, would have forgotten, in her loss of so much that had been between them. That Bettie was still allowed to bring it out incongruously was more a mark of condescension to her than a privilege accorded. Despite her house-training in awareness of her own dignity, she had her lapses into the manner of Jethro, which perhaps needed less of an effort against the grain of their identical definition as servants.

The absent Carole went in and out of what was now the home of Alpheus and his family, and often brought the baby over to the main house. She and Alpheus's girl made clothes for it on Pauline's sewing machine that Carole had taken to the garage. Sometimes she shared a meal there. But Hillela showed no interest in the inhabitants across the yard, and Alpheus was some sort of issue between Sasha and his mother that nobody but the two of them was aware of; when he came home for holidays there was expectation that he would go to talk to Alpheus as he liked to renew acquaintance each time with all that was familiar.

—What about?— He knew she naturally assumed that the kind of school community he was privileged to live in must provide an ease of communication with the young man she herself could not have. She wouldn't say it, but he wouldn't let her off. —I live with black boys all the time, I've got nothing particular in common with Alpheus.—

Neither he nor Hillela had been in the garage since it had become a family home. Frilly curtains on a sagging wire, smell of burned cooking and the sweetish cloy of confined human occupation, a hi-fi installation hanging the festoons of luxury over napkins, bed and cooker—its existence became real around their presence as strangers; bringing a sense of this not only here, but in the house across the yard where they had moved in from night streets.

Alpheus was a soft-voiced helper as he and Sasha dismantled a single electrical outlet whose plastic had melted and melded

with the overload of plugs connected through an adaptor. —You
need a separate outlet now that you have a hi-fi as well. They'll
have to get an electrician to install another lead from the main.—
Alpheus took the advice as if it were something he could follow in
the practical course of things. But both knew he had bought what
he did not want his benefactors to know about, because he had
no business spending money on such things as hi-fi equipment,
any more than he should have burdened himself with a family.
Alpheus's girl hanging about in the background acknowledged
Hillela with the same gazing politeness—gone completely still,
as if in the children's game where the leader turns suddenly to
confront those moving up secretly behind him—that she had had
when the white girl, carrying torn-up letters, had come upon her
carrying her pregnant belly in the yard. The girl was wearing
one of Carole's favourite dresses Hillela now realized she had not
seen for some time; she had worn it herself, she and Carole often
exchanged clothes. There was something else whose disappearance she had not noticed. In the little home where the functions
of all rooms were reduced to fit into one, there were no ornaments
except a few plastic toys and, on a straw mat on the hi-fi player,
the undamaged Imari cat.

In many ways it was more than the distance of a back yard
from the house to Alpheus's garage. It was the only outing
they took, that Saturday. Hillela did not use the telephone.
This was a day before them, all around them, untouched either
at beginning or end by the week that preceded it or the week
that would follow when on Sunday night, familiarity, a family
would return. The luxury of its wholeness extended the ordinary
course of a day, measured time differently, as Hillela's breath
had measured it in the night. The cat followed and stayed with
them everywhere, perhaps only because they did not know it
was accustomed to getting trimmings from Bettie. It kneaded
Sasha's thighs and Hillela kissed one by one the four sneakers of

white fur for which it had got its name, Tackie. What they took for affection, weaving them into its caresses, was only greed. They themselves did not touch. There were several chess lessons that ended in laughter, they even quarrelled a little; it was impossible to have Hillela to oneself, at one's mercy, without frustration at her lack of adolescent apprehension, envy of her— what? Adults begin to predicate from the time children are very small. What do you want to be when you grow up? What are you going to do when you leave school? What career are you interested in? This predication was not an answer to anything about life it was needed to know. These questions, formulae put absently by men and women preoccupied by financial take-overs, property speculation, divorces, political manoeuvres, Sasha knew were lies. From the beginning: —They knew you were never going to be an engine driver ... not if they could help it. They despise engine drivers. They know it's not what you want to *be*, it's what they've already decided you'll settle for, so they can say *they've* done all they could for you.—

—You should do whatever you want to do.—

—Can't you understand?—

—You wrangle away at it too much. You'll get hungry, you'll have to eat; you'll have to work.—

—I don't understand you. You're the one who's had a lousy time, you've been pushed around as it suited them, and you—I don't know ... you seem to feel free. No-one's less free than you! What's going to happen when you leave school next year? Are they going to pass the hat round to send you to university?—

—Now don't be unfair, you know they would.—

—Or are they thinking that for you it's a secretarial course and a useful job through influence at the Institute of Race Relations, and someone will pay for a degree by correspondence, on the cheap, like for Alpheus.—

—Well, maybe I'll go to Rhodesia.—

—You've just thought of that for something to say, this minute.—

She laughed; they were eating apples and the juice trickled down her chin.

—Maybe I'll get a job.—

—What job?—

—Oh journalism, or maybe nursing.—

—For pete's sake! The difference is … tremendous, total. You'd think it was choosing between chocolate or vanilla. When do you suppose you'll decide?—

—Then. I'll say, then. Nursing; newspaper.—

—Hilly, Rhodesia's a horrible place, there's going to be a war there.—

—Len never says anything.—

—When he writes you a birthday card, no.—

With regular bites, she was shaping a spool out of the apple core.

—Sasha … Why d'you let everything make you so angry. Sasha …—

He felt a fresh surge of what she called anger. —Because you forgive them.—

The castaway raft that was carrying the day dropped out of rapids into quiet water. She played the guitar to herself, bent over cradling it to save him from disturbance. Out of his week's pay at the liquor store he had bought himself some books, and had begun one this weekend. *The Brothers Karamazov* was in the house in the old red hardback uniform edition of Dostoevsky along with all the other books under whose influence he had been reared without knowing it or having read them, but he had bought the paperback as if the other had not been there all his life, on one of the shelves that narrowed every passage as well as stretched up the walls in every room, and made the odours he associated with home compound with the smell of paper and the livingroom fruit bowl. He wanted to read the book because he had heard one of the masters at school mention, in a debate on capital punishment (the school tried hard to introduce issues that schoolboys could not be expected to think about), that the writer Dostoevsky had stood before a firing squad and found himself suddenly reprieved instead of dead. The extremity of this experience attracted Sasha, who sometimes was secretly drawn to the possibility of committing suicide. One of the reasons for the anger which Hillela had gently mocked was that he felt his mother had wormed this secret out of him—not in words, but in the concentration of signs only she and he could read: the way he left a room, the shift in his attention when someone was speaking—he could not stop her adding these things up. But he was safe from that secret now. Hillela was there. It was not possible to think of nonexistence while she was close by, her bare foot with the one funny toe stretched towards the afternoon fire they had made for themselves.

He was disappointed with the visit to the holy Zossima (rationalism was one of the influences he was unaware of; religious mysticism bored him) until Fyodor Pavlovitch Karamazov embarrassed his sons by making a ridiculous scene, but after that the new reader entered the novel as millions had done before him, although to him it seemed its knowledge of all he needed to know, that nobody would ever tell him—even though everything was discussed, talk never stopped—was part of the possession of the house boarded this silent weekend when it was lit-up and empty. As he read his absorption deepened like the stages of sleep; and he was aware of his companion only the way the cat, actually asleep, showed awareness of the comfort of human presence and the fire's warmth by now and then flexing thorns through the white fur of a paw. Then he fell into a passage that seemed to surround and isolate him. 'I am that insect, brother, and it is said of me specially. All we Karamazovs are such insects, and, angel as you are, that insect lives in you, too, and will stir up a tempest in your blood. Tempests, because sensual lust is a tempest! Beauty is a terrible and awful thing! It is terrible because it has not been fathomed and never can be fathomed, for God sets us nothing but riddles. Here the boundaries meet and all contradictions exist side by side. I am not a cultivated man, brother, but I've thought a lot about this. It's terrible what mysteries there are!'

He did not know Hillela had stopped playing her guitar; he had not been listening. She wandered out of the room, and that she was not there any longer he felt immediately. He thought he heard her calling. Some other sound, the susurrus of the shower; perhaps he imagined the voice, like the voices heard under a waterfall. He went to the bathroom door and rapped a mock drum-roll. She did call something. He rapped again. Hillela opened the door, pink paths showing all over her drenched head, streams of water licking her breasts, the springy stamens of her pubic hair brilliant with shaking drops. A hollow of pale mauve shadow went from each lean hip-bone down to the groin. —I boiled myself by the fire.— He looked at her. Not at her face; and she was watching him, both encouraging and anxious, a kind of happiness. He kissed the breasts, letting them wet his face. He knelt down and pressed closed eyes and mouth against that wet moss that poor boys at school had tried to represent in ugly drawings in the lavatories. She reached for a sponge and squeezed it over his head. The water ran down his hair and plastered it. She teased: —Just like an old mango pip.— They played, through the open door the house was filled with shouts and laughter. The shower was still plashing. They fought and slithered in the steam. She pulled him under the fall of water and he struggled out of his wet clothes and imprisoned her, cool and ungraspable. The water found the meeting of their bellies and poured down their thighs. She la-la-la-ed, he pushed her head under the full force of the jet.

They dried their hair by the fire. He towelled hers vigorously, but her resistance was weak and laughing, the game was running down; the smell of Hillela's hair was identifiable as the source of the intimations of her he had found, over several years now, in her jacket that hung in the jumble behind a door, or on a cushion on the old sofa, in a jersey left inside-out, as it had been pulled off, sleeves holding the shape of her impatient push up to elbows.

Hunger was also a happiness. He cooked up a rich red-and-yellow mess of tinned tomatoes and mushrooms, tuna fish and cheese, an expert in clandestine boarding-school cuisine. They carried it to the fire and camped on the floor. The cat filched bits of fish with the club of a curved paw and spat out each morsel several times to get rid of the tomato coating. Sasha put her through the window, Hillela let her in again. Sasha suggested he would take another bottle of wine but neither wanted it. The telephone rang; Hillela was sopping up sauce with a piece of bread, he put down his plate, she waved the crust, and he did not know whether it was a signal that he should answer. She cleaned her plate with conscientious gusto, making figures of eight while he counted the rings, nine, ten, eleven, and the last cut off in the middle. Within such content so many things seem possible, even easy. —All you need is enough for a cheap one-way ticket. If you can get that together, then you can work your way round Europe. There must be people we know we could stay with … connections.—

—Billie—she's got family in London. You know—my step-mother.—

—I want to keep away from youth hostels. I've had enough of living in dormitories. They say in France, if you go to the South where so many rich people are, you can get taken on as crew for a yacht. Girls too. There's someone at school, his brother went all the way to the Bahamas—fantastic. The trouble is, we'll finish school in the December of next year—

—November.—

—Same thing; it's winter in Europe. But we could work in ski resorts for a bit.—

Hillela mimed a shiver.

—No, you'll love it. The way you can dance, I'll bet you'll ski well. Good co-ordination.—

—Cold places.— A fearful intake of breath.

—That's because it's something you can't even imagine. The sun is hot, the snow is cold—it's like eating sorbet and drinking hot black coffee.—

She smiled praisingly. —How do you know.—

He caught her hand, patted himself on the head with it. —I know, I just know.—

—And Carole could join up with us somewhere.—

—Carole?—

He stared at her. She looked back with the face of someone practical, considering ways and means.

—But she'll still be at school.—

—In the holidays. It'll be fun. The three of us. Like here.—

Orange and blue liquid pulsed in the coals; measured perhaps a minute. He picked up his book again, and, as the cat would look about fastidiously for a place to lie, slowly settled his head in her lap, where the plate had been. She grabbed a cushion, lifted his head, and put the cushion beneath it. He had been reading, on and off, all day. She looked to see how far along he was by now: more than two hundred pages.

—What about the bathroom.—

Only the pilot light of his conscious attention burned. —There's all day tomorrow.—

She began to read over his head; when he got to the end of a page before her, her hand went down to hold him back. As she caught up with the sense of the narrative their pace drew even, so that they were reading at the same instant the same passage; 'I want you to know me. And then to say goodbye. I believe it's always best to get to know people just before leaving them.'

Sasha closed the book and put it aside without marking his place with the torn bus ticket he used, but the spine of the paperback, bent as far as he had read, lifted the pages apart from the rest at that point. After a while her hand stirred as if about to touch his hair, but did not. She bent over, smiling, but his eyes were closed.

—Sasha?—

—Sasha?—

He waited, once again, to hear her call softly, again.

—Sasha?—

He opened his eyes and suddenly began to yawn, yawned till his eyes watered, full of tears.

They got up. She stood a moment, waiting for him.

—I would never go to Rhodesia.—

She was moving her head very slowly. Feeling him looking at her, a smile turned the edges of her mouth; she might have been being photographed. He approached her very shyly, and kissed her. They wandered through the house, arms about each other's waist, following the trail of their inhabitation: among the papers on the study desk, a packet of chocolate broken into, from which she took a square, records among the open tins in the kitchen, his telescope that he had been tinkering with (last year's birthday present for a boy interested in phenomena beyond his orbit) on the dining-table.

He took the telescope into his room and for a long time, until they got too cold, they drew the moon and stars near through the open window, just as their talk drew near ski resorts, the Bahamas, the anonymous freedom of foreign cities.

They were in the deep sleep of midnight when Pauline came quietly into her son's room and saw that there were two in his bed. She turned on the light. The room was cold and stuffy; warm in the core of it was the smell of a body she had known since she gave birth to him, unmistakable to her as the scent that leads a bitch to her puppy, and it was mingled with the scents of sexuality caressed from the female nectary. The cat was a rolled fur glove in an angle made by Sasha's bent knees. The two in the bed opened their eyes; they focussed out of sleep and saw Pauline. She was looking at them, at their naked shoulders above the covers, and she called, as if she had come upon intruders in the house— *Joe.* She turned and walked out.

They did not move. Something grasped Sasha's innards and was shaking him; he trembled against Hillela. Her body was calm as sun-warmed stone. He spoke. —It's not Sunday.— Hillela said nothing. Her soft, clean, curly hair lay against his neck, the last sensation he had been conscious of as he fell asleep. Hillela was there. Now that terrified him.

Pauline came back with Joe, she was clutching his upper arm, taking protection. She stopped him in the doorway, against some danger. Sensing attention, the cat began to purr. Pauline's splendid head rose like an archaic representation of the sun, aureoled with wild filaments, blinding them and holding them in her gaze. —*Joe. Joe.*— Sasha's mother was imploring his father to tell the intruders not to be there. The cat stretched, jutted rump and tail and jumped off the bed.

The greatest shock was the confusion. It was days before Sasha (and Hillela, for all he knew) understood why his parents had come home on Saturday night. And Pauline and Joe had to grasp a total displacement of apprehension. They returned because of a crisis they knew how to deal with, in an anxiety not unexpected in the context of their lives. Someone had brought that curse upon peace, a radio, to the camping ground in the Drakensberg. He took the thing, the size of a cigarette pack, along with him when the party of friends went on a climb, and under another kind of waterfall (of static) its cackle told of the arrest of Joe's partner in the early hours of Saturday morning. Joe and Pauline left

Carole with the party and tramped back in the silence of shared preoccupation along the hikers' trail where, a few hours before, they had noticed the minute beauties of every fern and flower, and the grand surveillance of eagles. What both feared most, on the long drive back, was that their house had been raided while the other two members of the family were left alone there. —Well ... they're not children ... they'll know how to behave sensibly.— Pauline accepted the reassurance, but a mile or two farther on, while she was taking her turn to drive, allowed herself: —How d'you behave with those bastards raking through a house? It's all very well ... but it hasn't happened to us. I'm not sure what my reactions would be. If I could shut up. And Sasha ...—

—Sasha knows the drill.— They were travelling in the car in which Pauline had taken the Masuku family to escape over the border. Police investigations into such things often took a long time when they were preparing a case pertaining to state security and involving many people. Both were thinking about this, but said nothing. When Pauline was not driving there was no other claim to distract her attention, and foreboding built within her a whole construct of consequences from a single act, made by her, it now seemed on impulse, that would trap the considered, continuing usefulness of Joe and his kind. She experienced a new guilt; through her, hands that should never touch, eyes that should never see the papers in Joe's modest study might have been going through them.

That was the first room in the house she went to, and there was some evidence of disorder—Joe's rug was not under the desk, files were on the floor, the chess set was not in its usual place. She could not wait to verify if anything had been taken but ran at once to be reassured that the children were all right, that Sasha was in his room.

Joe was already on the telephone, waking up his partner's wife.

Coming back from that room, Pauline waited a full minute, standing there looking at Joe, not hearing what he was saying, unable to understand anything, neither what she had just seen nor the purport of his expression as he asked questions and received answers.

And in the days that followed, which was one to think about, how could one grapple with the one, the always-to-be-expected crisis, while the other ... how was one to think of anything but the other? Joe had no choice. He was preparing applications, making representations, following procedures and looking (always looking) for the loopholes in Acts through which he could reach the detained man, while at the office doing the work of both of them. He phoned Pauline at odd moments of day, as a busy man will find time to do usually only to keep contact with a mistress. A few murmured, elliptical words, to which the response was equally laconic. Everything all right? Anything happened?

Yes. Nothing.

After Pauline had pushed past Joe that night, gone over to the bed and hit Sasha across the face, hit him for the first time in her life, hit him twice, jolting his head first this way then that, what could be all right. But outside that room where he lay naked, smelling of sex, with his sister—outside that house, all over the country, there were parents whose sons were in prison, whose sons had had to flee, like Donsi Masuku, and whom they would never see again.

For the first time, what there was could not be talked over 'frankly and openly' between the parents and children. There was no formula of confidence that would do. Pauline and Joe searched for one, as he searched for loopholes in the law. The attraction that had overcome taboo was something no-one could be asked to explain. Could one ask the fifteen-year-old Carole if she had noticed anything about—what? Could a father collude with his daughter in the old adult euphemism for sexual relations, 'something between' her siblings? The incident—how would one phrase it to Sasha, to the girl—was it an incident, a piece of sexual bravado (there was the empty wine bottle as a clue) in the defining family's absence, or was it something—

—Oh worse, worse.— Pauline stopped Joe. —Love, then, incest, going on who knows how long.—

Joe told her again and again, she shouldn't call Hillela Sasha's 'sister'.

—Not in actual terms of kinship, no, but in fact, how they've been brought up, how we live, they are brother and sister, they are, they know they are. And she is his first cousin. My sister shares my blood, doesn't she! Their mothers are one!—

—In some countries even marriages between cousins were not illegal. Until very recently. Where your grandfather was born, lots of Jews married cousins. Not only secular, but religious law allowed it.— Joe offered the information not to comfort his wife and himself, but to defuse emotion that they might apply reason to the unspeakable.

In the end, Joe closed the door in his study as was customary when he and Sasha wanted to be left in peace to play chess, and said to him as Len once said to Hillela: —I don't understand, either.— He was concurring, perhaps, with the state of mind of Pauline, who never before had excluded herself from any discussion concerning her son. —We're prepared to accept that you yourself do not understand. So let us put it behind us. Forget it.—

Such abject desolation burned over the boy that Joe sensed this like a fever emanating from him.

—Come. Set up the men. I've had a hellish day in court. Let's play.—

Sasha would go back to school, but Hillela would remain there, in the house.

Carole, younger and impressionable, shared a room with her. Already the parents could sense a protective hostility in Carole: ganging up for, rather than with, the old triumvirate, because Sasha was withdrawn, he spoke to the two girls only when others were present, in the conventional exchanges at table, and Hillela—no-one had confronted Hillela with anything. One of the things Hillela had done— Sasha and Hillela had done—was to take away from Pauline the single area where Pauline was certain always to know what to do, the area where she had been sure nothing could shock her, nothing elude understanding or alienate love. Joe had to shut himself up, alone, with Sasha; she could not bring herself to take on Hillela. When Hillela came over quietly—astonishingly—to kiss her goodnight as usual (this was a house where affection was displayed, normal emotions had never been suppressed) every evening of the very week that followed what had happened, Pauline touched that young cheek with lips like charred paper. Hillela went to her holiday job, Carole to hers, and in the evenings, if Hillela did not go out with those friends of hers (and god knows who they were, what ideas she had picked up from them and brought home) she was shut up with Carole in their shared room in schoolgirl intimacy— creaming faces, squeezing blackheads, pushing back cuticles; whatever they were doing or saying concealed by the music they played. Some of the nights of that week Pauline wept in the dark beside Joe, after they had talked in bed about the things that really mattered in the world, the clandestine investigations Joe was making, through contacts in the police, to find out whether his partner was going to be charged with subversion, and the progress of the trial of others, already in session. He patted her back, stroked her hip; uncertain whether it would be a good thing to go on to make love to her. Once, when his caress of comfort began to change, she spoke. —I have the feeling Carole knew all along ...—

—Oh surely not. Hillela will have told her? Not possible. I can't believe that— He did not say it: even of Hillela.

—Not *told*, nobody will have said anything, but you know how she adores the girl. More than any sister. Sensed it. Whatever Hillela does is always right, for her. You remember the Durban business. How she lied for her?—

It was because of Carole that a decision had to be made. Hillela had caused Pauline to strike her son, Hillela had used him as a man while he was still his mother's son, Hillela, made a sister out of Pauline's love for a sister, had misused the status granted her, but it was because of Carole that the petty domestic normality of the house, the goodnight kisses and cosy chess games that persisted binder danger and political upheaval, could not be allowed to return under this kind of threat. Carole was exposed; even supposing what happened were to have been an isolated incident, and when Sasha came back from school for other holidays it would not be necessary to wonder, every time one went out for a few hours, whether one should have locked grown children in their rooms ... Carole was exposed.

No decision could be made by Pauline and Joe alone. She did not know whether to write to the father, to Len. It was not proposed to pack the girl off to Rhodesia, to end up a glorified waitress, like the new wife. —She's still Ruthie's child.— For Pauline, if love failed, became incomprehensible, there was still justice. It was necessary to speak to Olga. It had to be done; hadn't Olga always said she had as much right to Hillela as Pauline? Olga, too, bore the charge of Ruthie's child. Olga must face facts, like anyone else, once or twice in her life.

Everything Pauline found it impossible to be, at home, now, she was restored to the moment she found herself in Olga's presence, in Olga's room with the Carpeaux *Reclining Nude* and (an acquisition she noted with the subliminal attention that stores such things) a gilt-turbanned Blackamoor holding up a lamp. —Sasha and Hillela have been sleeping together. Don't ask me the details. They don't help at all. It happened; we know; that's all there is to it.—

Olga didn't want to believe what she was told so bluntly; Olga wanted to get out of believing. They almost quarrelled. How could Pauline say such a thing, and about her own child, too—as if it were nothing! Matter-of-fact! *That's all there is to it.* Pauline was so *hard.* Pauline grinned shockingly at her sister. —What do you want me to say? Weep and wail? I've come to discuss what we ought to do next, as Ruthie's sisters. These things happen, they happen within closed walls, like these, you can't shut them out as you do so much else. They are in the family, Olga.—

—To think she grew up with Clive! And they're still together quite often! He's teaching her to drive—but Clive's a very steady, sensible boy—

—Of course, all parents are quite positive that the way *they've* brought up their children has produced models of virtue. I don't excuse Sasha, I don't exonerate him, it's all beside the point. And he's no concern of yours. We're talking about Hillela.—

Olga had a loose cashmere jacket over her shoulders, there was underfloor heating in her house and no need for the bulky winter clothing Pauline wore. Olga stood up giddily, taking courage in one certainty. —I can't take her, Pauline.— Pauline watched her pressing her oval red nails into the flesh of her slim arms.

—Even though Clive is so sensible. But Olga, no-one expects it, you handed her over to me the moment adolescence arrived, don't you remember? But now I'm asking you: what about her future? What do you suggest?—

Olga dug her nails testingly into her flesh because she was afraid of telling Arthur. All the time she was talking to her sister, she was anticipating the dread of telling Arthur. She feared something from him, and did not know what it was until it came: —A little tart, like her mother. I could always see it. Bad blood.—

Olga, who had tears of excitement in her eyes when she bid successfully at an art auction, who cried at school prize-givings, did not burst into tears but took on the force that appalled her in Pauline. —Like me. My bad blood. My sister, you bastard. You talk about breeding. I had to teach you how to hold a knife and fork properly. This house is full of beautiful things I work so hard to find and you never even look at. You bring people here you don't know how to talk to. D'you know how many times I'm ashamed of you?——

Pauline and Olga met again, with Joe as adviser; Arthur had business engagements and did not appear. Olga clung to the idea of getting Len to come down from Salisbury; this was not something to be discussed over the telephone, and a letter would be such a shock to him, poor devil, because he wouldn't be able to respond immediately, ask questions. Pauline and Joe were sceptical—Olga was stalling, as to be expected. Len would come, perhaps the solution already existing would be found; maybe boarding-school, once again, was the answer that would serve. Ah, and in the holidays? Where would she go in the holidays?

But Hillela herself provided the solution. She was leaving school. Yes. She had a job, 'somewhere to stay'; she was going to move in with other young people who had rented a house.

It was Joe she told. Joe who had bought her a guitar during the court lunch-break in Pretoria. She knocked and came into his study, as she had done so many times, with a cup of tea, and when he murmured thanks, she told him.

——Not before matric! What can you do without matric? Your whole life, Hillela. You'll prejudice your whole life! You can't do that! For god's sake, what do you want to become of you! It's only just over another year——

She gave him a schoolgirl's answer that made it easy for them both: ——I'm sick of school.——

The pen he held between second and third fingers seesawed, tapping at the desk. There was a strange sad echo between them. ——You're in a hurry to live, Hillela. You don't stop to think.——

She chewed at the inside of her cheek, and looked at him boldly, openly, appealingly—he never decided which it had been. He was ashamed to see she understood that although he used the present tense, he was referring to what he and she could not talk of, in the immediate past.

What could they be expected to have done about Hillela at that time? Her father had been reached after some difficulty; he no longer lived at the flat, his second wife had left him and he was working as a mine storeman up in Ndola. Len was clearly in no position or state of mind to take any responsibility. So there was nothing for it but to let a seventeen-year-old girl think she was the one who knew what to do.

Pauline believed it her duty, for Ruthie's sake, whatever might have happened, to see the place where the girl was going to live. Hillela took her obediently to an old house with peeling wall-paper, sash windows propped open with rolled newspapers, and in the bathroom (Pauline asked to see the bathroom) a lavatory bowl stained the colour of iodine. Olga, through Pauline, offered a small monthly allowance, to be sure the girl would have a roof over her head. The girl did not refuse; it was arranged that Olga would open a bank account in her name. It is unlikely that she ever saw Olga again; Olga could not very well invite her to Friday evening dinners at Arthur's house. Pauline telephoned, for Ruthie's sake, every week or two, while she could reach Hillela where she worked in some mail-order business, but she did not last long in that job and there was no information about where she was to be found next. She had been told that if ever she had any problems, she should come to Joe—problems were Joe's profession, he could deal with them disinterestedly; that was the one advantage she had left them to offer her. It would have been against Pauline's principles to forbid any child of hers anything, but Carole was kept so busy between school and the communal activities she shared with her mother that there couldn't have been much time or opportunity for her to seek out her cousin. And Sasha—Sasha was out of the way at school. When he came home for the Christmas holidays, Hillela had left her first job, moved from the old house, and—unless she had written to him? Hillela had never been known to write—it was unlikely he could seek her out, even if he had 'had the heart to'.

That was Joe's phrase, when they worried about the probability, and Pauline was somehow offended by it. What harm had been done Hillela? In that house, Pauline and Joe's, she had been treated like one of their own, as long as this was possible. Pauline could not resorb into mental balance the confusion of that Saturday night's return from the mountains—the eagles' air, so easily invaded by cackle of a cheap little radio, the fear of the State and police that roused a whole resource of heightened alertness, craft and strategy working above daily life, and then the unbelievable sight that stared from within the safety and familiarity of that daily life—a child's bed with the cheerful blanket crocheted by a black women's self-help group, on the floor the shirt she chose for him only last week, the telescope bought and kept concealed as a loving surprise for a birthday; the house cat purring in the aghast vacuum. Pauline did not allow herself to think about the last time in her life she had felt a like confusion. That was the sort of trite matching for Olga to go in for—Pauline had a lifetime of clear-headedness, passionate desire to face facts, in between, separating her from the ancient history when she was a young woman and their sister Ruth forsook them all, everything they knew, for a dockside nightclub in Lourengo Marques. Let Olga and Arthur compare the mother and daughter, if it would make them feel any better. Pauline loathed sanctimonious self-justification. She never abrogated her responsibility for that stage in Hillela's life. Never. It was not because of Ruthie they had failed with Ruthie's daughter.

The girl brought no problem to Joe, so she must have been all right. Whatever that meant in the way she must be living.

It is not easily understood why Pauline did not think about what the problem might be, if there were to be one. Perhaps she assumed that a girl who could do what Hillela had done would know how to look after herself. And that practical conclusion, in itself, referred to all that was unthinkable, must be forgotten.

It had to be forgotten for Sasha's sake, so that he could come back, always come back, without sensing the restraint of tolerance in the feel of home, come back to looking at the stars, chess games with his father and fierce political arguments with his mother. Sasha wrote letters but he never asked about Hillela, even in those addressed to Carole. *Forget it.* He had always, since it began, forgotten 'it' when he was at school; put it away, folded very small, and in code, in the centre of himself where no-one could get at it. Whether it was shameful or precious he had not needed to know until Pauline and Joe looked at it. Now he knew it had to be forgotten. It was all right at school; he feared the feel of home, the having to come back to its smell of fruit and Hillela's hair that was home; to sensing the odour of that hair that wasn't there anymore.

At school there was nothing to fear, until one weekend that term a girl in his class hanged herself in the gym. It was a Sunday, those who wanted to go to church had been in the town, others, including himself, had gone to help build a village school for the children of black peasants. She was a white Catholic girl and had stayed behind from church that day to hang herself; one of the juniors went into the gym to fetch cricket stumps and saw her dangling from the wall bars. She was not a particularly popular or pretty girl—people laughed behind her back at the dark hair that made her upper lip look dirty—but she had her little group, played tennis in the second team, was not left out at the Saturday night disco in the school hall. Sasha was among those brought running into the gym by the screams of the small boy, and her body hanging there was something without explanation. Another girl gave it to him: their classmate was pregnant. Her terror of her parents had been greater than her fear of death.

Sasha wrote in his weekly letter home about the brick-laying he was doing, building the village school.

Sasha had no fear of his parents. They were enlightened people. They had only looked. His mother had tried to hurt simply because she was hurt. He had not been afraid until now; he had only now remembered, discovered, there was something to be afraid of. This was the time when he would telephone home apparently for no reason; was there anything he wanted sent, anything he needed? They were always cheerful, pleased to hear from him. He tried, whenever he had a chance, to reach Carole when they were out, but never succeeded. The immense shock of curiosity with which he had seen the body of the girl turned into an obsession that blocked his co-ordination in the science laboratory and at games. He was able to bury himself in sleep the moment he went to bed at night in his senior boy's private cubicle, but he woke very early in the morning, as if something had taken him by the shoulder and shaken him. Or slapped him this way and that across the face. He did not open his eyes but was wide awake behind this sham of sleep, and what he saw was not a dream but like a film he had never seen yet remembered, or the images accompanying the reading of a book. He saw the carcasses he had passed so many times unremarked, hanging from hooks in the country butcher shop near the school, where *dagga* could be bought from old women in the yard behind. The pigs and sheep dangled; the girl dangled, the laces of one of her shoes untied. Her face was the face of Hillela with head drooped to one side, like the plaster statues of Christ on the cross. How many weeks passed? How soon did girls know for sure what was going on in their bodies? With the knowledgeable girl who was his friend he brought up the subject of their dead classmate, for whom prayers had been said at school assembly. —She could have had an abortion. I'm sure we'd have found someone to do it. Poor stupid, thing. It's not the end of the world ...—

How many weeks to half-term? At last he could wander into Carole's room. She was putting safety-pins round the torn hem of a skirt; he watched for a while. —Any news.—

She kept her head down.

—You haven't seen her?—

The head nodded, so that no-one other than he would witness, by the spoken word, an admission.

—What's she doing.—

—She wanted to leave the job she had, I don't know what she's found now.—

—You do know.—

Carole's hair hung over her face, a little long-haired dog whose muzzle can't be seen.

—Is she okay?—

A splotch fell on Carole's hands, and another. —She's okay, but I'm not going to talk about her with you.—

There came from him, riled by her tears of loss: —It's not the end of the world.—

Yet what sort of assurance was Carole's 'okay'. Who would confide trouble to little Carole? He spent a great deal of that weekend searching: the old haunts he remembered, the warehouse where Hillela had played her guitar, and the kind of places he thought she might frequent now, Hillbrow discos, pizza joints, jazz clubs. He ended up, the Saturday night of his half-term break, alone in one of the cinemas where they had sat on autumn afternoons.

Sasha never saw her, not then or any other weekend or in the school holidays. It was not that she was not to be found; she was there, in the city, all right, but not for him, or surely he would have seen her somewhere, as he constantly encountered others he knew. How many months passed? Slowly, he became used to the fear. He lived with it all the time. And then too much time had gone by; if what he feared really had been, something terrible already would have come to pass, by now. And so this meant she was safe. She would not hang from a butcher's hook with one shoelace untied. *It's not the end of the world. Forget it.*

This is not a period well-documented in anyone's memory, even, it seems, Hillela's own. For others, one passes into a half-presence (alive somewhere in the city, or the world) because of lack of objective evidence and information; for oneself, the lack of documentation is deliberate. And if, later, no-one is sure you are really the same person, what—that is certain to be relevant—is there to document? Everyone is familiar with memories others claim to have about oneself that have nothing to do with oneself.

In the lives of the greatest, there are such lacunae—Christ and Shakespeare disappear from and then reappear in the chronicles that documentation and human memory provide. It is not difficult for a girl of seventeen (out of sight of the witness of family and friends) to be absent from the focuses of a woman's own mnemonic attention in later life: to be abandoned, to disappear.

Time Off for a Love-Letter

Where was the seventeen-year-old on the Day of the Covenant, 16th December 1961, when bombs exploded in a post office, the Resettlement Board Headquarters, and the Bantu Affairs Commissioner's offices?

The public holiday of that date had only recently been renamed. On the 16th December 1838, the Boers defeated the *impis* of the Zulu king, Dingane (tradition misspelt his name), in revenge for his attempt to save his land and independence. Some months before, Dingane, pressed into trading for a token of cattle a vast tract of his kingdom, had first agreed and then killed the Boer, Piet Retief, and his parleying party, routed the Boer settlements already established in the kingdom, and chased the other whites, the British, from what they called Port Natal. At the cost of three white men wounded, the Boers slaughtered three thousand Zulus. Dingaan's Day curiously was then named for the vanquished rather than the victors. It was perhaps this aspect of the commemoration that moved the government to shift the dedication of the holiday to a biblical, less equivocal focus. The Covenant had been made, before the battle, with God—another piece of cattle-trading; in return for victory over the blacks, the whites would vow to hold an annual service of thanksgiving for the preservation of white civilization as carried into Africa by the guns of the Boers.

Whatever the holiday was dubbed, those white South Africans who did not gather to pray for their civilization in churches, or to listen at rallies to political speeches on the subject, traditionally went picnicking. So did many blacks, if they could find some place where they were allowed upon the grass—riversides, lakes and resorts were reserved for whites; it was only this year, as a consequence of the formation of the organization, Umkhonto we Sizwe, announced by Mandela and so troubling to Pauline, that the spear of Dingane's resistance had been taken up by blacks to mark the day as his and theirs.

If it hadn't been Dingaan's Day and if the first bombings in Johannesburg had not been reported to have taken place that very day, the psychiatrist's wife would not have been able to claim with the certainty of historical confirmation that she actually had met and could even recognize the girl subsumed beneath the woman's face in newspaper photographs seen many years later. The picnic itself was like many other picnics. The psychiatrist was newly qualified, in junior partnership, and not yet prosperous; the young couple had twin babies, lived in a small flat, and got out into the fresh air every Sunday. Hillela was with them on that picnic because she was now working as his receptionist; her third job— count can be kept at least that far. She had come to the consulting rooms he shared with his senior, peddling *The World Atlas and Encyclopaedia of Modern Knowledge* on ten per cent commission. The receptionist turned her away and she was taking advantage of the privacy of the corridor outside the rooms to eat a hamburger she had brought into the building, when the psychiatrist came out and punched all the lift buttons in turn. His impatience had no effect, and while he was waiting she looked for somewhere to put down her hamburger, could not, and so approached him with sample Volume I of the encyclopaedia and a half-eaten bun in her hands. They both laughed. He refused the bargain offer of the encyclopaedia and sympathetically told the girl nobody really ever wanted to buy that sort of thing; in fact, he explained, going down in the lift with her, the fraudulent offer of encapsulated knowledge was a survival of post First World War aspirations, long before television provided popular culture among the poor in Europe, England particularly, when unemployment rose and people hoped to survive by 'bettering themselves'. —It's pretty heavy to lug around, anyway.— That was all the young sales-woman knew. He asked if she wouldn't prefer some other job? She was swallowing the last of her hamburger but—with a hand over her mouth—eyes that attracted attention with their dark opacity signalled eagerly. Fortunately practical Pauline had made sure all three children had learned to type. And of course, on those visits to Olga Hillela had learned to drive a car; it wasn't neces-sary to add to her qualifications by saying she had no licence. The psychiatrist did not need a driver, but he told her to see the receptionist about a vacancy at his rooms. She dumped the sample encyclopaedia on a bench at a city bus stop. Somewhere in forgot-ten records her name appears, written off to the percentage of bad debts the publishing company expected from those who answered their advertisement: 'Would you like to earn up to R500 a week in your spare time?'

Because she had first approached him with an encyclopaedia and a hamburger with a big bite taken out of it, the profession-ally-regulated contact of learned doctor and unskilled employee had an element of shared amusement that held good through working days. He asked her if she was Jewish, too. —I suppose so.— Her reply amused him, once again; he felt the same about his Jewishness—at least he thought he did. But there was the occupational habit of asking gentle, insistent questions. —Why do you 'suppose'?— —My father was Portuguese.— He did not yet have the experienced insight to recognize a fantasy instantly. —It doesn't necessarily follow. There are Portuguese Jews. What did he do?— Even if she had been found traipsing around hawk-ing educational 'lines', it was evident in her style and the way she spoke that the girl was from the educated middle-class. —He was a dancer.— —Oh, that's interesting?—Not surprising that this—how had he described her to his wife?—'striking-looking kid'—should have a strain of artistic heredity.

—A dancing-partner in a nightclub.—

Now he laughed; she laughed; he did not exactly believe her but respected what he interpreted as a surprisingly mature way of reminding that a humble receptionist's private life was her own business. He suspected some history of running away from home, some chosen displacement, here; she was clearly of his and his young wife's milieu, so he suggested out of kindness that she join them on a picnic one day. She brought a guitar along, with charming innocent assurance that she could contribute something to the enjoyment of the outing, and his wife, seated under the willows with a baby tugging each breast sideways, was delighted with her. No girlish friendship developed, however; although his wife asked him to many times, he never brought them together again. He sent his junior receptionist out for hamburgers, as the kind of service her position was expected to fulfil, and then shared them with her in his consulting room while everyone else was out for lunch. On the picnic, first names had been adopted, though she understood without having to be told that he must never be addressed as 'Ben' before the receptionist or patients. In his room they sat together on the couch he kept as barbers keep a painted pole—he preferred to have his patients upright across the desk from him in a comfortable chair of contemporary design. She amused him greatly with her comments on patients. —They all sit in the waitingroom trying to look as if they're not there.—

—That's it. They don't want to be there. They're all people on the run from something.—

She smiled, unconvinced, her mouth full again. A healthy appetite. —I knew someone on the run, laughing and joking all the time. He wanted beer and music.—

—On the run from what?— He did not deal with criminal cases.

—Security police. And he got away, safely over the border. We knew he had because he sent such a ridiculous letter—he asked for a pair of brown lace-up shoes, *size twelve,* and then signed the letter, your loving sister Violet!—

—Asked whom?—

—I can't tell you. Well, you're used to secrets.— It was her job. to take each patient's file from the office cabinets and, preceding the patient silently into the doctor's room, place it before him.

He left off using a medicated toothpick to warn her, in collusion, smiling. —You're not supposed to read them, you know.—

—But Ben, I'd never believe anyone would have the thoughts they have!—

—You're a naughty girl. You know that?—

He insisted that she use toothpicks, too, to take care of her pretty teeth which were marred by only one misalignment. He often drove her, after work, to her room in the second commune she had joined. None of the other occupants would have recognized him, or cared, if they did. All brought men or girls home for a night or as long as an attraction lasted. After a few afternoon rides, he asked if he could see her room. She invited him in without fuss. But she would not make love. Was it because it would be her first time? Ah no—sexual knowingness proclaimed itself in her laugh, from the very day she approached him with the bun and the book, in the unselfconscious ease with which she was at home with her body in a way that none of his patients, poor things, were, squeezing her soft breasts past the hard metal filing cabinets, swivelling her little behind as she bent to pick up the pen that wouldn't stay efficiently clipped to the pocket of her white coat.

—You've got a boy you want to keep yourself for.—

Her answers were always so unmistakably hers. —No, Ben, not at the moment.—

Like a chemical change in the blood, he felt his attempt to put himself in his place with fatherliness turn to jealousy. Yesterday, tomorrow, another man; not today. —Why, Hillela?— He could not delude himself that hers was a moral objection, his wife etc.

She spoke kindly, it sounded like a privilege: —I don't want to with you, Ben.—

He bought her an expensive leather sling bag, a gooseneck reading lamp (had noticed there was only a central naked bulb on a cord in her hole of a room) and an anthology of poetry in which one of the names of contributors was his nom de plume. He did not confess authorship until he had asked for and been given her reaction to the poems. She said she liked one of them very much, it reminded her ... —Of what? Oh, something she'd once read in a book by that Russian ...

So she read Dostoevsky? What a pleasure to talk with her about Dostoevsky, to give her some psychoanalytic insights into the irrationality of his characters.

No, not exactly—she'd looked into the book while someone else was reading it.

—Who?—

—A cousin of mine.—

He wrote poems to her in which she did not recognize herself. In his professional experience of human vanity, her lack of it was amazing. He learnt something he didn't know; it is difficult to make oneself necessary to one who is free of vanity. He offered something better than hamburgers on the couch where nobody ever lay; they began going to lunch at Chinese restaurants down in Commissioner Street, the Indians' and coloureds' end of town, where no colleagues would be likely to be met with. They drank white wine and she teased him. He was treating some patients for alcoholism: —What about your drunks? You, breathing at them across the desk!—

—Doesn't matter. I can control my impulses within the pleasure principle, they can't! You'd better worry about Mrs Rawdon—if she gets a whiff of you in the office ...—

In the little shops of the restaurant neighbourhood he bought her a slippery satin dressing-gown with a gold dragon embroidered down the back, and incense she liked to burn in the hole of a room where she would take a man yesterday and tomorrow. —You're going to get more money from next month. Then you can move out of that place.—

—More money?—

—I'm going to raise your magnificent salary. And in six months, I shall do so again. I'm beginning to get the kind of patients who'll stick with me for years.—

She shook her head as if refusing a chocolate or another glass of wine. —I won't stay much longer, Ben. They're so solemn and miserable there in the waitingroom. Those ladies with perfect hairdos, those horribly skinny girls, those sulky kids who look as if they're handcuffed between mothers and fathers. And there's nothing wrong with them! Any of them! It's all made up, imagination? Isn't it? Those kids go to nice schools, they have toys and bicycles. Those girls can have as much food as they want, they're not starving, they just don't eat. Those men who talk to you for hours about sex—they never even take a glance at any woman who happens to be in the waitingroom ... just sit there looking at the same old ratty magazines Rawdon arranges every morning.—

For the moment, fascination distracted him from the shock of her casual farewell. —Oh my god, Hillela, you are so healthy it appals me! It's wonderful. I don't know where they got you from!—

Indeed, he literally never knew who 'they' might be, apart from that one piece of absurd information about her father. She was there, for him, without a past before yesterday and a future beyond tomorrow (she had just announced it), unlike those bowed under the past and in such anticipatory dread that they were, as she rightly observed, unable to look up and eat, learn, fuck in the present at all.

The psychiatrist never again suggested that he might make love to her. They sat at lunch in a Lebanese restaurant also unlikely to

134

be frequented by the medical profession. —I am going to divorce Elaine and we're going to get married. You and I are perfectly matched. It would be a terrible waste of my life and yours to leave things as they are. It would be unfair to Elaine for me to go on living with her; you are the only woman I can live with. So you don't have to see my patients ever again. You don't have to go, away.—

But she went; the darling girl with the hamburger and the book, the only woman, the one who was not a beauty but completely desirable to him, the one who was not an intellectual but whose intelligence was a wonderful mystery to him. She walked out the way she had walked in, the little tramp, clever cock-teaser, taker of free lunches and presents, bitch—she became these successively as he treated himself for the morbid obsession of his passion for her. And when in London, all those years later, his wife recognized her with Indira Gandhi in a newspaper photograph, he could not admit to remembering her because she had once reduced him to the condition of being one of his own patients.

Carole saw her suddenly, at the Easter industrial and agricultural fair. Hillela, in red shorts, black boots and a Stetson, handing out publicity at a stand displaying stereo equipment. Carole was with a boy; Pauline and Joe, the family, did not patronise this fair, which at that time was still segregated, for whites only. Carole squeezed the hand of the cowgirl, but the cowgirl hugged her. The pamphlets took flight and Carole's beau gathered them up. The beat of the music was so loud that speech appeared as mouthing. Hillela wrote an address on the back of one of the pamphlets. So Carole saw another one of the places in which Hillela lived at that period. (She had visited her at the first commune.) Carole arrived at an old flat with leaded light panes in the front door. She rang the bell for a long time, looking at the dead swordferns and empty milk and beer bottles in the corridor. The bell didn't work but when she rapped on the glass Hillela came. Carole had in her hands the record player from their shared bedroom; Carole had brought it to give to Hillela because the music at the stereo equipment stand reminded her that Hillela had no player; just as she had seen Alpheus and his wife had nothing beautiful in their garage home, and had given them the Imari cat she treasured, her gift from Hillela.

At the Resettlement Board Headquarters it was decided from where and when black people—African, Indian and of mixed blood—would be moved away from areas declared for whites only. At the Bantu Affairs Commissioner's offices it was decided for how long and in what capacity black people could live and work in the city. In the city, during the eighteen months Hillela was somewhere about (at least there was the evidence that Olga's stipend was drawn regularly, and under the circumstances, in all good conscience, there was nothing else her mother's family could do for her) there were thirty-one other targets. Most were hit by incendiary bombs. It was long before the Underground organizations were to have limpet mines, SAM missiles and AK 47s; these bombs were homemade, with petrol bought in cans from any service station. Letter boxes, electrical installations, beerhalls owned by the white administration boards in the black townships and railway carriages owned by the State monopoly—explosions attacked what represented the white man's power where blacks could get at it: in the places where blacks themselves lived. A man named Bruno Mtolo, a traitor to the liberation movement who turned State witness at a treason trial, said that 'recruitment presented no difficulty' if volunteers were promised they would be allowed to undertake sabotage immediately. And Joe was right; it was not possible to adhere completely to the intention to avoid bloodshed. Timing devices or the indiscipline of recruits caused things to go wrong. In the beerhalls and railway carriages black people were killed or hurt.

White people did not hear the blast, smell the fires; not then, not yet. In another part of the country, black policemen regarded as collaborators with the government were killed, and so were a few white ones, but no white suburbanite or farmer was harmed; not then, not yet. Somewhere about, Hillela worked—probably not in this order—as an apprentice hairdresser, in a car-hire firm (until it was discovered that when she had to deliver a car to a client she was driving without a licence) and in an advertising agency. She was the kind of girl whom people, on very short acquaintance, invite to parties. The advertising personnel drank white wine, their symbol of the good life, instead of tea at the usual breaks in the working day; they had many parties. It was certainly at one of these that she must have met her Australian, Canadian, or what-ever he was. Categories were never relevant to her ordering of life. He stared out of beard, eyebrows, brown curls. —So I suppose you're one of the great 'creative team' that persuades people to buy beer and dog-food.— She was not; she was hardly more than a messenger, she carried copy about and opened bottles of white wine. As soon as he realized she was working to eat, not out of devotion to the art of advertising campaigns, he began to assume a scornful collusion with her.

—Oh you mustn't be so hard on them. They're very easy-going people. They're fun.—

—You're quite wrong. They take themselves absolutely seri-ously. They believe they're writers and artists. The muse of consumerism is the new Apollo. Look at that androgynous crea-ture with his pink shoes and little boy's braces. He epitomises the whole crowd. I don't mean because he's queer. They're all neither one thing nor the other. Not workers, not artists. All the exhibi-tionism they imagine is unconventional—meanwhile they are the paid jesters of the establishment, selling the conditioning of the masses on billboards showing girls big as whales.— His yellow eyes rested amiably here and there in the room while he said these things; he even waved a hand at someone in the semaphore of this set that signalled 'I'm making it over here'. —I'd rather watch a snake swallowing a rat, a cat stalking a bird for a meal. I'm for lives lived by necessity.—

This turn of phrase came back to Hillela as the language of childhood, from the voices in Pauline's house. Since his manner contradicted the content of what he was saying, she thought, that first night, he might be drunk. Everyone at these parties was always drunk to some degree, with the consequent rapid changes of mood and disoriented awareness that made them so lively— they called it 'letting your hair down'.

She smiled. —Why do you come, then.—

He turned his face away from the company, an actor going offstage, and spoke as if he half-hoped she would not catch it: —It's necessary for me to be seen in places like this.—

He danced with her and stood in uproariously-laughing groups, an arm around her neck as a casual sexual claim understood in this circle, while jokes were told about copywriters, Afrikaners and Jews, who were present to laugh at themselves, and about blacks, who were not. It was usual for people to pair off after these parties, slipping away; outside she ran with him through the blows of a rain so strong it seemed to be attempting to strip off their clothes. It was so black and close around them that it was not until next morning she saw the outside of the house where they made love and slept the night together. It was the converted servants' quarters of a larger house whose occupants, he said, were 'all right'. She understood the inference, and also that she must not ask why it was necessary for him to have vetted them. (That was the advantage of having lived with Pauline and Joe.) It is doubtful if she was ever quite sure why. Everyone called him Rey, Andrew Rey, but he showed her, once she had moved in with him, a passport in another name with which he had entered the country. That was not his real name; 'too long a story' to explain why if he entered the country under a false identity he lived there under yet another persona. He worked as a free-lance journalist for several newspapers, including a black one, though his byline appeared only in one that was regarded as liberal while at the same time being a respectable part of the economic establishment. —Editorials full of fine phrases about the fight for freedom of the press, but when I bring in my copy on the Mineworkers' Union Congress, the brave editor puts the red pencil through the fact that blacks are seventy-five per cent of the labour force, and they weren't there—they can't be members. And why does the bastard slash my piece? Because the consortiums with their half-dozen company aliases who own the mines, who own everything here, also own the paper, and they don't want any ideas put into the blacks' heads. It's okay to 'deplore' the bombs, to be 'horrified' at the murder of white people in their holiday caravan by blacks who've turned to the Xhosa ruler of the spirits because the white man's Christ hangs on his cross in a segregated church. But it's not done to be 'horrified' and 'deplore' the fact that the only say blacks have is the choice between working on the white man's terms or starving.—

Under his good-time image in the kind of company in which she had met him, his sullen watchfulness from an out-of-the-way seat at the bar where journalists drank and talked sport as nois-ily as politics, his different, insider's watchfulness drinking in the dens of blacks (where he would soon catch a particular eye and turn aside for murmured, monosyllabic privacy) there was a resentment like oil under the earth, welling constantly, flammable in him. Since he could not let it blow before editors and other hypocrites, it found another path, heating him sexually. He would be withdrawn and bitter, and tell her he couldn't tell her why—another one, perhaps, who thought her too stupid to understand. But out of this mood he would make love to her with

the mastery of means, single-mindedness and passionate manipu-
lation of human responses he could not muster in another, his
chosen field of endeavour. This one didn't make love like a boy.
He might not confide, but he knew how to make bodies speak.
People who saw Hillela at that time might recall the nerve-alive
brightness of a young face, where he took her among people and
dumped her for others to talk to; at each stage in life a face in
repose, neglectful of composure, sets in the current dominant
experience of the individual whose face it is—her expression was,
in fact, amazement. She was aware, all the time, of the orches-
tration of her body conducted by him. The art director whose
pink shoes had annoyed her lover complimented her kindly: You
look well-fucked, darling. And she laughed and at the same time
burned with embarrassment—for Olga, for Pauline; and for Joe.

She was, perhaps, happy; she would not remember. The happiness may have been partly to do with something she was not
conscious of: working in an advertising agency, living with this
man, she achieved a balance. A balance between leaving them
all, the advantages they had offered—released by putting them
in a position where they had to put her out—and rejoining *without them* what each had offered: Olga, after all, would approve
of an artistic career in the fashionable advertising industry; the
lover was someone she could have taken home to Pauline's house.
Not that the girl did; not that she wanted to. But this life, even
though it was lived in an out-house like that Alpheus occupied,
was not the dropout's ramshackle of sleazy clubs and fairground
jobs they believed she had left them for.

It might have been a kindness to let them know where she was
and what she was doing: A single letter was found some years
later among Len's 'effects'—two bottles of vodka, a pot of peanut
butter and several copies of *The S.A. Commercial Traveller* in which
he appeared, as a young man, in a group photograph—when he
died in a home for the chronically sick in what had since become

Zimbabwe. *Dear Len, You probably know I'm working now, I've got a fun job in advertising?! I hope to make a career. It's great to be independent and I'm lucky not to be alone. I have a wonderful boyfriend, quite a bit older, he's about thirty and a writer. Nothing to do with advertising—he doesn't approve of that! We may leave the country; he is half Canadian, with—he says—some Red Indian blood from way back. But we won't go to Canada, thank goodness, I don't like the idea of cold countries. And he's never lived there. Maybe we'll pass your way. I know you're in the North now, and it's soon going to be a separate country from Rhodesia, they say. But maybe you'll come back down to Salisbury?*

I don't know whether or not to say I'm sorry about Billie, but I am. I'll send this, with love, to the old address, in the hope someone will post it on.

Five majuscular X kisses and the signature: *Hillela*

It was not quite true that she was independent at that time: she still collected her stipend supplied by what her lover called her 'rich aunt', putting that aunt at a further remove by the loss of a name. It was justified, though an eighteen-year-old's boastfulness, to make some claim for him as a writer. The yard cottage was padded with cuttings. The suitcases under the bed were so heavy with manuscript notes they could not be shifted by Hillela when she wanted to clean the floor—an immense physical gratitude moved her, she was quite housewifely, doing for him all the things—washing shirts, sewing on buttons—Olga's males had done for them by servants, and Pauline's males (in the case of loose buttons and holes in socks) were expected to do for themselves.

He talked about 'his book' as a companion and a leg-iron by which he had been shackled a long time, dragging it around the world with him. It depended before whom its existence was confirmed or denied; sometimes he said five years' work was already virtually completed, at others he said dismissingly he was going to scrap all that, events had overtaken him (in Marxist company, the version was History had done this), corrected perspective, and at other times he would lug out a suitcase and spend a whole night rewriting a sheaf of its contents, while she slept. Next morning the result would be pitched into the suitcase along with older papers flattened under their own weight. He never discussed 'his book' with her and she did not expect him to, assuming its political nature gave it the status of classified: after an enjoyable day in the white-wine camaraderie where a shampoo was being transformed by lyrical images into an elixir of youth, or smoking a particular brand of cigarette was in the process of becoming a ritual of success and distinction, she came home to someone who was almost certainly doing the kind of things most admired and seldom successfully aspired to, in the Pauline home. There, they would have regarded 'his book' as something more important than himself, than his girl, than the lovers together; for her, it was present as someone he had known before her, before she was even grown up, with claims she must walk round on the quiet rubber soles of respect.

Of course—correcting perspective—hadn't she always lived in the eye of the storm? That eye that meteorologists say is safe, a ball of security rolled up in fury, that eye that was whiteness. Pauline, given away by wild-blown hair, put her head out into the cyclone briefly. Others went out and did not come back. But fixedly, the white eye was on itself; Mandela came up from Underground that year with the gales of August that sandpapered the city with mine dust, while white children were waiting for the segregated swimming pools to be opened on September 1st. He went on trial in October for inciting the strike of the previous year and for leaving the country illegally; by then Olga was already planning ahead for December holidays at Plettenberg Bay, phoning friends who, like her, had houses there, to make sure there would be enough young company to keep her sons amused. Fire-bombs continued to explode, according to the news. There had been that ghastly murder of whites in their caravan at Bashee Bridge; but the numerous well-organized caravan camps throughout the official recreation areas of the country were whites-only and perfectly safe. As for the murders of headmen in the Transkei who collaborated with government officials—who knew a headman? All that was ignored as tribal unrest among black peasants. It was satisfactorily reassuring that the last communist front organization, the Congress of Democrats, had been banned in September. And the Sabotage Act was passed, defined widely to include strikes as acts of sabotage—restoring confidence to industrialists while Pauline and Carole had eggs thrown at them from a city balcony when taking part in the last public protest march before the Act put an end to such demonstrations for the duration—of what? The regime was then already in its fifteenth year.

That year when Hillela was living in the city with some man was the same year when torture began to be used by the police. Political suspects—mostly black—who, defended by lawyers like Joe, made such allegations when and if they could get to the courts, were dismissed from any concern of most white people, put out of mind as isolated agitators, left-overs of communist influence who had to be dealt with somehow; liars by ideology, who either invented injury or—looking at the issue paradoxically but righteously—deserved it anyway. And even those who were humanely and morally opposed, on principle, to beatings, applications of electric shocks, disorientation by extended denial of sleep, generally took their stand from under the centre of the white eye's hypnotic gaze. A doctor who had given vital testimony of torture that won the case Joe's team brought on behalf of a black man in a provincial town, described over a drink in the Pauline house his appalling findings on the man's body, and concluded: —By the way, Joe ... while you were appearing in Durban, were you ever invited to the Club? I was given a surprisingly good lunch there ... a charming place, lovely old colonial style ... I really enjoyed it.—

Pauline stared into her glass. —How did you reconcile the two?—

He smiled and quizzed, not following.

She read the dregs of wine as if they were tea-leaves. —Your morning in court. Your evidence. What you'd seen. And the Club.—

He smiled again, broadening the understanding to encompass Joe, anyone. —But they had nothing to do with each other!—

Easy then, with hindsight, to sneer at what was only a young girl excited by the exhibitionism she was too naive to distinguish from concomitant courage; the ex go-go dancer nested amid testimony of horror, happy in the midst of torture. By day she chilled the white wine, at night she was in the alternating current of the man's frustration and resolve, the thrilling tension into which, in his command of her body, he converted the dreadful happenings around her. He raged through a thinned line of mouth at the poor press coverage of revolutionary actions. He disappeared from the yard cottage for days. She was to tell no-one he had gone away; if anyone phoned or called in, he was simply out for a while. This was an important task she had. His reports of what he had seen of the scale of resistance coming from blacks pushed back to starve in the Bantustans, of the violence used by the police against rural people, of the sour and lethal misery this caused between government-paid headmen and desperate villagers—she watched him tear up these reports (rejected by his editors) in a tantrum and throw them into the big bin that served the main house as well as the cottage. She had once cast certain papers in other people's dirt, like that. But, these bits of paper she helped pick out again from under eggshells and vegetable peelings. They taped facts together; he sat down and wrote an article using the same material, but in the context of an accusation—press collusion with white domination. This, like the articles he wrote on concealed evidence of torture, she took in her elegant souvenir sling bag to the advertising agency; although the piece would be published under an alias abroad, its author might be traced by the identification of his typewriter with the typescript—it had happened to other journalists, before: envelopes addressed to newspapers, or even to cover addresses, were opened at the post office before despatch and photocopied for the secret police. It was another important task for her: the sipping and banter of copy-writers and models going on around her, she made her fair copy of subversive documents on one of the agency typewriters. —Time off for a love-letter? I don't blame you, love, they work us to extinction in this loony bin, can't call a thought your own.— It was with this (genuinely female) art director whose yellow-veined blue eyes stood out like an octopus's from a mound of forehead that the girl fell to the childish, vain temptation one day to hint that she was 'sometimes scared' on behalf of Rey, with whom, it was generally known in temporary pairings-off hardly kept count of, the little junior assistant had 'got together' at an agency lush. The woman whose loose, black-dyed hair was designed to make her look more like an elder sister than a mother not only picked up at once the scent of political danger holed up in its love-nest, was stirred by it and passed it on as a rill of risk to touch the agency with daring-by-association; she was also the one who kept absolute discretion when the girl's confidence was taken further. What Sasha had feared did come to pass, but not when he was looking for his cousin in the cinemas where they had spent autumn afternoons. While electric currents were passing through the reproductive organs of others, Hillela had an abortion. It was arranged for her in good hands, by the kindness and understand-ing of the woman art director. Hillela was nineteen. It happened inside her; her body, her life: and the torture was one of the things he—Rey—had ways of knowing about, outside.

On his birthday they took wine along to the house where, lately, they often met the same group of black men. Rey didn't take any notice of birthdays, but it was somebody-or-other's birthday every few days at the agency, and Hillela had acquired a style of adult celebration from there. She wrapped both serious and jokey presents elaborately, bought wine and a cake. The sexy card he glanced at without comment. The witty present (a beard-comb stuck into the orange whiskers of a toy orangoutang) he unwrapped and ignored, and the real elephant-hide attaché case with gilt fittings he looked at, lying there, as one does at something one is confused to see anyone could think one would want.

The wine was drunk, anyway. That was all right. The black men were not those African National Congress Youth Leaguers she had met with him when first she had moved into the yard cottage. He was perhaps collecting other material; they talked closely with him, watching him, some with moving, responsive eyes, others with the in-turned glaze between lids that sometimes dropped, with which blacks keep themselves intact from the invasion of white presences. He was telling them about his 'quiet trips': whom he saw, where he had got himself into, in the Transkei, in Tembuland and Pondoland. He brought messages they tested in silence. She felt indignation welling in her as it did permanently, from another source, in him: *Trust him!* Trust him! But she was not expected to speak. Halfway through the evening a white man came in, apparently from having been only in some other part of the house. His murmured upper-class courtesies and round face that in its texture and tender colouring appeared to be stripped down of several outer skins, seemed to belong to an English climate, yet his recognition of the younger white man signalled acceptance to the blacks: —Of course— you interviewed me in Cape Town, at my house. Some Swedish or German paper ... ?—

The free-lancer changes journalistic alliances too often to be expected to remember or to answer. This one grasped the fingerhold of credentials to press his own questions both stoutly and humbly, in the manner of whites demonstrating loyal support for

146

a black cause and aware of the superiority of the blacks' inner circle of involvement, drawn by experience, language and blood. About 'Qamata'—it had been described to him, in these rural inner circles in which his familiarity suggested he had been received, as a sort of church?

They took their time. There was a spokesman from out of the lazy, acquired deadpan: —It's their god, there. He comes from the sea.—

—One of our gods, Xhosa gods... our religion we had, before.—

—I was told he was the 'ruler of the spirits', a kind of Pantokrator ... top man among the gods ... ?

—Yes, ruler of our other spirits... them all. Those country people, they still believe those things.—

The journalist, with a movement of legs and behind, shifted his chair nearer the spokesman. —Or believe in them again? Weren't they all dosed with Christianity at school?—

Shrugs, and everyone waited for someone else to speak.

—Many people were Christians, but they kept the old customs.—

—Oh I know—I've been among the young *abakwetha* hidden away in the circumcision camps. That's not quite the same thing. I mean, Qamata, as I understand, isn't a hero who once lived, a warrior from precolonial or early colonial times. The old days. He's a different thing, different kind of inspiration, isn't he? A spirit that makes people fearless? Tells them what to do? White people are saying Poqo is like Mau Mau—of course you know that, it's inevitable. But is the idea that Qamata ... an African god, a Xhosa god is something that can chase away the god of submission, the Christian god who says 'thou shalt not kill', and make killing a sacrifice for freedom?—

—What's new with that? The Christian god's killed plenty, plenty! Here and in the world! He gives his blessing to the wars of white people.—

—You're right! So how will he give it to blacks! That's where Qamata comes in.—

The spokesman's broad, relaxed chest, naked under a football jersey, heaved to life. He kept everyone waiting while he dropped his head to one side, rolled it against the sofa back. —The Qamata thing ... it's really among the rural people, man, you must understand that. It's not policy. But regionally ... the people work out a lot of things for themselves, we don't interfere unless ...—

—But it's useful, it brings people together where political concepts like constitutions and programmes don't reach?— The lover put his fist on his breast.

—If you want to know about the Xhosa religion, man, you should talk to a guy like Prof here, I don't go along too much with that kind of stuff.—

—I just want to understand what I've seen, what I've been told. I don't want to misinform anybody—and that's for your sake... You don't want people believing, that Mau Mau story. Then tell me—

A small man who had been listening with distended nostrils, an alertness displaced from his ears, blew words like cigarette smoke across her face.—Let them believe. Kenyatta won. He's getting the country. Without Kimathi, the Queen of England would still have it. Let them believe.—

Rey was laughing, rubbing his taut palms along his thighs. —Qamata!— He drew himself into a knot of the white man, the man they called Prof, the spokesman and a very young man whose upper body danced up and down as he tried to interject and sometimes laughed harshly with frustration. The white girl was accustomed to being left to occupy or entertain herself until, as she saw it, 'his book' had garnered what was wanted for it. The black men around her began talking in their own language. It grew long, the night of the uncelebrated birthday. She dozed off, sitting on the sofa with the cadences and exclamations of an African language flying round her, accumulating in layers between the layers of smoke, wavering away and towards her ears; the lullaby without words, for her, surrounding all her childhood. The *platteland* towns where the commercial traveller took his little sweetheart, the Rhodesian boarding-school, the rich aunt's villa at the sea, the old church path where children sang picking their way past excreta, the shop window where schoolgirls danced, the kitchen where a former trumpet player with the Extra Strongs took refuge.

When they got back at two in the morning the cottage was in darkness as they had left it, but the door stood open as if they were expected. He felt round the jamb for the light switch. Again, there was the shock of light on a disorder; a blinding exposure. This time, it was she herself who called out: *Rey!* And he was beside her, but could not make what was there fly back to the way it was before—clothes, paper-spewing suitcases, books, the stuffing from eviscerated cushions—as a film run in reverse. There was no-one waiting. This was confirmed at once; the cottage was small. Whoever had ransacked it had found or not found what they wanted and gone. But this time, this exposure, was different. What had been turned up in the middle of the night had no context of other lives to resorb it. They went back to the house they had left and threw pebbles at the windows until the gentle-complexioned white man came down in a handsome towelling gown and took them in. Next day they went to stay with other friends-of-friends. Every day, her lover believed, must be lived at a further remove from the cottage. Nothing was ever to be restored of the life she lived there. Only the object that he himself had thrown aside, the toy orang-outang with the beard-comb, had become something in place, lying on the floor where it was dropped among its torn gold wrappings as if it had drawn down everything about it.

He was convinced that he was going to be arrested. Whether this was so or not nobody can say. Many premises are raided; there are not always consequences of the kind he foresaw, building up for her and for those who sheltered them a case against himself. Fear and self-esteem—his conviction of his own threat to others confirmed as it could be only by the assumption of himself being in danger—burned his old resentments as the fuel of elation. He made love more often than ever, and each race to the finish might be the last. His face presented itself as the face that must be looked at as a last look, at any ordinary moment of the day. She opened white-wine bottles and no-one knew the other tipsiness that animated her, now. She confided in no-one; no longer, not she. Sitting a moment on someone's desk, swinging her legs and chattering; no-one knew that next day she might not be there, one day soon would simply not be there. She and he: gone.

He did not even risk going back for what might be left of 'his book'. A friend-of-a-friend would go to the cottage and send later whatever papers were there. He—and the little girl, of course—would bum a few clothes (friends who weren't in danger surely owed them that much) and disappear as they were. The only problem was money. —I can manage, I don't care. But with you ... Maybe you should follow.—

For the first time, there was fear to be seen in her shining, opaque black eyes. —I'll get money. For both.—

It must have been in June 1963, exact date unknown, she left South Africa. Whether by air under assumed names, or by some Underground route overland, they were gone, she and whoever the man was. His name does not appear in any accounts of resistance during the period, his book seems never to have been published. No-one even gives him the credit for having been the one who, however reluctantly, moved her on.

*

It was to Joe Hillela went so that she wouldn't be left behind. To his rooms, asking to see him and sitting in the waitingroom among clients. These were blacks as well as whites, sharing the same chairs and journals, *The Motorist* and *Time* passed on, perhaps, from the household of one of Joe's new partners, the English *Guardian* and local liberal reviews she recognized as from the stacks in Pauline's livingroom. She didn't have to pass time with any of these. Joe appeared as soon as her name was taken in to him. Being Joe, there was no demonstration of surprise, pleasure or displeasure. He simply put up a hand and flagged a quiet, coaxing movement. He stood back to let her pass before him through his doorway: Joe, the smell of the shaving cream standing like a tongue'd icecream cone on the bathroom shelf, the buzzing cello voice sustained behind the high babble at family meals. He kissed her gently and held a moment the fingers of the hand she awkwardly took back.

—How have you been?— Even when she and his own daughter were children he had always treated them like grown-up ladies; she was under an old guidance, taking a chair he displaced from where clients customarily faced him across his desk. He drew up another, leaving his professional place empty. Her face was ready to fawn in parrying smiles, culpability, girlish charm at the formula of insincere reproaches that did not come; *months and months, not a word, thought you'd forgotten us!*

—Oh fine. I'm working in an advertising agency. Oh yes, and they haven't kicked me out yet, marvel of marvels. I've actually been there—what—about six months or so.—

She knew his pace. He didn't pretend not to be studying her. The last season of good clothes Olga used to supply was lost, along with the cottage, but friends who had offered her 'something to wear' had not failed to notice she took the best garments, not the most ordinary, hanging in their modest cupboards. For this visit she had picked a full black skirt that sank round from her small waist as she made herself comfortable, and an Indian shirt of thin red silk slit from a high collar down her brown neck to her wide-set breasts. Thin chains slid in and out of the opening as she gestured.

—There were quite a few jobs before then? Turnover pretty high?— They laughed together, after so long, she and Joe.

—Don't tell me! You were right about qualifications … you have to be prepared to take anything.—

—Anything?—

—Well, just about.—

After a moment, he spoke. —You didn't take 'anything'.—

There was the 'on my honour' tone of childhood. —I didn't—

He confirmed with his slow turn of the head, aside.

—We don't have the right to ask, anyway.— But he saw she was still so young that she was afraid of references to the family's rejection of her; the taboo she had broken made responsibility towards her a taboo subject, as well. Her mouth opened a moment, in unease. It seemed to him to contradict the new maturity, clenched hardness, of the way her cheekbones stood out. (She had lost weight after the abortion.) The eyes, without the differentiation between iris and pupil that makes it possible to read eyes' expression, were drawn miserably half-closed and then opened again, full on him. Her concern and confusion jumped at him like the attention of an affectionate puppy. —Of course, of course you've got the right, of course you have! You'll always have, I promise you!—

He was able to turn the emotion to a gentle, shared joke that gracefully accepted bonds between him and her, belonging to but surviving the past. —Now that's the correct way with the verb! Future tense! You and Carole used to drive us crazy by using it in the context of something already achieved: 'I did my homework last night, I promise you'—

—So you see I have learnt something … a little.—

—A lot, Hillela, a lot. You have earned your own living and lived your own life, without help from any of us.— Olga's hand-out was not worth his mention.

Joe's silences were comfortable. At the end of them, there was always some sort of understanding, as if, coming from him as the thread the spider issues from its body and uses to draw a connection from leaf to leaf across space, some private form of communication had been spun.

—So ... here I am.—

—And so you should be.—

—I'm going to ask you something. Something big. It's a lot to ask for. I won't blame you at all if you won't—can't.—

His old gesture: he rested an elbow on the arm of the chair and pressed a finger into the sag of his cheek. —Go on.—

She smiled with calculation, innocent in knowing, showing it to be so. —Not the others, just you.—

—What is said in these professional rooms is naturally confidential.— Dear Joe, teasing her a little while giving another, serious assurance—whatever she was going to ask, he would grant by the default of those whom she could not ask. —Go on, Hillela.—

The small taut fold of skin that formed beneath each eye sank away, drawn back over her cheekbones. It was a feature of her particular image she had had since childhood. She looked at him out of childhood, her darkness, where the natural moisture of her eyes made a shining line along the membrane of each lower lid.

—It's money.—

Slowly as he watched, her face changed; the molecules of this girl's being rearranged themselves into the exact aspect they had had when she lay under the sudden bright light, his gaze and Pauline's, calm in bed beside his son.

Joe judged himself, in the end, no more trustworthy than anyone else. He did tell Pauline. Pauline heard of the escapade—flight, defection, or whatever it was supposed to be—from Olga, of all people. Olga, who herself had long had contingency plans, was the first to hear that her niece had been out of the country for some weeks. The news came to her through the husband of a friend, a client of the advertising agency where, apparently, the girl had had the latest in a series of all kinds of jobs. The husband was told in confidence; the agency's directors did not want to shake clients' confidence by allowing any suggestion that their advertising portfolios would be handled by politically suspect people. The girl in question had no position of access to the creative process—she was described (euphemistically) as hardly more than a tea-maker. But the husband remembered his wife talking of her friend Olga's adoptive daughter of that unusual name; so he was able to supply a piece of gossip for dinner parties. His wife came out with it tactlessly in the presence of Arthur. Olga, from across the table, had to make a quick correction: —We'd never actually *adopted*—no—she has her father ... She already hadn't lived with us for some years—we've been completely out of touch—

Pauline burst the news to Joe: —That's a laugh! Hillela, 'having to flee the country'! That's how my sister puts it, I could feel her trembling in her boots, at the other end of the phone ... What could Hillela have done, she didn't even have any interest in helping black schoolchildren on Saturday mornings! Smoking pot in a coffee bar, that was more in that little girl's line.— Joe's customary considered reactions meant that Pauline did not notice he already knew what she had just learned. But he told her, then, of the girl's visit to his rooms because he saw that jealousy was mixed, in distress, with guilt, for Pauline. He made the mistake of phrasing it: —She came to me.—

—Came to *you*!—

How expressive these faces of his women were, how frightening in their importunity: the dyes of hurt, resentment, indignation

154

were always so quickly there to flood the cheeks and brow of Pauline.

—It was what she was told to do, you know.—

—But this kind of trouble! Hillela! She has no political sense, no convictions, not the faintest idea, that child! Hillela a political refugee—from what, I'd like to know! Now no-one can keep an eye on her. None of us can do anything, she's made sure of that. We've let it happen. Hillela a political refugee. What idiocy. What a final mess. God knows what will become of her.—

—She has the money. In good foreign currency.—

—And how did you get *that* for her?—

But what was arranged within the walls of professional confidence was not to be divulged further; his wife knew that he must have done what the ethics of that profession did not allow, and that he had never done before—contravened currency restrictions in some shady way. Hillela, of course, would not stop to think of consequences for others, then as at any other time. Yet suddenly anger became tears in Pauline's eyes.

—How long will it last.—

At least Joe's breach of confidence enabled her to telephone Olga and let her know that no-one in Pauline's family was trembling in their boots; on the contrary, Joe had done the practical thing, Joe had seen to it that the girl had funds of some sort for whatever predicament, real or imaginary, she had got herself into.

In July a country estate, in the area near the city where the rich lived to escape suburbia, was raided by the police. The people living at the evocatively-named Lilliesleaf Farm were not enjoying their gardens and stables but were the High Command of liberation movements planning to put an end to the subjection of blacks by whites by whatever means whites might finally make necessary. Walter Sisulu, Govan Mbeki, Ahmed Kathrada and a whole bold houseparty of others, white and black, were arrested, and Nelson Mandela was brought from prison to be tried with them on new charges. Olga—by now afraid to talk over the telephone; the girl was a blood relation, after all, it couldn't be denied if the police should make enquiries—came to see her sister. Was there anything to the story that it was known at the agency Hillela had gone with a man? Only a month earlier? Maybe he was mixed up in the Farm affair, perhaps it had been just in time … ? Pauline gave a light laugh at this—*flattery;* at Olga. But the idea provided the base for some sort of explanation that slowly came to serve, in the end. Attached herself to some man—that's what it was all about. *He* was the one who had to go.

Pauline and Olga were only two of three sisters, after all; still.

Attached herself to some man.

My poor Ruthie.

I, me.

Time, now. They had always, they went on fitting that self into their conjugations, leaving out the first person singular. Except one of the cousins, poor boy; he didn't.

It's not possible to move about in the house of their lives. A china cat survived two centuries and was broken. Awful.

Intelligence

Tamarisk Beach in the late afternoons was the place of resurrection. Those who had disappeared from their countries while on bail, while on the run, while under house arrest; that non-criminal caste of people from all classes and of all colours strangely forced to the subterfuge of real criminals evading justice—they reappeared on foreign sand in swimming shorts and two-piece swimsuits. While they swam, their towels, shoes, cigarettes were dumped for safety in numbers under the three etiolated tamarisks for which the British colonial families had named the beach once reserved for their use. Now hungry, raucous local youths hung about there all day, acrobatically light-fingered. If those of the new caste—big men, some of them, cultivated on distant soccer fields—looked warningly at the boys, they jacked themselves swiftly up palm boles and laughed, jeering from the top in their own language, that not even the strangers who were black as they were understood. Sometimes a coconut came down from there like a dud bomb, unexploded, from the countries left behind; the local boys fought over it just the way the scorpions they would set against one another in a sand arena fought, and the victor hawked it round for sale.

There was no respite from heat in weeks passing, months passing. Like exile itself, a sameness of time without the trim and shape of home and work, the heat was unattached to any restraints of changing seasons. Only in the late afternoons did something stir sameness: a breath blew in under it, every afternoon, one of those trade winds that had set history on course towards prehistory, bringing first the Chinese and then the Arabs to that coast.

It brought to Tamarisk Beach the men from alley offices with unpaid telephone bills and liberation posters, from the ante-rooms of European legations where they waited to ask for arms and money, and from the comings and goings between taken-over colonial residences and ex-governors' offices where rival political groups struggled to keep their credentials acceptable to their host country, lobbying, placing themselves in view of the powerful, watching who in the first independent black government there was on his way up to further favour, and worth cultivating, and who was dangerous to be associated with because he might be on his way down.

The exile caste came to the beach for air. And then the original impulse—to breathe!—became part of a social ritual, a forma-tion of a new regularity, a necessary ordering of a place where other needs that cannot be done without might be met. Many had experienced this kind of formation even in jail. On Tamarisk Beach they strolled through the colonnades of palms, avoiding or meeting each other, eyeing across a stretch of sand faces sepa-rated by the distance of alliances dividing Moscow and Peking, East Germany and the United States, or the desert distance of solitary confinement and the stony alienation that succeeds screams in those who have known torture since last meeting. They paused to pick tar and oil-slick from the soles of their feet, and scratched the hair on their chests, smoked, shook water from their ears—just for those hours in the late afternoon could have been holiday-makers anywhere. There were some women among them, political lags, like the men, and defiantly feminine, keep-ing up with curled, home-tinted hair, ingenious cut of local cotton robes as sun-dresses, and cheap silver-wire jewellery from the market craftsmen, the high self-image needed to defeat the humiliations of prison. There was sensuality on Tamarisk Beach. It came back with the relief of a breeze; it came back with the freeing of bodies from the few clothes thrust into a suitcase for exile and worn in the waitingrooms and makeshift living quarters of exile. It became a pattern of human scale made by strollers in the monumental arcade of palms and swimmers dabbling in the great Indian Ocean at the edge of a continent.

There were hangers-on, at Tamarisk. Not only the thieving urchins, but friends and acquaintances picked up by the exiles, and the appendages of love affairs and casual dependencies of all kinds. There were also those who passed as these and were suspected, found out or never discovered to be part-time informers for the governments whose enemies the exiles were. Most of the 'beach rats', as they were known, were themselves expatriates —black and white—who had been expelled from or broken with a series of schismatic groups in the exile community; others had become misfits, easy to recruit for pocket-money spying, in a survival of the old European tradition of black sheep. In imperialist times, these whites were 'sent out' to the colonies; in the break-up of colonial empires, their counterparts took advantage of transitional opportunities to get by, far away from the censure of home, in some warm place whose different mores didn't concern them. It would have been difficult to distinguish impostors from the genuine, those afternoons on the beach. The tall Jew whose incipient tyre around the waistline was being prodded at by a wobbly-breasted blonde girl—what was there to show, in his mock affront, that the black beard he still wore he had grown in order to escape across a border disguised as one of the White Father missionaries, dangling cross, breviary and all? Who could tell the difference between the credentials of a little beauty with a Huguenot delicacy of face-structure, speaking Afrikaans, and the black man, her fellow countryman, talking trade union shop with her in the same language? Hadn't both served their apprenticeship as jailbirds, back there? Suspect everybody or nobody. Leaning on an elbow in the sand, talking to an intimate, wandering to borrow a cigarette and join this group or that, resting one's back, in sudden depression, against a palm-pillar in this place of littered sand and urine-tepid shallows—gossip and guarded tongues erratically mingled with the long-held breaths expelled by the ocean on a coral reef. Among the regulars, every afternoon, there was a girl who looked as if she had slept in her clothes and hadn't combed her hair. Probably true; many, through obscure quarrels of doctrine and discipline, found themselves not provided for by any liberation movement housed up rotting stairs. This one (a man who was doing his best, without funds, to drink himself to death on local gin) had left his country before receiving permission from his cadre to do so. That one (staring at the sea as if to blind himself with its light) belonged to another organization and had defied its policy: recognized the validity of the white courts by accepting *pro deo* legal defence.

The Afrikaner woman noticed the girl about: she was clean, the hair naturally like that, tangled because in need of a cut—just living through hard times, as everyone was, more or less. She seemed a loner, but not lonely; at least, the men appeared to know that she was approachable. She came by herself to the beach, but as soon as her presence was noted there was always some man, arms crossed over his chest, digging a toe in the sand, chatting to her. The tamarisks cast no more than a fishnet of shade. She sat there beside other people's possessions the way the stray dogs came to settle themselves just beyond cuffs and blows.

When the Afrikaner woman saw the big safety-pin that held together the waistband of the girl's jeans above a broken zipper, she had one of the contractions in her chest just where, whatever rational explanation there was, she knew there to be some organ capable of keener feeling than the brain. It was this organ, taking over from all the revolutionary theory she had studied since recruitment at seventeen in a jam factory, that had been responsible for her arrest along with black women protesting against the pass laws, and her bouts of imprisonment as an organizer of illegal strikes and defier of laws decreeing what race might live where. She asked about the girl. The story was doing the rounds, by then: that was the girl who had come with that Andrew Rey fellow, the journalist. The man who had disappeared, dumped her, now. The one who was found to be politically unreliable (the informant was a member of the Command in exile and had the authority to decide such things). As for his girl ... what was anyone to do with her. She clearly didn't belong to any movement at all; his camp-follower, pretty little floozy. But he had misrepresented himself, and she must have moved about with him in all his unacceptable contacts, so she wasn't *their* responsibility, really.

Yet the Afrikaner woman brought her a pair of her own jeans, concealed in one of the straw bags from the market so the girl wouldn't be embarrassed by receiving charity in front of everyone at the beach. As she became accepted—because Rey had betrayed her, too—as one at least by implication belonging to the cause Rey was suspected of double-crossing, the member of the Command was among the men on the beach, far from their wives and likely to be for many years, with whom she slept.

Certainly she had no place to sleep in alone. Not until the Afrikaner woman decided something must be done about her. Christa Zeederburg, urged to reminisce at the end of her life, never forgot the safety-pin. —Just an ordinary safety-pin, the kind you buy on a card, for babies' nappies. That's all she had, then!—

If you have lived your young life with Jethro and Bettie to feed you and at worst always an aunt's stipend deposited monthly, it must be difficult to believe there is nothing for you in the houses you pass and the banks in their pan-colonial classical grey stone with brass fittings. For many weeks she was waiting for Rey to come back; that was her status. She was living in their room in an old hotel from British times which now functioned only as a bar; his radio was on the wicker table and his pyjamas were still under the pillows. He had gone on a quick trip to Sweden about a communications development project they wanted him to start in East Africa, or (depending to whom he was talking) to Germany to tie up a television documentary based on a book he was writing. She knew she could not go along. Already there had been problems; when the vehicle that took them from Northern Rhodesia arrived at their country of refuge, it turned out that although she had no passport he—quite properly, a professional in these matters—had an Irish one. He went with his companions to the local hotel in the small frontier town; she spent the night in the local jail—well, on an old sofa in the, chief warder's office, they couldn't put a white girl in the sort of cells they had. It was quite fun, really, she could sleep anywhere and wake up fresh. Her experience was something they joked about together, next day, all very exciting, like the leopard they saw crossing a red road at dawn. It disappeared into the bush as they themselves were doing, hour after hour, mile after mile, beyond pursuit.

He had taken only half the money. He wouldn't hear of taking more than that; he was going to come back with grants that would keep them for two or three years, they were going to look for a flat—or an old house, why not occupy one of the nice old houses with gardens the colonists had fled when independence came to this country? She was in one, once, while he was away. Some people from the beach took her along to a party given by the representative of a European press agency. The agency operated comfortably; there was a telex chattering in what had been a children's playroom, and the agency chief could refresh himself in the leaking swimming pool. She would have written immediately to tell what a good idea it would be to have a house like that from which the development project could be run, and the television documentary planned, but she had no address. She thought of looking round for such a house, in preparation. But the suburb along the sea was a long walk from town, and soon the taxis, reassuringly humble with their missing doorhandles and rust-gnawed mudguards, had become expensive in relation to the money she had left.

Unlike observers, she expected him back any day. She passed the days wandering purposefully about, looking, listening, smelling, tasting. The ancient town was a Mardi Gras for her, everybody in fancy dress that could not possibly be daily familiar: the glossy black men in braided cotton robes and punch-embroidered skull caps, the Arab women with all their being in their eyes, blotted out over body, mouth and head by dark veils, the skinny, over-dressed Indian children, bright and finicky as fishing-flies, the stumps of things that were beggars, and the smooth-suited, smooth-jowled Lebanese merchants touched with mauve around the mouth who sat as deities in the dark of stifling shops. Her watch was stolen in the hotel and she kept track of time by a grand public clock-face and the regular call of the muezzins from the mosques. There were no laws—nothing to prevent her going down into the black quarters of the town, here, except the rotting vegetables and sewer mud that had to be stepped through, and the little claws of beggar children that fastened on her whenever she smiled a greeting, not knowing that every day she had less and less to give away. She bought pawpaws and big, mealy plantains, more filling than ordinary bananas, down there; cheaper than in the markets. She picked them from the small pyramid of some woman whose stock and livelihood they were, arranged among the garbage, spittle, and babies scaled with glittering flies. She ate the fruit in place of lunch and dinner on a broken bench on the esplanade and did not get sick.

Olga, Pauline, even Len—they had never given her the advantage of knowing what to say to someone to whom one owes money and can't pay. The wife of the hotel proprietor stopped her as she came along the verandah where her room was, and broke her silence.

—Going on for six weeks, and rates are strictly weekly, dear. You know that, don't you? We aren't running a charity. *We* have to pay even the yard boys the fancy new minimum wage this government's set down, I don't know how much longer we're gonna be prepared to carry on, anyway.— A drop of water run down to one of the spiral ends of the girl's hair had fallen on the dry suncancer of the woman's forearm. —*We* have to pay for the water you're using for those lovely cold showers you take whenever you fancy.— From the day that fellow went off with his briefcase, never mind the pyjamas left under the pillows, the proprietor had not been happy about the situation. There'd been bad experiences before with that CCC lot who'd taken over Tamarisk for themselves. That's what the regular white residents from the old days called them: commies, coons and coolies. She looked at this cocky miss who played the guitar in her room as if the world owed her a living; looked in a way that made the girl feel she would be physically prevented, by the barrier of a scaly arm, from getting past her.

—I haven't any money.—

She didn't think of assuring that she was only waiting for 'her friend' to come back; of promising all would be set right and paid then—soon. It was only when she knew, quite simply, what to say that with that truthful statement another became true: she was not waiting. She was now one of the regular coterie of Tamarisk Beach, making out. She packed her bag and hung the room key on the board behind the unattended reception desk. The pyjamas she left under the pillows.

How are things? Oh, I'm making out. At best, the phrase used on the beach meant one had found somewhere 'to stay' ('to live' belonged to a kind of claim left behind in the home country) or that a relevant liberation organization had created a title, *Education Officer, Publicity Secretary, Liaison Assistant,* that provided a chair, if not a desk, in an office, and a stipend even more modest than that of a rich aunt. She had neither job, nor stipend, nor anywhere to stay unless the beach was somewhere, until Christa Zeederburg (her name should be recorded along with that of the woman art director with the octopus eyes) provided a sleeping bag on the floor of some other people's flat. It is possible the girl actually did sleep out at Tamarisk a couple of nights, taking the warmth of the sand and the thick air for harmlessness, recklessly unaware of danger, as in one of those anecdotes about small children who are found happily unharmed, playing with a snake. More likely that whomever she drifted away from the beach with in the evening found themselves saddled with her for the night. And it was quite customary for people who had a place to stay to allow others to dump their suitcases and duffle bags there. One might live out of such a base, calling in when one needed a change of clothes. Why did she have only one pair of jeans, with a broken zipper? What had happened to the clothes, most of them quite good, she had appropriated by right of a hunted status before she fled with her lover? Clothing of 'European' cut and style was short in a poor country trying to save foreign exchange; probably, to buy herself pawpaws and plantains, she sold the clothes in the wrong places (Christa Zeederburg reminisces) at poor prices, foolish girl, compared with what could have been obtained on the other kind of black market. Oh if Pauline, if Olga had known how little one could make out on, in money, comfort, calculation, principles and respectability, and stay healthy and lively, with good digestion and regular menstruation!

But they were never to know, and no doubt she who had been their charge was to make sure she herself would forget.

Poor countries provide for poverty. There was not only cheap over-ripe fruit that had improved her figure—Christa, of course, had found a swimsuit and sewn in the sag, so that those who had not slept with the girl watched with the envious desire to know more the sucking movement of the flat belly under wet yellow knit, and the deep rift of breasts into which sea water trickled down out of sight. There were all kinds of vendors of goods and services without the surcharge of overheads. She was outside one of those stone-and-polished-brass banks she had no more business to enter than the old crippled black man who sat on the pavement with his portable workshop spread neatly handy. For days she had been flapping along with a broken thong on her only pair of sandals; for a coin the shoemaker repaired the sandal while she leaned against the bank walls with a bare foot tucked up beneath her. The sun on Tamarisk had provided her with the free cosmetics of a dark, fruit-skin tan and a natural bleach of her hair. The heat made her languid and patient; she was enjoying the sureness with which hands like black roots snipped a little patch of leather to size, folded and sewed it, attached it to the broken thong and hammered flat to the sole the nail that was to hold it in place. It was just then that she experienced a surge of something, a falling into place of people passing that came from the unfamiliar moments of standing still while all flowed, as if one belonged there like the shoemaker, instead of being in passage. And the Africans, the Arabs, the Lebanese, and the Europeans from embassies, economic missions and multinational companies wearing tropical-weight trousers wrinkled at buttocks and knees by sweat, no longer were a spectacle but motes in a kind of suspension, a fluid in which she was sustained.

A man among passersby noticed her in that moment; she did not distinguish him. But he had come into her orbit as others had done and were to do. A few days later Christa took her along to a friend's flat. A free meal was never to be by-passed; on the way, she scarcely bothered to listen to Christa: —German fellow, I think he used to be in import and export, now he's going to represent a trade union foundation that's helping to organize in industry here. He got friendly with Mapetla and that crowd from home. That's how I know him, and now he's after me all the time, you know how persistent Germans are, wants me to teach him how to organize among blacks! He's a very generous fellow. He keeps giving me books, newspaper cuttings, I don't know what else. You'll see what a lunch we'll have ... he's got a cook and everything.—

He wasn't one of the beach people. Hillela had never before seen their host, with his deep T-shaped transverse and vertical clefts where the razor could not reach properly in the stubby chin, the red underlip with dark patches like tea-leaves he had forgotten to wipe away, and imprisoned behind thick glasses in that botched face, magnified grey eyes with ferny lashes. They changed at once when he saw her. For him there was no need of introduction. —You can stand like a flamingo on one leg. With your bright pink skirt.—

—Udi, what on earth are you talking about—this is Hillela, you don't mind me bringing her along—

—I am de-lighted ... also, you are very welcome to bring along anyone of your friends ... any time. I am glad her shoes are mended. But I wish she would be wearing her lovely pink skirt.— He held in his diaphragm with an almost military courtesy as he showed them into his livingroom.

—I couldn't. It's Christa's. Don't you notice, she's got it on?—

—So? Oh you're right... she has ... So ... But two legs, that's not the same thing, *that's a bird of a different feather* ... how could I be expected ...—

There was fish cooked in green coconut milk, then the cook brought in a dessert called *Zitronencréme* he had been taught to make. Alsatian wine revived trade union anecdotes in Christa and set flowing one of those instant friendships of tipsy laughter. —Isn't she wonderful, our Christa, with her funny oohs and aahs and her thick Boer accent?— —Hillela, do you hear that! From zat Cherman!— Even the mock insults were pleasing and approving. —Well, I've just heard him speaking Swahili to the cook, and I don't hear you saying anything but *jambo, jambo* after how long? You've been here a year?—

—And you?— The man's attention raced flatteringly between the woman and the girl. —How long are you going to go on saying only *jambo?*—

—Oh well, Hillela's right about me ... but she doesn't need any Swahili, she's on her way to Canada.—

The atmosphere was not one in which kindly lies were necessary.—No, I'm not. Christa, you know I'm not.— The man smiled sadly at the charming head shaking curls in a disclaimer. —Good. You stay here. This's a nice place. Hot, dull, poor, nice. Isn't it, Christa. Let's keep her here.—

—Then will you give her somewhere to stay? You've got this big flat... how many rooms ...— Christa tucked her head back to her shoulder, a child looking up round a palace. —All this to yourself. She's sleeping under a kitchen table. I'm telling you! And there are cockroaches—oooe, I hate those filthy things—

The other two laughed at her expression of horror, she laughed at herself; she who had survived interrogations and prison cells.

—That is your Room 101, Christa. Now we know.— But neither of the women caught the reference to Orwell.

Finishing the wine extended lunch. Hillela was not seen on Tamarisk that afternoon; they went off for a drive in his car, Christa still entertaining them, he solicitous and even momentarily authoritarian: —Fasten that strap across you, please. Now, this is how it opens—you try it once or twice, please— Hillela had not worn a seat-belt before. They were not compulsory back where she came from. —I feel like a kid in a pram.—

—All right. I'll adopt you.— It was said dryly, inattentively; he was turning out of his parking space into the street. Bicycles shot zigzag past and he called after them in Swahili, black-robed women congealed together out of the way. His lips pursed thickly on that chin, the chin pressed on the shirt-collar; he had about him the stubborn weariness of one who lives as a spectator.

Udi Stück demanded nothing. Christa came home—she had a job as a part-time receptionist to an Indian doctor as well as her title as some kind of welfare officer at Congress headquarters—not sure whether or not to be pleased with herself. —I was only fooling, that day ... But I bumped into Udi this morning, and you'll never guess, he's taken me seriously—he says he'll give you a place to stay in the meantime. I was only fooling ... I feel a bit bad ... as if I pushed him to it, taking advantage because he's so generous.—
Hillela used the schoolgirl phrase. —Is he keen on you?—
Christa's burst of laughter that shook her like a cough: —Me? Oooe, I hope not! No-oo-o. That's why I like him, poor old Udi, he's not like the others who think once you're on your own here, got nobody, no family ... you can't get away from them. That Dr Khan—I don't know how much longer I'll be able to keep on that job. He's always coming in and making some excuse to lean over to see what I'm doing. He presses his soft tummy against me. Oh it's no fun being a woman. Sometimes.— She wriggled her shoulders in one of her exaggerated exhibitions of revulsion. —I can't get over Udi taking me seriously ... Oh I think he feels guilty, us with nothing, living all over the place, and he didn't even have to leave Germany because of Hitler, he's not a Jew. He's got that lovely flat—didn't you like the way the sittingroom has open brick-work at the top of the wall so's the air comes in? And at night, there's always a breeze from the bay, he's so high up, it must be cool to sleep there. I only feel bad because of his wife—apparently his wife died last year and he sort of doesn't want to have people around, he wants his privacy. But you must jump at it! You'll have a room to yourself. Fish in coconut milk. That whatsis-zitron pudding—oh my god, I could eat that every day— She hugged the girl while they laughed.

—But don't *you* want to take the room, then?—

—No, no-ooe, I'm okay here with the Manakas, I couldn't leave Sophie and Njabulo. They'd be terribly hurt.— Christa, the real refugee, one who knew prison just as did the black refugee couple with whom she and her protégée were staying.

It would surely be a relief to the Manakas not to have their tiny kitchen doubling as a bedroom any longer, but Sophie kissed the girl she had given shelter and was gracious as any Olga with a private bathroom and a rose to offer. —A-ny time. Bring your blankets and come back to us a-ny time. We always find a place for you. We must help each other in these strange countries. It is terrible, terrible to be far from home. But we must stick together, fight together, and we are going back!—

So it was not for long that Hillela as a young girl slept on the beach or a kitchen floor and lived on over-ripe fruit and Sophie Manaka's mealie-meal with cabbage. *Trust her.* That was the observation that went around on Tamarisk Beach. She was still seen there most afternoons, in the yellow swimsuit. She was part of the company that lay like a fisherman's catch spread out on the sand, holding post-mortems on political strategies used back home, exchanging political rumours and sometimes roused, as a displacement of the self each had accustomed to living like this, by the arrival of a new member for their ranks, standing there urgently vertical to their horizontals, dazed, the tension of escape seeming to throb in the throat like the life pulsating in some sea creature taken from its element and peddled round the beach before them in the sun. Arnold of the Command or one of his designates usually accompanied such people; a bodyguard not against any physical dangers but to ensure that the relief of being 'out' and bringing firsthand news from home would not result in loose talk. A Beach Rat was sure to be grooming its whiskers in every group. It must be assumed that everything that was said on Tamarisk became what is known in the vocabulary of police files and interrogation rooms as intelligence, and would result back home in more arrests; more valuable people forced out to approach slowly, over the sand, to join the company.

Arnold would walk up the beach with newcomers; they sat apart, and the flash of his rimless glasses was enough to keep away anyone who might think of joining them. Their absorption was intense as can be only in those in whom singleness of purpose has taken hold of every faculty of intellect and feeling, so that even if that purpose is to be frustrated for a lifetime in prison, or to be exercised far removed from the people and places where its realization begins to take place, all other purposes in life are set aside, perhaps for ever, because each in some way contradicts the single one. Arnold was a lawyer—like Joe—who would never practise law again; the law in his country enforced the very social order his purpose was to end. He had a wife—like Pauline?—with whom he would never set up home again in the house where only white people could live. His children would grow up here and there—like Hillela herself—without his knowing them; there could be no family life for whites, with blacks, at best, illegally given a place in their converted garages. Christa's brother with his farm on land from which blacks had been removed could not be her brother while Sophie and Njabulo were her family. Mothering girls without a decent pair of jeans to their names, she could not have married the Afrikaner doctor in Brits who was in love with her, and mothered children he would take to the segregated Dutch Reformed Church every Sunday.

Arnold, rising from a conclave, paused on the beach as a bee holds, in mid-air. At the signal of the flower-yellow swimsuit, he waded into the water. There was no surf. A transparent grass-green was a huge lens placed from shore to reef over sand like ground crystal. He kept his own glasses on when he swam; the image of the girl's body under water swayed and shone, broke and reformed. His hairy toes struck him as ugly as crabs. He and she began to swim around each other. He had a soft way of speaking, conspiratorial rather than sexually modulated. —So you've got yourself nicely fixed up.—

—Oh ... ? Yes. Somewhere to stay.—

—Clever girl. Lucky Udi.—

—I was fine with Sophie and Njabulo but it was hard on them.—

—Left the beach—high and dry.—

She pinched her nose between thumb and forefinger and submerged herself, like a child at a swimming pool. When she came up, smiling, he was still talking.'

—You'd better watch out, with him.—

—He's a good friend of Christa's, really nice. I've got a room as big as Sophie's whole flat! You can see the town and the bay.—

—Are you sure it's to yourself?—

She turned like a porpoise, floated on her back, water beaded her flesh with light in the sun, in his sight.

—Well of course. I want Christa to come and share, but she won't leave the Manakas.—

—He won't need an invitation in his own house.—

She turned her head; not understanding, or thinking she ought to pretend not to? He took off his glasses, which she had splashed. The little beach girl was a lovely blur. He put them back again. —You'd better keep the door locked. Or maybe it hasn't got one?—

—Arnold ... he's an old man ... old as my uncle ...— It was in character with the footlooseness of this pretty girl, the ruptured kinships and displaced, marginal emotions of exile that, to his ears, made a slip of the tongue where the usual comparison would have been with a father.

—You don't know old men. The older we get, the younger we like 'em.—

—Well how would you know, you're not old.—

173

—Thank you for those kind words, obvious as they are. Isn't there anything you know without experiencing it for yourself?—

Both floated on their backs now, and it was not only the water-jewelled breasts, down to where the yellow swimsuit just covered stiff nipples, that surfaced, but also the thick index finger and fist of his penis and testicles under their pouch of wet blue nylon. They saw what there was to be seen of each other, while feeling identical delicious coolness and heat—the water on submerged and the sun on exposed flesh.

—Didn't you hear what I asked?—

—I thought you were telling me something.— A figure of such authority on Tamarisk; she had seen how the appearance of a line above the bridge of his nose made a voice stop short in mid-sentence, and how, when he was asked the kind of question that was not to be asked in such circles, his evasion of an answer came from complete intelligence of all that happened, was thought, discussed, investigated and decided there. What could he be interested in that she could tell him? The odd hours they had spent together (he worked very hard, even on Tamarisk he had time to take pleasure only when he left the last sandy foothold of the continent and entered the neutrality of the non-human element, the water) those times—caresses, the universal intelligence of pleasurable sensations, a rill from it present in wet coolness and heat, now—were the exchange with him in which she could take part.

—I don't know. Let me think.— Her eyes were closed against the sun; her smiling lips moved, he saw her so seriously young that she spelled out thoughts to herself the way children learning to read silently mouth words. The giant of desire woke in him to kiss her while she saw nothing but the red awning of her eyelids, and he slew him with the sling of priorities. Sexual pleasure was everyone's right; dalliance when he had simply taken a breather from the discussion on shore was not something he himself or those who could watch from Tamarisk should tolerate.

—No. Not really. No.— She kept her eyes closed, screwed up; the sun was making her see fire. —How can anyone know what hasn't happened to them? People like you, who've been in prison ... and once or twice others, I'd heard talking, back there. You can describe what it was like, but I ... I never, I don't really believe it's *all* it's like. The same with leaving the country. I was always hearing about it. I even once saw someone on his last night. But it's only now that I've done it ... it's different from what you're told, what you imagine. *You* are all different, all of you ... from the speeches. Where I lived—at home, when I was still in what was my home—everything was read out from newspapers, everything was discussed, I went to a court once and there was another kind of talk, another way of words dealing with things that had happened ... somewhere else, to somebody else ... I couldn't know. I can know what happens to me.—

—You'll burn your eyelids. Turn over. —But what you read, what you learn, what people tell you, what you observe—good god, that's what happens to you, as well! Not everything can be understood only through yourself—what do you mean?—and anyway, isn't your comprehension, your mind, yourself? What are you saying? You don't trust anything but your own body? It's a nice one, my god, certainly—but I don't believe you know what you're saying.—

—Thinking about what happens to myself—yes, of course, that I can *know*.—

—Someone needs to take you in hand, my girl. You are not a fully conscious being. I wish I had the time. And it would be quite pleasant ... I can imagine the sort of home you come from. Girls the ornaments who spoil their decorative qualities and betray their class as soon as they begin to think. How in god's name did you get here? I mean I know— but how'd you ever take up with that fellow? You know he was a liar and a double-dealer? He was for us and at the same time he was really working for

PAC*? And maybe if we'd not run him out of here he would be working for the government back there, as well.—

—He was collecting material for a book. That's why he went all over the show, he had to talk to all kinds of people.—

—And you believed that? What did you believe? That he was really one of us?—

A pair of talking heads, buoys bobbing on the water, tethered to lazy fin-movements of hidden arms and legs. —Yes.—

Impatiently, he gave her a chance to explain herself. She would not or could not. What a thicket of roses surrounded the power-drugged intelligence of the white sleepers; even dragged out through the thorns by some would-be prince turned betrayer, she could not recognize the lesson of wounds.

—Why?—

—I'd have to tell you too many things … Well, the family where I used to live—I just naturally thought, because of them, if white people were mixed up in that sort of thing at all, it was on your side. When I met his black friends, I didn't take much notice … whether there was any difference. Between them, I mean. Whether they were yours or some, others'. It was part of his work to know them all.—

—Yes, his work!—

—And he was in danger—

—Danger!— He scoffed.

—The police came and raided, you know that, they turned out all our things, took all the stuff for his book … He was writing for the papers under different names—

—And pushed different politics—

—Really, I think you've got it wrong. He told me, he had to have cover, that's why. Even his name. He even had to show up at parties given by people where I worked—and nobody talked about politics. Just there for a good time. Nobody gave a damn.—

*Pan Africanist Congress

176

—Not you, either.— It was said in the tone of one wanting her to be otherwise.

A man was swimming out towards them, his flailing arms black and defined in the heat-hazy radiance as the wings of a cormorant that skimmed the water.

Their voices changed key with the approach of a third presence. —So you see ... well, if you're right, what I think is true: I believed him because I believed what he was telling me; and none of it was happening to me.—

The swimmer was almost upon them; he didn't wave; he might not be making for them at all, just setting for himself the limit of his own horizon.

—Until the police came and gave you a big fright, ay?—

Wet hair slapped her throat as she shook her head. —Until I came here.—

By saying 'I' and not 'we' he saw she had begun to promise better human material. The girl was no longer jetsam on Tamarisk Beach. His desire for human dignity was gratified, his desire for the beach girl twinged with apprehension of loss. There was just time, before the black man, his sideways regard turned regularly upon them and away as his face was alternately hidden in water and lifted for breath in the movements of strong over-arm strokes, was upon them: —Don't suppose I'll be seeing you again.—

Low enough, but she heard. —Why?—

—Your elderly benefactor might object.—

—I've told you.—

—You'll come?—

As she slowly smiled the gestures and nod became a polite greeting for the head of the black man, now among them. To eyes accustomed to the radiance above water his blackness was a blow, pure hardness against dissolving light, his head a meteorite fallen between them into the sea, or a water-smoothed head of antiquity brought up from the depths, intact; basalt blackness the concentration of time, not pigment. Even the hair—black man's kind of hair—had resisted water and remained classically in place as a seabird's feathers or the lie of a fish's scales.

The man's urgency did not acknowledge the girl. —Nwabueze's been killed. A bomb in the car.—

Neither man noticed her go, the siren turning yellow tail and diving away from the navigators of the world's courses for whom, at that moment, in that ocean, she was no more than a distraction totally out of place.

A series of mini-biographies of outstanding women cites the news of the assassination of an important West African leader as the turning-point in her political development. Why should it ever have been contradicted?

But in that hour she was gliding and turning through water as perfectly tempered to the body as amniotic fluid, she heard no commotion but the sound of water getting into her ears and air breaking free in them through bubbles; the dead leader was a name. The real significance of the moment when the news was announced within a coral reef of the Indian Ocean was there, in another man, corporeal.

They love you. They tell you they love you. Len when making the neces-
sary despatch from Rhodesia because of that boy being coloured, Olga when
handing over to Pauline, Joe—dear Joe—when he gave the money with
which to escape them. When he called his son a bastard because nothing
was said in that bed, not about love of fellow man, not about family love,
not about sisterly, brotherly love, but it was done. Loved, let love. Used
what you have to love with, you know? It is there, you feel it, it happens
all over and inside you and there is no difference between you and the one
you're doing it with, you don't have to try to reach him, help him, teach
him—you can't lie, or spy or kill, so what could ever be wrong about it?
Left behind by my mother, they say, because of it; because they told her it
was wrong. The man they call a double-dealer, who lied about Sweden
and Germany: the place he told the truth was in bed, with his lovely
body, the feelings he gave me were not his fantasies or his boasts. Those
others, on the beach; they have no home—not out of clumsiness, a tendency
to break what is precious—but because they are brave and believe in the
other kinds of love, justice, fellow man—and inside each other, making
love, that's the only place we can make, here, that's not just a place to stay.

Trust Her!

The young guest did a little typing—a task invented by her host to make her feel useful—and some evenings played the guitar for him and sang those old coffee-bar songs, 'We Shall Overcome' and 'House of the Rising Sun', while swallows flew in and out of mud nests they had made in the brick lattice of his livingroom. He would not come to Tamarisk to swim; would not accept her casual invitation to join her, any time, when she went to the Manakas'. Njabulo Manaka had permission from the Command in exile to live outside the camp provided for refugees, but his friends were those who still lived in the camp. Some on their way to refuge had been captured in Northern Rhodesia and repatriated by the British colonial authorities; they had had to escape from the police at home, once again. Some were from the areas, at home, of hut-burnings and rural police posts whose methods of interrogation, the sjambok, suffocating plastic bag over the head, heavy boot on the spine, were less sophisticated than city facilities of electric shock. The office space up rotting stairs, the administrative titles, the few chairs were not sufficient to accommodate everyone who got away, even at that early stage, and neither did everyone have the education to be of use there. Along with other rank and file, from the cities, these men waited in the camp to be sent to the countries where the Command was negotiating for them to receive military training for their future as freedom fighters. A world refugee organization fed them meagerly, and although the host government made it a condition of refuge that they should not take jobs from local inhabitants, a few, like Njabulo himself, while waiting clandestinely made use of skills they had that most local inhabitants didn't have: he worked as a garage mechanic.

The smell of mealie-meal and cabbage that never cleared from the Manaka flat wafted out a signal: food and privacy among friends, with a woman in charge. The cushions of the old sofa that had one wooden arm missing never recovered shape from the impress of one trio of behinds before another flattened them. The snorting gulp of the lavatory emptying was as constant a punctuation of talk as laughter, argument, and the greetings of new arrivals. In the company of Christa and Sophie there was no question of women being ignored; and hadn't the girl slept there, on the kitchen floor, like any one of them? Many did not frequent Tamarisk Beach, feeling out of place in that high-ranking, half-naked, intellectual colloquy, and did not know the difference between the status of this white girl and that of Christa the revolutionary, one of themselves.

Newspaper cuttings and smuggled reports on the Lilliesleaf trial were coming to the office. —It's a white man who betrayed everything, all of us! Terrible, terr-ible. That's what I always said, we whites in the movement must be ve-ery careful, if anything happens through one of us, what is our position with blacks? Who's going to accept us? We going to isolate ourselves, we not going to be trusted ever again ... I *thought* when I met that Gotz fellow ... I don't know ... He was too eager to tell you all about himself, make a clean breast of it, you know—*ek is 'n ware Afrikaner, plaas seuntjie, maar*—like some religious conversion he wanted you to be convinced of. Ag, man, I felt like telling him, I'm an Afrikaner, too, *plaas meisie*, it's not such a big deal that you've come over to the movement. But some of them, they did think he was a catch for us—

—Meantime, they were on the hook— Christa's soprano distress was counterpointed by the low, black bass.

—Oh my god, they were. And the way he went for the women! Well, you see what one of them let herself in for ... Oh he tried something with me, but I never liked him, I never trusted him, he was clever all right, he smelled out that I didn't and then he kept clear. Terr-ible. Terrible fellow. And look what he's done. A white's blown the whole High Command.—

The volubility of high spirits that was Christa had changed to hysteria. In the silence of the black men on the old sofa she struggled against some kind of responsibility that suddenly had come between them and her.

—And in Umkhonto? There's infiltration there already. And Lilliesleaf, you'll see, as the State brings them into the witness box, there're blacks who were mixed up with informing there, too. Just the same, Christa. A thing we don't know how to deal with. A pro-blem.— In this company the euphemism took on weight with a long, round African O.

—But not right among the High Command. Close to them, eating with them, talking to them about important things with a tape-recorder going under his clothes or wherever it was, even under a pillow in bed, ugh, it disgusts me. Look, Njabulo, ever since I read that this morning my hands have been shaking—look, Elias—

—No, man, traitors are traitors. He's right. But the brothers at home will know what to do with them, don't worry.—

—With the High Command in jail? With life, if they don't get hanged? Not worry?—

—Anyway, those bastards who put them there, they won't live to get old.—

—Who's going to get Gotz in a location alley, the way they'll get the black ones? I'll bet he'll live a long life of promotion in the police or become a successful private detective, spying for divorce cases. I know the *Boere*. He can use his tape-recorder under some more pillows.—

—Is there anything new from Umtata and Engcobo?—

—I don't know, I didn't see …—

—Oh I asked Johnny. He showed something from the *Star*, just said the usual, 'peasant unrest' still going on among the Tembus. 'Agitators' are still at work.—

—Man! Tax was almost doubled for us there from nineteen-fifty-five up to nineteen-fifty-nine. You know? Ever since, how we have been suffering! You remember Dalindyebo's meeting in sixty-one against the rehabilitation scheme? That thing that took our land and pushed us tight together like cattle? A thousand chiefs came to that meeting. By the time I was grown up, Influx Control wouldn't let us out to find jobs. My uncle was chief in our place, he didn't want us forced back into the reserves, so the government made another man chief in his place. They do those things! My uncle was the one who said, They just want us chiefs to sign a piece of paper that says, *destroy me, baas.* He said, Let them destroy us without our signatures.—

—You know, we should have been better organized in the Western Cape, man. Too many Tembus who were working on contract around Cape Town joined Poqo instead of us.—

—Well! What do you know about the unions? ANC-affiliated unions were pretty active, I was working in one.— Christa shed her self-assumed burden at the turn towards a subject where the integrity of her contribution could not be questioned, even by herself.

Among such talk her protégée must have felt at ease, even if she were an impostor in its implied status. She had listened for years to people talking about these people; now they were real, the daily strategies of survival preoccupied them also, as these did her. There was much grumbling talk to which, at least, she could contribute, of where to get ordinary comforts they had taken for granted under oppression at home—soap and razor blades, batteries and insecticide sprays, in short supply here. People from the Command office might not meet these men on Tamarisk, but they kept close to them beneath barriers of sophistication and education through that other place in themselves nothing could alienate, where no bane of conquest, law or exile had ever touched them—the relationships codified in their language, the common embrace of their own tongue. People from the office ran classes in political and general subjects in the camp, and often one or the other would come on to Njabulo and Ma Sophie's to continue a point of discussion that would ravel into small-talk in English and their own language. Johnny Kgomani was there a few times, when the girl was; the one who had swum out with bad news. —We are spoiled, man, that's what it is. We all had it too soft. Wilkinson's Sword, passes in our pockets, first-class prisons ...— He watched faces waver from solemn acceptance or resentment to laughter. He had a way of drawing his lips to a line and giving a twitch to his nostrils, the skull mocking himself within the tight modelling of his face. Sophie translated for Christa and Hillela what the laughter was about.

There were not enough tin spoons or forks to go round at the Manakas'. Everyone got a plate piled by Ma and ate neatly African-style with their fingers, balling stiff pap the way a dung-beetle efficiently rolls together its cargo with the tips of prehensile legs. It was easier to learn to do that than to handle chopsticks at a Commissioner Street Chinese restaurant; and further than a few streets away from the embroidered place-mats, Bavarian crystal glasses and *Zitronencréme* where Hillela had herself nicely fixed up, now. There was not much chatter to join, round Udi's table. He sometimes went out to dinner but the impression left with her was that while she was staying with him they had always been alone at meals; the servant, with that air servants have (even Bettie, Jethro) of suppressing judgments that await their time, passed behind the two chairs, presenting each dish silently to the master of the establishment before dispensing the interloper's share. After she had been occupying her large, cool room for a few days, Udi asked her not to continue making her own bed in the mornings. —Mohammed thinks you don't sleep in it. It upsets him.—

Her laughter, her guitar, the slap of her sandals, the clear-struck notes of her voice—each time these sounded they seemed to make a splash into the stillness of those rooms.—Does he think I liked sleeping on the floor so much I can't give it up?—

—I don't think he knows you slept on the floor. Though I could be quite wrong … in the kitchens, they know everything about all of us, it's all picked up in the markets.—

—So where does he think I sleep?—

The ferny, magnified lashes moved dismissingly. Udi did not quite smile. —That's the trouble.—

Arnold had warned her. But if this was the to-be-expected approach, broached in a European way she was supposed to interpret, she could always appear not to understand. And it would not be Udi's way to be obliged to be explicit; although there were many things she did not know or understand that he did explain. Why wouldn't he get up out of his eternal chair and turn off his eternal Bach and Penderecki (the latter had to be explained, his music had not been among the records in Joe's collection) and come along to the Manakas'? He had said Christa's friends were his friends, *any time.* Christa had invited him again and again. The flat was only just down the road, in the old part of town.

—I am not lonely. A dear girl to worry … I am alone, that's different. Like the difference between the pink flamingo balanced on one leg and someone else wearing a pink skirt.—

She told him he was a stick-in-the-mud, coaxingly. Alone *must be* lonely. —To have another meaning for 'alone' there have to be two of you.—

—One can love one's neighbours at a distance, but at close quarters it's almost impossible. D'you know who said that true thing? Said it for me. A man named Ivan to his brother Alyosha, in a book called *The Brothers Karamazov.*—

Among all the possessions he had in that deep room with the frieze of live swallows, the African drums each with its ashtray and pipe beside each chair, the collection of Malian and Nigerian masks on the walls, the Fon hangings, the rugs from Khartoum with their counter-pattern of his pipe-burnings, the wall covered with shelves of damp books that gave the place its own body-smell—there must have been that same novel. Again that novel. He didn't have to explain about that! —I've read it, long ago.— She wouldn't be expected to remember the whole of such a long book, even if she had.

—That's why, although I believe all this (the room was kept dim against heat, the spines on the shelves shone titles of studies of revolutions, of colonialism, communism, social democratic theory)—all that Christa goes to prison for, I sit here in this chair ... I can't take part. That's why I'm worried about this trade-union foundation thing ... nearly as bad as politics. If only what Teacher—you know that's what the people call him, our President?—says could be true: 'People, not money' make development. The trouble is, I'm stupid enough to believe in what is being attempted in this place since the British got out ... and anyway... I can't go away. And I can't just sit here and approve out of books. So there you are ... at this time in my life ... It's funny, some people open the bible to see what message a page has for them. I find my message any-old-where. Listen to this I've just read, here. 'He avoided all the confusion and absurdity present in the efforts of those who say they are living for others'—now it goes on—'but in fact are living on others—on their gratitude, their opinions, their recognition'. The first part of that sentence— that used to be me. The second half— that's what I am now. The president invites me. The minister thanks me.—

—We all thank you.— She pulled a prim, pert face, her aubergine-coloured, shining eyes contradicting it. He saw that he amused her; she would not say 'I thank you for taking me off the beach, off the kitchen floor, using your influence with the immigration men to let me stay on in this town that has no place for me, where, if I have a reason to be, it is not the kind provided for on application forms!' Impossible for this girl not to be flirtatiously elusive, even with someone as clearly out of the running as himself; it came naturally from her as the sweat that, with the rising humidity of midday, painted on her lip a little moustache of wet that must taste salty to her lovers.

Udi showed Hillela something of the country. Around about that time—just before she started working in the curio shop,—he drove her along the coast for the weekend. —I am going to take you to Bagamoyo, where Livingstone started out to cross Africa from east to west.— But when they got as far as the new hotel where he had intended they should return to spend the night on the near side of the historical destination he had in mind, she hung back irresistibly. She ran to marvel at it from all perspectives, from sand so hot she danced across it as a fakir over the white ash of a bed of coals, to the cool of palms, remnants of the oil plantation the site once had been, now reified by a Scandinavian landscape gardener into his idea of a tropical garden. Her benefactor took his first photograph of Hillela there; the shadow of a palm tree falling before her. It could be measured for progress, like notches on a doorpost, against that other souvenir image under a palm.

He didn't insist on continuing the drive according to schedule; was content to study, as one standing back in a museum from a canvas whose conception he could not share but was fascinated by, her greedy pleasure in the post-colonial kitsch of the place— a Holiday Inn pervasion of piped music over poolside bars and buffets composed of a German-Swiss chef's attempt at reproducing his kind of food out of unidentifiable flesh and fowl decked with hibiscus flowers—all housed within a facsimile, as Udi informed her, of the 13th-century palace of Sultan al-Hassam Ibn Sulaiman. She ate the food with appetite. She had seen there were boats for hire and did not want to waste time accompanying the Arabian Nights-garbed black boy who would show them to their rooms. Under the sun of two in the afternoon, that was not in the sky but was the sky, had consumed both sky and sea in a stare of pure and terrible light, the black boat with the thin black oarsman slid away into dazzling evanescence. They sat side by side in the stern. The only detail to cling to in this total blankness of light was the legs of the oarsman, dark and sparsely hairy as the dried skin of a mummy. But when they reached the limit of the reef, heard the ocean open the roar of its surf at them, and the boat turned back, he, Udi, saw in the distance the entrancing pleasure palace she had been able to see all along, a mirage of the coast's past, shimmering there.

He took his hetaira to see something he could show her, even if she wasn't interested in Bagamoyo. They drove along narrow parallel tracks with grass stroking the underside of the car and thick shrubs running screeching thumbnails along the windows. Wind-maimed trees closed over, and they left the car. He led the way. At first she saw only the butterflies, so many they softly pulsated the still, dense air. Small white flowers scented it. She buried her face where the butterflies did. The competitive selection of nature—shiny, thick-tongued trees that had starved scrub from beneath them to make a clearing for plants and grasses; creepers and lianas closing off arbors where other trees had made the mistake of flourishing too close together—had created what seemed a garden; or there was the pattern of a human rearrangement of nature, far back, still faintly discernible under the natural aesthetic of growth, as the outline of a lost city may be traced from the height of an aircraft. Then she saw the pieces of china among the green; who had lived here, once, and owned beautiful things that got broken and were thrown away? But these were not broken vessels—they were tiles? Their azure, their unfaded brilliant designs were not designs but fragments of Arabic script? She had seen it, in her adoptive city. Wait, wait; he took her hand. With his other, he pushed aside creepers, lianas and webs: gravestones were sunken there, leaning; they were faced with the tiles, ornately embellished by their scrolling colours, like the pages of an illuminated manuscript. What was written? But he did not know the language, he couldn't tell her. ——Nothing out of the ordinary, I'm sure. Christians have a line from the bible on their tombstones, these will be the same sort of quotation, consolation from the Koran. The only interesting thing to make out would be the dates, if there are dates. I've always meant to come with someone who could read Arabic ... This cemetery is probably six hundred years old. Under the Imams of Muscat in the Persian Gulf, this whole coast from Mogadishu to Mozambique was ruled by the Sultan of Zanzibar.——

The butterflies mistook the ceramic colours for those of flowers, they touched at the hands of the two humans as the hands touched the stones. She tried to read the braille of the past: ——They lived here, there was a real palace? A town? It must have been lovely!——

——For them, yes. Many palaces. Not necessarily lived in; they moved from one to the other. They traded, in slaves principally. It wasn't lovely for the blacks. And after the Arabs came the Germans, and then the British. No more slaves taken, but not much difference otherwise: Now Teacher—he's about to join this country to the island as one republic. God knows what will happen. Zanzibar is still Zanzibar; the people who rule don't have the same ideas as Teacher, the Arabs there are still the rich and the blacks the poor. I think the blacks are ready to kill the rich and try to take over... I don't know how the combined republic's going to work, if they don't. But you see how it all looks as if it's buried, like this, in another few years these elaborate tombstones of powerful people will be covered entirely, like many others, we won't be able to find this place if ever we come back here——

——Oh I'd keep it clear, if I were the government, it's so beautiful—— the most beautiful place I've seen——

——For picnickers, yes? For people like you and me, out for a drive? The only monuments preserved in Africa are those of people who conquered Africans; no-one wants to keep such memories. But they will only be buried ... the old patterns of power, which were based on eternals like trade winds, that have no influence in the technological world, they remain as some kind of instinct from long ago, far back. Strange, uh? So that little island and this country will be called one again, under his African socialism, as they were by the old invaders, the Imams of Muscat.—

She sat on a tombstone. —They could be taken away from here, put in a museum, at least.—

He spread his hands. —No-one wants to interfere with a site that may have religious significance for some people.—

—Then why don't they keep it up?—

—It's here. So long as nobody disturbs it. That is what matters. It'll always be here, even when it's completely overgrown. It's not only the religious ones. We all have things like that, that will always be there. So long as nobody touches. But you are still too young.—

Immobile as the stone she rested on, she was hoping for a butterfly, hovering nearer and nearer, to land on her bare knee.

—You've been here often, then.—

—Yes. But not recently. And this will be the last time.—

If he wanted her to ask why, he swiftly changed his mind. —Come. We are thirsty.—

—Can I take just a small chip?— The fragment a half-stroke of script, in deep orange and blue.

—No. Take nothing.— But he laughed. —You want to make a museum out of this and yet you steal its treasures.—

They drove away, lost the site in a wake of swaying branches and stripped leaves. As they reached the main road, she called out. He braked for her. —Oh look! They're feeding on something!— There were the butterflies again; dozens of them, settled on a splatch in the road. —It's cow-shit! I always thought they lived on flowers.—

That was what he had brought her along for, her eager responses, her lack of pretension—to amuse him. —My poor Hillela! The most beautiful place she finds turns out to be a graveyard full of slave-dealers, and her wonderful butterflies eat dung!— But he saw that irony and disillusion could not tarnish her; pessimism a pleasantry, a manner of speaking associated with him. She was innocent: that is all anybody has ever been able to draw out of him when he has been approached by the curious as one who apparently knew her, once—rather well. He says it with a sense of discovery, adamant and unexplained.

Now at the hotel she was ready to go to her room and change into the yellow knit rag for a swim. The pink heels of the black boy in Arabian Nights dress led the way; there was one room, a large, beautiful room on two levels, with keyhole openings onto the sea, sofas, lamps, a bar corner, and one bed. Udi's bag and hers were already in place on a luggage rack.

She was looking at the bed. A strange bed, wide, low, and enthroned on a carpeted area between the two levels. She did not turn to her companion. The corners of her mouth dented a moment, then with a flick of the head, as if a fly had been encircling it, she went over and snapped open the elegant overnight bag the rich aunt had given her for one of the holidays to Cape Town—it was all she had had time to snatch from the cottage. She took out her yellow swimsuit.

Udi left the room. When he came back they saw one another first in the mirror she was standing before, tying a piece of Kanga cloth round her breasts over the yellow suit. He felt himself a voyeur thrust in to replace the figure in a favourite painting in one of his damp-rippled books, Manet's *Nana* watched at her toilet by a gross man. His face showed it; but dismay was all the girl read. Hillela smiled at him in the mirror.

—I've been to tell them we must have two rooms. I'm terribly sorry. I kicked up a fuss but it doesn't help. They are completely full tonight, they've promised that if we stay tomorrow ... Anyway, I can sleep on the sofa, they will bring bedding. Or in this climate ... look at the carpet, how thick (now he was able to smile, and distance himself in one of his pleasantries)—my turn to sleep on the floor. Everyone has his chance, in this life, good and bad. —I'm really sorry, Hillela, that idiot on the phone got the booking wrong. Believe me, I didn't expect this.—

—Oh it doesn't matter. Are you coming to swim? I'll wait for you.— She was wiggling her toes in the white sheepskin carpet; he saw one little crooked toe folded over a straight one.

He came out of the bathroom bearing his familiar unattractive head on an unfamiliar body; taken out of its wrappings, a hidden self appeared. It belonged to a younger, happier man, this well-made thick body with finely-turned muscular thighs and calves, and tight buttocks in black trunks. She had not been able to coax him out of his chair, but now he emerged of his own accord—or rather out of the volition of that hidden body—from the avuncular category in which a young girl would regard him. He hired skin-diving equipment and they laughed and clowned with Chaplin-flippered feet. He swam better than she did and led her into the green and purple-dark of passages undersea; be-goggled and rubber-finned, they were companionably identified with each other, the human species among other species that glowed with phosphorescence, steered past—hundreds of striped, ovoid discs making up one living streamer—or felt timidly with twiddling antennae from nests of rock, the blind silently tapping their way across the ocean bed. At sunset they walked on the beach like any other oddly-assorted couple seeking the retreat of a place like this: laughing black government Ministers from neighbouring states with their away-from-home girls, Greeks and Lebanese with their women, the wives sourly carrying their high-heeled shoes and trailing children, the mistresses hanging on the men's arms and inclining their heads with animated affection, earning the trip.

At dinner he ordered grilled fish. Again she ate with appetite the dubious food he avoided. —If I keel over and die during the night, you aren't responsible.—

—Don't say that. I brought you here. I am responsible.—

His sudden moments of solemnity were something she ignored, like an embarrassing tic disturbing someone's face.

A band shook and plucked at rattles and electric guitars. She did not seem to expect him to go so far as to dance with her; they drank wine, intensifying sea-laved well-being and the little, delightful shudders that puckered their sunburned bare arms with the night breath off the ocean. When a young olive-coloured man came across and asked her to dance, Udi watched her enjoying herself. The young man was a good dancer, someone transformed from obscurity by the grace and skill—perhaps the only skill?—he knew he had. She did more than follow; she moved as one body with the man she had never seen before in her life. Watching her, Udi had the impression she might never stop, that she might dance away, return night after night to the dance, to the man because he was the dance, something someone so young could mistake . . *dance her life away.* My poor Hillela. An echo sounded from him, of another country and another time, set off by a body, moving thighs, embracing arms inherited from another dancer. That was what was unexplained, to himself as well, when he said it always adamantly, bluntly: —She was innocent.—

But she came back. This dancer was not one to make mistakes. *Trust her!*—that was what others said of her. She came back and asked for soda and ice, took a cube out of the drink with her fingers and passed it over her forehead and neck. When the young man approached again to take her away she shook her head, smiling as if he knew very well why she was smiling; *no, no.*

They walked on the dark beach again, late. A fine luminous mist made an element neither air nor sea; they could barely see each other. He did not speak and—a small vessel calling out at sea—she spoke only once. —I wish I had my guitar.— He knew she was happy.

In the room with its ridiculous harem-bed he found Hillela lying plumb in the middle, a sheet over her shape up to the armpits. He came out of the bathroom in pyjamas. She gave an exaggerated sigh at her luxury. Then she shifted over to one side of the bed. He stood there with the spare bedding he had picked up from a chair. She patted the empty side of the bed.

He went over to the higher section of the room and started arranging the bedding on the floor. When he turned her hand was lying palm up, rejected, where she had patted the bed.

He came and picked up a pillow for himself. But could not walk away and leave her: her generosity, her honesty. He sat down on the bed and slowly took the sunburned empty hand. Her head was sunk deeply in the billows of down, her curly hair bleached the colour of bronze-brown seaweed and sticky with damp. Against cheeks shiny, reddened and slightly puffy with the fever of sun her eyes were glistening convex black in whose expression he saw only himself, himself as she must be seeing him.

She smiled, in spite of that. —Mohammed won't know.—

He kissed the hand with his sad, marked lips and, not familiar with the old-fashioned gesture, she casually pulled the hand away. On his back, laying himself out straight beside the body of the girl that was volume and weight and softness, the angle of each flexed and relaxed limb rounded-off by the soft bed as a Matisse odalisque has no angles or Picassos of a certain period have no joints in the continuous curved lines of bodies in a bacchanal, he took the hand again. The odd-assorted couple were now figures on a tomb; he put an end to the image in himself by gently coming alive to turn and give her a child's goodnight kiss on the cheek. But it was a long time since one of her surrogate parents sent her to sleep like that; she turned obediently, as a woman, so that he kissed her on the mouth, and was received by her mouth. She drew close to him and although she did not touch him with her hands, her body laid its caress along his side. For a long time he stroked her hair while she waited for the next well-known moves in love-making, and he waited to speak.

—Hillela.— Try out the possibility by pronouncing her, invoking her. Take again the hand, the empty hand he could not fill. —I can't, Hillela. Since my wife died it's finished.—

Of course he saw the girl misunderstood: so this was the famous love you read about in books, the eternal faithfulness, remote as the love religious people know for a god you can't see or touch.

—It's not out of some vow or conviction, some such nonsense. It's not at all even what Petra would want. She wasn't that kind, trying for promises 'you'll never marry another woman'. My god no. From time to time, we both ... we had others, and neither of us made a fuss. It wasn't important for us while we were together; it only concerned each of us separately, you know. So it's not that.—

—Oh it doesn't matter.—The phrase had served for the discovery there was only one bed; it served just as well for the decision that there was to be no obligation to make love. And in its banality—its innocence! yes—it absolved from humiliation, from loss of manhood, even from the pricklings of impotent desire, the shame of wanting what one was not able to take. He did not have to repeat with this child who by some instinct understood the male, loved men as one is allowed to say a man 'loves women', the panting and seesawing and desperate, hang-head feebleness (oh to take a knife and cut the useless thing off) that the bodies of bought women had abetted while bored and pitying, despising. Her ordinary little phrase brought about something else, if she could not—bless her—bring sexual relief. He could tell her. You could tell her anything; it suddenly became possible just because Hillela was there, lying beside him. —It's because I killed her.—

There could be no experience available to make it possible for the girl to deal with such a statement. She corrected him mechanically from a source that was all she had: something mentioned by Christa.:—No, no, she died in an accident.—

—Yes. I was driving and I killed her. It was just before dawn and I'd insisted we drive all night to get home from a trip. I must've fallen asleep a moment, she didn't have the seat-belt on, she was asleep. She never woke up, she was flung out and when I looked for her everywhere, the road, the bushes, she was dead, there. I'd hit a buck that must have jumped out into the road. Headlights blind them. She was quite dead. And the buck was still alive. Dying, but alive. I had no gun to shoot it. I'd killed her but I couldn't kill the buck. I sat with the buck, because she was dead … and the buck knew there was someone there with it. That night was over, light came, and it looked at me all the time while her eyes were closed. It was a female, too. It looked at me until I slowly saw the sight going from its big eyes. I can tell you, I followed it wherever it was going, dying out. I followed all the way. And then. They were both dead and I was hours alone on the road with them.—

He was stroking her hair again, comforting her for what he had told her.

—I've never seen a dead person.—

—I know. I can see it in your face.—

—But you didn't kill her. That's not killing.—

—I was driving, I'm alive, I killed her. Dead asleep. And the buck, the buck was witness. My body seems to know. So there it is. Since then, my body calls me murderer.—

She made no routine protestations, offered no platitudes of sympathy. They lay a while; what had now been put into words for the first time must find its level in consciousness. Then she got up and went over to the miniature refrigerator and bent to choose. The short spotted cotton shift she wore hitched over her rump as she came back to the bed with a bottle whose label's lettering had run with condensation. —I think it's beer.— She took a swig and handed it to him. —You should go and live somewhere else. Then it will be all right again.—

He pulled himself up against the pillows to drink. —The murderer can't leave the scene of the crime.—

—Udi, it wasn't this road?—

—No.— But she would never know; intimacy and confidence come and go between an odd-assorted couple like the moon passing in and out of clouds.

She sat cross-legged on the bed, schoolgirl style.

—I'd go away if something terrible like that happened to me. Somebody of mine dead. Nothing really terrible's happened to me, so I suppose ... Something that did—something *I* did—it seemed awful at the time, everyone said how awful ... but ... not like dying! D'you know why I had to leave home? Where I lived with one of my aunts? My cousin and I used to make love. He was a bit younger than I was. For a long time, we made love.—

—A real cousin? First cousin?—

—Our mothers are sisters.—

—How did it come about?—:

—My fault.— The moon passed behind a cloud again. He respected that. He leaned over and put his arm round her, shared the beer turn-about. Hillela choked because she had begun to laugh while drinking. —When they found us.— She gasped, laughing. —It was like the three bears. Who's been sleeping in *my* bed?—

The Diplomatic Bag

Leopard skins mounted on scalloped green felt, dead snakes converted into briefcases, elephants turned into ivory filigree carvings, bracelets, necklaces and paper knives, and table-legs with a copper rim decorating what was once a pachyderm foot—the AFRICAN ARTS ATRIUM did not sell powdered rhino horn, however; that sort of disgusting stuff was for local people in the magic and medicine trade down the road. Hillela wore—'modelled', as Archie Harper, the old Africa hand of a special kind, who employed her, insisted—the dashikis or galabiya-inspired dresses of African cloth her employer had made up by his 'connection' of Indian piece-workers who sat at their machines on the earth pavements all over the old town. The long dresses became bizarrely slit— some from the first vertebra to the small of the back, as well as to the thigh on both sides—during the period of her employment, because Archie found his assistant-cum-model so 'innocently inspiring'. He was not himself attracted to women, but had the homosexual's shrewd and kindly understanding of how they like to make themselves attractive to men: this girl (a real poppet; he knew from the beginning she would go far) inside his one-of-a-kind creations was the best way to encourage customers to clear the racks.

Business was torpid (—No tourists where you can't buy contraceptives or whisky, my dear—) but this expatriate, an Englishman, couldn't leave, either. He was quickly on girlish confiding terms with his assistant: he wouldn't leave his two young Arab lovers, twin brothers they were, he'd brought them up in his own house since they were fourteen. —You will never find anything ne-early like them in England. Ne-ever. Guardsmen with smelly feet who're only after what's in your pocket, that's all. Revolting.—

He had other connections, anyway, that made it possible for him to keep the shop open more or less for fun. Among them were sources of supply for his restaurant, ARCHIE'S ATRIUM TOO, which was the only one in town where French and Italian wine was still obtainable. The connections with airline personnel, Lebanese, Greek and Arab traders kept him, a coloured balloon-figure in one of his own extra-outsize unisex dashikis, moving about from rendezvous to rendezvous all day; his assistant was most often alone in the shop.

It was there that Marie-Claude—but Hillela did not think of her as that, then, of course—Madame Mézières found her. Picked her up, as Madame Mézières explained her luck to other diplomatic wives. She came in with a visitor from Europe who wanted gifts to take home; after several years in this posting, Madame Mézières was herself not interested in tourist kitsch, but the young girl assistant looked so charming in a cotton robe that she actually did buy one for herself, for wear around the pool—impossible to go to the beach now that it was full of all sorts of strange people. The girl said the thigh-slit certainly could be reduced as Madame Mézières wished, by five inches; the visitor could not speak English and the girl equally accommodatingly (even bravely) spoke to her in ill-pronounced schoolgirl French. When Madame Mézières came back a week later to fetch her altered robe, she invited the girl to have a swim at the Embassy, where she met the children, but not the Ambassador.

However Olga might be regarding her niece, of whose whereabouts sitting on a camel-saddle transformed into a chair Olga had no knowledge at that time; whether she might have felt occasional anguish at what had not been done for her sister's daughter, or regretted the waste of all that had been done for her, it is clear that the advantage of having been sent at Olga's expense to a school where she had learnt the elements of a foreign language was the deciding factor in her becoming part of an embassy household. There were very few customers at the shop. When she had occupied herself for an hour a day with disentangling the silver-wire jewellery webbed together by the hands of those who picked over but didn't buy, Hillela sat on the camel-saddle chair in the chrysalis of her long slit dress as if she would have to be carried from there by force. She had been twice called to the Immigration Offices and warned that she would be deported if she did not leave of her own accord, or produce refugee status supplied by an accredited organization. Udi's few words in the right quarter apparently had reached the limit of audibility; they did not carry far enough. Arnold, no doubt, she would not have scrupled to ask to intercede for her. Perhaps she had asked, and been refused because Arnold could not put the integrity of the cause at risk for any personal reason whatever; or, more likely, she was—clever enough?—to understand this and did not approach him, in the sense of seeking some advantage, although there is reason to believe—Udi had reason—she still spent Arnold's rare leisure hour somewhere with him from time to time.

So the move from the care of an Udi willing but unable to advance her status, via the camel-saddle chair in Archie Harper's shop to an embassy, with the Ambassador arranging residence papers for her to answer his wife's convenience, was rescue. Arnold, with her for what he had a feeling would be the last time, saw it differently, even distantly admiring: —And now you've got yourself really nicely fixed up.— She was vague about what her capacity was to be in the ambassadorial household but certain of one thing. —I'm not going to be deported.—

Malice has it that she was once a nanny; but she was much more than that.

Here, once more, there were flowers in her bedroom and silver on the dining-table. Pauline would have smiled confirming this 'refugee' hardship, and Olga would have been relieved. Madame Mézières' lucky find helped the children with their homework

(they were disadvantaged at an English-medium school), supervised their safety while they played in the pool, shopped for their
bothersome childish needs; it seemed that through the contacts
of her friend and former employer she could get commodities the
ambassadorial staff no longer had the trouble of ordering from
Europe. She blow-dried Madame Mézières' hair so creditably that
it looked better than it ever had while Madame Mézières had
suffered the heat and din of piped music in Salon Roma under
the hands of an Italian from Somalia. She ran errands on foot, not
fussy about where she went in this filthy town, and proved much
more compatible as a driver than the Embassy's black chauffeur.
—Emile, he smokes kif, or whatever they call it here, I don't
know; I smell it on him.—

The Ambassador did not exert himself to deny any of Marie-
Claude's obsessive fantasies directly. —One smells drink on
people's breath, not drugs. You've got Hillela to drive you.—
Marie-Claude could not pass on to her lucky find the oppressive
responsibility that was compounded with the oppressive heat,
in this posting: every afternoon, she had to sit over her children
while they whiningly completed a daily quota of schoolwork from
the syllabus and in the language of their home country. Here,
however, positions were reversed for an hour; instead of receiving services from the girl, she did her a service. Hillela sat in on
the lessons and improved her knowledge of the language along
with the children. Now, because she joined in with them, the
children tackled the task as if it were another of the games they
played with her. —She's my big sister.— —Idiot, I'm your sister.
She didn't come out of maman.— —Then she's our cousin, like
Albert and Hélène at home.—

It was a relationship in which Hillela had had plenty of experience, to explain her success.

Not only a find; she was a blessing. —Look at me, Emile, I'm
myself again. I don't have a headache all the time, that twitch in

my eyelid was driving me crazy—it's gone. Don't I look like your Marie-Claude again?—

Eating a mango, licking her fingers, the girl was the amiable witness of private bonds recalled between the couple. With his usual indirection, the Ambassador addressed himself to the cause rather than gave the opinion of the result that was expected of him. He was slitting the wrappers on European newspapers with a fruit-knife. —Hillela has changed the life of this house.—

It was in that first ambassadorial residence, behind gates where black guards strait-jacketed in gabardine and braid slouched on homemade stools, and sometimes a visiting wife and children squatted humbly behind the hibiscus, that she must have picked up, just as Marie-Claude had picked her up, much that has made her assurance so provocatively perfect. Olga, looking through a magnifying glass years later at a newspaper cutting in which she is told she will be able to identify the hostess sitting between Yasir Arafat and the President of a European country, cannot take more than half the credit for having sat down that hostess, as a child, at a dinner table the way a dinner table should look. The duty of helping Marie-Claude arrange official dinners would have been what instructed Hillela so usefully in protocol, and her own usefulness as a personable dinner-table partner to fill a place beside a bachelor, or someone whose wife was not present, was what has given her the range of safe subjects and the permissible limits of response, the appropriate lies, level of voice and laughter between guests at official gatherings. In true tradition, her youth and bountiful bodily confidence, not modesty, made the run-up Archie Harper cottons pass among the formal clothes white diplomatic wives equipped themselves with in Europe. They had the jewellery they wore as the badge of an occasion, as men wear decorations; but she was unadorned by the nervous tensions that redrew their faces like tribal markings. Hers was the real, not the fairy story of Cinderella and the sisters.

With the corporate female sense of protection, Marie-Claude imperceptibly intervened when she saw among her guests men reading the wrong signal in the shining cheeks and market cottons. —Don't worry, you won't sit next to Frédéric again. And Henning Knudsen, too! I was watching ... And he's got a daughter your age.—

Hillela laughed. —He told me he could arrange for me to finish my studies in Denmark.—

—What studies?—

—I don't know. Don't you think he meant it?—

—I know what he meant. When we first arrived here, and Emile was recalled for a few weeks, he kept coming in to see if I was all right. Then I realized ... what he meant, by looking after me ...— And Marie-Claude herself gave the sexual beckon of the patchy blush she seemed able to summon at will from the warmth of her breasts in low-necked dresses, deepening the Old Masters' pearl-pink of her skin against her Flemish gold hair.

—But you're so pretty, Madame Mezieres!—

—Pretty! Is it our fault? We women. Can we help it?—

—You put a lot of work and money into it, *mijn skatteke*.— The Ambassador liked to tease his wife, and never simply; she did not like being reminded, even by an endearment, that she was a Fleming and not French-speaking by birth.

In the confidence that grew between her and her find, the secret mother tongue became a relaxation and a bond. Hillela could understand her when, alone together lying at the pool, no-one about to hear, she took up Flemish like a homely garment; Hillela could even answer, in a fashion, through her knowledge of Afrikaans. It was not possible to go on being addressed as Madame Mézières; as if she were old. When they were lying there, two young women in bikinis! (She had at once replaced the yellow knit rag with something from her own wardrobe.) And talking about Emile—how they had met, variously-edited versions of decisions they had made together about his career, etc., the Ambassador quite naturally became referred to and addressed as 'Emile' by the girl, as well.

Hillela's old benefactor, Udi, would have agreed with Arnold on one point, at least: a prediction that she would never look back. Udi probably meant it in both senses. She was nicely fixed up, for a penniless, deserted girl whose refugee status no-one would vouch for. From the kitchen floor through a guest bedroom to an ambassadorial residence; no need to return, ever, with her blankets to the hospitality of the Manaka flat. When she met Christa and Sophie as she came out of the bank one morning (Emile insisted that her salary be paid into a bank account, not left lying about as a temptation to the black staff in the Residence) she had not seen them for months. Being Hillela, she made no apologies or excuses; but she clung to them and kissed them in a different way from the bird-necked dart from cheek to cheek, grazing contact, she had learnt to exchange with the ambassadorial family. Christa looked after her affectionately: Poor Hillela! Sophie's cheeks concertinaed up against her eyes: —Are you mad? Oh I'm glad she's so okay in this bad place.— Archie Harper was encountered at British diplomatic cocktail parties that included local person- alities from the old regime. He would put his arm round her and squeeze her to his enormous globe of a body; but nobody could interpret this as predatory on his behalf or a sign of availability on hers. Only after she had gone were there stories that although she dropped her political refugee friends once she'd installed herself at the Embassy, she still used to spend afternoons at Archie's house, when he would dress up in women's clothes, some elephantine duchess or brothel madam (that was how people could imagine it), and they'd dance with his Arab boys and drink black market champagne. The stories originated with Mohammed, who knew the boys, and had made her bed; the details were visualized by gossip among white people. While she was still in that country, a letter came from Canada to the hotel where her lover had left her. The proprietress propped it up, visible, in the bar for a few days, then threw it away. The girl's other lover (his rivals and political enemies among the gathering on Tamarisk said) was seen entering the garden of an old house where the ambassadorial car that the girl was allowed to drive was parked, even after it was well known she had become the Ambassador's mistress.

Those who have choices have morals, he says, after love-making, smelling home in the flesh, the rank sweetness of polished floors and gardener-tended roses, the leather-scent of three-car family garages beside backyard rooms with their clandestine fug of beer and cold pap. The smell of all things lost and repugnant, that is home, and that must be destroyed. It prompts him to talk of acts people are having to go through with, back there—the bombs and grenades whose targets are monolithic but whose shrapnel may pierce, three centuries of murderers cry, an innocent white. Who is innocent, after more than three centuries, among more than twelve generations of people who have paid for labour with a bag of mealies a month, beaten, imprisoned, banished, starved and killed? Those who can choose a candidate for a parliament—they can have their morals. The others have no choice but to meet, after three centuries, violence done to them with a violence of their own.

And all this while lying in the house that serves as a foreign news agency, the foreign correspondent himself out interviewing the Minister of Agriculture about a collective scheme for coffee farmers.

No mention, ever, of what is planned up the rotting stairs, only what already has been done. Because how can there be trust? What is there to go by? One who left that home uninstructed, ignorant, like most of her kind—for personal reasons which are no reason, in the measure of what has to be done. What credibility has she to show for herself, now, but the protection of yet another man?

Without a cause is without a home; lying here. I've learned that. Without a cause is without a reason to be. That's all decreed by others, as elsewhere everything was decreed by the absence of one sister, the decisions made by two more, and the long-distance authority of a putative father on the road. Looking at him; gazed at by him. How well does he see, how well does he see into the other self, this man who swims and makes love with his glasses on to see better—this man in whose narrow crowded face is concentrated the pull of a gravity that excites while it excludes.

What choice is there?

He could take her in hand, maybe, with help from Christa and others. She might be made useful. But the real life of exile isn't giving the boys an eyeful on Tamarisk Beach, you know.

Ah no, I'll tell about that, the real life of exile is, for your whole life, going home for the holidays wherever it's been decided you're to go.

Exile is the inevitable—for whites like us, he is instructing. But the claim doesn't enter, the way his body does; it talk away from her without purchase, the way she now slides off his body. This one won't accept to be a humble apprentice to the only objective worth living for. Who does she think she is? Unreliable: and this judgment tantalizes him to come back into the flesh again, to find that just consolation, that peace and freedom that is certain, and lasts only minutes.

The glisten of black eyes opening again.

Why don't you go back? Let them deport you. Probably you'd be let in; your lawyer uncle could maybe get you off prosecution for having come out illegally: you're still under age. You've got a guardian or something? At worst you'll get a suspended sentence and a fine—your rich aunt'll pay, won't she?

But he is nibbling, kissing, feeding on me, his face wet with me, exasperated. Because if she isn't the right material, she isn't one of that kind, either. God knows what will happen to her—it is not his affair— but she has one sound instinct to share with him, it's expressed in her laughter if not in conviction, it's dense in her flesh: she will never go back to the dying life there, never.

What choice? When the Ambassador and his family are posted to another country, of course I'll go with them. Of course; the credentials of the household contingent of such people are never disputed by immigration officials.

*

At certain times, in certain places, harmony settles over a human nucleus like the wings of some unseen sheltering bird. Marie-Claude was a woman who had constantly to be going through the wardrobe of her blessings before others. Sometimes her actual wardrobe was invoked: —Emile insists he must give me a fur coat for leave in Europe, but I'm not the kind of woman who needs that sort of present, I'm not repressed in *any* way, not deprived of *any* kind of satisfaction, I mean, far from it— Hillela was so responsive; she stroked the fur against her cheek, so that Marie-Claude knew, could see the present was beautiful and rich in meaning; that she lacked for nothing; And in this country on the other side of Africa the language of the former colonists was her children's mother tongue, and she was freed of the tedious after-noon hour of acting schoolteacher. She could sleep, sleep, for that hour after lunch, knowing the children were not left in the care of some local black or half-caste. Her breasts released from straps and lace, her waist free of elastic, she lay naked in the shuttered dark of their room—hers and her husband's. Sometimes—now that she didn't have to shut herself up over schoolbooks—when he came in quietly to fetch something on his way back to the office, she murmured, so that he would come over to her, and then deliciously tense but playing sleepy, she could put his hand on her soft, heat-dampened pubic hair, and after merely submitting for a moment (of course, she knew he was thinking he ought to be going back to his office) he would silently and efficiently take off his clothes (of course, he had to keep them uncreased to put on again immediately for the office) and make love to her. It was years, and several postings, since they had made love like lovers, in the middle of a working day. No child would burst in; they were safely with Hillela.

He came from the office—merely across a loggia in another part of the Embassy complex, all of their life was securely under one roof—and saw Hillela, many afternoons, sitting among a tumble of children and cushions, the children's limbs tangled close about her, their hands playing with her hair or fingers.

—Come, papa, it's a guessing game. Come and play.—

—Papa, there's a lion and two hippos and they want to eat him up but he won't come into the water—Hillela's telling that story again because it's such a nice one ...—

Smiling at him from among his children, her face as firm and clear as theirs; with his arrival, domestic content was perfectly rounded.

She did not have many duties—duty being what does not come naturally—in that posting, where the Ambassador was temporarily relieving a colleague recalled. In a French-speaking city, Marie-Claude had found more friends, liked to do her own shopping in boutiques run by French people who had stayed on under a black government civilisedly tempered, it was felt, by the fact that the President had a white French wife. Some people said the young girl in the Ambassador's household was a housekeeper, others assumed she was a relative of Marie-Claude—and Marie-Claude did not deny, only corrected this: —No, no, no relation at all! But it's true, she's like a young sister, a member of the family. The children adore her.— Certainly she played tennis, took part in sightseeing and dining-out parties, as any visiting favourite from Europe experiences Africa in pursuits imported long before her.

But there were times when the surrogate was alone in the house with only the half-awareness of the presence somewhere of servants that is like the sound of her own heart to any white brought up in Africa. Alone as if she were an ambassador's wife in a succession of interleading rooms, passing furnishings and objects with which she has no connection, interchangeable from Residence to Residence. If the Ambassador happened to come in he seized her sufferingly. Under his elegantly-hung suit his body swelled and prodded her; but that presence outside the beating of blood reminded that nothing further was permissible, not here, not now. —Look what you do to me.— He was handsome, proud. She would shake that curly head, not culpable. —You know just what you do, my little girl, don't you.—

Sultan al-Hassam Ibn Sulaiman had never been here but the town floated as flower and palm fragments, islands and isthmus, on lagoons covered with a mail of waterlilies; a breeze touched, as if it were the black rags of bats themselves, flapping the air round the streetlamps as lights threaded on across bridges. She was seen in the town, where the cry of Edith Piaf came from the bistros, but mostly she kept to the quarter of embassies, villas and hotels. Regularly a young First Secretary from the British Embassy ran to meet her at an open-air bar for their six o'clock rendezvous. —You had better be seen with one or two young men—believe me, my treasure, no-one will believe you haven't got a man *somewhere*, if they don't see him.— A First Secretary was eminently suitable. —But you won't sleep with him, will you?— She was such a sensible girl, she understood a man has to sleep with his wife; that was different. —You won't, will you, eh?— When there was a sortie to a nightclub, where the presence of wealthy local blacks and the strident sexual beauty of black prostitutes was the amusement, Marie-Claude appointed the young First Secretary to partner her protégée. Emile danced with her dutifully once or twice, flirting publicly in exactly the harmless degree expected of the married males in homage to the irresistibility of the female sex that had, of course, delivered them to their wives.

Boutique, bistro, bar, nightclub—these were the marked routes of the diplomatic and expatriate community. There was a path of her own drawn through the grass; the grass closed it away behind her. It led across one of those stretches of ground that are called vacant lots in the cities of other continents; here it was a vacant patch in history, a place where once manioc had been grown and goats had wandered, now appearing on some urban development plan as a sports or cultural centre that would never be built. A tiny scratching of planted maize was hidden in the grass, like a memory. Her path crossed those made by the feet of fishermen, and servants moving from and to where she was going, the enormous hotel that multiplied itself, up and up, storey by storey, shelf by shelf of identically-jutting balconies and windows that eventually had nothing to reflect but sky. There was no other structure to give it scale, nothing to dissimulate its giant intrusion on the low horizons of islands and water, that drew the eye laterally. Even the great silk cotton tree and the palms left as a sign of its acculturation when the site was cleared were reduced to the level of undergrowth beside its concrete trunk.

Inside, the scale of unrelation, of disjuncture continued; through ceremonial purplish corridors she walked, past buried bars outlined like burning eyelids with neon, reception rooms named for African political heroes holding a silent assembly of stacked gilt chairs, crates of empty bottles and abandoned mattresses, sudden encounters with restaurant stage-props—plastic palm trees and stuffed monkeys from some Tropicana Room, rolled-up carpets from the Persian Garden. At the white grand piano outside a locked entrance where photographs of girls whom gilt text dated the previous year announced as direct from the Crazy Horse in Paris, she turned to a bank of elevator doors like the reredos of some cathedral. Her path was always the same; through the grass, through the carpeted tunnels of corridors, the soughing ascent to the same floor. She had her key to the room; the bed was big as the one in Sultan al-Hassam Ibn Sulaiman's fake palace. The Ambassador came by some path of his own through this dark ziggurat, pyramid, Eiffel Tower, Empire State Building raised to the gods of development; he could arrange everything as he arranged immigration papers. He shed the Ambassador. What a pleasure to be able to give so much pleasure! Enough to turn any young person's head. One day when he made love to her he smelled his children on her. It was a great sweetness to him; it brought the two halves of his life together as they had never been before. An annealment, wholeness; a new eroticism.

—You have simplified everything.—

—Why me?— He had not concealed, despite the risk at the beginning that a young girl might have been shocked or even jealous, and withdrawn herself, that he had had many love affairs.

—I don't know, I don't want to know. Simplicity is the one thing that can't be explained. Not that you are simple, Hillela. You won't get away with that, my little girl! But that you are clever enough to make things simple.—

—Emile, why do you like other women so much?— She knew that was her category.

—Oh you are young, Hillela, you are still at the stage when you ask all the questions, you don't propose any answers.—

—Marie-Claude is so beautiful.—

—To have one beautiful woman. Once she is always there—it makes no difference. It doesn't help, you understand? Didn't she say it herself, about women: 'Is it our fault'—well it's not their fault they are beautiful, so many of them, and how can I not … try? As soon as I have one, or sometimes two at once—although they don't know it—I see another and I have to prove to myself I can possess her. And so it goes on … gets worse as I get older. I'm forty-seven …— The birthday was recognized between them in a different context from that of the children's performance, arranged by Hillela, that marked it the week before. If he had ever met Udi Stück, he could have curiously confirmed the possibility of telling this girl *anything,* confiding *amour propre* to her stranger's hands.

He was smoking; this one smoked after love-making, the member of the Command in exile had drunk water, and far back, there was the one who had shed sibling tears. The smoke seemed to be drawn down all through his body as it was through his nose; his toes flexed, and his hand bent hers. —I need it like I need smoking.—

He turned and looked at her. He was silenced by what he saw, by what she understood beneath the crude and paltry words. Her black eyes gave him back his meaning in yet another question, unspoken: is life terrible as that?

After the room was left empty he went away to his secretary, attachés, telex messages and distinguished callers, with the smooth look round the eyes of a man in harmony with his body and free to be alert; any experienced staff recognizes the signs of a successful love affair and is thankful for the calm it generates. Hillela did not make her path to the Residence. She wandered; her body moved with the suppleness limbered by love-making, the pretty loll of breasts and the rhythm of her thighs were a confidence that made another kind of path through people in the streets. Men turned, as if at a reminder, to look at her; it was not her fault. Where the European city grid of right angles was overgrown and broken up by the purposeful tangle of African pursuits—the shortest point-to-point meander taken on foot between barbers and fruit-sellers, scribes and bicycle repairers—to be white was to feel invisible; only a sensuous self-assurance, while it lasted, could counter that. Hillela came to the docks. Her nostrils widened to snuff in the spice of cargoes swinging out on cranes overhead—coffee and cocoa beans—and the scrubbed smell of tar, the grassy scents of wet rope and putrid whiff of fish guts. The sun sank and flung colours up the sky. The black labourers who did not see her in their inward gaze of weariness, their self-image of religion and race, suddenly unrolled mats towards the East and bowed their heads to the ground. Their seamed heels were raised, naked, as they kneeled, their feet tense. The draped fishnets enlaced the sunset like the leads of stained-glass windows. A flock of prayers rose murmuring, vibrating, buzzing all round her, a groan of appeal and answer, supplication and release.

There are many kinds of consolation. Not all can be orthodox, in the ritualistic or other, social, sense. Before the invisible bird lifted off as capriciously as it had settled, the Ambassador sometimes came to her room late at night and slid into her bed. He was breathing fast, with fear as much as passion; yet the moment he felt her small warm solidity he was sure no-one would discover them. She was proof against his recklessness; at the same time he was sure, in contradiction: she would go without fuss, if Marie-Claude found him out. It was a scandal, of course, among the white community, who followed the appearance of such phenomena through the spy-glass of their mores: a tranquil household, a whole family content, in its way, as few families ever are.

Credentials

The men who had shared pap and cabbage with her at Ma Sophie's went to Algeria and the Soviet Union instead of China, now. Alliances changed; she moved on.

It may have been because she was back in a country where she could speak her own language and therefore range more widely, but she is difficult to keep track of once the Ambassador's extended family moved yet again and settled in his next West African posting. So there is another lacuna; she is somewhere, of course, in momentary glances stored in those who must have passed her in the streets of Accra on a Saturday, colliding as she jostled between the mammy wagons and the street vendors' jingling dinner-bells, the shouts and the splurt of tyres through overflowing drains, but there is little to attach in a contiguous, concrete identity. Her good friends in Dar es Salaam had no word. The passport her Aunt Olga carried was not recognized in the African countries Olga overflew on her way to Israel or Europe; anyone in that blank bush down there between the clouds was lost. Pauline would have written if she had known where to find her niece, as she would have sought out Ruthie. Carole once made the suggestion that enquiries might be made through the African National Congress—that idea surely could not have been little Carole's own; could Sasha have been behind it? But Sasha never spoke of his cousin, he was bored by family connections, and now that his schooldays were over, lived at home in Pauline's presence like an estranged lover, turning away from her assertion of their bonds as affines and spending all his time with friends made at the university. As he had predicted, his name had come up in the ballot; but Joe arranged a deferment of military service. Joe had Afrikaner nationalist colleagues whom, although they knew he and his big-mouthed wife disagreed with them politically, professional buddyhood obliged to put in a word for his son. Carole's suggestion was out of the question (typically Sasha). The ANC was a banned organization with which any connection that could be traced was treasonable; its leaders from the Lilliesleaf house-party had been sentenced to life imprisonment, and the only man who might have been trusted with such an enquiry, the advocate Bram Fischer—whom Joe, like everyone who abhorred racism, loved and admired but would not go so far as to emulate—had been arrested, gone Underground, been recaptured and sentenced to life imprisonment, declaring that his conscience didn't permit him to recognize laws enacted by a body in which three-quarters of the people of the country had no voice. In any case, Pauline was dourly, depressedly amused by the romantic notion that Hillela was a revolutionary. More likely she had fallen on her feet in some way: Pauline never saw her as Olga did, as lost—Hillela was not the helpless Ruthie. After all, hadn't she had the advantage of being brought up to independence and self-respect along with Pauline's own children? There was nothing vulnerable in that persistent image of the girl lying beside, the trembling school-boy, composed in a—distorted, wrong—manifestation of the self-respect she had been taught.

Hillela herself, as they knew her, disappears in the version of a marriage that has a line in the *curriculum vitae* devoted to Whaila Kgomani in a *Who's Who* of black 20th-century political figures. *In 1965 he married in Ghana, and had a daughter.* From this accident of geography reports assume he married a Ghanaian; a suitable alliance with a citizen of the first country in modern Africa to gain independence, a citizen of Nkrumah's capital. With the fall, the following year, of the father of Pan-Africanism, the concept upon which black political exiles everywhere were dependent for their shelter, and the disarray of Umkhonto We Sizwe through police infiltration, back at home, exiles themselves had no heart to bother about which of them found consolation with (or even married) which girl. That this one was white and South African was slow to filter to those far away for whom such details had a gossip-column interest not extended to the great and terrible events happening in their midst and on the shared continent they overflew.

The girl is mother to the woman, of course; she has been acknowledged. In fact, the woman has generally chosen to begin her existence there, when asked about her early life: —I was very young, working at an embassy in Accra when I met Whaila at a reception given by the late Kwame Nkrumah.—

Well, it's not impossible.

Though in conversation with Madame Sadat after the assassination of President Sadat, speaking as one who has known widowhood among so many other experiences, it was recalled differently: —You always remember the beginning, not the end. Fortunately. It was in Accra, a man passed me in the street and then turned around—Whaila: we recognized each other.—

Hillela was at least once taken to a reception at Christiansborg Castle, although by then Nkrumah's party was in decline, even the adoring market women—his brides, he called them—had turned against him, and he seldom appeared in public. But after the break-up of the united front of four South African liberation movements, the Nkrumah regime favoured the Pan Africanist Congress, not the African National Congress; it seems unlikely that Kgomani would have been a fellow guest. The Ambassador and his wife took her everywhere—no party was complete without her, it is said. And she did go about with zest in the gregarious uproar of Accra streets. On Saturdays she was regularly at one of the hotels where, about eleven in the morning, a high-life band began to play for the weekend; everyone drank beer and danced among pretty prostitutes in wigs, children stuffing groundnuts, black businessmen in the company of the real financial establishment of the city, the huge female tycoons with their brilliant robes of plenty, sweat-gilded faces, weaponry of gold jewellery and imposingly planted feet. She may have sung and played the guitar in a nightclub; she would soon have picked up the West African beat. She does appear to have left the ambassadorial employ at some point before or not long after she began to be seen with the black South African revolutionary envoy; and she must have had to earn a living somehow.

The same kind of worn stairs. She went up that day while about town on an errand for Marie-Claude. As she approached the building she had passed many times without interest since being told some members of the organization—which did not yet have official representation—had an office there, that day she walked in as she might have turned aside into a shop that attracted her. Whether it was a sudden echo of the accents of Sophie's and Njabulo's flat, a flipping back of the pages of self, or whether it was a stir of something that couldn't be sickness for a 'home' that was exile, she went up to be there, among the same posters and drawing-pin-stabbed cuttings, the framed Freedom Charter and photographs of the old Chief (of whom, a secret between them, she had the private picture of a stout black man in an army overcoat, met at dawn) and the younger leader whose voice Pauline had brought into the house on tape and who was now an even further-disembodied presence, looking down on second-hand filing cabinets from a distant prison island.

She did not know either of the two young men sitting in the room. She introduced herself through her familiarity with Njabulo, Sophie, Christa and the names of others who used to come to the flat; she had lived with them, it clearly was not a false claim. Yet the two were cautious, and not only because she was white: because she was from back home. What had she come for? Who was it she'd come to see? No-one. —Just to say hello.—

It was dangerous to believe anything open, while holed up in refugee status where everything is ulterior. They stared past, willing her to go. Then someone walked in whom she did know. She began from that moment to have credibility of her own: he came back, the man who had appeared so black, so defined, so substantial from out of water running mercurial with light. He had come between them, a girl and man in the sea, paling them in the assertion of his blackness, bearing news whose weight of reality was the obsidian of his form. A slight acquaintance seems more than it was when two people meet again in an unexpected place. Although he had not acknowledged her when he rose from the sea, and she had only put in a word here and there in the conversations he had led at Ma Sophie's, he took her by the shoulders in greeting, shook her a little, comradely, and she was close enough to see the lines made by dealing with the white man, down from either side of his mouth, and the faint nicked scars near the ears made by blacks in some anterior life. —How did you find out I'd just arrived?— The shaking of her head, over the sweet warm drinks from a cupboard, became a sign to them both; she must have known without knowing. He was a man who did not laugh loosely but had a slow-developing strong smile when confirming something he was sure of.

He was not curious about her presence in the country; the norms of exile were constant displacement and emplacement on orders not to be questioned, or by circumstances over which the one in refuge had no control, either. The fact that she did have a refuge also gave her some credibility for him—what black man would believe a white girl would leave the luxuries of home without reasons valid for refuge? She wanted to introduce him to the people who had taken her in. But he had no use for diplomatic contacts with countries hostile to the organization, or which did not have, at least, an enlightened group which campaigned on its behalf. —I don't know about their *country* ... They've been wonderful to me.— And so, as Whaila (the white diminutives that diminished a black man in another way were being discarded, an African who spoke for his people before the United Nations Commission on Human Rights could not be called Johnny) assumed her loyalty to the cause, this became assumed by her as the reason for her presence, and the fact that the Ambassador's family had taken her in both confirmed that she was an exile and that her protectors had some humanistic partisanship that might be useful. There followed a period when Whaila Kgomani was something of a prize guest. Emile and Marie-Claude did not usually entertain blacks other than those who were unavoidable through protocol—members and officials of Nkrumah's government, and the representatives of other black states. —What pleasure is there? I don't see the point of mixing just because they are black. What can you talk about with them? They serve us up the platitudes they think we want to hear because that's what white people taught them. You never know what they think. Never give anything of themselves ...—

Marie-Claude had a correction for her husband, this time. —Except when they are dancing. Or drunk.— She enjoyed the occasional boldness of one who didn't know or chose not to know that European custom confines men and women to partners within their own party at a nightclub, and with a smile and flourish no-one could take offence to, sauntered her off into the rhythmical mob.

But this man from the south of the continent—her husband himself was the one who said it—he was a man with an intellect. —They may treat them badly down there in your country, Hillela, but it seems to sharpen their minds, mmh?— (The Ambassador always aimed exactly the right tone of banter at her, at the family table.) This one did not need wine to loosen his tongue but he knew how to drink it in a civilised manner, not swilled down because it was provided, free, by a white. His look, narrow eyes decoding the appearances of an embassy room, was not beguiled by the knick-knacks of European power—the coat-of-arms table silver, the humidor in which cigars were wheeled in, the royal portrait in which the face of the current incumbent fitted into the cut-out of medals and braid like the faces of revellers who have themselves photographed at a fairground. There was no predictable rhetoric, either. Hillela's compatriot stood before the portrait, turned with the battle-lines of his mouth curving a civil smile. —That must be a great-great-grandson? His ancestor was the one who cut off hands when the workers in the plantations didn't bring in enough rubber.—

Emile put up his own hands in mutual admission of the sins of the great-great-grandfathers. —Awful things happened on this side of Africa.—

—Well, he made his country estate over here, didn't he ...—

—It was only for a very short time. Then the other European powers got jealous, of course.—

—Of course. They were all the same family weren't they? Cousins, uncles and that... Him, the English queen, the German king ... we were their family property, man. But they were a cartel, really ... We were talking about multinational companies just now; what's new? Except that it's not aunties and uncles banded together to own us, now, it's foreign national economies. The extended family of the West ...—

Here was a black man with whom one could talk of contentious matters in the European mode of scepticism and irony that makes communication possible between the social irreconcilables of power and powerlessness. In that mode, one can say anything, if one knows how to say it. The Ambassador, putting one arm round his beautiful wife and one round the girl: —I don't know about the other whites in your country, but this one—we love her—

She went to them ('almost as if to parents' Marie-Claude remarked to her husband) and said she wanted to help the organization—clerical work. Never said right out that she was going away, leaving him; but the Ambassador knew her, knew it. He at once gave his wife a lead in generosity. —But Hillela can continue to live here. She has her room. We don't need it ... there's no reason ...— She did not stay on long. Just as well. It was not, after all, the right thing for the Embassy to open itself to complaints from her country that it was harbouring political dissidents from that country; wherever she went, it was not to diplomatic parties, now, and constantly in the company of the members of a banned organization.

Njabulo Manaka, under whose kitchen table she had been accommodated, had moved on again; he was on trial in the home country for having infiltrated after military training in Algeria. Sne moved on. As customary now with her, once she was no longer even a lodger at the Embassy, she did not go to visit the family there. The Ambassador saw her as he was passing the market; her profile with the light catching the cheekbone, her breasts swinging forward as she bent to test the ripeness of some fruit; her old poverty diet she had told him about in the sweet, light confidences of bed. He put a hand on his driver's shoulder, the car drew up in the swill of the gutter. —Get in.— She paid for her mangoes, first.

She sat angled towards him, knees neatly together, presenting herself, smiling as if she had been at the Embassy only yesterday.

—Where are you living?—

They spoke behind the driver's ears open to them under his braided cap.

—There's a house where we all live.—

—So you're with him.—

—We're all together.—

—Tell me. Hillela? ... Well, if it hasn't happened yet, it will. You're like me. You'll try ... It's quite a novelty, isn't it. I've had a few of his kind, myself. I always was attracted. And of course where I come from, it's no crime. No, to be fair, it's still (he made a familiar damping-down signal with his fine caresser's hand)—not done ...—

She took the hand. Her own was sticky with the juice and dirt that had dried on the fruit in her lap, her cheeks were the colour and smoothness of the rose-brown mango skin, the black eyes were those that had opened under him many times, holding for his reassurance the depth of pleasure he could plumb.

—I'm pregnant.—

—Oh my God.—

She saw the pain that slid its blade into him; her face was that of a child confronted with the middle-aged rictus of an angina.

Not his! Not from him! Could not be from him. But what a regret? If it had happened when it would have been his, he would have been irritated by her, as usual with women, for not being more efficient.

But of course she was not like other women. He knew that. Young as she was, she understood her field. He had even reinterpreted an aphorism once, for her, but she probably hadn't known the original and couldn't really appreciate the point: —The proper study of woman is man.—

—Do you want me to arrange something?— He spoke now as he would to a friend who had got a girl into trouble; it was only natural to stand together when these nuisances occurred. He had to grant it to her, Hillela's attitude to sex was that of an honorary man.

She shook her head. Then she lifted her throat; strangely, like a bird about to sing. Happiness is always embarrassing to onlookers. He gave her the mimed kiss, small sharp blows on either cheek, that marked both farewells and felicitations among people of his own kind.

Funerals and weddings are identical occasions when it comes to disguising in a generally-accepted façade of sorrow or celebration any previous state of relations between those taking part. If there was what can be called a wedding party at all when the black man married her (and there is no doubt that they were legally married, whatever the status of her other alliances) it was given by the Ambassador and his wife at their Residence. Because of the political implications represented by the bridegroom, it was not more than a small unofficial cocktail party, where the children who were so excited to be associated with their beloved Hillela in public kept racing up to touch her dress or lean against her, and the closer and less stuffy friends among the diplomatic corps came to make a show of wishing her well, no matter how they doubted this would help. The young First Secretary, coincidentally in the country on leave from the post elsewhere where he had been useful as a suitable public partner, was able to be present. He cut short any critical speculation among the champagne drinkers with a term that, in its particular British sense, was a high compliment. —We had a lot of fun together. She's a really good sport.—

And it was Marie-Claude, pulling down the sides of her lovely mouth in dismissal, who had the last word when later the rumour went round that the man had another wife—and children—somewhere, probably back where he and the girl came from. —To be one wife among several, the way the Africans do it—that's to be a mistress, isn't it? So she fits in, in her way, with a black man's family. Hillela's a natural mistress, not a wife.—

Lying beside him, looking at pale hands, thighs, belly: seeing herself as unfinished, left off, somewhere. She examines his body minutely and without shame, and he wakes to see her at it, and smiles without telling her why: she is the first not to pretend the different colours and textures of their being is not an awesome fascination. How can it be otherwise? The laws that have determined the course of life for them are made of skin and hair, the relative thickness and thinness of lips and the relative height of the bridge of the nose. That is all; that is everything. The Lilliesleaf houseparty is in prison for life because of it. Those with whom she ate pap and cabbage are in Algeria and the Soviet Union learning how to man guns and make bombs because of it. He is outlawed and plotting because of it. Christianity against other gods, the indigenous against the foreign invader, the masses against the ruling class—where he and she come from all these become interpretative meanings of the differences seen, touched and felt, of skin and hair. The laws made of skin and hair fill the statute books in Pretoria; their gaudy savagery paints the bodies of Afrikaner diplomats under three-piece American suits and Italian silk ties. The stinking fetish made of contrasting bits of skin and hair, the scalping of millions of lives, dangles on the cross in place of Christ. Skin and hair. It has mattered more than anything else in the world.

—When you touched me at the beginning (she takes his black hand and spreads it on her hip) this was a glove. Really. The blackness was a glove. And everywhere, all over you, the black was a cover. Something God gave you to wear. Underneath, you must be white like me. —Or pale brownish, it's my Portuguese blood.— White like me; because that's what I was told, when I was being taught not to be prejudiced: underneath, they are all just like us. Nobody said we are just like *you*.—

The smile deepens. —That wouldn't be true either. Then you'd have a skin missing.—

—If you are white, there, there's always a skin missing. They never say it.—

She says everything now. —When we are together, when you're inside me, nothing is missing.— The train leaving Rhodesia behind, the Imari cat, the expectations of benefactors, the deserted beds—everything broken off, unanswered, abandoned, is made whole. She never tires of looking at his hands. —Not wearing anything. They're you. And they're not black, they're all the flesh colours. D'you know, in shops— and in books!—'flesh colour' is Europeans' colour! Not the colour of any other flesh. Nothing else! Look at your nails, they're pinkish-mauve because under them the skin's pink. And (turning the palms) here the colour's like the inside of one of those big shells they sell on Tamarisk. And this—the lovely, silky black skin I can slide up and down (his penis in her hand), when the tip comes out, it's also a sort of amber-pink. There's always a lot of sniggering about the size of a black man's thing, but no-one's ever said they weren't entirely black.—

—And what d'you think of the size, now?—

—I suppose they vary, same as whites' ones.— While he laughs, she is even franker. —I still don't much like African hair. I couldn't say that there, either. Once when I was with my cousins on holiday, some hairs from the black cleaner's head had somehow dropped into the bath, and my Aunt Pauline was furious with me because I pulled a face and wouldn't bathe. I don't know why I felt like that... all sorts of muddled feelings—the kind you get down there, you know? I suppose they haven't all worn off ... I like the feel of your hair in the dark, oh I like it very much, but I don't think African hair is as beautiful to look at as whites' hair can be, d'you? Long blonde shiny hair?—

—I want you to grow your hair long, very long ...—

—Then you also think European hair is nicer, on the whole? But you won't dare say it!—

—What if the baby has my hair?—

—I told you, I love your hair. I wonder what colour the baby will come out, Whaila?—

—What colour do you want?— Len had let her choose her cold drink with that gentle indulgence.

—I love not knowing what it will be. What colour it is, already, here inside me. Our colour.— She buries her head on his belly.

Our colour. She cannot see the dolour that relaxes his face, closes his eyes and leaves only his mouth drawn tight by lines on either side. Our colour. A category that doesn't exist: she would invent it. There are Hotnots and half-castes, two-coffee-one-milk, touch-of-the-tar-brush, pure white, black is beautiful—but a creature made of love, without a label; that's a freak.

One of her protectors took his texts not from the bible but from whatever book he chanced on in his library. Riding in a Ghanaian taxi she saw a legend placed for her on the dashboard: IT CHANGES. She was too big, for the time being, for the high-life on Saturdays. The dance of life didn't have to be performed in a shop window: at that moment the jolting of the vehicle without shock-absorbers caused the foetus to turn turtle inside her. A queer feeling. *It changes:* exhilaration surfaced, as a wave turns over a bright treasure.

James and Busewe were suspicious of her when she appeared up the stairs; now she was installed among them, in their makeshift office, in their house. But it was not as they had thought it would be: teach me, she said, not only in words but in her whole being, that body of hers. And as she had picked up protocol in an ambassador's Residence she picked up the conventions to be observed, signs to be read, manoeuvres to be concealed in refugee politics. She cultivated friendships at the university so that she could borrow the standard works of revolutionary theory she could have taken advantage of in Joe's study, and whose titles had shone at her in vain in Udi's livingroom. The application and shrewdness with which she studied all cuttings, reports, papers, journals, manifestos brought an intimate aside from Whaila: —Never mind Portuguese—that's your Jewish blood. Studious people.—

—Is it bad for you … I mean, that I'm white?—

—But you know there are whites with us, Hillela—Arnold, Christa, the Hodgsons, Slovo—

—Yes but it's agreed, 'the leaders will come from our loins'. It's written. It means black. It must.—

Comically, she put a hand on either side of her hard, high belly. He leaned over, felt the warmth and liveliness that always came to her face at his approach, and stroked the belly as if over a child's head. —Hillela, Hillela, I can see you're ambitious for your children, you're worried in case you can't make a future prime minister in there.—

228

Her mouth bunched in derision of herself. —No, no, I only wonder about you. You're one of those who decided that. 'From our loins.' You've told me you were only eighteen when you joined the Youth League. And you're still an Africanist, you've always been one, haven't you?—

He was accustomed to a woman becoming placid while carrying a child; there were times when he did not know what to say to this one, in whom sexual energy was not quieted but instead fired a physical and mental zest that kept her working all day, racing about through the crowds in the stunning heat, and questioning him at night. He wanted to say: what have I done to you? What am I to you, that you transform yourself?

—If you look for contradictions in individuals you'll always find them. I'm not any different. There's never been anything laid down about marrying a white. It's of no importance.—

—What about the people in the camps. The things that are being said by some of them about the way the leaders are living.—

He smiled to catch her out. —So it's a luxury and a privilege to have a white woman?—

Her black eyes shamed him. —Like whisky and nice houses and big cars—the things white men have at home. People can't help judging by the way it was for them at home.—

—Well I haven't got any whisky or big house and posh car, I've only got you. There are plenty of real problems to worry about. I don't know what we'll find when we go to Morogoro next week... The trouble is, the life in the camps is so monotonous, and we can't send many people back down South to infiltrate yet. We're not ready. The men want to get out and get on with it. That's the real dissatisfaction. It's not whether the leaders eat meat while they get food they don't like. And Tanzania's own people are poor, you can't expect them to give ours more than they have for themselves ... It's the isolation. There's nothing to do every day when the training's over. You're miles from anywhere. Think of being in a remote hole like Bagamoyo.—

—I was almost there. It was beautiful.— She smiled at an old life where one caught butterflies.

Arnold was the first to meet, hatched from the cocoon of the little tramp on Tamarisk Beach, Mrs Whaila Kgomani. There she was in the office, sitting on the edge of the head-of-mission's table, arguing over the telephone with the owner of the building about responsibility for unblocking a drain. Huge, her belly and those wonderful breasts like elaborate vestments serving to emphasize the alert composure of that bright head, and those black eyes that absorbed all gazes, as they did his. Pregnancy did not blunt but made more powerful the physical presence that had once drawn him after her into the sea. On the bare boards of this no-place, no-time, she was an assertion of *here* and *now* in the provisionality of exile, whose inhabitants are strung between the rejected past and a future fashioned like a paper aeroplane out of manifestos and declarations. She got up and she and the dignitary from the Command kissed, not in the style of a foreign embassy, but as comrades in the cause, smiling.

—Whaila has taken you in hand.—

Once up the old splintered staircase, Whaila became again the obsidian of single purpose against which any personal attachment glanced off. He and Arnold were at one. She was not between them. There is no way of telling, ever, whether Whaila knew about the attachments of the girl on Tamarisk, because that kind of knowledge had no place in the purpose. The form of Hillela's presence was Praetorian—the only way an outsider could describe it. Not only did she keep people at bay (her eyes flicking a warning when she handed over to Whaila a suspect telephone caller), she could be felt (some emanation of her, from the concentration of human destiny going on inside her, the creature turning from fish to biped) willing the direction of a discussion, seeing, moves ahead, what would put Whaila at a disadvantage. Her presence paced the borders, of his sense of self. She was there, with an intense fixing of her black eyes upon him, sometimes with an insignificant gesture—breath taken, hand filling a glass with water—a fidget over which his concentration tripped a moment and was regained with a new awareness. The alarm that closed her face when Arnold made a point Whaila might have made, amused Arnold: how slyly and expertly she turned him away, too—from his amusement and advantage, this time— by a relaxing of her lips and a resting of her gaze upon him that belonged to the borrowed room in a foreign news agency. She was not present at the most important discussions, of course; not yet, but she was there, outside the door, so to speak. When Arnold was back from his tour of Cairo, Algiers, Accra and Lusaka, Christa asked—How did you find Hillela?— A smile, confirming a private prediction: —Ambitious.— She laughed. —What do you mean, 'ambitious'!— —Well, she'd like to see Whaila where Tambo is.— —That's not too likely... yes. But Whaila's a splendid fellow. He'll go far. She's right about that.—

There was a space round Whaila in the office even when the company were not his peers; James and Busewe were beguiled by Hillela, the three drank beer together while, entranced, her face tilted up at them from folded arms, she listened to the stories of their youth and childhood—the childhood of the children left at home by Bettie and Jethro when they came to work in white people's houses. But they were conscious that a task requested by Whaila and scamped by them, a half-hour when they kept him waiting, a hesitation in carrying out anything he expected of them, came under her scrutiny. Feet put up unthinkingly on his table were withdrawn. Cigarettes stubbed in the ashtray, there, would stop her as she walked by. With her Busewe and James were familiar; whatever the balance had been before she came, there was no familiarity with Whaila, after. Yet they have said of her: *She was okay, man. It didn't matter.* The denial is taken to refer to her being white. But it is more likely to have been an acceptance of her exigence; that it was the cause there was insistence on being served meticulously through Whaila: *their* cause, whatever her motive or impetus was.

Whaila liked to make statements that were really propositions to set off the others. He had the will to make everyone around him 'think things through' that ran beneath the perfectly orthodox version of policy and events he presented in public. He wanted to keep an historical perspective. —Tambo said the Defiance Campaign was 'aggressive pressure'—it wasn't just lying around waiting to be arrested, you know.—

Busewe pocked the dirty wood of his chair-arm with the point of a pencil. —But what did you really do, man? Going into locations without a permit, walking around after curfew, sitting on *Blankes Alleen* benches, trying to get served at the white counter in the post office. Je-suss! The only good result was the chance to use the courtrooms to make speeches.—

—Four months of keeping the police occupied, keeping a high profile for resistance? That amounts to nothing?— James was old enough to have boarded a Whites Only coach on a train when he was hardly more than a boy.

—I'm not saying *nothing*. Where did it get us? When everybody with the strength to carry on was in jail, that was the end. It was feeble, man! When the government made the sentences too heavy, people didn't want to keep on any longer. If you start defying you can't give up. You can't say, go ahead, arrest me, and then say—but only if I don't go to jail for too long. It was too much the idea of the Indians, that campaign ... with the English in India, the whole thing had rules, man, the Indians would go so far, the English would give in so far. They knew they were getting out of India in the end. The *Boere* don't accept any idea of giving over power, ever. Never. We know that, from the start. Why should we use campaigns that were worked out for a different kind of place?—

The ideas of others worked in Hillela's blood like alcohol; when she was stirred or puzzled by or disagreed with what was being said she would breathe faster and faster until at last she broke in. —If the blacks won't fight, it's the government that makes them fight.—

—That's it exactly.— Whaila acknowledged with a chairman's impartiality; the interjection might just as well have come from James or Busewe. —That's the stage we reached after the Defiance Campaign. The realization that we are forced to fight. But it doesn't make the campaign a failure. The campaign simply proved that there is no way but to fight, because the government doesn't know how to respond to anything else. It was a phase we had to complete, to convince ourselves, hey? Over fifty years passed before Umkhonto! Hell—maybe we needed too long for convincing! They were too slow, the old ones ... More than fifty years! We might not even live that long!—

Busewe had punched a cross that was turning into a tree. —If they'd changed strategy earlier it would have meant Congress would've been banned earlier. And then? ... But maybe before the Nats took over in forty-eight we'd have had a better chance of remaining above ground.—

Whaila had an unconscious habit of abruptly changing position in his chair when he had to correct an error of judgment. —D'you imagine Smuts would have been less tough with us than Verwoerd! Look at history, man. The English made an English gentleman out of a Boer general; but you know what the great Englishman Rhodes said: 'I prefer land to niggers'. No. The problem of tactics and results is very much a question of timing. Timing. It worries me. We need to think a lot about the timing in any situation where we launch new tactics.—

—'People in a privileged position never voluntarily give up that position'.— Hillela took opportunities to test the platitudes of her reading. She turned to the stranger, Whaila. —So there'll never be a right time for that? D'you think there'll be a right time for tactics to *make them give up?*—

—There'll be many times along the way to that one ... Many years, perhaps. That's the side of strategy I'm talking about. Tactics must always be first matched against the situation. Taking too long before making a decision can be a disaster. You can miss out... But it's no good getting frantic because nothing much is happening at home just now. What fits the present situation is to concentrate on getting support outside—foreign powers and international organizations are absolutely crucial to us, more important than activity down there. The whole movement will die without support. Collapse. So we have to run about ... The front line is this end.—

—Man, I still think they have to keep up the sabotage down there somehow. Even if it's with wire-cutters and choppers.—

—What *I* think—symbolic targets are the idea—all right. But sabotage is correct tactically for another reason. What is sabotage?— James was quoting a formulation, too. —Sabotage is violence to property. And whites are the ones with property—it's something blacks don't have. So sabotage is dead right in the situation. The results can be calculated, hey, Whaila; you're talking to whites in a language they're going to understand.—

—Well yes. But it's a tactic that's not going to have much chance to succeed from the point of view of timing. We just don't have the manpower to do the job. Too many in prison, or here, outside. Our people are getting arrested and rearrested all the time. You've got a hundred-and-eighty days' detention, now, not just ninety. And the sentences—they're getting five or ten years for nothing. We don't have the sophisticated weapons to be effective. Have to keep running about ... we need new sources of supply. The government has all the weapons, all the spies to make the sabotage campaign fail, as things stand now ... I don't know ... and maybe we haven't thought enough about the way the enemy will react. We know the reaction to mass action, okay, since Sharpeville—but the type of action the

234

government will take against a sabotage campaign, not only against our Underground but also the people ... the people! How much more repression can the townships take without expecting more positive results from us? There's also the question of training.— He stopped himself. —How much training our men have had and how good it was. In real military battles experts decide which weapons are right for which purpose, their striking power and so on. It's something I want to go into ... When it comes to guerrilla operations in the bush, the throw-outs from other countries' hardware aren't going to do.— They knew this must be what they had heard as a blur of voices when he and Arnold were behind a closed door. —And then there's timing again ... Things'll be easier next year when Basutoland and Bechuanaland become independent. If we can get in there, we'll be just over the fence from our people ...—

—Only Smith to worry about, then; our men will be able to come with ZAPU* down from Zambia right to Gaborone. You can just about wave over to the folks from there!—

—Not yet, Bra James, not quite yet.:—

Hillela took the freedom under turns of talk, to follow any aspect of the kind for which, as her cousin had complained in childish confidences long ago, all the advantages she had shared with him never gave an explanation. She would surface suddenly with her preoccupation, laying it before them. —There are people who have given up being white.—

Busewe pretended to be jolted from his chair. All three men laughed at her.

—You know exactly what I mean. What it means, there. Bram Fischer, the Weinbergs, Slovos, Christa, Arnold. And there are others ... another kind. I knew them, I was in a family ... they wanted to but they didn't seem to know how?—

*

*Zimbabwe African People's Union

235

—It solves nothing.— Pauline served her family at table. Carole had her boyfriend to lunch. Sasha was there but he did not bring girls home. —Back here his kind still carry a pass. Feeling free to sleep with a black man doesn't set him free.—

Carole's boyfriend knew one mustn't expect small-talk at that table. And the merciless intimacy with which each member of the family knew the context of subjects raised meant that he could not expect to follow anything more specific than the emotions roused. Carole squeezed his thigh comfortingly under the table. Her mother lifted her head, two streaks of grey, now, at the hairline, like Mosaic horns, to challenge; but no-one was drawn. Carole had told Bettie the news in the kitchen. —Hillela? A black man? What, is that girl mad? Black men are no good for husbands. He'll run away, you'll see. Ah, poor Hilly. We must bring her back home to us.—

Sasha in his room tore some sheets out of an exam pad and began to write: *She's jealous. Saturday classes for kids. Reformers are (take pride in being) totally rational, but the dynamic of real change is always utopian. The original impetus may get modified—even messed up—in the result, but it has to be there no matter how far from utopia that result may be.*

Utopia is unattainable; without aiming for it—taking a chance!—you can never hope even to fall far short of it.

Instinct is utopian. Emotion is utopian. But reformers can't imagine any other way. *They want to adapt what is. You move around, don't you, bumping up against—brought up short every time!—by the same old walls. If you reform the laws, the economy defeats the reforms. (That's what my father tells you, so you must admit it's true), If you reform the economy, the laws defeat the reforms (out of your own mouth, to him, a hundred times, when you're on that war-path of yours with a neat hedge Alpheus clips on either side). Don't you see? It's all got to come down, mother. Without utopia—the idea of utopia— there's a failure of the imagination—and that's a failure to know how to go on living. It will*

take another kind of being to stay on, here. A new white person. Not us.
The chance is a wild chance—like falling in love.

Sasha did not know what it was he had written: a letter? He did not keep a diary, having too frequently a revulsion against his own thoughts to want to be able to turn back to them. He would not tear up the pages. He would put them away yet at the same time leave them around somewhere easily come upon. She might read them. She was always so eager, secretly, to understand what she couldn't, ever; so nosey.

A Perfect Circle of Sand

Hillela was conscious throughout. But the hard work going on in her body, which usually performed its functions without bothering her, engaged her completely during the birth. As if in a train crossing at full speed a landscape in the dark, she saw and heard nothing outside that body until the sudden cessation, the light moment after part of her body slipped free of her. There was a great uproar of shouting and rejoicing. The yelling sway of voices chanting, singing, at different distances. It was all for her; she put the heel of her hand on her trembling empty belly and tried to sit up, smiling. She had come all alone to the hospital and now everyone was celebrating her, everyone.

Whaila was away in their home country, his and hers, when his baby was born. Nkrumah was in Peking, and the celebration in the streets was a real one: the crowds rejoicing an army coup, and his fall.

She knew where Whaila was but no-one else did, not even Busewe and James—or if they did, acknowledgement was not made. They were supposed to accept that he was somewhere in Europe at a meeting of the alliance he had helped form, a few years earlier, with liberation groups from the Portuguese-colonised countries, FRELIMO from Mozambique, MPLA from Angola, PAIGC from Guinea. The father of Ruthie's grandchild moved in the streets of South African cities within passing distance of Olga (in Cape Town at the tail-end of her summer holiday), Pauline and Joe (on their way to a lecture at the Institute of Race Relations in Johannesburg) and Sasha (leaving the city's reference library and taking a detour into the black end of town to buy an African jazz record for a girl-friend's birthday). Whaila was just as close, at one time or another, to his children by his divorced wife, and to his mother's house, 8965

Block D, in a black location. But he was also just as far, because he could make no attempt to see them; he carried a forged passbook with a false name, and that persona was under orders to see what could be done to revive the internal structure of the movement and accelerate recruitment of men for military training outside.

Hillela seems to have had no realization he might never come back. That he might be discovered or betrayed, and arrested, as Njabulo was when he infiltrated. Busewe had come to visit her bringing the standard African gift for a hospital patient, a bottle of orange squash. She rather mischievously wheedled to see if she could get out of him where she might send a letter that would reach Whaila 'in Europe'. She wanted, above all considerations of life and death, to tell Whaila how the baby had come out: like him, like him. The white American nurse had been embarrassed when she was asked, amid the cheers in the streets pressing against the hospital windows, whether the baby would grow black?—of course it was pinkish-yellow, newly-hatched. The black nurse giggled and gave expert opinion. —It never be white (jutting her scarred chin). When they born that colour, nothing you can do to make it white. She goin' to be a black girl.— —Oh you think so? It is always like that? Are you sure?—

The American turned away in further embarrassment at the patient's confusing joy, which was surely vulgar if not, in some peculiar way, racist?

Whaila came back, and saw that Hillela had never feared for him. She might be white, but she was the right wife for a revolutionary, who, ideally, shouldn't have such ties at all. She greeted him with desire, not questions. Her eyes were on him impatiently when other people were around, drawing him to their bed. The baby had slept with her until he returned but she turned it out to a cot to yield him his place. She wanted him to 'give her'—that was how she put it—another baby at once. He said it was too soon and added what he thought would be the last word for any woman he had known: —Anyway, I don't want to see you swollen up all the time, I like you slim.— No, no she must have more children. There were distracting caresses for a while. —You don't really want a whole lot of kids to cart around with us from country to country. God knows where we'll have to go next.— Her open gaze contracted and dilated, holding him steadily. —An African wife isn't a wife if she doesn't produce children.— —Oh my god, Hillela, is that what's on your mind!— He kissed her for the foolishness. —I've got enough children, already, that I never see. I'm satisfied to have just this one here with us.—

She was not offended by the reminder that another woman had supplied him with sons. Had it really been impossible somehow to meet them, down there? —I'm sure *I* would have found a way.— He took the opportunity to teach her something she would have to learn, once and for all. —There are always ways. To do what you have to do, you have to forget about those ways.—

Nkrumah would never come back. When she went to show Marie-Claude the baby, the talk round the Ambassador's lunch table was of relief. Condemnation rose as the drawn corks squeaked out of bottles of wine. The Ambassador and his colleagues discussed the disasters of Nkrumah's economic policy, the grandiloquent development projects that could be paid for only by borrowing at exorbitant rates of interest from overseas creditors, the catastrophic rise of Ghana's external debt since 1963, the pretensions of the state buildings he put up to his glory. —This National Liberation Council can't be worse; at least the military aren't a bunch of romantic African Marxists like him.— The Ambassador did not look once at the baby, only at Hillela, as if its existence had no significance other than to wound him. He went on talking while looking at her, with his old skill at communicating in two different modes at once, the voice that belonged with the distinguished exterior shaped by the tailoring of his three-piece grey suit, and the other, speechless message from the body beneath it. —There was no choice between an army coup and complete anarchy. When the ordinary black can't afford to buy food because of inflation, that's good riddance to your Nkrumahs. But it's not the end of the phenomenon. Ah, not at all, not at all. He has left behind the particular form mega-lomania is going to continue taking, in blacks, all over Africa. You'll see. Inventing isms, quasi-religions with neo-colonialism as hellfire and a succession of Osagyefos as saviours leading the continent to starvation—but in unity, my friends, of course, in the name of African unity, and his famous way of life that ensures security, abundance, prosperity (a ladder climbed by a fluttering hand)—all through brotherly love!—

In the office up the splintering stairs the despotic decline of the man had been discussed in troubled private. Whaila, Busewe and James did not know what the attitude of the new rulers would be to their own movement. They had reason to expect that it might now come into full recognition and favour; some reason to celebrate. Yet they were quieted, retreated into themselves in a way they could not discuss even with one another by a defeat for something that was there, inside them. To them, the unity of Africa was not another ism; it was the dignity in brotherhood they had found, at last, in a world that had always denied them any other. However its prophet had destroyed himself, whatever he had denied their own organization, however quarrelsome the brotherhood, they mourned him for what he had given Africa, and what they could never denigrate, however many times or by whom it was to be betrayed. Whaila did not talk about this with his young wife, either; and she did what she had learned to do all her life—assumed instinctively from observance of those with whom she lived the appropriate attitude. The celebration outside the hospital windows was not acceptable. The only cause for rejoicing had been, as she in her dazed state had mistaken it for, her having given birth to Whaila's daughter.

Nkrumah had not been seen in the streets when he was still Osagyefo and President, since she had been in Ghana. That single evening alone had he been an embodied personage, appearing for five minutes among the guests at Christiansborg Castle. He had not fallen, for her, as he had within themselves for the three men with whom she lived. It was when she was wheeling the baby about town for the first time and came upon a public square that he fell. A statue lay smashed upon the ground. People had brought him down. His people. She felt a strange dissolution; she suddenly understood fear, fear of the plans, orders, missions, the suppressed conflicts, the ambitions (her own) in the huge upheaval which she had placed herself astride as when a child she had revelled in the wild bucking of a playground's mythological bull. Another had risen, out of the sea, Zeus disguised to capture Europa, coming between her and her sometime lover, Arnold, and carried her off, clinging to its legendary black back. Power, people said. Pauline said Olga (half-remembered; the children half-listened when Pauline talked of these things) was afraid of it. Olga was not afraid of the power within which she lived, but of the other one, that would heave under it and bring it down. But power could not be contained for that purpose alone—the just purpose of the plans, orders, missions; it shook and toppled those who wielded it, too. Hillela steered the pram away through the crowds in whose close streams of gregariousriess she had roamed so at ease when she had been alone in African towns; his people.

The pram was a present from Marie-Claude, specially imported from Europe. The baby went about like the offspring of diplomats, in a shiny navy-blue carriage with white-walled tyres, the infantine equivalent of an ambassadorial Mercedes-Benz. Whaila approved; this kind of comfort and safety was far preferable to Hillela's first notion, that she would carry the baby tied on her back as he must have been carried as a child. She had begged to be allowed to choose the name. Since this was a girl, and, for her, the first child, he was amused to indulge her. So the baby was named after Nelson Mandela's wife, Nomzamo.

As Hillela passed through stalls where she paused to buy vegetables and fruit, market women to whom she was a familiar customer touched and admired the pram, the tasselled braid round the hood and the brown baby with the tiny, ivory-edged nostrils lying there. They teased her about motherly pride, compared the child's progress with that of their own babies, exchanged complaints about childbirth, and asked what the child was called. They did not know who Mrs Mandela was; they knew about seasonal produce, prices, making money, and pregnancy, birth, death—the female Free Masonry or other tribalism that drew her into their warm shelter. She laughed, teased back, and folded the pram's hood to show off the namesake to them.

The office car was old and shared between those who now officially staffed the mission. Busewe and James used it at night when they went off after girls; on Sundays, now that Whaila was a family man, it was understood that its use would be reserved to him—the old South African custom for black and white, whether on foot or by car, of the Sunday family outing, somehow finding its way into exile through trails of uprooted habit. Hillela liked to go to the beach. She formed a routine of scooping out of the sand a little bed for the baby. From that Whaila got the idea of digging a bowl big enough to shelter all three of them. The sand was cool and damp under its desert surface. An umbrella held off a sun that would put out their eyes. They lay there together, joined wherever they touched by the moisture of the sea evaporating on their flesh, the baby stirring the air with its toes and fingers like the small sea creatures themselves feeling at the currents of water. These Sundays at the beach were intensely private as the afternoons at Tamarisk had been public. In the house—it was the organization's house, no-one's home—the three were never without the contingent presence of Busewe and James, and transients who came and went;

on the beach they were complete, Hillela and her man and their baby; in the hot shade, contained within their bowl of sand whose circle had no ingress for anyone or anything else and no egress by which oneself could be cast out. And each Sunday fitted over the last in an unbroken and indistinguishable circle.

One Sunday that was not to run together with the others, they drove to a beach she had once swum at with the Ambassador's family. When she and Whaila got out of the car they saw it was deserted except for stick-figures, far enough off to be taken for driftwood until they bent to gather something when the surf drew back. The burning blue sea running its curling tongues over brown sugar sand was as she remembered, but there was a sign staked against the lovely sight she ran towards: CHOLERA AREA, NO BATHING. This was also the period when, like many young women with a first child, Hillela was obsessed with the idea of infections threatening this creature she had made. She raced back and would not touch the baby until Whaila had driven to a service station where she could wash her feet. She kept shuddering, beside him.

In place of the beach, they went to Tema. Without formulating this for himself or her, Whaila wanted them to see something that had been almost realized, a monument not fallen. They drove on an unfinished landscape model, a planners' maquette. Splendid wide roads looped and bent round buildings and features that were not there. The cardboard trees, toy cars and plastic people of the planners' board were missing; the roads debouched into weeds. Near the walls of an aluminium smelter there was life, the old familiar teem; a shanty town made of crates that had held the machinery imported for the plant. —An American company runs it, and the bauxite's imported from Jamaica and Australia. We used to be only the suppliers of the world's raw materials, and the buyers of the same stuff we'd dug for, as the finished product—if we could afford the price. Now even the raw material from other countries is brought to us to be partly processed by our cheap labour; we still have to buy back the finished product from someone else.— But the deep-water harbour was achieved, there under their feet. They were walking along great stone platforms that held half-circled the power of the sea. The waters tilted massively at them. The baby in her canvas carrier swung from Whaila's hand over groundnuts spilled from a cargo; fangs of cranes were bared to the sky, their dragon necks crossed. The docks were deserted of workers on a Sunday, but the cargo ships in harbour from all over the world were tethered to something Africans had conceived and realized. The harbour dominated the sea as only foreigners' fortresses—Christiansborg, the forts of Luanda and Mombasa—had done for centuries. Whaila stood before the sea as no black man could before the harbour was built. The salt-laden humidity in late sunlight was a golden dust on him, risen from the victory over those years. His closed lips were drawn back in the thin line that was the price of such victories, as well as failures. What Hillela saw at those times was how awesomely aged by experience he was, and at once how passionately attractive to her, how grandly handsome (it was the Hollywood word for male beauty she knew) he had been made, without knowing by what destiny. With him she went back to Christiansborg. They took the baby for an airing, walking around outside the walls. It was nobody's castle, now, neither the Danes' nor the Osagyefo's; some kind of administrative block? He found the grave of Du Bois, that American black whose bones at least, as he believed they would, had witnessed an Africa rid of white masters. Whaila's thin, strong black hands tugged out last year's dry grasses that swagged across the tombstone. —D'you know a poem he wrote, long before he left America to come home to his forefathers in Africa? I've forgotten the beginning … it ends 'I felt the blazing glory of the sun; I heard the song of children crying "Free!"; I saw the face of freedom … and I died.'—

*

245

The namesake grew up very black. This has been an advantage for Nomzamo although she does not live in Africa, since the vogue for black models, which had begun esoterically in Paris when Ruthie, Olga and Pauline were playing with golden-haired Shirley Temple dolls in Johannesburg, spread to the United States and Britain during African decolonisation and coincided with the period in which she took up modelling at sixteen. She also grew as beautiful as the woman she was named for. Her mother has never been one to make mistakes when following her instincts. Trust her, as her enemies would remark. The girl, described in an agency's portfolio as exotic, is known as all the most success-ful models are simply by a single name—hers is Nomo—easily pronounceable by French, Italian, German, American and English couturiers and readers of fashion journals. An international model does not hamper her image with national politics; to the rich people who buy the clothes she displays or the luxuries her face and body promote, she is a symbol of Africa, anyway; one prefer-able to those children in the advertisements of aid organizations begging money to keep them from starving. She has not made use of the origin of her diminutive except, during a certain period, on occasions when she was hired by a committee giving a fashion show benefit for a cause such as aid for South African political prisoners—then she had a byline in the sponsored programme: 'Appropriately, top model Nomo is named for the black leader, Mrs Nomzamo Winnie Mandela, wife of Nelson Mandela'.

The baby became perfectly black. A year old, she would try to climb out of the perfect circle, the bowl her father dug out of sand with fingers strong as the tines of a gardener's tool. Then she would tumble back, again and again, and fall asleep across the limbs of her parents. Hillela put the tiny cushion of a black hand, like something she had come upon, into her own pale palm; with her own pale foot dusted the sand off the little black wedge of a foot not yet shaped by the muscles used in walking. Satisfaction sank deep as the cool moisture that existed under the parched sand: not to have reproduced herself, not to have produced a third generation of the mother who danced away into the dark of a nightclub, the child before whom certain advantages lay like the shadow of a palm tree, the aunts who offered what they had to offer.

It was the reversal of parental feeling as it is supposed to be. Naturally! Trust Hillela! Incommunicable to the one who had fathered the child because no matter where in the world he was removed physically and no matter how his way of life diverged, he was in his line—the house-servant mother, the butcher's 'boy' Sunday preacher father, the night-class alumni—teachers and nurses and welfare workers—who were his brothers and sisters, the Second Class taxi drivers, watchmen and farm labourers who were his uncles and cousins; all the people without advantages for whom he had become what he was. From the first words a parent speaks down to the new-born whose sensory responses are still attuned only to the sound of the mother's heartbeat and gut noises, Whaila spoke to the baby in his language—theirs. Hillela picked up a little from them, as the child learned to speak; but the child always, from her first words, spoke to her mother in English. When he was away, the child never spoke their African language, even in the games she played with herself; later she lost it altogether at a nursery-school in Eastern Europe. It would not be much of an advantage, anyway, now when she flies out to spend a week with her mother at State House, because the African language spoken there is a different one.

Where Hillela appears next, of course, is where her husband was sent. For a time they were based in London. It was not more than that; Whaila came and went across borders, barriers of a kind that divided Europe insurmountably in the minds of most Britons and Europeans.

Her aunt—the rich one—had had every intention of taking Hillela to London. She certainly would have given the girl the chance to go abroad at least once. She would have seen the West End shows and the special art exhibitions at the Royal Academy and she would have stayed at the Royal Garden Hotel, where Olga herself always did. Whaila came and went, leaving Hillela in the kind of basement flat buried under a terrace of identical Victorian houses, contiguous as the street run along in a dream, that has been the traditional habitation for political exiles since the 19th century. Heirs to kingdoms and the revolutionaries who plotted their downfall—they have climbed the area steps to put out the dustbin, and have gone to the British Museum to read, out of the cold. She walked with a bundle of wool on two stubby legs that was her child, among other people whose features showed from what countries they were exiled. But—with her knack for such things—she did not stay among them long. Although the British government, like that of the Americans, would not give to the movement the backing in money and arms it needed, so that Whaila was constantly absent seeking this in the Soviet Union and other countries not so easy to guess, there were charming English people who supported the cause person-ally and socially. Some were even influential in the press, Labour or Liberal Party, useful friends of Whaila. To them, Hillela as a white South African was part of the scatter of white revolutionar-ies from that country they invited to parties, although, in fact, for these exiles the girl was a nobody. As a white South African actually married to a black South African, she remained for her hosts at these same gatherings an embodiment of their politi-cal and ethical credo, non-racial unity against the oppression of one race. Whenever they came across a white South African a black had taken as mate, there was to be seen in the union assur-ance that they, too, could be given absolution for their country's colonial past. Hillela became the favourite of that alternative court, the shabby-affluent liberal livingroom, filled with books and generous with wine and food. She was also, of course, very pretty—vivacious, the women called it, sexy, the men agreed, amused at their concurrence. Once again, no party was complete without her. She was not slow to make use of these contacts; someone got her child into a private day-care centre and paid the fees; she and the child were rescued from the basement flat and moved into the guest room of a Holland Park house, with the run of it. It was the least one could do, the television producer told his lawyer wife, and repeated in the bedroom quarrels (it was the only place where their guest or her child would not walk in on them) when the wife wanted to know if they were never to have their home to themselves again, without someone constantly chattering on the telephone and baby food boiling over on the Aga. Whether or not Hillela was aware of the tensions she caused, she gave no sign of understanding what, in their English way, presuming upon the coded communication of their own kind, had been an offer only of temporary hospitality. Some people claim to remember that particular young woman with her black baby (an updated chocolate-box image for people proud of being without colour revulsion) as one who made a play for the men. But in those years there were so many young women, white and black, from Poland and Czechoslovakia and Hungary as well as from Africa, who fluttered into the livingrooms for a while like escaped birds in whose faces there were to be read the descriptive plaques of their distant, caged origins, and found their quickest welcome in the eyes of appreciative men present. It is easy—when it seems one of these girls can be matched with another image, and so comes up out of the obscurity into which all have moved on—to confuse Hillela with someone else.

Thick-skinned. And even the husband, defending her against the accusation, shaming his wife for making it, is mistaken:

—Think of the danger and suffering that poor girl has been through under that bloody government. No wonder she can't be *sensitive* like you, no wonder she doesn't understand that people like us could be selfish enough to begrudge her a corner of our soft lives.—

Tensions behind closed doors; nothing new to breathe, coming from there. Sometimes Olga and Arthur are quarrelling, sometimes it's Pauline and Joe analysing, even once Len and Billie, and, maybe, when they were left behind, the sibling cousins—all discussing what is to be done about the one they took in. As for the men; is it the fault of women that they are, or seem, beautiful? That the African cottons over breasts that no longer are hot, tingling, and heavy with milk, but still keep the shape and fullness of it, draw more attention than Liberty silks? That one who has been a beach girl never loses what she found durable in herself while making out? And it was a mentor, not lover, who once remarked that every movement, look, turn of phrase, was flirtatious whether or not innocently so.

No one else knows—maybe not even the disguised god from the sea himself, who is wise enough (or too preoccupied with matters greater than themselves) not to suspect his wife—that although this invitation of the body is written in eyes and mouth and stance, it keeps no rendezvous in London with any man but him.

Only—something new has been learned, on the side, in the context of making out. One can offer, without giving. It's a form of power.

Casualties

If Pauline and Joe had known it, the daughter of feckless Ruthie had what they couldn't find: a sign in her marriage, a sure and certain instruction to which one could attach oneself and feel the tug of history. Pauline, for one, would have doubted Hillela was capable of appreciating this, while the irony of it was that her own children—Sasha and Carole—what direction had been given them, each with the highly-developed social conscience they had? Carole was jeered at by her brother for joining an all-white progressive youth group; Sasha himself, in his maddening changes of mood, had not allowed his father to arrange a further deferment for him to continue his study of law, but had gone into the army after graduating with a useless Bachelor of Arts degree. On weekend leaves he sat beside his mother at the family table in the murderous silence of a prisoner with his jailer. The love between them was a crude weapon each wanted to wrest from the other.

Early in 1967 the men in the camps in Tanzania were transferred to a camp in Zambia. Whaila was sent to Lusaka. It was the end of waiting about in the anterooms of Europe and Africa, for him. —No more running around. We'll be in Lusaka a long time.— Hillela took it as her instruction to find something other than temporary hospitality. The headquarters were not up any rotting staircase, this time, but a row of prefabricated huts in what had been a builder's supply yard, with a high fence of hammered oildrums and access only from a lane. Whaila told her dryly; South Africa was too near for safety. He and his family moved into a cement-grey flat in Britannia Court; streets had been renamed since independence but the buildings where white people had gathered to live apart bore still the claim of their nostalgia. Families of black minor officials in the Zambian government and civil service were Hillela's neighbours. The ivy of Africa, noisy-coloured bougainvillea, overran what had been a garden kept clipped by a Scottish caretaker's 'boy' for a residents' association; what associated the residents now was the cheerful tolerance of baby strollers, plastic tricycles and crates blocking the corridors, the day-long banging of the blistered glass front doors that led straight into the kitchens, the tramping up and down stairs of relatives from the country who had to be taken in, and the make-shift accommodation for these rigged up on egg-box balconies. The first nostalgia of her life began for Hillela with the smell of pap and cabbage; she was back in Njabulo and Sophie's flat in Dar.

Nostalgia implies the possibility of a home-coming. She had that, too, for the first time; a black husband in her bed, like anybody else behind the thin walls of Britannia Court, her baby exchanging snot and red earth with the other small children in the trampled garden; black, the same as they were. She tricked Whaila and soon was pregnant again, like any other young woman among her neighbours. She would not tell Whaila—there was still that expression round his mouth that set him apart from her, and that she did not want to provoke—until the right moment came, the moment when she had him beguiled. After all, he had said they would be in Lusaka for a long time. Christa had news of her and told Udi. —She's settled down.— He smiled, as if Hillela were there and he were appraising her to herself. —Settled down. Mutter Courage, at home in war.—

Christa took it as a compliment for the protégée who had held survival together with nothing but a large safety-pin.

Afterwards, it seemed perfect, but it was not. It was happiness, it was life. There were people who noticed them criticise each other in those marital half-jests that surface in company. There were closer contacts with home, here, for Whaila—individuals who had emigrated rather than fled from there and were settled as doctors, teachers and clerks, and Zambians who in the colonial period had gone South to Fort Hare in the Cape to study, at a time when there were no universities in British-ruled territories. He spent evenings in male company, in the bars of what were still black working-class quarters of the town. She was disappointed at being left behind. He came home slightly drunk, sometimes— vulnerable, that expression of his gone from his mouth. They made love then in splendid tenderness. She pleased him so greatly that she was childishly proud of herself; and he delighted in this. They quarrelled when she told him she was expecting another child—then her childishness in tricking him annoyed him, she was 'a spoilt little white girl without proper responsibility to the discipline of the struggle'—at which she looked as if she were going to cry but the tears spurted into a splutter of laughter at the pomposity so alien to his nature. —The struggle in bed?— —No, seriously, seriously, Hillela, this isn't the time to go ahead with your big ideas of an African family—that's what I mean.— But it was done, another one was on the way, so they might as well—what?

—What is it now, Hillela?— She buried her head in his neck, her hair settled like a soft hand hushing his mouth. —Might as well make love, because we don't have to bother about my getting pregnant.—

Nevertheless the novelty of the first child gave way to inat-tentiveness, sometimes. She would leave her (everyone *here* knew the little girl was dedicated by name to the cause) with one of the other women—that was the easy African fashion, children sharing each other's mothers. She went about with Whaila in the aura of closeness within which lovers move among rooms full of people, the personal pronoun of her conversation 'we' and never 'I', their appearance together consciously striking: the spare, obsidian dignity of the man and the miniature voluptuousness of a young girl whose pregnancy by him does not yet show in any other way. There are always women who resent such happiness, which they have never had, or have lost; it was remarked among white women: —Of course, she was there—displaying her black husband, full of herself.—

Whaila had for her, beyond sensuality, a concentration within himself that kept her steadily magnetized. The presence of a power. It was related to, but not, in effect, the awareness she had had before the fallen statue. It did not bring fear. The concentration was like that a woman must feel when a general comes to her on the nights before a great offensive begins. A long culmination of tension was not only in his face, his lowered lids, but particularly in the lines of his back when she looked up and saw him standing dead still with urgency. So she shared, in the high emotion of some extraordinary purchase being taken on events, what he did not tell her: there was a decision to join military forces with Joshua Nkomo's guerrillas fighting Smith's army in Rhodesia. What Bra James had foreseen was about to be attempted. Umkhonto men would pass down Rhodesia guided by the guerrillas through the game park of the Western border, and hope to infiltrate South Africa by way of Botswana without encountering the Rhodesian army. It was the ultimate journey for which there had been years of others; for which the gatherings on Tamarisk, the discussions up rotting stairs and in the Manaka flat, the long wait in strangers' lands, the missions to the cold hemisphere had been the victualling. Knowledge of it was growing in Whaila while he lay beside her at night, as the foetus was growing in her. After caresses were over she would clasp his hand tightly in friendship.

The trees in the streets wore puttees of whitewash, the clay-piped calves of the Governor's guard, petrified, left behind. Splashes of blood in garden green were the poinsettias the *songololo* wound past in Salisbury. But Len was dead and his little sweetheart did not know that he was buried, would stay for ever, in this country to the North where she, too, had been assured she was going to be for a long time. The moment of falling into place that had come to her while a street shoemaker mended her only pair of sandals had been an assurance rather than a premonition of how she moved among the people in this town. The skill of the watchmaker, at his fruit-crate table in the push and flow of the pavement, whose concentration on the ordering of a confetti of wheels and screws was fine as the minute tools that handled them, made her marvel as skills that put a man to walk in space did not. She would pause to see him drop each tiny component of his whole exactly where it must go, and he and she had a greeting for each other; he gave the child the present of an old pocket watch as a plaything. Although she never had her shoes shined, she was acquainted with the man whose violent-coloured home-concocted polishes were ranged at the kerb in old medicine bottles. The opportunity taken by taxi drivers to wash their cars with water from a broken main was the kind of making out, stepping across the streams, she understood. When the little girl lagged against her mother's hand, whining to play in the mud, the men reproached her. —You want to make your nice dress dirty? Why you want to make work for your mother? She so nice to you.— So, in laughter, Hillela became their acquaintance, too. A sign painter whose workshop was the hulk of an old truck parked on the route she walked from Britannia Court past Sandringham Mansions and Avonlea Place to town, was closer to her sense of reality than the dispensation of white wine at an advertising agency. She jostled and pushed along with the gaiety of the women who lined up in a soft-breasted, loud-mouthed army when a supermarket received supplies of cooking oil, and she was at ease in the caper with which they at once set up their own economy of distribution, getting their children to pour the oil from cans into small bottles for resale at the profit of a coin, and leaving the mess—broken bottles, spilt oil—of their defiance of the supermarket's distribution on its doorstep; A young man made furtive by poverty and the unfamiliarity of a town tried to sell her a 'stick'—a single cigarette from the packet which was his capital and stock-in-trade. —I don't smoke.— When the white girl smiled and spoke instead of seeming not to see him, as he quickly had understood white women usually did, he begged for work. —I don't have people working for me. — —I can be good for kitchen, garden boy. Please madam.— She did not know if he had enough English to understand, but she was moved by some overflow, pride or plenty, to tell him. —I'm not a madam. We are refugees from down South. My husband's like you ...— Not quite true, of course; but if Whaila, the son of a Bettie or a Jethro, had not had a spirit resistant and brain bright as obsidian, it might have been.

The fullness overflowed into her friendships with women. She fell in love—the young mother's equivalent of the school-girl pash—with this one or that, spent her days in the bosom company of the favourite and their pooled children, while Whaila was behind the tin security fence in town or out at the camp conferring with Nkomo's men. Sela is the only one who has ever heard from her again. At one time, Hillela left Whaila's bed only to walk down to Sela's house. The children played in the garden, looked after by Sela's relatives, and the two women settled in the cosy dark cool of the livingroom. Sela had her own car but her lively friend scarcely ever could get her to go out; she sat in calm and stillness, strangely like an object of contemplation rather than in contemplation. Before it, everything could spill over, spill out. There must have been many things about Hillela which she alone could tell; she has never offered them to anybody.

Selina Montgomery and Hillela Kgomani—personages in some race joke: there was this black woman married to a white man, and this white woman married to a black man ... The quartet would have made a neat quadrilateral relationship if not a perfect circle, had Whaila had time for social life that did not in some way further the cause, and if Russell Montgomery had been materially present. Among the crocheted doilies of missionary artisanship and hammered copper plates representing idealized tribal maidens or trumpeting elephants that were African bourgeois taste, there hung in the dimness Edward Lear watercolours of Italy and Stubbs sporting prints swollen with humidity and spotted as blighted leaves. Russell St. John Montgomery was an engineer whose family made a colonial fortune two generations earlier in those raw materials that were exported and sold back, transformed, to those who could afford them. He himself was transformed; he came back to Africa as the member of the family who married a black girl instead of paying her forebears a few British pence a day to labour in field, plantation or mine. She was older than Hillela and had been married twelve years; his engineering projects, begun before independence to help build her new Africa, were more and more delegated to other hands and he spent more and more of his time attending to inherited interests in England and Scotland.

The children with whom Nomzamo played, decorating mud pies with the torn bloody strips of poinsettias and serving them on the split giant pods of the mahogany tree, were not really Sela's but those of her relatives—she had no servants but many collateral retainers who lived in the back yard and the empty rooms of the house, and brought in at eleven and four o'clock cucumber sandwiches or soda-tasting scones on the tea-tray. A photograph of two coloured boys in kilts stood on the piano. (They had not come out beautifully black as the namesake.) A schoolgirl in a pork-pie hat smiling obediently to a photographer's command over the crinkly plait fallen across her shoulder, looked down at her mother from the wall. Sela's children were in England at the schools Russell and his sisters had attended. —He entered them when they were born.— She had a way of stopping to reflect after a short statement; and then saying something that, perhaps, was not what she might have said. —It's very hard to get into those schools, apparently.—

—I wish I'd known you when we were in England! A house in London and one in Scotland! But you weren't there, Sela, were you— why aren't you ever there?—

Sela's heavy and beautiful head was coiffured in sculptural wedges that seemed carved not combed into place, like those of the wooden figures vendors from Zaïre hawked in Cairo Road. She wore the gold, garnet and diamond Victorian ear-rings of Russell's family jewels dangling to her neck, and from there down the matronly dresses and, no matter how great the heat, the tight varnish of stockings and the high-heeled shoes of a colonial generation of white women who had been her teachers. —When I was studying for my thesis, I stayed there. When I was young. The children were small. But Russell will invite you to his house. Russell has a lot of visitors, his friends. When you go back, you'll see him.—

—Oh no, we're here for good. Well, quite a long time. However long it takes, Whaila says.—

Sela had great delicacy. Her manner stopped any indiscretion that might be coming from Hillela about what it was rumoured was being planned behind the tin security fence; whatever indiscreet fantasy of imminent triumph and freedom, down South, the young girl was about to flaunt.

—But don't you like London, Sela? I had such a good time. To have a house in London, of your own! I've never been to Scotland, but I suppose that must be something, too. Why don't you spend part of the year there? Isn't it lonely for Russell? I was so often alone in London when Whaila had to go away—I couldn't stand it, I moved in with friends.—

—There's this house to see to. My family. Always a lot of problems with our families, such big families ... now my father is dead and my mother has to deal with the uncles. The children come out for the holidays—in their summer, over there. And there's the garden.—

If Hillela did not find her friend in the dark house within its cave of towering trees, she was in her garden, the tightly-stockinged legs kneeling on a sack and the other family's jewels looping forward over her flesh-ringed soft neck. Sela talked of her gardening as she might have been expected to talk of her profession as a physicist—with the achievement and concomitant responsibility of a vocation. She was the first woman in her country to graduate with a Master's degree in science, one of the first to have a university education at all, let alone at an Ivy League American institution. She was not teaching at the local university 'at present', she said, in the tone of an official communiqué, and had not for a length of time she did not mention. On one of the few occasions when she appeared at a gathering, Hillela heard her respond to the reproachful bonhomie of one of the deans of the university. —It wouldn't be fair for me to take a teaching post, I am away so much, you see, in England.— Her little white friend came up to her and embraced her, and Sela did not know why; well, she was an impulsively affectionate girl and the atmosphere at parties went to her head.

An odd couple. The women friends, not the Montgomerys or the Kgomanis. But while Hillela chattered and Sela, silent, attentive, overcast the seams of tiny dresses Hillela was sewing for her daughter, they complemented each other in a way nobody saw. Hillela, who had been like a daughter, had no longer a comparative status; was at the centre of a life in her marriage to a black man. Sela, in her marriage to a white man, for all her dowager dignity assumed at thirty-six was only making out; and Hillela had been a prodigy at that.

*

259

Yes, she knew them all. Except Mandela and the others with him. Mandela remained the voice on tape heard when she was a schoolgirl. Mandela was in prison down South, off the very last peninsula of Africa, pushed out to an island in the Atlantic by white men who frightened themselves with rhetoric that his kind would cast them back into the sea by which they came. Her old friendship with Tambo dates from those days when she used to serve him tea at Britannia Court and somehow produce enough food to go round whomever Whaila brought home. There hasn't been anything she hasn't profited by, at one period or another; the cuisine at the Manaka flat stood her in good stead, in its day. Oliver Tambo, even then, had the eyes of sleepless nights behind his thick glasses, and the opacity of flesh that, as it did in Whaila, marks the faces behind which decisions must be made: loosed boulders whose thundering echoes a passage out of sight, into consequences that cannot fully be foreseen. Tennyson Makiwane was one of those who came to Britannia Court, too—another name-sake; inheritor of Victoriana—who was there in a Xhosa family who admired Tennyson? Tennyson Makiwane gave Nomzamo a stray kitten he had taken in—Makiwane who outcast himself, years later, from the cause for which, like the other frequenters of Britannia Court, he lived then; a man whose shame was obliter-ated for him by a traitor's death.

Whaila knew at least an edited version of his young wife's life; she had told him how she had got to Tamarisk Beach via Rey; and when she had expressed wonder that anyone (Rey) who seemed so committed to the cause had abandoned it (she had this wider interpretation, now), Whaila gave one of his held-back sighs that became a grunt. —We'll have them, too. Casualties. And not only operational ones... There'll always be some who won't go the whole way.—

On the 8th of August 1967, he told her. The little girl had climbed into bed with them, early in the morning. She sat astride her father's chest and he spoke it straight at her, who couldn't understand and couldn't betray. —Umkhonto is crossing the Zambezi today.—

Hillela turned her head to him, he saw her eyes, that were never bleary in the morning but opened from sleep directly into acceptance of the world as it is. —It's begun?—

—It's begun. Two parties. Nothing big in numbers.—

—How many?—

But even in the telling there was some instinct to hold back. —Enough.— The little girl rode him as her mother had loved to ride the playground's mythical bull. —There'd be no hope of getting through with a whole company. I only hope the ZAPU crowd really know what they're doing. Ours have to depend on them to find their way hundreds of miles through the bush. It's all the way sticking to Wankie.—

—What about animals? Can you just walk about among lions and elephants?—

—That's not the problem. Lions don't come looking for men and if you sight a herd of elephants you can turn and head the other way for a bit. The danger is running into the Rhodesian army patrols; Wankie's the only route you've got a chance against that.—

The child bounced her laughter into gurgles, thumping him. He lifted her gently under the arms, to regain his breath, gently put her down again.

Hillela sat up with one of her surges of energy, her sunburned breasts juggled between tightened arms. She took his hand, hard. Then she was out of bed and moving about the room as on the morning of some festival. She rushed back to kiss him, holding his head, her possession, between open palms. She rolled on the floor in play with the child and trod by mistake on the kitten. Amid laughter and miaowing he watched from the bed the excitement she felt, for him.

While he shaved she lay in the bath trickling water from a sponge onto her navel. Her belly was coming up; the creature in there was beginning to show its presence. She did not ask him, this time, what colour he thought it would be; they would be a rainbow, their children, their many children.

—What will happen when they get to South Africa?—

The sound of the razor scraping. —They'll split, into smaller groups and operate in different areas. They'll join up with people inside. There are specified targets to go for.—

—In the towns or in the country? Where they cross the border it'll be farmland, won't it? Are they going to attack white farms? Or is it going to be pylons and things like that, in the cities?—

—Military installations, power stations—hard targets.—

—There won't be bombs in cafés and office buildings, or in the street? I can't imagine what that would be like—

He dried his hands, ridding them of something more than shaving foam. He was aware of her waiting for him to tell her what she should be feeling about the unimaginable. —If the government goes on doing what it does, torturing and killing in the townships, in time ... well, we'll have to turn to soft targets as well.—

—Soft targets. You mean ordinary people. People in the streets.— Pressing her fingers into her belly, testing for a response from the life in there. She thought she felt a faint return of pressure and he mistook, with a flicker of displeasure, the beginnings of a smile relaxing her lips as lack of understanding of what she really had said.

—Ordinary people? What ordinary people? Our ordinary people have always been the soft targets. Our bodies, hey? Our minds. The police use violence on us every day and white people think they keep out of it, although the beatings-up and the killings are done on their behalf, they've let it happen for so many years. One day the blacks will have to carry the struggle into white areas.

It's inevitable. The violence came from there. Violence will hit back there. It must be, we know it. But not yet. Not now.—

—Innocent people?—

The answer echoed from another bed, another time. —Are there really any innocent people in our country?—

She was communicating in nudges with the third person present, inside her. —And me?—

Down on him came all the sorrow of pain and destruction that his people had endured, were suffering, and would endure no longer, and all the suffering they might have to inflict in consequence, in the knowing horror of victim turned perpetrator. Of course she brought it upon him; he had brought it upon himself by making such a marriage. Sometimes her lack of any identification with her own people dismayed him, he who lived for everything that touched upon the lives of his; there was something missing in her at such times, like a limb or an organ.—This secretly felt, paradoxically, in spite of the fact that he saw their own closeness as a sign; the human cause, the human identity that should be possible, once the race and class struggle were won. With her, it was already one world; what could be. And yet he looked at her lying pearly under water, the body prettily shaded and marbled as white flesh in its uncertain pigment and peculiarly naked nakedness is, and had to say what there was to say. —Yes, you too. If you happened to be there. You were born in sin, my love, the sins of your white people.—

But saved. She knows how to look after herself. She climbed out of the bath and he wrapped her in a towel tenderly, as if she had just been baptised.

Through the still heat before the rains men moved as the wild animals moved in the bush where tourists used to follow game rangers' advice about the best areas to find and photograph them. There was silence. Whaila was silent about the silence. The occasional news that came back to the offices behind the tin security

263

fence was confused in a way that did not allow an interpretation that was anything but bad. The maps had turned out to be inaccurate in a territory where the only true maps are the migratory paths of wild creatures drawn by the imperatives of the propagation of life, not the campaigns of war. The two parties lost their way, and the journey took much longer than provided for; they ran out of food. Moving like wild creatures in the bush, they were spotted like wild creatures by game rangers. On August 14th fighting with the Rhodesian army began. It was easier to hear the Rhodesian version of the combat over the radio than to keep up with how Umkhonto actually was faring. The Rhodesians, who lied so consistently in their own favour about every campaign in their civil war, claimed 'overwhelming victories' against the ZAPU and Umkhonto guerrillas. When news did come through from the freedom fighters, they claimed victories, too; and after two weeks they were still fighting.

Hillela searched Whaila's face for news each time he entered the flat: still fighting! If certain people had thought her 'full of herself' before, what could they have said of her now! She went about with the beginnings of her big African family—the one by the hand, the other swelling her like a bellying sail—in animated confidence that she was escorting the first generation that would go home in freedom. She would deliver what she had heard discussed there at suburban tables, what had been aborted by hesitations and doubts, the shilly-shallying of what was more effective between this commitment or that, this second-hand protest or that. Her blood was up, the colour of her skin warmed her eyes, darker with what she saw in the inner eye. —Pregnancy suits you, you're lucky.— Her friend Sela envied her energy, mistaking its source. Mutter Courage, as her older friend Udi knew, survived on war as well as survived it.

No-one reached home down South. By mid-September there was defeat; most of the guerrillas were either killed or captured by the Rhodesian army, and the few who had managed to get as far as Botswana were imprisoned for illegal entry. But one of the parties had been successful in mobilizing black Rhodesian villages as support bases for future attempts; planning must already have begun for a new incursion. The huge weight of Joshua Nkomo was lowered once or twice onto the cheap furniture at Britannia Court, the little namesake welcomed to sit on whatever space there was between his enormous stomach and knees—he, too, could have been regarded as an old friend, later; but Hillela has never lost her instinct for avoiding losers. Christmas had a significance other than the traditional when the time came; Sela invited the Kgomani family to the traditional kind of dinner Russell Montgomery would have expected had he been there, with a tinselled tree, presents and plum pudding, but over the wine Hillela grasped Whaila's hand in covenant with another occasion—at the end of December brothers from the camp were going into Rhodesia once again.

Whaila was with Tambo and his other colleagues eighteen hours a day; she saw him, usually, only when she opened her eyes as he came into the bedroom late at night. She did not ask questions but behaved with her friend Sela as if she knew everything and was saying nothing. This empty boast became real when Whaila, in some inexplicable urge to honour the clasp of the hand in the way that his possession of her body could never do, in some certainty of trust that would transform both him and her and their relationship, told her the plans in detail. This time Umkhonto men were a much larger force, and under their own command. —We've learned our lesson. We've gone over the logistics again and again, this time. Nothing left to chance. One of the main objectives is going to be to help ZAPU prepare rural people for an uprising. It's all one struggle. Their war's ours.—

The handclasp held. She had more concealed inside her than a baby; weeks went by and the men in the bush moved about undetected, hidden by the local people down there. The nature of time changed. With each day, each week, it was something gained, not passed. Each morning, when she and the man beside her woke together, their first thought was the same. The intimacy was an entry into one of the locked rooms of existence. No-one could ever surprise them there; no-one could ever appear in that doorway and look upon them, judge them. He was lover and brother to her in the great family of a cause.

And all around, the marvel of daily life went on weaving continuity as the birds in the rampant bougainvillea threaded shreds of bright cloth, human hair combings, twigs and leaves into their nests. On the twenty-sixth morning in January Hillela smelt the scent of the frangipani as the breath of her own body, the thick pollen in the hibiscus trumpets as her own secretion, as she stretched, the baby inside lifting with her, to hang washing in the old garden of Britannia Court. Whaila came down from the building on his way to the office—that banal summing-up of an ordinary man's day that had so little to do with the row of prefabricated huts behind the tin security fence. He strolled over to say goodbye and they laughed because her belly (her Nkomo, they called it) got in the way of an embrace, and instead he turned her about and crossed his arms over her breasts from the back, bending round her neck to kiss her cheek. His bare arms in a short-sleeved shirt were, for an instant, the black shining arms that had flailed the sea, coming towards her from the shore. She recognized now, in the heady oxygen of a morning after rain, that she had even then noticed that watch he still wore, flashing on the swimmer's left arm.

Ten past eight when he left for 'the office'. She went to the market in the afternoon. Sela was persuaded to come with her; —But leave Nomzamo at the house, Hillela. You know you'll say you'll only be half-an-hour there, and then you expect that little kid to trail around for two or three.— Sela was right; the smells

and colours and sounds of the market were the adornments Hillela
wore as brightness and bells of an extended self, and she could
not pass any stall or squatting vendor without stopping to finger,
admire, question and talk. What she was supposed to have come
to buy she forgot, once in among the cloth-hung alleys, the yards
with their pyramids of rape, cabbages, oranges, okra, bananas,
groundnuts; she could not be kept to any purpose or time limit.
They went through the sheds where dried split fish and grasshop-
pers were laid out neat and stiff as if lacquered. Sela had to ask, for
her, the names of roots big as torn-off heads or fanged like drawn
teeth. Hillela had dozens of lengths of Kanga cloth hooked down
from the stallholders' rails and draped them, one after another,
over Sela's crêpe two-piece. Wonderful, wonderful: a Nubian
queen! As if Sela could be persuaded to wear such things; but
she was stirred by some old familiarity that afternoon. The questions she was urged to ask on behalf of her friend, in the language
she shared with the market people, developed into conversations,
laughter, and even an insider's scepticism about prices. —No, no.
That's far too much; don't give it to him.— Sela was bargaining, with all the pauses of feigned loss of interest, the African
organ-note hums required. Sela's white shoes were splashed with
the mud and scales from around the fish-vendors' tables and the
spurt underfoot of rotting vegetables studded with flies; a young
madman naked except for a sack he held over himself did not beg
but rooted in the mess: yet Hillela that day saw only wholeness.
—Everything's here. Everything in the world that you really need.
Come and see.— There was furniture that delighted her with its
parody, in cane and grass, of suburban coffee tables, and its brave
approximation of white middle-class ugliness in sofas and chairs
covered with acrylic-coloured plastic and hammered together,
out of the memory of something seen in a white man's house, in
the cubist angles of the Thirties. She liked best the tinsmiths'
section set out under trees with exposed club-foot roots. —Come

and see!— She followed every process of the ancient craft adapted to the waste materials a modern industrial society throws away. Here a man was cleaning the paint off tin containers and drums; there another was hammering them out into sheets. Others were cutting shapes from the sheets as she cut out dresses for her child. Saucepans, pots, funnels, buckets, ladles, braziers for the charcoal most blacks used for cooking were set out for sale. —Those pots burn the food if you put them on electric stoves, Hillela, I'm telling you.— —Oh come and see these funny little things!— Hillela did make one purchase, in spite of Sela's good sense. She held up a tiny object formed as an inverted, hollow pyramid, with a handle like that of a cup soldered to it. —What's this?— —You must have seen the women selling groundnuts in Cairo Road. They're measures—for a handful, when you buy. What will you do with it, Hillela? Don't give it to Nomzamo to play with—these things are not well finished, they've got sharp edges.—

The children belonging to Sela's relatives made a doll out of the namesake and never wanted to part with her. This was one of the many evenings when they wandered back with Hillela to Britannia Court. Hillela taught them songs the *songololo* had sung, as they walked home with her past Sandringham Mansions and Avonlea Place; a sunset first stamped out every coarse leaf of the flamboyant trees against translucent lakes of sky and then clotted the black metallic cut-outs into a cage of earthly dark. The little straggle of woman and children made their cheerful chorus far beneath, and stumped up the stairs to the flat. When Whaila came home, the streetlight that could be seen from the kitchen window was on, bats circling it like the rings round a planet. He held his little daughter up to look, but she wriggled away to the other children. There was the static of frying behind loud play; Hillela, barefoot in her broad stance of pregnancy, was cooking chips for their supper. The eldest girl had made herself at home with the radio playing monotonous African music; on one of those sudden impulses children have, all scrambled out of the room to some game in the bathroom but the music wound on. The level of noise was raised by a tumble of running water. Neither Hillela nor Whaila was sure, for a moment, whether or not the doorbell was ringing. He said something she didn't catch, where she bent at the open refrigerator to fetch a carton of milk, but she was aware that he had passed behind her to go to the door and she took off the shelves a couple of cans of beer as well—it was the time in the evening when one or another of the men from the office or camp would call in. The door was swollen by summer damp and she seemed to hear all at once the prelude of its scrape along the linoleum, a pause in which she had no time to grasp that there were no greetings exchanged, and then a crack that splintered the thick homely hubbub against the thin walls of the flat. Something fell. As she turned there was another crack and a bolt of force hit the refrigerator door she stood behind. Someone— one, more than one—ran clattering down the corridor of Britannia Court; the doorway was open and empty: and Whaila? Whaila? As she came out from behind the shield of the refrigerator, he was there, on the floor. Whaila was flung before her, red flowing from the side of his head, his neck, under the shirt pocket where his pen still was hooked. His open eyes faced the wall and his lips stretched finely in that expression drawn by his life.

His life running away in red like the muddy filth in the gutters of the market.

There was a wrenching upheaval inside her as the foetus convulsed and turned. The bullet that was lodged in the refrigerator door penetrated her consciousness in the bullets' disorientation of sequence; she felt she was shot. She backed away from death, from death ebbing away Whaila. Backed away, backed away. Her shoulder hit the jamb of the doorway leading to the internal passage of the flat. She opened her mouth to wail but terror blocked her throat and instead of her cry there was the voice of a radio commercial enthusing over a brand of beer. She burst into the bathroom in the path of a plastic duck one child had thrown at another; the children saw in her terrible face grown-up anger at their game. She grasped the thirteen-year-old girl in charge. She dragged her to the kitchen, but when they reached the doorway, she herself turned to the wall and pressed her bent arms tight against her head, screaming.

It was the child who went in, and began to heave small, hard breasts in deep breaths that became sobs, and slowly went up to the dead man who had been Whaila, and touched him.

There have been others since then. They received parcels of death in mail from their home country. It seems that in the case of Whaila Kgomani, one of the first, the agents employed by the South African government might have bungled their mission. It was said in Lusaka that they were meant to kill Oliver Tambo, but came to the wrong address. Seeing a man through the blistered glass door, they did not wait to verify any identity; there is no margin for hesitation in such tasks. Others said the government's instructions were carried out: Whaila was a key man in the planning of armed infiltration. In South Africa itself, of course, the death was reported as the result of rivalry and a power struggle within the movement; as any statements from the organization itself were banned and could not be published, that version became the accepted one for most white people, if they were aware of the assassination at all.

It was not surprising that news of Hillela's whereabouts at that time should have come to the families of her aunts by way of violence. Trouble. She was always trouble. Olga hoped nobody would tell Arthur, recovering from a coronary on a low-fat diet with instructions that he should not be subjected to stress or annoyance. Anyway, there was no unpleasant publicity, fortunately, because no-one made the connection between Hillela and Ruthie's sisters—it was merely mentioned that the ANC man had a white wife. Carole was about to be married, herself, to a young journalist. A simple wedding in the garden, no big Jewish show for Pauline's daughter. He could have written a Sunday paper scoop that would have given him a byline, and Pauline certainly didn't give a damn whether or not Arthur was upset by the family's political connections, but Carole asked her boy not to. He would soon be her husband; she tried to imagine how it would be to have him killed, taken away from her. She could not have borne to have had her life with him taken away, as well, exposed in a newspaper. Perhaps a sign, already, nobody read: she was not the wife for a newspaperman.

Pauline knew Hillela was not little Carole. —Whatever else Hillela has lacked, it's never been guts. She won't shut herself away somewhere.—

—What'll she do? She's got a small child. So the paper said— he had a wife and daughter. But maybe that's from a previous marriage— his child?—

Carole's father reassured her. —People will look after Hillela and her child, the organization will take care of that. There are resources.— And of course Joe, through his legal cases, was in touch with the circumstances of political exiles—some of his clients became them.

—I want to write to Hillela, Daddy.—

Sasha, silent among them, was suddenly present. —What about? Your bridesmaids' dresses?—

Carole was still emotional on the subject of Hillela. —Don't you care about anybody anymore? What's the matter with you? Maybe she'll come home, now, maybe she can come home.—

The future husband had never seen Carole, of all people, shrill and angry. There were still so many currents in this family he couldn't follow.

Her bastard of a brother looked as if she had slapped him across both sides of his face. —Don't you understand anything about anything? What are you the product of, for Christ' sake?—

And now the mother lifted her head and narrowed one eye, as if in pain.

There have been others. There were to be others. To begin with— O, what was grief, could anyone have guessed, explained, prepared for this—anyone, a quiet, wise lawyer-uncle, the father of the little sweetheart, for only a man can comfort for the loss of a man, only a man's arms, the smell of a man's shaven skin can make it possible to believe that a man actually came to an end, that it happens in a kitchen, on an evening like any other ordinary evening, and that there will never be another ordinary evening like that one again. If there had been a mother, if she had turned up the lights in the nightclub and seen the cockroaches and the dirty neck of the ageing fado *singer, would she have been able to provide the advantage: to prepare the daughter against the lights going up on her romance of defiance and danger? Who knew about this? Who could bear to know about this? So that if it happened to someone, that one feared to tell what it was, and everyone feared to ask.*

And what about the other survivor who had done the killing himself, driving his wife home on the road to Bagambyo? His body rejected life, afterwards, could not accept what had happened. The baby rejected life, wrenching itself from the body it was anchored in. It loosed with it the waters of grief: the longing of the body the man would never enter again, the untouched breasts, empty vagina, empty clothes in the cupboard, rooms without a voice: desertion. What am I without him? And if, without him, I am nothing, what was I? The loving gone, the African family of rainbow-coloured children gone, the innocent boast of the striking couple gone—

What was left behind was the handclasp. Because the handclasp belongs to tragedy, not grief. Udi explained it, once, not knowing the explanation would ever come to be understood. —No, the fact that I killed my wife is not a tragedy. I must not call it that. A tragedy, Hillela, is when a human

272

being is destroyed engaging himself with events greater than personal relationships. Tragedy is an idea from the ancient Greeks; from the gods. A tragic death results from the struggle between good and evil. And it has results that outlast grief. Grief is a rot, it belongs with the dead, but tragedy is a sign that that struggle must go on. If I had experienced tragedy, I'd be all right... but it has nothing to do with someone like me.—

Whaila is dead. There have been others. There will be others.

When the police had gone away Sela brought an old relative to scrub Whaila's blood from the linoleum. The man rolled up his trousers and carefully took off his laceless shoes so that they might not be spoiled, but he worked reverently, intoning some kind of lament to himself, or perhaps it was a hymn he was breathing. Hillela and her child were taken into the empty rooms of Sela's house, dark as if they had been waiting for the occasion of such occupancy.

The obsidian god from the waves, the comrade was buried in the gold, green and black flag he died for. Tambo spoke of him, at an oblong hole in red earth that had been dug. *Woza, woza,* rose the responses to the verses of the national anthem that came from home and belongs to all Africa. Hillela's bare feet in shabby sandals carried away red earth on the toes. Sela was correctly dressed in a black tailored skirt and jacket and she led from among the women in her band of relatives the traditional ululation. The high, unearthly, ancient sound is produced to release sorrow or hail triumph; it is both grief and tragedy.

Hillela stood, huge, at the graveside, like Joshua Nkomo, who had been the subject of a private joke. Her pregnancy appeared to have risen to her flushed and swollen face. But nobody seems to know what happened to that child. She was close to her term, then. It might have been born dead, or it died shortly after birth. The namesake who looks out from magazine covers, unsmiling with charming haughtiness, nostrils dilated, is her only child, her daughter.

Under The Snow

Saved by a refrigerator door. In the undeclared wars that maim and kill without battlefields or boundaries, in the streets, cafés and houses of foreign towns, on tourist planes and cruise ships, it was a campaign ribbon from a front that is anywhere and everywhere. In her confusion, she had felt herself hit; and, indeed, the story went round that the baby had been killed by a bullet inside its mother's belly at the same time as its father was shot. She kept to herself the true story, telling only Sela: —It died because I cheated Whaila into making it. So it went with him.— Sela calmed these fantasies of shock; she knew her friend was young and healthy and would regain an equilibrium.

And it was also true that the persistent rumour that she had seen not only her husband but his child, as well, sacrificed to the cause, provided her with credentials of the highest order. There are lacunae again, mainly because she was deployed in Eastern Europe and Western hysteria over such contacts made it necessary for her to ignore, in one period, the existence of another. But it is certain that the organization accepted full responsibility for Whaila's wife and daughter. She went first back to London, where she worked in its office. Personality clashes with other white women employed there, some of them the veterans of political imprisonment and exile who remembered her from Tamarisk Beach, cut short that posting.

They did not understand that even if she had not been hit, the little beach girl was buried.

The fiery surf of veld fires was the last Mrs Hillela Kgomani saw of Africa, leaving it, and the first she saw of it, coming home to Africa. Whaila Kgomani's widow flew back to be present at a memorial-day ceremony held for him and others a year after his death. Twenty-five years old, very thin except for her breasts, the cheekbones prominent beneath black eyes, she wore African dress and headcloth and made a speech on behalf of wives and mothers who had given husbands and sons to the cause of liberation. It was clear from her delivery that this was not the first time she had spoken in public, and the emotion she conveyed was not only private but also skilfully drawn from that generated by the crowd. A day or two after the ceremony, she changed into the duffle coat and boots of a European winter and flew away again to the other hemisphere, to an ancient Eastern European city whose gothic and baroque and art nouveau buildings, so beautiful and strange to her, were poxed with the acne of gunfire from generations of wars and revolutions. Muffled in clothing that gave a new dimension to her body (—It's like driving a bus when you've been used to a racing bicycle.— Her observations of things they took for granted amused local citizens) she came out of the steamy fug of an apartment into a seizure of cold every morning. She took her child to a nursery-school, and then walked to her place of work. It was along gangrene corridors whose colour had nothing to do with forgotten summers of trees and grass, and—when the dented lift did not work—up flights of cold stairs. The room itself was like the others above rotting stairs in hot climates thousands of kilometres away: the old typewriters, the posters and banners, framed declarations and newspaper collages, with the addition of photographs of the host country's heroes displayed like a shop-keeper's licence to trade. She typed letters and was brought into negotiations as a translator when there were people who could speak French, which was not their language any more than it was hers, but which served as a means of communication if they had no English. She apologized briskly for her poor ability: —I was nursemaid to French-speaking kids, once, in Ghana, that's all.—

Sela was right, Mrs Kgomani had gained an equilibrium that discarded girlish fantasies. She was also discovered to have an ability to talk to women's worker-groups, herself through a translator. She crossed borders to the North, was useful in still colder places, Stockholm, Oslo, Moscow— everywhere that Whaila had gone, on journeys for which she now needed no proxy. Most of these were taken with Citagele Koza, head of mission, who had been Whaila's close friend, but several times she was deputed to accompany Arnold, who came back and forth between Africa and Europe. She kept notes for him. Perhaps he had asked specifically to have her assistance; the decision would have to be Citagele's. Alone together in dusty hotels like the museums of the Europe before the war and revolutions, afternoons in the colonial house rapped out in memory by a press agency's telex were never resumed. Arnold grieved for the loss of the beach girl. In her place was a young woman who had experienced tragedy and who did not have the same appeal for him. She was no longer a distraction to catch the eye. She was part of the preoccupation she once had disrupted so naturally. They were concentrated together in a struggle within the struggle, bargaining or begging (there was only the collateral of an uncertain future to offer) for arms and money. He did not need to take her in hand, although he had the opportunity to do so, now. The education Whaila had begun, she completed alone. She taught herself not the old theories of ends, but the diplomacy and technicalities of means, that were immediate. She mastered specifications of guns and missiles and their relative suitability for the conditions under which they would have to be used. The men who had crossed the Zambezi again before Whaila was killed in his ambush had lasted out three months in the bush, lugging these weapons towards home, towards the army, the police, power lines and government buildings— Soft targets. No. Not yet. But the other side, they were not waiting, they had no distinction between steel-and-concrete and human bodies. Whaila's warm black flesh dissolved red.

She toured factories where women with kerchiefs on their heads made parts for guns as neat as the components the street watchmaker put together in perfect functional harmony. On flights between one city and the next, liquid shudders in glasses and, watching it, thoughts surface. —If Whaila had had a gun he might have got them before they got him. We should all be armed with Parabellums.—

Arnold has told people, over the years: —If things had turned out differently, she was the type to have become a terrorist, a hijacker. A Leila Khaled. She had it in her, at one time. I don't think we'd have been able to contain her. It wasn't that she was undisciplined; no discipline was demanding enough for her— you know the sort of thing.— When he himself spoke out of his drowsiness in a plane, he asked a question. —What happened to the yellow swimsuit?— She did not seem to find the reference odd or suggestive. —In this climate?—

Other men had no beach girl to regret, of course. A man she was known to be associated with, eventually, had—like everybody else in that city—experienced tragedy and survived grief. Among such people she was not changed; they knew no other state of being. She was sent to a meeting for cultural solidarity of the Eastern bloc with the Third World, one day—contacts at all levels had to be kept up—and the chairman had a big, Balkan head with thick, grey-black hair rising from a peak like a dart set in a broad low forehead, a short, humorously-obstinate nose, and a brush moustache to show off well-worn lips and teeth. The details remain because the head was all that was visible of him above the rostrum; the head of handsome maturity to which years cannot be accurately attributed. When the meeting was over she saw that he was heavy and had the sideways gait of ageing. She went up dutifully to present her credentials and he asked her to stay on and allow his committee to take the opportunity to discuss African literature in English with her over a glass of wine. She knew much less about the subject than he, but when his committee members had all left and he and she were still talking, he took her to dinner at a restaurant she would not have known still existed in that city. They crossed the river and walked a long way in the cold. His left leg swayed him and he was short of breath, never stopped talking. Until then, all the city had run together for her in the overlapping stone statements, destruction, reconstruction, of its past; such density impenetrable, not only by reason of the ignorance of the historical significance of architecture in which the advantage of a colonial education had left her, but because she was accustomed to a thin layer of human settlement in countries where cities are a recent form of social focus. Underneath the skyscrapers of Johannesburg were only the buried gin-bottles of a mining camp where her great-grandfather Hillel had hawked second-hand clothing to blacks who came in their blankets to earn hut-tax. And she was not even aware that he had had this role in history. Under Britannia Court were the migratory trails by which Whaila's and the namesake's ancestors had explored their continent, begetting living monuments in their descendants rather than marking their generations in stone. The European read off to her as they walked the history of his city that he knew by heart, in marble stumps of Roman ruins, the iron rings embedded in medieval walls, the church with the bombed tower, the scaffolding round the restoration of a 17th-century palace, the piles stroked by the flow of water where a bridge was blown up, the withering forbidden wreaths placed at an empty lot where victims of the last uprising were shot down.

—They'll never build anything on that spot. They know if we can't have a monument there, there must be nothing else.— A rough bronchial laugh. —So they just let the weeds grow. It's a way of dealing with realities you can't handle: neglect. Not such a bad way. It works with other things, too.— He pointed at a red star which hung crookedly from the pinnacle of a public building and was lit up only on three neon points.

—You were mixed up in it? That uprising? Nobody else mentions it.—

—No. Because it's not, how do you say, my dear, healthy … if you were in it, it's better to keep quiet. And if you were not, well, some people have a reason to be ashamed because of that. It did bring some benefits, you see. Apparent lost causes always do … Mixed up! Yes, I was in prison for thirteen months. But I have friends … The President and I were at the *gymnasium* together— young boys, we joined the youth group of the Party while it was still an Underground movement… One night, they come for me, in my cell. (It wasn't so bad, that time, I was allowed books, I worked on my translations of Neruda.) I thought, they've changed their minds, they're going to shoot me. I'm on the journey to the river, where they threw the others. But they push me into a car and the next thing, I'm in the State chambers. He's there in his windowless study—it's like the last of the Chinese boxes, nothing can get at him once he's inside there. A big fire burning, and a chair with a glass of brandy beside it. For me. He reads me a lecture, and then he comes over and gives me a push in the chest, like this, the way we used to start to wrestle when we were boys. Then he said to me, he pleaded with me, 'You know I can't do what you people asked. *You* know that. "Freedom"—we used that kind of talk when we were waving banners at sixteen. We give them our coal at their price, and they close their eyes to our trade union independence. We never criticise them in our newspapers, and they ignore the books we publish here by writers they ban. That's freedom. We didn't know it would be like that, when we were young. But *you*, Karel, *you* know, now.' So they let me out. Again. Each time I've been rescued by someone different; the Russians let me out when the Germans imprisoned me as a communist, our first communist

279

government let me out after the Russians imprisoned me as a nationalist. Oh, and our fascists had to let me out, of course, when the war came, and I was sent to the army.—

He took her gloveless hand and tucked it under his arm between the thicknesses of his enormous coat, laughing. How old could he be? Old enough to be her father, her grandfather, in terms of the wars, invasions, military occupations, uprisings, imprisonments he had lived. The restaurant was warm, warm. A conservatory. It had palms under its glass dome and the waiters were crook-backed and wispy-haired. So was the violinist who played from table to table. Her host ordered little packets made of stuffed vegetable leaves, fish soup, a duck dish and a veal dish, and 'a wine that isn't exactly champagne, but it will make you happy tomorrow'. He touched his big head; no headache. He tasted from her plate and encouraged her to taste from his. The wan violinist, bent in one curve with his instrument, came over and played passionately to her, and her new friend was delighted to see that she was not embarrassed, as so many women would think it necessary to be, but listened as if receiving what was her due as a rather beautiful young woman—whether it was the cold they had tramped through, or some private mood, she gave the impression of a coursing of new blood through the vessels of her being, a brilliance of colouring and brightness of gaze, a flow of words. —I've been rescued, too. A few times. A bullet went into a door instead of me. But nothing like you ... More like a beetle that's flicked out of a swimming pool. I used to lie on my stomach and do that, as a kid. There'd be rose beetles that had fallen into my aunt's pool, and I'd flip out one, and let the others drown. Why that one?—

—Someone may just be passing by—that's the only chance. Two boys teased the girls together in the school yard; then he happened to be President, and I was in jail. So I got flicked out. What are you looking round for? Is there a man you don't want to see you with another man? But look at my grey hair.—

—No ... Is it all right to talk about anything, here?—

He laughed. —Oh I know what's worrying you, there have been times when we couldn't talk, either ... but it's all right—everybody talks, everybody says what they think, it doesn't change anything, now ...—

—What do you believe?—

—Ah, that's the kind of talk my friend the President says we used to have at sixteen! But you're not much more than that your-self—no, no, I'm insulting you when I think I'm paying you a compliment. You are a woman. Nothing less.— He had asked about a husband, children, and she had told him, walking across the bridge.

—You were against the old regime, you were a socialist when you were young.—

He signalled with a full mouth; he enjoyed his food. —Like everyone. Like you, yes?—

—No. No. I didn't know what it meant. Everybody told me, explained—but I was white, you see.—

—What has that to do with it? There are white, black and yellow socialists, millions of them ...—

—White made it impossible to understand. For me, anyway. Everybody talked and argued, and I thought about other things. And whenever I heard them again, they were still talking and arguing, living the same way in the same place. Liberalism, socialism, communism.—

—What other things? I don't know what life must be like, down there.—

She sat back against her chair, smiling for herself; the move-ment drew him to lean towards her across the table in the familiar invitation and approach between a woman and a man.

—Someone to love. A man. Somewhere to go.—

—Where there would be—what?—

—What the others didn't know about.—

—And did you know what that was?—

—No. But I knew it wasn't to be found in their talk, they would never find it. Oh it sounds such rubbish—but I've never tried to tell anyone before. Oh and now I'm getting like them, all the people I behaved so badly to, I'm talking, talking.—

—You weren't asking me about God, were you? For god's sake, my dear! Here religion has been allowed again to offer its soporific until you wake up in the next world, as even we can't seem to get this one right. But I stick to my cigarettes and wine.—

—Not that. Can I ask you something—you were in that uprising, and this is a communist regime; does that mean you're no longer a communist? If that's so, how could you be running that meeting this afternoon? For the Ministry of Culture?—

He put up a large, long-fingered hand with a thin seal-ring on the third finger. He made to comb down the moustache but stopped himself fastidiously as if a gesture might trivialise seriousness or honesty. —It's right that you should ask me. Don't be afraid. If we are going to be friends, in your position you must know about me, my dear.—

—My position?—

—Your somewhere to go is right at the centre of this century. In my country you've come to ask for backing from the regime, and you've got to get that backing. That must be your one and only objective. You must be careful not to give any impression that you have fraternising connections with dissatisfied, critical elements in our population.—

—So you're no longer a communist.—

—I have been a Marxist since I was sixteen and I'll die one. That's what I've spent years of my life in prison for, whether it was the fascists or capitalists who put me there, or whether it was the comrades who called me a revisionist. I don't want this to come back.— He made a conductor's gesture, taking in the palms, the chipped gilding, the weary servility of the old waiters.

—I don't want my grandfather's estate with its illiterate peasants dying of tuberculosis. People like me are run down, I can't afford to buy foreign books anymore, I have to burn them—excuse me, I learnt that from the British, during the war—through boring myself stiff in cultural organizations, I can travel to Rome to see my beloved Piranesi wall only by getting myself invited to conferences—(short of breath or caught by laughter)—bourgeois hardships! But life is better for people who were wretchedly poor before. I wanted that. I still want it. That's freedom, too. You see, it's turned out that freedom is divisible. My schoolfriend is right. And I still prefer the way it's divided here to the way it's divided in the great riches of the West.—

A moment later he filled her glass and put a hand on her wrist. —But don't go asking your kind of question among people here.—

—Oh I should keep my mouth shut! But—again—you see, being in this kind of country's not like talking about it. Reading about it. I read quite a lot, in Ghana—the university library ... because Whaila—he hadn't been brought up in a house with books, the way I was, but he'd managed somehow to know so much; so much you need to know. For me, everything happens for the first time, for him everything grew out of what had already happened. I just think about how to manage; the way people do it, wherever you find yourself.—

—It's all right with me. With me you don't have to worry.—

—No, but I shouldn't have. I shouldn't have started asking. I don't even know you.—

—There are some people who have never been strangers.—

No need to explain why some subjects were invaded out of sequence by others; talk between them wove back and forth closely a pattern of its own; their pattern. While he was examining the bill, spectacles balanced on his nose but not hooked behind the ears, she set out firmly before herself like a hand at cards to be read:—You have an empty place where they were shot, we … Some are buried in the veld, nobody knows where, maybe hyenas have dug them up. He died on the kitchen floor. Another family eats there, now, there's a housing shortage.—

He was querying an item, kindly, with the wraith-faced waiter, and counted out notes in their language, but he knew what she was saying to him. —Yes, we are lucky. Yours is the hardest kind of struggle, in its worst phase—a battle going on in exile, with no place that belongs even to the dead. That is the greatest dispossession there is. Even to be in prison in your own country is to have a place there. I know.— As a cat sees the movement of a mouse while apparently not looking its way, he noticed the bottom of her glass was still coloured, and drank off the mouthful of wine left. A drop shone on the brush of moustache. She thought she felt it, although that was ridiculous, it must have been the frost of the streets, the wind across the river, when he kissed her goodnight under the statue without a nose above her apartment building's entrance. It was a kiss on either cheek, but not the butterfly flit of the Ambassador's household. It was of the order of the handclasp; to which she belonged, held by the hand of the dead.

A warning was not necessary for a good worker like Hillela. She had—she made—all the right connections. Citagele has always admitted he never anywhere had anyone more energetic (even if she was a woman, even if she was white). And watchful; as if life depended on never forgetting for a moment what they were there for. She entered various circles, or drew from these a certain circle around her—it is not possible that one did not attract people, whether she had the heart to or not. From among them she cultivated the most useful—nothing new in that, for her, but the focus was different, and calculated, as it had not been. So she disappears. She disappears into what is known about the mission, in that country at that time. No history of her really can be personal

284

history, then; its ends were all apparently outside herself. There was someone named Pavel—he was not a native of that country but an envoy or expert sent from outside; Karel had told her there used to be many of them, 'experts' watching even members of the government, but now they were fewer—only their army units remained stationed in certain parts of the country.

Pavel was young and did not limp. Surely more to her taste, but how can anyone know? He had the wild face associated with ballet dancers who defect to the West, and that face was the centre of a group of State officials and press functionaries who met often in the same café or at the apartment of a painter. —From Africa. You are strange to us like a giraffe.— She had the answer for this first remark addressed to her. The namesake was with her: — Today I went to the hairdresser, and the girl who was cutting my hair spoke a few words of English. She gave Nomzamo chocolate and pointed at her—'Where did you get that?'—

—Maybe she thinks at hard currency shop, like any other luxury she knows foreigners can buy.—

The café was for repartee, the painter's apartment for discussion where attitudes outside the insulation of book-and-canvas stacked walls, between other, official walls, could be gauged, and the movements up and down the ladder of influence and favour traced, even advanced or retarded. They made conclaves there, in their own language, but broke into English in the company of English-speakers. She heard Karel referred to as 'the hero of the revolution'. Why was he called that? —Because that's what he is, we have One Hundred Heroes of The Revolution, old boys who fought the Germans and were honoured by our first communist government after the war. The trouble is, some of them think that's a free pass to grab everything that's going, for the rest of their lives.— —Well, the Minister knows all about the Hero, so there's no danger he'll get the Embassy appointment in London.— —Oh but he's got a friend higher up than that.— —Maybe. But there are jobs younger men need to do, it's not nineteen-fifty, you know. Attitudes have changed. Our representatives in the West shouldn't be people who are remembering instead of thinking— that's all forgotten now, it's nuclear warheads not the Nazis we're talking about with Western Europe and America. There is a new style of diplomacy entirely—

—Time to get rid of these old men. You have even more of them, Pavel.—

The other foreigner swallowed, the Adam's apple bobbing almost humorously above his sweater. —His translations of Neruda are excellent. We'll invite him to a conference with Latin American scholars at our institute. Nice old man. Let him stay happy with his Neruda and his chasing girls. That is heroic too for him.—

There was laughter.

—Well, he must be kept out of the West. He has the wrong friends in the West, he is here and there with the enemies of this country. You'll invite him to a conference? What for? He'll expect to see reactionaries like Borges there! Our hero … that house of his, how is he allowed to have such a house for two old people?—

Mrs Kgomani said nothing to defend her friend or correct misinformation. She continued to take the bus to the old suburb where most houses, withdrawn up green drives like the houses in the white suburbs where she had lived as a daughter, had been converted into institutions. Her friend lived in the house that had been vacated in a hurry by a general of occupying forces, and he had no wife alive but two very old aunts and several sons and daughters with their wives and husbands living with him. There were neat beds behind rigged-up curtains in passages, and a warped grand piano in an entrance hall where four carved dining chairs that had somehow survived being chopped up for firewood during bad times were oddly-assorted round a plush-clothed table in anticipation of a vanished occasion. The aunts sat there and did not speak, even in their own language. Karel had a room at the top of the house with french windows and a balcony. —But don't step out, it's unsafe.—

Grass up there, growing from blown seeds between cracks in the cement. Inside, so much was safe. The room was perhaps meant for a reception room or studio, in the days when people like him had separate rooms for each function of living, and his grandfather's peasants were crowded into huts like the ones where Whaila's people lived now. Karel worked, slept and ate there, in the middle of an entire, assembled life. It was abundance of a kind she had not known existed, a fullness beyond money, although here and there was a fragment of something costly but damaged, like the Imari cat. She wandered about this life of his. A photograph when young; handsome as she had never seen a man to be, with the wing of black hair pointing back from the brow, and a cigarette holder between beautiful lips. Plaster maquettes of vanished structures; a piece of thick embroidery detached from its ceremonial occasion, hanging on a cord, dictionaries in five languages, solid as furniture, step-pyramids of journals shedding press cuttings, a plate of smooth stones, the painting of a man in braid and medals, dated 1848, who looked like Karel in fancy dress, framed letters in foreign languages signed 'Lukács Gyorgy' and 'Thomas Mann', scrap-paper drawings and sheets of music manuscript with dedications, old lamps that had scorched their shades, long fixing with an amber eye among books one left open at a poem or an engraving, a child's clumsy posy of dried flowers, a draped flag worn thin as an old dress, theatre programmes, abstract paintings of the modest size presented by artists themselves, even a tin canister—What's this?—

He looked at her hand for a moment as if it held one of the grenades whose features and performances she was studying. He came over to her. —Don't you see? The label is still there. Like a can of beans. It's Zyklon B, the gas the Nazis used in their death chambers. It was issued with—what d'you call it—rations to the camp commandants.— He translated from the German: —'For the control of vermin'—and there are instructions to be careful not to contaminate yourself when using it. —

He took the canister slowly from her and replaced it on a scroll-ended bibelot shelf stained with circles made by wine glasses at long-past parties. He adjusted the position so that the label would not be obscured. —I was with the Russians who went in when Berlin fell. Most of Hitler's men had fled but we opened doors and found some. One had this can on his desk.— His head seemed too heavy for him and under raised eyebrows his face sagged before her. —A sample. Something to (he ran his fingers round some invisible gadget) play with, while talking on the phone. I put the can in my pocket. That was the looting I did. And I keep it here where I can see it every day among the books, and the photographs of the women and children and friends because that's where it belongs, that's how it was used, as some ordinary ... commodity—

An urge came upon her crudely as an urge to vomit or void her bowels. She began to tremble and to flush. Her eyes were huge with burning liquid she could not hold back. She wept in his arms, blotted against the solid body thick with life in which the constricted breathing of age was like a great cat's purr. He knew she was not weeping for the man he had shot dead at his desk, or even for the innocents for whom death was opened like a can of beans. The kitchen floor; it was the kitchen floor.

She came from so far away, down there in a remote country, belonging to a privileged class at home, and far, far from the bombardments, the childhood existence on frozen potatoes, the firing squads for partisans set to dig their own graves, and the gas chambers for families. The necessity to deal in death, no way out of it, meeting death with death, not flowers and memorials, was just coming to the people among whom she had grown up.

*

Where the city of the intermediate thousand years had been bombed to rubble in the war, excavations for a new subway line had unearthed Roman baths belonging to a garrison from the first foreign occupation of the country. With enough time, foreign occupations become part of a treasured history which is threatened by the latest foreign power: asserting national heritage in stone restored everywhere, the local authorities raised the marble columns in a park laid out above the subway. Behind, at the distance of a crowd from a spectacle, was the solid horizon of workers' housing blocks. The nursery-school teacher who lived there took Nomzamo's mother home for coffee to what she called 'The Great Wall'. In a kilometre of ten-storey buildings with windows set like close type she pointed at one she alone could distinguish from all others. —That's where we are.—

The mythical wooden beasts of a children's playground were furred with snow, here. The women and their small children moved at once into the hot, echoing concrete walks beyond double doors. —Everybody in this block has not less than three children. That's the way housing is allotted. In the school holidays you can't think, you can't hear yourself speak … your own children are among them, and they make a hell.— The teacher was studying to improve her qualifications and become an official translator for a State publishing house. —I'm lucky, my two eldest can look after themselves and my mother takes the little one, so I can go and work at night in a library.— Here, too, were neat beds disguised as livingroom furniture; the preoccupations of different members of the household staked out in corners and shelves of territory: musical instruments and reference books (the husband taught in a college of music), children's sports banners and bicycles, models on box-lids, an ironing board before a television set. —D'you want to go away?—

She was a soft-voiced blonde with all her tension and emotion in her neck. —Only to a better apartment. That's all. To have another room! I know very well why we can't have it, it'll take another generation to make up what was destroyed and provide for all the people who have come to the towns. But I want it. If I had money, I know I'd try and buy the way ... although I think it's wrong.—

—Can people do that?—

—Always, everywhere, people do that. It can't be stopped, altogether.—

—We've got something ... a charter. Something like this '... the people shall have the right to live where they choose, to be decently housed'.—

The coffee cups were special ones, the teacher's laugh rang from the cupboard where she sought them. —Oh yes, that's what the leaders say, but when they are in power, they have to do it ... that's the trouble. But it's a rich country down there? You didn't have wars. Maybe you can.—

There was no African family here in which the namesake was common responsibility. Mrs Kgomani could not go out at night unless she could find a baby-sitter. Pavel took up the instruction begun long ago by a naughty boy and girl in Joe's study among documentary evidence of the kind of activity she was engaged in now. Pavel came to the apartment and taught her chess. Snow did not keep him away; looking out the window at the expected hour she saw him in his fur boots and elegant coat, moving through the white like one of those antlered creatures in his own latitude who graze in cold wastes, digging for nourishment only they know is there.

—The longer the revolution takes to come in your country, more danger there is to be a bourgeois revolution. That is what people like your lady friend—she wants to have here. She will tell you she is glad the big estates are gone. State has taken over banks and capitalist industry. She is glad for that, because she was not big land-owner, not factory owner. So she is glad those people have not got what she did not never have.— —'Never had'.— —Yes, never have.

But she wants, wants to get house to leave to her children, and then it's a shop, and so it must go on ... She's dreaming of unearned income—no good for the old regime, but good for her ... Do you know that those apartments are heated, free? Maybe that's nothing for her, she was always living in a heated house. But generations of peasants, and those who became proletariat with industrialization in nineteenth century, they never knew what it is to have heat, electric light! Danger is, for your country, with industrialization maybe there is coming a class—blacks—like here. They want the little house, the little shop, the little farm, for their children. Even some who come here ... Bourgeois in the heart. What does Citagele care for landless peasants? He doesn't need land, he wants a fine office. Kotane, J. B. Marks, Tambo, Nzo, Makatini—they care for the people. But him ... You must not forget what kind of a life, what kind of an education does a little black kid get on your farms, and in your ghettos, before you tell us in Eastern Europe we haven't solved the housing problem for the masses.—

She needed no reminder. —I've got a little black one of my own, you know.—

—Yes, and I love her. She is just like her mother, only nicer—

Laughter at the double-edged compliment. —Only darker.—

—Why you don't let me finish? Nicer to me.—

The change of subject stopped the laughter.

—What have you to complain of, Pavel.—

—When you are tired with your work, it's time for me for an hour. And even that time—you are working, maybe.—

—For Christ' sake, what do you think I am—a spy? An agent of the South African government?— The laughter came back.

—No. But you are working too much. And I don't know ... if you are right for what you are doing.—

—I know what I'm working for, Pavel.—

—All right. I believe it. You are good material, yes. But I'm not sure you should be typist and translator—things like that.

Sitting in an office. Oh yes, don't be offended, yes I know you make a speech to women sometimes ... But it's not for you ... A functionary. I feel it. You try to be, what is it in English—not 'nice'—careful, no, 'tactful' that is it, but you can be something different! You got your own talent.—

—What are you talking about? I get on very well with the others. With Citagele. With Arnold. So what are you talking about?—

—How to live. We've got some people like you. In the end, valuable if they are, you can't do much with them in bureaucracy, and even freedom movement, it has bureaucracy. You can say: dangerous individualism; you shut them away. Because if they know something, it's not what other people can know. So what is use? But you are too clever for anything to happen to you, Hillela.—

Winter is burial. The days are shorter and shorter intervals between longer and longer nights. Everything that had opened, everything that was full to overflowing has contracted. The snow falls like the clods of red earth, on the living. Layer by layer, month by month, frozen then sodden then frozen, buried deeper. How to emerge from it, from the yellow ceiling-bulb that is daylight and the suffocation of human and cooking smells that is the warmth of their sun. There is no rainbow-coloured family. Only the one who came out black; there remains, black-to-white, the little foot that feels for the comfort of the white thigh, under covers, while steam in the pipes hisses; the small, open-mouthed face that is all there is on the other pillow. No rainbow-coloured family; that kind of love can't be got away with, it's cornered, it's easily done away with in two shots from a 9-mm Parabellum pistol. Happiness dancing in a shop window behind glass, while outside there are hungry crowds in the street, looking on. Not for long. The glass explodes; their arms reach up to drag, to claim. The only love that counts is owed to them. Waves of resentment towards him, for not firing first, for not saving himself for the rainbow-coloured family, the only love made flesh, man gloved inside woman, child emerging to suck the breast the man caressed: the perfect circle, cycle. But he never belonged to it, the beloved—the bastard!—he belonged to the crowd outside and he died for them. The other wife, whom he left behind in Krugersdorp location, would not be lying in bed alone reproaching him. She was one of the crowd, she knew what belonged to them. The balancing rocks seen through a rep's car window; embraces fall at the soundwaves of the next word spoken, the first crack of a bullet discharged.

The dear old one says, White people who settled in other countries have no past, so you're not surrounded, like me ... but you tried to live—there's *something von Kleist wrote—'in a time that hasn't yet come'! Ridiculous, crazy, but I like it.*

And the other one: You're too clever for anything to happen to you. Repeats it, another night, adding, Oh I know, I smell it on your skin.

What you smell is the black market perfume you bought for me.

The handclasp is the only love made flesh. Learn that. Read the handclasp, learning the kind of love in the calibre and striking power of hardware.

The slums along the river destroyed by bombardment had made way for a park and as the snow melted it was there: sheen on the grass and the namesake running after a ball. Pale sun unrolled slanting rugs. Water trickled under remnants of ice like cracked wine glasses. An age of winter remained shut up in apartments, offices, and on the other side of restaurant doors. Perhaps it would never leave, it would store next winter there as it did the one before. Pavel took Mrs Kgomani and her child to the woods to pick early snowdrops. He made boats out of sticks and leaves and the three of them raced these vessels on a stream. He lay on wet ground with his pure-pale wild face and delicate eyelids up to the weak sun as if it were blinding; this was the 'they' many people in that country resented and feared, this young man to whom the season of emergence from snow was a worshipful ceremonial. Karel, following the same impulse to share pleasure that the young woman brought out in people, drove her and the child to the town where the country's first king had had his palace, in the 13th century. The ruins of European feudalism were the namesake's playground, that day; she rode worn heraldic lions and griffins. Near the town was a garrison with the red star over the barbed wire at the sentry gates. —Poor devils, the men are kept shut up for the whole time they're posted here, only the officers are allowed to mix in the town.— —Pavel Grushko says they help people with the harvests.— Karel turned to look at her with sleepy-eyed compassion for the soldiers, for the youth of all men. —Once a year, in autumn? Never to see a girl for the rest of the year? Mr Grushko doesn't deprive himself of anything, does he.—

They must have missed her when she emerged from her winter as the park did, as the woods did, as the streams did. The old man for quite a long time, whether as a lover (no-one knows) or more likely—once again, for her—as if she had been a daughter. Pavel not for long, because he was young and very attractive to women. Karel did not live to hear of the times that have come, for her.

295

Grushko—his position merits that he be referred to by surname alone—has surprised nobody by making a career for himself, first as a diplomat in English-speaking and Arab countries, then as his country's representative at United Nations, where, at a reception recently, he recognized her instantly. He remembers her, in their youth, with an English phrase he does not know is long out of date: a good sort.

Why she left the Eastern European mission is a matter for speculation. It happened very abruptly: one week she was in the thick of the midday clique at the café, already gathered at outside tables for the touch of the spring sun. The next week people were asking where she was. Suppositions were carried by particular turns of phrase in their language that had gathered ironies from dour discretion under many foreign occupations. —Pavel has flown her off for a weekend at his dacha.— But while they were laughing (and what was there to laugh at? He was to have his dacha before long, and his chauffeur-driven limousine) he arrived with his quick, wide stride and flying scarf and joined the table. Where was Hillela Kgomani? Nobody could tell him.

When Citagele was approached in the office, his raised brows lifted his bald pate, through which he felt, he had complained to his efficient assistant, the cold reached right into his brain in winter. (She had found for him—maybe knitted it herself?—a cap like those black workmen wear down to the eyebrows in all weathers, at home, and it comforted him when they were alone in the office and there was no-one to see.) —Her time was up. She'd been here what—two years?—

—You should know, of course. But not two years.—

—Okay, about … well, nearly.—

—Why did she not say? She never told me.—

Citagele clasped his hands and looked at Grushko to see what he might know. Then he spoke within the four walls, as he would wear the knitted cap. —It wasn't what I wanted. But there you are. You'll hear about it eventually, I suppose. There has been some discussion, we're making some changes.—

A quirk dented one corner of the European-tailored mouth, so different from the soft African one that was looking for words that would say nothing.

—Personnel being shifted around in accordance with needs.—

—She has gone where?—

—To the United States. Eventually. Oh she might be in London now.—

—America! You get nothing from them!—(the laugh that has made him popular in Western diplomatic circles)— Where are your friends there! You've got rid of her!—

—I've told you. Transferred. Maybe somewhere else. I don't make these decisions alone.—

One version of her departure was that she had left in a fit of temperament because she had quarrelled with a Russian lover she expected to marry her. This seems gossip's inversion of the other, political theory, that the Africanists in the organization wanted to oust the influence of white communists, and, somehow, because she was white and was too close to the Russians living in the country that was hosting her, she had got swept up. Not in a purge, exactly; the worst that happened to Arnold—one of the important figures—for example, was that he temporarily lost his place on the Revolutionary Council.

Some gossip found the second story unlikely: for heaven's sake, Whaila leaned towards the Africanist wing, why should his widow suddenly have become a communist? But there was the rumour that she had joined the South African Communist Party in London, on which of her stays there rumour could not specify: never mind 'Whaila Kgomani's widow', she had her life in her own hands, apparently she had done well in Eastern Europe, even learned something of the cursedly difficult language. If that wasn't devotion to the cause! Oh, maybe it was some other kind of devotion—the young widow had intimate friendships, it was said; she would never lack admirers, or the means of communicating with them.

These generalities have gathered the velvet of the years, befitting the past of someone who has achieved a certain position. Her Russian lover kept a house for her in a Black Sea resort where she would join him from all over the world, under an assumed name and false passport; or, if you prefer, the government of the host country had told Citagele's mission she must leave because she had become the mistress of one of the dissident intellectuals intent on overthrowing the regime.

Who knows.

She has always been loyal, whatever (as Pauline might say) her lack of other qualities. A child in a Salisbury park, she quit the company of her buddies but did not betray the secrets of the shrubbery to the schoolmistress under the *mnondo* tree. She has never given a reason (even one that would reflect well on her!) for her sudden departure from the Eastern European mission. Maybe she left as she had hitched a lift to Durban one afternoon after school. That is a judgment that has to be considered. A harsh one.

Special Interests

Everything is known about her movements. Americans are such industrious documenters: the proof of her presence among them, like that of their own existence, is ensured by reports of symposia and conferences, prospectuses of institutes and foundations, *curricula vitae,* group photographs, videos, tapes, transcripts of television interviews. She and her child came to the United States under the auspices (that's the vocabulary) of a political scientist who roved Africa as a new kind of white hunter. Dr Leonie Adlestrop's trophies were causes, exiles, aid programmes and black political intrigues. In her sixties, in socks and sandals, floral dresses scoop-necked for the climate showing the weathered hide of her bosom as two worn leather cushions crumpled together, she bore her trophies from Nigeria, Ghana, Angola, Mozambique, from Tanzania and Kenya, from little Swaziland and Lesotho, back to America. The university where she had tenure as a Distinguished Professor was merely a base. On first-name terms with the Presidents of African states already independent and the leaders of black liberation movements who would one day be presidents, she was also able to make herself accepted, motherly yet sexless (perhaps in the precedence of those post-menopausal women who are given a special, almost male, status in certain tribal rituals), into the confidence of all kinds of ordinary groups—religious, political, educational. These attributes brought her, first, lecture tours round African studies departments, then fellowships from foundation-funded institutes for social and political research, co-option to para-governmental commissions on international affairs, and finally a status where her name listed among trustees, executive members, advisers meant she was a consultant to a succession of Assistant Secretaries of State for African Affairs, and an influence on lobbyists in Congress.

There was not much American popular interest in Africa in the late Sixties. Preoccupation with the war in Vietnam, the neo-Gothic thrills of Weathermen terrorism and even with the great black civil rights pilgrimages to Washington did not distract Ma Leonie; she took up Africa long before the students and black Americans did, and maybe without her it would have taken even longer for America to do so. Her government did not recognize the liberation movements for whose exiles she obtained entry visas and totally unorthodox admission to her own and other universities. Those who were academically qualified had teaching niches made for them; others were given scholarships she could expect on demand from a roster of sources her secretary did not even have to call up on the computer—Dr Adlestrop had them all, under the first names of their directors, at hand in her head.

A beach girl would have been too marginal to have met Dr Adlestrop in Dar es Salaam. But Dr Adlestrop—Leonie, she asked at once that you call her Leonie—passing through Accra to add the officers of Ghana's new National Liberation Council to her rotary card file, of course had called Whaila, and met his new wife. Leonie and Whaila made the easy elliptical exchanges of old acquaintances. She had just seen Julius in Dar, spent an hour at the airport with K.K. when he arrived from a state visit to Yugoslavia, unfortunately missed Oliver— and, landing in Accra, was quite overcome with grief to realize Kwame was no more ... Whaila was anti-American as a matter of policy, since the United States government supported the South African government and gave neither overt recognition nor covert encouragement to the African National Congress. But apparently Leonie was different; Leonie was with him. She was supplying funds in a small way through some of her numerous private organizations, opening cracks that might widen into future access. —I'm keeping at it, Whaila, I'll go on beavering away.— Like most Americans highly critical of their government, she was at the same time patriotic and anti-communist. —You know that I've never been able to stand the idea that you're going to have to be grateful to the Eastern bloc.—

He teased her; she loved it. —But look at all those Marxists you smuggle into the USA.—

—He's a great flirt, your man. We're always like this together.— She bridled happily to the new wife. —Don't you know, Whaila, it's because I'm really intending to have the FBI brainwash them?—

The documentation begins only with arrival in the United States. Whether Hillela remembered Dr Adlestrop and got in touch with her from London, or if it was Leonie who made the approach, is not known. Whichever it was, Hillela's instinct for calculation or Dr Adlestrop's nose for a trophy, another form of power—the power of Leonie Adlestrop's kindness—could be counted on. Without adequate papers, with a history of residence in an Eastern European country, Hillela Kgomani and child slipped in easily under the armpit of the Statue.

If she had no passport, no money, few marketable qualifications, in a country more concerned with shoring-up repressive regimes than providing so much as working space for those whose professional skills were to oppose them, she had the qualification of tragedy. There is no-one so safe, so secure, so frivolous or hard-headed as to be able to be unaware of that. Leonie knew Americans would be impressed, even intimidated by her presentation: a white widow and her fatherless black child, the black husband assassinated before the wife's eyes by a racist regime. The namesake's small black hand in her mother's white one: the shame of the slave yard, of the years of the Klan, the centuries-long march before Washington had been reached, the bullet that lodged in the dream of Luther King—this simple sight brought it all to them. For them, Hillela came straight from the kitchen where Whaila died on the floor. It was all of her they needed to know. She began there. It was the signature of her life; what she had been, what she was, and would be.

Dr Adlestrop commandeered the frame house of a professor on sabbatical and a place in the primary school for faculty members' children. These facts are recorded in the yearly newsletter, released at Commencement, Leonie had distributed by her Department to colleagues on the campus, to alumnae, and pandemically to friends and contacts. 'Ms Hillela Kgomani and her delightful small daughter, Nomzamo (named for Ms Nomzamo Winnie Mandela, wife of Nelson Mandela), joined us early this spring semester. I had the privilege of knowing, for some years, Ms Kgomani's late husband, Whaila Kgomani, who was tragically killed in Lusaka. Ms Kgomani has been seconded to the Robert and Elsie McCray Program for African-American Social Research. REMASOR will make her available to special interest organizations—African studies, women's studies, international relations and refugee studies—throughout the state. Her personal experience in having lived close to the needs of the people in a number of African countries will be invaluable to us. She and Nomzamo are presently occupying Professor Herbert Kleinschmidt's house on College Walk, and Nomzamo has settled happily at our excellent school. We welcome mother and daughter most heartily.'

Nomo, when interviewed about her increasingly successful modelling career, sometimes varies replies to questions about her background by adding that she was, in fact, partly educated in America. Hillela stood at the double-glazed window in Professor Kleinschmidt's study and watched the little girl chase squirrels with the stooping gallop of Groucho Marx. She couldn't get the window open but she knew before she saw the parade that

the child, forgetting the squirrels and turning her face in curious amazement, had heard something pleasing. Then through
the glass it came, the singing and the wavering blare of music,
as it had rejoiced the birth of the one who had come out just
like him—him, lying on the kitchen floor. The alumnae parade
advanced from under lettuce-green of spring elm trees and the
little black face kept glancing back to her mother in bliss to
confirm proudly what small children feel about all phenomena
passing before them for the first time—that it was for her, for her
delectation, the college band and the bannered ranks, class of '40
grey-haired and smiling on false teeth, '52 wearing well through
sensible diet and exercise, '60s, some pregnant, some got up in a
kind of retrogression to college days, some lovely with the flying-
haired zest of having been qualified adult for a whole year.

The alumnae were the first group Hillela addressed in America.
Her audience was mostly the classes of the '40s and '50s; the
younger ones, her own age, were with their husbands and children
on the lawns or drinking beer with their boyfriends. What should
she talk about? —Oh, my dear, you have so much to tell them!
The role of women in the new Africa, a few personal touches
to lighten things up ... but you know, lordy, you know— The
winter-pink or cruise-tanned faces, the perfect coiffures and gold
costume jewellery quickly made the lecturer change, as she went
along, the talk that had been prepared for factory workers in peasant kerchiefs. Dr Adlestrop, mistress of the broadcasting medium
of discretion, had ensured in undertone asides that everyone knew
about this young woman; she stood there on the podium touched
by eyes that wanted to search out the mark—suffering's grace or
Cain's slash—that set her apart, as the eyes of larger crowds still
did with the widow of their assassinated president. The college
had acquired its own house-version widow: was endowed with
her, this year, along with a poet-in-residence and a Japanese
garden established in previous ones.

Americans take in each other's children the way Africans do. The namesake had many temporary brothers and sisters, was made free of all the bunk-beds and milk-and-cookie sustenance she could possibly need. As Hillela had adapted her subject to the kind of expectations she sensed available in the alumnae, so she moved on to more exacting forums around the Eastern Seaboard, the Middle West and even California. The exaction was not only exercised upon her; it soon was exercised by her upon those who brought her among them. She had to go back to libraries (Leonie's houseful of abstract Africa in words and statistics that shared the shelves with displaced ritual carvings and vessels, ceremonial beadwork and artisans' tools) to find the supplement she had always said she could not trust: what she had not experienced for herself. It was necessary, for the practice of exaction. She had moved not merely on, but up; over academic elms to the Foundations and Committees with money to spend. People running development projects in Ghana were surprised to receive under her name, with the title of co-ordinating assistant or deputy director of this or that programme, letters offering and outlining the conditions of grants. (Good god, Hillela. Well! —Trust her.) Some working in Tanzania corresponded on these matters without making the connection between the colleague of Democratic congressmen and senators and the girl in the yellow swim-suit on Tamarisk Beach. It might have taken even old friends, old intimates, a moment or two to recognize her, if they could have come upon her at a conference table or head-down over an open briefcase on a shuttle flight. Christa, Sophie, Marie-Claude, Busewe—would they have found Hillela in this cropped-headed girl who had adopted Leonie's practical socks and sandals, walked official corridors instead of dancing high-life, and carried reports, agendas and minutes instead of a guitar? Even Emile. He might have been tricked by the absence of obvious beauty women can't help having. Only Udi would have known her instantly, for the signals this particular one could not help giving. And Sasha. Sasha would have known her anywhere, at any stage or age in any life.

It was at this stage that he wrote the first letter. *Seven years since you left this country. Not that I saw you for the year or so before that, but at least you were here. We could always still have bumped into each other somewhere.*

I can imagine—or I think I can—something of what your life is like, extrapolate from what I pick up in newspapers and books and even in the office about the kind of situation(s?) you must be living in. (I work with Joe, articled—I didn't go back to university after the army.) I imagine it quite well but there's a sort of cut-out shape in the middle—I can't quite put you in. But I suppose you've changed enough, outwardly anyway, to fit.

They heard you'd got married—the family. You'll be able to read off the predictable reactions like a hand of cards. The queen declared: It solves nothing. The king isn't played; he always loved you for yourself, as the saying goes, didn't want anything else of you. Loved you more than he does our namby-pamby sister but could not show it. I knew, though.

I know your husband was killed. Hillela's husband. I was angry with the others because I was the one who should have felt the most for you and I couldn't feel anything. It was because I couldn't believe in his wife. If you really haven't changed, you'll laugh at that, at me. I don't know what's the matter with me, Hillela, that's the fact of it. I'm sorry Whaila Kgomani was killed. That's lame but what other way is there to approach what happened to you, one can't walk right up to it. Pauline pronounced you'd be all right. And of course what Pauline says is definitive. On the other hand, you're the only one of us who didn't let it be. So I don't know. But my mother's no fool, and you made her respect you. No matter what she did. No, 'made' is not true; you never entered into the wrestling game she and I have, to the last gasp—she or me. You never recognized its existence, so you didn't have to. I continue to wound her savagely. I've told her: she sneers at her sister Olga, the Jewish mother, and certainly she herself is no Jewish mother, she's the Medusa. I live with a girl but I keep going back to the house. Pauline is not the explanation for this.

305

*What would you want to know? I went with my girl to England,
France and Italy last year but I don't suppose you were there. Or we
might have bumped into one another. I have part of a house with her on
the old Crown Mines property—you might remember Crown Mines, no
longer being worked, although I'm not sure the former staff houses were
for rent when you were still around. Seven of us share, two more— nice
queers—live in what were the servants' quarters. No prejudice involved,
just that they wanted to fix up their own place in housewifely style, everything just so. The seventh tenant has an unofficial eighth, a black girl
who works for some church organization—so we have our token or totem
or whatever you want to call it. Big whoopee, as we used to say to bring
each other down a peg or two, when we were kids. Alpheus had three more
children and had to leave the garage. He never completed his articles with
Joe, but him I did bump into recently, and he's making a good living as
a furniture salesman. I won't complete my articles, either. You probably
won't read this (I haven't any address for you) so you won't be able to
tell anyone, even supposing there were to be someone around who might be
remotely interested. I'm a champion at writing letters that never get sent.*

*What else? Well, I still read a lot. The other day l read a story, a
translation from the Hungarian writer, Dezsö Kosztolányi, where the
girl dies and the man longs for her for years, wants to see her again for
only half-an-hour. His concentration is so fervent that he actually brings
her back from the dead. There she is, just as she was, in his room, and they
have nothing to say to each other. All they can think about is how much of
the half-hour is still to pass. Eventually, she leaves after twenty minutes.*

*Why can't I end off? I never know how to end off. I did my year in the
army, you know. A good thing. Good thing to learn how easy it is to be
one of them. To you, one of those who killed him; I can come up very close to
that fact. My god, that story about the dead was tactless; I didn't think.
Another thing I won't do—I won't go to the army camps I'm supposed to
spend a month in each year. So far I've managed by lying, aided and abetted by my girl, by Pauline and Joe, who approve finding ways of getting
round things. When the call-up telegram comes my girl replies I'm no*

306

longer at this address, and when another comes to Pauline's, she does the same. I disappear for a while, and the army calls up a substitute, putting my name down for the next camp. So far, military police came round only once, and my girl put on the innocent act and dealt with them. So that's where I am: between call-ups. The alternative is to be like the Seventh Day Adventists and go to jail for conscientious objection on holy-roller grounds. But we kids were brought up without all that mumbo-jumbo, weren't we, to cope with this world, not the next. I'm doing useful work helping prepare defence material for Joe's cases, when I'm not hiding away. He has had a coronary but still slaves in that study night after night. He has pale moon-rings round his pupils although he's only about sixty.

I remember when we read it: 'I want to know you, and then to say goodbye'.

Sasha

They say you did have a baby. I can't remember whether you liked children.

There were no scandals. Memoranda carefully prepared, files of cuttings up-to-date. No-one could catch her out in inaccurate statistics; she could always support her strongest and most challenged assertions, breaking down in a way new to her any resistance she encountered. At finger-suppers she convinced minority-report dissenters. Before a Senate committee she placed the long-term consequences, for United States interests, of backing repressive regimes in Angola, South Africa, Namibia, when these countries inevitably would become independent black states before the end of the century—and to whom would they supply their oil, gold, platinum, uranium, titanium, then? Those who had recognized them in their struggle for human rights ('freedom struggle' was not in the preferred vocabulary for the West) or those who had 'actively ignored' them? She showed a quick aptitude for the invention of euphemisms so like that the State Department could have taken them for their own; this one was to be understood to mean that although it might have to be accepted that no 'military hardware' would be forthcoming, no 'humanitarian aid' was being given, either.

A senator, seated beside her drawing right-angled shapes while she talked, flourished a circle round them. —Mr Chairman, experience has shown that there is no way of controlling how so-called humanitarian aid is used. If it's given in the form of money, it goes to buy arms, not medicine. We are meddling in destabilization. If it's given in kind—look what happened to the famous Congo chickens: I'm told it's a fact that the 'starving' Congolese sold the cans to specialty stores down in Rhodesia.—

But the circle was not closed. Hillela took something out of the wallet in her attaché case. —Mr Chairman, may I have permission to pass this round?—

They had already received from her several information sheets; the bush schools run by FRELIMO in the area of Mozambique where it was in control; clinics run for the refugees in Tanzania; figures for the number of villagers harassed out of their homes by the South African army in Namibia. But this was a photograph of the family kind those present themselves had in their wallets. The spokesman for the Assistant Secretary of State for African Affairs twitched his small moustache like a scenting rabbit; the namesake, her ecstatic black face under a stocking cap, looked out at him from snow. She went politely from hand to hand. What on earth was the purpose? The company was able to glance over human features as if over statistics, as accustomed to concealing embarrassment as to concealing lack of interest. The speaker's dark and brilliant eyes let her colleagues off nothing. She looked at them all with an acceptance of what they were thinking; with a confidence against which there was no defence. —That black child is plump and cared-for in the United States. She was born a refugee who has never seen her father's and mother's country. She's mine, so she's lucky. If she were one of those in Africa, her

308

life would depend on a handout of soup powder, the installation of a well to give her clean water, and a clinic to immunise her against disease.—

Leonie embraced her after such triumphs. Though it was not at all certain whether it was this emotional retrogression— intentional or not—or the hard work that went into the rational case presented, that succeeded. Funds were voted. Hank (as the Assistant Secretary of State's African Affairs man was known to his friends) was quoted at cocktail parties: —Lust is the best aid raiser.—

Not the breath of a scandal, nevertheless. Hank never had the good fortune to pursue further the possibilities he was sensitive to in Mrs Kgomani. Professor Kleinschmidt, a divorced man, returned from his sabbatical and would have liked to let the young woman stay on in the house but could not tolerate the noise of the child. The child was over-indulged by everybody, precocious and spoiled. The brat already knew how to exploit being black. So he had to make the choice. People invited him as Hillela's dinner partner from time to time but it was apparent that those who schemed to match them failed. Herbert Kleinschmidt was lonely, yes; but who could think of Hillela Kgomani as lonely? She was Leonie's promotion, Leonie's working partner; and Leonie's friend- ships were thickly gathered in, Leonie's emotions ran grandly as cables under the oceans back and forth between the developed and underdeveloped worlds. Leonie and Hillela had no nuclear family but their distant ties, obligations, dependants, held them fast.

Of course Hillela had the body. The old, like Leonie, have no body except in its necessities for food, drink and shelter, and its creakings of pain. The body quickly knows—is the first to know—it has not been shot. It is still alive, alive in the Eastern European snow as in the tropical sand-bed. But it also knows when it is being ignored. Neglect of the body doesn't mean not washing or cutting toe-nails. It's a turning away from its powers.

It's using it like a briefcase, to carry oneself around, instead of living through it.

Hillela Kgomani travelled; even to Africa sometimes with Dr Adlestrop, those years; the interests of their commissions coincided or Leonie contrived that they should. With the pride of a teacher leading a school outing Leonie arranged for unmarked planes, boarded on hidden airstrips shaved out of the bush, to take them behind the guerrilla lines in several countries. They ate with bearded commanders who were old (scholarship) students of Leonie, but had had to finish the kind of education they needed in the Soviet Union, Cuba or China, depending on the alliances of their movements. Some had known Whaila; the grip of the hand, when Leonie introduced the young woman, tightened; she had been taken out of the ranks of useful onlookers and silently accepted among the commanders in their garb composed of distinguishing styles of many liberations, from the Risorgimento to the Thousand Days, from Liebknecht to Castro. She watched men—like those who had shared the hospitality of the Manaka flat, drinking beer and grumbling because they couldn't buy the brand of razor blade they had used in Soweto—drilling in a mismatch of captured fatigue dress, and sitting about tending their weapons, talkative and expert as the tinsmiths in Lusaka market fashioning their buckets and braziers. There were women among them. Enclosed in third-hand battledress, the generous breasts (like her own) characteristic of black girls seemed to have atrophied to meet conditions; their chests were the hard shields of males'. Only their feet escaped, bare. Hillela pushed off her sandals and socks while she sat in the hot, paper-bag glow of a tent, writing notes for a report. All became typed paper. The voices that brightly skimmed the surface above sleep in the early morning were at first puzzling, then—again, as always—the most familiar assurance; words that meant nothing (a language not understood), and everything; the rep's 'boy' talking in a dorp street outside the car, Jethro heard while face-down beside the pool, and the spill of harassed chatter flying through the service doors as the waiters served the schoolgirls. It was a home. An audile, sensory home like that soundmen provide for the sequences of film where there is no human speech, holding up their microphones in an empty room where the quality of silence contains vanished voices, vanished heartbeats.

Single-file paths behind the training camp had been made by bare soles and the brush of heads against twigs. They were so tentative they disappeared into the bush here and there or came to a stop at the obstacle of a red earth funnel higher than a man, built by ants. There was no concept of 'place' in this wilderness, fiercely undefined in reconquest by its original inhabitants of territory defined on maps of colonial possessions. She and Leonie found their way not to a place but a presence of several hundred people there in the bush like companies of storks or cranes come upon when insects surface in one area or another. They had no more possessions than scavengers. They waited; or at least the only aspect they had was that of waiting; as Hillela saw human beings do when they have lost everything of the past, have no hold upon the present, no sign that there is a future. They appear to be waiting because there is no state appropriate to their existence. Leonie picked a baby like a phoenix from ashes of a small fire; its whole small being was fascinated by the gingerish hairs, flashing with sweat, at either corner of her smiling lips. Family love casts out squeamishness. She touched scabby heads and called out cheerfully. —Scurvy. And look at the belly—oh you potbelly, you—kwashiorkor as well.—

Hillela returned with the freedom fighters who brought maize porridge or beans by way of the paths, once a day. When the children had eaten, they roused from the dust and began to play; they slowly began to chase and laugh, make weapons out of sticks. When she smiled at them, they pointed the sticks and stuttered machine-gun fire. And then the fuel of food was burnt up, they lay about on their mothers again, and the women searched for lice in their hair, whether there were lice or not. The ritual was all that was left of providing for their children's needs. A feeble old man fought the children for the roll of peppermints Hillela found in her pocket. She grabbed the stick he was wielding—but whom was she to defend? He was so thin that pulses beat visibly at his temples and jumped beneath the skin on his hands.

Leonie knew better. —First your peppermints, then your clothes, then your malaria prophylactics—and what use will you be to anybody, then? What they need is what we're going to go back and get sent out here, high-protein foods and basic medicines. What they need is for the U.S. to stop giving covert aid to keep those gangsters down in the capital in power.—

One of the freedom fighters who perhaps understood a little English watched the old woman with something of the incredulity with which the filthy children had surrounded the distributor of small discs sweet and strong, the taste of a whole other existence. His gaze fingered Dr Adlestrop's assurance as if she were a magic crone from a life he used to know—someone who brushed with others in city streets, who saw clothes in shop windows, travelled in taxis, drew pay once a week and walked into the fanfare of talk and music in the rich fermented scent of bars.

'In addition to the large number of fighting personnel, which includes women as well as men (no figures available because these would provide useful information to the government forces), there is the added logistical burden of feeding and providing minimal care for hundreds of refugee families. These have been victimised by the government forces for aiding freedom fighters, or in some cases were simply caught up in areas where fighting was intense and no normal life—planting of crops etc.—was possible.' In hotels and planes all was transformed into reports, studies and working papers. The phrasing of a banality could make the difference between approval or rejection in a committee room thousands of miles away from the bush, the dry seams of river-beds, the deserted sands and green-massed forests passing under the plane's belly. The inclusion of an observation better left out could give the high-minded (Lord save us! Those are the danger-ous ones, worse than the open reactionaries, my dear Hillela) the chance to carry a 'no' vote.

The self-same sight of people in a place that was no place, wait-ing: these were over the border where they had fled to another country, saying they had been beaten and robbed of their cattle when they would not help the freedom fighters. That sight would not be transformed into typescript and serve as self-righteousness for people who experience nothing for themselves and have not the courage to distinguish between ends, only to condemn the ugly necessities to which means are driven. Lines crossed out, the sight crossed out with a finger tapping on the upper case X. If she could have found the ones who ran away down the corridor of Britannia Court, would she not have shot them with her souvenir Makarov?

Leonie Adlestrop's special position in Africa made it possible for her to move with ease back and forth from conservative to radical regimes, in fact, everywhere except to South Africa and Namibia, where she had been declared a prohibited immigrant— and so proudly joined the status of political refugees from that country. —We can't get in, but we can kick up a heck of a lot of dust outside, can't we, Hillela?— They were in Dar es Salaam for a day or two, and Hillela, keeper of the papers and briefcases, was part of Dr Adlestrop's gatherings of useful contacts in the bar of the Agip Hotel. Neither Udi nor Christa encountered her, she was not available—in meetings, when Christa phoned—and Udi she called from the airport only just before she left; a voice he could attach only to the flamingo-girl in the pink skirt.

—How do you look now?— It was his way of asking many things.

—I don't know.— The line drew a long hum of passing time between them. —I really don't know. I'm so busy.—

—I didn't know where to reach you—well, I could easily have found out from the office here. But I just wanted to tell you you'd be all right. That time. And it might have been the last thing you could bear to hear.—

—Udi, I've got to go now.—

—Yes of course. But if you suddenly phone when you know the flight is going to be called, it means you want to say something, Hillela.—

—Udi? No ... just to say hello. I'm too tired to think of anything—and there are meetings to prepare for the moment we arrive back in the U.S. So much I haven't written up.—

—You, a bureaucrat. I didn't think that was the way you'd be all right. Well.

—What other way is there. If you're not carrying a gun in the bush you have to do it with documents and committees. I'm not a bureaucrat, I have to use bureaucracy.—

—You must be formidable. You sound it. But I can't imagine ... Hillela, your voice is just the same, you know.—

—You have to dig up bad consciences and good intentions and put them both on the line. Give them no out. Confront them with the way you've calculated they can give you what you want while they're using this in their own interests. That may be to build up one of their 'caring images' before some election or get them promoted to responsibility for a funded project. You have no idea what it's like, Udi.—

—I hope not. You didn't ever use those kinds of words ... And your child, the little boy—

—Nomzamo. For Nelson's wife. Oh she's got the Americans wound round her fat finger, all of five years old now ...—

314

—She must be just like you.—

—The time I wasted. I should have learned the things I need now. I've had to teach myself how to prepare budgets and estimates—

—What are you going to do, Hillela?—

—What d'you mean?—

—You know what I mean. Is it going to be for the rest of your life ... oh Hillela.—

—Do what I'm doing. Looking for ways to free Whaila.—

That was why she had not been able to go away without reaching him: he was the one who would understand what she had just said. That was his place. He was ashamed to think she could hear the weakness of emotion that changed his voice. —That drudgery ... for you ... and what can that sort of thing achieve. It will be the big powers who'll decide what happens to blacks. And the power of other black heads of state influencing the big powers. A waste, yes... it's *this* that's a waste of your life— The line cut off. He waited, but she did not ring again. She must be walking to the plane with that old ghoul who grinned as if from a bridal group in newspaper photographs of people who would kill or be killed when she had gone.

If Hillela Kgomani had not a spare moment to see old friends, she found time to meet people from the African National Congress. Not in their office (which was why she missed running into Christa) but at a private house. This suggests that if it were true she had been expelled from the movement while in Eastern Europe, she was back in favour. Maybe had earned her way by turning some of the paper-rustling drudgery to the organization's advantage in the unpromising conditions of the United States. It is also possible she was never expelled at all, but that this was a planned pretext to get her into the States in the status of disaffection (as the euphemism for defection goes) so that she could work secretly on the prospects of getting a mission opened there.

315

Certainly in the early Seventies offices were opened in New York, for the first time. Probably she was working for the organization all along, under the spread breast-feathers of mother hen Leonie and her aid and research projects in many African countries. Bradley Burns, who is given to quiet analysis of the time when he was the man in a position to know, says she confused him. Deliberately. At times it was clear that for her only sexual love— and oddly this included her feeling for the little girl— was to be trusted. All the rest (his phrase) was shit and lies. And he did not know whether she was thinking of the killing of her husband, or some other kind of treachery that happened to her while she was in exile politics in Eastern Europe. Then at other times she could also say love 'can't be got away with'; or it wasn't 'enough'. What she seemed to mean by this last was that in spite of all evidence against it, another kind of love had to be risked.

Acronyms the language of love. United States Institute for African-American Cooperation, USIFACO; Third World Committee for Africa, TWOCA; Operation Africa Education, OPAD; Co-ordinating Committee for Africa, COCA; Commission for Research into Under-development, CORUD; Foundation for Free People, FOFREP. The child plays with alphabetical blocks on the floor, builds houses with them. A career can be built out of acronyms; everyone here must have a career, you fulfil yourself with a career, there are books that specify what a career is by listing what is available. Pauline would be happy, she was more than willing to supply the advantage of a career, whatever Sasha said. Leonie couldn't have done more if it had been for her own daughter; Leonie will go on with her promotion, beavering away. Leonie knew him. Leonie is the only person in the board rooms, at the working breakfasts in motels, at the Thanksgiving dinner, who knew him—the one who came out just like him does not remember. Not even a trauma to know him by; she was carried away with a towel across her eyes so that she would not see what was on the kitchen floor.

Twenty, forty years after they have received the advantages of a career they still form their version of a songololo, *singing their songs as they stride along under the same elm trees in the same avenue. Everything remains in place, for them. The storm windows will be put up, as theirs are, every late autumn and removed to let the smell of spring in. The namesake will grow up as a little black American with civil rights and equal opportunity to protect her, like everybody else, and the distinction of her African names to assert that individuality everyone here says is so important in making a career. She won't have to have engraved on her bracelet,* I am me; *she'll say,* I'm Nomzamo Kgomani, *and that will impress.*

No need ever to run out of acronyms. There is a career of continued useful service ahead; there is the example of Leonie, loverless lover of all those she is entitled to call by their first names, fulfilment (as they sum up, here) shining out of every group photograph in which she appears. But no need to emulate entirely. The documentation will be read in bed beside a young man advancing well in his own career, ready to help with the dishes and to perform—woman, man, and the little black daughter he regards as his own—the safe and pleasant rituals of a family, here; parent-teacher co-operation, playing games, going to the lake shack and Cape Cod house.

The real family, how they smell. The real rainbow family. The real rainbow family stinks. The dried liquid of dysentery streaks the legs of babies and old men and the women smell of their monthly blood. They smell of lack of water. They smell of lack of food. They smell of bodies blown up by the expanding gases of their corpses' innards, lying in the bush in the sun. Find the acronym for her real family.

Housewarming

Bradley was her own age, like the men the young alumnae had. He was an economist with a promising position in a multinational company. His grandfather had been one of the editors of *The New Republic,* an associate of Edmund Wilson, and a victim of the McCarthy hearings. The leftist tradition was a family heirloom sufficient in itself; a claim to a way of life that no longer actually need be practised, just as the painting of an ecclesiast ancestor in ermine on the wall is prestige enough for descendants who never go to church. It was adequate for the family image to be brushed up from generation to generation during the youthful period when the social conscience, along with spontaneous erections, naturally evinces itself. Brad had done his stint—in opposition to the Vietnam war, and a year with an aid agency in India. Now he could settle down with the complete set of *The New Republic* published during his grandfather's years, on display in his study—handed down to him as a housewarming present when he found his own brownstone.

Of course people with his parents' background would not show any reaction to the appearance of a black child with their son's new friend. And when the explanation came, bringing into the big living-room with its grand piano (Brad and his mother played), New England samplers and bowls of tulips, distant horrors the Burnses were accustomed to being able to shrink with the flick of a switch to blank on the face of the television, this provided proof by association that they were still on the right side, just as, conversely, guilt by association provided danger for those other parents, Pauline and Joe. The parents' house was a generous thoroughfare where the adult children made their long-distance telephone calls, cooked, borrowed cars and electrical equipment, used the basement laundry, slept over with friends or lovers; snatches of their independent lives were enacted there—before Hillela, or even drawing her in—whose contexts were elsewhere. Brad's 'find', brought home (good for him!), was just such a snatch of his life. The brothers and sisters chattered with her, regaled themselves with laughter when they encouraged her cute little black girl to be sassy, and were lavish with invitations for brother to bring her along to jazz clubs, sailing trips, cinemas and parties.

Only Brad was quiet. He watched and listened to the girl and her child he had contributed, getting on so well with his siblings. The pair represented him in the way he could not represent himself, now that these brothers and sisters were no longer children.

He was quiet when he made love the first time. Nothing in the room, in the world, would distract him from the act of worship now approached, and his trance produced blind excitement in which only the body knew its way. When she was seeing with her eyes again she smiled appreciatively, cheekbones lifting a little fold under her dark, lazy gaze. And he spoke.

—Was it the first thing you saw.—

—Yes. I thought of a puppy, the kind with a velvety patch over one eye.— She withdrew her lax hand from between his arm and side and stroked the dark birth-blot that all his life others pretended was not there.

This man talked after love-making. Not the mumblings of dreams and names in a Slav language, but a wide-awake fluency, entered by way of her body. He told again and again: —Hillela, I don't care how many lovers you've had, no-one can have loved you as I do.—

She did not ask how he knew she had had many lovers; it was simply one of his qualities that he knew things about her without troubling her with questions, sensitive to the repetition of certain names in her conversation and able to read changes in her expression when certain subjects arose. She did not answer; sometimes smiled at him as she did at her child, but never in disparagement or disbelief. The fact that she believed him, when all that he could find to express so great a conviction was something like the line from a stupid song—this tortured him. He had to try and follow her reasoning; there must be a reasoning, and the reasoning would establish the state of the emotions between them.

—I'm not saying anything about him ... And not just because he's dead. (A gesture, acknowledging that unchallengeable rivalry.) I'll never pry into your feelings for each other. Whatever they were. I'm talking about the nature of mine. That's what I mean.— But then he saw to what he might be leading. —No, no, it's not because of what you think, Hillela. The puppy isn't licking your hand.—

And again, in her apartment, with the door slightly ajar because the small girl in the next room insisted it be so: —Hillela, I really cannot live without you again. Not what you think, no. It's because there's something a bit frightening in you; it's that I can't do without.—

This time she laughed.

—How can I say that to you. You'll tell me one can live without anyone. You know. Lying here in bed with me, you're the proof, aren't you—

She was propped on one elbow, listening to him. She fell upon him and he rolled over with her.

Without explanation, there were times when she took up something he had approached in some other room, some other night.

—Whaila had another wife. Nomzamo's got brothers and sisters she hasn't seen yet.—

—A divorced wife.—

—I don't know if they were divorced, really.—

320

—What if he'd lived, and one day gone back to her and the other children? That's the kind of living without I mean.—

—We had our time together. She must have had hers ... If we had been able to go back!— She stopped and slowly her hands made fists, came to rest on her naked thighs; the unselfconsciousness with which she accepted her nudity in moods and situations now removed from sex reminded him strangely of the women in Pascin and Lautrec brothel drawings seen in art galleries. —If he had lived to go back—oh, that would have been another time, that would have been ... that would have been ...—

—More than *love*.—

—Oh why this measuring, how can you measure?—

—Yes. Something I'll never know: exaltation. And awfulness. The way you have. Yes, you are a bit frightening. But I'll get used to you. No—I don't want to get used to you, I never shall.—

He had a long face with a slender nose the everted curve of whose nostrils was exactly repeated in the upward and downward curves of his upper lip. The skin of his throat below the shaving line was tender and fine down to the breastbone and its cup where a few glossy curls of chest hair began. The pulse in the throat was always visible and the network of nerves round the mouth and nose seemed like those of some sensitive plant—every face has them, but they are sluggish or hampered by a layer of fat or a thickened hide, while his changed his expression with every nuance of atmosphere generated by the people around him.

So he was beautiful—except for *that,* it had always been said with suitable regret. Among the commissioned pastel portraits of each of the Burns sons and daughters as children, his was in profile—the 'good' side. His mother, when he was small, had made a habit of kissing him goodnight on the birthmark, so that the imprint of the kiss became for him the disfigurement; later, a vague forgiveness for what he did not know he had done—forgiveness for the 'bad' side. Now the two sides had come together by the unimaginable means of a rather tactless and childish remark. *I thought of a puppy, the kind with a velvety patch over one eye.* It had happened as a Zen sage flings enlightenment at disciples in the form of an outrageous and flippant half-sentence.

He sat in the audience listening to her speak on public platforms, sometimes with the namesake on his lap. The young woman up there was scarcely to be distinguished from the other men and women on the panels of the committed, wearing with them the much-washed clothing, varied only by slogans printed across backs or breasts, with which they showed their identification with the causes of the poor and oppressed by assuming their characteristic markings, as a certain kind of moth disguises the fact that it is alive and free by keeping perfectly still and exhibiting the lineaments of a skull on its wingspread. The blunt-cut nails of her clenched hands, as she opened them to emphasize a fact, were short as those of women she had walked with as they scratched for roots to eat, and her curly hair was cropped without consideration for looks but as it was done as a mass precaution for hygiene in refugee camps, among the lice-ridden. Now she was talking not of refugee camps but of three political trials that had taken place in South Africa in a year. —All real opposition is on trial as terrorist and communist. Four people were sentenced to five years' imprisonment for smuggling anti-apartheid pamphlets and records into the country; only four, because the fifth accused, a schoolteacher, thirty years old, Ahmed Timol, died by falling from the tenth floor of police headquarters while the police were interrogating him. In the Mzimela trial, a young man was sentenced to fifteen years in prison. What had he done? He left the country secretly and fought with the Rhodesian freedom fighters against Smith's illegal white regime, he attended the Morogoro liberation conference, and he re-entered his home country to organize support for the banned African National Congress. Are these people, risking their lives to be free of racial oppression, criminals? I knew

Mzimela in Tanzania. Yes, he was like many others; he went to the Soviet Union and to East Germany for military training because the West, which created South Africa militarily and economically, does nothing to influence the South African government to free people like him, neither will it help them to free themselves. Did any of these people on trial kill anyone in South Africa? There was one act of violence involved—and one only: when Timol's life, in the care of the South African police, smashed on concrete—

The namesake sang softly in his ear; she did not like attention to be on her mother instead of herself. Her breathy buzzing was warm on his skin; it roused him alarmingly, it was the warmth and humidity of Hillela, who—difficult to believe—existed within the specifications of an impersonal function, up there, the simplified, line-drawn figure from a banner or poster, among the ritualistic paraphernalia of water carafes and glasses, microphone and tape-recorders, scratchpads and pencils stamped with the acronym appropriate to the occasion.

She continued with the work although it kept them apart too often; it had more, even, than the connotations of a career, and commanded more respect from him and others. He had frequently to explain she couldn't accompany him because she was put of town or even out of the country. When there was mumps or measles in the namesake's usual surrogate homes, he took her into his calm bachelor brownstone during her mother's absence, and called in one of his willing sisters to help take care of her. Hillela often brought Leonie's trophies into his company, along with Leonie. He met all kinds of interesting people he never would have met, without Hillela; more than he had known since India. They carried with them demands that stretched muscles of response which atrophy where a common background provides always foreseeable demands and appropriate ways of meeting them. There was the supercilious black journalist from South Africa, a Nieman fellow, who tried to provoke him into academic quarrels over economic theory when sober, but with whom he got rather happily drunk whenever the fellow came over from Cambridge for a weekend. There was the black woman with purplish hollows under her eyes—combined with the bewilderment in her face, these appeared to be the marks of unseen blows— who flung herself in tears to embrace Hillela. That woman drank only Coke. It was another kind of intoxication that compelled her to explain to everyone: —She was just a kid, when we slept at her people's place that night we left the country. I'll never forget those people, they did everything for us. And look—how she's grown up just as good as her mother! How can I forget how her mother drove us to the border in her own car? Packed up food for the children. I always say it to Donsi.—

—We danced with him, that night, my cousin and I. It wasn't my mother, it was my aunt who drove you.—

Bradley followed attentively the stumbling, laughing excursion into Hillela's adolescence, which he had tried to explore for himself— wrongly, he knew—in terms of his own.

—Look at her! Even though politically we're not on the same side—

Leonie put an arm round the woman. —Bongi dear, we don't recognize any split in the liberation movement, PAC or ANC, in my house. We're a bit premature, we know, but here we have African unity!—

—Just like her mother, not like other whites at home, she's in the struggle, like a real black girl.—

—Where's your *real* black girl, Hillela?— Leonie gleefully stage-managed her party. —Somebody go get Nomzamo to meet her mother's old friend Bongi.—

Samora Machel came to the brownstone with Leonie and Hillela, though it was kept out of the papers that he was in the U.S.; Leonie was on such close terms with FRELIMO that she was now a prohibited immigrant in Mozambique as well as

South Africa. SWAPO Ovambos from Namibia bent their heads, huge with great beards meeting their thick hair, in comradely embrace of Whaila Kgomani's widow. Patrice M'ba, slender, neatly-shod and elegant as the French masters who had a price on his head in his own country, talked with another Hillela, one who spoke the language with softness, as if it had been learnt in some intimacy whose cadence it kept. With others, there was no nuance for Bradley to pick up—Marc Nzōkou, the Cameroonian who had been in prison in four countries, having each time sought refuge just before coups that changed Pan-African alliances; disaffected Ghanaians; a Somali novelist for whom Leonie had found a publisher; another exile, Reuel (surname unpronounceable), who always sat aloofly in a room as if there only for someone influential he'd been promised and who wasn't present. These were the material or rather the subjects of the Work; merely associated in her future husband's mind with the purposeful young woman's dedication to their cause.

It was taken for granted by everyone that that was what he was going to be—Leonie's fine young woman's new husband. His father thought she was very lucky to have caught his son. He said so to the boy's mother—fine young woman without much of a background, from all appearances, and saddled with a small child; Brad was so young. The mother was the one who played Schubert with Brad. —*Appearances.* He isn't concerned with appearances. If he had been, his life would have been spoiled, wouldn't it? Have you forgotten that? Brad is used to difficulties, he's not shallow like some of our other children. He wouldn't be satisfied with one of the girls he went to college with. He's like my father.—

Hillela moved again in the spring of the third year in the United States; but not on. Merely a practical domestic move, just down the road from the apartment where the namesake would never allow a door to be shut, to the brownstone whose mortgage was being regularly paid off. It was foolish to waste a monthly sum for housing in two places. That was how he broached it. She was delighted. He saw she was delighted. She was shelling peas; she took him by the shoulders, at arms' length, and her eyes held him in that gaze of hers. —Brad, you're so good to us. It'll be so much more convenient, when I have to be away. Nomo loves the yard. Will you put up a swing for her?— And then the kisses, tasting green of the vegetable she ate while she shelled. *She* was so good, so generous with herself, as if the bountiful pleasures welled up in her, the more she gave—here, here, Brad—the more she had to give. Nomzamo, possessive about her new room, reversed her edict about doors: all had to be closed. And all was open, to him, the pale mushroom flesh discovered under sunburned breasts, the little twirled butter-curl of the navel, the cleft of buttocks, the hollow beside the poor crooked toe, the satin-walled cave of the mouth, the triumphal way between thighs. Usual enough to become erect, alone in an office thinking back on the night or early morning; but he found himself actually trembling.

The brownstone investment contained the imbalance of luxury and austerity common in the household of a bachelor in the intellectual professions. The floors had been sanded and the bookshelves put up from floor to ceiling when he moved in, but some rooms were empty of anything else, and others had pieces of inherited furniture for which no definitive location had yet been found. There was a bed of the size that can be bought only in America, hemmed in by hi-fi installations and towers of books and newspapers. There was a large empty freezer but few pots, a microwave oven and lattice wine-rack, but no cupboard for basic supplies. Some of the empty rooms quickly filled up with the child's possessions—bicycle and doll's house in the livingroom, construction sets fragmented all over what was supposed to be the study; in the bathroom, drawings of happy houses with smoking chimneys, moons and suns, and a male, female and child, figures whose faces sometimes were all crayoned black, and sometimes pink.

The bachelor and the child; there was still no provision for the median mode of living. —We've got to decide how we want it all to be. What suits us. We must sit together and make a list, room by room—

Hillela took his hand. —What's wrong with the way it is? I like your house.—

—Yes, but it's our house. There're things we need that I didn't. What kind of furniture did you like—where you lived ... What are the sort of things you miss?—

She was at once, in the new familiarity of the kitchen, in her nightgown, a stranger to him, smiling. —From where? My one aunt had antiques—rather like your parents', but more elaborate. She collected. In the Embassy where I worked, everything was a diplomatic issue—gilt this and that—standard, nobody chose it.—

—I mean, when I think ... I have had my paternal grandfather's desk since I was fourteen.—

—I had a pair of Japanese china cats. I gave one away, I don't know where the other is.—

—I'll get you a real cat. Much nicer. We ought to have a cat sitting here on the window-sill.—

—In Lusaka the flat was furnished.—

—I see.—

—And in Europe.—

—Well, now we're going to find out the kind of thing you really like. We can mix contemporary styles with my stuff, or we can hunt around for the same Early American period. Whatever you want.—

On Saturdays they went to antique fairs and bric-à-brac shops crowded with the continuity of his past—the cigar-store Indians as well as the samplers—and to the clinical, glassy spaces where contemporary Japanese- and Italian-designed furniture looked ready to accommodate extraterrestrials only. They bought a child's

19th-century naïvely-painted bed and modern Czech lamps, absolutely functional. She chose an old patchwork bedcover whose price he concealed from her (she might be thinking how many antibiotics for wounded freedom fighters in Machel's, Mugabe's or Reuel's country those dollars would buy). They found a New England farmhouse table to go with the six chairs he had inherited from Big Uncle Robert (not to be confused, he explained dryly, making fun of the hierarchy, with Boston Uncle Robert, the offshoot of another Burns branch). Laughing and staggering, with the namesake running wild around them, they lugged heavy pots of decorative plants to the windows. They were always within touch and happiness came simply, like sweat from activity; he looked across at her while they paused to drink coffee, and saw the faint lift of the flesh at the corners of the eyes; for him. She was, as Leonie remarked, 'blooming'.

The house had turned out rather like the parents' house. The objects from the past gave it the soft patina of somewhere long lived in and the products of high technology brought it alive in the current phase of the Burns chronology. Mrs Burns told Brad's future wife secretly that she was going to give him the piano; it was not only for him, the little Nomzamo was old enough to begin taking lessons. Every Burns child started at the age of six or seven. She never forgot how the girl, Hillela, embraced her, moving—a stranger's—curly head against her shoulder, as if she could not find words. There was no doubt that the emotion was genuine, no doubt at all. That girl understood, all right, that with the piano Brad was being given into her hands; as a secret between two women who loved him.

There was certainty, waking up in the morning. It flowed in with the light every day. Depend on it. The beautiful young man sleeping beside her; a pale body like her own, the body familiar as that of a brother. He would get up soon and go to his office—a real office, glass rearing up to the open sky confidently without need of protection—and come back safely every evening when the glass became a giant painting of the sunset. The huge bed into which they slid as an envelope of warmth and comfort was not on loan; nobody else's clothes would hang in the cupboard. No need to watch out about how to manage—make out, the way people do it; not here. No caution necessary about whom you are seen with, because their factions are all announced out loud with brass bands and rosettes. No need to watch for what can be traded—searching pockets for attributes: martyr's wife, expressive Latin eyes and large breasts, the probably unacceptable currency of avowal to a revolutionary cause—in exchange for a stamp on a piece of paper. Once married to a bona fide citizen of a country already existing and not still to be won back, there is full citizenship of the present.

She lay following the flaxen and gold threads shaded horizontally in the hand-woven curtains they'd chosen. —Like a field of grass.—

—Yes, they're a real success. What do we still need?—

—Nothing. Nothing.—

—There's always something you discover you still need.—

—Stop it. Stop measuring.—

His slender hand moved over her head as over a piece of sculpture. He received her fastidiously through all the senses.

—I want you to grow your hair.—

Softly stroking, now and then stiffening his fingers to press the plates of the skull.

She said nothing, perhaps took the request merely as a murmured endearment, along with the caress.

—No.— Her eyes moved rapidly under the thin skin of closed lids. —No, it's not practical.—

She jumped out of bed and then stood stock-still as if she had suddenly discovered where she was; then busied herself, drawing the curtains, picking up discarded clothing.

He closed his eyes for the pleasure of hearing her moving about near him. He put out a hand where he thought she was passing, but it caught at air.

The wedding of Mrs Hillela Kgomani and Bradley Burns was delayed several times—not through her, one would never have suspected anything capricious about her. For family reasons. The death of Mr Burns's brother; the absence of two of the sisters at summer school in Florence. She was always understanding about such things, not selfish the way most young women would have been. And his mother knew why. —She's lived. She's been through a lot in her young life.— The future husband accepted the family claims because Hillela did—Hillela had never known what it was to be at the centre of a family (future wife of the eldest son); the comfort and protection of its place in a homogeneous society. Anyway she was his wife already, they had made a home together in the brownstone that would never have been one without her. His only unease—not a fear, half-developed—was again that he might be changing her by the cherishing; whereas he wanted to be transformed by her. And so the one time the marriage was delayed for her reasons this was an opportunity for self-testing. She was going with Leonie to the country from which one of Leonie's trophies, Reuel, was exiled, where the civil war had produced a terrible exodus of Southerners to refuge in the North. He knew it was dangerous although Leonie's vocabulary turned bullets to water and blunted spears—they would 'liaise' with the U.N. High Commissioner for Refugees, the 'logistics' provided for military escorts and 'safe conducts'. The cholera areas would be no go. The prophylactics were standard prescription. —We'll most likely meet a lot of great people and have an inspirational time, Brad, the horror stories you keep hearing are months old, it's always like that. I'd have spent my life on my front porch and never been any use to anyone if I'd listened to people's disinformation.—

He delivered Hillela to the airport an hour after making love at five in the morning. He had said nothing, but the fear and anguish in the transparent control of his face had made her suddenly notice, and come back to the bed from folding something into her suitcase, smiling to blot out his wretchedness. He let her go. Greater than the reassurance in his body was the reassurance that he could pass the test. He would risk her, to keep her as she was.

She drank the water and ate the forbidden fruit. Of course she returned safely. These trips to misery under the sun grotesquely produced the sunburnished forehead and wind-scoured hair others brought back from Florida or the Bahamas. It was difficult to believe where she had been, what she had seen. Frightening; he embraced it all in her. It seemed the hair was a little longer, she had not cut it again, but he didn't make any remark for fear of spoiling a slow surprise that was being prepared for him. She was working very hard at her reports and papers, consulting people here, hopping on local planes there (back to him by evening). In their bed, or drinking wine in deck-chairs under their yard elm, he shared it all. Everything was recounted. Over the forest the burned villages seen from a helicopter like black holes in a green blanket, and as the craft swooped low, the pink palms upturned from black arms, beckoning for help— —And what could you do, for Christ' sake?— —Oh the surveyor with us pinpointed each place on a special map, supplies were dropped to them within the next few days.— —Some would die before then. Some of the hands wouldn't be there to take the food.— —Yes, some would die.— Those steady black eyes held; turned away from nothing.

—It couldn't simply have been a matter of what you grab first from all that must be left behind; not the things I saw. A woman with a mincer, one of those old-fashioned ones with a handle to turn, you know? She had nothing else—in rags; she must have abandoned or bartered for food everything else she'd managed to salvage. Those people had walked two hundred miles from their village. Another one had a heart-shaped mirror with a little wire stand at the back. And her baby. I saw her looking at herself. I saw a man almost kill another because that one wanted to kill the rabbit—no, must have been a hare, there aren't any wild rabbits in Africa—he'd carried god knows how far in a cage made of twigs. They were both starving. There're things people can't live without.—

He stared and half-smiled.

But she had forgotten. Only he would measure the stature of his claim, diminished to nothing beside the kind of needs she knew.

There were women who had been raped by soldiers, and school-children abducted for military training. —By which side?— She wasn't always clear. —And some lied.— She opened up under their feet the pit of wretchedness where what was true and what was not hardly had any meaning. How could she stand such ugly confusion? —But if they had been raped and mutilated?— —Yes, but some were being fed and looked after by other soldiers. They gave them their own rations. We saw that, too.— —It's sicken-ing. And what kind of decent regime can come out of people like that, even if they do win. From what you say, half the time they behave like the crowd they're trying to get rid of.— —Just as both sides have always done in every war. That crowd has to be fought with its own tactics—what else is war? You're a victim, or you fight and make victims. There's no other way. European coun-tries are training that crowd, giving them planes and arms. The others can fight back only if the rural people support them—even if they have to force them sometimes.—

Frightening. She took sides in the general horror, she condoned means for ends; but at the same time she wasn't looking on, no-one could say that of her, she was at home with polluted water and mined roads as well as in their brownstone. When he swelled with desire for her, he swelled also with admiration for her. Where is the line between lust and esteem? Hillela confused him, for ever.

She told him with true kindness, the impulse with which her guerrillas cared for some of the homeless and starving in their war. —Brad, I don't think you should marry me. I've been with Reuel, on and off, when I was in Africa. I don't think you'd be able to—well, to manage with that.—

He did not know where in the brownstone to go to get away from what he had heard, and he knew would never be unsaid, withdrawn by her. He blundered into the bathroom because there was a bolt on that door. Fixed to the tiles with plastic putty were the drawings of the stick-limbed, smiling symbols of Hillela, himself and the child, the happy family outside the house whose boldly smoking chimney signifies the security of the fireside.

A Face for a Postage Stamp

Reuel was the General—the General who had led an army coup in his country, returned it to civilian rule under his presidency, and then escaped when the former colonial power sent in paratroopers to restore the regime it favoured. Escaped with his life—the phrase goes; how manifest this was, in him. If he were in reach of a swimming pool, a river, the sea, he swam in all weathers in all countries, he could still run a mile (in his fifties, perhaps—he was discreet as an actress about his age), like all men who lead crowds and must be constantly visible, he needed only three or four hours' sleep a night, and he ate and drank greedily or could manage as well without sustenance for days. His wide and fleshy chest under barathea or blue lounge suit moved grandly with deep breaths, as if always fresh from some exhilaration.

The General did not tell her he could not live without her. It was in his face, and hers—they recognized it in each other without ever having it stated: each could live as long as individual life lasted, independent of anyone, in the momentum of moving on.

He did not take much notice of her, nor she of him, in the brownstone. Leonie was useful but he was too large in every way to be anyone's trophy. At finger-suppers and colloquies, boredom dulled his male responses and the efflorescence of his strong ability to attract. It was far away from that, on an evening in Nairobi when he and Hillela were having a drink after Leonie had retired to write up her journal, that the recognition was there. —The only old women I like around me are my mother and my grandmother. They made me, êh, Hillela? D'you know what name my mother gave me, my African name—it means 'God has done very well'.— Hillela laughed at his own estimate of himself, and he with her, confidently. —Isn't it a good thing to have a name to live up to? We Africans always give names that mean something, not your Marys and Johns—what does it mean to be a Mary, that you'll give birth without a man? Is that something you'd want for a daughter?—

—Good god, no. That's why I called her after Mandela's wife.—

—So you want to influence her to be an African liberationist, you want her to be a heroine?—

—God may have done very well with you ... but it doesn't always work out the way the parents intended. I'm named for a Zionist great-grandfather.—

—We'll give you an African name—oh I know you have one, I mean the first name. What can we call you?—

—Well, what do you suggest?—

—I'd have to know you better to find out. You know that the name has to do with many things, the circumstances when it is given. Whether there's been a drought, or a war.—

—What has already happened.—

—No, more important, what is going to happen. What the name will make happen.— The atmosphere between them took these swallow dips into seriousness, instantly skimming away. —D'you think I'd still be alive if God hadn't done so well!— The commanding shine that was always on his full face and majestic jowl used the dim theatrical lighting of the bar as a star performer attracts the following beam of a spotlight. A big hand with a thick ring embedded in the little finger covered hers a moment in the pleasure of laughter. —We're going to celebrate something—I don't know what.— He ordered champagne; she read the label—South African. But they didn't send the bottle back. They drank—to Mandela, to freedom. —Amandla!— The language was different from that of his people, but the meaning was the same: power. Their talk burrowed deeper and deeper into the night, safe from interruption. This was not West Africa, where a woman could be picked from any table as a dancing partner. —This kind of place isn't Africanised—you see that? Dull. It's still the European style, it belongs to the new white compound, businessmen, safari tourists, journalists instead of settlers, that's all—and the local bureaucrats—what does Leonie call them?—fat cats—for them it's just an extension of business lunches with foreigners at the Norfolk, it's got nothing to do with having a good time our way. West Africans haven't let the Muslims or the Christians tie them up inside themselves as they did on this side … That's why I like them. You know how it is in West Africa, if some fellows spread a mat and pray five times a day, there's still high-life in Ghana; if the nuns teach little black girls their catechism, there're still girls in Brazzaville who know how a woman should show herself off to a man—and the places where you can dance and drink! The blacks have taken over the European nightclub and made an African party out of it, êh. But here. It's the Arab religion more than the Christians. Can't drink, hide the women behind that ugly black cloth. It wasn't our way in Africa, we've always known how to enjoy life … even when they took us to sell as slaves, we sang and danced and the Arabs and the Christians only watched.—

—But you like the whites' champagne.—

—Why not. Even what the Boers make.— He emptied his glass.

—But you don't like the Arabs. That must be a difficulty.—

—Of course, we're allies—and at the U.N., as you know, without them … they're the ones who count with the European countries, East and West, and the Americans. What could we hope to do, on our own. But I'll tell you … their style doesn't appeal to me … not politically, either. Religious fatalism becomes fanaticism in politics. We Africans, we don't go in for jihads and suicide missions. We'll fight our enemies and die if we have to, but we'd rather kill and get away with it, êh, stay alive!— He laughed and filled their glasses with froth. —I don't mix politics and religion.

They didn't get me and I'm going back to fight for my people, no gods. God changes sides too often, for me. The people can worship whatever they like—sacred crocodiles, Mohammed—we are all men and women, êh. We don't know why we are in this world; we have religions to tell us why. So I'm a Catholic.—

—You're a Catholic?— Her face kept changing with enjoyment, curiosity, flashes of disagreement or fellow-feeling.

—Of course I'm a Catholic. Brought up in it. I was going to train for the priesthood, at one time. That's a fact! But once in this world, you have to decide what you are doing here. I became an African nationalist; but it wasn't the church, it was Marx who told me why that was. So I'm a Marxist. My own kind. A Catholic Nationalist Marxist— African-made—

—Like the nightclubs in West Africa.—

—No, don't laugh—it's part of the same thing. Whether I'm inside, in our bush headquarters, or outside, making deals with our brothers (oh of course, Arab brothers, too) or in bed with a woman, it's all part of my African-made—work, love-making, religion, politics, economics. We've taken all the things the world keeps in compartments, boxes, and brought them together. A new combination, that's us. That's why the world doesn't understand. We don't please the West and we don't please the East. We never will. We don't keep things separate. Isn't that what orthodoxy is—separation? We make our own mess of things. They interfere; we ask them to interfere—what else am I doing? What else were you doing in Europe? I don't know what you're doing in the United States—

She turned her face towards her palm, covering her mouth in a gesture as if to grant whatever he thought. He passed his ringed hand absently, without intimacy, down her cheek.

—We *ask* them to interfere because power—the question of power—always divides again the combination that it brought together, looks for strength outside the unity, breaking it. Then

337

the old gang— they come in again. The world powers. We fight their battles for them with our own. Everyone knows that. They send us guns and soup powder, êh. Some get the guns. That's the important thing, to be the side that gets the guns. You will never come to power on soup powder.—

—So I'm wasting my time.— A swig of evidence, she swallowed the champagne.

—If it's really only on soup powder ... That's all right for Leonie, people are suffering. But it won't stop the wars, and the wars make the refugees—

—Leonie knows that.—

—When I get back to the capital in my country, this time I'll have not only the arms to take power again, I'll have the money for development the other side can't get. You have to be in power to be able to feed your own people. You get there with guns and you stay there with money.—

A crowded bar has no attentive faces, no ballpoints moving over scratchpads ready to record. Someone with fibre coarse enough to grasp at the high-tension cable of power will not be distressed by what would fuse the gentle lamplight by which evenings pass in a brownstone. —What I thought I was doing ... I wanted to get rid of the people who came to the flat and shot Whaila. I knew who they were, by then. From him, and even before that, in Dar ... although I didn't realize. The farmers and businessmen and doctors and lawyers in parliament, sitting in that lovely old building at the Cape Town Gardens under the Mount Nelson Hotel, where I had such a good time as a kid, staying there with my aunt. The teachers in the girls' school I went to, the people I worked for in Johannesburg, the doctor, the advertising agency ones. Even the others. My other aunt and her husband—Joe, he was so wonderful to me—who tried to show me I ought to resist what was going to kill Whaila. Although it was no good. Not only because I treated them badly—but because all of them, *they let it happen.* I never understood my life until there he was. In the kitchen. It happened in the kitchen.—

He was listening without embarrassment or the simulated horror that invariably hid embarrassment when the subject came up; without the fatherly shelter of a Karel, the distraction of a Pavel, without even the perfect tender acceptance of the young man she was going to marry. He was looking at her, and he offered the cautery of desire for her: in her raw sorrow, far away, buried under the snow and the brownstone, she had felt that only a man could comfort for the loss of a man, only the smell of a man could make it impossible to disbelieve that a man actually came to an end on the kitchen floor.

When he spoke it was back on the level of conventional indiscretions that could be ignored in the light of day; he and she knew that when the bar closes and the music stops there are cockroaches and the sweat of cleaners. —And now? When did you marry the American fellow?—

—We're not married.—

—He seems—okay. Nice house. Leonie and her crowd. Good people.—

They smiled—at his dismissal or approval.

—It's been postponed a couple of times. Now until September.—

—What'd you actually mean by 'get rid'?—

—The same as you mean—when you talk about power. But now it's soup powder I've been doling out. Most of the time. Since Europe. When you see everything reduced to hunger, nothing, nothing but the terrible way eyes look at you, men, women, children, cattle, dogs—the eyes become the same—you can't remember anything else. You only want to find something to stuff in those mouths. You lose all sense of what you wanted to do. And the same thing with pain. You just want to stop it, for them, for the hour you're there with them. There's no other purpose you can even think about.—

His nostrils widened and his big mouth creased down in emotional rebuttal. —It's not for you. It's not for you to spend your young life with those poor devils—and I can call them that because they're my people, I've been one of them, I'm telling you, I've been without food or a place to go … That's not *getting rid*. I'm going to tell you something— But he glanced up away from her rapidly as if at some sudden presence invisible to her, and returned with a change of mind and tone. —Come along with me to Mombasa tomorrow, you need a day off. All that misery, it gets on a person's nerves.—

—Oh I can't, we're seeing Mzee in the morning.—

—Leonie will see the old Man. She'll do all the talking, anyway, you won't get a word in. You're not really necessary.—

—Of course not!— She laughed at the airy offence. —But she expects me, and it might be useful for me to know him.—

—He'd see you any time, as soon as he recognized your name. Come for the ride.—

—I've never been to Mombasa.—

—Beautiful. I'll drop you at the beach or the hotel—don't you want to swim? Bring your things… I'll be busy, you can do what you like. But we leave early, êh—five-thirty in the morning, can you get up?—

—I'll be up!—

—Of course you'll be up!—

—When would we get back?—

—Late tomorrow night. If it gets too late, we can find somewhere to sleep on the road. I have to be here by lunch-time, whichever way.—

—To see Mombasa! Why not?—

—But you better put on another dress …—

She amusedly presented herself, stretching her back upright against her chair, palms open. He gave her a quick, up-and-down military inspection. —Haven't you got something else? It's a five star, the hotel where we'll have lunch.—

The General saw in her, that first evening, someone who could keep abreast of him; moving on.

Shoved, the sliding doors of the wardrobe in her hotel room rolled back, lighting the interior. There hung the few garments of those who wear the sackcloth rejection of the West's plenty or the battledress of identification with an eternal guerrilla struggle of humans against the evil in themselves. She put on the garments every day, replacing dirty with clean. There was nothing that would please an exiled Third World general preparing his liberation army for reinvasion. She felt a sudden impatience with these jeans worn white at the knees and these baggy shifts. If the shops had been open—she had the impulse to buy that splashy African cotton and wrap herself in the fancy-dress 'confections' the beach girl had displayed on the camel-saddle chair at Archie's Atrium. She put out a shift and found some sort of token adornment in a necklace made of red seeds and porcupine quills—a tourist thing she had in her suitcase to take back as a gift for one of the Burns sisters who was looking after the child. The traveller's alarm clock beside her bed was set for five o'clock. This time, before she went off on a jaunt to the sea, she left a note. It was pushed under Leonie's door at dawn.

A navy-blue blazer with gold buttons swayed on a hook provided between the front and back windows of the hired car. The General wore pale beige tropical trousers with a crease ruled exactly down each monumental thigh, hand-stitched Italian brogues on high-arched feet, and a batiste shirt whose placket and buttons strained to contain the rise of a punchbag-hard belly and the spread of pectoral muscles. His big head almost grazed the roof; his presence filled the car, giving off the pleasant scent of good soap and after-shave cologne. When he got out and went into the bush to have a pee, his passenger felt the weight of that presence emphasized by its absence. The moments scarcely interrupted their talk; within the landscape they were cleaving— villages, cyclists, roaming children, distorted crones with loads of wood or produce supported by a thong across the forehead—they were in the familiar territory of exile, that knows no hemispheres; a globe of blank spaces between those areas where one has been allowed in, whose climates are characterised not by rainfall and temperature but by whether one is tolerated only in inactivity or may seek alliances, support, and bases. There was no need to censor. Each knew the social and personal codes and morality of that territory, which those who had never been there could not, need not, know. —How can you ever explain?— He knew she was talking of the finger-supper questions, silences (of judgment), assumptions of understanding that understood nothing. —I don't answer about Europe because no-one who hasn't worked that way there can follow. It's like when my little girl asks me where babies come from. I tell her. They grow in the mother's tummy. That's as far as she can go. Her innocence makes it unthinkable she could grasp how they get there—and more important, why. She doesn't know enough to want to ask. The questions aren't even ever the right questions—you know what I mean? In each society there's a different way of putting things, a different way of interpreting what happens or what's been said. What seems a lie to someone at Leonie's wouldn't be one somewhere where relations between people take place in completely different circumstances—politically, socially, oh, every way there is. Every way they can't imagine.—

—That's what makes the easy life tough in the States.— A glance, to see her laugh. —It's happened to me, too. But what about the other way round? The other side of the world? Got to wear a different hat there, êh.—

—People seem—older.—

—Not so much innocence and icecream.—

—The trouble there's more likely to be they're on to everything you haven't said, when you ask or answer ... But *your* hat's always the one with gold braid, everywhere.—

—The best place is here and now, on this road in Africa, with no hat on at all. Bare head, bare-foot. The chance doesn't come too often. (His passenger had taken off her sandals and was lying back with her feet up on the dashboard.) D'you want to drive for a bit? The road will be passing through the Tsavo reserve soon and we can't change over among the lions.—

In command of a hired car, alone in the front with a casual acquaintance asleep on the rear seat (—I need to be fresh for what I have to do when we arrive—) there was in this trivial and marginal circumstance a sense of being that really belonged with permanence, not a day-trip. He rumbled a little, an inactive but not extinct volcano, back there. She snuffed at the old hot smells of grass digested and excreted, of wet grass growing, blowing with the wind-flow of her speed, that flushed away the scent of after-shave. The road was empty; the rump of a buck or two whom the approach of the car startled long before she was close enough to see more. At a detour she scarcely slowed down on the loop of sand road. The car sang a different tune, shuddering softly over corrugations beneath a fluffy surface. Then the wheel was wrenched away under her hands—she clutched at it, shocked, almost laughing, on a roller-coaster—and the space that enclosed her and the sleeping man went wild, displaced fiercely this way and that, back and forth across the road. She had her foot down on the brake as if on the stirrup of a bucking monster, the wheel twirled uselessly, the enclosed space tilted sideways, righted, tilted completely, she was upside-down, struck on the head, feeling at the same instant a huge thud at her back.

The car landed on its four wheels and careered away through grass and trees, hitting nothing and coming to a stop where its own momentum ended. She had been thrown into the empty seat beside her. She saw him struggling up from the floor behind with the grouchy clumsiness of someone inconsiderately woken by a shake on the arm. He must have unfastened the buckle of his elegant belt for ease before he took a nap, and his first instinct was to close it dignifiedly. She began to laugh. He saw her laughing at him with eyes shaking and glittering with tears. The tears splashed onto her mouth: he laughed at her. —My God, what did you do? What did you do?—

She could not stop laughing. —Woke you up. Sorry I woke you up.—

—My God, what did you do?—

Their amazement at being unhurt turned to euphoria. The doors were not jammed; they got out of the car and examined each other, knees, arms, heads. —Are you sure you're all right? You can't be all right?— —But I am! Maybe a bump'll come up here on my head.— He took her head entirely between his hands and felt it all over. —Does it hurt here? Here? —No. No. Just a little there, where I told you.—

—No sign of a cut. You should let your hair grow, it's a protection.— —Idiot, idiot I am, I braked. Everyone's taught never to brake in a skid. I knew it, but I didn't do it.—

He got into the car and it started at the turn of the ignition key. Their faces exchanged triumph as he looked up at her through the window. —I've never before believed in miracles.— —But I'm a Catholic, so I do.—

Slowly rolling back to the road; she gave a little shudder and put her hand, as if to steady herself, on his broad knee as he drove. It was the touch with which they had examined each other for hurt. Quiet and emptiness of the landscape closed over the startling rupture as if it had never happened. A few hundred yards from where they had broken into the environment with their steel capsule gone amuck, he stopped the car, took up her hand and pointed it into the trees. Five or six elephants were browsing there at various distances, to be made out, patiently, one by one, by the fan of ears like giant leaves among dark foliage or the stir of a tree-trunk become a huge foot; had been there in their vast and dreamy existence, outside the short violent incident taking place in human time. If the skid had happened a few hundred yards farther along the road, the car would have burst down upon the beasts with an alien present. The car and its occupants could have been crumpled like a chocolate wrapper under their rage. The travellers sat in silence watching life on this grand scale of size and time. —It's not so easy to kill me. It's been tried three times.— He was looking out turned half-towards her with his elbow leaning on the open window and his hand hanging on the steering wheel: a face composed always to be observed, ambivalent nuance erased, features boldly and definitively simplified for emphasis. A face for a postage stamp.

—Shall I tell you something?— From the moving car the forest scrub they were passing through again appeared uninhabited. They were alone as human beings are alone only among animals. —What I'm going to do when we get there? Certain people I'm going to meet? Nobody else in the world knows this, it's going to happen in Mombasa because in Nairobi everyone's got big ears. I'm going to meet people who are willing to kidnap my son.—

Willing? But she asked nothing, her attention fixed hovering on the hieroglyph of a profile. The small nose, whose nostrils rested low and broad seen full-face, was curved, polished along an arch of bone like a weapon lodged in the flesh.

—My son, that I trained in my own army, he was one of those who threw over my government. Yes, he was willing to have me killed. Now he's going to have his chance: they'll bring him to our bush headquarters and there, in the North, where we're in control again, I'll give him the choice—to defect to us.—

He was waiting to see if there was any need to explain what could not be said, whether the experience of this white girl with

345

whom nothing had needed an explanation so far, went so far as to 'follow him' as she would put it.

She did not ask the question. Without moving his head he slid his glance. Her head was cocked back as if she had taken a deep breath, but the full lovely breasts were stirred only regularly, calmly, shallowly. She asked a different question; and that was his answer. —Your only son?—

—No. The eldest—by the second wife. The first has daughters. My eldest—and the best of them. Right from the day he began to walk.—

Alone on an East African beach again, among strangers. The General dropped her where there was no tamarisk but the same cloisters of palms to stroll along, and a swim was a gentle engulfment through ghost-pale shallows until the body was taken, like the streak of another substance into the watery layers of an agate, into the still, clear sea. Lusaka was landlocked, Eastern Europe and the brownstone locked each year in snow, in West Africa the open surf flung high and hissing upon sand tainted with cholera. She went back into the Indian Ocean through groups of tourists talking German, English children squealing, and a few black rocks, stepped round, that were African bodies. She floated and recalled without pain the yellow swimsuit and the emergence of the obsidian arms, head and torso from the sea. The water itself washed pain away; there was only the sensuality with which it did. She floated, and had nothing in the world but a pair of jeans held together with a safety-pin.

The General did not arrive for lunch at the five-star hotel. She waited at the terrace bar, as arranged, and lazily refused the approaches of a handsome young German who had noticed her on the beach and now offered a Pimm's Cup. As the bar emptied towards two o'clock, he did not believe she was really expecting any particular man (a girl like her would not be waiting for a woman) and came up to her again, his flat pink ears gristly clean and his blond hair marked round the hairline with dried salt. She shook her head, but with a smile that softened offence. —Anozzer time, maybe?— She ate a sandwich in place of the five-star lunch and gave the barman a note, describing to whom it was to be handed: —A large man in a blue blazer and beige pants. African.—

In the hotel's glossy gallery of shops she amused herself. There were the carved tusks and cotton galabiyas she had once sold but there was also a jeweller's with amber from the Persian Gulf and a boutique displaying silk tunics and suède jackets: she went in and suddenly was trying on the kind of clothes she had not worn since Olga had taken her shopping each change of season. The adjustable mirrors showed a triptych of anxious concentration, making decisions between garments she was not going to buy anyway. With this or that one, she met—stopped dead by, as it were—herself, remarkably elegant; a possibility never considered. A whole hour in the booth smelling of other women's perfume! Agitated, she fished her shift and spiky necklace from behind the layers of fancy dress, but as she was about to leave the shop, came back and did buy something, a French bikini swimsuit she had seen in the window before she first entered. She had brought a traveller's cheque along with her because the jaunt was in the company of someone she hardly knew, and Mrs Whaila Kgomani was no longer a beach girl.

The General came onto the terrace a moment after she was back there. He was carrying the blazer looped by one finger over his shoulder and his tie was loosened, but whatever experience he was fresh from left him unmarked in contrast with the attack of lust whose evidence was beside her in a black-and-gold plastic bag and the tendrils of hair stuck in sweat on her forehead. He was unperturbed at having missed lunch, or having been kept waiting by her when he did arrive: —I went to freshen up.— At ease with the rituals of five-star hotels, he looked a moment at his nails, twisting into place the ring that had been turned by a towel. The long time they had known each other—all that had passed since five-thirty that morning—made apologies understood, as between partners preoccupied in a joint enterprise not to be trivialised.

—Is everything all right?— Her words were almost those they had used to assure no bones were broken.

—That depends on him.— His eyes moved rapidly in confirmation of orders gone over. —Whether he resists—really.— The eyes fixed on her. —I've told them to be careful.—

She did not arrive back in Nairobi that night. Leonie was not worried; she had found the note, Hillela was safe with Reuel, splendid fellow, Leonie herself would be confident to go to the end of the world with him. If only she could convince the State Department to be as confident that *he* was the man to support.

They came to a country hotel. The wooden building stood on stilts among fever trees whose slender trunks gleamed phosphorescent green in a dark roaring with insect song. An old nightwatchman gave them a key attached to a slab of wood marked Room 8. They stood on a rickety gallery that was supposed to allow tourists to watch hippos come out of the river down below, but nothing moved in the frantically vibrating humidity. In Room 8 there was a fan that turned its face, clicking and creaking, this way and that over them as they lay naked. They had already touched and felt one another, that morning, and that kind of familiarity was natural to turn into the other between a sexually-experienced man and woman. Yet she was a surprise to the General as his big body blotted hers from the face of the fan and the chilled layer of his skin and hers melted in his heat. She bore his weight vigorously and gave him great joy. And he could see in the dark the river-shine of eyes and the white of teeth—she

348

kept her eyes open and was smiling—and when he had done with her he had the best feeling of all, that all he had felt was only the possibility of what she could make him feel.

She was not sentimental in the morning, either. Each lay, before the other was aware, wakened by the farting grunts of hippos. —I thought it was you, snoring.— She leapt up, breasts jumping, wrapped the giraffe-printed bedcover round herself and went out to see the animals. He lay in the smell of her body, already specifically identifiable to him, and thought about the man who was his son.

Leonie had to admit: if the State Department wouldn't, Hillela had the nous to take up with the General when he was on the up-and-up again. She must have had a pretty good inkling he was sure of getting back into power. Perhaps she even knew something conventionally well-informed circles on African affairs didn't? The love affair with Reuel went on for several months, after it apparently had started—that time when they went to Mombasa together—before she broke off with Brad. She was back in Africa on two or three working trips during the period; though nobody but she and Brad themselves knew for sure when the break actually came? Brad's mother—who couldn't believe anyone could do such a thing—said it seemed she had stayed on in the brownstone (presumably platonically?) quite a while after she told Brad. And he never said a word to anyone. Probably ashamed to.

It was said she wanted to marry Brad to qualify automatically for American citizenship. That theory fell away as malicious gossip—she didn't marry him, that was the point! Leonie defended her spiritedly, romantically; among the protégés two had 'found each other', there was a new career opening if the one in the brownstone had been abandoned. But the young white widow and her African child, ikon of liberation and reconciliation between the Third World and the Western World, taken on by a local Joseph who found room for her in a house with storm windows like their own, had no options, for others. In Committee, the ikon could only be turned to the wall. She ended there, for them. She had not even given the opportunity for an embarrassed farewell presentation.

At a bookshop in London Pauline met a friend who passed on news of Hillela she was not aware was already out of date. The friend had been to a seminar in Boston while on a visit to her daughter, married to a professor of International Relations, and actually heard Hillela speak. The name 'Kgomani' had meant she expected a black, and then she realized who this white girl must be. Pauline's niece spoke very well, very knowledgeably, it turned out she was quite a figure in circles concerned with African problems, now. Somebody said her husband had been assassinated by the South African secret service, in Zambia? Yes, Pauline could confirm something like that had happened; the South Africans had denied it, of course, put the blame on rivalry among his own exiled comrades—sickening.

Pauline herself—Pauline and Joe—had left all that, left South Africa. She was defiantly miserable in London, with its civilised pleasures of parks and ponds, art galleries and theatres, pubs where house painters, advertising men and middle-class women up for a day's shopping reached over each other's shoulders for draught beer—democratic pleasures she had so enjoyed on the few visits as a tourist she, unlike her rich sister, had been able to afford. It was Pauline who had persuaded Joe they should leave. His offices had been broken into and some evidence stolen—who but the security police could have done that? The evidence was vital in a case he was defending; being Joe, he went doggedly through the proper channels, seeking an indictment against the police, working himself to death as a detective rather than a lawyer to find the individual culprits. And being successful, of course; exposing the false alibis, the cover-ups by one department of the police hierarchy for another, in cross-examination. For what? The men he was defending were members of the Black Consciousness movement, who rejected white participation in the liberation of the country. She burst out laughing every time she reminded him of this; she did so before friends as well as when they were alone. Her Saturday classes in the church had closed down. The South African Students' Organization didn't want black children to take white charity education, and what SASO said dwindled attendance as the students' authority grew. The children sang freedom songs instead of the songs of gratitude they used to offer to Pauline and her helpers. One of the parents came to her to ask whether madam couldn't make the children come back to her Saturday mornings?

But there was nothing madam or the Soweto woman could do; that was exactly what the students, even quite small children, were saying: they had done nothing, they could do nothing, together. The other non-racial groups to which Pauline belonged had gone white. It was the only advice to be got out of Black Consciousness. Work to change your own people, not us. Joe kept suggesting there was still plenty to be done that was worthwhile at the Black Sash advice bureaux, where some women with views just as politically advanced as Pauline's helped blacks resist by asserting to the limit such rights as they had. But Pauline could not take the place assigned to her, among whites. The revolutionary temperament that had been unsuccessful in driving her Underground more than ten years before became vanity that would accept black rejection only as some schism within the central movement towards liberation, not as the exclusion of whites like herself who were ready to opt out of their colour and class. —If it's not simply a revival of the old split between the ANC and PAC, then what is it? If it's not a revival that favours the others, because the ANC's at a low ebb in influence within the country, at the moment?—

Joe had to remind her that when she drove a certain friend of hers and his family to the border one night years ago, the friend was one of those who, at that time, merely put it another way: 'did not want to dance with whites'. Her theatrical laugh spluttered upon him again. —What are you saying? And we found him dancing with our daughters!—

So they sold the house and he took Pauline away to London. She was convinced they could stay only as collaborators with the whites, now, whatever they did, however many legalistic triumphs he had. All conversations or arguments with her ended in reiteration of this. Their divorced daughter Carole and her small boy left the country with them, the elder boy had been given into the custody of his father. Joe found a position with a firm of solicitors who employed him mainly on litigation over football-team disputes. He worked as conscientiously as he had done against charges of treason, the documentation of which he had taken with him to Frognal Green, where it occupied one whole wall of bookshelves in the livingroom (the flat was too small to provide him with a study) and was available to the Anti-Apartheid Movement, the African National Congress, the Defence and Aid Fund, the International Commission of Jurists, the National Council for Civil Liberties—Pauline went out as soon as someone from any of these arrived, or shut herself in the kitchen and cooked. Carole—at this stage in her life, after having two children and emigrating—had decided she wanted to study law, after all, and was articled to her father's firm; he helped her with the degree course at London University she studied at night. On the other hand, Sasha, of course, had given up law; he was the only member of Hillela's adoptive family who had stayed behind. Unless she would have counted (who knew, with her) Olga and the other cousins.

The one who had contingency plans had not left. Olga had had both breasts amputated and was no longer afraid of blacks. She went courageously to the knife and would do so again if the cancer were to recur elsewhere in her well-cared-for body; she had had fitted artificial breasts that couldn't be told from her old shapely ones, even in a swimsuit, and she lived on in the house with her antiques—that selection from the past only of what is beautiful, lifted cleanly from the context of its bloody revolutions— her étagére, guéridon, George IV dining table and gilded Blackamoor. She lay beside her pool; only Jethro was gone; one of Jethro's sons, a cook in a resort hotel in the Vumba Mountains in Rhodesia, was imprisoned for provisioning and hiding freedom fighters, and Jethro went home. Her own sons had all been commissioned during their military service in another kind of army. There was no correspondence between the two sisters after Pauline left and it is unlikely Olga received hearsay about the platform career of the girl she would have brought up to a different life as her own daughter.

Sasha heard because Pauline passed on the news to him. They could not leave one another be, Sasha and his mother. Pauline phoned once a month and he spoke to her. Before she went into the bedroom and shut the door and dialled the long-distance call, she washed her hands and combed her thick-streaked grey hair at the bathroom mirror: still not too much the old hag. The haughty eyes in the mirror saw Sasha—many Sashas, after even a few months had passed, the last sight of him became a reconstruction out of many, many, like the changing face produced by riffling the pages of one of those booklets of 'moving pictures'—the expression on the same face drawn on each page different from that of the previous page—that are supposed to have led to the invention of cinematography. There was never much to say to each other. Not 'What are you doing?'; god knows what he was doing with himself. At least it was something to relate: —I bumped into a woman I know who heard Hillela speak, in Boston recently. Apparently she's working with some institute concerned with refugees in Africa. It was a seminar at M.I.T. This woman said she was good—knowledgeable. I'd hardly think it was Hillela's field.— Sasha didn't respond; what could one find to talk about that would rouse his interest. That old childish fuss over Hillela was forgotten long ago, otherwise Pauline herself couldn't have brought up her name, to him, so easily. But maybe it was just as well he was crossing her voice with his own, asking whether an acquaintance of his could look up Joe for advice, in London. If she had annoyed him by a judgment in her remark (didn't she know they annoyed each other always, unavoidably, inevitably, making judgments) and he had pressed her over the implication of what she *did* think was Hillela's field, then she would only have made things worse by coming out with it: Hillela's field was, surely, men.

Liberated Territory

What has been, what was, what will be: nobody else can decide.
That was understood, lying tenderly apart in the biggest bed in
America. His choice, to lie apart; he could have been comforted, why not,
he knew he was still loved the way he had been loved. It was never any
different. Staying would not have made this house safe for him.

But that is what is always said by the one who is going.

No need to leave yet—nobody knew, and nobody could know there was
happiness in that house, yes, still there, during those months. Like brother
and sister lying there, tempting—but he thought it was wrong. Not for
us. Sometimes he panted in his sleep, from his wound. But nothing to be
done; tenderness only salts. There would have been many more wounds,
because that love would never be any different.

That's what is always said.

He was thinking about the other one all the time—nearly all the time;
sometimes both forgot, in the little American family of three, playing in
pyjamas in the tropical warmth of the brownstone's insulation. What's
he like? What's he like? You were thinking of nothing else but never
said it. You sweated it. The child sensed something; tugged uneasily at
those frizzy plaits. You tweaked her ear or nose—What' you staring at,
Nomikins, what's the matter.

Nothing like. With all the intelligence and willingness and understanding shining the golden-brown lantern so steadily from the dark
side of your gaze, you would not be able to follow. Because of that, he
could never have told you what he told me. And because he could tell me,
and I could follow—no, you'll never follow, it can't be done in this old
house full of heirlooms, the things handed by fathers to sons. A desk, a
complete set of The New Republic, and soon a piano; that's heritage,

here. Possible only to stroke your hair, if you'll allow it, and let them say what they like; you will never explain to anyone why we stayed on a while, your first little family (you'll play the piano, one of the tall, hunch-shouldered American girls will give you more brothers and sisters for your first Nomikins), and although you'll never follow what he's like, what she's like, the one who is going, you did know, oh you did know—no-one can draw a proxy signature beneath a life.

The other will not die. Not even a herd of elephant will trample him out. He is not beautiful, he carries his Parabellum, he knows how to deal with sons, in him the handclasp compresses the pan-pipe bones of the hand with which it makes convenant; it is, on recognition, irresistible.

The General did not marry her for some time—or Hillela did not marry him. They moved about Africa, warp and weft of purpose, trading decisions and carrying out, separately and together, the actions these required. He made the decision over the namesake: —Send her to a decent school in England. An eight-year-old child can't be dragged around the place, she needs a settled life, and that schooling is still the best in the world. I have two kids there. Give her the advantage. I'll pay.— He meant it, but it was not necessary; Hillela had her connections to revive on behalf of Whaila Kgomani's daughter. If Nomo doesn't know her father's tongue, she hasn't grown up speaking the colonial-accented English of her mother; she was educated at Bedales.

It became evident afterwards that Hillela went on several missions for the General, to countries where he could not go, and to which, on her decision, he could not trust anyone else to go. At the beginning she had the unique advantage: no-one in Africa yet connected her with him. If he had been seen to spend the night in an hotel with a young white woman—well, he had never been known to be able to resist a pretty girl, particularly a white one. Such girls have no names. People who came across Hillela in various African states knew her as one of the aid functionaries whose criss-crossing of closed frontiers was tolerated by all sides for reason of what they could hope to get. She looked up old friends without their realizing she was no longer doling out soup powder; and if they did, as perhaps on the night she dined with Tambo, Amojd and Busewe (upgraded) in Algiers, maybe it was the mission itself, on that occasion, to do so. It has never been clear what her position with the African National Congress was, beyond that of Whaila Kgomani's widow, at that period. And the uncertainty of future political alliances between countries makes it always wiser for references other than 'she played her role in active support of her husband's determination to restore peace, prosperity and justice to his country' to be excluded from data available at the General's Ministry of Information and Public Relations.

Anyway, he took her with him to Mozambique in 1975 when he attended the independence ceremonies and saw another of the community of exiles return to his own country as President. The official invitation was in itself a political statement; his old friend Machel showed by it his country's non-recognition of the regime that had ousted the General from his. If the General brought along a consort who was not his wife—she was the widow of a martyr to the cause of African liberation, and Machel had known her personally as one of Leonie's American lobby. And if once she drove in some official car past the old Penguin Nightclub where her mother had danced night after night, she did not know that that was the place, that it had ever existed: closed up, along with all the other nightclubs, and the prostitutes whose kind of freedom had excited poor Ruthie were being re-educated for occupations more useful to a country than the sexual relief of white South African tourists. She could not search for any face among the crowds. It belonged to the recollection of the child beneath the palm tree, and that was overlaid by so many shadows.

In Africa the General wore a black beret bound with leather in place of the gold-braided cap. He grew a beard. It was not only to the great occasions of flag-raisings she accompanied him, sitting there with the growing feeling—binding them together more than if their flesh had been in contact—that next time, or the year after that, he would be the one making the victory speech. Her experience in Africa made it possible to take her even to his bush capital in the expanding area his army was able to declare liberated territory. She was as accustomed to drinking contaminated water and eating off the land as she was to making dinner-table conversation with a Minister. He took her everywhere; a characteristic of the qualities developed by a mistress that she should be, unlike a wife, someone who can be taken everywhere. The language of their intimacy was as much the terse anguish when supply lines of ammunition broke down or a go-between dealer failed to deliver the Stalin organs, Kalashnikovs, Israeli UZI submachine guns, Belgian FAL assault rifles dearly paid for in trade-offs and money, as it was love-talk. Her sexuality, evident to every man watching her pass as he sat in the bush oiling his gun, or stood at attention for review before the General, was part of the General's Command. For him it seemed to grow, to be revealed with the success of his push towards the real capital. Her small, generous, urging, inventive body was the deserts of success; some bodies are made only for consolation, their sweetness touches with decay. But he had known from the first time he made love with her that that was only an experience of her possibilities—without realizing exactly what these would turn out to be.

Everyone has some cache of trust, while everything else— family love, love of fellow man—takes on suspect interpretations. In her, it seemed to be sexuality. However devious she might have to be (he realized he did not know why she should have wanted to be chosen by him) and however she had to accept deviousness in others, in himself— she drew upon the surety of her sexuality as the bread of her being.

You cannot run a country, in exile you cannot equip and train an insurgent army, augment it with villagers, local recruits, establish safe houses both within and without your country, without having an instinct for finding the right people to whom responsibility may boldly be delegated. Right at the start of their relationship he offered this bedfellow a mission for which she was an unlikely candidate—by anyone else's judgment. But he did not solicit any. It was Hillela, on one of those working trips to Africa while she and the namesake were still living with Brad, who went to the safe house in a country to which the General's eldest son had been taken when he was successfully kidnapped. It was an Arab country that had agreed to this hospitality. He had to disappear; a strategy to confuse the General's enemies, with whom his son had allied himself, by not transporting him directly to the bush capital. Hillela was sent because she would be so unexpected an envoy that the hit men who had had to be employed for the job would be uncertain what interests beyond the General's her presence might represent, and therefore would be more likely (the General repeated the phrase without elaboration) to be careful with the young man they had abducted.

Her arrival also threw the defiance, anger and fear of the young man into confusion. All he had prepared for the confrontation with his father was become a set of cumbersome armour of which this feminine apparition was not worthy; for which his posture was useless. Whatever explanations she gave, he was sure he did not really know who she was and why she was there. She could not be from the CIA, because the CIA had helped oust his father. Was she from the KGB? Or from Castro?

She said his father had sent her to see if he was 'all right'. They were figured-over, the two of them and his guards, like patterned cloth, by lozenges of orange and purple light that came through closed velvet curtains in a suburban villa. He would not speak to her. She told him that what he had been hearing in the capital for the past six months was the regime's propaganda: the General was not routed and in retreat, the whole of the Northern region was liberated territory, he was now receiving massive material and other support from outside, village after village was welcoming his men. Within the year he would be in the capital. —Whatever happens to the government people, he can't leave you to be among them. He wants you to know that is why you are here. I know you don't believe it, yet, but he doesn't want you to come to any harm.—

A servant interrupted with coffee and sweetmeats glazed with honey. The General's son ate. He had the air of unreality of one taking the last meal before execution, unable to imagine the actuality of what he dreaded. She could not open her mouth to reassure him.

Back in her hotel room between visits to the villa, she lay following the screen of the television with the sound switched off; she did not know, so far removed now from the General's presence, whether there was any reassurance to be given. How long had she known the General? Behind the shared territory of exile, the shared beds in safe houses and Intercontinental Hotels, there was a whole lifetime of which not even the testimony of souvenirs, as in a beautiful room in Eastern Europe, was open to her.

She bought jeans and T-shirts and took them to the villa. The heat hammered at the walls. It was a prison—the General's prison—with marble-topped tables, thick hot carpets, and pictures, to be made out in the moted stuffiness, someone must have chosen. Furniture can be anonymous but someone has always chosen the pictures. The General's son did not speak to her during those days but they experienced together, a drowsy gaze, over and over, on the Swiss alpine view and the Belle Epoque woman in a carriage at the Place de l'Opéra; the room buzzed with prayers being said in the adjoining one by the off-duty guards, who were not allowed to leave the house for the mosque. After a few days he still did not speak but appeared in the clean clothes looking like one of the black students, eager to demonstrate to free somebody, who came to hear her speak on American campuses. He was slim, with a bunched mouth and delicate pointed jaw; no resemblance to his father, his fingers were long and tentative in their movements. The favourite must have been a fragile child. Even though she had a child of her own, the abstract relations of her own childhood—Len the Other Man, Ruthie dancing, dancing in a nightclub—meant she had no understanding, was free of the patricidal and infanticidal loves between parents and children. It was another advantage her aunts had not intended.

In her hotel room, piped music instead of prayer came through the back of the bedhead from the room next door while she telephoned Reuel. There was no direct dialling to the safe house he was in, in another country. A chocolate had been placed on a paper doily inscribed: *The Management Wishes You Goodnight.* She was eating it by the time the connection was established, and he heard that her mouth was full, a signal of calm audacity that reassured and at the same time delighted him.

—Not a mark on him. But it's an awful place.—

—How's that? I arranged for a house, a nice house!—

—It's hot and ugly, and the curtains are kept closed all the time.—

He was laughing thunder down in his deep chest. —If he's got any sense, he'll never be in a worse place, my God, if you call that awful ... ! You've been a lucky girl.—

She told his father he wouldn't speak to her. But the day she was to leave and explained he would be following, separately, to his father's bush headquarters, he stood up—for a moment she thought he was going to clutch at her physically, not wanting to be left. —Who are you?—

He knew her name; she had given it to him the first time she saw him, and seen disbelief in his face.

—I'm your father's lover. My husband was assassinated seven years ago.—

He looked at her; appeared to be looking at her dark eyes, all shining pupil, her tight-skinned cheeks, mouth with the beginnings of the lines of her most habitual expression—generous, wary confidence—overprinting the relaxation at the corners of her lips, but he was following something else. Every feature of her—the breasts slung from the angle of bare collarbones, the dent of her navel visible under the thin cotton of her skirt, the ringless brown hands and dabs of red paint on her toenails—all these, of face and body, were markers and footholds showing the way. He had enough of his father in him to recognize this one not only knew the need to move on, but also what she would not reveal to his father: what it was necessary to do, to bring this about.

I see, he said.

He saw.

By the time the General was ready to eliminate the government's border outposts and push his forces, at last sufficiently large, properly clothed and well-equipped, to attack the second largest town in his country, his son had a black beret and a beard that broadened his face. His breast was crossed from shoulder to waist, on either side, by a sash like an Order made of the pointed steel teeth of machine-gun bullets. It is true that Hillela worked beside him for four weeks, that dry season of the General's advance. They were with the General in an abandoned farmhouse that had once belonged to a white settler before the first war there, the old war of independence. It was the supply depot closest to the fighting; the farthermost point of a road able to carry heavy transport vehicles. The General's men unloaded their cargo and stored the boxes in the house. The son was the best of them, yes; he worked until dawn. Hillela had a kitchen table at which she sat typing the serial number of each gun before distribution so that the General would know exactly what weapons were being deployed where. The specifications were not unfamiliar to her; her trips with Arnold stood her in good stead, as the Manaka cuisine once had done in other circumstances.

The house with its curtainless windows was a creature who has witnessed so much that its eyes can never close. But everyone slept there during the day. It was stacked with grenades. If one were to have been faulty all would have gone off as a bundle of deadly firecrackers, blowing up the whole place. At midday the sun stripped the walls bare, ransacking yet again: bare boards, shelves of dead insects. At the same hour every day a bar of light rested on the eyelids of the General. He woke, and often made love to her and then would stroll with her in what must have been the settler's farmhouse garden. Among the mud huts, like burned broken pottery, of the peasants who had moved in when there was redistribution of land and then, in turn, fled from the new war, there was still the remains of a swimming pool. In it were skeletons of frogs and a dead snake lying like a lost leather belt, stranded from the last rainy season. The General wished there were some way of filling the pool; he would have liked to do his twenty lengths a day.

The small airport was taken with the town. When the General sent her out during the mopping-up operations (which included the looting of bars and brothels by some of his long-deprived troops) it was from his stance on this strategic bit of liberated territory that he saw her off in one of his Libyan planes. The son, now with the rank of colonel, was alongside his father. Not customary, among these people, to kiss when not making love, and so she did not offer any dab on either cheek to the young man, but they clasped hands and the corner of his bearded mouth went up in a smile, slowly exchanged. It was as if, at last, they had turned to acknowledge together the view of the Swiss Alps and the lady in the carriage on the Place de l'Opéra.

*

Agostinho Neto was another friend of the General who had become President of his country. Hillela waited safely in Angola while the General and his son advanced, captured airstrip by airstrip, village by village and town by town, towards the capital she had never seen. She must have lived for seven or eight months in that hotel in Neto's capital, with one trip to England to see the namesake. She took Nomo to visit the Holland Park couple with whom they had stayed when she was small—at ten, what long thin black legs she had! The wife babbled on about her surely going to be a dancer or a model, she kept talking, afraid Hillela would take advantage of any gap to ask if she and her child could occupy the guest room again. But Hillela was in no need of being taken in; she had been provided with a flat by some organization or other, she didn't name it, and, as the husband remarked, it was idiotic to be nervous, so obvious Hillela was not short of money, the child was at Bedales, and how well Hillela looked, prettier than ever. She was vague when asked what she was doing in Africa—Luanda, of all places. She had worked with various refugee organizations but now was not sure what would come next. From the way she got into the taxi he found for her when she left, from the way she settled herself and quickly remembered to smile through the window, her mind already discarding the visit like a used ticket, he knew—he couldn't say why—what had come next was a new lover, and whatever role that meant. Once she had gone, the wife agreed: there was nobody quite like her; awful and rather marvellous.

The General came to Luanda expectedly unexpectedly, every few weeks. It was not only to fill with the scent of his after-shave, the grunts as he did his twenty morning push-ups on the carpet, the glowing weight of his body in bed, a room registered in the name of Mrs Hillela Kgomani, but also to consult with Neto and others in the Organization of African Unity. Alliances must be negotiated with foresight. Self-assured of winning his war, he was already looking towards his stature in peace. She always knew if he had arrived and entered the room while she was absent; his presence expanded it before she noticed his bag or the newspapers spilled on the bed. She was alone in that presence—he had been in town since the previous night and was out at a meeting—on a day when the telephone rang and it was not he ready to say where to join him for lunch. There was someone to see her, downstairs. Who? A woman asking for her.

What woman? —The lady won't give her name.—

A strange hackle of fear rose from somewhere long quieted. She stood for an instant once again behind the refrigerator door and felt the thud of her own death.

—I don't see people who won't say who they are.—

The telephone rang again and it was the General. The young man behind the reception desk came running out on his two-inch-heeled shoes, bum-tight black pants waggling, to open the lobby doors as she passed. Colonists never leave; they leave their blood and style behind. He wore a pendant on a glossy chain dipping down into his open-necked shirt, like any Portuguese dandy, and in his watered-down African face his eyes were the polished aubergine-coloured ones—like her own. —That 'oman, she speak Portuguese to me.— But he saw madam was not interested, she had the face of someone who has just come from her bath and her mirror and is ready to be received by company that commands the best table in the restaurant.

The next afternoon the persistent caller was there again. —I tell her, without she says the name (a shrug in the voice)—she say, Mrs Nunes.—

A General's consort meets many people and does not always remember doing so, particularly if they are wives, who appear only in marginal social contexts and usually don't have much to say. It might be that this was one of those whose offers of invitations to visit she had accepted without any intention of pursuing.

Hillela came down into the lobby, thirty-three next birthday, not grown tall, grown to be a young woman with deep breasts and a curly head well-balanced on a straight neck, shiny cheeks without make-up, a black, brightly-suffused gaze.

A woman was sitting on the plastic-covered bench where only the nightwatchman ever sat. Her skirt was arranged round her knees and her feet were neatly together, pushed up by high-heeled sandals. She pressed the heel of her palms on the bench and got up. She came slowly nearer; stopped.

—I'm Ruth.—

The young woman tilted her head a moment; but the other was right, there was no need to make any other claim.

—The housekeeper here's a friend of mine, she often talks about the people who come to stay, it's only natural. She said there was someone with an unusual, pretty name—'Hillela'. She'd never heard of anyone called that before—I didn't say anything but I thought, what a great coincidence. So I asked what you were like, about how old ...—

—Won't you have some tea or something cool to drink.—

As if this were one of the wives to whom politeness was due. That's what came out. That's all. She heard the slither and clip of high heels behind her. They sat down between potted palms. No-one appeared to serve them. A long, long silence, twenty-nine years of silence uncoiled around the two women, it stretched and stretched to its own horizon, like the horizon drawn by a landscape of cloud rimmed by space, seen from a plane thousands of feet removed from the earth, from reality. Silence was another dimension: 'mother', 'daughter'.

—You don't mind my coming.—

The remark did not break the silence, it was nothing, swallowed up by it. She shook her head.

She got up and pressed a bell on the wall.

—Really—I'm not thirsty. Don't bother.—

But she was pressing the bell again and again, it could be heard shrilling from behind the louvres of the patio bar.

Even for one so used to adapting to others, so skilled and quick to adjust, how does one talk when one doesn't know to whom one is talking—acquaintance, secret friend, someone standing in a relationship never tried out? There was at least something in the silence, something to say:—You live in Mozambique.—

—I did, in Lourenço Marques—used to be, Maputo now ... We moved here in the late Sixties, my husband thought there was more opportunity. With the oil, you know.—

Vasco. The name torn in pieces and stuffed into a bin with the crusts of school sandwiches. *To have inside me a man who has nothing to do with being introduced: this is my wife, this is my child, my dog.* The woman had the creamy opaque skin of the generation that used face powder, the skin of Olga. The high brow of Pauline was still smooth and the neck unlined but its fullness quilted. The beautiful painted mouth, shiny as tar in the photograph beside the silver dish of Liquorice All-Sorts, opened on false teeth. —How is Pauline? Is she still married to old Joe? And Olga? I don't suppose I'd recognize them, now—or them me (acknowledging good-humouredly the hair dyed red). Olga must be sixty!—she's the eldest, and I'm fifty-three, I was twenty-one when you were born. Sixty! But I'm sure she won't look it, she was always afraid of using herself up—you know? Precautions. 'Don't cry, it makes your eyes red.' Even when we were children, she used to cream her elbows and knees when she got out of the bath. She was so pretty and so afraid—at fourteen, of wrinkles! I threw her into terrible confusion when we were young girls and I read somewhere that if you shaved your legs you lost your sex appeal —she was always perfectly depilated. Well, anyway, all she got was Arthur ... I suppose he's still around—

That circumcised ox, and he did become rich enough for her to buy a pair of Imari cats and an 18th-century Blackamoor holding up a globe, and Jethro carrying cream scones to her swimming pool.

—My darling Pauline ... has she stuck with Joe? I've often wondered ... though I didn't write often ... No, well, that's not true, I didn't write at all after about a year. I'm not going to lie to you. I can't picture Pauline living a whole lifetime with that nice deadpan stuffed with legal documents, he was like a suit of old clothes filled with paper to keep birds away. I always knew, I *hoped* she'd still have some other life, she could have done anything—She wasn't like Olga or me. And all she had was Joe and her drunken black friends sponging on her. How is Pauline?—

But she knew no more than this woman, about the sisters, the aunts. She had been gone since she was nineteen.

—And you don't write?—

—No.— Gone, like Ruthie.

A black man in a waiter's suit that gaped between the buttons on jacket and fly stood by with a tin tray. An icecream was ordered—Well, all right, I'll have something!—and a soda.

—Did you live with Olga or with Pauline? In the end?—

Now it was two schoolgirls meeting years later; the icecream was being smoothed, tiny cardboard spoonful by spoonful, between sentences.

—With both. At different times. I went to boarding-school in Rhodesia and I used to spend the holidays with Olga.—

—She had only the three boys? She always envied me, getting a girl.—

—Clive, Mark and Brian.—

—And Pauline?— Ruthie had never written and now this woman wanted to register a preference for Pauline to have been the surrogate.

—Oh, I used to be invited a lot to Pauline's. And then when I left Rhodesia, I went to live with her and Joe.—

A smile. —Len. It was he who didn't want me to write, you know. You were too small to read, anyway.—

But not later. *I've had a husband, I've given birth, these things were done to me, but with you I do things, I'm all over my body, I'm there wherever you touch me, my tongue in your ear, your armpit fur and your sweet backside.*

—Pauline had only the two, didn't she, Alexander—Sasha—and the little girl, just a baby, when I went away.—

—Carole, we went to school together.—

—Sasha was a darling little boy. Did you get on well? You and Pauline's children?—

—Yes, it was fine.—

—No jealousy? We sisters never quarrelled, we were very, very close.—

—I know. They were always talking about you.—

Sideways on the iron café-chair, the legs were arranged exposed from the knees as they had been on the lobby bench; elegant legs narrow at knee and ankle, displayed as all that was left to display by a woman whose fine breasts (breasts of Hillela) now met, where a waist like Hillela's had been, a solid bolster that was diaphragm, belly and hips in one. —You wonder why I came. Why I've bothered you. Hillela.—

She was smiling without admission or reproach. —No I don't. Curiosity. It's natural.—

Offended, all the same; and the momentary twitching expression of one who is used to enduring the carelessness of others. —It's a bit different from my friend who happens to work here, I think. Not just 'curiosity'; couldn't be, could it? If you'd known I was here, would you have looked for me?—

—I don't know, really. I wouldn't have known whom to look for.— A lie. Resemblances, sisterly and filial, can't be avoided. But the General's consort did not look where she thought they were to be found, in Mozambique.

The red mouth opened a little, the hands with the puffiness round the nails that results from some sort of manual work drew ringed fingers slowly down the powdered cheeks in preparation: —So you don't remember me at all.—

—I think I was only—how old?—about two. There's a photograph in Lourenço Marques. I was there with you but I don't remember—not where it was taken, not the palm tree, not being there with you. Olga framed a photograph—of you—one taken during the war.—

—Nothing later?— Laughter. —That's Len. He must have torn them up. You had no other idea of me?—

—None.— No pictures, but letters. All sensations alive in the body, breasts, lips of the mouth and the vagina, thorax, thighs. *Vasco.* A thirst of the skin.

—What'd they tell you? Len?—

—That you'd made another life.—

—Was that all? What could that mean to a child? How ridiculous. Len's phrase.—

—It didn't really matter what he said, he was talking about someone I didn't know, bringing up a subject that didn't exist, you see. I travelled about with him when I was little, in the car.— And now remorse. —Oh my God.—

—It was wonderful! I remember it all, sleeping on a teddy-bear cloth blanket in the back, between the sample boxes. We stayed together at hotels in little dorps; slept in the same room with him.—

—'Another life'. Sounds as if I'd gone into a convent. Len just never could face facts. Wouldn't let me write, you know. And my sisters? When you were bigger?—

—Pauline explained.—

—That I'd gone away with a man.—

Oh more than that. To another life—Len's phrase wasn't a euphemism. To look for passion and tragedy. The wrong place; when it really happens it happens on the kitchen floor.

But a daughter cannot instruct a mother. —Yes, that you hadn't been—right—for Len, and you'd fallen in love with someone else.—

—So you were old enough to understand, by then.—

—Oh yes. Some of my friends' parents were divorced.—

Vasco, my Vasco, the taste of you! You are still in my mouth. I read somewhere it's supposed to be the taste of bitter almonds. Not true, not for yours, anyway. Like strawberries, like lemon rind, I always did eat the rind of the slice of lemon people put in drinks.

The silence came back. The woman braved it. —He left me two years after we moved here.—

—You're not with Vasco anymore?—

Ruthie, childish, self-absorbed Ruthie, never able to be aware of anything outside her own skin, that's her charm in a way—doesn't notice that if nothing else is remembered, the man's name is known.

—Oh, a long time. Things didn't work out, here. We had nothing left. Neither of us had a job, so he went to Europe to look for something. He was going to send for me in Lisbon, but it's never happened.—

Mrs Nunes. —You're married to someone else, now.—

The woman shook her head slowly, smoothing into silence the remoteness of that possibility. —Not married. When I was still young ... younger... I was fooled again a few times. I didn't understand what men were.— A little late to begin explaining the facts of life. No doubt someone did that; so far as Pauline and Olga could be said to know them. Or poor Len.

But the young woman was smiling at Ruthie as if she were the one capable of giving instruction.

—And I hear you've got a daughter, too. I'm a grandmother!—

—Yes, ten years old, she's called Nomzamo and she's at school in England.—

—My friend saw the photograph in your room. Is she from this husband you're with here?—

—She's a black child. But not from the man your friend's described.—

They laughed together for the first time. —Oh I've lived among them so long, it's nothing to me, although I've never really had anything to do with them. And now, of course, they've taken over everything—I believe it's the same in Mozambique—not like it was when I was there, there's nothing in the shops, no water, even, half the time, in the old Polana. It was such a beautiful hotel. People used to say better than anything on the French Riviera—of course, you stayed there once with me! You did! When you were tiny! That's where the photograph must have been ... There were all the outdoor cafés, the nightclubs ... and now nothing left. Just the same here; look at this dump of a hotel. They took over everything, but without the experience ... that's what happens. I often think, Pauline ought to be here, and see what it's like—I was always supposed to be the impractical one, I lived in dreams, but what about Pauline ... ! I work for them. Yes, I do.— The mouth moved half-humorously, half-emotionally. —I'm a housekeeper, too. At the Hotel Continental. They want white or at least half-caste people for the job because the other poor things always fall to the temptation to steal towels and sheets. Of course—these things are such luxuries to them! What will Olga say when she hears her sister's a glorified maid in a hotel!— But Olga will never know; neither mother nor daughter has any contact with her. —Are you a professional? Did my sisters send you to a university? There was no shortage of money, my father must have left a pile, and Arthur's a money-making machine. The more I ask, the less I find I know about you.—

—No. They would have—Olga would have paid—but I left when I'd finished school. Left where I'd been living—at Pauline and Joe's. I've done all sorts of things, doctor's receptionist, sung in discos, served in a shop, been a kind of governess in Ghana, once; and then political work in Europe, and jobs with aid organizations—in Africa, in America.—

Ruthie followed as if she had planned it all herself. Now she could put a hand out and place it over Hillela's, a parental blessing bestowed upon a bowed head. —Hillela, I'm so glad you've really lived. I knew you'd be well taken care of by my family but at the same time I felt ashamed that it would mean you'd grow up like them, and never know anything different. Every time I remembered you I thought that. It would come upon me suddenly in the most unlikely moments, moments when it seemed that the things I was doing, the things that were happening to me—they made it impossible that what I left behind in Johannesburg had ever existed, that I had ever been Olga and Pauline's sister and Grandpa Hillel's favourite granddaughter and married someone under a canopy.—

The first touch in twenty-nine years. Her hand was trapped under the stranger's palm and neither turned to let the palms meet nor slid away.

—I know it couldn't have been all honey. But I can see—you wouldn't expect it to be. I don't know you—don't think I'm pretending to know you, I can't—but I am your mother. The blood's the same. You have a child of your own. And this man, I hear he's some kind of politician, someone important—does he love you? Do things go well between you?—

If you never have had a mother you never have been asked such questions. She was smiling, conceding a right that didn't exist. —Things go very well. We'll soon be living in his own country.—

—You've turned out so good-looking, Hillela. And clever, I can tell. You remind me of Pauline when she was young—a certain look around the eyes.—

The eyes: that was the moment to ask the question. But did it matter, any longer, whether she was Len's daughter or the child of Vasco; abandoned or abandoner, both were gone. No need to invent a reason for her particular kind of existence taken in among antiques or bedding down with a cousin (the blood the same),

374

when for her, too, all that had happened to her made it impossible that what was left behind, there, had ever existed?

—Will you show me the photograph of the little girl? I need proof to believe I'm a grandmother!—

—Of course. I'll fetch it for you.—

She ignored the elevator, raced up the stairs and the room was staring at her as she burst in and took the leather frame from the dressing-table. It was a double frame that balanced ajar like a book; on the side facing the namesake, laughter-dents in her cheeks and her arms raised joyfully, was a photograph of Hillela and Whaila with the baby in the crook of his arm. It had not been looked at for a long time, although it was there on the dressing- or bedside-table in every hotel room and in the duffle bag that lay among the guns and grenades in. the farmhouse. Whaila, thirty-eight years old for ever in the garden of Britannia Court, the light catching his strong slender forearm with the watch there, distinctly, and the lines of pain in his smile that struck deep and never faded from the print. She slipped the photograph out from beneath the plastic window and clumsily, tremblingly, put it in a drawer. The veins of her neck swelled and for a moment the room lurched in tears.

The woman had the good family manners to know she had stayed long enough; she had left the patio and was waiting in the lobby. She studied the namesake, considering fondly; maybe considering what to say, it was hard to find resemblances not blotted out by blackness. —She's an adorable little girl.—

They stood seeing together the daughter's daughter, smiling politely.

Hillela took back the photograph only for a moment. —Here, Ruthie, you have it.—

The General said of course she must come and live with them. —Your mother is our mother. She will have her own quarters in our house, or her own house, same as my mother.—

—She's Ruthie. I don't know her, I've never lived with her. I might as well take in anyone.—

This had no significance for the General. Among his people most children were brought up by grandmothers or other kin as well as or in place of their mothers—anyone who performed the function shared the title: the mother remained the mother. —Hillela, you're not adopted?—

—Well, I was—but not by Ruthie.—

—Then she's your mother, even if you don't know her face. I don't care. We look after our elders.—

—But even if we had a house—

—You will have a house soon, a house you can't imagine, a house with I forget how many—fifteen, sixteen rooms— And the thought of regaining his official residence roused him, so that he pressed the breath out of her and kissed her with his hands encompassing her head, as he had held it at the beginning, to examine it for hurt.

—If we really want to do something …—

—Of course. You must look after your mother.—

—D'you think we could get a cheap ticket to Europe? I don't believe she's ever been. Even if it were only to Portugal—she Speaks Portuguese, apparently.—

—That's easy, if that's what you want. Airlines must make sure all eventualities are covered.— He was laughing, zestfully packing his bag to go back to his bush capital. —TAP wants to keep its landing rights if a change of regime is coming.—

Hillela had no address; it had not been pressed upon her, must have been clear in her face or manner that she would not know how to find any reason for another meeting. She went to the housekeeper to ask where Mrs Nunes lived. —You can h'ask for 'er at the Continental, madam, that's where she works.— —No, her address at home. Do you know when her day off is?— —Like me, she's off work Thursdays—tomorrow, you see, I'm not 'ere.— The housekeeper wrote a few lines on the torn-off border of a newspaper. —Is it far? — —There's a bus, madam— but you take a taxi.—

The General had left by the time the crows were squabbling on the balcony ledge in the early morning. It always was a day or so before she took possession of the deserted room again. The hearth-fire of the bed had gone out, cold. Hillela dressed, approached the/couple of taxis that leaned night and day against the kerb outside the hotel; and then went on walking. The heat of the day had not yet risen; there was a shimmer of humidity and the smell of salty wet stone and oil from the docks; the concrete of Tema rose from the waves, underfoot again, and sank away. She meant to walk in the direction of the fort, which she vaguely knew was that of the quarter indicated on the slip of newspaper in her bag, and pick up a taxi after she had had a breath of air, but she kept walking while the cross-wind on the causeway road that connected the town with the *restinga,* where the beaches were, blew about her its scarves and veils. The road to the fort hung as a slack, snaked rope from the walls. The Portuguese built their fortresses as indestructibly as the Danes and they have survived to be put to use everywhere on the coasts of Africa by successive powers, housing governors-general or colonial militia, and, at last, black heads of state or their army headquarters: the stony armour fits everyone, imperialist and revolutionary, capitalist and Marxist. She saw the fort up ahead with its great incongruously voluptuous bouquet of bougainvillea at the portal, then passed beneath it, and looked back once at it high behind her. She had not been up there, although she moved in official circles; Neto did not live in his palace as Nkrumah had done in Christiansborg, outside whose walls grass covered a grave: *I saw the face of freedom ... and I died.* Military vehicles were tilting down the steep road and showering her with dust: this was army headquarters.

At the other end of the causeway road she stopped some-one riding a bicycle and showed him the slip of newspaper. He gabbled directions in Portuguese, but her vivid incomprehen-sion and feminine friendliness roused him to make further efforts and he drew her a map in the dust. She turned left, and then left again, passing rows of tiny pink, bright blue, acid-green and yellow facades like children's, iced birthday-cake houses. Pastel picket fences enclosed minute spaces of sand. The streets seemed deserted; row after row, pink, blue, green, yellow. Pleasure houses; places to store surfboards and waterskis and barbecue grills for prawns, doll's houses where one could keep a girl, even, and visit her during the week when families were back in town.

Ruthie lived in one of these. The address was correct. The chalk-blue door was opened by a small girl with black eyes and thin gold rings in her baby ears—Hillela herself, if she had not been left behind twenty-nine years ago. Perhaps Ruthie owned or rented the house, perhaps she hired a room there; perhaps it was Vasco's pleasure house in which Ruthie had been left behind, and she hired it out to share with others? The child ran away to the kitchen, which could be smelled (green peppers and coffee, the odours released when Pauline was preparing a treat lunch), and there were voices talking across each other in Portuguese.

Ruthie must have just washed her hair. She wore a towel turban that pulled firm the skin of her temples and cheeks; the lost beauty her sisters talked of almost emerged—useless beauty thrown away so cheap on the first man to take it up in a night-club. It was her turn to lead the way, chattering and apologizing for her dressing-gown. They went into what must have been the communal room: paper flowers before a plaster Virgin Mary, piles of gritty records, a photograph of a frock-coated man and a woman in a high collar under oval convex glass. They sat on a sofa protected by crocheted headrests and arm-mats. The curtains were closed against the sun and again what was said was said in patterned dimness, twenty-nine years submerging their faces under the dissolving play of depths.

Ruthie's chatter stopped instantly. —Europe. But what would I do there. I mean, I don't know anybody.—

—We've got friends who would look after you.—

—Oh no. Thank you, it's very generous, tell your husband, I don't know what to say ... No, I'd better stay. I'm used to it, now. I speak the language pretty well, you know. After such a long time. Some of the whites who went away when it was all finished for them, they've come back, they can't settle down there, after here—even though everything's changed so much. And would I get my job back ... Europe. I'd better stay where I'm used to.—

Five weeks after a certain telephone call from his mother Sasha followed the impulse, and wrote to the Department of Political Science at M.I.T. asking whether the Department would be good enough to supply him with the address of Mrs Hillela Kgomani, who had taken part in a seminar on Africa (he apologized for not being able to be more precise) the previous spring. It was necessary for him to contact Mrs Kgomani for reasons of research. He requested that if it appeared that his letter was directed to the wrong department, it might be passed on to the appropriate one. He received a courteous reply, and the address of the brownstone. But although Hillela wrote several times to Brad over the next year, she never gave any address other than that which would place her in a city at the moment of writing: 'Algiers', 'Luanda'. If there is nowhere to reply to, of course, the one to whom a letter is addressed cannot fall to the temptation to write back, and cannot deliver any slight through not doing so. Trust her to protect herself ... She would not know the joy and pain her handwriting caused.

Brad wrote across the envelope from South Africa: return to sender.

Unwanted, unopened, dead letters come back slowly, by sea mail. Sasha opened his and could not stop himself from beginning to read: ... *my "field" (as my mother says, as if we were sheep she'd like to keep corralled chewing on this bit of grass or that) turns out to be not so different from yours, after all. I suppose that's why I'm writing. I chucked up law (again, the first time was for the army) and I'm working with a black trade union in Durban, the place you once ran away to with your friend, I've forgotten her name, and left the whole house in a state of shock ... I'm relieved to be away from JHB, I'm no longer with that girl, either. And the house is gone, they sold it before they left. But I hate the climate. I've never liked lying about on beaches, which is what everyone finds the compensation for breathing warm soup instead of air, night and day, in summer. I haven't had a winter here, yet. What I do: I'm helping to organize workers. It's as simple as that but of course it's not simple at all here. You would have gone off to take a shower or gossip on the phone if I'd talked about such things, but now I suppose you'll know something of them. Maybe more than I do. Pauline said you lecture. African problems—she didn't know the details, she thought it was refugees, but anyway, refugees are ex-employees, potential labour, an unemployment problem among other things, so you're certain to have picked up a lot from them. As you must know, blacks' unions here at home still aren't allowed to participate in the official industrial conciliation process, but this won't be able to go on for much longer, whatever the government would like. As blacks have become the main work force, not only traditionally in mining, but in the engineering, construction and other secondary industries, being able to negotiate directly only with whites has left the bosses a fraction of the labour force to parley with. The recognized trade unions are a farce, and these pragmatic capitalists have to deal with reality. So it's certain that in a year or two black unions will have to be recognized. And there's the question of mixed ones—but I won't go into all that. The only thing that was alive for me in law was labour legislation, and now at least I'm doing something practical with all that stuff I mugged up. Black workers have little or no experience of the kind of organizing skills they're going to need, or the kind of structures, right from the shop floor, they have to set up. Not that there's always a shop floor—I'm mostly concerned with dockworkers, at present. All I ever knew about them when I started was that they invented (should I say 'choreographed') the gumboot dance, you know, the calf-slapping-and-stamping performance, tin whistles shrieking between their teeth—teams of them used to be brought to put on for Pauline's indigenous art shows. It's not much of a career; I only mind for Joe—but believe it or not, Carole has taken up where I dropped out, she's articled to the firm he joined in London! So that's good, for him. He didn't want to leave but my mother decided he was useless here. And that was that.*

I don't know what you want to know. If anything. But I imagine that you are back in a family now; you have your own family, a professor husband, a child (I know that's not his, that's from another marriage).

I've never been to Uncle Sam's great U.S. but I can choose and furnish your house from the movies ... how else? And you in it. No movie to supply that one.

I suppose that house and you in it is a good idea. So that with it you may want to know the sort of things people want to know when they have family houses. The other cousins: maybe you'd like to hear about them. They all three have careers. Mark's a urologist, a neighbor of yours, more or less, in Philadelphia. Brian's in banking: Clive—I'm not sure what he's doing, can't remember for the moment, but whatever it is he's very successful—I met him once, on a plane going to Cape Town. He gave me a card which I lost. Maybe you have a card now: Professor and Ms Hillela—what? Pauline didn't say; you keep your other name when you lecture.

It's wonderful to be with blacks. Working with blacks. Already there are some who are senior to me, one or two who have been, for training, to England and West Germany. I take my orders from them. So I suppose I'm like Pauline, really. Where I get my thrills. It's wonderful and sometimes it's a terrible let-down. Alpheus's garage was luxury compared with the flat near the Point I'm living in, but I'm still cut off from the vigorous ugliness of the life they live, different from my ugliness; what they find to talk about in their endless dialectic—no, synthesis—of laughter, anger and mimicry, their Sunday booze-ups, the childhood loyalties they never seem to give up—it's not in a manner of speaking that they call each other brother.

But what am I saying. You were married to a black. It must have been different, for you. Perhaps I should marry a black girl—if that were possible. (By the way, the law against that is going to go, too, one of these days. They're looking for ways they can trim off the straggly edges without harming white power.) But I have to tell you I'm not attracted to black girls. Not so far. As if they could care.

The kind of job I do—it's neither legal nor illegal. It's not really new, either. I'm making no great break-through for progress. It was done before we were born or when we were little kids by people whose names I've learned, Afrikaners like the Cornelius sisters and Bettie du Toit, and Jews like me, Solly Sachs and Eli Weinberg. Before the laws put a stop to it. Some of them landed in jail and exile, and others gave in and settled for working in white unions. So now it has to be begun over again, but this time there'll be no stopping it. The gumboot dance won't be hustled off the arena when the whites have had enough for their amusement. Our offices have been raided a few times; the police seem bewildered by what they find, might as well be reading upside-down. I've been questioned, along with another white involved. But they don't seem to know what to do about us, yet.

It was not prying, to read the letter meant for Hillela. As he read he saw that when he was writing to her, he was writing to himself. He tore up his letter and dropped it into the office waste basket among memoranda, spoilt photocopies, and the Coke cans his colleagues aimed there.

The signals from the General's free radio stations became stronger and stronger. His pilots, training in Bulgaria to fly MIGs, qualified and came back to the bush to operate from the captured provincial towns with their airports or airstrips. The government troops were fighting from besieged towns. The General rocket-attacked and bombed military bases but gave strict instructions that the oil refinery and the country's two ports were not to be touched, nor were there to be any but unavoidable civilian targets. —I'm not going to walk into a ruined city and take on a wrecked economy.— But in the end there was fighting in the streets in which his former comrades, his neighbours when he was a young officer, his friends and perhaps even some members of his own family would be killed. Only the best of them was safe by his side, and no-one dared to recall that the Colonel had once belonged with the enemies his father had overcome. The General did not have to explain to Hillela his feelings about this; she had seen the homeless wanderers between army and army, war and war, sitting in the bush, she had brought the soup powder that comes after shrapnel.

Some time before the army headquarters, police headquarters, broadcasting station and telecommunications centre in the real capital were taken by the General's troops, and he entered the capital in a procession of armoured cars and tanks whose engine power was quickly superseded by the lava of crowds that carried them forward in battered, ecstatic eruption, the marriage took place in some Hilton or Intercontinental hotel where he flew to join Hillela for twenty-four hours. It was then that the General gave her her African name. She had forgotten the promise, taken as one of the kind offered her meaninglessly so often in the playfulness of sexual advances. —You'll be there on the register: Chiemeka Hillela.— Now she remembered. —What does it mean?— He took a smiling breath that expanded the muscles of his neck as well as his big chest. —It's not a name in my language, it comes from another country, but it means the same as my real name does. 'God has done very well'.—

His bell of laughter broke and reverberated, back and forth. She embraced him, the accolade of victorious commanders, her arms hardly able to reach around his shoulders.

She had drawn back. The shine of her one cheekbone was impressed with the ridges of the insignia he bore, her eyes were inescapable; he found the challenge very attractive. —Why in another language? Because I'm a stranger?—

—Now, now. Wait a minute. It's an Igbo name, from Nigeria. I had a good friend there, I stayed with him and his mother, she treated me like her son. It's in her honour I call you. She fed me, she clothed me the first time I was in exile, as a youngster. And her name was the same as mine, a female version; a name that was fated ...—

The name that was ready for her has been hers for official purposes ever since, but between the couple she remained Hillela, as he remained for her Reuel, his colonial baptismal name at the Catholic font. So that 'Hillela' has become the name of intimacy, withdrawn from the currency of general use and thereby confusing her identity and whereabouts, for others, further than these already had been. It was only by her face that Olga recognized the President's wife in the newspaper photograph, that time, sitting there right next to Yasir Arafat.

State Houses

A leopard stands in the entrance of State House. When Nomo has a week to spare between seasonal haute couture presentations in Paris, Rome, New York and London, and flies out to Africa, the moment of arrival for her is when she passes an elongated hand over the creature's head in recognition of the way the namesake climbed on its back the first time she was brought to visit, as an eleven-year-old child. She has a leopard-skin coat at home in her Trastevere apartment or London mews flat (depending where she passes the winter). It was designed for her by one of the Japanese couturiers who have superseded the French since Chanel and Dior died.

This other, a taxidermist's, version of the leopard gives it flanks hard and hollow to the touch as cardboard under the bright-patterned tight silky fur, and a tongue like congealed sealing-wax in its snarling mouth. There are a small rock and clumps of dried grasses glued to the plinth with which it was supplied; the whole tableau a gift of homage to the State given by the oil concession-aires when the country became independent and the General was President for the first time, before the civil war. The entrance is an atrium, with wings of the house led to by open, white-pillared passages on either side. State House was originally Government House, and built to the standard design of one of the sovereign-ties of hot climates in the imperial era which, of course, flourished and declined before that of airconditioning. The President has wanted to brick up walls and extend to the whole place the airconditioning system he long ago installed in the public and private rooms, but Hillela's early exposure to the stylistic graces and charms of the past, spending school holidays with a collector aunt, left latent in her an appreciation that has emerged in the mistress of the Presidential residence. She has insisted that State House appropriate Government House, not destroy its architectural character. She has been in charge of all extensions and structural alterations. A style of living commensurate with the dignity of the State, she persuaded the President, is not expressed in the idiom of the Hilton and Intercontinental (with which both have a strong emotional tie as the places where his return into his own was bargained for and planned). As for luxury—a measure of which every Head of State, even one as determined to live as close to his people as Nyerere was, must have in order to symbolize some estate now attainable to the people, since every head of a black state was once one of its oppressed people—real luxury is expressed in gardens and the indulgence of individual notions of comfort, idiosyncratic possessions. Behind the leopard of black independence, the atrium opens across the reception area from which official visitors waiting to be received by the President can watch, in the park, peacocks from the last governor's tenancy trailing worn tails. Hillela would not touch, either, the collection of votary objects that surrounds the coat-of-arms that has replaced an imperial one: plaques beaten out of the country's copper, the carvings by local artists of heroic agrarian couples, faithfully but subconsciously reproducing as an aesthetic mode the oversize head and spindly legs of undernourishment, and the toadying gifts of white visiting artists or the multinational firms who commission them—heroic animals, more leopards, elephants, lions—paintings as subconsciously reproducing the white man's yearning for Africa to be a picture-book bestiary instead of the continent of black humans ruling themselves. She knows the strings of cheap pearls and pressed-tin miniature human limbs that encrust walls round the ikon in Eastern Europe called the Black Virgin— whether 14th-century anticipation of Black Theology or time and the grime of worshippers' breath had made her so, the admirer who took Hillela on a weekend expedition to the shrine could not say.

The President's passage of heroes is also intact. Strangely, even his usurper did not remove them during the period of the counter-coup. When one of the aides with the thick squeaky shoes of policemen leads an official visitor to the President's study, they pass under the photographed eyes of Lenin, Makarios, Gandhi, Chou En-lai, Mao Tse-tung, Patrice Lumumba, Nkrumah and Kennedy.

The first few years could not have been all honey—to appropriate Ruthie's phrase. Power is like freedom, it has to be fought for anew every day. The ousted president found refuge with Mobutu Sese Seko in Zaire. He was far enough off not to be able to gather supporters in any number around him—and Mobutu knew he couldn't get away with allowing that; it was by a secret accommodation, arrived at between the OAU and the General, that Zaïre had become an agreed place of exile for that gangster. But the now rebel forces—government forces when the General's had been the rebel army—regrouped under the command of three ambitious officers who had escaped imprisonment by the General. They established themselves in the South-West of the country and for a time the civil war burned on. The General—now President—could contain it but not put it out. Not militarily. Now he had the advantages of the solid bases and heavy equipment of a conventional army (his former rebel one, enlarged by a sullen 'reconciliation' with and absorption of large numbers of surrendered troops) and the rebels had the disadvantages of makeshift command posts in the bush; but in the pursuance of guerrilla war the unconventional fighting conditions—as the President as General had so victoriously proved—often favour the apparently disadvantaged. The President thickened in the sedentary obligations of State House; in every way, he was not as quick on his feet as he was when he slept among grenades in the farmhouse. He had to begin to go abroad a lot, again; not as an exile, but as Head of State with an entourage in his private jet aircraft, he had still to seek friends, to importune, and to trade in the currencies of power. His white wife was no ordinary wife who would go along just to take advantage of a European shopping trip. She had the experience that fitted her for conclave; long ago, when she was very young, she had developed, along with the love-child inside her, a feminine skill of guardianship, an ability to see, moves ahead, what the opposition tactics were revealing themselves to be, and to intervene warning with the signal of a gesture or a look. Later, empty of love, taking notes of negotiations in cold countries, she had learnt to read more in the ellipses than the dictation. The President's trusted advisers knew that the most trusted, the only one indispensable so far as the President was concerned, was one not of their number.

She did perhaps find the odd hour to shop, as well. Quite soon after their alliance began the President had made it clear that his companion could not go about with him in cotton shifts, jeans, and sandals made by street cobblers. Fortunately, she knew fine fabric and good cut; as a child performed the equinoctial rites of storage, carrying silk and suède garments against her cheek.

The collapse of the rebel forces which finally ended the war was brought about not by the President's military victory but by the victories in conclave. The French were persuaded into embarrassment over the arms that were being supplied to the rebels through Chad; the Americans debated in Congress a cul-off of their ambiguous aid to the rebels, aid which at first the Under Secretary of State defended as a policy of bringing peace to the region. The cut-off was implemented and after the shortest decent interval the President successfully negotiated a $3 billion loan from the United States for the rehabilitation of war-devastated areas in his country. It was all as he had said: he had to win his war with arms from the East, and to win his peace with money from the West. The world press was amazed to report that only a rainy season after his troops still had been monitoring the physical surrender of arms in the South-West, his Ministry of Agriculture held an agricultural show in the region and the President was rapturously received when he addressed rallies there. His pithy style of comment on the event made a good quote: —My popularity comes from the full stomachs of my people.— He was accompanied by a military brass band from the capital, but not by Hillela. Absent in exile and occupied by war, he had not visited the people in the South-West for a long time, and it would not have been wise to reinforce any sense of his having alienated himself by bringing to them a white wife.

He did not, however, take along one of the other two wives, the black ones, either. Hillela's place, for him, cannot be filled by anyone else. The first wife resented her but scarcely had any opportunity to demonstrate that resentment. She was already fifty when the President brought Hillela to his capital, and more because of her venerable position as his first wife than her age, regarded as in retirement. She had her house and retainers in the village where she had spent her childhood. The President took Hillela to be presented to her; his escort keeping its distance, they drove alone as they had when they encountered the elephants but his monumental profile with the curved chip of nose was heavily sad: he would have wished to be taking her to his mother, but she had died while he was winning his war in the bush, and he had not even been able to be at her funeral. He repeated, as people do for themselves rather than the one to whom the observation has been addressed again and again: —The eldest is the best of them. All my children. And this one gave birth only to girls. She was very annoyed ... blamed me! And then I had five sons with the other. That was worse, because since then she hasn't been able to blame anyone but herself. Poor woman, she's all right with her house and her farm, plenty of relations to work it for her. But I think she drinks. When our women drink, their faces get dead-dark and the red from inside their mouths begins to grow out to their lips. She was never a pretty girl, but lively.—

She lived among altar-like pieces of 19th-century furniture which must have come down to her not only from her father—a chief—but from some European missionary family before him. The room was dark and the silences long as Sela's; the first wife was put out rather than disarmed by the ease with which the white woman made herself at home where she should have been ill at ease in strange surroundings, feeling the reserve of a way of life that doesn't belong to white people. In the kitchen with the relatives, she got talking as if she were back somewhere she knew well, and tasted the wild spinach being cooked to go with the maize porridge as if it were a treat. When asked whether she had any children: oh yes, a daughter. —A black child.— The old wife took the President's smiling remark as a boast: this one was young enough to bear him black children.

But the old wife did not live to see whether this would happen. The news came to State House that she had died; as customary with Africans, the President said, there were a half-dozen versions of the apparent cause. He gave her a funeral in keeping with her status. There are many sides to the President no-one would suspect but that Hillela seems to know through some matching in herself, although outwardly they have always appeared an incongruous pair—it is not the matching of beauty in the couple of the Britannia Court photograph. Sadness, like every other emotion, is diffused powerfully by the President's physical presence: after the funeral it was again in the lament of the rhythm of his breathing, the lie of his hands and the look of the nape of his neck, so broad that the delicate, tiny ears appear stamped back into it. He was ashamed because he could not manage to weep at the funeral. (Hillela was listening, if he wanted to talk.) It was his first woman he was burying, the mother of his daughters; the young man who had been her husband was going down into the grave, too. Yet he had no tears.

Hillela lay in bed and patted the place beside her. He padded over the cool marble floor of what had been the governor's bedroom, reluctantly; but took her nightgown off over her head and gazed at what he had revealed to himself. He moved in beside her; moved on.

The mother of the Colonel, the second wife, has treated Hillela with respect that Hillela has sometimes been able to cajole into some kind of affection—but the second wife cannot make a sister out of a white woman. The respect—for her usurper, a foreigner, it's not as if the President had done the normal thing and simply taken a third wife from among his own people—probably comes about because the second wife knows Hillela went to protect the eldest son in some far country, after he had done a wicked thing and joined the people who wanted to kill his father. The Colonel himself must have told his mother; and told her never to talk about it, because it has never been mentioned between Hillela and her. She does not live in State House but has a large house of her own, in town, and maybe the President still visits her occasionally; she was married at fifteen and is not much older than Hillela. Visitors entertained at State House in the last few years have come upon charming young children chasing the peacocks and tame guinea-fowl from their roosting places in the flamboyant trees, and riding bicycles over the lawns. The visitors presume these are the children of the President by his present wife (although they look quite black—it is said those genes prevail in mixed progeniture). But no-one knows for sure whether Hillela has had any children as the President's wife; whether she ever had any child other than the namesake. It seems unlikely; the President has seen her in a light other than that of perpetuator of a blood-line. Any woman could be that. In fact, no man wanted Hillela to be like any other woman, would allow her to be even if it had been possible for her, herself. Not even the one who supplied a brown-stone. The charming children, who have the composure and good manners of black and the precocity of white upper-class children, dressed by Hillela and educated at schools chosen by her, probably have been born to the President since his third marriage, by the second wife. Anyway, that one will never lose her position as mother of the best of them. That is something between the President and her no other woman will ever have. It would not trouble Hillela. What others perceive as character is often what has been practised long as necessity; the President's highly intelligent intuition, that has made him so successful in his allocation of portfolios in his government, recognized the day she hopped into the hired car and set off for Mombasa with him that Hillela is a past mistress of adaptation. But Hillela has not been taken in by this African family; she has disposed it around her. Hers is the non-matrilineal centre that no-one resents because no-one has known it could exist. She has invented it. This is not the rainbow family.

The President and his wife were hosts to experts from Bulgaria, Czechoslovakia, Rumania, Hungary, East Germany and the Soviet Union attending a workshop on his country's trade and economic links with Eastern European countries (Hillela entertained some old friends at State House). The President succeeded in obtaining a loan from the World Bank to form his Rural Development Corporation for the upgrading of provincial towns. Abdu Diouf of Senegal (an old friend of the President, this one), then Chairman of the OAU, paid the President's country a state visit. It was also the year Pauline was back in Africa.

The monthly telephone calls to her son had tailed off several years earlier. But at least he made the effort to reply to her letters irregularly, and she wrote regularly although the letters were about people he did not know and a life far removed from what mother and son had experienced together. That was childhood and adolescence; their battleground, to be avoided.

There were no letters from him and when she tried to telephone, she heard the plaintive siren of disconnection. It was a voice that was no voice; an alarm. Joe got in touch with his old colleagues in Johannesburg and they investigated. It was as Pauline had known, as she had told Joe, she knew from that mindless voice—Sasha was in detention. It was logical for Joe to be the one to fly back, since he was the man to deal with the law, legal representation, prisoners' rights—

—What law? What rights? They're holding him under Section 29. What lawyer among your friends has been able to get permission to see him? They can keep him in solitary confinement indefinitely. The only ways of getting to him, helping him, must be other ways, and I'm the one to find them.—

Her face surrounded by stiff grey hair was incandescent with the manic excitation of anxiety he had seen sometimes in clients whose mental balance was threatened; Joe understood that if he tried to make Pauline wait in London, take a bus every day at ten o'clock to her pleasant job at a Kensington Church Street book shop, she would simply go mad. Not just in a manner of speaking.

They flew together to Johannesburg, awake all night on the plane, silent together, as they had once hurried back along the footpaths in the Drakensberg. But that time they had not found an arrest, what they had found that time was nothing, nothing, child's play, this time was the real horror that hung over your life, all your life, if you belonged in that country, no matter where you ran to.

Joe did what lawyers can do; and that was a lot, despite Pauline's dismissals. Applications for the parents who had come from abroad to see the detainee were finally approved after Joe reached, link by link of connections—members of parliament, judges, influential friends-of-friends—the Minister himself.

The meeting was terrible. Pauline's blazing red face, steamy with tears, relived it for hours in the Rosebank flat friends had lent them. It was Sasha's fault, it was Joe's and hers: there he stood behind the cage and faced them as if he expected them to be facing him as a criminal, prisons are for criminals, aren't they?— and that wasn't the way they had come at all, that long distance to find him, endured that sycophantic struggle to get to see him!

He was all right. What was 'all right'? He was not ill or apparently depressed. No thinner if paler than they remembered him on his last visit to London. No more difficult to talk to, taking into consideration that the awkward platitudes exchanged, which were one part of the customary mode of communication between them, couldn't have been anything more, anyway, in present circumstances, with a warder on either side of him listening in, and the other part of their family communication, the clashes between mother and son, were too preciously intimate for a non-contact visit. What was 'all right' about his being led away by two louts back to solitary confinement, a bible and a sanitary bucket? 'All right' was the report given by white liberal members of parliament when they received parliamentary privilege to visit such prisoners: it meant that prisoners were still alive, in possession of their senses and with no immediately apparent evidence of the wounds, bruises and burns of torture. One was supposed to be grateful to the prison authorities, the Minister of Justice, the government, for that? As an aside, there was also the routine Opposition condemnation of the principle of preventive detention. That was 'all right', too. That was all the conventions of justice, of humanitarian concern meant in this country Pauline had rejected but where she had left a hostage. Joe went back to London because—she let him know—these were his conventions, in all good faith they represented all he could do; she stayed to do what she had failed to after the Maritzburg All-In African Conference more than twenty years before; to find what else there was for her, beyond them.

She went to the house of another couple whose child—a daughter, this one, a student and not a trade unionist—was in detention. Being Pauline she had neither sought an introduction through anybody nor telephoned first; just was there, with her great quick eyes ready to stare down timidity, scepticism or distrust, on the doorstep and then in the livingroom. The professor of chemistry and his wife found she had burst in not to commiserate in misfortune but to share action against it. Out of this intrusion on meek despair she became one of the founders of a committee of detainees' parents; the professor and his wife became numbered among those who did not beg for mercy for their sons and daughters but demanded justice, and by justice meant nothing less than the abolition of laws, opposition to which had sent their young and thousands of others to prison—laws that in those years removed whole populations of black people from their homes and dumped them elsewhere at the will of whites; divided blacks' own country into enclaves under dummy flags from beneath which blacks could not move about freely; kept education segregated in favour of white privilege; tried for treason leaders of non-violent opposition, turning it to violence; attacked black trade union action with mass dismissals, police intimidation, banning and imprisonment of officials; and created the last institution and edifice of white domination, the Parliament with three Houses provided by the State, one for Indians, one for people of mixed blood, one for whites—and none for the mass of the people, the blacks.

The Committee members, too, respected no conventions of how things were being done in the official best interests of the country. They would not be turned away from State doorsteps; they unearthed facts and figures—how many people were detained each month, each week, each day, and who they were—that were not revealed by the police or the Minister of Law and Order. They learnt to use Underground—or rather under-prison-wall—means by which they were able to inform the newspapers of a hunger strike among detainees anywhere in the country, while the police denied such a strike was taking place. They followed word-of-mouth to find the evidence of parents of black schoolchildren who were scooped into police vans and detained, in that long period of boycotts; they produced at public meetings in church halls (the only assembly places where there was some chance of proceeding without a ministerial ban) children of nine and ten whose precocity, here, was a terrible fluency to describe their experience of the cell, the solitude, the plate of pap pushed across the floor, the sanitary bucket and the beatings.

Black parents' committees set up in the segregated townships, but they did not keep themselves apart from whites and the whites did not confine their concern to the smaller number of their own in detention but were active on behalf of the thousands of black sons and daughters; with her son shut away, Pauline received back the acceptance she had been deprived of when the Saturday morning children ceased to come singing up the brick-lined path in the garden laid waste with broken bottles and human shit.

The acceptance was happening at the same time as petrol bombs and limpet mines began to explode in streets where whites went by. Countless black children (even Pauline's colleagues could not keep tally in the burning townships) had been killed; now the first white children were. This was the kind of bond between white and black the whites had not foreseen and were never to recognize.

Sasha also found ways and means. It was from Maximum Security that he wrote the last letter to his sibling cousin.

I am incommunicado, so might as well try to reach you. That's not so much more hopeless than trying for anyone else now. Little Hendrik who comes on duty at night has smuggled in this paper for me. He had it under the plastic lining of his warder's cap; just now, when he took off the cap, there it was. He's about nineteen and has a double crown, the hair stood up all bright yellow and sticky-shiny He always wants to get out of my cell quickly because he's agitated—he likes me, and is afraid of that. He likes me because I don't curse him—gaan kak, Boer— the way the brave ones do. These maledictions are scratched into the walls where I'm kept.

I suppose there are prisons like this where you are, too. That's a ridiculous thing to say—I'm not quite crazy, don't decide that—of course there are prisons, but I mean ones where politicals are held. There surely have to be those. Every power has to put away what threatens it—that's where the just and unjust causes meet. Okay, I know that, I accept it. Not cynically. I still believe. But I hope you don't think about these places. Because it's no good, you can't imagine what it's like. I had read so much—the Count of Monte Cristo to Dostoevsky to Gramsci!— and I thought I had a maximum security Baedeker in my head, I knew my way around every 7-by-7 cell, along every caged catwalk, saw the bit of sky through bars and had ready-paced-out the exercise yard, had my ingenuity kit to keep track of days with bits of unpicked thread. And the mouse or cockroach that would become a friend. (Sources: from Ruth First to Jeremy Cronin and Breytenbach.)

Even the business of the thread is wrong. I know every day when I wake up what day it is and whatever else has gone out of my head in seven months the calendar beside the phone in Point road is there, with the volk's holidays figured in red, Day of the Vow that if Dingane killed Piet Retief it would be only whites killing blacks from then on, Family Day when the whites picnic and the dockworkers and miners get drunk alone in their single-sex hostels. Today is the 214th day I've been incommunicado.

Oh my mother has seen me, and Joe was here, there were two visits with him before he went back to London. But what is there to say. The reasons I'm here are not negotiable (as Joe would put it). I'm where I have to be. Yes, Joe, I want to overthrow the State, I can't find a way to live in it and see others suffer in it, the way it is or the way it revises its names and its institutions—it's still the same evil genie changing shapes, you have to smash the bottle from which it rises. Rhetoric. That's the fancy language of my speechifying to unions that the Major reads back to me in interrogation. But I am my fancy language. I used to read a lot of poetry—as you know. Well, that's my poetry. That's the meaning of my life.

Oh I tell him: it's fancy to you because even now when you can see it's all up with white-man-baas, you see the real end as a 'fancy' you'll knock out of the heads of a horde of ignorant blacks incited by romantic white radicals. The Major snorts with laughter (every mannerism these interrogators have that one wouldn't notice in anyone else becomes piggish) when I say there is unbeatable purpose expressed in the horrible mishmash of Marxism, Castroism, Gandhism, Fanonism, Hyde Park tub-thumping (colonial heritage), Gawd-on-our-sideism (missionary heritage), Black Consciousness jargon, Sandinistism, Christian liberation theology with which we formulate. He thinks he's getting somewhere with me. He thinks I'm beginning to have doubts, and they'll soon be able to produce me as a State witness at somebody's trial. He's not getting anywhere. I have no doubts; I only see better than he does that if the means are confused, the end is not.

Gaan kak, Boer. I've always died a thousand deaths. You remember how when we went to the dentist as kids, I couldn't eat breakfast, my knees and elbows were pressed together, I wanted my steps to take me backwards when the nurse called me to the chair. And the big fuss about the army I was always scared stiff I wouldn't be able to stand things.

But that was dread, which is fear of something that hasn't yet happened. There are times when I'd do anything to get out. I'm craven. But never when I'm with the Major or his team. All the things you've read about have happened to me; even if my feet are swollen from standing and I have a thirst for sleep that's the strongest desire I've ever known—Hillela, forget about sex—even then when they lead me back here I always have the feeling I've won.

There's nothing more to dread. Is there? If they put me on trial and the skills of all Joe's colleagues can't get me off, I've stood it for seven months in prison, if I go in for years, I won't have to die that death again.

I'm going to tell you that at first Pauline actually had the idea you might be able to 'do something' about me! Olga recognized you in a newspaper photograph, Hillela is Madame la Prèsidente. How you got there, that's confusing, too. When I wrote some years ago you were supposed to be married to an American professor, but the letter came back. Pauline was in one of her hyped-up states when she arrived here: you would get your President to pull strings. What strings? Through the OAU; she had rushed off to one other old chums still teaching African Politics at Wits and checked your husband's standing, which proved high. Joe had to point out that the OAU was not exactly influential with the South African security police. It was only a lapse; my mother's really always been cleverer than Joe, we know. She's still here. I realize she'll never go back while I'm inside. She's tremendously active with a group that supports us—detainees, and politicals on trial. It's possible she might land up inside, too. She looks wonderful. I'll tell you: happy. She's the only person I see except the Major's team, and Hendrik and his mates in uniform. The visits are in the presence of warders, you can't say much, but all Pauline and I have to say to each other is political and we've come to some strange kind of intuition between us, a private language by which we're able to convey information back and forth in a form Hendrik and co. can't follow. Family sayings, childhood expressions—we have access through them.

Then why do I say I'm incommunicado.

*You couldn't experience it, of course, being more or less a lucky orphan,
but hearing from outside exclusively in the voice of your mother, it's like
being thrust up back again into the womb.*

*I can never guess whether you'll be interested or not. Because I can't
imagine what your life is. If I think of you in the morning, for instance,
I can't imagine where you get up out of bed as you used to in your short
pyjamas, that kind of baby dress with bikini pants, you having breakfast—what sort of room, not a kitchen!—you going off to do what? What
do you do all day in a President's house? State House—Groote Schuur's
the only one I've ever seen, and I'll bet yours isn't Cape Dutch-gabled. I'm
lodged with the State, myself, so we've both landed up in the same boat,
but you're at the Captain's table, and I'm pulling the oars down in the
galley. That's supposed to be funny, in case you think I'm dramatizing
myself. I was going to say—I don't know if you're interested in how I got
here. I don't think it will be any surprise to you that I am. I was on my
way while we were still kids, although I made a kind of nihilistic show
of kicking against it. Pauline's Great Search for Meaning. It was a pain
in the arse. You went off and plink-plonked on your guitar. I sneered at
her. My school—the one she chose for me, did Joe ever decide anything
for us?—its Swazi name meant 'the world', one of those great African
omnibus concepts (I love them), the nearest synonym in our language is
a microcosm, I suppose. Nobody at home knew how happy I was there—
certainly not you. Carole may have suspected. It was the world (and the
world's South Africa for us) the way we wanted it to be, the way Pauline
longed for it to be, and into which she projected me. But it had no reality
in the world we had to grow up into, less and less, now none at all. It
was all back-to-front. When I went to school, I went* home *—to that
'world'; when I came to the house in Johannesburg, I was cast out. Good
god, even you were more at home in that house than I was. Alpheus in the
garage, Pauline and Joe's pals bemoaning the latest oppressive law on the
terrace under that creeper with the orange trumpet flowers. At Kamhlaba
blacks were just other boys in the same class, in the dormitory beds, you
could fight with them or confide in them, masturbate with them, they were*

friends or schoolboy enemies. At the house, my mother's blacks were like Aunt Olga's whatnots, they were handled with such care not to say or do anything that might chip the friendship they allowed her to claim—and she had some awful layabouts and spivs among them. I smelt them out, because where I was at 'home', that sort of relationship, carrying its own death, didn't have to exist. Poor Pauline. I hated South Africa so much.

When I was older—by the time you left the house—I hated them all, or I thought I did. Maybe even Joe. I expected them to have solutions but they only had questions. Do you realize I was the only answer Pauline ever had? She knew what to do about me: sent me to Kamhlaba, 'the world'. But I had to come back. Joe half-believed his answer: the kind of work he was doing, but you know how she was the one who took away half the certainty. And she was right, in her way, you can't find justice in a country with our kind of laws. I feel as Bram Fischer did, that if I come to trial it's going to be before a court whose authority I don't recognize, under laws made by a minority government of whites. I'd like to reject that white privilege, too, but how can I take away from Joe the half he believes in? It's all my father has. And of course if I can get off and live to fight another day, so to speak, I want that. No sense in a white being a martyr. There's not enough popular appeal involved.

I've no way of knowing how much you know. I mean, you certainly know the facts of what has happened in this country since you left. After all, you were married to a revolutionary. You probably knew more about it, from a politico-analytical point of view, than I did, at least during the years you were with him—and that's why I can't imagine you, Hillela, that's it, I can't imagine you living your life in the tremendous preoccupation that is liberation politics. Yet it seems this has been your solution, in your own way—and I never thought of you as in need of a solution at all, I still don't, I never shall. You know, in these places one suffers from something called sensory deprivation (Pauline's crowd apparently have published an extensive study of this which has horrified even people who think those like me ought to be kept locked up: they've revised their punitive premise, they think we deserve all we get, but nobody deserves quite that). I have it, too, 'sensory deprivation', I won't go into the symptoms but the incoherent jumps in this letter are well known to be one. As I said, I'm not really crazy, and they won't get me that way. Thoughts are wonderfully free when you're in this state of sensory deprivation. Some hallucinate but it's not that with me. It makes me know things I didn't know. About you, Hillela. You were always in the opposite state. You received everything through your skin, understood everything that way. I suppose you still do. One can't judge change in others by change in oneself.

They said you went because of the journalist chap. A solution. D'you know he was almost certainly working for the security police? The whole business of raiding the cottage where you lived with him was a put-up job, to keep his credibility and make him appear to have to flee the country so he could carry on his slimy trade in Dar es Salaam? Apparently the ANC blew his cover there, I heard the whole story only recently. Well, at least nothing happened to you. What do you look like, Hillela. I didn't see the newspaper photograph with you sitting next to Yasir Arafat (imagine Olga's face).

I got lost somewhere a few pages back. Even now—specially now—you must know just about everything, in terms of events, and the reactions of white power to events, here; and the precipitation of events by that power. But you can't know what it has been to live here, I hated everyone in the house for not having a solution, because I was like Pauline, I was looking for one myself. Pretending not to be. Not arriving at one, through my skin. I've always been afraid to feel too much, the only time I did it was all so painful, such a mess. But in the Seventies everything changed. Pauline and her crowd were told they could not look for a solution—it was not for them: something like a state of grace, they couldn't attain it. You knew that, before then. Long before. Well, whatever your view of the Black Consciousness movement (you may be politically sympathetic or not, for all I know, it'll be a matter of alliances, now, although you were a loyal kid in your own way and surely your ANC ties prevail, whichever way your President/husband inclines)—whatever you think, Black Consciousness, black withdrawal freed us whites as much as it reduced us to despair. Despair for my mother; she packed up Joe and Carole and went to London.

Me—it freed me. There was nothing a white could do in '76 when the black students had the brilliant idea of beginning the revolution at the beginning of blacks' lives: in school. Don't believe anybody who claims to know who exactly should take the credit. SASO has a good share, underground ANC has some, but there were so many little groups with long titles that became proper nouns in the acronymic language we communicate in now. It was spontaneity that created its own structures, but the form action took was old as revolt itself, as oppression itself. The demands arose first from the apparently narrow orbit of children's lives—the third-rate education, the prohibition of students' councils, the objection to Afrikaans as a medium of instruction. But this was another Kamhlaba—'a world' of a different kind from Pauline's failed solution for me, a real microcosm of real social conditions under which blacks live. These childish demands could be met only by adult answers. What the young really were doing was beginning to put their small or half-formed bodies under the centuries' millstone. And they have lifted it as no adult was able to do, by the process of growing under the weight, something so elemental that it can no more be stopped than time can be turned back. They have lifted it by the measure of more than ten years of continuous revolt—pausing to take breath in one part of the country, heaving with a surge of energy in another—and by showing their parents how it can be done, making room through the '80s for new adult liberation organizations—you've heard about the UDF*—for militancy in the trade unions and churches.

That's where I come in—came in. If you couldn't wait, I suppose you had to go: Pauline went. There was nothing for whites to do but wait to see what blacks might want them to do. There was a lot of shit to take from them—blacks. Why should I be called whitey? I didn't ever say 'kaffir' in my life. Not being needed at all is the biggest shit of the lot. But everything was changing—no, the main thing was changing. Not the laws, the whites were only tinselling them up for travel brochures. (You could marry your black husband here, now, but you couldn't buy

---

*United Democratic Front

our old house and move in. Though you could live illegally in a Hillbrow that and get away with it; apartheid is breaking down strangely where everyone said it never would—among the less affluent whose jobs are at risk from black competition . . .) The main other thing was changing, the thing far more important than the laws, in the end. Blacks of all kinds and ages were deciding what had to be done and how to do it. Even the white communists, people like Fischer and Lionel Burger, hadn't recognized quite that degree of initiative in blacks, before, they'd always at least told blacks how they thought it could be done; and even the ANC in its mass campaigns had responded to what whites had done rather than forced whites into situations where they were the ones who had to respond to blacks. Now it didn't matter whether it was one of the black bourgeoisie the radicals said were being co-opted by the white system, a businessman like Sam Motsuenyane getting British banks to make their South African operation acceptable by putting up capital for a black bank and training blacks to run it, or whether it was kids willing to be shot rather than educated for exploitation, or whether, from '79, it was the bosses forced to admit they couldn't run industry without a majority of unionised labour with which to negotiate. It wasn't any longer a question of justice, it was a question of power the whites were confronted with. Justice is high-minded and relative, hey. You can give people justice or withhold it, but power they find out how to take for themselves. There are precedents for them to go by—and whites on the black side had tried to establish these— but no rules except those that arise pragmalically from the circumstances of people's lives. That's why text-book revolutions fail, and this one won't. Castro made a revolution with fifteen followers. Marcos was driven out to exile by Filipinos who simply swarmed around his military vehicles like ants carrying away dead vermin—they'd judged by then he couldn't will his soldiers to fire into crowds. I know it's said that Reagan saw the game was up for Marcos and that's why the troops didn't shoot—but that's not the whole story. The slave knows best how to test his chains, the prisoner knows best his jailer. (How did I persuade Hendrik to bring me this paper!) The way we've lived here hasn't been quite like anything anywhere else in the world. The blacks came to understand that to over-throw that South African way of life they'd have to find methods not quite like anything that's succeeded anywhere else in the world.

What a lucid patch I've struck. But where I came in: I wrote you about that, in the letter that was returned. I saw no point in becoming Joe (though I still admire my father) but the legal studies I'd been dragging myself through were a good background for what did come up. Something blacks did turn out to want was whites to work for them in the formation of unions, people with a knowledge of industrial legislation. They gave me a job. When the United Democratic Front was launched, and the unions I was working for affiliated, I got drawn in along with them, by then, blacks had sufficient confidence to invite whites to join the liberation struggle with them, again. They have no fear it'll ever be on the old terms. Those've gone for good. So you're not the only one who's spoken on public platforms. I was up there, too. There's not much corporate unionism among blacks—you know what that means? Unions that stick to negotiating wage agreements, safety, canteen facilities and so on. Our unions don't see their responsibility for the worker ending when he leaves the factory gates every day. Their demands aren't only for the baas, they're addressed to the government, black worker power confronting white economic power, and they're for an end to the South African way of life.

There've been a great many funerals. The law can stop the public meet-ings but not always the rallies at funerals of riot dead—although the law tries. Sometimes the police Casspirs and the army follow people back to the washing of the hands at the family's house, and the crowd gathered there is angry at the intrusion on this custom and throws stones, and the army or police fire. Then there is another funeral. This has become a country where the dead breed more dead. But you've seen these scenes of home on your television in State House. There were plenty of television crews to record them before the law banned coverage. And clandestine filming still goes on. I can imagine that, Hillela—you sitting watching us—but of course you look about eighteen years old, and now—good god, you must be forty. You also see the madness that this long-drawn-out struggle has bred. Your traitor was lucky, he was white and he flitted long ago. The blacks who inform have roused madness in ordinary people. Necklaces of burning tyres placed over informers' heads, collaborators' heads, and packs turning on a suspect among themselves and kicking him to death. 'Her', too; I was at a funeral of a unionist, shot by the police, and some youngsters followed the cry that a girl had been recognized as an informer and each brought down upon her blows that combined to kill her. You know how people come up to a grave one by one and throw their flower in, as a tribute? Well, each gave their blow. Mistakes are made sometimes; that is sure. I don't know if that girl was what the crowd thought she was, or if she just happened to resemble a culprit. And the manner of dealing with culprits. What happened to the smiling grateful kids who used to come to free classes at the old church on Saturdays—even you gave them a Saturday or two, didn't you, before you found there were better things to pass the time. They boycotted the Bantu Education that made it necessary for them to receive white charity coaching, they got shot at and tear-gassed after you'd gone, there've been funerals for many of them. Does bravery, awesome contempt for your own death take away all feeling? (White kids don't even know what death is, we were kept away from funerals for fear of upsetting us psychologically.) Can you kill others as you may be killed—and do even worse? And is this death really worse than death by police torture? Whites don't call their fellow whites savages for what goes on in this building.

No-one is on record for feeling any remorse. Neither the police and soldiers who shoot blacks every day, nor the blacks who kill—no, not their own people, which is what whites are saying—but those who are not their own, anymore: who have lost all identity but that of enemy. There's colour-blindness for you, at last ...

What excuse is there for that? The madness. How do you feel about that? The whites want the madness to be the last, the final, triumphant vindication of all they themselves have done to blacks for hundreds of years.

There's no excuse.

There's only the evidence: if over hundreds of years you distort law and order as repression, you get frenzy. If you won't attempt to do justice, you cut morality, human feeling, pity—you cut the heart out.

White kids are being killed in landmine explosions and supermarket bombings, on Sunday rides and shopping trips with their loving parents. The mines and petrol bombs are planted by blacks, but it's the whites who have killed their own children. The loving parents and grandparents and great-grandparents. The white family tree.

How is it possible to live like that; well, how was it possible to have lived like that. They can go away from what's happening now, but they can never go away from the way we lived for so many generations. On little floating islands, it exists still, that life like patches of blue water hyacinths that used to choke the rivers, broken from their moorings now and being carried out by heavy seas. (Sentence sounds odd because, in fact, it's the beginning of a poem I tried to write; break up the lines and you'll see it's not so bad.) I hired a cottage—only eighteen months ago—along the North Coast. It was on, wooden stilts and built of corrugated iron with a wooden stoep and a water-tank. White miners used to save up and retire on pension in little pondokkies like that, but they've nearly all been pulled down for time-sharing condominiums for richer whites. This one was in an area the Indians have got declared for them since they've had a House in Parliament, and their development scheme hasn't started yet—so an Indian friend found it for me. (You see, there's privilege even among revolutionaries.) Between the strikes and the funerals I was going there regularly whenever I could. It was my Safe House. The Gandhi settlement nearby was burned down and Buthelezi's government-approved private army was fighting our United Democratic Front people in a black township just over the hills. In my cottage there was perfect peace. The wasps buzzed their mantras. I ate the shad I caught and drank my Lion lager like every South African male. At night I sat out in what the darkness reverted to the miner's garden. I couldn't see the weeds and broken chairs and rusted pots, and the frangipani trees, that had survived neglect and the black women's search for firewood, were a constellation of scented stars just at my head. *The frogs throbbing on and the sea hissing. I'd walk down to the beach. Nothing. Nothing but gentleness, you know how the Indian Ocean seems to evaporate into the sky at night. In the middle of my witness of the horror of this country, I experienced the white man's peace. I did. I woke up at night and heard the heavy sea, the other sea, pounding on the land. But that was only a line for the ending of the poem; although I was being carried out on it, it was bringing me here.*

There has been madness since the beginning, in the whites. Our great-grandfather Hillel was in it from the moment he came up from the steerage deck in Cape Town harbour with his cardboard suitcase, landing anywhere to get away from the Little Father's quotas and the cossacks' pogroms. It's in the blood you and I share. Since the beginning. Whites couldn't have done what they've done, otherwise. Madness has appeared among blacks in the final stage of repression. It is, in fact, the unrecognized last act of repression, transferred to them to enact upon themselves. *It is the horrible end of all whites have done.*

The Major is triumphant. Well, how do you feel about your blacks now? What about your savages hacking each other to death? What about the end of capitalist exploitation and the great dawn of freedom and peace?

But my position is sane. I'm without doubts about that.

This cell, at this moment, seems full to me, brimming, this empty cell is fuller than the other rooms I've had. My room in the house always looked as if Bettie had just cleared someone's stuff away. I never hung it with sports pennants and school photographs and pop stars the way you girls did yours. I didn't keep things, didn't want to remember. What have I got of my life? Only what is here. D'you remember the toy car? It belonged to that kid. I kept that.

Hendrik/Mercury/Icarus, don't fall into the sea with this. From jail, from here I'm free to say everything. I love you.

Sasha

Whaila's Country

The letter was produced at Sasha's trial.

He must have bribed the young son of a farmer ruined by the '80s drought in the Koster district who had said there were opportunities for advancement in the prison services. But what could the prisoner have had to offer? It is the wretched thieves and prostitutes, not the politicals, who traffic in the prison economy of drugs. Maybe he had even tried to convert the boy to the cause; it is known to prison officers that those trained by the Left are taught to subvert the Christian values inculcated by the Dutch Reformed Church.

Hendrik Gerhardus Munnik had never written a letter in his life, except as a school exercise. The letter he smuggled out of prison (it was 'under the plastic' in his warder's cap, he told the court) was very thick, he didn't know what was inside. He kept it for three days before handing it over to the Commandant. And why did he decide to surrender it to prison authorities?

Because he was afraid of what his father would say if he lost his job.

Did the prisoner promise him any reward or remuneration for smuggling the letter?

No.

Why did he agree to take it?

Because he thought it was a love-letter.

Sasha was accused with three others, Burtwell Nyaka, Makekene Conco, Thabo Poswao, on five counts, which the Defence conducted by Joe's most distinguished colleagues succeeded in getting reduced to the two principal ones: conspiring to overthrow the State and furthering the aims of the African National

410

Congress. The 'love-letter', the Prosecution submitted, contained a clear statement of the accused's intention to commit high treason. The passage was read out and the exhibit, numbered 14, passed to the judge: 'Yes ... I want to overthrow the State ... that is the meaning of my life'. The whole tenor of the letter, the Prosecution continued, made clear that for the accused the 'solution' to South Africa's problems was revolution. In this context, he lauded violent uprisings, lawlessness in the black townships, strikes and boycotts, as the blacks' understanding of means to 'overthrow that (the) South African way of life'. He blamed whites for the murder of white children. These sentiments he had already expressed on public platforms, in the trade union and other journals to which he contributed, in the pamphlets it would be alleged he had conspired to distribute by pamphlet bombs, in fact in his record of revolutionary activities that could be proved as far back as 1979. And his convictions were so strong that he would even risk sending subversive material out of prison by clandestine means—some love-letter!

The Defence submitted that the letter was, in fact, 'a moving credo' from a man whose sense of justice and humanity had found no structures within which to redress the misery he was aware of in South Africa. He had been brought up in a family where a social conscience was the foundation of personal morality, his father had been for many years what would be known in Western countries as a civil rights lawyer, his mother had been an active liberal; their son had seen them leave their country in despair at the fruitlessness of their efforts to assist meaningful constitutional changes. It was, indeed, out of love—love for fellow human beings, for the poorest and most disadvantaged, the majority of the South African population, that the son had given up the promise of a lucrative career in law and a high social and economic position among whites in order to put his life at the service of black workers.

Exhibit 14 included two envelopes. Within the first there was another: State House, the name of the capital, the country, this surely should have been an adequate address to have reached the one for whom it was intended. Exhibit 14 did not even reach the cover address on the outer envelope; but although Hendrik had failed to deliver it there, it had led the police to the friend Sasha had hoped would get it taken to England and forwarded. The friend was arrested and detained as another possible co-conspirator, but released after a week of interrogation.

There was a stir of comment in the public gallery the day Hendrik gave his reason for accepting the letter; typically soppy, probably thinking of his Koster *meisie* back on the farm. These backveld boys, *plaasja-pies!* His brother-in-law, a cartage contractor from Pretoria and not to be patronised, who had accompanied Hendrik's mother to court, turned angrily on the faces behind him. No, a *boereseun* was no match for a Jewboy communist. The mother grasped his hand in a vice to quiet him; never looked up from under her hat.

The Defence disputed the Prosecution's interpretation of the letter. The person to whom it was addressed was like a sister to the accused. She was a relative who had been brought up by the accused's parents as one of their own children. He had been deeply attached to her, she was apparently his confidante through child-hood and adolescence. It was not surprising that under conditions of sensory deprivation in solitary confinement, where time loses its normal dimension and partings of many years may seem the same as partings that took place a few weeks or months previously, he should have turned to her, in imagination, to review his life and set out his commitment to serve others. In no way could the intimate confidences of this letter be regarded as constituting a revolutionary document. And whom could it have been planned to incite? The intended recipient had lived abroad for a long time. Defence requested that the letter be read out in its entirety, not quoted from selectively.

The other mother was beside her husband and they heard it all. There were flashes in Pauline's face. Joe made no move to touch her. There was the sense around them, in them, that the matings, the birth of children, the quarrels, the convictions that didn't lie together, the unsaid, the spoken that should never have been said, the right questions, the wrong answers, the trust and distrust, the blame and the forgiveness were casting them in the bronze of a single fused figure. For them, there was nobody else in the court; the mass of their feeling occupied it, it would not have been surprising if everyone on the adjoining benches had edged away or silently trooped out with a bow to the judge.

Olga was very supportive. Whether Arthur liked it or not, she insisted that Pauline and Joe move out of that pokey flat and into her house, where they would be properly fed and looked after during their ordeal. After all, the two sisters had only each other—they had lost Ruthie, she might be dead, for all they knew. But Olga did not attend the trial. Pauline would not expect that of her. She had never been in court in her life; police vans from which hands clung through the diamond-mesh guard, men in shackles led to the dock, a red-robed protector with the authority—thank God—to lock away burglars, rapists, embezzlers, car thieves, murderers where they couldn't threaten decent people any longer—all that belonged to the criminals and the poor. Poor devils, the latter; a matter of environment. Certainly not the environment to which the sisters belonged, and in which even Pauline's children had been brought up. Poor Pauline, she hadn't deserved Sasha. Olga's Clive, hardly a year older, was consultant to exporters and importers in the wine industry, an authority on vintages, with a 'nose' equal to that of some of the great experts in France; sad for Pauline: when Clive's name appeared in the newspapers it was not as an accused in a trial for treason but as author of his syndicated column for wine lovers. But Olga was loyal to her sisters, never would have heard a bad word said about the other one, and would not tolerate any condemnatory remarks about Pauline's son. Once or twice she invited carefully-selected friends to dinner—her sister and brother-in-law surely needed some distraction, sitting day after day in what she imagined a court must be like. Olga deliberately did not avoid the subject that was in the guests' minds, like a death in the family. Sasha was not disgraced; he was wronged. He had somehow fallen through one of the man-holes of life into an environment that wasn't his; there had been criminal carelessness somewhere, on somebody's part, mainte-nance was a scandal, what did one pay taxes for if no-one was secure any longer. Her own nephew had been locked away by these Afrikaners, put on trial by them, arid he was a young man of good family, intelligent, cultivated. If Arthur wanted to (he didn't look as if he wanted to, he was spitting out fish-bones without even putting his hand over his mouth) he could tell some tales about the real criminals, the swindling and fina-gling that went on high up in the financial world in connivance with members of the government. Whom had her nephew swin-dled? Whom had he cheated or hurt? —He's done nothing! The government is mad!—

There was an abrupt change of atmospheric pressure which all felt without for a moment knowing why.

Pauline put down her knife and fork, stood up and flattened her hands on Olga's Georgian table so that the wine jumped in the glasses. Then she lifted the hands and dug the spread fingers up through that wild head of hair that needed the attention of a good stylist. Her eyes held their audience as they had always sought to. —Olga, Sasha did not do *nothing*. Understand that. He did every-thing he could to bring down this government, and the power of white people who made it, and all their white governments before it. *They* recognize the danger he represents to their evil; don't you sit here and minimize that. This trial is a sign of his effectiveness. *He did something.*— And she sat down to her plate while others did not know how to take up again the normal flow of the evening;

for a few moments only she and Arthur were eating—he never listened when Pauline spoke, and had not been interrupted.

Since Olga did not come to court she did not hear the letter read out. There was merely a mention of its existence as evidence, no extract of its contents or mention of the name of the individual to whom it was written, in the day's newspaper reports of the trial. When Joe's colleagues, the team defending Sasha and his co-accused, came to confer with Joe and Pauline, Olga sent in Jethro's successor with tea and cream scones (Olga's servants stayed with her faithfully until pensioned; the old cook had been retired to KwaZulu—the recipe remained) but she ensured there would be absolute privacy for the discussion going on in her little sittingroom, where some of her favourite pieces were gathered, including the Blackamoor lamp that used to stand in the main lounge. When she walked past the door she rose on tiptoe.

Pauline did not talk of the letter to Olga. And Joe did not need to be told not to. So Olga was not caused pain by any unearthing of what else had been out of place in the environment of the family. Anyway, it was none of her business, never had been, she had not taken any responsibility for Ruthie's child beyond buying her a new outfit every six months.

Pain was caused to the girl with whom Sasha lived for several years up to a short while before he was detained. They were parted by then, but although he never mentioned her in the letter, she had been with him in the tin cottage with the water-tank and the frangipani. She had married someone else while he was in detention; the husband was a friend of Sasha and the couple came up from Durban, in solidarity with those on trial, at least once to attend part of the proceedings. When the letter was read out she realized that for its writer she never had been in the cottage, that was what was wrong that she hadn't understood, all the time they were together. There was no need to laugh at Hendrik, the *boereseun*, the *plaasjapie*.

The letter was merely one exhibit in a dossier of incriminating evidence that took months to be led. Burtwell Nyaka and Makekene Conco received varying sentences. Sasha was found guilty on both counts of the indictment and given a lengthy sentence, along with Thabo Poswao, although the period of punishment on each count was to run concurrently. Joe's colleagues decided against an appeal to a higher court, for Sasha. There was the danger that instead of the result being a reduction of sentence the State might cross-appeal for a heavier one. There were some aspects of the case where the Defence, all things considered, had been lucky. The matter of the letter was an example: because of Hillela's new names and some-what unlikely and exotic status, perhaps, the Prosecution never made use of her strong association with the African National Congress, the fact that she was the same woman who had been the wife of the assassinated Whaila Kgomani, and who after his death had worked for the Congress in Eastern Europe as well as Africa. If the Prosecution had chosen to exploit these links, it wouldn't have been too credible to attempt to establish Exhibit 14 as any kind of love-letter.

When sentence was passed, Sasha suddenly did not belong to them—Pauline and Joe and Carole (who had flown out to be with her parents for the verdict). The blacks in the gallery began to sing and stamp over calls for order and as the police hustled them out they went stamping, waving fists at the four men being led down to the well of the court whose fists were raised to them, and already there were new verses for the refrain of their song: *woza Luthuli, woza Mandela, woza Tambo, woza Sisulu, woza Mbeki, woza Slovo, woza Kgomani*—to those names they added the names of the four men, the three blacks and their white brother, descending to prison. For the first time in his life Sasha resembled Pauline—turning, pausing before he was pushed down to the well—his face public, blazing, exalted, open to the chanting crowd dragging and tramping their feet heavily along the boards as they left the gallery. Then he was gone.

Outside in the street his family was passed from arms to arms in the huge embrace that is the reverse of the hostility a mob can generate. The mother of Thabo was clinging to Joe, weeping with pride and sorrow, and he held her head to him, like a lover. *Viva!*, coming by way of Cuba, Mozambique and Nicaragua, had joined the old litany of freedom cries. They flew back and forth, exciting the police dogs and bringing the white shop assistants to the doors of the chainstore and Greek-owned supermarket in the maize-belt town. Political trials were no longer held in the cities, in order to avoid mass gatherings of blacks, but trade unionists had come by the busload and they were joined by local black delivery men wheeling their bicycles, farm workers with their small purchases of soap and sugar, unemployed youths—all those people from a nearby 'homeland' who gravitated towards the streets of the town where they were forbidden to live. Petrified among them was the equestrian statue that stands in every Transvaal dorp, the Boer War general with the trunk of a stone tree growing up into his horse's belly to solve the sculptor's problem of supporting his work. Press cars and several chauffeur-driven ones with diplomatic number plates (these cases attracted foreign observers at a high level) made through the crowd a passage which flowed closed again. Pauline was swept away but Joe heard her: —Those sentences don't mean anything! They're not going to be all those years inside! The end to all this will come long before then!—

Trust Hillela; she chose well. The President was able to achieve in his one-party state what the handbooks on and surveys of Africa concede as 'impressive development' during the years when oil prices were high, and by the time oil resources were no longer such a profitable source of revenue had succeeded in diversifying the economy so that, in comparison with most neighbouring countries, his people are reasonably well off and there has been no serious 'crisis of expectation' to threaten the stability of the regime. The oil fields, mining industry and banks are nationalized, land has been redistributed and there are co-operative farms, but agriculture, learning from the disasters elsewhere, has not been collectivized. The General within the President has never forgotten the subversive power of hunger. The petty shopkeepers have not been touched. The Lebanese still constitute what is best referred to as an informal banking structure; so long as the back-of-the-shop deals in foreign currency stay within reason, it is best to ignore them. The country rarely has any entry under the list of violations of human rights published by Amnesty International; imprisoned cabinet ministers and officials of the previous regime were amnestied one by one in the yearly celebrations of the President's reaccession to power which take place in State House, country-wide sports stadia and schools. Of course there is a prison where individuals designated Enemies of The People are held. As a prisoner in another country once wrote, there surely have to be such places? The rendezvous just and unjust keep, in turn. Every power has to put away what threatens it? *Habeas corpus* is entrenched in the constitution, and the occasional expulsion of a miscreant foreign journalist intent on finding a story discreditable to African regimes in grievances of the sort malcontents and anti-social elements have in all societies, scarcely is to be regarded as suppression of freedom of the press. The President's son, the Colonel, is Director of National Security. But no-one can accuse the President of nepotism in this case; the Colonel is immensely capable, a man with a particular silence suited to conscientious discharge of his duty. It is a silence that came to him in the room of an Arab house, developing with the pattern of light and dark that played over him there, as a photographic negative fixes a phenomenon of place, time and experience. He is greatly feared and known by the designated Enemies of The People as the President's hit man. There is no amnesty from his surveillance. He is married to a young woman from the Ministry of Works and has provided the President with the eldest son of an eldest son—in his less formal photographs the President in an open-neck shirt is often shown with his good-looking white wife (or is she half-caste, she has an African name), and this favourite grandson on his knee or restrained by the hand—he's an exuberant child.

The President has some unwelcome guests in his country. It is not only in Africa, of course, that there are deposed tyrants nobody, not even their former friends, wishes to harbour. And even the just men among the Amins, Bokassas, Shahs, Baby Docs and Marcoses can be an embarrassment in terms of international relations. When the President has had no choice but to grant asylum, those whose statues have been brought down in their former capitals are confined to residence in one of his provincial towns and know they are under the surveillance of the Colonel: It's not an ideal life, but one can manage, as both the President and the President's wife know, having experienced it in previous existences. Since the beginning—that is to say, the beginning of the President's second access to power, with his new wife (he likes to joke and call it the Second Empire)—there have been some taking refuge, however, who seem to be in a special category. His country is too far removed, geographically, to have been any use as a base for incursion to South Africa; not even the government there in its wildest accusations against him could have suggested that. But safe houses were provided and the experienced lobbying ability and growing prestige of the President were brought into play in the world to obtain increasing support for those who temporarily occupied the safe houses. The President's wife—never has been like other presidents' wives among members of the OAU, even the other white ones, such as old President Senghor's—was always present at these negotiations, whether they were with the American Assistant Secretary of State for African Affairs, the director for Africa from the French Foreign Office, the East German Ambassador or the heads of African states: a small but quite voluptuous, bold-eyed woman, one mustn't be misled, by her perfect grooming and elegant clothes, into dismissing her as the ornament of the President's sexual tastes and prowess. She offers hospitality to many old friends at State House. She understands well the exhaustion of exiles, flying from country to country with the responsibility of arguments, strategies, methods of presentation and persuasion to be carried from offices up rickety stairs to State anterooms, from bush camps to Intercontinental Hotels. There are many who have found a day's revival—a moment recovered from responses put aside—in the swimming pool at State House which she has had made private even from the peacocks and guinea-fowl by a surrounding trellis covered with the orange-flowered bignonia that grows at all latitudes in Africa. Tambo came but did not swim; neither did Thabo Mbeki. Arnold was there at State House sometimes, between planes, and Busewe, and young people who were not at the Lusaka headquarters before the assassination took place. The President's wife and Arnold were in the water together, again, he saw the shape of her body, her legs and arms wavering under water like coloured flags and streamers, then rolled up into flesh and a bright swimsuit as she surfaced, pushing back from her face her long, wet curly hair. Only it was dark bronze now—something fashionable, no doubt. The year he was the Nobel Laureate, Bishop Tutu and his wife Leah were guests and walked in the gardens with her. The Bishop's laugh sounded from out of the animated chatter, a trumpet from home; he would not have known anyone there the President's wife remembered, it was too long ago, but he and his wife had about them the kind of bloom of a particular air and place that is unmistakable and that those in exile had lost.

To be with such people is like opening a cupboard and burying a nose in the folds of a forgotten garment.

Despite—or more likely because of?—the sometimes unseemly prominence of the woman the President brought with him when he came back to power, theirs appears to be what is called a happy marriage. Which, in the curiously mysterious while too public sense of the relationship between symbolic figures, surely means a good combination of accommodation. She is said, by the small faction in the South of the country who still support their leader exiled to Zaïre, to have unnatural powers over the President and—a foreigner—too much say in the ruling of a country which is not her country and a people who are not her people. More sophisticated circles remark that she sees herself as a Madame de Pompadour if not an Evita Perón; but no-one who really knows anything about the President believes he would allow anyone, or needs anyone, to be more than his peer; his choice wisely has been a woman who can keep up with him in the reality of the position his power, like that of every country in Africa, straddles—between Africa and the world, neither of which can do without the other.

After a few years, the President was known to have a passing fancy. Another foreigner, far more foreign. The Scots wife of the Swedish Ambassador. Nomo, when she was out on a visit, dubbed her The Albino or The Bloodhound—she was unrelievedly blonde, with blue eyes that showed a wet pink rim at the lower lids and a skin so fair it shone in the dark gardens of State House in the evening, when receptions spilled outdoors. Nomo could not understand why her mother laughed so much at the names. In due course, the Swedish Ambassador's tour of duty was up, and a successor took his place, a bachelor.

The President has never deserted his wife's bed, even during the pursuit of passing fancies; and she has never ceased to please and, still, surprise him—for him, there is no one like her. She must have had several affairs of her own—some people would even give names—but the skill of discretion, like any other, comes with the experience of adaptation to circumstance. She travels alone to visit her daughter in Rome, London and Paris, she is invited as an honoured guest to gatherings of socialist women's organizations in Eastern Europe and feminist congresses in Africa and the West; the Colonel knows better than to keep her under surveillance. And if, after all, the President has some idea that a woman he continues to find so attractive may attract and not resist another man, from time to time—well, Chiemeka is not like other women, she is a match for him in this way as in all others.

Burtwell Nyaka, Makekene Conco, Thabo Poswao and Sasha served their full sentences. The end to it all did not come before then.

During the years Sasha was in prison Joe died one summer night in London while preparing a case for Manchester United. Pauline was in their small garden, restlessly pacing it out; she was due to leave for South Africa next day for a contact visit with Sasha. She came inside under the clematis tapping on the open glass doors and saw the figure dropped sideways in the desk chair. She called him:—*Joe*—exactly as she had called at Sasha's bedroom door, her voice as a young woman was back in her throat.

Olga died. Arthur remarried. He became richer than ever, during those years, as a subcontractor to Armscor, the South African government's armament corporation. His new companies made parts for the four-barrelled 7.62-mm cannon, one of the variants of the GA 1 Servo-Controlled aircraft weapons system, and the CB cluster bomb system which could fire 40 six-kilogram bombs like ping-pong balls from its apertures. He was invited to Chile to exhibit home-grown skills South Africa had developed in response to arms embargoes. He did not care for these tropical countries full of half-Redskin, half-Latin coloureds, but to be an honoured industrialist in Chile or Paraguay, almost an official emissary for South Africa, was not like being there as any ordinary tourist.

Neither the four barrels of the cannon nor the deadly juggler was any protection. When the time came, he realized it and went with his wife not to the villa his cultured wife Olga had wanted in Italy (the new woman was a simple person who agreed that as in America there were no servants it was best to put up for auction at Sotheby's all those fancy things that needed dusting daily), nor, God forbid, to one of those dirty, run-down republics where he had displayed his achievements, but to California, where one of his sons, the eminent urologist, had moved.

Sasha came out of prison, was banned from resuming his trade-union activities, and worked clandestinely with the liberation front, going Underground every time there were new waves of arrests and reappearing whenever one might be able to count on a respite; he, too, became experienced in adaptation to his circumstances, although nothing in the advantages of his youth had prepared him for them. The death of his father was part of the deaths all around him. A country where the dead breed more dead—that was written in the letter that had become only a document, addressed to nobody, a testament, an exhibit among pamphlets. And death was still breeding. The whites wouldn't see that their structures were bursting at the joints with the pressure of massed bodies, alive and dead: a country courtroom (this one in a town smaller than the one where Sasha had stood trial) was built to hold only thirty people, and three thousand came to the trial of a few rebellious schoolchildren. The fences fell, the municipal gardens were trampled, the walls shook with the press of the living, the edifice of white justice, big enough only for a minority, could not hold. The police shot into the three thousand as they had shot before, year after year, as they were shooting day after day, hopelessly killing, unable to keep back the living who kept coming on and on, endlessly replacing the dead. The petrol bombs that burned the wives and children of traitors, the stones that hit tourist buses, the limpet mines that blew up police stations and the AK 47s that bred with the dead—the homemade and the smuggled instruments of death could not be kept out, even by a Servo-Controlled weapons system and the cluster bomb. Against her own wishes, Pauline stayed in London after Joe's death. She understood that her presence in the last days of the old South Africa would place a strain on Sasha that would be at the cost of the work he had to do; for which he had gone to prison, and for which he had now emerged. One day he telephoned Pauline from Amsterdam. Sasha had no passport, she knew he must have come out the way she had helped a black family escape when he was a schoolboy— not by the same route, for a long time there had been no safe houses in Botswana that the South African army hadn't destroyed—but with the help of someone like herself. She had seen on television the bombed walls of police headquarters in two cities. A limpet mine had been placed in the women's lavatory, in one, and in the men's lavatory in the other. Pauline thought how obvious it was that the first must have been placed by a woman, and the other by a man; an error on the part of the saboteurs to give away this clue. Then she read that a young woman had, indeed, been arrested, a white woman. When her son called from Amsterdam she believed she knew the identity of the man.

This year, the President is Chairman of the OAU. It is an honour at which some say he (and his ambitious wife) set his braided cap and his black, leather-bound beret from the beginning of his second regime. The fact is that he was an almost unanimous choice of a body known for its dissension: thrice-over victor in the anti-colonialist struggle, first against the colonial occupation, then in his coup against the government that colluded with the former colonial power, and finally against Europe's and America's covert backing of his usurpers; a professed socialist with a mixed economy in his own country, a man of high intelligence whose emotional style makes him popular in Africa and the Eastern bloc, and whose humour and sophistication do the same for him with the West.

One of his first official duties is to attend the proclamation of the new African state that used to be South Africa. It is fitting that this should have come about during his year of office, because he was part of the negotiations that continued outside the country concurrently with undeclared civil war there even when the black leaders were finally released from prison and brought back from exile, the liberation movements unbanned, and apartheid legislation abolished (a formality, the country had become ungovernable under it), but a section of whites, led by the white military command and a portion of the army, tried to retain a power base—they called it the white homeland—in the Orange Free State and part of the Transvaal. The role of the Frontline States in the independence of Namibia some years before was revived to facilitate the establishment of black liberation in the last and most important of the southern African countries ruled by white power, and the composition of the Frontline States was enlarged accordingly by greater representation of the black power of the continent. The white corporations who owned the mineral wealth of the country have been eager, ever since they saw that the whites were going to lose political power, to ensure that they will have some future—say, 49%?—under black rule. The present incumbent of the OAU chairmanship has been an extremely useful adviser to the black liberation leaders in their determination to make use of the executive and managerial skills of the corporations in order to maintain the economy while nationalizing the mining industry: his experience in driving such hard bargains has been invaluable. So, in many ways, he can be regarded as a brother who has been part of the South African liberation struggle in accordance with the old Pan-African ideal that sometimes seems forgotten.

There will be many ceremonies to mark the birth of an African republic where there have been a number of kinds of colonial occupation disguised as republics: the Boer republics of the Orange Free State and Transvaal, the Republic of South Africa. There are many historic sites sacred to the black people that were trampled over by white interests and now will be restored to honour by the celebrations to be held on this ground. These sites are everywhere; in the Cape, in Natal, in the Orange Free State, in the Transvaal—and it is all one country now, there are no homelands but only a homeland. (Some observers speculate it may be difficult to keep it that way; there are former 'national state' and 'independent state' leaders whose addiction to sectional power won't be easily cured or accommodated.) But the actual ceremony of declaration can take place, it has been decided, only where white power sat immoveably and apparently unassailable for so long: in Cape Town. The House of Parliament is too small; it never was enlarged to take in representatives of the whole population, merely provided with Outhouses to accommodate the failed experiment of annexing the Indian and 'Coloured' people to save apartheid. The Gardens adjoining parliament could have provided the site to become the most sacred of all, the one on which the ancestral country itself will be returned to its people; van Riebeeck's gardens where the first fence was put up, centuries ago, to keep out the indigenous people. But that would have meant destroying the old trees and flowering groves—as in Harare, that was once Salisbury, the public gardens are a relic of the colonial style worth keeping.

A stadium has been built, or rather an existing one has been greatly enlarged and completely refurbished. It has been surrounded, since early last evening, from the foreshore to its six gates of access, as if the ocean itself has flooded up from Table Bay, as if the flanks of Table Mountain itself have crumbled down in a moving mass to the city, by hundreds of thousands of people wanting to get in to occupy the stands open to the public. A cordon of police and the liberation army keeps out the huge crowd for whom there is not room within; the stadium was filled as soon as the gates were opened at ten in the morning for the ceremony that is to take place at noon. There is a sense that the liberation army is protecting the police from the crowd; for many years these black policemen took part in the raids upon these people's homes and on migrant workers' hostels, broke down squatters' shacks, sjambokked schoolchildren and manhandled strikers: every now and then they cannot avoid meeting a certain gaze from eyes in the crowd that once burned with tear gas.

The enormous faces of those who have not lived to see this day sway, honoured on lofty placards. Special contingents overflow the stands packed with those of the liberation organizations and the trade unions. There are student, church and women's groups, all with their uniforms, T-shirts and banners, there are choirs, musicians with traditional instruments and dancers in the national dress of the amaXhosa, amaZulu, Bapedi, Basotho, VhaVenda, amaPondo, Batswana. Gold, green and black bunting swathes every stand, dais, barrier and pole. The flags of many countries clap at the air in the force of the south-easter blowing. The blue, white and orange flag of the white

428

Republic of South Africa was on the flag-pole in the middle of the arena ready, according to the instructions of some stickler for procedure, to be ceremonially lowered for ever, but during the night someone has got into the stadium despite the heavy guard maintained, and hauled it down. It lies, ripped by a knife, wrapped by the wind round the base of its pole. The television crews from all over the world are filming this image with the same idea in mind: it will provide a striking opening shot for their coverage.

For hours the great swell of singing and chanting has been carried back and forth between the mountain and the sea by the south-easter. When the band in gold, green and black leads in the military escort and motorcade with the first black President and Prime Minister of the country, his wife and his cabinet—all people whose faces were for years not even permitted to be published in newspapers, whose words were banned, and who were banished to exile or prison—the swell rises to a roar that strikes the mountain, and jets above it to the domain of eagles, ululating shrills of ecstasy. The mountain may crack like a great dark glass shattered by a giant's note never sung before. The instruments of the band, continuing to play as dignitaries and foreign guests are seated on the dais covered with velvet in liberation colours, are obliterated by the human voice; no trumpet or flute can blow against that resonance from half a million breasts, and the Western-style military drums are shallow, beaten out by the tremendous blows of African drums.

Diplomats, white and black, white churchmen and individuals or representatives of organizations who actively supported the liberation Struggle sit among black dignitaries; there are one or two white industries representing the mining corporations. The Chairman of the OAU and his wife are in a place of honour. She is a white woman, but she is wearing African dress today, the striped, hand-woven robes and high-swathed headcloth that is the national dress of the women of the President's country. Those who know about such things would recognize that the gold earrings suspended from the tip of each lobe that just shows, beneath the headdress, are not of the workmanship of that country, but probably of Ghana. She is a beautiful woman—at least, the splendid outfit makes her appear so; there are not many whites who could carry it off. She has imposing stature despite her lack of height—in the forties, one would say, and rounder than she must have been when she was a girl. Her very large, brilliant black eyes are made-up but unlined—the crease that appears as she smiles and greets people to whom she is being presented, at her husband's side, is to do with the structure of her face, her high, tight-fleshed cheekbones, which look scrubbed, without artifice. Not possible to see what the colour of her hair may be, now, because of the headcloth. She is embraced by and embraces the wife of the first black President of the country, whom she has never before met; a real beauty, that one once was, and the distinction is still to be discerned despite and perhaps because of the suffering that has aged her to fulfil a different title.

Sasha has not yet come back home. His Dutch wife has twins and she is nervous of going to an unfamiliar country with small children too soon after the long struggle down there has ended. She has been accustomed to the kind of health and welfare facilities taken for granted in Amsterdam. There is also the unsolved problem of Pauline. No longer comrades of war, she and her son have been unable not to resume their own congenital war, but she is certain to want to follow him if he returns. Olga's sons, Clive and Brian, are the only members of the sisters' family left in the country. Clive already has been approached by the new Ministry of Agriculture to serve in a consultative capacity on the adaptation of the wine industry to the new social order. He sees no reason to leave. There is no black man with his specialised knowledge in this field, not anywhere. Brian, as the Foreign Exchange economist of one of the largest banks, has been appointed on a commission to review the activities of the Reserve Bank in consideration of the broadening of trade alliances with the world from which the old white regime was excluded, in particular the Afro-Asian and Eastern blocs. So he sees no reason—at present—to leave. Neither brother is in the crowd at the stadium, although there are thousands of whites among the blacks, some wearing the T-shirts that bear the face of the new President. (Clive, with a loan from the Afrikaner bank and in partnership with an Indian clothing manufacturer, was enterprising enough even as a very young man to have had a side-line in the production of such shirts for the liberation movements.) The brothers have always kept away from all that sort of thing, they wouldn't get mixed up in any mob. The struggle was not their struggle. The celebration is not their celebration.

Now the surface of the living mass has changed, instead of heads it has become fists waving like spores. The wife of the Chairman of the OAU has slowly risen alongside her husband, beside the first black President and Prime Minister, his wife and the other leaders of a new nation, and the Presidents, Prime Ministers, party and union leaders of many others, in practised observance of her training in attendance at great and solemn occasions. She takes a breath, perhaps to ease her shoulders in the robe, and her hands hang at her sides a moment and then are lightly enlaced in front of her thighs in the correct position. Her face is the public face assumed, along with appropriate dress, for exposure.

If it is true that the voice of a life is always addressing someone—for the religiously devout it is a god, for the politically devout it is the human mass—there is a stage in middle life, if that life is fully engaged with the world and the present, when there is no space or need for reflection. The past is not a haunting, but was a preparation, put into use.

It also may be true that a life is always moving—without being aware of this, or what the moment may be, and by a compass not available to others—towards a moment.

Cannons ejaculate from the Castle.

It is noon.

Hillela is watching a flag slowly climb, still in its pupa folds, a crumpled wing emerging, and—now!—it writhes one last time and flares wide in the wind, is smoothed taut by the fist of the wind, the flag of Whaila's country.

Nighthawk

CLIVE CUSSLER
and GRAHAM BROWN

PENGUIN BOOKS

PENGUIN BOOKS

UK | USA | Canada | Ireland | Australia
India | New Zealand | South Africa

Penguin Books is part of the Penguin Random House group of companies
whose addresses can be found at global.penguinrandomhouse.com.

First published in the United States of America by G. P. Putnam's Sons 2017
Published in Great Britain by Michael Joseph 2017
Published in Penguin Books 2018

001

Set in 11.5/13.68 pt Garamond MT Std
Typeset by Jouve (UK), Milton Keynes

Printed and bound in Great Britain by Clays Ltd, Elcograf S.p.A.

A CIP catalogue record for this book is available from the British Library

PAPERBACK ISBN: 978–024–15078–27
OM PAPERBACK ISBN: 978–1–405–92386–6

www.greenpenguin.co.uk

Cast of Characters

Spanish Expedition of 1525

Diego Alvarado Spanish soldier and leader of an expedition into South America 1525, contemporary and competitor of Francisco Pizarro.

Costa Spanish nobleman and financier, bankrolled Alvarado's expedition.

National Underwater and Marine Agency

Rudi Gunn Assistant Director of NUMA.

Kurt Austin Head of NUMA's Special Projects division, world-class diver and salvage expert, once worked for the CIA.

Joe Zavala Kurt's right-hand man, mechanical expert, also an accomplished helicopter pilot and amateur boxer.

Hiram Yaeger NUMA's resident computer genius, owner of many patents relating to computer design.

Priya Kashmir Hiram Yaeger's assistant, was supposed to join a NUMA field team, before a car accident left her unable to walk, instead joined the computer technologies department.

Paul Trout Tallest member of the Special Projects division, at six foot eight, married to Gamay. Has a Ph.D. in Ocean Sciences. Quiet and steady.

Gamay Trout Marine biologist, married to Paul, Gamay is a fitness aficionado, an accomplished diver and an excellent marksman.

Ed Callahan Captain of the NUMA vessel *Catalina*.

National Security Agency

Steve Gowdy Head of Extra-Atmospheric projects at the NSA, director of the *Nighthawk* program.

Emma Townsend Former NASA scientist, astrophysics expert, integral part of the *Nighthawk* program. Coworkers refer to her as *Hurricane Emma*.

Agent Hurns NSA field agent.

Agent Rodriguez NSA field agent.

United States Air Force

Colonel Frank Hansen Commander of the 9th Space Operations Squadron, based at Vandenberg Air Force Base, California.

Russian Federation

Constantin Davidov Special executive at the FSB, successor to the KGB, in charge of *technology retrieval* for the Kremlin.

Rear Admiral Sergei Borozdin Old friend of Davidov's, commander of the Russian 1st Salvage Flotilla (Pacific).

Victor Tovarich Captain of the TK-17 Typhoon-class submarine.

Major Yuri Timonovski Commander and pilot of *Blackjack 2*.

People's Republic of China

General Zhang Highest-ranking officer at the Chinese Ministry of State Security.

Daiyu (Black Jade) Special operative for the Ministry, one of the 'children that were never born'.

Jian Daiyu's partner, also one of the 'children that were never born'.

Li Ying Liaison officer, Beijing.

Lieutenant Wu Field officer for the Ministry of State Security.

Falconer Code name of an anonymous asset connected with the NSA's *Nighthawk* program.

MS *Reunion*

Buck Kamphausen Captain of the MS *Reunion*.

Peru

Urco Archaeologist studying the origins and disappearance of the Chachapoya people.

Vargas One of Urco's volunteers.

Reyes Another of the volunteers.

Washington DC

Collin Kane Bomb disposal expert.

Prologue
The Burning Point

South America, January 1525

The spear hit Diego Alvarado in the chest. A jarring blow that knocked him to the ground but failed to puncture the strong Castilian armor he'd carried all the way from Spain.

He rolled, took a position on one knee and leveled his crossbow. Spotting movement in the trees, he let the bolt fly. It sliced into the foliage, drawing an anguished scream.

'In the trees to the right!' he yelled to his men.

A cloud of blue smoke exploded over the narrow trail as several large-bored muskets, known as harquebuses, fired simultaneously. The shots tore into the forest, severing small tree limbs and ripping through the lush green leaves.

A wave of arrows flew back at them in response. Two of Alvarado's men went down and he felt a spike of pain in his calf as an obsidian-tipped dart punctured it.

'They have us surrounded,' one of the men shouted.

'Hold your line,' Alvarado ordered. He limped forward instead of back, ignoring the pain and reloading his weapon.

After a long hike into the foothills, they'd been

ambushed, lured down a path and attacked from both sides. Another group of men might have broken ranks under the assault, but Alvarado's men had once been soldiers. They stood like a wall and didn't waste their precious ammunition. Several drew their swords while the others steadied their heavy firearms.

The natives were drawing themselves together to attack once again. With a shrill cry, they charged from the trees. They broke into the clearing only to be struck down by Spanish thunder as a second wave of black-powder explosions shook the air.

Half their number fell, others turned and ran, only two continued the attack. They rushed toward Alvarado, charging through the smoke, their dark, reddish faces and blazing white eyes highlighted by streaks of war paint.

Alvarado took the first one with the crossbow, dropping the man in his tracks, but the second lunged with a spear. The tip of the crude weapon deflected off the angled chest plate of Alvarado's silver armor. Impervious to such crude blades, Alvarado reached toward his assailant without fear. He grabbed the man, shifted his weight and flung him to the ground.

Falling on him, Alvarado finished the native with a dagger.

By the time he looked up, the rest of them had fled.

'Reload,' he shouted to the men. 'They'll be back soon.'

As the men began the laborious process of packing powder charges in their weapons, Alvarado tried to remove the native's arrow from his calf. He dug at his own flesh with the tip of his dagger and then eased the arrow out. He looked at it and then tossed it aside. It was nothing new. He'd been told these 'people of the clouds' were different than the Inca and the other tribes of the area. That they were brave in combat, there was no doubt, but they had no greater weapons than any of the other natives. They had nothing to their advantage but raw numbers.

Alvarado poured some wine from a small flask on the wound. It stung, but helped numb the pain – and, he hoped, clean out any poison. He then wrapped his calf in a cloth and watched as the blood soaked it, spreading from a central spot, until the entire cloth was stained crimson.

'We have to fall back,' he said, struggling to get up on his feet.

'How far?' one of his men shouted.

'All the way,' Alvarado said. 'Back to the village.'

None of them argued. In fact, they looked relieved to hear the order.

They formed up and began to move. Alvarado managed to walk for the first mile, but the heavy armor and the pain in his leg soon became too much. One of his men came to help, supporting him and leading him to the sturdy packhorse they'd used to carry in supplies. The strap was loosened and the goods dumped on the ground. With a boost, Alvarado was lifted up onto the horse. He held on tightly, and the entire party continued quickly, heading downhill, back toward their camp.

After several hours Alvarado and his men reached the village they'd left early that morning. Night had fallen, but warm fires stoked by the soldiers he'd left behind welcomed them.

A nobleman named Costa helped Alvarado down from the horse. 'What happened?' he asked, blanching at the wound.

Costa was an aristocrat of the middle tier. He'd agreed to fund the expedition in return for a third of all treasure recovered. Why he'd come along personally was anyone's guess, perhaps for the adventure, or more likely to ensure he wasn't cheated out of his profits. So far, he'd done little but complain.

'We've been tricked,' Alvarado said. 'These people of the cloud are not amenable to our presence. They would rather kill us than join us, even if it means they remain enslaved to other masters.'

'But what about Pizarro?' Costa asked. 'These are his marks. He came this way. He said we would find allies.'

Alvarado knew all about Pizarro's marks. The would-be conquistador had carved inscriptions into some of the trees alongside the trail so that Alvarado and his reinforcements could catch up with Pizarro and his advanced guard.

He knew about Pizarro's plans as well, to turn other natives against the ruling group. It had worked in other places, but not here.

'Something must have happened to him,' Alvarado said. 'Either Francisco has been killed or . . .'

4

He didn't have to finish. None of them really trusted Pizarro. He kept talking of gold, which no one had yet seen, kept promising wealth, which had yet to appear. He was a little man with big dreams. He'd been turned down by the Governor twice when requesting funds to assist his expeditions and in desperation had finally turned to Costa, and to his rival: Alvarado.

While Alvarado didn't like or trust Pizarro, he did understand the man. Both of them were cut from the same cloth. They were men of inauspicious birth, both had come from Spain to make a name for themselves. But they'd been enemies only months before, and it was entirely possible that Pizarro had agreed to partner with them only to lead them to their doom.

'We must leave for the coast immediately,' Alvarado said.

Costa looked sick at the thought.

'Something wrong with that order, my friend?'

'No,' Costa said. 'It's just that . . .'

'Spit it out.'

Costa hesitated. 'Some of the men have fallen ill. Fever. It may be the pox.'

Alvarado could not imagine worse news. 'Show me.'

Costa led him to the largest of the native huts, made of mud and grass, that might have been a communal gathering place. A fire in the center burned brightly, venting smoke through a hole in the roof. A group of Alvarado's soldiers lay on the dirt floor around it, each of them in various states of distress.

'When did this begin?'

'Shortly after you left to find Pizarro.'

In the flickering light, Alvarado kneeled beside one of the men. The soldier was little more than a boy; he lay on his back with his eyes closed and his face toward the thatched ceiling above. His shirt was soaked with perspiration and small red sores had begun to appear on his neck, face and chest. His temperature was so high that kneeling over him felt like standing too close to an open flame.

'Smallpox,' Alvarado said, confirming the diagnosis. 'How many are like this?'

'Eight are in the grips of it. Three others are less ill, but they can barely stand. They certainly can't walk ten miles to the coast.'

With eleven of his men sick, several wounded and two dead, Alvarado had only twenty left who could fight. 'We'll have to leave them.'

'But Diego . . .'

'They're too sick to walk and too heavy to carry,' Alvarado insisted. 'And we're greatly outnumbered. I count thirty huts around us. Each big enough for a large family. There must have been more than two hundred people living here before Pizarro came through. Even if half are women and children, we'll never hold out. And who's to say other villages are not allied with this one.'

Costa took the estimate grimly. 'Perhaps Francisco will turn back and bring help.'

'It's too late to pin our hopes on rescue,' Alvarado said. 'You and the others must go while there's still time.'

6

'*Me and the others,*' Costa repeated, suspiciously. 'Surely you don't intend to stay?'

Alvarado put a hand to his forehead and wiped a sheen of sweat from it. It might have been the heat or the wound in his leg, but he suspected it was the beginnings of the disease that was ravaging his men. 'I would only hold you back. Now, round up the men and head for the ship. Sail with the current until you're clear of the coast, then turn north and head back to Panama.'

Costa stared for a short moment, then abruptly turned to leave.

Alvarado grabbed him by the wrist, gripping it with such strength that Costa thought his bones might break. 'Pay my family what you owe me or I will haunt you till the end of your days.'

Costa nodded. It might have been the only promise he'd ever made that he was honestly afraid to break.

As the men departed, Alvarado grew feverish. He'd armed himself with two preloaded muskets and his crossbow. The other men who could hold weapons were each given a loaded pistol and several helpings of rum.

With the fires still burning in the night and the smoke drifting thick and low, they waited and watched. It seemed forever, but eventually the natives appeared.

Through a gap in the thatched wall, Alvarado saw them approach. When they were close enough, he fired into the nearest group.

The blast scattered them, but others came from different directions. They burst into the huts from all sides.

The pistols fired and several natives went down, but the horde raced across the bodies of their dead brethren, while others crashed through the flimsy walls to join the attack.

Alvarado fired the second harquebus, killing two more natives. He clubbed a third attacker with the smoking barrel, but was knocked to the ground an instant later.

Resorting to his crossbow, he fired the bolt into the melee. He was reaching for his dagger when a stone axe came down upon his wrist and hacked off his hand.

He shouted in agony and gripped instinctively at the bleeding stump. But a spear through his back paralyzed him, ending his cry and leaving him on the ground unable to move or even to call out to his men.

Lying there, Alvarado watched as the natives massacred his sick and dying men; hacking at them and stabbing them repeatedly. The frenzy lasted for several minutes, with blood, sweat and saliva flying in all directions.

In the aftermath, Alvarado was left for dead. As the light faded from his eyes, he watched the natives dragging a few surviving men into the forest. He would never know what became of them.

Invisible and unseen in the mayhem, the tiny pathogens that carried smallpox and measles had been spread with every breath and every splattering of blood and saliva. The natives of this New World had never been exposed to them before. They had no resistance to the invisible enemy.

In a week, most of the warriors involved in the attack would be sick and dying. In a month, their entire village would be stricken. By the year's end, scores of other settlements would be suffering as well, and, in a decade, the entire region would be wilting under the strains of the epidemic.

Unchecked, smallpox would ravage the Incan empire, pave the way for the Spanish conquest and ultimately kill over ninety percent of the native population of South America. An entire continent laid to waste by a weapon no one could see.

I

Steve Gowdy sat in a comfortable chair on the top level of a darkened control room in the heart of Vandenberg Air Force Base. The setting resembled the NASA command centers in Houston and at Cape Canaveral, but was smaller and stocked with military personnel instead of civilians.

Gowdy was in his late forties. He wore a gray polo shirt and black slacks, his thin covering of sandy brown hair perfectly coiffed but too thin to conceal his scalp beneath. He looked like a golfer ready to play eighteen holes at the local country club, a visitor on a day tour or a bored middle manager stuck in another endless meeting. Only the tightly bunched wrinkles around his eyes and the unconscious drumming of his finger on the arm of the chair suggested he was paying close attention.

Gowdy hadn't come to Vandenberg for a tour of the place, or to marvel at the technology, but to oversee the final stage of a mission so secret only forty people in the entire world knew of its existence.

The project was called *Ruby Snow*, which meant nothing, of course, but had a poetic ring to it that Gowdy appreciated. It involved an aircraft funded by the

National Security Agency and operated by the Air Force and other members of the Defense Department.

Aircraft was the wrong word, he reminded himself. The *Nighthawk* was a hybrid vehicle, part aircraft, part spacecraft. The latest in a long line of platforms descended from the space shuttle. It was the most advanced machine ever flown and was finally returning to Earth after three long years in orbit.

A large storm brewing over the Pacific had caused the NSA to move the reentry up by a full week, but, other than that, everything had gone according to plan.

Watching the reentry live, Gowdy stared at the huge, high-definition screens that made up the front wall of the room. One showed a column of numbers and symbols that honestly meant nothing to him, except that all of them remained green.

A second display showed a chart with a line that dove sharply from the upper-left-hand corner before leveling out across the middle and then beginning to drop again on the right side. Labeled *Nighthawk Descent Profile*, the chart had something to do with the altitude, speed and distance of the aircraft. But he kept his attention glued to the central display, where a global satellite map showed the Pacific Ocean and the west coasts of North, South and Central America.

Icons representing the *Nighthawk* and lines tracing its path were drawn in bright colors. Because the *Nighthawk* flew in an unusual polar orbit, the reentry path originated over Antarctica, cutting across the globe at a diagonal angle. It had flown past New Zealand, passing to the east by less than a hundred miles, and from there it drew a line directly over the top of the Cook Islands and Tahiti. It passed south of Hawaii, and its projection continued toward Vandenberg and the high deserts of California. It still had several thousand miles to go, but traveling at over five thousand miles per hour meant less than forty minutes before touchdown.

An echoing call rang out over the loudspeaker system, known as the loop. 'Vehicle has cleared Max Q,' an anonymous voice said. 'Heat shield secure. Temperatures dropping.'

Max Q. That was a term Gowdy knew. *A danger point – the point of maximum aerodynamic stress on the craft. A point where any weakness or damage would likely result in structural failure and loss of the craft.*

Hearing that the *Nighthawk* had passed Max Q reduced Gowdy's anxiety a bit. Many things could still go wrong, catastrophically wrong, but the largest hurdle had been cleared.

He glanced down to the middle tier of the amphitheater-style room. That level was the domain of the flight director. In this case, an Air Force Colonel named Frank Hansen. Hansen was a steely-eyed veteran of thirty years, a former fighter jock and test pilot who'd survived two ejections and a crash in his time and was now head of the 9th Space Operations Squadron.

Hansen turned, made eye contact and offered a nod. So far, so good.

Among all the controllers and system specialists and

experts, Hansen was the only man in the room – aside from Gowdy himself – who understood just what a monumental risk they were taking. And if Gowdy measured him right, Hansen was just as nervous.

Hansen pressed his intercom switch. 'Give me a status update,' his calm voice called out.

Down on the lowest level of the room, the individual systems controllers went into action. Each of them had one thing to worry about; guidance, telemetry, propulsion, etc. Like the front row in a movie theater, their positions made watching the main screen a neck-craning exercise, but since every bit of information they needed was displayed on smaller monitors directly in front of them, they rarely looked up until their tasks were done.

Gowdy sat back and listened as the stream of replies poured in over the loop, his finger continuing to drum.

'Telemetry: Go.'

'Electrical: Go.'

'Flight controls: Go.'

On it went, each man or woman reporting, confirming good news, until all the controllers had reported in but one.

An awkward pause ensued. Down below, Hansen waited and then pressed the button on his transmitter. 'Guidance, what's your status?'

There was no response.

'Guidance?'

The room went deathly quiet. Gowdy's finger stopped its tapping. In all the simulations, he'd never heard a delay, not even a few seconds. He stood up, gazing down over the rail toward the bottom row, where the guidance controller sat.

A young airman with a crew cut was working furiously, typing and tapping things on his keyboard, switching screens.

'Guidance?' Hansen called out. 'I need a response.'

'Guidance is go,' the airman finally replied, 'but we're seeing a delay in the repeat.'

Because the *Nighthawk* was a pilotless craft and controlled remotely from Vandenberg, the system had been designed to repeat every instruction back to control center before executing a maneuver, much in the way a pilot repeated the instructions to air traffic control to make sure everyone was on the same page.

Gowdy tapped his own intercom button, which went directly, and privately, to Hansen. 'What's happening? What does it mean?'

'A delay in the repeat could be anything,' Hansen replied. He spoke with a practiced indifference. 'It could mean a problem processing the command, an error on our end, or even —'

Before anything else could be said, the telemetry controller spoke up. 'Telemetry is yellow. Signal intermittent.'

On the big screen with the numbers, two boxes had begun flashing yellow alarms; a third began to flash red.

'Course deviation detected,' the tracking controller said. 'Two degrees south and turning . . . Five degrees and turning . . .'

Gowdy felt his throat clench up. He buzzed Hansen again. 'What's happening?'

Hansen was too busy to reply and Gowdy turned his gaze back to the screen. The *Nighthawk*'s projected line had begun to curve, angling to the right, away from California and toward Central America.

'Eleven degrees south and still turning,' the guidance controller said. 'Speed dropping, descent arrested. Altitude maintaining nine-one thousand.'

Gowdy could hardly believe his eyes. Instead of descending as planned, the *Nighthawk* was leveling off at ninety-one thousand feet and losing speed because of it. Since the craft was a glider at this point, it was imperative that it maintain the proper descent profile; otherwise, it would bleed off so much speed that it would no longer be able to reach California.

Gowdy felt his legs shaking. He gripped the rail in front of him with one hand while the other went into his pocket, fumbling for a key.

'Reissue directional commands,' Hansen called out tersely.

'No effect,' the controller said.

'Reboot command program.'

'Reboot initiated . . . Stand by.'

Gowdy descended the stairs to Hansen's level and held his position. He was sweating now, his hands trembling, his fingers on the key he hoped never to use.

How could it all be going wrong now? A decade of research and three years in space. How could the effort possibly be failing here at the end?

'Twenty-one degrees south,' the guidance controller said. 'Altitude still nine-one thousand, speed dropping to four thousand.'

'What's happening?' Gowdy shouted to Hansen, no longer bothering with the intercom or the pretense of calm.

'We've lost control.'

'I can see that,' Gowdy replied. 'Why?'

'Impossible to tell,' Hansen said. 'It seems to be a constant right turn. There may be damage to the wing or vertical stabilizer. But that wouldn't explain the telemetry problems or the delay on the command repeat.'

Gowdy fumbled with the key in his pocket, turning it over and over in his hand. It was his responsibility to terminate the mission if it became too dangerous; his call. To act early before all hope was gone would be a mistake, but to act too late . . . could be disastrous.

He stepped forward, barging into Hansen's personal space. 'Get this damned thing back on track.'

Hansen pushed past him, all but shoving Gowdy into a seat. The two men had never liked each other. Hansen felt Gowdy didn't know enough about physics and astronautics to be attached to the program, and Gowdy considered the Air Force Colonel to be arrogant and condescending to his authority. The higher-ups had ordered them to get along; it had worked for a while, but not now.

'Transponder data intermittent,' the telemetry controller said. 'We're losing the signal.'

'Reboot the transponder,' Hansen called out. 'If the

transponder goes out, we'll lose track of the vehicle. It's not in primary radar coverage.'

Gowdy sat, immobile. His body went numb and he listened to the desperate exchange as if in a trance. It wouldn't matter if they were in radar coverage, the *Nighthawk* was designed with a complete stealth covering. Unlike other spacecraft, it was black in color, invisible to telescopes. It was covered with the most advanced radar-absorbent material ever developed.

He looked up. The vehicle was now streaking toward the coast of South America at thirty-five hundred miles per hour. Its turn was moderating, its speed continuing to drop. Its maximum glide path, marked by a shaded orange circle on the map, was shrinking with each second and moving south. It no longer reached the United States.

Gowdy knew what he had to do. There was no more reason to wait.

He pulled the red key out of his pocket and inserted it into a slot on the panel in front of him. A turn of the key opened a compartment just above it and a small pedestal rose up and locked in place. The pedestal was marked with yellow and black chevrons. In the center loomed a red button protected by raised metal bars that prevented it from being pressed by accident.

Gowdy looked up at the screen. They were now getting erroneous position data indicating the *Nighthawk* was in several different places at the same time. Returns blinked on and off, but the main line continued to head south, heading straight for the Galápagos Islands and the coast of Ecuador beyond.

'Guidance reboot completed,' the controller said.

'And?!' Hansen asked.

'No response.'

'That's it,' Gowdy whispered. He turned the key to the right and the red button lit up.

'*Self-destruct, armed,*' a computer voice called out.

Letting go of the key, Gowdy reached for the button.

A firm hand intercepted him, grabbing his wrist and yanking it away.

Hansen had appeared at his side. 'Are you insane?' the Air Force Colonel growled.

'It's gone off course,' Gowdy said. 'We can't have it coming down in a populated area, the risk is too great that the worst will happen.'

Hansen continued to hold Gowdy's arm back. '*The worst* has already happened. It happened the moment we brought the *Nighthawk* and its cargo back into the atmosphere. Destroying it now will only trigger the catastrophe.'

Gowdy blinked, confused. He felt a sense of vertigo. He truly didn't understand. But then, this was what Hansen had complained about all along. The science was beyond him.

The *Nighthawk* suddenly vanished from the screen. The graph showing its descent profile went blank and all the numbers in the far screen froze and began to blink red.

'Telemetry is down,' another controller reported with little emotion. '*Nighthawk* contact lost.'

A murmur swept through the room. It sounded like fear. Gowdy stared at the screen, waiting and hoping the course line would reappear. He sat in silence as repeated attempts to reestablish the link between Vandenberg and the aircraft failed.

Eventually, a new number appeared on the screen and began rapidly counting toward zero.

'What's that?' Gowdy asked.

'Surface interface time,' Hansen said with grim honesty. 'The longest possible time the *Nighthawk* can remain aloft before reaching zero altitude.'

The number ticked down without mercy, going from minutes to seconds and then stopping implacably at 0:00:00.

'Now what?' Gowdy asked.

'Give me live satellite coverage,' Hansen ordered. 'Wide-angle. South Pacific and western South America.'

The controllers did as ordered. No one asked why.

One by one, the satellite views came up. Gowdy stared at the peaceful scene. Clouds drifted over the Pacific. The west coast of South America ran hard against the blue waters of the ocean. The tropical disturbance in the Pacific swirled like a peaceful merry-go-round.

Everything appeared calm.

'What are you looking for?' Gowdy asked.

The stern Air Force Colonel turned to the NSA bureaucrat he'd put up with for so long and exhaled. It was more relief than frustration.

'Absent a command from the ground, the *Nighthawk* will enter an autonomous mode, thinking for itself. When it determines its own position and computes that it can't reach Vandenberg, the craft will execute emergency descent procedures, slow to an appropriate speed and then land safely . . . by parachute.'

'How do you know it hasn't broken up already?' Gowdy replied, trying to reassert his aura of authority. 'How do you know the autoland system hasn't failed like everything else?'

'Because,' Hansen said, 'we're still here.'

It took a moment, but Gowdy began to understand. He looked up at the live satellite view and all the normal things it displayed. 'How long do we have?'

Hansen performed a quick mental calculation. 'Seven days,' he said. 'Less, if the fuel cells, solar panels or the battery packs were damaged.'

Gowdy turned back to the screen and the massive expanse of the South Pacific on display. Seven days to search all that ocean and find a needle in its watery haystack. Seven days to find and shut off a ticking bomb that could shake the very foundations of the Earth.

2

Kohala Point, Hawaii

Kurt Austin straddled a surfboard in the tropical waters a half mile from the Kohala Lighthouse on the Big Island of Hawaii. The strong Pacific sun warmed his tanned skin and the swells rolled beneath him in a constant rhythm. His muscles were taut and his mind quiet as he watched a fifteen-foot wave build toward the beach and then curl into a perfect left-hand break.

White foam zipped along the top of the wave, racing to catch up to the surfer riding it, but he kept his speed up, turned out and accelerated toward the beach just before the crest surged and crashed down behind him.

The sheer power of the wave sent a thunderclap echo off the lava rocks at the south end of the beach. There was a timbre to that symphony. 'I could listen to that sound forever,' Kurt said.

'That's because you're *Kaikane*,' a surfer beside him replied in a distinct Hawaiian accent. *'Born from the sea.'*

Kurt glanced to his right, where a solidly built Hawaiian man straddled a short board. Polynesian-style tattoos on his arms and chest nearly matched a pattern painted on the board. He had shaggy black hair, a warm smile and a soft face. His name was Ika, but everyone called him Ike.

Kurt grinned. 'You might be right about that.'

Now in his thirties, Kurt Austin had grown up in the Pacific Northwest where he'd spent most of his time boating, fishing or swimming. Years working in his father's marine salvage business meant he learned to dive as a teenager. He'd spent countless hours underwater since, working for his father first, before a stint in the Navy and several years with a special CIA unit that did subsurface recovery and engineering.

Since leaving the CIA, he'd been with NUMA, the National Underwater and Marine Agency, a branch of the federal government focused on the exploration, study and preservation of the world's oceans.

Strangely, the farther he'd gone on his journey, the more technology came between him and the water. Skin diving gave way to wet suits and then to dry suits. Those layers gave way to hard-shelled, deep-diving units, which encased him like an undersea astronaut. More often than not, he now used submersibles, either robotic units piloted from the surface or manned subs that were pressurized and heated and comfortable enough to wear shorts and T-shirts. And so, after finishing a project on Oahu, Kurt had decided to get back in touch with the water and the rhythms of the sea.

Being in Hawaii, that meant surfing, and over a period of weeks Kurt pushed himself to tackle larger and faster waves with a relentless desire to improve.

After several weeks, he was almost as good as the

local guides he'd grown to be friends with. His skin was so tanned he might have passed as a Hawaiian – except for a mop of prematurely silver hair.

'The rhythm of the sea is changing,' Ike said, turning and gazing out behind them. 'Can you feel it?'

Kurt nodded. 'Swells coming through faster. Closer together.'

There was a storm out there. It was beyond the horizon but growing toward cyclone strength. The waves pushed ahead of it were starting to line up.

'Gonna get too rough to ride soon,' Ike said.

'Let's make the best of it, then,' Kurt said.

He dropped forward on his board and began paddling toward the break zone.

Ike did the same and they moved closer to shore, increasing their pace and separating. One huge swell after another rolled beneath them until Kurt sensed a monster wave, the largest of the day.

This was the wave he wanted, the one that carried danger and power in equal measures. He paddled faster, began to roll up the face of the swell and got to one knee. He stood and turned with perfect timing, dropping in and accelerating just as the top of the wave began to curl.

Ike was up ahead of him, already slicing a white wake in the water as if his board were powered by rockets. Kurt cut across the wave behind him and couldn't help but grin at the incredible feeling that poured through him as if he'd tapped into the power of the sea itself.

Accelerating down the face and cutting to the left,

he stayed just ahead of the curling top that was forming a pipeline behind him. He dropped his hand and trailed his fingers in the water, drifting back until all he saw around him was a tube of translucent blue, a sheet of liquid glass.

The wave roared like a living thing and began to close on him like Scylla and Charybdis. Just before it was about to crush him, Kurt turned out and zipped into the open again.

He saw Ike up ahead and another surfer who'd picked the same wave. They maneuvered a little too closely and Ike had to cut back. His turn was sharp enough to avoid contact, but the other surfer was overmatched by the speed and power of the breaker and he went down.

Kurt turned to avoid him, but then the sea surprised them all as the wave peaked suddenly and closed out all at once.

The entire front crashed simultaneously, a change from the long, curling break they'd been enjoying. A mountain of water landed on Kurt's shoulders, knocking him from his board and driving him under.

He was forced deep and slammed into the sand. An outcropping of lava rock gashed his arm and he felt the snap of the surf leash attached to his ankle as his board was ripped away.

The huge wave held him down, but Kurt's experience diving prevented any panic. He steadied himself as the undertow returned and the swirling sediment around him cleared enough to see the light from above. He planted his feet and pushed off the bottom.

Breaking the surface, Kurt immediately glanced around. Another wave was barreling down on him and his board had been flung into the shallows and tossed onto the beach. Ike was there in the shallows as well, pulling himself back onto his board and paddling frantically to get back out into the water.

Kurt quickly realized why: the other surfer was nowhere to be seen. He'd gone down and stayed down.

Kurt took a deep breath and dove just as the following wave crashed over him. He felt the surge rushing by, lifting him and then releasing him as if he was just beyond its grasp. He heard the muted rumble of the wave crashing up ahead and fought to see through the sand that exploded and swirled back toward him.

In the gloom ahead, he spied a flash of color, yellow and red, dimmed by the water's hue and blurred by the limitations of human vision underwater. He kicked hard and used his arms in a powerful stroke, lunging forward, until he grasped the surfer's board. It was wedged into a gap in the lava rock, stuck tight. Feeling along the board, Kurt found the leash, used it to pull the unconscious wave rider toward him and ripped the Velcro cuff that held him.

The undertow returned. The next wave was coming. He pulled the limp surfer to him, pushed off the bottom once more and emerged beyond the crest of the wave.

He swam toward the shore; the next wave crashed behind them and shoved them forward in a burst of foam and spray.

As they cruised into the shallows, several other surfers rushed out to help. They grabbed the injured man by his arms and legs and hauled him onto the sand.

Ike helped Kurt to his feet and onto the beach, where he stood with his hands on his hips, drawing in as much oxygen as his lungs would allow. 'Is he okay?'

A few feet away, the other surfer was on his side, coughing and spitting out water. One of the men with him nodded.

Ike grinned and held up the broken end of Kurt's leash. 'Look at this. You broke your leash. You're a *real* big-wave surfer, now.'

Ike laughed at his own joke and gave Kurt a playful shove.

'Not exactly how I wanted the ride to end,' Kurt said. 'What happened with that wave? Everything seemed fine and then . . .'

Ike shrugged. 'Every wave is different, bro. It's part of the deal. *Moana* will let you play, but from time to time she reminds you *I'm dangerous. I'm unpredictable. One day, I'll turn on you. And in that moment of truth, you'll find you can't control me. You'll find you're at my mercy and only I will decide whether to hold you down or set you free.*'

Kurt enjoyed the poetry of the statement, enough that he didn't labor the point with anything but a respectful nod and a glance back out to the sea. The waves were still growing, the storm was coming on. Moana *would not let them play anymore today.*

A shout from higher up the beach broke his reverie. 'Kurt Austin,' a voice called.

There was an official tone to the address, sharp and clear. A tone very out of place on a beach with so much local flavor.

Kurt looked up and saw a man coming down from the road. He wore black slacks, dress shoes and a white, button-down shirt. He had narrow shoulders and hips but stood ramrod straight and moved with a purpose. He'd come from a white SUV parked on the road up above.

'Kurt?' the man shouted, getting closer.

Ike leaned in. 'I wouldn't answer, if I was you,' he whispered. 'Looks like Five-O to me.'

'I should be so lucky,' Kurt said. He recognized a government official when he saw one, and he recognized this one in particular. 'Rudi Gunn,' he said, extending a hand to NUMA's number two official. 'I didn't know you were on the island. I'd have brought you surfing with me.'

'I only arrived a few hours ago,' Rudi said, shaking Kurt's hand, 'but, considering the wipeout I just saw, I'd have to consider any future invitations as part of a plan to get rid of me and take my job.'

'And handle paperwork all day long? No thanks. What are you doing here?'

'I've been trying to reach you,' Rudi said. 'Must have left a dozen messages on your phone.'

'Phones and surfing don't exactly mix,' Kurt said. 'What's the emergency?'

'Who says there's an emergency?'

Kurt offered an incredulous look.

'Okay,' Rudi said. 'There probably is an emergency – otherwise, they wouldn't have sent me to pick you up – but I don't know what it is. I'm just lucky the valet at your hotel remembered you loading up a surfboard and heading this way.'

'That kid just lost his tip,' Kurt said.

'He'll survive on what I paid him,' Rudi said. 'Trust me.'

Kurt knew it was time to go. He looked over at the surfer he'd pulled out of the sea. The young man was smiling now; he offered the hang-loose sign: a twist of the wrist with his thumb and pinky extended.

Kurt returned the gesture and then turned to Ike. 'The sea isn't the only thing that's unpredictable. Looks like I have work to do.'

He pulled a black T-shirt over his shoulders and grabbed the backpack he'd brought with him. Hiking up toward the waiting SUV, he asked the obvious question. 'So what can you tell me? Now that we're out of earshot.'

Gunn shook his head. 'Only the obvious,' he said. 'That time is of the essence.'

Kurt figured Rudi knew more than that, but he was as tight-lipped as anyone at NUMA. Being number one in your class at West Point tended to come with that kind of self-discipline. 'Don't suppose I have time to shower and change?'

Gunn shook his head. 'No, I don't suppose you do.'

3

Rudi drove to Upolu Airport, a small strip on the northern tip of the island. A gleaming turquoise Gulfstream waited on the tarmac with engines running. It was a NUMA aircraft, one Kurt recognized as a model with extended range.

The aircraft was buttoned up as soon as Kurt and Rudi took their seats. Moments later, they were screaming down the runway. After a long takeoff roll, the Gulfstream clawed its way skyward and turned east.

As they climbed, Kurt stared out the window. Off in the distance he saw the dark clouds of the tropical depression that had sent the swells barreling to the shore. After a tip of the imaginary hat to the storm, he turned his attention back to Rudi.

Of all the men at NUMA, Rudi was the closest thing to an enigma. Now in his late forties, he had lost none of the intensity and precision that were his trademark. Fiery but close-lipped, Rudi could be jocular and fun but never quite let down his guard. His mind was always active. Even now, as he sat in silence contemplating whatever it was they would soon talk about, Kurt could sense that Rudi was planning, coordinating and rearranging things. He was a logistical genius with a knack for getting things set up in the most efficient order.

Kurt let him be. Twenty minutes went by before either of them spoke. 'Are we going to see a flight attendant sometime soon? I could use a drink.'

'You know alcohol is not allowed on NUMA aircraft anymore,' Rudi said.

Kurt chuckled. *By the book, as always.* 'I was thinking a bottle of water or a nice, cold Coke.'

'Oh,' Rudi said. 'Sorry. Help yourself.' He pointed to a fridge.

Kurt unbuckled his seat belt and went to the minifridge. He opened it and plucked two bottles of Coke from the back, where they'd be coolest. Glass, not plastic, and he noticed the fine print on the label. It was written in Spanish, suggesting the plane had been restocked somewhere south of the border. Turning the bottle in his hand, Kurt found the bottler's address, nodded to himself and closed the fridge.

He returned to his seat, opened both bottles and slid one toward Rudi. 'Time to talk,' he said. 'Judging by the long takeoff roll and the slow climb, I can tell we're carrying a lot of fuel. By our course, I can safely assume we're not going to Oahu or Los Angeles; and by the wrinkles in your shirt, I'm assuming you've been on this plane a long time. Just came to get me and to bring me back, I'd suspect. So where are we headed? Somewhere in South America?'

Rudi was in the process of pouring the Coke into a glass as Kurt spoke. 'South America?' he said. 'Is that your guess?'

'It is.'

'A rather large place,' Rudi replied with a grin. 'Maybe you'd care to be more specific.'

Kurt hemmed and hawed for a second as though thinking deeply on the subject, though he already knew exactly what he was going to say. 'Ecuador.'

Gunn's eyebrows went up.

'Guayaquil,' Kurt added, 'to be precise.'

Gunn looked truly shocked. 'With all due respect to the great Johnny Carson, Carnac has nothing on you.'

'Not really,' Kurt said, grinning and pointing to the Coke bottle. 'These were filled in Quito. But that's a landlocked city. The largest port in Ecuador is in Guayaquil. And we tend to work on the sea.'

'Hmm,' Gunn said. 'Not sure whether to be more impressed or less.'

A red phone buzzed beside Gunn's chair. He picked up the receiver and listened for a moment. 'We're ready,' he said. 'Put them through.'

'If you're not giving the briefing, who is?'

'A colleague in the National Security Agency.'

'Am I working for the NSA now?' Kurt asked. He'd been loaned out before.

'Not just you,' Gunn replied. 'Every NUMA ship and team member within five thousand miles.'

Now Kurt's eyebrows went up. There could be only one reason for that. 'They've lost something.'

Gunn didn't confirm or deny. 'I'll let them explain.'

A flat-screen monitor on the bulkhead wall came to life. It displayed the confines of a briefing room with two men at a desk. The first was an Air Force officer with multiple ribbons on his blue jacket. The second wore a shirt and tie.

The man in the tie spoke first. 'Good afternoon,' he said. 'My name is Steve Gowdy. I'm the director of ExAt projects for the National Security Agency.'

'ExAt?' Kurt asked.

'Extra-atmospheric,' Gowdy replied. 'Basically, anything that takes place above the stratosphere. Including our satellite and maneuvering vehicle projects.'

Kurt nodded to indicate he understood and Gowdy leaned toward the camera like a TV reporter on the evening news. 'Before I begin, you have to understand that this project is of the utmost importance and is compartmentally classified on a highly restricted basis.'

Kurt had heard this speech before. 'There's not much in the NSA that isn't. But I understand.'

Gunn cracked a smile, but Gowdy didn't seem to get the joke.

'We've had our project go off the wire at the last moment,' Gowdy continued. 'An experimental craft on a reentry profile over the South Pacific.'

Kurt knew something about the NSA's space operations. 'X-37,' he said, referring to the well-known NSA craft that was launched on a rocket and returned to Earth by gliding back down similar to the space shuttle.

'No,' Gowdy said. 'A vehicle we call the *Nighthawk*. Its official designation is VXA-01. It's the first of its kind. In a way, the X-37B was a prototype, a test bed used to develop certain technologies. The new craft is twice the size of the X-37 and far more capable.'

'I'm impressed,' Kurt said. 'I've never heard of it. Not even a rumor.'

'We've done our work keeping it quiet,' Gowdy admitted. 'By flying the X-37 under mysterious circumstances, we've been able to occupy the public's attention and give them something to be suspicious about. In the meantime, we've built *Nighthawk* and had it up in space for over three years. Unfortunately, it went off course on reentry and failed to answer commands.'

'So . . . are we worried about losing the warp technology to the Klingons?' Kurt asked.

Gowdy sat in stony silence before answering. 'There are no warp drives,' Gowdy said without a trace of humor, 'but the *Nighthawk* is the most advanced aircraft ever built. It was constructed with materials and technology that are two generations beyond anything the European, Chinese or Russian space agencies are using. It's a revolutionary aircraft. I say *aircraft* because it looks like a plane, but, make no mistake, it is a spacecraft, capable of maneuvering in orbit, acting autonomously and completing missions the shuttle never dreamed of. And while it doesn't have a *warp drive*, it does possess a revolutionary *ion propulsion system* that could be used for Earth–Moon travel and cut our transit time to Mars in half.'

Kurt nodded. 'And you want us to look for it.'

'You'll be part of a team responsible for a specific sector in the search zone. Naval assets from Pearl and San Diego will be working close by.'

As Gowdy spoke, Rudi Gunn unlocked a briefcase, pulled out a file and passed it to Kurt.

Using the edge of his palm, Kurt broke the imprinted seal. Inside, he found information about the *Nighthawk*: trajectory data, time sequencing and a map.

'As you can see,' Gowdy continued, 'we lost track of it halfway between French Polynesia and the South American coastline. Based on the last telemetry response, and the vehicle's speed and altitude, we believe it came down somewhere east of the Galápagos Islands.'

Kurt studied a satellite photo with red lines overlaid upon it. The lines showed a widening cone of probability that began just east of the Galápagos. It stretched and widened in a sideways V toward Ecuador and Peru. A scale suggested the calculated odds of the *Nighthawk* coming down in any particular section.

'Does it have an emergency beacon?' Kurt asked, still studying the map.

'Yes,' Gowdy replied, 'but we're not receiving a signal.'

'So we'll be looking for debris,' Kurt concluded.

'No,' Gowdy said firmly.

Kurt looked up.

'We have reason to believe the *Nighthawk* landed intact,' Gowdy said.

Gowdy went on to explain the autoland system and how the internal processors would take over the flight controls once commands from the base at Vandenberg were cut off. He mentioned the word *confidence* at least three times but never gave a reason why the autoland system should be working when so many other systems on board had failed.

Kurt let it go. 'What resources do we have for the job?'

At this point, Gunn took over the conversation. 'Everything we could get our hands on,' he said. 'NUMA has three vessels in the area. One coming up from the Chilean coast and two coming through the Panama Canal from the Gulf of Mexico.'

Another sheet of paper came Kurt's way. It listed the various ships.

'Paul and Gamay Trout are already on the *Catalina*,' Gunn said, referring to two of the most trusted members of NUMA's Special Projects team. 'They were down off the coast of Chile doing an ecological study. They'll be within range in about fifteen hours.'

'That's fortunate,' Kurt said.

Rudi nodded. 'The *Jonestown* and the *Condor* will transit the canal and arrive thirty-six hours later.'

'Thirty-six hours sounds a little optimistic,' Kurt said, looking at the relative positions of the ships. 'It's nearly thirty hours' sailing time and the canal looks like a freeway at rush hour this time of year. Ships can wait as long as two days to transit.'

'They're getting a priority hall pass,' Rudi said. 'Since NUMA helped prevent the destruction of the canal a few years ago, we've had a gold star status anytime we stop by.'

'Ah,' Kurt said, recalling hearing about the operation from Dirk Pitt himself. The fact that NUMA's Director had been personally involved in thwarting the destruction paid dividends to them all.

Gowdy broke in. 'NUMA will be in charge of the

southern and eastern patrol areas. In three days, a salvage fleet from the Navy's 131st Salvage Squadron will arrive from San Diego to search the western half of the target zone, while additional vessels from the Pacific Fleet will cover the western edge of the search area.'

Kurt was looking at the list of vessels. Aside from two auxiliary ships out of San Diego, they were all warships. Destroyers and frigates. 'What's with all the firepower?'

'Unintentional consequence of logistics,' Gowdy said. 'This section of the Pacific is a long way from everywhere. Forty-five hundred miles from Pearl. Twenty-nine hundred miles from San Diego. These were the closest, fastest ships equipped to search for underwater targets. Additional salvage vessels are following, but they can't keep up and are being left behind. In addition, P-3 Orion and P-8A aircraft are crisscrossing the search zone, dropping sonobuoys and other autonomous units to assist the search.'

There was some logic to that, but it suggested panic. 'That's a large fleet,' Kurt said. 'Are you sure that's the best way to do this?'

'What do you mean?'

Kurt closed the folder and leaned back in his chair. 'I have to assume you want to keep this quiet. A dozen American ships and a swarm of aircraft surrounding the Galápagos Islands might be tipping your hand. The tortoises might think we're invading.'

Gowdy nodded appreciatively on-screen.

Kurt made a suggestion. 'We could always publish a story that NUMA's doing an ecological study. Put that out in the press and no one would think twice about a few extra research vessels moving into the area. Once they're on station, we could deploy their helicopters and survey boats and search to our hearts' content. All without drawing any attention to ourselves.'

'Not a bad idea,' Gowdy said. 'Except we think the Chinese and Russian intelligence services are already clued in. Within hours of the *Nighthawk*'s vanishing, we noted course changes from several vessels belonging to each country. We're tracking them. I think you can figure out where they're headed.'

'The Galápagos Islands,' Kurt said.

'Exactly,' Gowdy replied. 'Right for the heart of our search area.'

That suggested other complications. 'Do you think they'll interfere?'

Gowdy shrugged. 'I've given up trying to predict what our Chinese and Russian friends will do. My job is to keep them from doing it. But after that mess in Ukraine and all the problems in the South China Sea, I don't put anything past anyone. And once you understand how badly they want what we have, you'll come to the same conclusion. According to our studies, the Russians have fallen so far behind in technology that they're in danger of getting lapped. The Chinese are a little better off because they have an army of engineers over there and more spies than you can shake a stick at – but they still operate without much ingenuity and are probably a full decade behind our latest designs. Add in the fact that both countries prefer to catch up by stealing what we have rather than coming up with their own ideas and you can imagine them licking their chops.'

Kurt understood that concept quite well. Spying and stealing had always been a big part of Russian and Chinese research efforts. 'There's a reason the Russian space shuttle *Buran* looks exactly like the one we designed. A reason their *Blackjack* bomber is almost indistinguishable from the B-1.'

'Yes there is,' Gowdy said. 'In a way, I can't blame them. In their shoes, I'd do the same thing. But we're not in their shoes and there are no circumstances under which they're going to be allowed to get their hands on this vehicle.'

'What if they find it first?' Kurt asked, wondering if Gowdy was talking about a shooting war.

'No circumstances,' he repeated.

The words were cold and unyielding and Gowdy didn't bat an eye as he spoke them, but that brought to mind another question.

'So why didn't you just blow it up?' Kurt said, putting the folder away. 'Prevent any chance of them finding more than a fragment of the hull?'

Gowdy looked stricken.

'I have to assume it had a self-destruct mechanism?' Kurt asked. 'Why not blow it to pieces and avoid all this?'

'We tried,' Gowdy croaked. 'The self-destruct command failed. A review of the telemetry data shows a complete loss of communications just before the command was initiated.'

'A game of inches,' Rudi Gunn added. 'Or fractions of a second.'

Gowdy nodded.

Kurt turned his attention back to the effort. 'How many ships are the Chinese and Russians sending?'

'We count nine Russian vessels, including a few warships. Twelve Chinese ships. All military. Including their newly built aircraft carrier.'

'Thirty ships, from three different countries,' Kurt noted. 'All desperately looking for the same thing in a fairly restricted area. What could possibly go wrong?'

'Anything and everything,' Gowdy grunted. 'We're in a race against time. Every day that craft is missing, the danger increases.'

Something in Gowdy's tone struck Kurt oddly, as did the stony silence of the Air Force officer, who hadn't said a single word.

'We're the closest,' Gunn said, jumping in. 'NUMA will be on scene days before anyone else. I'll bet you a bottle of Don Julio tequila that NUMA locates the *Nighthawk* before either our Navy or the Russian and Chinese fleets.'

Gowdy nodded appreciatively. 'I'll see your bottle of Don Julio and raise you a box of Cuban cigars if you can find it before our adversaries arrive.'

Kurt was listening and thinking at the same time. With only three ships, two of which wouldn't be there until at least a day after his own arrival, chances of success were slim. But then, Kurt had spent a lifetime figuring out ways to change the odds. As he studied the map, an idea jumped out at him, a way to up his chances and deal a blow to the Russian and Chinese fleets all at the same time.

He looked up with a roguish grin on his face. 'In that case, someone better call Fidel and ask him to start picking out the best tobacco leaves on the island. Because if the *Nighthawk* is out there, I'm going to find it for you. And I'm going to do it before we see any foreign flags on the horizon.'

Gowdy looked on blankly, probably considering Kurt's boast nothing more than a false bravado. But Kurt had an ace up his sleeve. An ace and an elephant.

4

Constantin Davidov sat in the back of an American-made sedan as it moved along a crowded Chinese highway through a canyon of high-rise office towers built from Brazilian steel, Korean glass and cement imported from Australia.

Throngs of people moved along the sidewalks. Armies of them massed at each intersection like opposing battalions. They surged toward each other at the changing of a light but mixed and meshed and passed on through without incident as they traveled to a hundred different destinations.

Street vendors and shops by the hundreds catered to them with food brought in from the countryside. Construction engineers dug up the road to bury new pipelines that would feed the city's ever-growing need for water and natural gas, while smog from exhaust pipes and coal-fired power plants choked the air, blotting out the light of the noonday sun.

'How can you stand it?' Davidov muttered to himself.

A Chinese man sitting beside him overheard and looked appropriately offended. Li Ying was a liaison officer in the People's Liberation Army, a captain in a pea-green uniform with gold stars on his shoulder boards and a smattering of ribbons above his breast pocket. 'This is globalism,' Ying said. 'The engine that drives the Chinese economy.'

A look of disgust settled on Davidov's face. As far as he could tell, *globalism* and the interlinking of the world's economies was nothing but a disaster in the making, a disease slowly infecting the cells of the world's collective body. *Everything, everywhere, all the time.* At least that seemed to be the motto. Personally, he longed for simpler days.

The Chinese officer continued. 'China has transformed in a single generation from a backwater land to a global powerhouse. We're very proud of what we've built.'

'Pride goeth before the fall,' Davidov said.

The sentiment was lost on his host. And why not? Why should Ying worry? He was twenty-eight. A captain in the army of an ascending nation. Like his country, Ying was bold and brash at this point in his life, undaunted by decades of work that might lead nowhere.

'At least we move forward,' Ying said. 'Russia seems to do nothing but regress these days.'

Davidov couldn't argue with that. Forty years prior, he'd come to China with a group of Soviet officials. They found no cars on the street, few working phones and nowhere decent to stay – even by Moscow standards, which at the time were dreadfully low.

Back then, the Chinese bought Russian MiGs and patrol boats with borrowed rubles. Back then, Russian oil, coal and financial aid were a lifeline for Mao's hermit kingdom, but now . . . Now, even a pitiful, junior-grade officer could be rude to a Russian emissary.

The sedan pulled up to a modern, angular building. Walls of gray cement, broken by narrow, vertical bands of glass. The design was dramatic; it brought to mind a medieval castle, complete with slits in the wall for archers to fire through.

A white-gloved soldier stepped forward and opened the door. He stood at rigid attention as Ying climbed out and Davidov followed.

'This way,' Ying said.

'I know where to go,' Davidov said. 'Stay with the car.'

'Excuse me?'

'Trust me. This won't take long,' Davidov said. 'You can even keep the engine running,' he suggested, glancing up to the brownish sky. 'Add to your precious globalism.'

A minute later, Davidov was inside the building, his shoes making distinctive clicks on the cultured granite floor of the Ministry building. He was ushered into a conference room. The man he'd come to see waited for him.

'You're free to speak in here,' General Zhang, of the Chinese Ministry of State Security, insisted.

'Thank you for the reassurance,' Davidov said. He was quite certain the room was bugged. It didn't matter. He had no intention of disclosing anything General

Zhang didn't already know. 'We have word on the American space plane,' he announced. 'Confirmation.'

'And?' Zhang said excitedly. 'What happened? Did the Americans regain control?'

'They tried,' Davidov said. 'But our transmission was closer and more powerful than theirs. We overrode their commands. Unfortunately, it becomes difficult to ascertain what happened after that.'

'Difficult?' Zhang crossed his arms. 'Did the *Nighthawk* reach California or not?'

Davidov offered a subtle smile. 'You know the answer to that as well as I do, Zhang: the craft did not make it home. But our team was unsuccessful in tracking it to a final location.'

The two men stood quietly. The tall, lean Russian on one side, his shorter, stockier host on the other.

Davidov was a horseman whose ancestors had ridden the frozen tundra. He had long, flowing limbs and preferred speed and stealth over massed strength – a cavalryman at heart.

Zhang was shorter, stockier. His muscular build, thick neck and heavy hands creating the look of a powerhouse who could break down walls. A bulldog who moved with the grace of a tank, slowly but inexorably, grinding and pulverizing anything in its path.

Neither was superior or inferior to the other, but they were so different as to be opposites, unable to mix for long without combustion. It made everything tense.

'You expect me to believe that?' Zhang said, a practiced edge in his voice.

Davidov sat down. 'Not really. Though it is the truth. You had ships on the flight path. Spy trawlers in the area. You know as well as I do that the *Nighthawk* is invisible to radar.'

'You must have some data,' Zhang proposed, trying to pry anything out of the Russian. 'Some suggestion to the ultimate outcome.'

Davidov shrugged. 'Perhaps. But if there is anything else, the men in Moscow have not seen fit to share it with me.'

'Then why have you come?'

'To inform you that our partnership is over.'

This time, Zhang seemed surprised. Score one for the swiftness of the cavalry.

'The mission has failed,' Davidov added. 'All our efforts have been for naught. So, I've been sent to officially dissolve our joint enterprise.'

'Surely we don't need to part ways so quickly,' Zhang said. 'We could talk some more. Smooth out our differences. Over dinner, perhaps.'

'I would enjoy that,' Davidov said. 'Except that, as we speak, your salvage vessels continue at flank speed toward the possible crash site.'

'I don't know what you're talking about,' Zhang replied.

'Then I suggest you contact your naval chief of staff.'

Zhang's posture stiffened. 'Perhaps you're right. It seems this latest *bout* of teamwork has outlived its usefulness.'

'It was doomed from the start,' Davidov said. 'At least this way we have no spoils to argue over.'

Zhang moved to the head of the table and slid some papers together in a folder. In truth, he was pleased. Freed of the Russian shackles, his men could go to work immediately with no need to hide in the shadow of the Bear. 'So it's every nation for itself,' he said. 'I assume your ships will be looking for the wreckage?'

'Of course.'

'As will ours,' Zhang replied. 'I can only hope there will be no conflict.'

'I wouldn't expect any,' Davidov said, standing and drawing himself up to his full height. 'By the time your fleet reaches South American waters, the *Nighthawk* will be in a crate on its way to Moscow with a large red ribbon tied around it.'

Zhang scoffed at the boast and pressed an intercom button on the conference table. It buzzed his assistant. 'Comrade Davidov will be needing a ticket back to Moscow,' he said. 'Make sure it's first class, China Air.'

Davidov offered a bow of thanks and then turned for the door. Both of them knew he wasn't going to Moscow.

5

Hiram Yaeger walked through the air-conditioned computer bay on the eleventh floor of the NUMA building before heading for home. He made the same checks every night and thought of himself as a ship's captain inspecting his vessel, but it was really just a habit born from the early days of computing when things were not as reliable.

Back when he'd first started, Yaeger had to check and reset huge reel-to-reel tapes and inspect processing connections by hand. When they first looked for bugs, it meant actual insects that had a habit of seeking out warm, dark places, getting themselves zapped on fragile micro electric circuitry and burning out what passed for microchips in the process.

Years later, it was all about mainframe processing loads and hardwired connections. Now the computers did it all themselves, speaking to each other through Wi-Fi, checking and rechecking their own performance against preset parameters. All Yaeger *really* had to do was to make sure no one had unplugged the system from the electrical outlet.

He checked anyway.

Satisfied that everything was in order he made his way toward the outer office. 'Good night, Max,' he said, speaking to the computer.

'Night and day are the same thing to me,' the computer replied. *'Unlike you, I work twenty-four hours a day.'*

Hiram had designed Max and the rest of the computers in NUMA's state-of-the-art processing center. Years before Siri had begun talking, Yaeger had given Max voice processing and interactive capabilities. Why he'd ever added a sense of humor, he didn't know.

'No one likes a computer with a smart mouth,' Hiram said, pulling a light jacket over his shoulders and adjusting his wire-framed glasses.

'I don't have a mouth,' Max pointed out. *'But your point is well taken. FYI: you have a visitor in the outer office. My sensors indicate Priya Kashmir has just used her badge to enter the room.'*

'Thanks, Max. See you tomorrow.'

Hiram continued toward the outer office, grinning that he'd stumped Max by saying good-bye in a way Max could not correct or elaborate on. A small victory for the human race.

He stepped through the door and spotted a figure in a wheelchair waiting for him.

Priya Kashmir was Yaeger's new assistant. Born in southern India, raised in London, and schooled at MIT – where she'd graduated at the top of her class – Priya had been set to join one of NUMA's field teams when a three-car pileup left her paralyzed from the waist down.

NUMA had honored her contract despite her injuries, paid for her medical treatment and given her a pick of assignments including working in the field if she wanted, insisting they'd find a way to make it work.

By then, she'd already decided on a different path, asking if NUMA could use her skills in the computing department.

'Hello,' she said cheerfully. 'How are you this evening, Mr Yaeger?'

Her accent was a mix of British and Indian, with the slightest hint of a Boston Yankee thrown in for good measure.

'Please stop calling me that,' Hiram said. 'It makes me feel old.'

'Because your father was Mr Yaeger?'

'My grandfather.'

She laughed, brushed a strand of mahogany hair from her face and handed him a note. 'This just came in.'

Hiram took the note. It was written in flowing script that could have passed for calligraphy. 'Your Post-its should be in an art museum.'

'I had a few minutes on my hands while I waited for the elevator,' she said.

Hiram read the note. The message was far simpler than the writing. It was from Kurt Austin.

'"Need you to make Dumbo fly,"' Hiram read aloud. '"Use those big ears and find me a splash-down site. And I need it quickly. Otherwise, you're going to cost Rudi Gunn a bottle of Don Julio and box of hand-rolled Cuban cigars."'

A puzzled look settled on Hiram's face. 'Curious.'

Priya had to agree. 'I didn't understand when Kurt rattled it off in the first place,' she admitted. 'And I don't honestly understand it now. But Kurt insisted you would know what he meant. I assume it's some type of code.'

Hiram sighed, took off his jacket and draped it over the back of the chair. 'Sort of. It's Kurtspeak for: can you pull an all-nighter and find me a miracle?'

'Really? What's the Dumbo reference? Isn't that a flying elephant from the Disney cartoons?'

'*D*ynamic *U*nderwater *M*onitoring *B*and,' Hiram said. 'We added the *O* for fun. It's a series of highly sensitive subsurface listening posts NUMA has set up throughout the Pacific. There are several hundred major stations and five thousand tethered buoys. They listen for seismic activity.'

'P-waves and S-waves,' Priya said.

Hiram nodded. 'With DUMBO, we can detect a large earthquake and pinpoint its location far earlier than the existing tsunami monitoring network, but we're also able to monitor the smallest tectonic movements. Deep earthquakes that wouldn't wake a light sleeper if he was dozing next to the china cabinet. We learn a lot more about deep-earth geology that way. We can even predict when a big one is coming by the prevalence or absence of tiny tremors.'

Priya nodded, but she still looked confused. 'What does that have to do with his mission and why does he want DUMBO to fly?'

'The flying part is just Kurt being Kurt,' Hiram explained. 'He thinks he's funny. I warn you: *do not laugh at his jokes.* It'll only encourage him and you'll never hear the end of them. But the idea is top-notch as usual.'

From there, Hiram went on to explain about the missing *Nighthawk* and the rapid naval buildup to search for it. He tied the DUMBO project in as he finished. 'Kurt wants us to listen to the tapes in case the seismic sensors picked up any sign of the crash. If they did, we can triangulate a location and save everyone a lot of time searching the South Pacific.'

Priya's eyes seemed to catch the light as she smiled. 'That's brilliant,' she said. 'If it works. Can seismic detectors really be that sensitive?'

Hiram hedged. 'The network is far more sensitive than we thought it would be. We learned shortly after setting it up that other sounds from the ocean were being recorded. Subsurface mining off Taiwan, torpedo and artillery explosions at military test sites around the Pacific and even the last desperate groans of sinking ships. As those go down, they tend to break up, often accompanied by subtle explosions as the hull ruptures and trapped air is released. We were able to pinpoint the exact location of nine missing ships in the first six months of operations. But the *Nighthawk* is much smaller than your average seagoing vessel.'

'Better than nothing,' Priya said, grinning.

'Exactly,' he said. 'It's just unlikely to be easy, especially given this time frame.'

She eased her chair forward. 'How can I help?'

'The first thing we have to do is download all the recorded data,' Hiram said. 'Then we have to cross-reference it and begin the slow, painful process of weeding out the background noise, the magma and seismic activity that the sensors are designed to pick up and anything that doesn't emanate from the search area. After that, we have to identify and remove shipping static, biological sources of interference like whale songs and schools of tuna, and at least a hundred other extraneous forms of underwater vibration.'

The lights in the office brightened and the coffeepot in the corner switched on automatically and started brewing.

'More precisely, he means I have to do all that,' Max announced over a speaker. *'Looks like we're all working through the night together.'*

Priya laughed. 'I swear, sometimes she misses you,' she said.

Hiram noticed a sense of glee in the computer voice that he'd have sworn he never programmed into it. 'Eavesdropping again, Max. That's another bad habit.'

'All in the name of efficiency,' Max replied. *'Seismic data accessed, commencing download. Also, please advise Kurt that machine-rolled cigars are every bit the equal of – if not superior to – human, hand-rolled products.'*

Priya laughed. 'Have you been smoking again, Max? You know that's a bad habit.'

'No,' Max said. *'Just stating a verifiable factual principle.'*

Hiram chuckled. 'You're an expert at most things, Max, but I'm going to leave cigars and liquor to Kurt.'

'*Very well,*' Max said. '*Beginning audio analysis.*'

Hiram walked over to the coffeepot and poured two cups. When Max finished the grunt work, he and Priya would have to make the final choices regarding what frequencies would be allowed to remain in the recording. Not much to do until then.

'Cream and sugar?' he said to Priya.

'Two cubes, please. And, thank you.'

Hiram dropped a sugar cube into the dark liquid. It made a tiny splash and almost no sound at all. The way he reckoned it, the *Nighthawk* parachuting into the ocean would do something similar, although it would be the equivalent of tossing a sugar cube into an Olympic swimming pool. He put their chances of hearing it, even with the network of sensors, at ten-to-one.

He dropped the second cube in, stirred the coffee and watched the small block of sugar dissolve and disappear. At least the *Nighthawk* couldn't do that.

6

Guayaquil, Ecuador

After touching down in Ecuador, Kurt checked into the hotel and allowed himself a quick shower and a change of clothes. Refreshed, he caught a cab to a dockside warehouse on the outskirts of Guayaquil's bustling port.

Passing through a security checkpoint, he entered the cavernous building and quickly found his way to the section NUMA had taken over. There, hidden among towers of stacked shipping containers, he found a rack of hard-shelled diving suits, stacks of torpedo-shaped sonar emitters, a pair of small ROVs and several sleds with cameras and lights on them.

Perched in the center of this collection, like a mad scientist amid his creations, was Joe Zavala.

A few inches shorter than Kurt, Joe had dark, close-cropped hair, high cheekbones and deep, brown eyes that seemed soft and contemplative at times, fierce at others. As Joe moved among the crowded stacks of equipment with a checklist in his hand, he displayed the qualities of a cat. Never once looking up from the clipboard and yet never putting a foot wrong or hitting his head on the overhanging arms, jutting fins or brass propellers that surrounded him.

Joe had been Kurt's closest friend at NUMA for years. He was an amateur boxer, the most gregarious member of the Special Projects team and an avowed bachelor. He was also a mechanical genius and had built many of NUMA's more advanced submersibles.

'You look like the proverbial kid in the toy store,' Kurt said, alerting Joe to his presence.

'It's a *candy store* in that proverb, amigo.'

'So I did a little rewrite,' Kurt said. 'Looks like Rudi really came through. Where'd he get all this stuff? Aside from the hard suits, I don't recognize any of this equipment.'

'You shouldn't,' Joe said. 'Those submersibles came from an oil exploration firm. These sonar buoys are cast-offs from the Ecuadorian Navy – I have no idea if they even work yet – and those camera sleds came from the movie company that produced *Megalodon Versus the Giant Squid*.'

'A classic, if ever there was one,' Kurt said.

'So I've heard,' Joe replied.

Kurt turned serious once more. 'Rudi told me he'd chartered a group of fishing boats to supplement the fleet. I assume this equipment is for them?'

Joe nodded. 'And I have twelve hours to get it all ready and send them out. At least we've got our own people flying in to run the systems once they're on board; otherwise, I'd have to teach everyone, too.'

'The more ships we have in the water, the faster we'll cover the search area,' Kurt said. 'But we're going to need more than a fishing fleet to make this work.'

Joe checked one more thing off of his list and put the clipboard down. 'What do you have in mind?'

'How much do you know about the DUMBO project?'

'Big ears in the sea,' Joe replied. 'You think you're going to hear the *Nighthawk* going down?'

'I was told those sensors could hear a pin drop,' Kurt said. 'In this case, a fifty-billion-dollar pin that fell from outer space.'

'That sounds like another bad movie,' Joe said.

Kurt laughed. 'The way I see it, if the *Nighthawk* hit the water hard enough, we might hear it. Even if it parachuted down and then sank, there are compartments that would implode from the pressure. The central core covering the cargo bay, fuel cells and control unit have been built to withstand a thousand atmospheres. Something about sending it to Venus one day. But there are other cavities that might rupture. Hollow spaces in the wings and tail. The wheel wells around the landing gear.'

'Good point,' Joe said. 'On top of that, parts of the heat shield would have been hitting a thousand degrees or more shortly prior to touchdown. There might be an identifiable hissing and cavitation as that surface came into contact with the water.'

'Never thought of that,' Kurt said. 'This is why you're in charge of building and repairing things.'

'So who's listening to the tapes?'

'Hiram and Max. I told him to contact you if he needs any more information.'

'Contact me?' Joe said. 'Why? What are you going to be doing?'

'I have to go meet a specialist from the NSA who'll be riding shotgun with us.'

'Are we really getting a chaperone?' Joe asked.

'Looks that way.'

Joe picked the clipboard up once again. 'Well, that ought to slow our progress by at least fifty percent. What the guy's name?'

'Emily Townsend,' Kurt said.

Joe's eyebrows went up. 'Strange name for a guy. Bet he got teased a lot growing up.'

Kurt laughed. 'From the profile they gave me, I don't think *Ms* Townsend gets teased much. Around the NSA, her nickname is *Hurricane Emma*.'

'You know what that means,' Joe said. 'Either we got stuck with her because we're the problem children or we got stuck with her because she is one and the Navy didn't want her on one of their ships.'

'She's got a background NASA would kill for,' Kurt said. 'A job with Rockwell right out of school, designing propulsion systems. Three years with Jet Propulsion Laboratory, and then the last five with the NSA. She's definitely an expert in her field.'

'An expert,' Joe said sarcastically, 'okay? I'm upping my estimate to a ninety percent reduction in progress.'

Kurt checked his watch. 'I'll do my best to charm her and turn her into an ally instead of an impediment. With a little luck, and some fine wine, all will turn out well. Trust me.'

'You seem to be in a very good mood,' Joe said. 'Nothing gets your blood up like a challenge.'

'Especially when someone else is doing all the hard work,' Kurt said. 'And all I have to do is charm an attractive woman.'

'Good luck with that,' Joe said, turning back to his inventory of equipment. 'But be careful. Some icebergs can't be thawed.'

Kurt left the warehouse and passed through the security gate unaware that he was being observed. Perched high in one of the oversized mobile cranes that moved the shipping containers around the port, two men were watching, one through binoculars.

He lowered them, revealing dark eyes and little else. A filtered mask covered his nose and mouth, the kind some athletes wore while training in high pollution areas. His voice was muffled as he spoke through it. 'When did they arrive?'

'Within six hours of the *Nighthawk* disappearing,' the man beside him said. 'They're already gathering equipment and chartering vessels to help them search.'

The masked man stared at the activity below him, like a chess master looking over the board. A slight wheezing could be heard in his lungs even with the filtered air to protect them. 'The Americans reacted faster than even I expected.'

'But you wanted them here,' the second man said. 'Didn't you?'

'Of course, but it'll do us no good if they learn too much too soon.'

'We could slow them down,' the second man suggested. 'Damage some of their equipment, scare off the charters, so they have to find new boats.'

The masked man pondered this and then shook his head. 'Not the kind of delay we need. In fact, I think giving them a push rather than holding them back would better serve our plans. Are you still in contact with the Chinese?'

'Yes.'

'Alert them to the presence of these Americans, suggest that they know something vital. Point out the array of equipment they've gathered. The Chinese agent's imagination will take it from there.'

'And if the Chinese kill them? What then?'

'The American government will send replacements and the race will begin anew.'

7

Emma Townsend sat in a cozy booth in the recesses of El Caracol, the four-star restaurant Kurt Austin had suggested as a meeting place.

Despite Joe's assessment, there was little about her that suggested ice or frost. In fact, warmth was the first thought her appearance brought to mind. Her auburn hair fell straight to her shoulders and shimmered with a copper hue in the subdued lighting. Her eyes were a soft, hazel color, flecked with green, her lips full and her skin just sun-kissed enough to bring out a smattering of freckles that made her look younger than her thirty-three years.

Entering the restaurant early and waiting for Kurt, she'd already garnered her fair share of second glances and lingering stares. She noticed the gazes but ignored them. It was no worse than Washington.

The restaurant itself was an architectural delight. Its design brought together several styles much the same way the menu did, and the clientele was a mix of hip, bohemian customers, obvious tourists and refined Ecuadorian couples. Perhaps that was due to its location in the hills of Las Peñas, a four-hundred-year-old section of Guayaquil, where brightly painted houses had been turned into art galleries, restaurants and wine bars.

Tourists and locals alike flocked there on warm evenings. They strolled the boulevards and galleries and enjoyed the views, which overlooked the city and the coastline. As night fell, the lights of the Malecón, a restored promenade on the waterfront that had once been the historic Simón Bolívar Pier, came into view.

With only a glass of water in front of her, Emma waited for Kurt and reread the NSA bio that had been sent to her phone.

A quick look told her Austin was a man of action. He and his second-in-command, Joe Zavala, were listed as the principal figures in a series of high-profile missions. They'd averted several international catastrophes, including the recent events in Egypt, where they'd prevented former members of the Mubarak regime from co-opting the sub-Saharan aquifer and establishing authority across all of North Africa.

Further reading made it clear that despite this record, both Austin and Zavala had rubbed plenty of officials the wrong way. It seemed they were not fond of authority, chains of command or doing things by the book. Perhaps that explained his position with NUMA, she thought. NUMA had always preferred to shoot from the hip, right from the day James Sandecker had founded it. Men like Kurt thrived there, while in other agencies they were shackled and held back.

Just as well, she decided. She preferred results over protocol. In fact, she preferred results over everything, including personal friendships, alliances and rules. This had made her something of an outcast in her years at the National Security Agency. It had also vaulted her up the chain of command as quickly as it made enemies. She knew her reputation. Few in the agency wanted to work with her. They were governed by fear, afraid to fail. Afraid to take a chance. In her opinion, it made them ineffective. Which made it far preferable to work with a man like Austin.

If she found the *Nighthawk* with his help, she would be untouchable. She could name her next position, most likely becoming the youngest department director in the agency's history. And if she failed . . . well, the odds were stacked against her anyway. And she could always blame it on NUMA.

She spotted Kurt as he entered the restaurant and spoke briefly with the host. From there, he walked directly to her table, seeming taller and more handsome than his photographs. It wasn't that his features were any different; if anything, they were a little more careworn and weathered, like a book cover that was slightly tattered and broken-in.

She put her phone away and introduced herself. 'Emily Townsend. You can call me Emma. Pleased to meet you,' she said. 'Finally.'

Austin sat down. 'Sorry to keep you waiting,' he said. 'I was checking on the preparations.'

'How much equipment do we have?' she asked.

'I meant, in the kitchen,' he said. 'I was making sure the chef was up to standards.'

He grinned at his own comment and Emma found his self-assurance a most attractive quality. One that could be used to manipulate, if need be. The small talk continued until the waiter arrived.

'Any preference?' he asked, perusing the wine list.

'Surprise me.'

He closed the list. 'We'll have a bottle of the 2007 Opus One.'

'Excellent choice,' the waiter said, moving off to retrieve the selection.

'An extravagant bottle of wine on the first night,' Emma noted. 'Your expense account or mine?'

'I'll pay this time,' Kurt said. 'Save yours for the big stuff.'

She couldn't resist smiling at his easy way and had to keep reminding herself why they were there. Before anything else was said, she pulled a small device from her purse. It was triangle-shaped, several inches long. She placed it on the table. At the touch of a button, it began emitting an audible hiss of static.

'Active noise cancellation,' she said, easing the device to the edge of the table. 'It listens to our words and distorts them with interfering frequencies as they pass out of this cozy little booth. Anyone trying to record or eavesdrop on us will pick up nothing but garbled static.'

'What about a bug on or under the table?' he asked.

'I've already swept for it. Trust me, we can talk freely.'

He seemed only half convinced, and based on their conversation throughout dinner, perhaps less than that.

She noticed that he kept glancing around, eyeing everyone in the restaurant, in particular a Chinese couple who had arrived shortly after he had and were now sitting directly across the main room. Every time she was about to get into specifics, he changed the subject to something innocuous. At one point, when she was ready to force the subject, he offered her a bite of his entrée, holding out a fork toward her.

She accepted and changed the subject. He must have his reasons.

'So how did you end up in NUMA after working for the agency?' she asked.

'Admiral James Sandecker shanghaied me,' he said. 'That's how he gathered all his best people.'

Sandecker was now the Vice President. She was impressed that Austin knew him well enough to joke about him. And that he hadn't name-dropped him earlier.

'And how did a sworn pacifist end up at the NSA?' he asked.

'I see you have your own sources.'

'In low places,' he insisted.

'I was a pacifist,' she insisted. 'That's why I joined NASA. To better the state of humanity by exploring the universe in the name of peace. Unfortunately, life doesn't conform to the ideas of a naïve twenty-four-year-old. Not for long anyway.'

'Something go wrong in paradise?'

'Doesn't it always?'

He offered a wry smile, obviously waiting for more.

'After a year at NASA, I was selected for a new team,' she said. 'A follow-up to the relatively famous Daedalus Project, which hoped to use nuclear explosions or some other form of exotic propulsion like matter-antimatter combustion to power future spacecraft at tremendous speeds. Much faster than we can achieve with chemical rockets. It was exciting. Intoxicating, really. The project demanded long hours, at close quarters. And as you might expect, with eight people spending almost all their waking time together, we became a very tight-knit group. Then, out of the blue, we began receiving threats.'

'Because of the work?'

'Apparently,' she said. 'A fringe group I'd never heard of began accusing us of militarizing space. At first we thought it was a bunch of nonsense. But the threats became deeper, more personal. We were sent pictures of ourselves in vulnerable areas, in our houses, in our cars, at restaurants with our colleagues. Whoever these people were, they were obviously stalking us.'

'I assume the FBI got involved,' he said.

'They did. And they were able to link the threats to an anti-American group that had killed two scientists in the Arctic and sent letter bombs to several high-tech companies. We thought with the FBI on the case, we'd be safe. Two weeks later, our team leader and a friend – a man named Beric – was killed.'

Across from her, Kurt nodded thoughtfully but said nothing.

'Beric was an incredibly kind man,' she told him, surprised at the emotion it brought up after all these years. 'If anyone needed anything, right down to the cafeteria workers and janitors, he made sure they had it. If there was an underdog cause without much hope, he championed it. And he was brilliant. A genius in several fields, everything from software development to astrophysics. Above all else, he was committed to NASA's mission of peace, committed to a world where all men and women treat each other with decency.'

She took a deep breath, gathered herself and then continued. 'That someone would target him, accuse him of being a militarist and kill him for it, was a disgusting irony. It affected me. Lifted the blinders from my eyes. It proved to me that the pacifist mind-set is nothing but a childish dream. Peace is fragile, not a natural state. It can only be secured through strength. And when that strength fails, disaster ensues.'

'In many ways, I'd agree with that,' he said. 'Mind if I ask how it happened?'

'Like many of us at NASA, Beric loved to fly. He owned his own plane. Took it up every chance he could. If we had to go somewhere, he'd fly himself instead of going commercial. One day, on the way to an astrophysics conference, his plane exploded. From the wreckage, the FBI was able to determine what we already knew: the explosion was caused by a bomb. Three of us were supposed to be on that plane. But, as it turned out, Beric went alone.'

'I'm sorry,' Kurt said.

'Anyway,' she continued, 'the propulsion study was cancelled a short time later and the whole project was eventually shut down. Feeling like I was drifting, I began casting around for something else to do. When the National Security Agency began recruiting scientists for their space program, I jumped at the opportunity.'

He nodded thoughtfully and then changed the subject to something more cheerful. But even as he spoke, her mind lingered on Beric. She hadn't thought of him in years. He wouldn't have approved of her career change.

She shook off the thought and focused on Kurt once more. They continued to chat and enjoy the meal. Halfway through the second glass of wine, he paused midsentence and then pulled his phone from his pocket to study a text that had just come in.

'Checking your phone,' she said. 'Am I really that dull?'

'Anything but,' he said, putting the phone away. 'In fact, I think it's time to see how adventurous you truly are.' He slid the triangular, noise-cancelling device toward her, pulled out several hundred dollars in cash and flagged the waiter down. 'For the meal. And a tour of the kitchen.'

The waiter examined the cash briefly. Then he smiled and said, 'This way.'

Emma stood and went along with whatever Austin was up to. If anything, she was interested in seeing how his mind worked.

They followed the waiter through the kitchen and out the back door, where Kurt gave the waiter another instruction. 'Block this door for a few minutes, if you can. Don't let anyone follow us.'

The waiter nodded and Kurt led her out into a dimly lit alley behind the restaurant.

'I think you've got this backward,' she said. 'People

normally sneak out of a restaurant when they realize they can't pay, not after overpaying. And never before dessert.'

'We were being watched,' he said, leading her down the alley toward the main street.

'We're American agents operating without cover in a foreign country,' she said, 'of course we're being watched. I'm sure the Ecuadorian government is following us, especially considering our last-minute travel and sudden arrival.'

'These weren't Ecuadorian police or federal agents,' he insisted. 'It was a young Chinese couple. They were waiting at the door and took a booth directly across from us. They never touched their food.'

'Chinese couple,' she said, remembering their features. 'I saw them. Not a big surprise either. We know the Chinese are looking. But I promise you, no one could hear what we were saying as long as the interference processor was running. Our best people haven't been able to crack it.'

He stopped. 'They didn't have to hear what you were saying. They were reading your lips.'

She froze for a second, trying to remember anything she might have accidentally said and suddenly thankful that he'd interrupted her at every turn. 'I was wondering why you kept asking me to try your dinner, even though we ordered the same thing.'

'Less talk, that way,' Kurt said. He continued to lead her down the street.

'I'm still not sure why we left,' she said. 'If you knew

they were watching us, it might have been a good chance to plant some false information.'

'Not a bad idea,' he admitted, 'but I'm more concerned with real information, some of which I've just received. And I'm not interested in letting them get their hands on it.'

'What kind of information?' she asked.

'The whereabouts of the *Nighthawk*,' Kurt said. 'I know where it landed.'

She looked at him suspiciously. 'Impossible.'

'Not the exact point. But I can narrow it down to less than a hundred square miles.'

'How?' she said.

He stopped in his tracks but didn't say a word. At the end of the alley, a trio of men had suddenly appeared. They stood there implacably, waiting under a streetlight and blocking the path.

Emma eyed them. 'Something tells me they're not tourists.'

'I'd have to agree,' he said, looking around. 'And they seem to have brought some backup.'

At the sound of a commotion, Emma turned around and glanced down the alley. The rear door of the restaurant had come flying open. The Chinese couple came rushing out, the man shouting something at the kitchen staff. The argument ended when he pulled out a gun and fired into the doorway. The staff scrambled to safety and the door was slammed shut.

'Didn't count on them having backup,' Kurt said, 'and probably shouldn't have counted on a waiter keeping two armed agents from making it through the back of the house.'

'Are you armed?' Emma asked.

'Afraid not,' he said.

'Me neither,' she replied. 'Not exactly an auspicious start to our relationship.'

In simultaneous precision, the two agents at the back of the restaurant and the three new arrivals began to close in on them from opposite sides.

8

Kurt held on to Emma's hand – as he had since they'd left the restaurant. He'd hoped to outflank the Chinese and get back to the boulevard and hail a taxi. But the additional Chinese agents had cut them off.

'Now what?' Emma asked.

The two groups were closing in slowly, moving relentlessly toward their prey, as if they were afraid any quick action might offer a weakness or a break in their lines for Kurt and Emma to escape through.

'I almost wish they'd rush,' Kurt said. 'At least we might be able to throw them off balance.'

'Think they'll shoot us?'

Kurt shook his head. 'Not to kill. More likely they'd rather capture us and torture us until we reveal everything we know.'

'How comforting,' she said. 'Tell me you have a plan?'

Kurt's eyes darted around. He saw a thin gap between two of the buildings almost directly across from them, but it was so narrow that he'd have to squeeze through to make it. And even from this distance he could see obstructions and cables in the way. If they were held up, they'd be instant easy targets.

He glanced to the left, where a trash dumpster with

a closed lid stood in the dark. The roof of the building behind was reachable. 'Can you climb?'

'And run and punch, if I have to.'

'Perfect,' he said. 'Follow me.'

Kurt raced to the dumpster with Emma right beside him. He gave her a boost and then climbed up beside her. Out in the alley, the Chinese agents delayed for a second and then started to charge.

'Keep going,' Kurt said.

Emma kicked off her shoes, reached for the edge of the low-slung roof and pulled herself up without needing any help. Kurt came up beside her.

'Get to the front. Look for a cab,' he said.

'What are you going to do?'

'A holding action.'

She left Kurt and sprinted up toward the peak of the building, staying low in case the Chinese agents started shooting.

Kurt lay flat on the roof and waited for their pursuers to arrive. The loud metallic banging of someone climbing on the dumpster came a few seconds later. Hands appeared on the edge of the rooftop, and then a face, as one of the Chinese men pulled himself up.

Kurt thrust a foot forward, slamming his heel into the man's face. Blood spurted from a shattered nose and the man's head jerked back. He fell, taking his partner to the ground in the process.

Without waiting for a rematch, Kurt turned and raced up toward the top of the roof and went over the other side. Emma was crouching there, waiting for him.

'I don't see any cabs,' she said.

'A little late to call Uber.'

They jumped down together, landing solidly on the deserted front walk. Almost immediately, the trio of men who'd been at the far end of the alley came racing back out onto the main boulevard and sprinted toward them.

'Go,' Kurt yelled.

They ran across the street and this time several shots came their way. No loud concussions, just soft pops from well-suppressed handguns, the impacts marked by a sudden shattering of car windows parked on the far side of the road.

Kurt dove across the hood of a classic BMW 2002 and took cover as the well-preserved machine took the brunt of a minor onslaught.

At the sound of the shooting, the few people still out on the street raced for cover.

'I thought you said they wouldn't shoot us?' Emma asked.

'It must be plan B: target elimination.'

To see without exposing himself to a well-placed shot, Kurt ripped the mirror off the side of the car. 'Sacrilege,' he whispered as he vandalized one of his favorite old machines.

Using the mirror as a periscope, he said, 'They're surrounding us again.'

'Can you hot-wire a car?'

'Not in the blink of an eye,' Kurt said. 'Especially with people shooting at me.'

He looked down the street. A pair of buses idled at a

quiet stop beside the next intersection. 'How to feel about public transportation?'

'It'll do in a pinch.'

'Let's see if we can make the crosstown express,' Kurt said.

They darted from the cover of the old BMW, cut diagonally across the lawn of a small church and ran toward the idling buses.

'Yuck,' Emma gasped as she ran.

'What?' Kurt said.

'Wet grass, bare feet.'

At least she didn't slow down.

They reached the bus stop just as the lead bus began to move out. Kurt crashed through the door with Emma right behind him. The driver instinctively slammed on the brakes.

Kurt lunged forward, pulled him from the seat and stomped on the gas pedal. The big diesel engine roared and the bus lurched forward and began to pick up speed. Kurt grabbed the wheel and steered to the left.

Behind him, the driver had pulled a can of Mace and aimed it. Kurt shut his eyes, turned away and kept his foot on the gas. A commotion followed and a loud thud. When Kurt looked up, Emma had disarmed the bus driver, flung him to the ground and taken posses-sion of his spray can.

'Nice work,' Kurt said.

She brandished the Mace in the driver's direction and pointed. He looked and then moved back to the first open seat.

'*No vamos a hacerle daño a nadie,*' Emma said in fluent Spanish. '*Estamos trabajando para el gobierno.*'

Kurt continued to drive the bus, swinging wide around a corner and down the next street. The crowd stayed put. The murmuring didn't end, but there were no uprisings. 'What did you tell them?'

'I said we're not going to hurt anyone and that we're working for the government,' she explained. 'It's true, if you think about it. I just didn't specify which government.'

'Works for me,' Kurt said, rotating the big steering wheel and guiding the bus down the road. The big rig was surprisingly easy to drive as long as he went straight. How the drivers traversed narrow cobblestone streets without taking out parked cars and the corners of buildings, Austin couldn't imagine.

And after a mile, they'd reached the outskirts of Las Peñas. Kurt figured they'd left the Chinese agents far enough behind. He began to slow, easing over to the shoulder and looking for a place to park.

A sudden jolt from behind whiplashed his neck and sent shivers through the bus. The passengers screamed and several were thrown from their seats. Emma fell against the front window before regaining her balance.

Stomping on the gas instinctively, Kurt checked the mirror. The problem was obvious: a second bus had raced up behind with its lights off and rammed them. It was now maneuvering to pull alongside. Kurt swerved to cut it off and kept accelerating, but they failed to leave the other bus behind.

'*Modelo nuevo*,' the bus driver shouted to Kurt. '*Más rápido.*'

Emma explained. 'He says that the other bus is a newer model and much faster.'

'I got the gist,' Kurt said, trying desperately to keep the other bus from getting beside them.

The two traveling monoliths continued to accelerate, roaring down the dark street and away from the brightly lit Las Peñas section of town. Other cars swerved from the road to get out of the way and Kurt accidentally took out a line of newspaper machines on the edge of the sidewalk, scattering a hundred copies of *El Telégrafo*, *El Universo* and *El Metro* into the air.

They careened through an intersection to a chorus of horns and onto a more deserted stretch of road that led down the hill and out toward the coast. With the pedal floored and heading downhill, the bus began to shudder; it wasn't built for speed.

'They're coming again!' Emma shouted.

Another hit from their pursuer rocked the bus. A third ramming attempt almost forced them off the road.

Fighting for control, Kurt had to slow down. In response, the other bus raced up beside them and swerved. The two buses crashed together, windows shattered and the passengers screamed. Some dove to the floor, others began to pray.

If there was going to be a beating, Kurt preferred to dish it out rather than take it. 'Get everyone on the left side,' he shouted.

Emma waved the passengers over. Once they'd taken new seats, Kurt rolled the wheel to the right. The buses crashed together again and separated and the newer model fell back.

As they reached a long straight section of road, it came up once again. This time, Kurt glanced at the driver. It was the Chinese man with the bloodied nose.

'Hang on,' Kurt said, expecting another cross-check.

Instead of hitting him, the other driver just pulled close and held formation. Two heavy thumps sounded on the roof above them.

'We've been boarded,' Kurt said.

One set of dents appeared directly above him and Kurt knew what was about to happen. He dove from the driver's seat as a collection of holes appeared in the sheet metal above and a spray of bullets perforated and the dashboard the seat where he'd been sitting.

Lunging to the floor, he slammed his palm into the brake pedal.

The air brakes clasped the wheels at full strength and the bus went into a skid. The man flew off the roof and landed on a spiked fence. Skewered, he passed from view.

Kurt jumped back into the driver's seat as a second man swung down from the roof, his hands grasping the luggage rack. He came in from the side, kicking the door open and grabbing for Kurt's throat.

Emma nailed him in the thigh with her knee. He fell back and she blasted him in the eyes with a burst of the pepper spray. He covered his eyes and dropped into the fetal position. She promptly kicked him out through the door.

'*Cambio exacto*,' she said.

To Kurt's surprise, the passengers cheered.

'*Exact change*,' she said. 'He didn't have it. So I had to kick him off the bus. Get it?'

Guiding the bus through a sweeping, high-speed turn, Kurt laughed. 'We're going to have to work on your delivery. But great work.'

For the next mile, Kurt was able to keep the other bus well behind them, but when the road straightened, the bus closed in once again. Another slam from behind almost sent them down the embankment, while the lights of the Malecón, and a sign depicting a boat being pulled out of the water by a trailer, whipped past.

'We're running out of road,' Emma said. 'Unless you can make this thing swim, we're going to need an exit strategy.'

'That's a brilliant idea,' Kurt said.

'No, actually, it wasn't,' she said.

'Seriously, it's genius,' Kurt replied.

'But buses don't swim.'

'Exactly!'

Kurt slowed around the next turn and edged to the left. The other bus pulled up once again, dutifully taking the right side. It came over and hit them once. Then did so again. Kurt held his ground and waited until he saw the opening for the boat ramp.

Spotting it, he turned hard and held it. The two

buses locked together, sections of sheet metal tearing loose and scraping the road.

Racing forward with a trail of sparks flaring out behind them, they came to the Y junction and the boat ramp.

Kurt gave the other bus a final shove and then spun the wheel back to the left. As the two buses separated, the one driven by the Chinese agent went down the boat ramp. The driver locked up the brakes, but the bus skidded on the wet, angled surface and slammed into the bay. A sheet of water flew up and crashed down around it. When the bus came to a stop, two-thirds of it was submerged.

Kurt brought his vehicle under control and continued down the road. Less than a mile later, he pulled into a bus stop on the outskirts of the Malecón.

Several people scattered, in shock at the condition of the bus. As Kurt parked, one of the front tires blew and the entire bus tilted to the side. Broken windows and paneling swung back and forth while chunks of glass dropped to the floor. When the air brakes hissed to release their pressure, the old bus gave up the ghost.

Kurt opened the door and waved a hand toward it as if delivering his passengers on a daily run. 'Welcome to the Malecón. Watch your step.'

The passengers just stared at him with blank and confused expressions. 'Tough crowd,' he said, switching the sign up front to *Sin Servicio – Out of Service*.

He and Emma stepped off the bus together and made their way toward the crowd of tourists down below on the promenade.

'Think they'll be back?' Emma asked, looking toward the boat ramp.

'Not tonight,' Kurt said. 'If they're not injured, they're probably running and hiding, like we should be doing. But I'm assuming your NSA friends can get us out of any trouble we encounter.'

'I think we'll be okay,' she said. 'So how'd I do?'

'Not bad, for a rookie,' he said.

'Not bad?' she replied. 'I totally saved you from some Mace in the face. *And* I got rid of the guy who tried to Tarzan into our crosstown express.'

Kurt laughed and the two of them eased into the flow of people, disappearing into the crowd and making their way to a secluded spot farther down on the pier.

'Okay, you did great,' Kurt admitted. 'Just don't let it go to your head.'

'I won't,' she promised. 'As long as I get appropriate credit in your report.'

'I'll make you look good,' he said, 'which won't be hard to do. But if you really want a gold star, you're going to have to take another risk. One that most of your NSA coworkers would have a meltdown even contemplating.'

She narrowed her gaze, looking suspicious and excited all at the same time. 'And that step would be . . .'

Kurt pulled out his phone, double-checked the message from Hiram Yaeger and made up his mind. 'We need to steal our own equipment and go rogue for a while.'

'Because stealing a bus wasn't enough excitement for one night?'

'We're being watched,' he said. 'The group we met tonight aren't the only agents we're going to have to deal with. And our problems won't end when we get to the open sea. According to a few satellite photos I looked at before dinner, some awfully suspicious-looking trawlers are already following the *Catalina* and our other vessels.'

'Chinese spy trawlers with tall masts and lots of antennas,' she said. 'I already know about them. But none of that matters if we can find the *Nighthawk* and pull it off the bottom before their salvage fleet gets here.'

'Which would be great if it was just sitting down there ready to be picked up like a stuffed bear in a carnival game. But I have information suggesting it didn't come down in one piece like your people think it did. In fact, it's probably sitting on the bottom in several large pieces and a thousand small ones.'

She folded her arms across her chest, a faraway look that suggested she was calculating something. 'Our people are adamant that the *Nighthawk* did not break up.'

'And my people have audio recordings from underwater listening posts that pinpoint an impact four minutes and seventeen seconds after you lost track of the *Nighthawk*. The particular sound signatures suggest a high-speed surface impact, mid-frequency noise consistent with sudden generation of superheated steam – which is to be expected when a thousand-degree surface touches seventy-degree waters – and low-volume implosions at deeper depths consistent with wreckage breaking up.'

'Where?' she asked.

'Approximately fifty miles east of the Galápagos Islands chain,' Kurt said. 'Right in the heart of your probability cone.'

'How sure are you?'

'Certain enough to risk a case of Don Julio tequila and a box of Cuban cigars,' he said. 'Trust me, this information is not wrong. Our subsurface listening posts are more advanced than the Navy's SOSUS line and our computers, and the guy who built them, are one of a kind.'

She seemed almost convinced. 'Share it with the NSA's central office and we'll confirm. I promise you'll get the credit.'

'I don't care about credit,' he said. 'And telling anyone at the NSA would be a major mistake.'

For the first time, she looked angry. 'You're working for us, remember?'

'Sure,' Kurt said. 'But what about everyone else who's working for you? Are you willing to bet no one's moonlighting?'

By the look on her face, she obviously got the implication. She clenched her jaw and stared at him, and Kurt wondered if Hurricane Emma was about to make an appearance. 'What are you getting at?'

'We've only been here for six hours, we've already been followed and attacked. There's a Chinese spy trawler following the *Catalina* and it's officially still doing an environmental survey. By the look of things, the Chinese are aware of every move we make almost before we make it. That tells me we have a leak.'

'It might not be the NSA,' she suggested. 'How can you be sure NUMA doesn't have a mole hiding in the woodwork somewhere?'

'I can't,' he admitted. 'That's why we tell no one about our next move. Not NUMA, not the NSA, no one. It's the only way to be sure this information doesn't end up in the daily briefing in Shanghai.'

She looked him in the eye. Once she'd accepted his logic, the path became clear. Her lips curved into a knowing smile. 'Okay,' she said. 'So we go rogue. I must admit, it has a certain appeal. Count me in.'

'Fantastic,' he said. 'Now . . . all we need is a helicopter and a ship big enough to operate from. One they would never suspect us to be using.'

9

The NUMA vessel *Catalina* continued through the night on a northerly heading, traveling at full speed. Two hundred and sixty feet long, the *Catalina* was sleek for a research vessel and she took to the high-speed run well, cutting through the waves and rolling only slightly with the crossing swells.

Gamay Trout was thankful for the ship's stability as she walked from the communications room to the bridge with an odd message to deliver.

Five foot ten and willowy in build, Gamay had dark red hair with a rich and ever-changing luster; her eyes and easy smile suggested a tough playfulness, brought about from growing up as a tomboy. She spoke in a clear, concise way, with few wasted words, a pattern she'd been told came from an uncluttered mind that moved with effortless speed.

At any rate, she had a never-flagging sense of urgency that had earned her several degrees, including a Doctorate in Marine Biology and a Master's in Marine Archaeology.

Most men found her attractive, but not in a superficial way that faded over time. The more time they spent with her, the more impressed they were, partly because she put them at ease. It was a gift, one she was trying to summon as she approached the bridge with a directive that had just come in from Kurt Austin.

She smiled as she entered the bridge, spotting Ed Callahan, the *Catalina*'s captain, his executive officer – or XO – and her husband, Paul, conversing near the radar scope.

'Good evening,' Callahan said. 'Sorry I've kept Paul up here for so long. We're discussing the scuttlebutt surrounding our change of plans. The fact that we were ordered off a study we'd spent five months prepping for has a few people concerned.'

She raised a single eyebrow. 'Gossiping around the water-cooler and I wasn't invited? Shame on both of you.'

'Inexcusable,' Callahan replied. 'Consider this an official request to join our party.'

The captain made space in the group for her to join and she slid in next to her husband. Paul was a towering man of six foot eight who spoke seriously and quietly. Gamay had met him at Scripps Institution, where Paul was getting his own Ph.D. in Ocean Sciences. They'd married soon after and had been inseparable ever since. After joining NUMA together and becoming part of the Special Projects team on the same day, rumor had it working together had been written into their employment contracts.

86

'Any idea what's going on?' Callahan asked.

'Not really, but . . .'

Ever the voice of reason, Paul spoke up. 'I told everyone to expect the unexpected when Kurt's involved. Though I'm sure it won't be anything too crazy.'

Gamay took a deep breath. 'I wouldn't put money on that.'

Callahan noticed the dispatch in her hand. 'What have you got for me?'

She handed Callahan the printed request and explained the order that had come in as calmly as possible.

His tone changed instantly. 'They want us to do *what*?'

'To dump our best submersible overboard and leave it behind,' Gamay repeated.

Callahan looked at Paul for some assistance. Paul held up his hands as if to say it had nothing to do with him.

'But that's absurd, on the face of it,' Callahan said. He was a two-year NUMA veteran, with stints in the Navy and Merchant Marine before that. He'd been on the receiving end of strange and questionable orders before, but this topped them all. 'The *Angler* is a thirty-million-dollar machine,' he reminded everyone. 'It's not some old rust bucket you sacrifice to Poseidon.'

'Did anyone explain why?' Paul asked. 'Are we getting a tax write-off?'

Gamay shook her head and read out the order word for word. '"Per Kurt Austin, Director of Special

Projects. Immediate directive. Under cover of darkness, submersible NSV-2 (*Angler*) is to be launched unmanned. Ensure all systems are fully charged and set depth to one hundred feet. Program the autopilot to surface the vessel in two hours. Immediately upon launch of *Angler*, *Catalina* is to change heading and proceed east, directly toward the Guaya river mouth, and await further orders. Be aware, *Catalina* is under surveillance. Make all efforts to conduct launch without drawing attention to your actions. Do not report launch of *Angler* to NUMA HQ. Do not reference this order on standard radio channels."'

'Are we sure this came from Kurt?' Callahan asked.

Gamay nodded. 'When I double-checked, I was told to *Make sure the lid was screwed on tight and don't get the velour seat covers wet.*'

Paul laughed. 'That's Kurt, all right.'

The XO chimed in. 'Maybe we should check with Rudi Gunn anyway. Just to be safe.'

Gamay shook her head. 'Trust me. You could call Rudi Gunn, Director Pitt or Vice President Sandecker himself and you'll get the same answer from all three: *If that's what Kurt wants, that's what Kurt gets.*'

Callahan glanced at the navigation panel and the chronometer. It was after ten p.m. The Moon would be up in an hour.

'No time like the present,' he said, turning to the XO. 'Issue the men night vision goggles and keep the deck lights off. Check the tech manuals and make sure dropping the *Angler* over the side at our current speed won't damage her. Otherwise, we'll slow down, make our turn and drop the penny then.'

'Yes, sir,' the XO said. 'I can only imagine what they'll ask for next.'

'I'm sure it won't get any crazier than this,' Callahan insisted.

Neither Paul nor Gamay commented, but they shared a knowing look. If history was any guide, Callahan would probably be proven wrong.

While Gamay returned to the communications room, Paul went with the deckhands to oversee the launching – or perhaps discarding – of the submersible.

Working on the fantail of the ship moving at full speed was not an easy task under the best of circumstances. Operating under blackout conditions with night vision goggles made it a surreal sight. The view was slightly distorted, and the sky was now lit by thousands of stars the naked eye could never spot, but the sea remained black and cold.

Despite the conditions, the crew operated smoothly and efficiently, with Paul stepping up to work the heavy crane himself.

The XO soon joined him. 'The quick-release hooks have been set. Feel free to lift away. Also, per the specs, the *Angler* should be fine dropping into the water at this speed.'

'Expected nothing less,' Paul said, 'considering Joe Zavala designed it.'

Joe was a top-notch engineer, he tended to overbuild,

making things far stronger than they had to be. A fact that had saved NUMA crews on more than one occasion.

The crane came to life and the white-painted submersible with a broad red stripe across its back rose up off the deck. As the boom extended, Paul noticed a problem. 'We're going to get creative with the launch.'

'How so?'

Paul pointed toward the rail. 'If you look over the side, you'll see that the slipstream of the bow wave curls back toward the ship at our position. If we drop the *Angler* straight down, it might get caught in the slipstream and be slammed back into the side of our hull or even get swept into the propellers.'

Paul extended the crane to its maximum length and began to raise it up, increasing the angle to thirty degrees.

'I'm not sure that's going to help,' the XO said. 'The sub is up higher but also closer to the side of the hull.'

'Haven't done much fly-fishing, have you?' Paul said.

'You're not serious?'

Without answering, Paul retracted the boom a few feet and then extended it. The *Angler* swung in and then out, moving farther each time Paul manipulated the controls.

'I don't know about this,' the XO said.

'Trust me,' Paul said, timing his motions perfectly.

He used a flashlight to signal one of the crewmen, who picked up a phone and called the bridge. Paul had already set up the plan with the captain. Upon receiving that call, Callahan would idle the props. They would reengage thirty seconds later. The reduction in speed would be almost unnoticeable. But with the props idled instead of spinning, a bulge of water would deflect off of them and out instead of being drawn through them.

A subtle change in the vibration told Paul the propellers had been feathered. The stern rode a little higher. The wake was smoother.

Paul pulled the controls back once more and the *Angler* swung toward them like a four-ton bob on a pendulum. The crane groaned, and the strain on the boom was noticeable, but it was designed to hold three times the weight.

Paul allowed one more arc and then, just as the *Angler* was swinging outward, he hit the release button. The cable disconnected with a sharp crack and the fish-shaped submersible flew outward, seeming weightless for a second, before dropping down.

It hit the water fifty feet from the ship's hull. A baritone thud resonated and its impact drew up a tower of water that spread out and splashed down behind the ship.

As the spray fell and the impact zone disappeared behind the *Catalina*, the engine vibration picked up once again.

The First Officer was standing with his mouth open. 'Very impressive. Crazy but impressive.'

Paul grinned. 'It's all in the wrist.'

By the time Paul had retracted the boom, the ship

was turning east and the multimillion-dollar submersible they'd dumped out behind them was nowhere to be seen.

Twenty miles behind the *Catalina*, a figure stood on the top deck of a small vessel made up to look like a fishing trawler. Tall, for a Chinese woman, though no more than five foot six, her black hair fell straight to her shoulders and cut across them in a perfect horizontal line. Her eyes were nearly as dark as her hair, and the skintight clothing she wore made it easy to see the lean, muscular build of a distance runner. Her given name was Daiyu, which in Mandarin meant *Black Jade*. She was twenty-eight years old and already a skilled and experienced operative for the Ministry of State Security. She was also one of the 'children that were never born'.

It was an awkward euphemism given to her and others who were victims – or perhaps beneficiaries – of China's drastic stand on procreation. Amid the fervor of the infamous 'one child' policy, most couples who conceived second children were strongly encouraged, if not forced, to endure abortions. If they skirted the state rules and hid the pregnancy, punishments were harsh and lasting.

When officials in Guangdong discovered that Daiyu's mother was pregnant for a second time, they initially insisted on the standard remedy: threatening prison for the deception if an abortion was not agreed to. Appeals for mercy fell on deaf ears until a mysterious man named Zhang arrived from Beijing carrying special paperwork and granting them an exception at a very high price.

It was a mixed blessing. By signing the papers, Daiyu's parents would be allowed to carry the birth to term, but only under the harshest condition imaginable: the child would be taken from the family at eighteen months and raised anonymously in a government orphanage.

With little choice, her mother and father had agreed to the terms. A year later – six months earlier than they'd agreed to – Zhang had returned to her village and taken Daiyu away.

She was sent inland, to an orphanage run by the military. Some might have thought it odd to see hulking sergeants and stern-faced officers caring for gaggles of young children, but the orphanage was in a forbidden zone carved out for military purposes. There was no one around to see anything that went on there.

Daiyu grew up in the military's care, never learning the real names of her parents. She was told they were special. Her mother had been a world-class athlete who'd competed for China in the Olympic Games. Her father was an athlete himself and a decorated soldier. After his military career, he became one of China's leading scientists.

It was explained to her that her parents' blend of attributes were the only reason her birth was allowed. In a godless country, her existence was a blessing bestowed upon her by the state. From birth, she and the others like her literally owed the nation their lives. This fact was drilled into their heads while they learned at the hands of their masters.

By age twenty, Daiyu was an expert marksman, a trained survivalist who could live off the land and a lethal opponent in hand-to-hand combat. She was also an electronics expert and was fluent in five languages.

She proved less adept at the more subtle arts of charm and deception. With rough edges that the Ministry could not sand off no matter how hard they tried, she was assigned to the field instead of a consulate position; she was tasked with projects that required physical work and lethal skill.

After a series of missions to Africa and Europe, she was transferred to South America, where Chinese influence and investment were growing by the day.

Now, standing on the top deck of the trawler, she stared at the distant navigation lights of the NUMA vessel they were following. It was dark, and the wind blew with a chill.

Behind her loomed a seventy-foot-tall mast that carried a radar dome, several antennas and a powerful set of cameras, which were watching the American ship for things no human eye could see.

On a video screen to her left, a tiny flare of white appeared and vanished. It looked to her as if it was a large splash, but it did not repeat itself, and all else remained normal.

'The Americans are up to something,' she said.

The statement was addressed to a man standing in the dark behind her.

Jian Feng had a sturdy, muscular build, a square face and short, dark hair. He had a very plain look except for his right ear, part of which had been torn off in a fight years before.

Another member of the unborn children, in an odd way Jian was her brother. Like her, he'd been raised to serve the state. 'They're turning,' he said.

'Turning?'

'Look at the radar track.'

Daiyu glanced at a separate screen. The Americans were indeed turning to the east. 'It makes no sense. The search area is to the north and west.'

'Maybe something's gone wrong,' Jian said. 'The nearest port is due east.'

Daiyu could only hope that the American ship had suffered a mechanical problem. Perhaps that was the cause of the brief flash she witnessed. 'They're continuing at full speed,' she said, noticing the new data on the radar plot. 'They've noticed us.'

Jian shook his head. 'I don't think so.'

'And why is that, Jian?'

'We're too low in the water and our signature is too indistinct. The vessel we're following is not equipped with military-band radar, only a simple weather-tracking set. There's been no radio traffic beyond the banal chatter that seems to permeate American culture. They know nothing of us.'

There were other ways to be spotted. Her instincts

told her the Americans had done just that. She resisted the urge to argue and instead checked the time. Her watch was over. It had been for almost an hour. She took a final look at the American ship and then turned to go inside.

With a curt good night, she left Jian to his ignorance, walked back along the deck of the dilapidated-looking trawler and entered a hatch.

The vessel itself was filthy. It smelled of diesel oil and fish guts – discomforts she took little notice of. Passing through the wheelhouse, she entered the control room, where the façade of the aging trawler gave way to a modern command center, complete with flickering screens, climate control and a row of technicians in military uniforms sitting at various consoles.

She looked over the latest reports and then put them down without comment. Only one of them was of any consequence: the operatives in Guayaquil had been given a tip regarding the American named Austin. Something to act on. But they'd failed to corral either Austin or the rather unimpressive woman (in Daiyu's opinion) named Townsend.

'Contact General Zhang,' she told the communications specialist. 'Inform him of the new course. And wake me if anything changes.'

The man nodded and Daiyu continued to her cabin.

She closed the door behind her and stripped off her outer layer, revealing a pistol in a holster, strapped across her flat stomach, and a series of tattoos across her back.

She removed the pistol, sliding it under her pillow on the narrow bed in her quarters, then placed the holster with her clothes.

Half dressed, she stood in front of the tarnished mirror and struck her first pose. With almost inhuman precision, she moved through a series of martial arts steps that were beautiful, well balanced and deadly.

As she turned from position to position, the ink on her skin seemed to change color with the light. On one shoulder blade, she wore the Chinese symbol for love; on the other, the symbol for punishment. In the middle, centered on her spine, a pair of black and white forms swirled together – a stylized version of the famous symbol for yin and yang.

In Chinese mythology, yin and yang were supposed to be complementary forces, each providing what the other cannot. But Daiyu rejected the notion. In her mind, they were antagonists. Yin would destroy yang, if it could; and yang would murder yin, if ever they met – for that's what opposites did. Because of this, she'd directed that an almost invisible line be left between the two curving symbols. A sliver of her own natural skin color remained there as if she was the buffer between the two warring forces, the only thing preventing the great destruction.

As the moves progressed in speed and intensity, the sweat began to trickle from her skin. A kick, a turn, an upward thrust of the hand that could break a neck. After a time, her hair, body and clothing were soaked. Her last move was a turn and sudden punch with an open palm that could kill any opponent it caught. She held it for several seconds, realizing she was staring directly at herself in the mirror, and then turned away.

The dance was over. She stripped off the rest of her clothes, threw them in the corner and stepped into the shower, blasting the water at its most icy cold.

Ecuador

The sleepy airport on the coast of Ecuador appeared abandoned in the middle of the night. A chain-link fence topped with razor wire and a few perimeter lights were the only efforts at security. Occasionally, a guard in a white pickup truck with a yellow rotating beacon on top would drive the taxiway and runway, but more out of boredom than anything else.

'Not exactly Fort Knox,' Emma noted from the driver's seat of a car she'd rented under an assumed name.

'Why do you think I chose it?' Kurt said, stepping out and walking to the gate. 'Under normal circumstances, there's nothing here worth stealing.'

Kurt found the gate unlocked and eased it back. He waved Emma through, closed the gate behind her and hopped back in the car. 'Over that way,' he said, pointing to the left.

Emma drove carefully, navigating by the moonlight and sticking to one side of the crumbling taxiway. They passed a few small planes tied down at the edge of the ramp: single-engine Cessnas and Pipers. Judging by the weeds growing up between them, few of the planes had moved in weeks, if not months.

'How did you even know about this place?' Emma asked.

Kurt pointed across the runway. 'On the other side of that fence, the waves of the Pacific are pounding the beach with rhythmic precision. This is one of the better surf spots in all of South America. I was going to come here when the season begins in a few months.'

They continued on, passing a small hangar and pulling up beside a mammoth orange helicopter that looked more like a giant mutant insect looming in the dark than a machine made by human hands.

The helicopter stood on spindly, outstretched legs, its long rotors drooping like a dragonfly's wings. A thin, pointed tail stretched out into the dark behind it, while its large, bulbous head bent near to the ground, giving the appearance of a locust gnawing the grass.

The Erickson Air-Crane was a modernized version of the famous Sikorsky Skycrane. It was seventy feet long, sported a huge, six-bladed rotor and was powered by two Pratt & Whitney turboshaft engines. It could carry a crew of five and a ten-ton payload. Most of the working models were used to haul heavy loads to places no truck could possibly reach or to battle forest fires. Its heavy-lifting capacity and precise maneuverability allowed it to drop tons of water or flame-retardant on hilltops, in box canyons and other tight spots normal firefighting planes could not target.

Since Erickson had taken over the design, each newly built helicopter was christened with a distinct name of its own. One named *Elvis* fought fires in Australia.

Another named *Jaws* ferried parts to oil rigs in the Gulf of Mexico. The craft sitting on the tarmac in front of them was named *Merlin* and had a small caricature of a wizard painted on the nose.

As Emma parked beside it, a light came on inside the cockpit and a figure stepped out through the door.

'About time you got here,' Joe Zavala said. 'This must be Hurricane Emma.'

Emma shot Kurt a suspicious look and then shook Joe's hand. 'I've been downgraded to a tropical storm. But don't make me angry.'

'Duly noted,' Joe said. 'Care to step on board?'

'I thought we'd have some loading to do,' Kurt said. 'Did you get all the equipment on the list?'

'Of course,' Joe said. 'It's stored away in the aft cargo container. We also have a drop tank filled with extra fuel.'

He pointed at two pods attached near the tail: the cargo container was black and had the aerodynamics of a brick; the drop tank was sleek and tapered, with the appearance of an orange bomb.

'Did you run into the security guard?'

'Of course,' Joe said. 'Who do you think helped me load this stuff?'

Kurt laughed. 'Joe has a way with people,' he explained to Emma. 'He was once pulled over for speeding and instead of getting a ticket, he wound up with a police escort to the Boston Pops.'

'I was late for a date,' Joe explained. 'The officer was very understanding.'

Kurt checked his watch. 'Getting late here, too. If we're ready, let's go.'

They boarded the Air-Crane through a door in the back of the cockpit. To reach it one had to walk under the fuselage, which was like walking beneath a small bridge. Even when they were standing straight up, the backbone of the craft was several feet above their heads.

Joe took the pilot's seat in the surprisingly tight cockpit and began to go through the start-up checklist. He had almost a thousand hours in helicopters of various types, but this was the first time he'd flown one this size.

'Are you sure you know how to fly this thing?' Kurt asked.

'They're all the same, more or less,' Joe replied.

'It's the *less* part that I'm worried about.'

'Trust me,' Joe said. 'Have I ever let you down?'

'I'm not going to answer that,' Kurt said.

He sat down and strapped himself into the copilot's seat while Emma took the third seat just behind them. As Joe finished his checklist, he turned on the navigation lights and a flashing red glow became visible out in the dark. He held the starter switch down and the rotors began to move slowly above their heads. Seconds later, the engines came to life with a throaty roar.

'Welcome aboard Zavala Flight 251 to nowhere,' he said. 'Please put your tray tables in the upright and locked position.'

'Should we call the tower?' Kurt asked.

'They went home hours ago,' Joe replied.

'In that case, I'd say you're cleared for takeoff.'

Joe ran the throttle up to full power and pulled steadily back on the collective, controlling lift. The weight came off the wheels and the helicopter began to roll forward. It lifted from the ground and turned into the wind.

Accelerating and climbing, Joe turned the Air-Crane toward the sea, and they crossed the beach and climbed out over the Pacific.

An hour later, they were nearing the spot where the *Catalina* had dropped off its submersible.

'I've got it,' Kurt said, looking through a set of night vision goggles. 'Two miles ahead, ten degrees right, bobbing up and down on the surface, right where it should be.'

A low-intensity light on the *Angler*'s hatch – no brighter than a handheld flashlight – appeared like a magnesium flare through the goggles.

'I see it,' Joe replied. He brought the helicopter down to fifty feet and hovered directly above the submersible.

Kurt removed the night vision goggles and switched positions. He moved past Emma to an aft-facing seat at the back of the cockpit, surrounded by a clear Plexiglas bubble, reminiscent of a tail-gunner's position in a World War II bomber.

The payload specialist's station offered a clear view of everything behind and beneath the Air-Crane. With the flip of a switch, several floodlights came on, illuminating the scene below. The white submersible with the broad red stripe rode low in the water, surrounded by a spiraling pattern created by the downwash of the Air-Crane's rotors.

'Back ten feet,' Kurt called out.

'Roger that,' Joe said, easing the helicopter backward.

Activating the winch controls on a panel in front of him, Kurt released a heavy steel hook and lowered it toward the *Angler*. His target was a prominent bar on top of the submersible's hull that resembled the roll cage of an off-road vehicle. The thick red band painted across the top of the submersible marked the attachment point.

'Right five,' Kurt said. 'Forward two.'

As Joe maneuvered the Air-Crane, Kurt made several attempts to hook the *Angler*, but the task wasn't as easy as it looked. If the submersible rose on a swell at the wrong moment, the hook bounced off its hull. Other times, the hook swung and missed as the attachment point dropped beneath it like a boxer ducking a slow punch.

Kurt was seriously considering getting wet and placing the hook by hand when a solid click and tension on the line told him he'd nabbed his catch.

'Got it!' he said, reeling in the slack. 'Dropping second cable.'

The second cable didn't attach to the submersible; it was already connected to the first cable, and also to a hardpoint near the nose gear. Its purpose was to act as a guide and keep the payload from twisting in the swirling downwash from the main rotor.

'Second cable locked.'

'Pull it up,' Joe said. 'Can't have NUMA getting fined for littering.'

Kurt set the winch control to retract and the braided steel cable went taut. The strain of lifting the four-ton submersible was felt instantly and the helicopter dipped several feet before Joe countered the effect. As the roar of the engines grew, the *Angler* came free of the Pacific and was soon locked in place, snugly up against *Merlin*'s belly.

'Outstanding,' Emma announced. 'Never let it be said that the men of NUMA fail to impress.'

'It's what we do,' Joe replied, a false tone of bravado purposely evident in his voice.

Kurt made one last check of the winch controls and turned back toward the cockpit. 'Onward.'

At Joe's command, the Air-Crane began to move forward once more, picking up speed and altitude more slowly this time as it thundered across the sea toward their next destination.

'How far to the ship?' Joe asked.

Emma checked the handheld GPS unit she carried. 'Ninety miles from here.'

'That gives us time to practice our sales pitch,' Kurt said.

'Have you decided what you want to tell them?'

'I was thinking I'd appeal to the most basic universal desire.'

'I don't think love is going to help us here,' Joe said.

'The *other* universal desire,' Kurt said. 'Money. Everyone wants to be rich.'

'But we have no money to give them,' Emma pointed out.

Kurt nodded. 'Who says we have to use our own?'

Both Emma and Joe gave him a quizzical look, but Kurt said no more; he was still working out the details.

I I

MS Reunion, *refrigerated cargo carrier, en route from Chile to San Diego*

The MS *Reunion* was running with a full complement of lights as it steamed north at eleven knots. Lit up like this, the ship was visible from miles away, a white beacon alone on the dark mat of the sea.

After a brief conversation with the *Reunion*'s night watch, the Air-Crane was cleared to land. Joe maneuvered toward the elevated pad near the bow of the ship and planted the big helicopter in the exact center of its yellow circle.

One of the ship's officers watched the landing and couldn't help but be impressed at the pilot's skill, especially since there was no more than ten feet to spare on either side and only two feet of clearance between the helipad deck and the bottom of . . . whatever the big orange machine was carrying.

With *Merlin* tied down, the officer led the new arrivals toward the bridge, stealing several glances at the attractive woman with auburn hair. It wasn't often they had female guests on board, and he couldn't recall ever having one this striking here for a visit.

In the lighted confines of the bridge, introductions

were made and pleasantries exchanged. That the captain of the *Reunion* was an American played into their hands. That he'd been woken in the middle of the night weighed against them, but that couldn't be helped.

Captain Buck Kamphausen arrived on the bridge dressed in his boxers and a T-shirt, with a jacket thrown over his shoulders. Six foot three, sporting a patchy brown beard with plenty of gray creeping in, he wore rectangular glasses, which he was constantly adjusting, often with a glance at Emma.

Kamphausen was an affable fellow; he knew of NUMA and considered himself a big fan. As they spoke, though, he looked like he might agree to anything as long as Emma promised to stay on board and dine with him.

'What we need,' Kurt summed up, 'is to use your ship as a floating base for a few days.'

Kamphausen scratched his beard. 'For what purpose?'

'I can't tell you that,' Kurt said.

Kamphausen's demeanor changed instantly. 'Let me get this straight,' he said gruffly. 'You land on my ship in the middle of the night, bringing god-knows-what on board; you ask me to change course, fake a mechanical problem and possibly miss my delivery schedule – but you won't tell me what you're attempting to do or explain what I'm getting involved in?'

'I know it sounds odd,' Kurt began.

'More like downright lunacy.'

'The thing is,' Kurt said, trying to keep the meeting on track, 'we – and by *we*, I mean the United States government – can make it worth your while.'

'Not worth my while to get fired or busted down to seaman first class,' the captain said.

'I don't know about that,' Kurt said. 'Depends on how much we recover.'

Interest sparked up in the captain's eyes. 'Recover?'

Kurt nodded.

Kamphausen's gaze narrowed. He adjusted his glasses once more and focused on Kurt. 'Go on.'

'You're familiar with NUMA,' Kurt said. 'You know what we do. We find things on the bottom of the ocean. At the risk of saying too much, that contraption we've got tucked up under our helicopter is a specially designed submersible, built to search for something that is extremely valuable.'

He was stretching it a bit here, but he needed to sound confident.

'Something the United States government wants to find very badly,' Emma added.

Kurt cleared his throat to get the captain's mind and eyes focused back in his direction. 'It's been my experience that the monetary rewards of helping the government can be quite substantial –'

'If I recall correctly,' Joe busted in, 'everyone who helped us find that lost U-boat received a percentage of the diamonds we recovered or the equivalent value in cash, if they preferred.'

'Diamonds?' Kamphausen said.

'On that mission,' Kurt cautioned.

'Percentage?' the First Officer asked eagerly. 'What kind of percentage?'

'Like in the old pirate days,' Joe said. 'One share for each crewman, two shares for the NCOs, three shares for commissioned officers and four for the captain.'

Kurt nodded in support of Joe's ad-lib as if it were standard practice. Captain Kamphausen and the First Officer exchanged a knowing look.

Emma chimed in to help the process. 'As the saying in government goes, a billion here, a billion there, and pretty soon you're talking real money. You don't need a large cut of that to buy a summer home in Tahiti.'

'But you can't tell us what you're looking for,' the captain repeated.

Kurt shook his head. 'I can't. But think about this: would we be here, in the dark of night, asking for your help, if it wasn't something *extremely* important?'

Knowing the plan would work best if the crew convinced themselves, Kurt let them run with their fantasy, until a voice of reason interrupted.

'Hold on a second,' a new arrival said. 'I'm supercargo on this run. I'm responsible for the entire shipment. We're carrying fresh fruit. Limes, apples, oranges and kiwis. If we're more than four days late, the shipment will be rejected. My company will be out several million dollars and I'll be out of a job.'

Kurt looked at Joe. 'What do you think?'

'I believe we can swing it,' Joe said.

Kurt nodded. 'We only need a couple of days,' he

said, turning to the fruit company's rep. 'But if we are delayed more than forty-eight hours, the United States government will buy the cargo. Lock, stock and barrel.'

'Or in this case, limes, apples and oranges,' Joe added.

'Don't forget the kiwis,' the representative said.

'How could I?'

The captain stroked his beard. 'Diamonds?'

'I didn't say that,' Kurt reminded everyone.

'Barrels full of 'em,' the First Officer said. 'I saw it on TV.'

'We'll need to have papers drawn up,' the captain added.

Kurt glanced at Emma as if she were in charge of such things.

'Of course,' she said. 'There will also be confidentiality agreements and required radio and electronic silence until we release the ship back into your custody. Any violation of which will terminate the profit-sharing agreement and result in criminal charges.'

The winds of Hurricane Emma had suddenly blown cold. But it did nothing to dampen the mood.

'We can keep quiet for a couple of days,' the First Officer said convincingly.

The fruit company rep looked suspicious. 'I want papers ASAP.'

'I'll contact Washington and have the papers drawn up first thing in the morning,' Kurt insisted.

Kamphausen grinned and offered Kurt a hand. 'I've always wanted to get in on an adventure like this one.'

'If history's any guide, you'll get more than you bargained for,' Kurt said. 'In the meantime, we should all get to work. We need to change headings.'

The captain took one last look as if wondering whether he might be losing his mind. He glanced out the window to the orange helicopter sitting on his deck and the high-tech submarine nestled beneath it and reminded himself of everything he knew about NUMA. 'Helmsman,' he called. 'Lay in a new course.'

'What heading?'

He turned to Kurt. 'Whatever direction our new partners want us to go.'

12

Kurt gave the helmsman a new heading and the ship veered to the northwest. In the interest of secrecy, Kurt had the captain shut down the AIS beacon so their position would not be reported automatically to the satellite system that tracked the world's seagoing vessels. That done, he returned to the main deck and used an encrypted satellite phone to call Rudi Gunn.

Rudi was still in Guayaquil, working the political angle and hoping to get some assistance from the Ecuadorian defense forces without telling them why. Despite it being the middle of the night, Rudi answered on the second ring. 'One of these days, you'll call me during normal business hours,' he grumbled.

'These are normal business hours,' Kurt said. 'NUMA never sleeps.'

'NUMA doesn't, but I do,' Rudi replied. 'What can I do for you, my insomnia-stricken friend?'

'I just wanted to give you an update,' Kurt said. 'I've left Ecuador, Joe and Emma are with me, but don't put it in any reports. The Chinese have agents everywhere, and we're not sure about the NSA right now. They may have been compromised.'

'Great,' Rudi said. 'Maybe I'll start sending them false information.'

'Not a bad idea,' Kurt said. 'At any rate, we're on our own. And we're not going to be checking back in for a while.'

'Then why bother to tell me?'

'I didn't want you to worry,' Kurt said as warmly as possible.

'Where are you?'

'On a refrigerated cargo ship. Only don't bother looking for us. We're temporarily invisible.'

Kurt heard what sounded like movement and a soft click. He imagined Rudi throwing back the covers of his bed, sitting up and switching on the light. The tone in Rudi's voice perked up instantly. 'You've found something?'

'Maybe,' Kurt said.

'Hot damn,' Rudi replied. 'Wake me with that kind of news anytime. What's the probability?'

'Fairly good. Check with Hiram for details and stand by. Also, keep the rest of the fleet doing their thing. The busier they look, the less likely anyone is to notice that we've gone off the map. Might even want to pretend you've found something back that way, it'll draw the heat in your direction.'

'Great idea. I'll get something in the works. I'll even put it in a report to the NSA.'

'Perfect,' Kurt said. He was about to sign off and hang up when another thought occurred to him. 'One more thing. If you happen to get any calls from the Malabar Shipping Line or the Golden Fruit Company of Valparaíso, Chile . . . I wouldn't answer them right away. Probably just a telemarketer.'

The gloom returned to Rudi's voice. 'Do I even want to know?'

'Put it this way,' Kurt said. 'If I don't find what we're looking for in the next two days, there will be no shortage of limes for your margaritas.'

Rudi acknowledged with a soft grunt and then hung up. Kurt switched off the phone and turned to see Emma approaching him.

'You have them eating out of your hand,' she said. 'But how do you intend to pay for this ship? Not to mention the cargo and the pirate's booty Joe promised them?'

Kurt shrugged and put the phone away. 'I figured we'd use that expense account of yours. I took care of dinner, remember?'

'Very funny,' she said. 'But I'm serious. We're either going to end up walking the plank here or being drawn and quartered on the Capitol steps.'

Kurt didn't think so. 'There's a ten-hour difference between here and Malaysia, where the shipping company has its headquarters. They're closed now. They won't be open again until tomorrow morning, Malaysian Standard Time. By then, it will be dark in DC and the phones will be forwarded to the answering service. Between that and the normal speed of bureaucracy, it'll be a week before anyone starts sorting out this mess. By then, we'll have found what we're looking for.'

'And when it doesn't turn out to be filled with barrels of uncut diamonds?'

'I never mentioned diamonds,' Kurt said.

'No, but the cargo you vouched for is worth fifty million dollars. And this ship is worth twice that much.'

'And how much did the *Nighthawk* cost?' he asked. 'Fifty *billion*? A hundred? How much would the NSA pay to keep it out of Russian hands? You're worrying about the pennies and forgetting about the thousand-dollar bills. Trust me, by the time this becomes a problem we'll have the *Nighthawk*'s actual position locked down and the most important parts of the aircraft on board. Instead of complaining about the cost of this ship and the cargo, someone will be pinning a medal on your chest and calling you a risk taker and bold leader and buying Captain Kamphausen and his friends their own ships, crewed by beautiful mermaids.'

She took a deep breath and looked away out over the dark sea. 'You really are crazy,' she whispered, before turning back to him with a smile. 'What sort of Pandora's Box have you opened for me?'

'Must be your inner rebel,' he replied with a grin.

'All I can say is, you'd better be right or we're going to end up partners in a fruit stand for the rest of our natural lives.'

'I could think of worse fates,' Kurt said. 'But, trust me. It's going to work out just fine.'

13

Paul Trout thought his wife was playing a practical joke on him as she read the latest order, this time from Rudi Gunn. It made as little sense as the previous one.

'"Proceed to specified coordinates and begin dropping sonar buoys on north–south line. After three hours and twenty-seven minutes, begin concentric circles. One hour later, at the captain's leisure, come to a full stop. At this point, make obvious preparations for deep-sea recovery operation, including launch of ROVs. Send coded transmissions and continue recovery operations until further orders."'

'Recovery of what?' Paul asked.

'It doesn't say,' Gamay insisted. 'Just that we need to make it look good.'

'With what?' he added. 'We just dumped our only manned submersible over the rail.'

'I suppose we'll have to improvise,' Gamay said.

Paul shook his head. 'Ours is not to reason why,' he said. 'Let's go give Callahan the news. Hopefully, his head won't explode.'

*

Four thousand miles away, Constantin Davidov thought his head might do just that. He'd been traveling in the passenger compartment of a Russian Mi-14 helicopter for the better part of a day. The huge blue-gray-painted craft was the newest, extended-range model, stripped of weapons and armor and given two large auxiliary fuel tanks. It was known to its pilots as the *Carrier Pigeon*, since it was used to ferry men and equipment over extremely long distances. The men on the ground called it the *Clay Pigeon* because it was filled with so much jet fuel that it was ponderous, heavy and slow, making it an easy target.

All Davidov knew was that nineteen hours in such a craft, including several air-to-air refueling passes, qualified as torture and should have been banned by the Geneva Conventions.

When the ungainly craft finally touched down on the deck of a Russian guided missile cruiser, he all but jumped from his seat to get off the torture machine. Not waiting for permission, he stepped through the door out into a pouring rain.

The weather was deteriorating in all directions as the guided missile cruiser *Varyag* and several other ships continued headlong into a storm halfway between Hawaii and the South American coast. Davidov didn't care. A ship in a Category 5 storm was preferable to another minute in the oversized eggbeater.

As the Mi-14 was strapped down, Davidov was led inside and shown to a cabin. By the time he'd showered and pulled on a clean uniform, the ship was pitching noticeably. He found he had to grip the rail to keep from losing his balance as he moved down the passageway.

He was escorted through 'officer country', to the quarters of Rear Admiral Sergei Borozdin, whose door was guarded by two Spetsnaz commandos. After displaying his credentials, he was shown in immediately.

Borozdin was sitting behind a desk, pretending not to notice the arrival of his old friend. It was a game they played. The two men had come up together, one through the Navy, the other in the party machinery itself – KGB, NKVD and the consular services. They rarely met these days but, when they did, the liquor flowed.

Despite the stereotype of vodka-drinking Russians, both men preferred scotch, specifically single malts from the highlands of Scotland, preferably aged at least fifteen years.

Davidov had brought with him a fine example. He offered it to Borozdin. *'Aberlour,'* he said. 'Gaelic for *Mouth of the Chattering Burn.* It's only a twelve-year-old, but it was aged in a Spanish sherry cask.'

Borozdin looked the bottle over with reverence. 'The least you could do for sending my fleet into this cyclone.'

Despite the gruff words, Borozdin was pleased. He grinned and reached for two glasses, pouring a taste. 'I swear to you, Constantin. If Putin ordered me to destroy Scotland with a nuke, I would refuse and take my chances with the firing squad.'

Davidov laughed and Borozdin filled both of their glasses. The aroma was unique, with a hint of raisins. The first sips were heavenly.

Even then, Davidov swore he could still hear the helicopter blades hacking at the air above him, could still feel his body shaking from nose to feet. 'It's too bad about this storm,' he said as the *Varyag* rolled appreciably to starboard.

With each swell, the ship rolled and nosed down and then came back up. The waves were hitting the fleet from the front quarter, and they were getting worse by the moment.

'If we weren't so far behind,' Borozdin said, 'I would let it pass and proceed in its wake. We've already had to send one of the tenders back; two of its hatches were damaged.'

The *Varyag* was shepherding a fleet of salvage ships and auxiliaries toward the search zone. It was larger, faster and heavier than the other ships. It was faring better, as a result.

'We must press on,' Davidov said. 'At least the storm is delaying the Chinese as well.'

'But what about the Americans?' Borozdin asked. 'They're our real problem. This damned cyclone has done nothing but aid them and ruin our plans. If it hadn't appeared, they wouldn't have brought the *Nighthawk* back early. We would have been in position to catch it when it fell. Now the storm delays us even as the Americans steam south from California in good weather.'

'Yes,' Davidov said wearily. 'I know. Not to worry. It shouldn't matter.'

Borozdin cocked his head and looked at his old friend suspiciously. 'Why wouldn't it?'

'It's true, the Americans seem to have this cyclone on their side,' Davidov said, smirking. 'But we have a Typhoon on ours.'

A few seconds passed before Borozdin got the reference. 'TK-17,' he said, referencing the ID number of the vessel in question.

Davidov nodded. 'She's gone right under the storm and is almost in position. By this time tomorrow, the *Nighthawk* will be in her hold and on its way to Kamchatka. The Chinese and Americans will never know we've taken her and her precious cargo. They will search forever . . . in vain.'

Borozdin looked pleased, but the smile quickly left his face. 'Then why are we plowing directly into a Force 5 gale?'

'Appearances,' Davidov said, finishing his tumbler of the Aberlour. 'They must be kept up. Otherwise, the Americans and the Chinese might begin to suspect something.'

Davidov finished, pushed his empty glass toward Borozdin and waited. His old friend broke into a toothy grin and gladly poured a second helping of the liquid fire. 'To the Typhoon,' he said, raising his glass.

Davidov did likewise. 'To the Typhoon.'

14

Kurt stood on the starboard bridge wing of the six-hundred-foot cargo vessel looking through a pair of large binoculars. In the distance, he could just make out four red-hulled boats on the blue ocean. They were lifeboats from the *Reunion*, repurposed to search for any sign of the *Nighthawk*.

Taking a page out of Rudi Gunn's plan, they'd put four boats in the water and sent them to the east in formation. Traveling abreast of one another and two miles apart, the small fleet covered an eight-mile-wide swath at a single pass. Each of them trailed a pair of *fish*: torpedo-shaped tubes packed with the most advanced sensing equipment in the NUMA catalog, including top-of-the-line side-scan sonar emitters and a sensitive magnetic alloy detector NUMA had only recently developed.

The new detectors were far more precise than the old magnetometers that simply scanned for iron content. According to Joe, they could tell not only what alloys it was examining but where the alloy was produced and the name of the shift supervisor on duty during the mixing.

The fact was, they were using the most advanced equipment in the world and covering forty square miles of ocean floor each hour. The pace had led Kurt to predict they'd locate the missing craft by lunchtime, though at half past breakfast they'd yet to find a thing.

Patient as Job, at least for now, Kurt turned to Emma. She sat in front of a high-definition screen, studying the results. As the four lifeboats moved in unison, they transmitted the data from the sonar emitters and other instruments back to the *Reunion*, where a special laptop computer processed the signals from all the different sensors into one image.

The resulting picture was a comprehensive, detailed view of the ocean floor, far sharper than any standard sonar scan. It was comparable to switching from an old tube TV to a modern high-definition display.

'This is incredible,' Emma said, using the controls to pan and zoom in on different sections of the image. 'No wonder Steve Gowdy wanted NUMA on the job.'

Kurt lowered the binoculars down and took a seat beside her. 'Something tells me our proximity and availability had more to do with it than our expertise. Had the seven sisters of the poor been out here with a fishing boat, he'd probably have hired them, too.'

'Maybe,' she said. 'But you definitely bring more than proximity to the table.'

Kurt accepted the compliment, sat back in the chair and watched the computer screen along with her. He knew the software would point out and highlight anything that didn't belong on the seafloor, but he liked to keep an eye on the scan as much as he could. For one thing, computers were not infallible. For another, until they found something, there was literally nothing else to do.

He leaned back and craned his neck around to alleviate the soreness that had set in. As he did, Captain Kamphausen strode over. He, too, was sensing the tedious nature of the search. 'Somehow, I thought looking for sunken treasure would be a little more exciting than this.'

'Mowing the lawn isn't my favorite exercise either,' Kurt replied. 'Never liked it as a kid and I don't like it any better now.'

The captain laughed, moved to the radio and checked in with his crew. Meanwhile, Joe came in, juggling three cups of coffee; he placed one in front of Kurt, handed one to Emma and kept one for himself. 'Find anything yet?'

'Nothing interesting,' Kurt said. 'The only real excitement turned out to be an old anchor that must have fallen off a ship sometime recently. Other than that, nothing but a few outcroppings of lava rock jutting from the abyssal plain.'

'That's to be expected,' Joe said. 'The Galápagos Islands *are* volcanic.'

Kurt reached for the coffee cup. He tested the heat and swallowed some coffee down, wincing in the aftermath. 'How much sugar did you put in there?'

'Only seven packets,' Joe said.

'*Only* seven?' Kurt replied.

'I figured a sugar rush would keep you on your toes.'

Kurt placed the cup into a holder. 'I'll be bouncing off the walls if I drink any more of that.'

Before Joe could reply, a soft tone and a flashing red highlight on the screen suggested they'd found something new.

'What is it?' Emma asked.

Kurt leaned over the keyboard and used the touch pad to zoom in on the highlighted area. 'I'm not sure.'

He adjusted the angle and allowed the computer to extrapolate the data. They soon got a closer view of the targets. In a wide swath there were several objects and a series of small craters and gouge marks in the otherwise flat expanse of sediment.

'Looks like something rained down from above,' Joe suggested.

Kurt nodded and checked the magnetometer. 'Can't be sure what we're looking at, but it's definitely man-made.'

Emma was not as easily convinced. 'How can you be sure? I don't see anything but holes in the mud.'

Kurt pointed to the reading of the alloy detector. 'Because those holes are hiding something built of high-strength stainless steel and magnesium.'

He pressed a button and the printer came to life, spitting out a chemical profile of the target in question. It was approximately twenty percent magnesium and fifty percent aluminum, with lower concentrations of iron and other metals.

As the boats continued to move along, the image on the screen changed slowly. Several additional targets appeared, but they were too small and too far off to be rendered in any kind of detail.

'Can we get in closer?' Emma asked.

Kurt was about to zoom in when the image blurred and a large swath of the screen went dark.

'What happened?'

'It's a shadow,' Joe said from behind them. 'The side-scan sonar is sending its pulse across the seafloor at a nearly flat angle, like the sun getting low on the horizon. When something gets in the way of the echo, it creates a long shadow, like those you see stretching across a street in the late afternoon.'

Kurt zoomed out and a jagged shape appeared. A ridge of volcanic material jutting up from the seafloor. Everything beyond it was invisible.

'We could have the boats circle back and get another scan from a different angle,' Joe suggested.

'I've got a better idea,' Kurt said. 'Let the boats continue on until they reach the edge of the search zone and then have them make the turn as planned. While they do that, we'll take the *Angler* down and check out what we've found. If it turns out to be anything important, we'll be able to confirm. And if not, we won't have brought the whole search to a halt in the process.'

'Makes sense,' Joe said. 'And it gives you something to do.'

Kurt grinned. 'There's a method to my madness.'

'You keep thinking that,' Joe quipped.

'I'm going with you,' Emma said. 'If it turns out to be debris, it's likely to be in rough condition: mostly small pieces and mangled and bent fragments. I'm the only one here who'll be able to make a positive ID.'

'You don't have to come down to do that,' Kurt said. 'You can watch on the monitors up here.'

'I prefer to see things in person,' she said. 'Besides, when am I going to get another chance to dive to the bottom of the sea in a high-tech submarine?'

'The lady has a point,' Joe said.

Kurt didn't mind the company. 'Okay,' he said. 'You've got one ticket to the bottom of the sea.'

Twenty minutes later, Kurt and Emma were sitting in the command seats of the *Angler* as Joe used the Air-Crane to lift them off the deck and carry them toward the target zone.

Though the submersible was hooked on securely, it still swayed beneath the fuselage of the orange-painted helicopter.

'I'll be glad when we get into the water,' Emma said. 'How close are we?'

'*Approaching the drop zone,*' Joe's voice replied over the intercom.

'You mean the *Lower us gently into the sea zone*, don't you?' Kurt replied.

'*Of course,*' Joe said. '*Wouldn't want to give you too much frustration for one day.*'

As they neared the drop zone, Joe slowed the helicopter to a hover and brought it down toward the surface. At the same time, Kurt ran one last check to ensure the *Angler* was watertight and that all systems were go.

'Ready for our bath,' Kurt said.

'*Roger that,*' Joe replied.

The submersible lurched downward as the cable began to unwind. It descended the rest of the way smoothly and then settled into passing swells, rising and falling softly, once it reached the sea.

A metallic clink sounded as the hook was detached and the line reeled in.

'*Catch-and-release program completed,*' Joe called out. '*You two are on your own.*'

'Roger that,' Kurt said. 'Deploying communications buoy and beginning descent. See you in a couple of hours.'

As Kurt flooded the ballast tanks, seawater crept up the curved glass of the canopy, bathing the cockpit in a blue-green light. As they submerged completely, the thundering racket of the helicopter diminished to a muted staccato beat.

Kurt vented the forward tanks and the nose of the *Angler* tilted downward to begin the submarine's plunge into the deep. A fiber-optic cable, connected to a floating buoy, trailed out behind them. All radio and video communications would be transmitted through it.

The water grew darker, and the pitch steepened until the nose was pointing downward at an eighty-degree angle.

Though she was strapped in, Emma instinctively put her hand on the console to compensate for the sensation of falling forward. 'It's like we're on a roller coaster and we just went over the crest of a hill.'

'I didn't want to bore you,' Kurt said.

'Is this why they call it the *Angler*?' she asked. 'Because it dives so steeply?'

'No,' Kurt said. 'But we are nose heavy. It's designed that way. By descending almost straight down like a raindrop, we travel faster and save on power and oxygen.'

'And sacrifice a little bit of comfort,' she said, hanging forward in the straps of her seat. 'How fast are we going?'

Kurt pointed to the depth gauge and a digital read-out that noted the rate of descent. 'About three hundred feet per minute. We could go faster, but this is a nice, safe speed. We'll level off before we hit the bottom, I promise.'

The submersible continued to dive. Aside from the odd creak and groan, all sounds vanished and the world outside the canopy grew rapidly darker, changing from sea green to indigo blue to a deep violet color. Finally, it became an impenetrable black curtain.

Kurt dimmed the interior lights to help their eyes adjust and soon they needed only the glow of the various switches, indicators and gauges to see comfortably inside the sub.

'There's a certain ambiance to this,' Emma said. 'Almost like candlelight.'

'And I forgot to bring the wine.'

'A huge oversight, in my opinion,' she replied.

With an eye on the depth gauge, Kurt began to trim the submarine. By using the ballast controls to pump air into the forward tanks, he raised the nose and decreased the rate of descent at the same time. 'Coming up on the seafloor. Or should I say down?'

'How about turning on the porch lights?' she said.

'Afraid of the dark?'

'No. Afraid of running into things in the dark.'

Kurt reached above his head and flipped a series of switches. A battery of lights around the base of the *Angler* came to life. Initially, they lit up nothing but the sedimentary particles flying upward past the windows.

The particles were actually stationary or moving slowly downward, but as the *Angler* was dropping at a much faster rate, the particles were more like snow-flakes moving in the wrong direction.

A yellow light began to flash. *'Terrain detected, one hundred feet,'* a computerized voice said.

Kurt pumped more air into the tanks and slowed the descent further. The gray sediment layer of the seafloor began to appear in the cone of light beneath them.

'Terrain, fifty feet,' the computer voice said.

'So much for *ambiance*,' he said, looking around for a way to switch the voice off. He'd never liked talking cars and he didn't want a talking submarine either.

'Terrain, thirty feet,' the computer said. *'Descent stopped.'*

They were now suspended in the water at a depth of nine hundred and seventeen feet.

Kurt pressed the radio switch. 'We're on the ground floor,' he said. 'Give me a bearing.'

Joe's voice came back, slightly distorted. *'Target should be no more than three hundred yards from you, on a heading of one-five-zero degrees.'*

Kurt dialed up the heading and the *Angler*'s inertial navigation system took over. The batteries kicked in and small thrusters on either side of the sub began to spin. Instead of propellers at the stern, which could only drive them forward, the *Angler* had two compact propulsion pods jutting out on stubby wings near its tail. They could be rotated to point forward, back, up or down, making it easy to move the sub in any direction.

For now, they drove the sub across a carpet of gray silt that stretched unbroken into the dark like a field of dirty snow.

'It's so bleak,' Emma said.

There were no colorful reefs or schools of fish, only the occasional tube worm and small outcroppings of volcanic rock that hadn't yet been buried by the marine *snow*.

'It always makes me think of the Moon,' Kurt said as he flicked another switch and the telescoping boom began to extend from the top of the submersible.

'What's that?' Emma asked.

'*That* is the reason they call this sub the *Angler*,' he said. 'Joe named it after the anglerfish. A well-known denizen of the deep with a very particular method of getting food.'

'I know all about those fish,' Emma said. 'They trick other fish into swimming near their mouths using a lighted antenna. When a smaller fish is attracted to the lure, they open their big mouths and chomp on it.'

'Exactly,' Kurt said. 'In fact, I'm fairly certain *chomp* is the exact term marine biologists use to describe it.'

She laughed.

Outside, the boom locked in place with a dull click; its tip was now extended out in front of the sub by fifty feet. Kurt flipped a switch and a slight electric buzz became audible in the speakers of the intercom system. But aside from the static, and an almost invisible halo around the boom, nothing else happened.

'Looks like someone forgot to change the light-bulbs,' Emma said.

Kurt flipped another switch and a pair of cameras on a lower part of the boom came to life. The video was displayed on a flat screen in the center panel between the two seats. It showed a view of the terrain stretching several hundred feet ahead of them. Undulations in the sediment were clearly visible; mounds of lava rock appeared here and there. In one spot, a deep-sea crab flared white and then vanished as it buried itself in the silt.

Looking through the canopy with the naked eye, none of this was visible.

'High-intensity violet and ultraviolet light,' Kurt said. 'It penetrates seawater far better than the visible spectrum, but since human eyes are not sensitive to UV frequencies —'

'You use cameras tuned to pick it up,' she said, finishing the thought for him. 'Ingenious.'

'It allows us to explore the dark much more efficiently,' he said. 'And if you're feeling a little pale, it doubles as a tanning salon. Though a minute or two in the beam would leave you burned.'

They continued across the flat expanse, dividing their attention between what they saw on the screen and the view through the curved front window. As they neared the target, Kurt took manual control of the sub and brought them in closer.

The first thing they came in contact with was a flat piece of metal that had been bent and twisted. On the screen, a second piece could be seen nearby, complete with a hinge and some wires attached to it.

Kurt moved closer and the two pieces of debris became visible in the normal light.

'You were right,' Emma said. 'Definitely man-made.'

Kurt eased up to the first target and held station against the current. 'See if you can grab it with the claw,' he said, pointing to a pair of joysticks in between the two seats.

'I warn you,' she said. 'I never get anything when I play this game at the carnival.'

'No one does,' he said. 'That's why the stuffed animals are covered in an inch of dust.'

Emma tested the controls, which resembled those of a miniature remote-controlled car. Pushing one of the sticks forward, she extended a metal arm with a claw-like pincer on the end. Manipulating the claw until it was directly over one of the targets, she plucked the four-foot strip of metal from the silt on the first try.

'Great job,' Kurt said.

'Now what?'

'Drop it in the bin,' he said, pointing to a twelve-foot-long bin attached to the *Angler*'s port side.

With a twist of the joystick, she drew the arm back in and positioned it over the recovery bin. 'Good?'

Kurt nodded.

She pressed the release button and the metal strip fell from the claw into the bin, hitting with a soft bump.

'If you fill that one up, we still have a second bin on the starboard side,' Kurt told her. 'They're detachable. We can send them topside by using inflatable air bags, if we need to, or we can keep them in place and carry them home when we surface.'

'Perfect for cleaning the ocean floor,' Emma said.

She retrieved the second piece of metal and then found a hydraulic strut.

'What do you think?' Kurt asked.

'I'm not sure,' she said. 'I have to admit these appear to be aircraft parts, but there's nothing definitive. Let's keep moving.'

Kurt nodded and took them farther to the south, tracking along a trail of small scars in the sediment.

'Are those impact points?' Emma asked.

Kurt nodded. 'A metal rain fell here. The smaller items buried themselves, leaving these marks. Only the bigger ones or those that came down with less speed remained on the surface.'

'So this is a debris field?'

He nodded.

Emma looked grim. 'If this is the *Nighthawk*, we'll need to find the core. All the technology our adversaries are after is hidden there.'

Kurt bumped the throttle, adjusted course and

guided them forward. They passed by a smattering of small parts and additional gouges in the silt, stopping only when they found another large section of shredded metal, which looked like torn and tattered paper.

'This isn't good,' Emma said. 'That looks like a fuselage section.'

'It must have hit the water at high speed,' Kurt said.

She shook her head. 'It shouldn't have,' she replied. 'Every simulation we've run suggests the onboard computer was still operating. It should have flared as it descended and then deployed its parachutes and come down softly.'

Kurt paused. He found it odd how strongly convinced everyone in the NSA was that the aircraft was in one piece. 'The evidence doesn't support that,' he said, tired of hearing about what *should have happened*.

'The core *must* still be intact,' Emma said urgently. 'Keep going. We need to find it.'

It sounded like wishful thinking to Kurt, but he moved on, guiding them in a zigzag pattern. Once he'd established the width of the debris field and the direction it ran, they made steady progress, with more and more debris appearing out of the darkness, eventually stopping when they discovered several large sections of what had to be an airframe, lengths of wire and insulation wafting in the current, and the unmistakable shape of a wheel still attached to a hydraulic strut.

'Landing gear assembly,' Emma said dejectedly.

The wheel hub lay on its side. Every shred of its tires had been ripped free and the hydraulic strut had been bent at a forty-degree angle. A curved section of blackened sheet metal that looked like part of the fuselage lay just beyond it.

'So much for the core being in one piece,' Kurt said.

Emma didn't respond. She was staring into the dark. The look on her face suggested anger and confusion. She focused on the wheel, squinting until a small furrow appeared in her brow. 'Go in closer.'

Kurt nudged the throttle and guided the *Angler* gently into position, trying not to stir up too much sediment.

As they closed in on what appeared to be the nose gear, Emma moved to the edge of her seat. The anger vanished. 'It's too big,' she said.

Kurt could see that. 'We can't carry it up,' he said. 'But we can attach a cable and winch it to the surface.'

'No,' she said, turning toward him. 'It's too big to come from the *Nighthawk*. To speed up development, we took the landing gear from the smaller X-37. It gave us more interior space and less weight, but it made the *Nighthawk* look odd when you saw it sitting on the ground. Like a big dog with short legs.'

She pointed back through the canopy. 'The diameter of that wheel is too large. The strut is too long, even though it's broken off.'

'We're looking through curved glass,' Kurt said. 'It magnifies things.'

Emma glanced at him and then back through the canopy. She scanned the wheel first and then turned her attention to the wreckage out beyond. 'There's too much debris,' she added. 'Too much material all together. I'm telling you, this isn't the *Nighthawk*.'

'Then what is it?'

'I don't know,' she admitted. 'Some other plane that crashed. Maybe it's that missing airliner from Malaysia. Maybe it's an old military transport that came down years ago.'

Kurt shook his head. 'The wreckage is pristine,' he said, quashing that theory. 'It's recent. If this material had been down here any length of time, it would be corroded and encrusted with marine life. The craters in the sediment where each piece made an impact would be filled in like footprints in a snowstorm. Besides, we heard this plane hit the water – it came down within twenty minutes of Vandenberg losing contact with the *Nighthawk*.'

'I'll take your word for that,' she said. 'But you have to take mine as well. The debris we're seeing is not from our vehicle.'

Kurt hadn't heard of any crashes in this part of the world. But there was no point in arguing. He clicked on the radio. '*Reunion*, are you getting all of this?'

'The video feed is good,' Joe said. 'Looks like you've hit the mother lode.'

'According to my copilot, it's fool's gold,' Kurt said. 'I'm going to haul some of the debris up for you to inspect; maybe you can figure out what kind of plane this came from.'

'Sounds good,' Joe said. 'Look for something definitive.'

Kurt scanned around them for a smaller piece of debris that might reveal the make and model of the wreck. 'What about that circuit board?' he said, pointing to a length of wiring attached to a green computer panel.

'Good idea,' Joe said over the radio. 'The electronics might be traceable.'

Kurt maneuvered the *Angler* into position, overshot just a bit and then cut the throttle, allowing the sub to drift back over the target.

With the thrusters off, the *Angler* was utterly silent. In the sudden quiet, he noticed something he hadn't heard before: a vibration in the water; a low, repetitive hum, coming from somewhere in the distance.

Emma heard it, too. 'What is that?'

It sounded like a ship to Kurt. He got back on the radio. '*Reunion*, are you on the move?'

'Negative,' Joe replied. 'We're full stop. Half the crew are out on deck, sunning themselves. Why?'

'Do you see any traffic?'

There was a slight delay before Joe replied again. 'Also negative. There's not a ship on the horizon.'

Despite that fact, Kurt was certain they were hearing a ship's propeller.

'If it's not up there . . .' Emma said.

She didn't have to finish. Kurt was thinking the same thing. He deployed a hydrophone. It wasn't a true sonar receiver – in fact, it was just a basic microphone encased in a waterproof container designed to record whales and other sounds of sea life – but by turning it a few degrees at a time, he was able to get a better fix on the strange hum.

Heard through the speakers, the sound was deep and ominous, and growing louder by the moment. 'It's coming from behind us,' Kurt said. 'And it's coming this way.'

15

Kurt nudged the thrusters and slowly spun the *Angler* until it was pointed in the direction of the approaching hum. He switched off the normal light, leaving only the UV system in place. Still they saw nothing.

'Maybe we should get out of here,' Emma said.

A sharp ping exploded through the water, reverberating in the hollow confines of the *Angler* like someone had struck the side with a hammer.

Emma put a hand to her ear. Kurt marveled at a ripple in the silt, caused by the power of the invisible sound wave.

'Someone just painted us,' Kurt said, meaning the sonar ping had found them and probably registered back to whatever submarine had issued it.

'Searching for wreckage like us?'

'Maybe, but you don't need a sonar pulse like that to search for wreckage,' Kurt replied. He left unsaid that powerful sonar pings were normally used to get targeting data for torpedoes.

With a smooth touch, he spun the *Angler* around, looking for the source of the ping. The thrumming sound grew louder, like a freight train barreling down on them.

'What are you waiting for?' Emma asked.

'We have to look both ways before we cross the

road,' he said, pivoting the nose of the submersible upward and turning the UV light to full intensity while simultaneously glancing toward the monitor.

At first there was nothing. Then, in the far distance a distortion appeared, like a portal to another dimension opening in the deep. Kurt knew it was the swirling water and the tiny sedimentary fragments being forced aside by a pressure wave. Behind the distortion, a shape began to form, emerging out of the darkness.

Huge, wide and bulbous, it was the curving nose of an approaching submarine. Not a small submersible like the *Angler*, or even a svelte attack submarine, but a monster of the deep, grinding toward them, its bow a wall of steel.

It was cruising slowly, perhaps a hundred feet off the seafloor.

'They're trying to run us down,' Emma said.

'No,' Kurt said. 'They're just following the same debris trail we did.'

'Then we should get out of the way.'

Kurt shook his head. 'Moving now would give them our location. As long as we remain still, we *should* appear no different than a rock formation or part of the wreckage.'

As Kurt spoke, another ear-splitting pulse came forth. The NUMA submersible rang like a bell and still Kurt held his ground.

A swirling cloud of sediment swelled forth, beneath and in front of the approaching vessel. It made it seem like the behemoth was riding on a cushion of dust.

'Hang on,' Kurt said.

The disturbance hit the *Angler* and the small submersible was spun around and swept to one side.

Kurt used the thrusters to straighten the sub out and watched in awe as a mountain of rust-colored steel passed over them, filling the view from one edge of the canopy to the other. It passed by slowly, almost endlessly. The submarine crossing above them was as wide and long as the cargo vessel floating on the surface.

Finally, the propellers came into view.

As they neared, the *Angler* was pulled off the bottom by the turbulence and drawn toward the spinning props. It was swept in close and then spat out behind the passing leviathan, tumbling in the submarine's baffles. Kurt fought to control the ride, but had little power against what was essentially an underwater tornado.

The *Angler* spun and rolled and banged against an outcropping of rock. Several warning lights blinked on. And then everything went black.

Up on the *Reunion*, Joe and Captain Kamphausen watched the events live until the video feed suddenly cut out. Without sound or commentary, it was hard to tell what happened. The last image caught on tape was a shot of the churning brass propellers.

'Did it hit them?' Kamphausen wondered aloud.

Joe picked up the microphone. '*Angler*, what's your status?'

He waited a few moments before making another attempt. 'Come in, *Angler*. Kurt, are you there?'

When he received nothing in response, Joe put the microphone down and played the video one more time, studying the blast of sediment and the last, ominous view.

'I don't think the props got them,' he said. 'A close call, nothing worse. But the communications line must have been cut.'

'Why didn't he move?' the captain asked. 'He just sat there like a deer in the headlights.'

'Kurt doesn't freeze up,' Joe replied. 'He must have felt it was safer to stay put. A tactic I would agree with. It's very surprising that a vessel that large would be traveling that close to the seafloor.'

Joe checked the last burst of telemetry data from the *Angler*'s control systems in hopes of gaining more insight. What he saw concerned him. A list of warning lights had come on right before the line was cut.

'Battery pack,' he said, reading off the labels. 'Pumps. Gyrostabilizer. They must have hit something pretty hard for all of those systems to go out at once.'

Kamphausen offered a grim look. 'What exactly does all that mean? Are they drowning?'

'I doubt it,' Joe said. 'The *Angler* has a strong hull, so I'm assuming they're dry. But they may be facing the submariner's worst nightmare.'

'Worse than drowning?'

'Being marooned alive on the bottom,' Joe said. 'With electrical problems and the pumps off-line, they may not be able to surface.'

'Is there any way we can help them?' Kamphausen asked. 'Or do we just have to wait and see?'

'Under normal circumstances, this wouldn't be a big problem,' Joe said. 'I'd just drop another sub in the water, hook a line on them and tow them back to the surface. Failing that, I'd don a hard suit and hook a cable to them and winch them up. But since we don't have either of those things, we're going to have to improvise.'

'What about that submarine that almost ran them over?' Kamphausen said. 'Judging by the rust on the hull and the general state of neglect, I'd say it was a Russian boat. Is it too much to assume they're after whatever you're after?'

'We'd be foolish to assume anything else,' Joe replied.

'Are we in any danger?'

'I doubt they'll torpedo a surface ship like the *Reunion*,' Joe said. 'That would be inviting war and their rapid destruction from our sub-hunting aircraft. But the depths of the sea are a different story.'

'How so?'

'To a large extent, *what happens down below, stays down below*,' Joe replied, co-opting the famous Las Vegas advertising slogan. 'They could easily eliminate the *Angler* by ramming it, or hitting it with a torpedo, or by sitting on it and crushing it down into the silt. In all cases, no one up here would ever know what happened. And that, I cannot allow.'

Kamphausen scratched his head. 'But how can we stop them?'

'By getting them off the bottom before anything else happens.'

Kamphausen nodded, looked around as if he was

thinking deeply and then turned back to Joe. 'I've got nothing.'

'Fortunately, I've got an idea,' Joe said. 'But it's going to take a little work. I assume you have a few generators on this ship.'

'Several.'

'Show me to the largest one you've got. And have your engineering team meet us there with a complete set of tools.'

Kamphausen looked at him suspiciously.

'Don't worry,' Joe said. 'I'll put it all back together when I'm done.'

Nine hundred feet below, Kurt and Emma sat in darkness. The huge submarine had passed over the top of them and continued on into the dark. The turbulent ride had slammed them against a ledge of volcanic rock, tripped a few circuit breakers and lit up several warning lights on the panel before shutting off all the lights.

Using a flashlight, Kurt found the main panel, pushed the circuit breakers back in and brought the *Angler* back to life. 'No real damage,' he determined.

'Listen,' Emma said.

The hydrophone was still picking up the sound of the propellers, but the intensity level had waned. Before long, it ceased altogether.

'They've come to a stop,' Kurt said.

'Better than having them double back.'

'Couldn't agree more,' Kurt replied. 'But what are they doing down here in the first place? Considering the size and shape of that sub, I make it out as a Russian Typhoon, a ballistic missile submarine. Not exactly cut out for search-and-rescue work.'

'Maybe it was the nearest vessel they had with sonar capability,' Emma suggested.

Kurt wasn't so sure. He straightened his headset and tried to reach Joe. 'Joe, are you out there? I'm hoping you got the number of the truck that almost ran us down.'

There was no answer. Not even static. 'I think the Typhoon cut our line as it passed overhead,' Kurt replied. 'We've lost communications with the surface.'

'Maybe we should count ourselves lucky and head up,' she suggested. 'See if Joe can identify this aircraft and let everyone know this is a dead end.'

Kurt considered that, but a curious mind and a sharpened sense of suspicion ran in his family, just like the silver-gray hair he'd inherited at a young age. 'That would be the smart thing to do,' he admitted. 'But something doesn't make any sense here. Did you report this location to anyone?'

She shook her head. 'I haven't told a soul.'

'Neither have I. So, there couldn't be a leak.'

'What about our *partners* on the *Reunion*?'

'I can't imagine a Russian agent being stowed away on a refrigerated agriculture ship I chose at random,' he replied. 'And even if we were *that* unlucky and someone up there did pass our location to the Russians, what are the odds they would have a Typhoon submarine within a few hours' sailing time of our location?'

'Astronomically low,' she said. 'The few Typhoons they have left spend most of their time in port, and when they do sail, they rarely venture far from home.'

Kurt knew that, too. He also knew the Typhoons were in the process of being retired from service. 'By all rights, that sub should not be here.'

'Maybe we should worry about it another day,' Emma said. 'They've already scanned the debris field with their sonar. If we're lucky, they'll bring their salvage fleet out here and spend a few days recovering aircraft parts off the bottom before they realize this wreckage doesn't come from the *Nighthawk*.'

Kurt was one step ahead of her. 'That's just it,' he said. 'I think they already know.'

His hand went back to the console and he raised the volume on the hydrophone. A new sound was emanating from the dark, a pulsing noise that sounded more like water running through a pipe.

'Bow and stern thrusters,' he said. 'They're keeping station out there in the dark. I suggest we go find out why.'

16

Are you afraid they'll see us?' Emma asked, commenting on their stealth approach.

'Submarines like the Typhoon don't have windows to look through,' Kurt said, 'but they might have cameras or ROVs and submersibles of their own to deploy. They also have passive listening devices that are highly sensitive. Hugging the bottom will absorb any sound we make.'

They both fell silent and Kurt continued tracking toward their target by making small adjustments to the hydrophone. When a rock formation appeared on the video screen, he weaved around it. When they came to a slope of sediment piled up against a wide ridge, he put the *Angler* into an ascent.

They tracked the slope upward and came over the top.

'Look,' Emma said.

Kurt looked up from the screen. An eerie blue glow loomed in the distance.

With enough light to navigate by, he switched off the UV system and retracted the *Angler*'s namesake boom. Continuing over the ridge and down the other side, they approached the lighted area.

From a distance, the glow was nothing more than a

shimmering orb of water, dark blue in color and revealing no details. As they moved closer, it turned green, and eventually took on a yellowish tint similar to natural light.

Because of the total darkness surrounding them and the weightless state of the submarine, it felt as if they were approaching a strange planet in the depths of space.

As they closed in, Kurt cut the throttle and allowed the *Angler* to drift. 'Our friends have set up shop.'

The glowing orb had become a swath of daylight that ran for several hundred feet. It was cast by row after row of high-powered floodlights on the underside of the Typhoon. The bulk of the huge submarine remained hidden in the inky black water, but the seafloor beneath was lit up like a stadium. The reflected light illuminated the underside of the Typhoon and the maroon-colored paint the Russian Navy preferred to use below the waterline.

Several pod-like shapes were visible beneath the keel.

'Divers in hard suits,' Kurt said.

They were descending toward the seafloor like tiny probes dropped from an alien vessel. Their destination was a large concentration of wreckage, including an upturned wing and the T-shaped tail of a large aircraft.

'Vertical stabilizer,' Emma said. 'Fuselage section over there. And that looks like an engine pod. I told you this wasn't the *Nighthawk.*'

A clanking sound came through the hydrophone and then a hiss of bubbles.

'Pressure door opening,' Kurt said. 'Most likely, the lockout room where those divers came from or a compartment from where they can release an ROV.'

More clanking sounds rang out through the hydrophone and a narrow slit of light appeared in the underside of the Typhoon. It grew wider as a pair of huge doors in the bottom of the hull drew back from each other. They locked in place, leaving a hundred-foot opening in the bottom of the submarine. As Kurt and Emma watched in amazement, a huge clamshell bucket descended from the center of it, its jaws stretched wide.

The bucket crashed into the wreckage with abandon. Sediment swirled in the light, and as the hydraulic jaws closed, the screech of rending metal cried out through the water.

Kurt watched intently as the tail section of the aircraft was hauled up into the open bay of the submarine. 'The Russians have built a submersible version of the *Glomar Explorer*.'

The *Glomar Explorer* was the most famous salvage vessel in the world. Built by the CIA, using the celebrity status of Howard Hughes as a cover, it had performed its secret task once, and only once, pulling most of a sunken Russian submarine off the bottom of the Pacific in 1974.

Disguised as a mining ship, the *Explorer* had moved into position, lowered a cradle, and hauled up three-fourths of what had been the K-129, bringing the wreckage through a huge door in the bottom of the hull and hiding it in what the engineers called the *moon pool*.

Russian spy ships watching from several miles away never knew what happened. When the truth leaked, the Russians were furious. They were also embarrassed and put on notice that anything in the sea was fair game. They'd maintained a large salvage fleet ever since – a substantial portion of which was currently sailing for the Galápagos – but this Typhoon, this huge submarine converted into a clandestine salvage vessel, was something new.

At least it was new to Kurt. 'You guys at the NSA know anything about this?'

'This is a surprise. But it makes perfect sense, if you think about it. Take the missile tubes out and the Typhoon has huge storage capacity. It can move about undetected, dive to twenty-five hundred feet and pluck things right off the bottom, all unseen by the world's satellites.'

'Wish we'd thought of it,' Kurt said. 'While we're tracking their surface fleet and telling ourselves we have several days before they get here, these guys are already on scene. Which begs the question: exactly what scene is this? If this wreckage isn't the *Nighthawk*, then what are we looking at? And why are the Russians so interested in it?'

'Maybe we should get a little closer and find out,' she said.

'Look who's become a risk taker,' Kurt replied, grinning.

'It's a risk-reward scenario,' she said. 'A few photos of this Typhoon will help soften the blow of not finding the *Nighthawk* out here.'

Kurt bumped the throttle forward once more. 'Who am I to stand in the way of shameless self-promotion?'

'I assure you,' she said, 'I'm thinking purely of the national interest.'

Kurt suppressed a laugh – on the odd chance it might have carried through the water to the Typhoon's hydrophones.

The closer they got, the louder the racket became. As they watched the effort from the darkness, it became clear that haste was the priority. As soon as the retrieval bucket deposited a load of wreckage in the Typhoon's cargo bay, it was run back out, repositioned and dropped once again. There was no caution to the work and no attempt to preserve or protect any technology they might be recovering.

The reason dawned on Kurt. 'They're not trying to *salvage* anything. They're trying to haul it away and hide the evidence before anyone else finds it here. Which means – '

'This is a Russian aircraft,' Emma said, finishing his thought. 'Maybe it's a recon flight that went down while searching for the *Nighthawk*.'

Kurt shook his head. 'This crash happened almost simultaneously with the *Nighthawk*'s disappearance.'

'A chase plane, then,' Emma suggested. 'The Russians have tried that before.'

By now, they were near enough to make out gearing and teeth on the inner part of the wing. He was maneuvering to get the camera focused when a brief flash caught his eye.

Kurt shut off what remained of the interior lighting and waited. A full minute ticked by before the light made another appearance. It was quick. Here and then gone. A white spark in the dark water of the sea.

'Low-powered strobe light,' he said.

'Black box,' Emma suggested, referencing the nearly indestructible data and voice recorders common on most military and commercial aircraft.

'Let's see if we can get at it without drawing too much attention to ourselves.'

He eased the submersible forward with a deft touch, traveling past that shattered wing and holding station near a tear in the forward part of the fuselage. The curved body of the aircraft had been opened and peeled back. The section beneath it was exposed. The tiny strobe flashed again from within.

'See if you can reach it.'

Emma went back to the controls and extended the arm to its maximum length. 'No,' she said. 'Can you get any closer?'

'Hang on,' Kurt said. He backed off and moved forward again, using a quick burst of the throttle. The *Angler* bumped against the wreckage, scraping against it and pushing a section of the airframe out of the way.

When the strobe flashed again it was brighter and closer and they were all but inside the airframe. Emma extended the arm once more. The claw at its end opened. The lower half slid underneath a metal handle on the housing of the data recorder and Emma closed it down tight.

'Got it,' she said, retracting the arm.

The black box – which was actually orange and covered with gray Cyrillic writing – came out of its slot with a little effort. Once it was clear, Emma retracted the arm and dropped it into the starboard cargo container.

'Good work,' Kurt said.

He put his hand on the throttle and prepared to back out but paused when the sound of the Typhoon's thrusters surged through the water with a different timbre.

Emma looked up. 'The Typhoon is repositioning.'

Kurt already knew that. He could see the lighted swath of ocean floor moving toward them.

He reversed thrust, trying to back out of the open section of the fuselage, but instead of moving in a straight line, the *Angler* was yanked to the side and pulled around.

'We're caught on something,' he said, craning his head around to see what had hooked them.

'I can see it from here,' Emma said. 'The frame around the retrieval container is snagged on the wreckage.'

Kurt moved the sub forward and then backed up

again, trying to pull free. But it was no use. The *Angler* was hooked.

A third try did nothing to free them, and the wreckage around them began to brighten as the peripheral light from the Typhoon reached the area.

Kurt had no choice. He rotated the thrusters and forced the *Angler* back into the wreckage, crashing down and shutting everything off.

'What are you doing?' Emma asked, in shock.

'Hiding,' he said. 'It's the only choice we have.'

The light around them grew brighter, filtering through gaps in the airframe like morning sun through high windows. The throbbing sound of the Typhoon's thrusters grew until the submarine appeared directly above them, rotating slowly until it was aligned into the current once again.

The maroon hull was marked with long scars of corrosion and algae while the lighted gap of the cargo bay shimmered with a sterile white glow.

Two divers in hard suits traveled up toward it, ascending with smaller pieces of debris in their nets and vanishing into the flooded hold. A moment later, the huge bucket reappeared. It traveled on rails in the cargo bay ceiling, stopping and locking into position almost directly above the *Angler*.

'This is not good,' Emma whispered.

Kurt couldn't have agreed more.

The bucket remained stationary for what seemed an eternity, its clamshell jaws opening slowly and locking into position. Finally, with nothing more than a pitiful squeak, it began to drop.

There was no mistaking its destination. The huge bucket was dropping straight for the wreckage pile and the NUMA submersible hiding in it.

17

The outstretched jaws of the retrieval bucket plunged downward, crashing into the wreckage surrounding the *Angler*. Metal screeched as it was torn and twisted. A cloud of silt erupted from the impact site and the *Angler* tilted over to one side.

With the teeth of the bucket embedded in the silt below, the powerful hydraulic struts activated. The jaws were forced together, burrowing through the silt, until they slammed shut beneath the heap of tangled metal.

The powerful winch in the Typhoon's cargo bay was engaged and the steel cables pulled taut, straining against the suction created by the sediment. The resistance didn't last. With a sudden lurch, the latest collection of wreckage was pulled from the seafloor to begin its journey upward.

Watching from the outside, the divers in hard suits saw nothing to differentiate this load of material from any other. It was just another stack of twisted metal being hauled away, with a long trail of silt pouring from the gaps and streaming in the current.

As the bucket neared the opening in the Typhoon's hull, a maneuver called *the shake* was performed. The ascent was halted and the jaws were opened a few inches. The tension on the cable was released and the bucket allowed to fall several feet before being stopped.

Each time the crane operator shook the bucket, a new cloud poured from the bottom. After several shakes, there was little sediment left. The jaws were closed once again. The winch was reactivated and the load drawn into the cargo bay.

Once it was fully retracted, the bucket began to move horizontally. At a predetermined position, it stopped and dumped the latest pile of wreckage on the inner deck.

Inside the *Angler*, Kurt and Emma were thrown about. They remained in their seats. When they were finally dropped inside the Typhoon, both of them were amazed to be alive. The claws had gone under and around them. The hull hadn't been punctured or even scratched; the acrylic of the canopy was free of cracks.

'Look at the size of this hold,' Emma said, gazing around.

'Used to be the missile bay,' Kurt said. 'In their original configuration, Typhoons carried twenty-four extremely large ICBMs. The largest ever deployed to sea.'

As Kurt spoke, he got his bearings. The bay was filled with water, which could be pumped out once the heavy doors were closed. At the moment, they were facing aft and tilted over at a thirty-degree angle. To get free, they'd have to rise up, make a U-turn and then dive out through the opening. Assuming, of course, that they *could* get free.

Leaning across the cockpit, Kurt spotted the offending piece of wreckage. 'I think I can cut us loose.'

'Better be quick,' Emma said. 'There's not much wreckage left down there.'

Kurt moved an acetylene torch into position. At the touch of a button, it snapped to life. He brought it up against the bent metal spar that had snagged them. The flame burned bright blue and the metal flared, red and molten, dropping away in burning fragments.

As he worked, the Typhoon repositioned itself and the retrieval bucket descended once again.

Emma watched the gearing above them spin. The cable let out for several seconds and then came to a rather abrupt stop. 'Now would be a good time,' she urged.

Kurt continued to burn through the length of metal, watching small bits melt and fall off. It seemed to be taking forever, as if the metal was made of something other than aluminum.

The gearing above began to spin as the cable was reeled in to bring the next load of wreckage on board.

'Hurry, Kurt,' Emma urged.

'I'm cutting as fast as I can.'

The torch finished its cut and a large triangular piece fell away. The *Angler* was free.

Kurt switched over to the throttle, tilted the thrusters and poured on the power. The *Angler* rose up out of the junk pile, shedding metallic debris and the coating of silt it had acquired.

Once they were above the wreckage, Kurt spun the submersible in a half circle and accelerated toward the open gap at the end of the cargo bay. They reached the edge, dove downward underneath the bucket just as it shook loose its next great cloud of silt.

Momentarily blinded, Kurt kept the throttle wide open. When they emerged on the far side, they were in the clear, headed for the darkness and safety beyond.

Sitting in the operations room of the Typhoon, Captain Victor Tovarich of the Russian 1st Salvage Flotilla watched the operation unfold on several screens, each linked to cameras on the underside of the Typhoon. An additional screen was divided into four quadrants and displayed the video feed from cameras mounted on the divers' hard suits.

He was proud of his men and his great machine but anxious to complete the project. He turned to his second-in-command. 'Progress report.'

'Eighty percent of main wreckage recovered,' the officer replied.

'Any sign of the *Nighthawk*?'

'No, sir,' the officer replied. 'I'm afraid not.'

'It has to be here,' he said, walking over to the monitor to study the grainy picture that was coming in. 'We know they had it in their grasp.'

'Permission to speak freely?' his First Officer said.

'Of course.'

'If the *Nighthawk* is not with the bomber, we should stop wasting our time on this recovery and get back to searching for the American craft.'

Tovarich resisted the urge to smile. His First Officer was a charger. He wanted the glory that came with plucking the American space plane off the bottom. He wasn't alone. 'I share your desire, Mikael. But they've decided in Moscow that this craft is a priority.'

The officer nodded.

'Besides,' Tovarich added. 'It could still be here. There was always a chance that the pilots managed to hold on to the *Nighthawk* even as they lost control.'

'A blind man's chance of catching a sparrow.'

'Perhaps,' Tovarich agreed. 'Only an airman could come up with such a plan. We should salute their bravery. Which reminds me, we'll need to search the wreckage in the cargo bay and recover the bodies.'

He reached over and tapped a button, switching one of the monitors to an internal camera view. 'Have one of the divers report to . . .'

Tovarich froze midsentence. Something on the screen caught his eye. A flickering light: *fire*. His first concern – that they'd brought something combustible on board – vanished as the firelight snapped off, but his confusion grew worse as he saw movement in the wreckage. 'What in the name of . . .'

Tovarich watched in disbelief as a white submersible with a broad red stripe rose out of the tangled metal and spun around. It came forward, heading right toward the camera, and then dove out through the open cargo bay doors, but not before Tovarich noticed the letters *NUMA* prominently displayed on the top of the submersible.

Rushing to the tactical section of his control room, Tovarich grabbed the sonar operator. 'We have an uninvited guest out there,' he said. 'American submersible. Find it!'

The sonar operator worked feverishly, pressing the earphones to his head and listening for the tiny, electric-powered submersible. With all the background noise, it proved impossible.

'It's no good, Captain. Too much interference from the salvage team and the thrusters.'

Tovarich turned to the navigation officer. 'Thrusters off. All stop. Shut down the salvage operation.'

The positioning thrusters were turned off and the vibration they produced began to fade. As the Typhoon began to drift, the work outside came to a halt as well. No one dared move.

'Anything?' Tovarich asked.

The sonar operator continued searching. Finally, a signal emerged.

'Small craft,' he said. 'Bearing zero-four-five. Depth seven-fifty and rising.'

'I want a positive range-and-firing solution,' Tovarich said.

The tactical officer looked surprised. 'Sir?'

'That's my order. Lock on and fire!'

Out in the dark, racing as fast as they could and heading for the surface, Kurt and Emma listened through the hydrophone as a strange silence grew up in their wake. 'They've shut down the thrusters,' Kurt said. 'It means they're listening for us.'

He considered shutting down as well and drifting on

the current, but if he did that, the Russians would just resort to active sonar and would find them eventually. The only way to be safe was to reach the surface. He doubted the Russians would do anything once they were out in the open.

He angled the nose of the sub higher and watched as the depth went below seven hundred feet. They still had a long way to go when the sound of the Typhoon's main engines coming back to life reached them.

The heavy pinging of a sonar sweep caught them seconds later, followed by the sound Kurt was dreading: a sudden rush of compressed air as a torpedo was thrust into the water to track them down and destroy them.

18

The NUMA submersible was maneuverable, but not very fast. Certainly not in comparison to the torpedo homing in on it.

'Use this to control the hydrophone,' Kurt said, placing Emma's hand on a large dial. 'Keep it focused on the torpedo. We need to hear it coming if we're going to have any chance to avoid it.'

'Torpedo?'

'Shouldn't have told you that,' Kurt said.

A different kind of sonar found them next: rapid clicks with short intervals and a higher-pitched sound.

'It's locked onto us,' Kurt said.

They'd put about a mile between themselves and the Typhoon by the time they were discovered. At that distance, and considering the comparative speeds, they might have forty seconds before getting obliterated.

'Can you take evasive action?' Emma said.

'We're making eight knots,' Kurt said. 'Nothing we do would be considered evasive. But we're not out of options.'

He reached past Emma to the cargo controls. 'If we can create a diversion, we might survive.'

Kurt had loaded the flight recorder into the right-hand cargo container. But the left-hand container was filled with nothing of real value, just junk from the wrecked bomber. Pressing one button, he unlocked the clasps that held it to the side of the *Angler*. Turning a pair of valves to full open, he inflated a pair of yellow bags attached to the container. The rush of bubbles drowned out all noise for several seconds and the bags expanded like hot-air balloons. They rose toward the surface and lifted the cargo container free.

At almost the same instant, Kurt blew the air from the ballast tank and pointed the submersible straight down, hoping the wall of bubbles and the ascending cargo container would draw the torpedo off course.

For several seconds, the water was too turbulent to hear anything, but as the disturbance cleared, Emma refocused the hydrophone. The sonar pings from the torpedo had changed pitch, becoming weaker.

'It's headed for the container,' Kurt said. 'It's lost us.'

He kept the nose of the submersible pointed down and the throttles full open, trying to put as much distance between the torpedo and themselves as possible.

'It's still going to hurt when it explodes,' Emma said.

She wasn't wrong. Ten seconds later, a white and orange flash lit up the dark water as the torpedo obliterated the cargo container. The explosion caused a shock wave that slammed the *Angler* and sent it tumbling end over end.

With his ears ringing, Kurt stabilized the sub. 'Now to make them think they hit us.'

He shut down the thrusters and blew the ballast tanks. The little sub righted itself and began moving upward, headed for the surface propelled by buoyancy alone.

'I'm borrowing a play out of the old U-boat text-book,' Kurt said. 'They would make their escape *after* the depth charges went off because the water was so turbulent it was impossible for sonar to hear through for several minutes.'

'Won't they just ping us again?' Emma asked.

'Maybe,' Kurt said. 'But I'm betting they'll just listen for wreckage first. And it'll be a while before the water settles down enough for them to hear anything. By then, I'm hoping to be on the surface and out in the bright light of day.'

The elevator ride picked up speed as the last drops of water were forced from the tanks. Kurt and Emma sat in silence, eyes locked on the slowly unwinding depth gauge.

'Anything?' the Typhoon's captain asked.

The sonar operator was listening, but all he could hear were the bubbles and cavitation left over from the explosion. It had rendered the passive sonar temporarily useless.

He waited and listened, keenly aware of the captain standing over his shoulder.

'Well?'

'Bubbles,' the sonar operator said. 'A moderate volume of released air traveling toward the surface. That would indicate a hit.'

'Any wreckage?' Tovarich asked.

'Wreckage?' the tactical officer said. 'Captain, that torpedo is designed to take out warships and American attack submarines. There won't be enough left of that submersible to qualify as wreckage.'

Tovarich understood, but he was a cautious man. 'Humor me,' he said. 'Use the active sonar. I want to be sure.'

The sonar was adjusted, another ping was released and the return echo examined. The results astonished everyone on board. 'Target zero-six-one,' the sonar operator said. 'Depth one hundred and twenty feet and headed for the surface.'

'Can we get them before they get there?'

The tactical operator made a few quick calculations. 'No, sir,' he said. 'They'll be up top before we can fire.'

Tovarich hesitated. He had standing orders not to allow any interference in the salvage, but he'd also been given similar – and now conflicting – orders to keep the mission clandestine. 'They know too much,' he said finally. 'Load and fire. And, this time, you'd better not miss.'

19

Joe Zavala sat in the cockpit of the Air-Crane as it rested quietly on the helipad near the bow of the *Reunion*. Captain Kamphausen was in the crane operator's seat, working the winch controls and reeling in a long section of cable. At the far end was a jury-rigged contraption Joe and the *Reunion*'s engineers had built to pluck *Angler* off the bottom of the sea.

'Are you sure this electromagnet is going to work?' Kamphausen asked.

'I used the best coils from your main generator,' Joe said. 'With the power from the Air-Crane's aux unit, it should have plenty of power.'

Still believing the *Angler* might be stuck on the bottom, Joe's plan was to find the submersible with the side-scan sonar, lower the magnet down on a cable and stick it to the steel hull of the sub. That done, he'd reel them in.

Kamphausen, who'd worked cranes for half his years at sea, would do the honors while Joe piloted the Air-Crane. He shut down the winch as soon as the final length of cable wrapped itself around the drum and the magnet locked in place. 'Now all we have to do is find them,' he said.

Before Joe could reply, a deep, echoing thud reached

them from the port side. Joe turned to see a momentary bulge on the surface of the sea. The circular displacement rose up and then fell back, releasing a tower of white water and foam from its center.

'Looks like someone else found them first,' Kamphausen said.

Joe turned around and rushed through the preflight in record time, hitting the starter and getting the rotors moving above them. 'Kurt and Emma must be on the move.'

'How do you know that?'

'Because there's no other reason to shoot at them.'

'At least we don't have to get them off the bottom,' Kamphausen said.

'I have a feeling they're still going to need our help,' Joe said.

As Kamphausen clicked his seat belt and the rotors flicked past at ever-increasing speed, Joe pulled on a headset and changed the frequency on the number one radio. He'd sent one of the small boats out on the water trailing the side-scan sonar and trying to pinpoint the location of the *Angler* without giving it away to the Russians. '*Survey 1*, did you catch that?'

The replay came loud and clear. 'We saw it on the surface. No idea what caused it, though.'

'Do you still have the Typhoon on the scan?'

'Yes, but the latest return is blurred.'

'The Typhoon is moving, too,' Joe concluded. 'They wouldn't be doing that unless they were chasing something.'

He turned his attention back to the instrument panel. Everything was operating in the green. With a firm twist of the throttle, Joe commanded full power. The weight came off the landing gear and the orange helicopter rose from the deck. With a kick of the rudder, Joe turned the nose to starboard and accelerated toward the widening circle of white water in the distance.

The *Angler* continued to ascend, moving upward at two hundred feet per minute. Kurt watched the light grow around them and Emma tried to pick up something, anything, on the hydrophone.

'It's blown out,' she said.

Kurt wasn't surprised; his ears felt as if they'd almost blown out as well. 'Never mind,' he said. 'Just get ready to abandon ship in case they fire another torpedo our way.'

She pulled a life jacket on as Kurt continued to pilot the submersible. They could see the surface now: a shimmering, waving mirror of silver that meant freedom.

As soon as the sub breached the surface, Kurt grabbed the radio. '*Reunion*, this is *Angler*,' he said. 'We're on the surface and need *immediate* pickup. Do you copy?'

'Let's just hope our antenna didn't get blown off,' Emma said.

Kurt pressed the transmit switch again. '*Reunion*, this is *Angler*, do you read?'

*

Joe was cruising across the water at an altitude of three hundred feet when he heard the radio call. Seconds later, he spotted the white and red submersible bobbing in the swells.

He turned the volume up. 'Kurt, this is Joe. I have you in sight. We'll be on you in thirty seconds.'

'Thirty seconds?' Kurt replied. He sounded shocked.

'We're already airborne. We thought you might need help.'

Joe brought the Air-Crane onto a matching course, setting up to grab the *Angler* off the water. As he finished the turn, he noticed something else: a long white trail of bubbles coming in from the west. 'Don't look now but you have a torpedo heading your way.'

'We'll bail out,' Kurt replied.

'Stay put,' Joe said. 'I think I can get you before it hits.'

'You'll never hook on in time,' Kurt said.

'We don't need a hook,' Joe said. 'We have a magnet.'

The submersible was moving, but it was ponderous on the surface. The white line of bubbles from the torpedo was tracking quickly toward them.

Joe cut in front of it, brought the Air-Crane down closer to the water. 'Lower the magnet.'

Kamphausen let out fifty feet of cable. The heavy, bell-shaped electromagnet trailed out behind them. He aimed for the red strip across the top.

'Activate the magnet,' Joe said. 'Full power. We're only going to get one shot at this.'

'Coils are powered,' Kamphausen shouted. 'Electro-magnet is live!'

From the corner of his eye, Joe saw the compass spin wildly as it picked up a new source of magnetism. They were thirty feet above the waves and closing in on the submarine at a shallow crossing angle. The torpedo trail was coming from directly behind them. Kamphausen could see it; Joe couldn't.

'It's going to be close,' he said.

Joe slowed as he came in behind the sub and matched its course. The magnet skipped across the water, and the cable scraped across the sub's back. The magnet came free of the water, hit the stern of the small sub and bounced.

It looked as if the impact might cause it to skip over the top, but the powered side of the magnet was drawn toward the flat iron spine of the submersible. It snapped onto the hull with a solid clunk. The winch strained and let out several feet of cable before the brake locked it tight. The Air-Crane was pulled downward as the tension on the cable threatened to whip the helicopter into the sea, but Joe countered the effect and the *Angler* surged forward, riding high in the water for a moment before pulling free. It swung forward underneath the Air-Crane, shedding curtains of seawater behind it.

Joe was too busy stabilizing the Air-Crane to worry about the torpedo. Kamphausen held his breath as it passed underneath.

Nothing happened. No explosion. No detonation. The torpedo didn't even turn to acquire a new target. It just continued on a straight line and traveled off into the distance.

Kamphausen watched it go and gave it a mock salute. 'Good riddance,' he said.

Joe laughed and turned back toward the *Reunion* with the *Angler* flying beneath them.

Nine hundred feet below, Tovarich and the rest of the Typhoon's crew waited for a detonation that never came.

'What happened?' Tovarich asked finally.

'Nothing, sir,' the sonar operator replied.

'I know that already,' Tovarich said, the fury barely restrained. 'What went wrong this time?'

'Nothing, sir,' the tactical officer said. 'Torpedo still running straight and true.'

'So it missed?'

'No, sir, it . . . it was right on target . . . It's just . . .' he replied, baffled by the situation.

'It's just *what*?' Tovarich demanded.

'It's just that the American submersible is gone.'

The captain stared at his sonarman in disbelief. 'What do you mean *gone*?'

'It's no longer in the water, Captain.'

Tovarich hauled the man out of his seat. He'd begun his career as a sonarman. He'd show these two amateurs how it worked. He snatched the headset and listened intently, adjusting the frequencies, the bearing and the sensitivity settings. He heard what they heard: the torpedo running but not the submersible.

'Give me an active ping!'

The emitter sounded almost immediately and the return came moments later. The torpedo was there, running off into the distance, as was the stationary freighter he assumed the NUMA submersible to be working from. But the submersible itself was gone.

Tovarich pulled the headset off. 'Detonate the torpedo,' he said. 'And return to the crash site. Once the cleanup is finished, set course for the deep. I'll be in my quarters. Alone.'

20

Kurt, Joe and Emma said their good-byes to the crew of the *Reunion* a few hours later. To their surprise, it was a warm send-off, despite the fact that no diamonds had been recovered. With the ship back on course and scheduled to make its delivery on time, even the fruit company rep stopped worrying. He took the ream of paperwork he'd been preparing for NUMA's lawyers and tossed it overboard.

Kamphausen, in particular, appeared sad to see them go. He all but crushed Joe in a bear hug. 'Haven't had this much excitement in years,' he insisted.

With Joe at the controls, the Air-Crane lifted off and turned east, headed for Guayaquil once again. Emma was in the copilot's seat and Kurt sat in the jump seat between the two of them.

Little was said as the flight progressed. Emma seemed pensive even before they took off and grew quiet during the flight, staring out the window for long stretches.

Kurt tapped her on the shoulder. 'Are you okay?'

She turned his way. Her eyes suggested she was troubled, but the look was quickly covered. 'Just disappointed,' she said. 'We're back to square one.'

He nodded. 'In a single day's work you uncovered a

pair of top secret Russian projects. That's got to be good for something – at least a smile.'

'Our mission was to find the *Nighthawk*,' she said.

'Relax,' he said. 'We'll find it.'

She glanced at her watch. 'We'd better.'

As she turned back to the window, Kurt considered her demeanor. She played it like she was feeling disappointment, but Kurt saw it differently. It was stress. She looked as if she was carrying the world on her shoulders and that the world was getting heavier.

He unlatched his harness, folded up the jump seat and moved aft. Their backpacks rested there, along with a hard-sided suitcase in which the flight data recorder from the Russian bomber had been stored. Next to the case lay an assortment of refreshments and a parting gift from the crew of the *Reunion*: a fruit bowl covered with plastic wrap. It held limes, apples, oranges and, of course, an assortment of kiwis.

Kurt grabbed an orange and then paused. He glanced over his shoulder toward the cockpit. Emma was still staring out the window. Joe was busy flying.

He hesitated for only a second and then did what he felt needed to be done. Finished, he returned to the cockpit with refreshments for everyone.

An hour later, they were on the ground. Two cars waited for them on the airport ramp. Standing in front of one vehicle was Rudi Gunn. Climbing out of the second were a pair of men in dark suits.

'Friends of yours?' Kurt said to Emma.

'Not friends,' she said. 'Colleagues. I recognize the

guy on the left. He works for Steve Gowdy. A personal right-hand man.'

Kurt had expected something like this. He grabbed the luggage and climbed out through the door.

The three groups met on the tarmac. Names were exchanged and ID badges flashed until everyone had been introduced.

Emma handed over the hard-sided case. 'Inside, you'll find a flight data recorder from a supersonic Russian bomber. Modified *Blackjack*, by the look of the wreckage.'

The lead agent, whose name was Hurns, took the case. 'What about the submarine?'

'Extensively modified Typhoon,' she said, handing over a portable hard drive. 'Photos and video are on here. We got some very clear shots.'

Hurns nodded. 'The brass are going to be thrilled. At this rate, you'll be a legend before you turn forty.'

His words didn't seem to affect Emma in the least. 'We all have our jobs to do,' she said. 'I'm staying on with the NUMA group until this mission is complete. Tell Steve I'll contact him as soon as I have anything else.'

Hurns nodded. Carried the case to the trunk of the car and placed it inside. 'We'll leave you to it,' he said.

As the two agents from the NSA drove off, Rudi Gunn took over. He leaned against the side of his car with his arms folded and a stern look on his face. He addressed Kurt. 'So what's this I hear about NUMA going into the vegetable business?'

'*Fruit* business,' Kurt corrected. 'It's an interesting story. If you'd like, I'll tell you on the way.'

'On the way to where?'

'Consulate building,' Kurt said. 'We need a secure satellite link so we can test a theory I've come up with.'

Rudi glanced Joe's way.

'First I've heard of it,' Joe said.

Emma shot Kurt a suspicious glance, but he just smiled.

'Okay,' Rudi said. 'I'm game. But this better be good. We're already getting a lot of flak from the NSA about your *methods*.'

'Give me a few hours and judge for yourself,' Kurt said.

Rudi raised an eyebrow of suspicion and opened the driver's door. 'I will.'

At the American consulate building in Guayaquil, Rudi spoke to the ranking official and clearance to use the communications suite was soon provided.

A quick look at the room revealed a high-tech masterpiece: consoles everywhere, flat-panel displays, computers and keyboards, even a virtual reality head-set. All connected through encoding and decoding machines.

Kurt explained. 'During my stint with the CIA, I had to use the consulates a few times. I was always impressed by the amount of technology they packed into one small space. It was often better than the stuff we were using on the outside since it didn't have to be portable.'

Joe and Emma sat down wearily. It had been a long forty-eight hours. Only Kurt seemed to have any spring in his step.

Rudi remained guarded. He hadn't slept much. When he wasn't deflecting questions about NUMA commandeering a cargo ship or fighting off pressure from Steve Gowdy and the NSA to rein Kurt in, he'd been ducking calls from the fruit company and NUMA's general counsel. So far, they had nothing to show for all the commotion. Eventually, order and sanity would have to be restored, if only to satisfy Rudi's own sense of discipline.

Kurt placed his backpack on the central table and unzipped the main compartment. He pulled out a scuffed and dented piece of equipment. It was a dull-orange color and plastered with Russian writing on all sides.

'What is that doing here?' Emma asked, jumping from her seat.

'I pulled it out of your case while we were flying,' Kurt said.

'Obviously,' she replied. 'But why? I was ordered to send it back to the lab. It's NSA property now.'

Kurt held up a cautioning finger. 'Actually, based on the law of Admiralty, this flight data recorder is the property of NUMA . . . Or, perhaps, the Russian Air Force, since it would be hard to prove they'd abandoned it or relinquished an ownership interest in it. But, as we're not sending it back to Moscow, I took it upon myself to assert NUMA's claim.'

Joe clenched his teeth and shrank down in his seat a bit.

Rudi sighed and looked up at the ceiling, perhaps wondering why the gods had placed Kurt Austin in his life.

Emma just stared at him. 'Gowdy is going to flip out.'

'We're protecting him,' Kurt said. 'There's a leak in his department. The bomber and the Typhoon prove it.'

'And you know this *how*?' Emma asked.

'Think about it,' Kurt said. 'The *Nighthawk* goes off course and vanishes. At the same time, in the same vicinity, a Russian supersonic bomber falls out of the sky and crashes into the sea. We mistake one crash for the other and race to the location only to find a top secret Russian submarine *already on the scene*. That's not a coincidence.'

Emma sat back. 'No, it's not. But I don't see how that indicates a breach of security.'

'Don't you?' Kurt said. 'To reach the search area when it did, that submarine had to leave Murmansk several weeks ago. And it's not the only vessel to end up in the right place at the right time. There are two separate fleets, one Russian, one Chinese, both steaming across the Pacific at flank speed right now. Both made up primarily of deepwater search-and-salvage vessels, both within a day's sailing of a crash site that didn't exist forty-eight hours ago, despite the fact that their home ports are *ten thousand miles* to the east.'

'The fleet movements are suspicious,' Emma admitted, 'but explainable. Both units were on maneuvers, training exercises. The Chinese and Russian liaison teams informed us about them months ago. It's a little thing we do to keep from starting World War III.'

Kurt didn't back off. 'Of course they informed you months ago. Because they knew the *Nighthawk* was going to go down months ago.'

'How could they know that?'

'Because they're the ones that brought it down.'

'Brought it down?'

He nodded. 'By hacking the *Nighthawk*'s command system. Codes that are jealously guarded by your NSA friends at Vandenberg. Which means the NSA has a mole, a very highly placed one, and that gives me every good reason not to share this flight data, or anything else, with them.'

She went silent. Kurt let the words sink in.

'You're out on a very long limb here,' Rudi said. 'Even if some of those assumptions are true, it doesn't . . .'

'No,' Emma said, interrupting him. 'Kurt's right.'

All eyes turned her way.

'It's the only thing that makes sense. We've never been able to figure out why the *Nighthawk* went off course in the first place. One technician noted that *Nighthawk* was having a problem trying to process *conflicting* commands. It made no sense at the time. We assumed it was a computer glitch. But the bomber, the Typhoon, the salvage fleets conveniently on the scene – it all suggests the Russians and/or the Chinese reprogrammed the *Nighthawk* and tried to get it to splash down in the ocean where they could pick it up with ease.'

Rudi said, 'But if that's the case, why wouldn't their fleets be *in* the crash zone instead of several days' sailing from it.'

'Because we brought it back early,' she said. 'The storm off Hawaii was tracking toward the California coast. It was expected to hit during the initial landing window. We didn't want to risk dealing with the weather, so we moved the reentry up a full week. Without that change, both salvage fleets would be within a hundred miles of the Galápagos Islands chain just waiting for the *Nighthawk* to drop out of the sky and into their hands.'

'Even the location makes sense,' Joe added. 'Aside from the terrain around the Galápagos, the sea is ten thousand feet deep for hundreds of miles in every direction.'

'And the bomber?' Rudi asked.

'Probably a chase plane,' Emma said. 'The *Nighthawk* is coated in third-generation stealth materials. It's completely invisible to radar. But coming through the atmosphere, its skin heats up to three thousand degrees. A supersonic bomber with an infrared tracking system could follow it for miles, zeroing in on its heat signature and following it until it slowed to landing speed and parachuted softly into the sea.'

Kurt nodded. 'Exactly what I was thinking. But something went wrong. And even though the bomber went down, there might be a clue to the *Nighthawk*'s whereabouts on the data recorder. A clue we don't want broadcast to Moscow or Beijing.'

'What if someone has found it already?'

'They haven't,' Kurt said, 'or their fleets would have turned around.'

Emma nodded. 'All right,' she said. 'Do your magic. Send the data back to NUMA and let's find out what the Russians were doing.'

Kurt presented the black box. 'Can you tap into it?'

Joe nodded. 'Dataports look fairly standard. I'll do some quick tests and then send the information to Hiram. Max will be able to decipher it better than we can.'

As Joe went to work, Rudi stepped out to make a call and Kurt took a seat next to Emma. The color had returned to her face. 'You like the game?' Kurt said.

'I like to win,' she replied.

'So do I.'

They sat for a moment. 'So what did you give them anyway?' she asked.

'Who?'

'My colleagues, Hurns and Rodriguez. When I lifted that case, there was something heavy in there.'

Kurt leaned back in his chair and put his feet up. 'A very nice parting gift. One I'm sure they'll appreciate on their long flight home.'

The NSA-owned Gulfstream was halfway to Houston before Agent Hurns let his curiosity get the better of him. On this mission he was a courier, assigned to pick up and deliver a package. He wasn't supposed to open it and have a look, but he couldn't help himself.

He suggested as much to Rodriguez.

'I'm game,' his partner said.

They left their seats, walked aft and lifted the metal-sided suitcase onto a table. With quick fingers, Hurns popped both latches and opened the case.

His face went blank. 'What the heck is this?'

Rodriguez stared over his shoulder. 'It appears to be a bowl of fruit,' he said, reaching in for a ripe kiwi.

A handwritten note was tucked in between two oranges. It read:

Feed these to the mole.

Best regards,
Kurt Austin

21

NUMA Headquarters, Washington DC

Hiram Yaeger had been part of many daring operations during his time with NUMA. But when the data from the black box was finally decoded, he could not help but tip an imaginary cap to the Russians for the sheer audacity of what they'd attempted.

With the full details revealed, he waited in the video conference room at NUMA Headquarters while the satellite connection to the consulate building in Guayaquil was secured.

The room was a mix of the old world and the new. Paintings of tall ships lined the walls while a mahogany table from a nineteenth-century yacht dominated the center of the room. It was surrounded on three sides by comfortable chairs, though one had been removed for Priya, who came into the room in her wheelchair. On the remaining side lay a wall of flat-panel screens on which the team in Ecuador soon appeared.

'Good to see you all,' Hiram said.

'Looking forward to being enlightened,' Rudi replied.

Hiram nodded. 'I have a feeling you won't be disappointed.'

He pressed a button on the remote and another

flat-screen display lit up. It was divided into three sections. The main part displayed a video image, taken from the Russian bomber's camera system; the second part of the screen displayed an overhead map view; and the third section displayed the bomber's cockpit and instrument panel as seen from a high-mounted camera over the pilots' shoulders. Their helmets and shoulders were partially in view.

'Are you seeing this on your screen?' Hiram asked.

'Yes,' Rudi said.

'Fantastic,' Hiram said. 'The Russians use one recorder to collect all vital information instead of two separate recorders for voice and data like the FAA requires. Their system worked well, but we only have the last twenty minutes of the flight. I think it'll be enough. For your convenience, Max has translated all the voices into English.'

The lights dimmed and the presentation began. The initial image was a gray-scale infrared video. On the right side were various numbers, indicating speed, course and altitude. In the distance, a tiny white dot flared and dimmed while tracking lines indicated it was above the bomber and thirty miles distant.

'Target acquired,' the translated voice said.

'Vehicle speed four thousand one hundred. Engaging scramjets.'

'Did he say *scramjets*?' Emma asked.

'He did,' Hiram replied. 'We double-checked the translation. They're using a different acronym, but the operation is the same. The bomber was powered by supersonic ramjets capable of taking them up to Mach 6.'

As the scramjets came to life, the video image began to shake and buzz. The Mach number climbed and the voices of the pilot, copilot and engineer were almost overridden by the ever-increasing roar of the engines.

The pilot called out the milestones. *'Passing Mach 3 . . . 3.5 . . . Mach 4 . . .'*

The acceleration continued for another minute and then slowed.

'Speed locked in at Mach 5.1.'

The copilot spoke next. *'Surface temperature within tolerance.'*

'He's referring to the outer skin of the aircraft,' Hiram said.

Emma nodded. She was the aviation expert. She understood instinctively. 'At Mach 5, the leading edges of the nose, wings and tail would be suffering tremendous heating. Regular steel would melt. The aircraft skin would have to be made of a special alloy, probably using extensive amounts of titanium.'

'Which explains why the alloy detector and the magnetometers locked onto the wheels and internal parts first,' Joe replied. 'More iron, easier to find.'

'Exactly.'

The video continued to play. *'Course matched,'* the pilot's voice said. *'Releasing controls to the computer.'*

The small dot they were tracking on the cameras grew larger as it moved closer until it became obvious they were looking at the *Nighthawk*. But they weren't catching up to it; they were allowing it to catch up to them.

'At this point, the bomber is in front of and below the *Nighthawk*,' Hiram said. 'Max, display the course lines.'

On a second part of the screen, the satellite view of the South Pacific and the South American coast sharpened. Two icons appeared, one red, one green. Thin lines stretched out behind them.

'The red line is the Russian bomber,' Hiram said. 'The green line is the *Nighthawk*.'

The two lines soon merged, with the Russian bomber slightly ahead of the unmanned spacecraft.

'*Course matched,*' the flight engineer's voice called out. '*Distance two miles and closing.*'

Another voice sounded on the cockpit recorder. '*Signal jamming complete. Vandenberg has been blocked.* Nighthawk is all yours.'

'*Roger that,* Blackjack 2.'

'A second bomber?' Joe asked.

Hiram nodded. 'Approximately a mile ahead of the first.'

On the infrared video, the *Nighthawk* continued to grow larger and move closer. A distance indicator and a series of vertical and horizontal bars appeared on the video feed.

'*Range one thousand feet and closing,*' the copilot called out.

The *Nighthawk* approached steadily, looming ever larger in the video. The camera tracked it moving past the bomber's tail and into a position directly above the Russian aircraft. At thirty-nine hundred miles an hour and ninety-one thousand feet, the two aircraft were now traveling in perfect formation.

The copilot's voice was calm. *'Speed matched. Course steady. We're in position for the capture.'*

'Deploying windbreak,' the pilot said.

A series of small spikes emerged from the back of the Russian bomber. They created a vortex and a low-pressure area across the bomber's spine that drew the *Nighthawk* downward. It dropped slowly, kissing the Russian plane gently. It was immediately trapped by a series of clamps that sprung up from the bomber's fuselage. They grabbed the *Nighthawk*'s wings and locked it in place.

'Contact made. Snares in place,' the copilot said.

'Deploying secondary windbreak,' the pilot announced.

A triangular wedge of metal rose up in front of the captured spacecraft. It deflected the wind around and away from it. A vapor trail streamed from the top of the windbreak, traveling up and over the nose of the delta-wing craft and back. The ride was smooth.

'They grabbed it,' Emma whispered. 'They snatched it right out of the sky.'

'I can't believe there's no turbulence,' Kurt said.

'The atmosphere is so thin at that altitude there isn't any turbulence,' Emma said.

'But they're traveling at four thousand miles an hour,' Rudi pointed out.

'Not in relation to each other,' Emma replied. 'We dock spacecraft in orbit all the time. On TV, it looks like they're barely moving, but in reality they're whipping around the Earth at 17K. In the sixties and seventies, the *Apollo* and *Gemini* pilots eyeballed it. I'm sure these guys have the most advanced computers in the Russian catalog at their disposal.'

'*Docking complete,*' the pilot reported. '*Tell Moscow we have the* Nighthawk.'

The sounds of a celebration could be heard on the tape, and the next few minutes were routine. A call went out to the second bomber. Tests were done, systems were checked and rechecked. All this time, the *Blackjack 1* continued on the same course, traveling at the same incredible speed.

'*Reducing power,*' the pilot said finally. '*Inform Caracas we'll need refueling.*'

'We're not sure if he means Caracas, Venezuela,' Hiram said, 'or if that's a code name for a refueling aircraft.'

'I'll bet on the former,' Rudi said. 'The Russians have plenty of friends where Hugo Chávez used to rule.'

As the aircraft slowed, there was a noticeable drop in the background noise. The speed fell below Mach 4 and then below Mach 3. At Mach 2.5, the bomber began a shallow turn to the north and, for the moment at least, it seemed as if the Russians had pulled off the world's greatest hijacking.

A flicker ran through the video, followed by a garbled communication.

A rhythmic vibration grew up and the aircraft began to shudder. Before long, the cameras were trembling.

'*Inertial dampers failing,*' the copilot said. '*Vibration reaching critical.*'

'*Where is this coming from?*'

'*We're getting a strain on the lockdown bolts,*' the flight engineer called out. '*It's the* Nighthawk; *there's a flutter in the control surfaces.*'

The pilot's next response was unintelligible. He was grunting and breathing hard as he fought the controls.

A call went through the radio. '*Blackjack 2, we have a problem.* Nighthawk *is trying to go active. I repeat, the* Nighthawk *has woken up. Falconer, use the alpha codes. Shut it down.*'

The return call was far calmer. '*Are you certain,* Blackjack 1? *We show no activity. Our board is green. You should not be having any issues.*'

The pilot shouted his response. '*I'm telling you that damned thing is trying to break free. Boost your signal and order it to shut down — now!*'

Whatever *Blackjack 2* did in response, the vibration only grew worse. The sound of alarms filled the cockpit. Warning lights came on all over the board.

'Hydraulics,' Priya said. 'Vertical stabilizer . . . Inertial dampers.'

The pilot's breathing was labored. His words marked by cursing and desperation. On the external video feed, the *Nighthawk* could be seen shaking violently in its locked-down position. Its own flight control surfaces could be seen fluttering. Ailerons moving up and down. Rudder snaking back and forth.

And then it was gone.

In the blink of an eye, the captured aircraft ripped free of its moorings and peeled away, taking a chunk of the bomber's fuselage with it. Hydraulic fluid and white vapor streamed from the gaping hole it left behind.

'*Mayday! Mayday! Mayday!*' the pilot called out. '*We have an emergency situation.*'

Despite his frantic efforts, the plane rolled over slowly and began corkscrewing dizzily toward the ocean. Mercifully, the camera failed a short time later. From that point, only the audio remained, filled with desperate shouts and garbled radio calls, until even the pilots went silent and all that could be heard was the aircraft's computer warning the pilots repeatedly to *Pull up . . . Pull up.* And then suddenly everything stopped.

Utter silence filled both rooms.

'We think they blacked out,' Hiram said.

'Why didn't they eject?' Emma asked.

No one knew the answer.

The Russians might have been their political adversaries and opponents, but the pilots were just men doing their jobs. Men taking a tremendous gamble, and almost pulling it off, before paying with their lives.

'You can't help but admire their guts,' Kurt said, breaking the silence. 'If it wasn't our plane they were trying to steal, I'd be sitting here wishing they'd succeeded.'

Everyone around him nodded.

'Any idea what went wrong?' Emma asked.

Hiram replied. 'As long as the Russian bomber continued on the *Nighthawk*'s original course, all went well. As soon as the pilot turned away from that course, the *Nighthawk* went active again, attempting to steer itself back onto the initial heading. That started the vibration which led to separation and the crash.'

'Why would it do that?' Kurt asked.

'We think the Russians hacked the navigation system,' Hiram replied. 'They reprogrammed it to head south and rendezvous with the bomber, but they forgot to shut the inertial navigation system off before they commenced the turn to the north.'

'*Alpha code* is the NSA term for a reboot command. The equivalent of hitting the *Ctrl–Alt–Delete* buttons on your computer. It's supposed to break everything and reset the operating system.'

'Any idea what they meant when they called out to the *Falconer*?'

Emma hesitated for a moment and then spoke. 'I'm not sure,' she admitted, 'but several years ago we received intel suggesting that the NSA's space program had been penetrated. Either by a mole working at Vandenberg or through a Trojan horse computer program. There was no way to confirm the information and there were few details in the lead itself. Just a suggestion that vast amounts of data were being passed on to either the Chinese or the Russians. Other than that, we had only the code name.'

'Falconer,' Rudi said, 'interesting choice. A falconer trains raptors to fly free and then return to him.'

'The concept was lost on no one,' Emma assured him, 'as that's exactly what we were trying to do with the *Nighthawk*. Even so, a thorough investigation revealed no evidence that the agency had been compromised. The idea was written off as a red herring. You'd be surprised how much bad and false information is passed along. Most of it deliberately. We do it, too. All part of the game.'

'Something tells me your boss might want to reopen the investigation,' Rudi said.

'Agreed.'

Kurt glanced at the dark screen and then back at Emma. 'Well, whoever he was, he failed. The real question is, why? Everything appeared to be firmly in hand.'

'Maybe a stray signal got through from Vandenberg?' Joe suggested.

'We don't think so,' Hiram replied. 'They were using the second bomber as a mobile transmitter, blasting a high-powered signal at the *Nighthawk* from close range. A setup like that would effectively drown out anything the NSA tried to send through.'

Emma agreed. 'Assuming the time on their clock was accurate, we'd already lost total contact with the vehicle when they caught it. It wasn't our doing. It must have been the autonomous programming. Not that it matters at this point.' She looked Kurt's way. 'For whatever it's worth, you were right about one thing: the NSA and Vandenberg have been compromised. If the Russians have the alpha codes, they have everything.'

'Not everything,' Kurt reminded her, before turning back to Hiram. 'Any idea where the *Nighthawk* went after this?'

'We're working on that now,' he replied. 'But it's difficult to say for sure. The intercept changes all the calculations. The Russians gave it a nine minute piggyback ride at Mach 5, keeping it at full speed and above ninety thousand feet when it was supposed to be slowing and descending. That helpful little boost added seven hundred miles to the maximum glide path. Complicating matters are several video frames where the *Nighthawk* appears to be turning and shedding tiles, suggesting it was damaged as it broke free. All of that could affect the course, speed and glide path.'

'I'm sure you have something,' Kurt prodded.

Hiram nodded. 'Max, show us the new course probability cone.'

An image appeared on the screen. This time, the Ecuadorian coast was much larger and closer. A widening yellow cone curved toward it, crossing southern Ecuador and continuing inland over the mountains and jungles of Peru.

'It could be anywhere in that area,' Hiram said. 'Or any other area if the flight controls were damaged.'

'So we *are* back to square one,' Emma said.

'Not quite,' Priya said. She wheeled over to a keyboard and tapped away on it for a few seconds. 'We have this. It's a video that was released on Peruvian television.'

The recording played for all to see. Shot by an amateur, it went in and out of focus but captured a glowing object crossing the night sky like a fireball. There was some shouting in the background and then the object disappeared beyond the top of a nearby hill.

The camera panned around, briefly capturing the edge of a solar panel and a pile of jumbled stones that looked like the ruins of a Neolithic building. A voice spoke off-camera. *'A sign from the gods,'* it said in accented English. *'The end must be near.'*

A few grins broke out among the NUMA staff, but Emma's lips remained tightly pursed. 'Who filmed this video?' she asked. 'And where?'

'According to the television network, it was taken by a Peruvian archaeologist named Urco. He's currently working in the Andes on a dig connected to the Chachapoya, the Cloud People of Peru.'

'Is there any way to authenticate it?' Kurt asked.

'No,' Priya said. 'It was shown a few hours ago. But it was allegedly filmed just before dawn on the morning of the *Nighthawk*'s disappearance. We've double-checked. The time frame is right and the location is within the *Nighthawk*'s newly extended glide path.'

Rudi spoke next. 'Any chance the video is a hoax?'

'A hoax of what?' Emma said. 'No one in the outside world knows the plane is missing.'

Priya added to that thought. 'If you notice, the man in the video doesn't claim he's seen a spacecraft. The text accompanying the video calls it a *meteor sighting*.'

'Can you calculate altitude and speed from the video?' Kurt asked.

'Not without more information,' Hiram said. 'Even if we could get a rough estimate, it wouldn't do any good without a precise direction.'

Joe chimed in. 'If we knew where he was standing and the exact location of that cliff dwelling behind him, we could get an accurate directional fix.'

Kurt nodded, glanced around the room and then

asked the question on everyone's mind: 'Do we have any other leads?'

Both rooms held silent.

'Then it's agreed,' Kurt said. 'Let the Russians and Chinese search the Pacific. We'll go inland and see if this archaeologist can point us in the right direction.'

'I say we move with all possible speed,' Emma added. 'We're not the only ones with access to Peruvian TV.'

22

Daiyu stood in the control room of the Chinese trawler. The swells had vanished and the sea was as dark as pitch. Everything quiet and still. Too quiet for her. Unnerving.

For three days, they'd kept the American vessel *Catalina* under surveillance. Over the last twenty-four hours, it appeared as if the crew of that ship had begun search-and-recovery operations. Daiyu had been planning an underwater reconnaissance mission to see what they'd found when the Ministry called it off.

General Zhang appeared on a video screen. 'The recovery effort of NUMA vessel *Catalina* has been determined to be a diversion.'

'So we've been wasting our time,' Daiyu said. There was an edge to her voice; it was always there, even speaking to a superior like Zhang. It was half the reason she'd been posted to such a backwater place.

'So it would appear,' Zhang replied. 'But that's not the only news. We have new information that suggests the *Nighthawk* escaped capture by the Russian bomber and did not come down at sea. A possible sighting has been reported over the mountains of Peru.'

'So our Russian friends failed to do their part,' she replied. 'I'm not surprised. You cannot trust a bear to dance with a sparrow.'

'Nor can you trust it to share its meal with you,' Zhang added. 'This is a blessing in disguise. Had the Russians succeeded, they would have taken the American aircraft home with them and given us as little as possible. Now we have a chance to take it all.'

Daiyu nodded. 'As it should have been from the start.'

She well knew that General Zhang felt the same way, though he would never say it. A slight curl of his lip was all she received. 'A helicopter is being sent,' he said. 'It'll be on deck within an hour. Be ready.'

'We shall,' she replied.

'Do not fail your country,' Zhang said and signed off.

Jian stood at her side. Where Daiyu was excited, he appeared solemn, apprehensive. 'Is something wrong?'

'The Americans will not be easy to eliminate,' he said. 'Our men had the advantage of surprise in Guayaquil, but they still failed. By the time we make contact, the Americans will be on guard.'

'There are methods beyond brute force,' she said. 'If we can't take them by direct action, we'll set a trap. All targets are susceptible to one form or another. If they're ready to run at the slightest sign of us, then we'll let them run headlong into disaster.'

23

Guided missile cruiser Varyag

The storm had passed. Or, rather, the Russian cruiser *Varyag* and salvage vessels accompanying it had passed through the worst of the weather. No one was happier about the sea change than Constantin Davidov. For the first time in days, he was sitting to a full breakfast without worrying that it would come back up.

Rear Admiral Borozdin sat across from him, his eggs smothered in hollandaise sauce. It kept the powdered taste down and passed for a delicacy in the Soviet Navy.

'You look different today,' Borozdin said between forkfuls of egg. 'I can't quite put my finger on it.'

'Yes you can,' Davidov said. 'I'm not three shades of green.'

Borozdin laughed. 'Yes, of course, that's it.'

A knock at the Admiral's door brought a courier. 'Captain Tovarich reporting on the satellite link,' the courier said.

'Have it patched through to us in here,' Davidov suggested.

Borozdin nodded to the courier and moments later they were listening to Tovarich.

Though his voice sounded tinny and distant, the

signal was clear enough to reveal disappointment. 'Recovery operations are complete,' Tovarich explained. 'We've pumped out the cargo bay and combed through the wreckage. Unfortunately, there's no sign of the American craft.'

'How can that be?' Davidov asked. *'Blackjack 1* reported the *Nighthawk* as captured and locked in long before the emergency.'

'I'm aware of that,' Tovarich said. 'But a preliminary examination of the wreckage reveals that the lockdown bolts have been sheared clean through. The *Nighthawk* must have broken free as the bomber lost control.'

Davidov sat back in frustration. Things were not going according to plan. When he'd dissolved the partnership with China and left Beijing, he'd done it thinking he had a bird in hand. At that moment, he'd been certain that Russia – and Russia alone – knew the whereabouts of the American craft because only Russia knew where the bomber had gone down.

'I'm afraid there's something else,' Tovarich added.

Davidov looked up. 'More bad news?'

'Of a sort,' Tovarich said. 'During the recovery operation, we encountered an American NUMA team in a small submersible. They seem to have arrived and surveyed the site just before we did. Their presence not only compromised the secrecy of this vessel but the airborne mission itself.'

'How so?'

'We have reason to believe they took *Blackjack 1*'s flight data recorder. We've searched the wreckage and the surrounding area. Despite detecting a signal when we first arrived, it's nowhere to be found. The only logical explanation is that the Americans have it.'

'NUMA,' Davidov grumbled. This wasn't the first time the American nautical organization had thwarted a Russian effort.

Across from him, Admiral Borozdin grew tense. 'If the Americans have the black box, they won't have any problem piecing together the entire mission. They'll know we tried to hijack their craft out of midair.'

Davidov waved off the concern. 'It's of little consequence. They can't reveal or complain about our actions without exposing their own secrets. The bigger issue – the only issue – is what happened to the spacecraft.'

The submarine captain assumed the question was for him. 'I have no answers, at this point.'

'Continue the search,' Davidov ordered. 'Follow the last known course. I want updates every hour.'

Tovarich signed off, and Davidov found he'd lost his appetite. His silver fork rattled against the Admiral's fine china as he put it down. 'We had it,' he said. 'We had it in our hands.'

Borozdin put his own knife and fork down and took a drink of water. 'Even if the *Nighthawk* broke free, it should have come down nearby.'

'Not necessarily,' Davidov said. 'Considering the speed and altitude at which they were traveling, it could literally be anywhere.'

Borozdin nodded. 'What orders did *Blackjack 2* have?'

'Its primary job was to override the signal from Vandenberg,' Davidov said.

'And in the event something went wrong?'

'To track the *Nighthawk* as long as possible and report final course, altitude and speed.'

'Do you have any reason to think they did otherwise?'

Davidov bristled. 'I have no reason to think anything, Sergei. We never heard from them again.'

'They were Russian officers,' Borozdin said. 'Highly trained. No doubt handpicked for their proficiency, loyalty and bravery. Unless you sent cadets up on your most secret of missions, I think we can assume they followed orders as long as possible. Right to the end.'

Davidov settled back. 'Fine. I agree. What good does it do us? We still don't know where they are.'

'We know where they aren't,' Borozdin noted. 'They're not in the sea.'

Davidov froze. For the first time, he realized Borozdin was not just toying with him. 'How can you be so sure?'

'Because the Americans would be pulling them out of the water already.'

'I think you overestimate – '

This time, Borozdin cut him off. 'We are loath to admit it, but their technology is far superior to ours.'

'Sergei, it doesn't help – '

Borozdin would not be interrupted. 'I've been thinking about this for a while,' he continued. 'I don't know how the Americans found *Blackjack 1* so quickly, but they did. They heard it, or saw it, or found it with a drone or with remote sonar or some other method we know nothing about. Whatever the case, they were on-site and picking the bones of our dead before we could get there, and we knew *exactly* where the plane had gone down. But now they're searching grids again. Back and forth, east and west. If *Blackjack 2* hit the water, they would have found it just as easily as they found *Blackjack 1*. But they haven't found it, which tells me it didn't come down in the ocean.'

Davidov considered this. 'So you think it made landfall. How does that help us?'

'If *Blackjack 2* was following the *Nighthawk* as ordered and then crashed on dry land, it stands to reason that the *Nighthawk* made landfall.'

It was a leap, but there was logic to it.

'And if we can find the wreckage of *Blackjack 2*,' Borozdin continued, 'even if it's burned to a cinder in the jungle somewhere, it will still be an arrow pointing us in the direction of the *Nighthawk*.'

Davidov warmed to the idea, in part because it was all they had. 'We need satellite data and we need it immediately.'

24

A long, pointed cone stuck out horizontally from beneath a tarp. It stood a dozen feet off the ground and was unmistakably the nose of a high-speed aircraft. Streaks of blackened oxidation swept back from the tip that suggested it had been through a fire, but the soot-colored stripes were caused by friction with the air and the heat of traveling at five times the speed of sound.

Several men with reddish brown skin hauled lines connected to the tarp and pulled it forward until it covered the entire aircraft.

'Stake that down,' someone yelled. 'I'll not have another windstorm pulling it free.'

While the first group of workers pulled the tarp taut, a second group moved into place with sledgehammers. With repeated blows, they pounded long spikes deep into the ground. When they'd finished, the tie-down rings at the edge of the tarp were hooked to the spikes and locked down.

As the men worked in the chilled mountain air, white vapors streamed from their mouths and noses. They wore colorful coats of alpaca wool, while the man who supervised them was dressed in modern black garb and wore a balaclava over his face.

'Two more spikes here,' he said.

As the section he'd pointed to was secured, another man came up to him. He had his long sleeves pushed up to the elbows, exposing an old scar that ran the length of his forearm. 'We've doubled the number of stakes,' he said. 'And the men are cutting more branches to lay across it.'

'Have them cut slits in the tarp as well,' the man wearing the balaclava said. 'Up high.'

'But won't that expose —'

'It will keep the tarp from lifting. Aerodynamics. Trust me, my friend. This is my business.'

The second man nodded. 'Do you think we've been noticed?'

'I checked the satellite tables,' the man in the balaclava said. 'Fortunately, we're in a remote part of the mountains. No one is flying spy satellites over this area. Not yet, at least. But, we can expect that to change soon. Another exposure could ruin everything.'

'But you want them to find the bomber?' the second man said, unsure and trying to follow his master's lead.

'Oh, yes. But on our schedule, not theirs.'

The man with the scar on his arm nodded and turned away, walking toward the forest. He made a whirling motion with his hand and chainsaws roared as the men began cutting down branches and felling entire trees, all of which would be dragged forward and used to disguise the landed treasure.

The man in the balaclava was pleased. With the aircraft covered again and the camouflage work progressing, he ducked under the edge of the tarp and walked beneath the bomber's sharply swept wing. He passed the squared-off engine pods and continued forward beneath the fuselage, careful not to bump any of the antennas or aerodynamic probes that stuck out beneath the plane. With its sharp edges and armored exterior, the aircraft seemed to him like a sleeping dragon. One that would wake and breathe fire soon enough.

He arrived at a ladder that dropped from the center of the fuselage just behind the nose gear. He climbed it slowly, arriving in the darkened crew compartment. Another of his men was inside. He wore fur-lined boots and a colorful poncho over his shoulders.

'What about them?' the man asked in his native tongue. 'Another night like the last and they'll freeze to death.'

He was referring to the Russian pilots, bound and gagged and sitting on the floor of the aircraft. Three nights in the frigid plane without food or much to drink had taken most of the fight out of them. A swath of dried and frozen blood beside them where another crewman's throat had been cut served as a warning not to argue.

'They bring disease,' the man wearing the balaclava said. 'But we'll need them when the time comes. Take them to the cave.'

The man in the poncho whistled down to several others and the prisoners were soon being taken down the ladder and hauled away.

With the tarp covering the aircraft, it was dark in the cockpit, but it would be darker for the prisoners in their cave. And darker still for the world to come.

'Keep everyone on alert,' the man in the balaclava replied. 'Things will happen at a rapid pace now. The lure has been set. The trap will not remain empty for long.'

25

Ecuador

They parted ways at the airport — Rudi boarding a flight for Washington to put out a growing series of political brush fires, Kurt and Emma boarding the NUMA Gulfstream for a ninety-minute flight to Cajamarca, Peru, where they would meet up with Paul and Gamay.

Joe would follow in the Erickson Air-Crane, but the helicopter's lumbering pace and the need to stop for fuel along the way meant it would be nine hours before the Air-Crane reached Cajamarca. It was a long delay, but if they were lucky enough to find the *Nighthawk* – or major pieces of it – they'd need some way to haul it out of the jungle or off the mountains.

Shortly after takeoff, Emma used the encrypted sat-ellite linkup to contact Steve Gowdy and give him a status update.

The NSA chief was blunt from the word go. 'So, what was all that business with the fruit bowl?'

'Complimentary gift,' Kurt said. 'We send one out to all the VIPs.'

'You're not helping,' Emma said.

Kurt put up a hand and remained quiet for the rest

of the call while Emma explained their new theory and vouched for Kurt's belief that the NSA had a leak.

On-screen, Gowdy's eyes narrowed, but instead of anger or defensive bluster, he said simply, 'Falconer. I thought we'd determined that to be an unfounded rumor.'

'Listen to the tapes,' Emma suggested. 'As they say, dead men tell no lies.'

Gowdy nodded. 'I'll start an immediate investigation. But if there is a mole in here somewhere, then you'd better be careful. Your move to Cajamarca might be front-page news already.'

'We haven't reported it to anyone but you,' Emma replied. 'But we'll keep our eyes open.'

'You're going to need more than that. I'm sending Hurns and Rodriguez back down to help you out. Don't brush them off this time.'

Emma shook her head. 'No deal,' she said. 'If the Falconer is real and has a contact inside the NSA, it could be anyone. Even one of them, for all we know.'

'They're field agents,' Gowdy said. 'They have no access to Vandenberg. They weren't even on the project until after the *Nighthawk* went missing. They're clean, I promise you.'

Emma sighed and looked at Kurt. He shrugged. With a little luck, they'd have the *Nighthawk* in hand by the time the two agents arrived.

'I still don't like it,' Emma said.

'And I don't care,' Gowdy said. 'They can stand by

in Cajamarca in case you need them, but I'm sending them.'

She couldn't argue with that. 'Fine. Anything else?'

'Just be quick about this,' Gowdy said. 'We're running out of time.'

Kurt saw a look pass between the two of them. Even on a video screen, even from five thousand miles away, it was obvious and intimate – the acknowledgment of something unsaid.

Without another word, Gowdy signed off.

As the screen faded to black, Emma sat quietly.

Kurt looked on. It was now obvious to him that she was concealing something – probably on direct orders from Gowdy – but, as the saying went, a lie is a lie is a lie. And, in this business, the lack of information tended to get people killed, people like Kurt and Joe.

They touched down in Cajamarca thirty minutes later and Kurt stepped from the plane into the brisk mountain air. Cajamarca sat at nearly seven thousand feet. This time of year, the midday temperatures hovered in the fifties. Quite a change from the steamy subtropical heat of Guayaquil. It was also overcast and, as any skier could attest, the difference between clouds and sunshine at high elevations was far more pronounced than at sea level.

Pulling a black sweater over his head, Kurt moved down the stairs and signed a rental car agreement for a burnt-orange four-wheel drive Range Rover Sport. It sat on the ramp beside the plane, where it would be easy to load up. As Emma swept the vehicle for bugs, Kurt walked inside the small terminal, where he spied a pair of friendly faces.

Paul and Gamay Trout had been airlifted in from the *Catalina* and then flown up commercial, arriving shortly before the NUMA jet.

'Great to see you guys,' Kurt said, giving both of them warm hugs.

'Glad to be back on the A-team,' Paul said. 'Not that it wasn't fun dumping millions of dollars of equipment over the side of the ship, but we're looking forward to being used as something other than a distraction.'

'Shall we go meet your new friend?' Gamay asked, shouldering her backpack.

'Not yet,' Kurt said. 'I have a change of assignment for you.'

The look of suspicion appeared in practiced unison. Gamay dropped her pack. 'What is it now? Shopping for alpaca sweaters?'

'I need you to do some research,' Kurt said. 'Find out everything you can about the *Nighthawk*, and I don't mean the surface-level stuff. They're hiding something from us, something big.'

'What makes you think that?' Gamay asked. 'Other than your general distrust of the NSA.'

'For one thing, they seem on the verge of panic,' he replied. 'It's felt like that to me right from the start. Losing the *Nighthawk* would be bad, but even at its worst all that would do is give whoever found it technologies they're probably already trying to develop.'

'It is the most advanced aircraft in the world,' Paul reminded him.

'*Was,*' Kurt corrected. 'The thing has been floating around up in space for three years. And they didn't design and build it in a day. At best, it's five or six years old. The plans were probably drawn up a decade ago. Even if the Russians or the Chinese found it in one perfect piece, they'd still have to take it apart, reverse-engineer every component and then build the factories and facilities to duplicate what we already possess. What we possessed years ago. By then, we'll be on to the next technological leap.'

Paul nodded. 'Like stealing a used car and watching the owner get a new model to replace it.'

'Couldn't have said it better myself,' Kurt said.

'It's still a big loss,' Gamay pointed out.

'If you saw their faces, you'd think it was the end of the world.'

Gamay nodded. Paul did the same.

'And it's not just our friends at the NSA; the Chinese and the Russians have gone over the top as well.'

'An opportunity comes up to get your hands on the adversaries' stuff, you take it,' Paul said. 'We always have; can't blame them for that.'

'I don't,' Kurt said. 'But it's not done like this. There are unwritten rules to the game. Boundaries that stop it from turning into outright war. None of those seem to be in effect here. The Chinese tried to kill us before we got to square one and the Russians tried to torpedo us twice. The second time, on the surface for everyone to see.'

'So the stakes are higher than they appear,' Paul said.

'Which is interesting, considering how high they seemed to begin with,' Gamay said.

Kurt nodded. 'And we're the only ones in the dark. That needs to change. I want to know what they're hiding. And I want to know as soon as possible. I need you to find out what you can by linking up with Hiram and Priya on the satellite. I'm sure they can dig something up.'

'And then what?' Paul asked.

Kurt checked his watch; it was a long drive to the archaeological site. 'We'll be out of satellite coverage on the way up the mountain,' Kurt said, 'but we should have a signal by the time we get there. That gives you four hours.'

'Four hours to do the impossible,' Gamay said.

Kurt was already on his way back out of the terminal. 'It's more time than I usually give you.'

'That doesn't make it okay,' Gamay called out.

Kurt pushed through the door and let it close behind him, crossing to the Range Rover and climbing into the driver's seat.

Emma was in the passenger seat. 'Aren't your friends joining us?'

'I need them to look into something,' Kurt said. 'They'll fly up with Joe, once he arrives.'

'So, it's just the two of us on a romantic drive in the country,' she said with a grin.

Kurt smiled and turned the key. The engine came to

life instantly, the finely tuned machine a symphony to his ears. 'Hope you brought a picnic basket.'

'Of a sort,' she said, opening the lid of a small plastic case.

Kurt peered inside. He saw a night vision scope, a black 9mm pistol and a belt with several spare magazines. Underneath, he saw a survival knife and several small demolition charges.

'You forgot the wine,' he said.

'That's your job,' she joked.

Kurt laughed. He might not have brought wine, but the back of the Range Rover was filled with hiking equipment and tackle, if they needed it. In addition, he'd brought his own weapon: a Heckler & Koch HK45. The weapon was a lightweight tactical .45 caliber pistol; it had a ten-round capacity, a mini-flashlight on the lower rail and tritium sights.

He had brought three spare magazines, each loaded with a separate type of ammunition. The first carried soft-tipped hollow-points; the second carried a mix of standard shells and minitracers, specially fabricated by a gunsmith Kurt knew. The third magazine held solid steel slugs coated with a thin layer of titanium and propelled by a more powerful blend of gunpowder; they traveled at higher velocity, and the titanium jacket kept them together at impact.

Kurt had never used them but was told they could punch through an inch of armor plating or two inches of regular steel. He was also warned that the pistol kicked like a mule when fired. He hoped he wouldn't have to find out, but they'd already been attacked twice and he wasn't interested in going a third round without punching back.

He dropped the transmission into drive and pulled away from the aircraft.

'So what's with the explosives?' he asked, getting his bearings and looking for a spot to exit the ramp.

She closed the lid and put the box away. 'If we find the *Nighthawk* and can't haul it out of the jungle, I have orders to blow the electronics package and the propulsion system.'

It made sense. But he took everything she said with a grain of salt now. From the size of the charges, he estimated each to be the rough equivalent of a grenade. 'Those should do the trick,' he said, pulling through the gate. 'Next stop, La Jalca and the Fortress in the Clouds.'

Daiyu stood on a low hill watching the burnt-orange SUV as it left the airport. The color and the metallic gloss made it easy to spot, especially against the gray road and the dusty mountains.

She tracked the vehicle as it passed through the airport's main gate and moved east. When it shifted into the right-hand lane and moved onto the mountain road, she lowered her binoculars and picked up a radio.

'Target moving,' she said, speaking into the radio. 'Route 6A, as expected. We'll follow at a distance. Be ready at the intercept point.'

'Affirmative,' a voice replied.

She clipped the radio to her belt and walked to a white Audi A8. Jian sat at the wheel, his broad shoulders filling the cockpit of the sleek car.

She climbed in the passenger's side, slammed the door and nodded. 'Go.'

26

The route from Cajamarca wound its way eastward, climbing higher into the mountains as it went. Paved at first, the road surface changed to a combination of gravel and hard-packed clay after an hour of driving. As the footing worsened, Kurt dialed back the speed. They continued to climb, curving around the switchbacks, while ducking in and out of patchy fog.

The higher they went, the cooler it got. Passing eight thousand feet, they found spitting rain. At nine thousand feet, they were in the clouds. At ninety-five hundred, they finally broke out into the sunlight.

A wide valley appeared on the left, its floor a thousand feet below. Successive layers of jagged mountains rose up behind it. The visibility was twenty miles or more.

'Welcome to the Andes,' Kurt said.

From this point on, the road clung to the shoulder of the mountains. It grew narrower out of necessity and, in certain spots, had been cut right into the cliffside, requiring the cars to drive beneath an overhang of solid rock.

While the terrain to the right-hand side changed often, the view to the left was constant, nothing but a sheer drop.

'They might have splurged on a guardrail,' Emma said.

'And ruin the view?' Kurt replied, laughing.

Instead of a barrier, the road sported a low curb, painted in alternating blocks of black and white. Not only wouldn't it stop anything larger than a model car, hitting it would be like catching one's foot on a tree root – more likely to tip a vehicle over the edge.

'Just be glad this isn't an English colony,' Kurt added. 'Otherwise, we'd be driving on that side.'

The mountain bulged outward and the road bent out around its waist, offering a view back in the direction they'd come. They were on the leeward side now and the slopes were tawny brown and spotted with patchy scrub brush and a smattering of gray rock. All of it tied together by the zigzagging ribbon of route 6A.

Kurt stole a quick glance. Emma shifted in her seat and took it all in.

'How much traffic do you think this road gets?' she asked casually.

'Not much,' he said. 'We've passed two trucks and an old Jeep in the last hour. Why?'

'I count three cars following us,' she said. 'Two black, one white. By the dust they're kicking up, I'd say they're moving a lot faster than they should be.'

Kurt set his jaw. 'I was hoping we'd left all that behind.'

Emma reached into the 'picnic basket' at her feet. She pulled out the 9mm Beretta, made sure it was loaded and switched the safety off.

Kurt drove faster, but there wasn't a turnoff until they hit the plateau. If the cars behind them proved to be trouble, they'd have to deal with them here and now.

It took several minutes but the trio of vehicles finally appeared in the rearview mirror. Between the vibration from the road and the dust streaming out behind them, it was a blurred image, but it was all Kurt needed. The two black cars were staggered up front in an attacking formation, the white car trailing a short distance behind. All of them charging up the hill in a cloud of dust.

'Here they come.'

Emma slipped out of her seat belt and lowered her window. Holding the Beretta on her lap, she poked her head outside and risked a look. She could see little inside the dark interiors, but when a man popped out through the side window, she knew what was about to happen.

He brought a submachine gun up and opened fire. Emma ducked back into the Rover as a series of tiny explosions raced along the dusty slope to the right. The first shots went wide, but a second burst clipped the driver's side-view mirror and shattered it. 'So much for our relaxing drive in the country.'

Kurt mashed the pedal to the floor. The super-charged engine answered and the Range Rover surged ahead.

For a moment, it seemed they might leave their enemies behind, but the cars following them were also high-performance models. They had the horses to answer and they quickly closed the gap.

Kurt crouched low on the wheel as another spread of bullets punched angry holes in the sheet metal. One blasted out the tail-light, while another hit the rear window, rendering it a mess of cracks and fissures that was impossible to see through.

Emma leaned out the window to return fire. She hit the lead BMW with several shots, but it drifted to Kurt's side and the back of the Rover blocked it from her view.

She turned in her seat and aimed for the back window. 'Cover your ears.'

There was no hope of that, but Kurt appreciated the warning. She opened fire, blasting out the remnants of the back window with her first shot and emptying the rest of the magazine into the nearest chase car. It dropped back for a moment but soon came on again.

Kurt pulled the .45 out of his shoulder holster and handed it to her. 'Try this.'

Emma took it and aimed. The first shot almost knocked her out of her seat. She righted herself and fired three more times.

The armor-piercing shells found their mark. Steam and smoke blasted from the punctured engine block of the BMW as its radiator exploded. The car swerved toward the cliff and then back the other way, going up the slope at an angle, rolling over onto its roof and then sliding back onto the road and coming to a stop just short of the cliff's edge.

The other cars passed and left it behind.

'I like this,' Emma shouted over the noise. 'Can I keep it?'

'Get rid of the two cars and it's yours.'

Emma climbed between the seats and into the back for a better spot to shoot from while Kurt did his best to present an elusive target. He kept the gas pedal pinned to the floor as long as possible, thundering toward each turn and then tapping the brakes before cutting the wheel and hitting the gas again.

On one inside turn, they banged an overhanging rock. It put a huge downward dent in the roof. A sharp outside turn came up quicker than Kurt had expected. As Kurt hit the brakes, the Rover started skidding.

Kurt released his tight grip on the steering wheel and stepped back on the gas. He'd raced in off-road rallies both in cars and on dirt bikes; he knew that getting through a turn like this required power to the wheels.

They hugged the edge, sliding and drifting and threatening to tip. From Kurt's position, all he could see was the drop, not an inch of road left. As if they'd gone over the edge and were already airborne. And then the heavy tread bit into the road once more, the tires spat dirt and the Rover surged back to the inside of the curve.

'That was close,' he shouted. 'Almost found out if man was truly meant to fly.'

Emma didn't reply. It was so loud inside the Rover that she didn't hear him. She was perched on the backseat, holding the .45 in a police grip with two hands.

The cars had fallen back as they refused to take the turns at full speed. But instead of closing in straightaway as they had before, they held their distance this time.

Emma watched the passenger emerge through the sunroof of the lead car, the upper half of his body visible. He brought out a long weapon with a pointed end.

'Go faster,' she called out.

'Can't go much faster,' he replied.

'Go faster, Kurt! They have an RPG.'

In the white Audi, Daiyu could see the Americans accelerating and weaving left and right, trying to present a difficult target. 'That's it,' she urged under her breath. 'Speed up.'

She pressed a button on the headset she wore. 'Push them,' she urged. 'Push them harder.'

'We have no shot,' one member of the kill squad called back.

'It doesn't matter,' Daiyu replied. 'Push them to the limit. We're almost there.'

The car ahead of them accelerated and Daiyu switched channels. 'Thirty seconds,' she said. 'Be ready to detonate.'

'Ready,' another voice replied.

'Blow the bridge as soon as they come out of the tunnel.'

Up ahead, Kurt was almost shocked to still be alive. Unfortunately, a long, straight tunnel loomed in front of them where this section of road had been carved into the side of the mountain. The overhanging rock closed down on the left and the road soon became dim and dark.

'They're coming again,' Emma said as the lead car began to close the gap.

'I see that,' Kurt said.

'The road is getting narrower.'

'I see that, too.'

Emma put the empty .45 down and grabbed her Beretta, ejecting the empty magazine and reloading. Kurt kept the pedal down as they roared through the tunnel. The growl of the engines reverberated off the walls. Headlights blazed behind them, daylight appeared in the distance. At any second, Emma expected to see the flare of the rocket coming their way.

But they raced out into the sunlight again still in one piece. The wall to their right softened into a hilly slope and the road angled downward toward an iron bridge that crossed a narrow chasm and looked as if it had been built in the forties or fifties. As they charged toward it, a series of detonations erupted along the bridge. Two larger blasts followed, one at each end.

Iron bent, rivets exploded and the bridge buckled and fell, collapsing in on itself and dropping into the depths of the gorge.

Traveling slightly downhill, on loose footing, at high speed, Kurt knew instantly that they couldn't stop in time.

He jammed his foot on the brake pedal, bled off half

the speed and then turned up the embankment, skidding, bouncing and nearly flipping the Range Rover in the process.

Traveling uphill, the Rover slowed rapidly and Kurt regained control. What had been a desperate maneuver to avoid a thousand-foot swan dive now became a possible way out.

He dropped the transmission into a lower gear and kept climbing. With a deft touch, he turned away from the gorge and traversed the slope at an angle. The four-wheel drive kept them moving, spinning the wheels in the soft gravel, bouncing them over the rocks and powering through the thorny bushes that clung to the incline.

Emma held on in the backseat. They were climbing so sharply that it felt like she would slide out the back. But the engine of the Rover was in the front, which kept the weight forward, and every time Kurt felt the front wheels lifting, he pulled off the gas for just a second.

They were still climbing the hill when their pursuers came out of the tunnel at a much slower pace. Emma watched as they stopped in the middle of the road, looking up at their escaping prey.

At first, they appeared confused, and the man holding the rocket-propelled grenade launcher steadied himself and aimed, leaning against the back edge of the sunroof.

Emma was faster, raising the Beretta and raining a hail of bullets down on them. She emptied the entire magazine, peppering both cars with multiple shots and hitting the rocket man in the shoulder.

He twisted with the impact and squeezed the trigger.

The RPG fired. Its smoke trail stretched upward across the terrain, drawing a line from the road below directly across the top of the Range Rover and into the ridge above them. It detonated amid a wall of weathered rock.

The mountain shook and a long section of the ridge broke loose and came tumbling toward them.

Kurt turned the wheel, angling to the right and fighting against gravity. He couldn't turn any sharper without rolling the vehicle, but even that would be better than being crushed in a landslide.

Fist-sized rocks bounced their way, pounding the doors and smashing the windshield. A wave of dust engulfed them. They pulled clear just as half the mountainside roared past behind them.

Daiyu stared upward from the passenger seat of the white Audi as man-made thunder echoed through the canyon. When the smoke from the explosion cleared, she spotted movement, but it wasn't the American Rover tumbling and burning, it was the mountain itself. With gathering speed, a large mass of gravel and heavy rock was surging their way.

'Move!' she shouted.

Jian slammed the car into reverse, looked over his shoulder. The transmission whined as the car sped backward. A hail of gravel pinged off their hood as they rushed into the tunnel.

The BMW driver reacted too slowly. Instead of backing up, he tried to turn, and his car had just begun moving when the main body of the avalanche thundered across the road, a tsunami of stone and sand. It hit with surprising speed, launching the car off the cliff like a child's toy swept angrily from a table.

The landslide continued for another few minutes. The large rocks settled first, but the sand and gravel continued to pour down, filling the entrance to the tunnel, until dust choked the air and all that could be seen was a hazy beam of light coming from the Audi's front end.

High above, Kurt and Emma had skirted the landslide, avoiding the worst of the damage. They picked their way upward toward the next section of the road, surging onto it with a final effort.

'I didn't think we were going to survive that,' Emma announced.

Stabilized on flat ground once again, Kurt stopped to look back. 'Never entered my mind.'

'Think that's the end of them?'

Looking down the embankment, he saw nothing but an impenetrable cloud of dust. 'No idea,' he said. 'Doesn't matter which way; even if they're gone, we'll have others to deal with soon enough.'

As Emma returned to the front seat, Kurt thumped

the shattered windshield with his palm. It fell away, peeling off the A-pillars like matted paper. Able to see clearly now, he donned a pair of sunglasses, put the Rover in gear and continued on.

They were twenty miles from La Jalca and every minute counted.

27

Kurt drove the rest of the way at a reduced speed because the suspension had been damaged in the climb and was groaning with every mile. An hour later, they were nearing the ruins.

'This is the turn,' Emma said.

Kurt pulled off the road. The new track was little more than two ruts in the ground, with a long furrow of stray grass standing knee-high between them. It took them into a narrowing valley past small herds of grazing animals and terraced fields abundant with crops. Both sights suggested a large community nearby, though Kurt saw no houses.

'I thought this was an archaeological site,' he said.

Emma nodded. 'As did I. Seems more like a working farm.'

As they continued into the valley, the ridges and peaks grew higher and the gorge became narrower. When an encampment of tents appeared in the distance, Kurt pulled over and parked.

'I suggest we walk from here,' he said. 'I don't really want to start off by explaining how our vehicle ended up like this.'

Emma laughed. 'You might want to practice that speech; you still have to turn this thing in.'

They climbed out of the battered Rover, pulled backpacks over their shoulders and began a short hike.

On foot, without the roofline of the SUV interfering, the view was spectacular. The excavation was taking place in the closed end of a box canyon. Three high peaks dominated the landscape, towering above the ridgeline around them. The cliffsides were honeycombed with caves and marked with several distinct layers of construction. They were also covered with a scaffolding of vertical and horizontal ropes. Another set of wires stretched across the sky like power lines, spanning the canyon from one peak to the next.

'Quite a setup,' Kurt noted.

Emma nodded but didn't reply. To her, the canyon felt tight and compressed – the kind of place a Western gunfighter might find himself surrounded and ambushed. She kept close to Kurt, aware that the Beretta in her pack would not be easy to reach if something did go wrong.

As they neared the tents, a group of men came out to meet them. They stood in the path, arms folded, eyes squinting, mouths tight.

'Hola,' Kurt said, thrusting out a hand toward the closest of them. 'My name is Kurt Austin. I'd like to speak with Urco, if I could.'

The man stood like a statue. He was shorter than Kurt but well built, with muscular forearms and bulbous shoulders. He had a different look from the Peruvians Kurt had known; broader and shorter, with a wider face; more indigenous, less European. His skin was a darker, copper shade and his eyes seemed larger.

He neither responded to the words nor reached for Kurt's hand.

Kurt lowered his arm and glanced at Emma. 'Maybe you'd better try.'

She repeated the greeting in Spanish. Adding something about them being interested in archaeology and the Chachapoya and mentioning that they'd seen Urco on the Internet.

This brought some chatter among the group, and the burly man nodded. *'Me llamo Vargas,'* he said, unfolding his arms and pointing to the cliff top. 'Urco,' he said, before adding in English, 'Up there.'

Vargas led them to the base of the cliff. Several ropes dangled down from above.

'I'm not great with heights,' Emma said. 'Maybe I'll just wait here.'

Looking at a climb of several hundred feet, Kurt wasn't all that excited himself. 'I don't suppose he could come down?'

Vargas just stared.

'Never mind.'

Kurt was given a safety harness and led to the nearest rope, where Vargas handed him a pair of well-used work gloves. They were loose and worn smooth – not exactly fit for gripping a nylon rope.

'To climb?' Kurt asked, making a hand-over-hand motion.

Vargas shook his head. 'No . . . fly.'

He placed Kurt's hands on the rope and then snapped the safety harness to a hook using a heavy carabiner.

Kurt saw instantly what was about to happen. He gripped the rope as Vargas released a cast-iron clamp attached to a second rope.

A heavy weight suspended up above began to fall and Kurt – whose rope was attached to that weight by means of a pulley – was lifted off the ground and hauled upward.

The initial launch was sudden, but after that the ride was smooth.

He passed small dwellings carved out of holes in the stone. Open rooms were empty except for ladders that went from one level to the next.

Above them, he passed a row of stone figures carved into the living rock; they looked almost bird-like, but with enlarged heads and human bodies and features. They reminded him of Egyptian hieroglyphs.

Higher up, in smaller niches and openings, he saw mummified bodies and weaponry; spears and morning stars. These were the mountaintop burial sites of the Chachapoya warriors.

He was approaching the block, tackle and pulley arrangement, which had allowed him to ascend so quickly, when Vargas applied the brake. He came to a stop ten feet from the crest of the mountain. A ladder affixed to the cliffside on his right led the rest of the way.

'You've made it this far,' a voice boomed from above. 'Now comes the tricky part.'

Kurt looked up to see a face peering over the edge at him. It was weathered and creased from years in the sun, topped by shaggy dark hair and half covered by a gray beard as thick as wool on a sheep. Gleeful, dark eyes focused on Kurt. The man chuckled as he pointed to the ladder.

'I see it,' Kurt said.

'And you see the dilemma?'

Kurt saw that, too. The ladder was several feet beyond his reach. And even if he could stretch out to touch it, he would have to disconnect the safety harness from the rope in order to transfer to the bottom few rungs.

He looked down for a moment and then wished he hadn't. 'Now I know what the window washers on the Freedom Tower feel like.'

He swung his feet toward the ladder, pulled them back in the other direction and then swung them again. The rope began to move, sliding side to side with his motion. On the third arc, Kurt stretched out and grasped the metal frame of the ladder. Pulling himself over to it, he set his feet, wrapped one arm around the closest available rung and then disconnected the harness. Keeping his gaze skyward, he climbed to the top and pulled himself onto solid ground.

The man with the gray beard offered a slight bow. 'I congratulate you. It takes most people several minutes before they figure out how to do that. And even then, many are reluctant to let go of the rope. Indeed, one reporter who came to interview me last year flat out refused. He just mumbled a few questions from the harness and then asked to be lowered to the ground as quickly as possible.'

The man allowed himself a belly laugh.

Kurt chuckled and turned to take in the view. They were standing on a platform in the sky, the highest spot for miles around. A major valley loomed to the east and north while the teeth of lower ridges loomed to the west. 'That reporter missed out,' he said. 'Reminds me of a spot called Eagle's Nest in Colorado.'

'There was a time when eagles made their homes on this aerie,' the man said. 'Long ago.'

Kurt noticed that the man spoke English far better than Vargas had. 'Since you're the only one up here, I'll assume you're Urco.' He offered a hand. 'Kurt Austin.'

The man looked at Kurt's outstretched palm and offered an uncomfortable grin. 'I am Urco,' he said without moving. 'Pleased to meet you.'

For the second time, Kurt pulled his arm back. 'Not too fond of shaking hands around here, are you? Is it some custom I'm unaware of?'

Urco shook his head. 'I'm afraid we are . . . germaphobes . . . of a sort.'

'Really?' Kurt said. 'You live out in the wild, dig around in the dirt, unearthing dead bodies, and you're afraid of germs?'

'I know it sounds strange,' Urco replied, 'but, in a

way, it's the bodies that remind us to be wary. These dwellings and burial chambers are from the last stronghold of the Chachapoya people. They held out against the might of the Inca for centuries. They even resisted the conquistadors after Pizarro and his one hundred and sixty-eight men defeated Atahualpa and his six thousand Inca warriors. Unfortunately, their next enemy was one they could not defeat.'

'Disease?' Kurt said.

Urco nodded. 'Smallpox. It ravaged the settlements, killing nearly everyone it found. Those who stayed died. Those who fled brought the disease with them, spreading the plague to other villages. I've found writings that describe a traveler coming home to a village of two thousand people to find no one alive. Most had died horribly, covered with pustules. Others had killed each other when fighting and chaos set in – as they always do when social order breaks down.'

Urco waved his arms about in a sweeping gesture. 'This place was a nation once. And then it was gone.'

Kurt nodded. He knew the grim statistics. European diseases had hit the New World hard. South America fared the worst. According to many experts, smallpox, influenza and measles wiped out ninety-five percent of the indigenous population.

Urco continued. 'The men and women who work on this project are all descendants of the Chachapoya. Some nearly pure-blooded. Others, like myself, have a mix of European and indigenous genes. Of course, we're not really afraid of disease anymore, but avoiding the touch of outsiders is one way we remind ourselves what happened to our ancestors.'

'I assure you,' Kurt said. 'I've had all my proper shots and inoculations.'

Urco stared at him for a second and then began to laugh. He waved Kurt over and sat down, leaning against a slight rise in the ridge that acted like a natural chair even if it was made of stone. Beside him was a laptop computer. A wire from the computer led to an exterior antenna propped up and pointed at an almost flat angle to the northwest.

Kurt recognized the antenna as a type used to communicate via satellite. 'Checking your e-mail?'

'Yes, actually,' Urco said. 'The satellite we use is very low on the horizon this time of year. You can't get a signal from the valley floor. So I come up here every day. Sometimes twice a day. I tell the workers I'm conversing with the gods. They remind me to check my battery level or the gods will never hear me.'

'I'm very impressed with the dig,' Kurt said. 'I assume all the ropes are to keep you from damaging the excavation sites.'

'Partly,' Urco said. 'The Peruvian government owns the site and they won't permit us to set foot in the burial areas – something I agree with. As a result, we have to learn what we can by looking in from the outside. That means being suspended midair like an acrobat. I must admit, it sometimes makes things tricky, especially if the wind gets up, which it often does. But after a while, it becomes second nature.'

Kurt studied the setup. Three high summits around the valley acted like the points of a jagged crown. The face of each peak was adorned with a rope and pulley system like the one that had lifted Kurt. The scaffolding ropes were offset from these, and the third set of taut cables stretched from one peak to the next. Highest to middle. Middle to lowest. And from there, back down to the camp below.

The heavy ropes reminded Kurt of the recreational zip line operations marketed to tourists all over the world.

'Your people use these lines to get from peak to peak,' Kurt said.

'Precisely,' Urco said. 'They allow quick access from one crest to the next without having to go all the way down and back up again. I make the circuit at least twice a day myself, inspecting the work. It's a one-way journey, of course – since those crests are lower than this one. But it's quite exhilarating.'

'I can imagine,' Kurt said. 'I'd like to try it.'

'You're more than welcome to,' Urco said. 'But something tells me you didn't come all this way to talk about ropes and zip lines.'

'No,' Kurt admitted. 'I'm looking for some information. But I'm not a reporter. I work for the American government, for an agency called NUMA.'

'Ah, yes,' Urco replied. 'I know of this organization.'

'You do?'

'When your work is dependent on grants, you become very familiar with the world's governmental organizations. Over the last ten years, I've applied to every department, of every agency, in every country, in the Americas. Or so it seems. I've petitioned NUMA several times. I'm afraid you've always turned me down.'

'That's unfortunate,' Kurt grunted.

Urco laughed. 'Not to worry. It's all part of the business. But tell me, why would an organization that studies the sea be interested in the mountains of Peru and the people who lived there?'

'It's complicated,' Kurt said. 'The other night, you posted a video of a meteor crossing the sky. We wanted to know more about it. Can you tell me what you saw? When exactly it happened? Which direction you were looking?'

'It was very early in the morning,' Urco said. 'I get up before dawn each day. The sunrise is my affirmation. That morning, we were going to film a new chamber we'd uncovered. I was checking the cameras to make sure the batteries were charged. As I went about my routine, I looked up and saw a light in the sky. At first I thought it was a star, but it was moving with great speed. I had the camera in my hand, so I pointed and filmed. Pure serendipity. I'm not even sure the video was focused.'

'It was slightly blurred,' Kurt admitted, 'but not too bad, considering the circumstances. Which way did it travel?'

Urco pointed to the north. 'It came in from that direction, crossed over the clearing and continued south.'

The time interval was right, but the direction seemed off. Although Hiram had suggested the *Nighthawk*'s right wing appeared to be damaged. That might account for the change.

Kurt chose his next words with care. Urco was obviously a man of great intelligence. He was worldly even if the people who worked for him were relatively simple. Kurt had found truth worked better with such people, better than even the most carefully crafted lies. 'What if I told you it wasn't a meteor in the sky that morning?'

Urco's face scrunched up, his weathered skin wrinkling, the beard shifting, but hiding any true expression. 'I would have to agree with you,' he said. 'Up here, one sees shooting stars on a regular basis. No city lights to blind us. I posted the video as a lark, but as the day wore on I couldn't stop thinking about it. I must admit, my later impression was of something larger and closer. Lower to the Earth, I think.'

'I think so, too,' Kurt said. 'I believe you saw an experimental American spacecraft that reentered the atmosphere and went off course. We – and by that I mean NUMA and the United States government – are very interested in finding the crash site. If you help us now, I can promise you, with a high degree of certainty, that you'll never be turned down for a grant again.'

Urco nodded as if considering the possibilities. 'Perhaps we can help each other,' he said. 'Have you ever heard of my theory?'

'Afraid not,' Kurt said.

Urco didn't take offense. 'It's called *Civilization Wave Theory*. It's adapted from a field known as cataclysmic evolution, which is the belief that a new form cannot prosper until the existing, dominant form subsides. Mammals, which rule the planet today, were nothing more than scurrying rodents for the first hundred million years of their existence. Surviving only because they were beneath the dinosaurs' majestic notice. But after the Chicxulub meteor impact, the dinosaurs fell. In the blink of an eye, the entire playing field was leveled; indeed, tilted toward small animals with warm blood and fur. And so the rise of the mammals began.'

Kurt nodded.

'My theory suggests that civilization changes in much the same way. Nothing new can rise until the old, dominant power is swept away. Usually by a catastrophe beyond its control.'

'For instance?'

'Being a man of the sea, I'm sure you're familiar with the sudden collapse of the Minoan empire.'

'Of course,' Kurt said. 'After dominating the Mediterranean for centuries, the Minoans were weakened by the tsunamis that hit their island after the eruption of Santorini.'

'Precisely,' Urco said, 'but they weren't wiped out. They still existed. They hung on for centuries in a diminished capacity. But the effect was a changing of the playing field; it was now tilted toward other civilizations of the region. The Mycenaean civilization in particular. Something that would never have happened were it not for the cataclysm.'

Kurt nodded again.

'You see the same thing here,' Urco told him. 'Originally, the Chachapoya were more powerful than the Inca, but catastrophe struck them from the outside – not once, but twice.'

Kurt settled in; he loved a good history lesson. 'How so?'

'At the end, it was the diseases,' Urco admitted. 'But long before that, these people faced another catastrophe. You can find the evidence in a body of water known as the Lake of the Condors, fifty miles from here.'

Kurt had heard something about Lake of the Condors when reading Urco's website. 'There are Chachapoya ruins there as well.'

'Indeed,' Urco said. 'Extensive ruins in the cliffs all around it. Everyone knows about these. But what I found is different. Evidence that a major settlement had once thrived on the valley floor, stretching from one side to the other and up into the foothills.'

'This I hadn't heard,' Kurt said.

'Few have,' Urco insisted. 'Thousands lived within the walls of this city, which made it a very large settlement for its day. They were protected by a strong warrior caste, with some of the finest weapons of the time. I assure you, these men shrank before no one, and for several centuries the Chachapoya were the power of the region, taking tribute from other groups. But then the disaster came upon them.'

'What happened?'

'The city was built in the sheltered area between the mountains. It received its water from the snowmelt and a mountain lake, higher up in the range,' Urco said. 'A massive earthquake in the eighth century released the contents of that lake all at once. A fifty-foot wall of water crashed into the city in the dark of night. It drowned the city. The people were trapped. They died by the thousands. It was Noah without any warning from God. Pompeii without the ash. By daybreak, there was nothing left. The wealth was gone; the warriors were gone. *The city itself was gone.* The reign of the Chachapoya, unbreakable at sunset, was swept away by morning. And in its aftermath the Inca began their storied rise.'

Kurt had no idea if there was any merit to the tale, but he found it fascinating. 'Were there any survivors?'

'A few hundred,' Urco said. 'Those who'd lived higher up in the hills. When they tried to rebuild their civilization, they did things differently, constructing their dwellings in the cliffs, instead of on the valley floors, where they felt they'd be safe from any future disaster. At first it was simple logic, but as time went by it became their way, their religion. They became the *People of the Clouds.*'

'Can't say I blame them,' Kurt added.

'Indeed,' Urco said. 'Who could sleep on the low ground after surviving a night like that?'

'Sounds like you've got it all worked out,' Kurt said. 'What do you need us for?'

'To help me prove it.'

'By exploring the lake,' Kurt surmised.

Urco nodded. 'The Peruvian government has given me a permit but denied all my requests for funding or help. They have a vested interest in not diminishing the appeal of the mighty Inca. And I lack the funds to mount a submerged expedition myself. But I tell you, at the bottom of that lake is a flooded city the likes of which no one has ever seen.'

The idea of unearthing something that would change the accepted history appealed to Kurt, but they had a more pressing issue. 'I'm sure something could be arranged,' he said. 'You help me, I'll help you.'

Urco stroked his bushy beard. 'I was hoping we could do it *the other way around*.'

'The problem is time,' Kurt said. 'I *have* to find this missing aircraft before I do anything else. I don't say this lightly, but everyone here is in danger until that plane is found.'

Urco looked at him with a powerful gaze. 'Why would *we* be in danger?'

'Because NUMA isn't the only group looking for the missing aircraft. Agents from several other countries are after it as well. They've tried to kill my partner and me several times already. Including on the way up here.'

'On the way up here?' Urco asked, suspicious.

'We were attacked on the road,' Kurt said.

'They could still be following you.'

'Not unless they can fly,' Kurt said. 'But others will come. And they're not the kind of people who are interested in striking deals. They won't hesitate to torture or kill everyone here to get what they're after.'

Urco sighed and looked away. 'I put nothing past selfish men,' he said. 'My research has shown it's our nature to fight and oppress. But how will helping you protect us? Wouldn't these other groups be more likely to resort to violence if they knew *we* had chosen sides?'

'All they care about is the missing aircraft,' Kurt said. 'Once we have it, they'll have no reason to be here. The danger will be gone.'

Urco took a minute to ponder Kurt's words. Finally, he looked Kurt in the eye once again. 'Nothing good happens to small people when they get in the way of the great powers. Better that this thing is found and taken away so we can continue on with our lives.'

'So you'll help us?'

'I will. What do you need?'

'Only for you to show me where you were standing when you took the video. Once we match up the surrounding peaks with what's on the recording, we can extrapolate the precise direction of the craft and make a good estimate of its speed and altitude. With that information, we'll be able to find the landing site in a matter of hours and haul it away.'

'And once that's done?' Urco asked.

'I'll make sure it's well known that we've recovered the vehicle intact,' Kurt promised. 'I'll even tell the world where we found it so that anyone who wants to look for themselves can bypass you and go straight to the crash site.'

Urco stroked his beard. 'Very well,' he said. 'Then I will help you gladly. But first . . . we eat.'

28

The mountain road to La Jalca had been blocked. The bridge was gone; its twisted metal frame now lay at the bottom of the canyon while the road itself was covered with a swath of gravel, boulders and rock ten feet deep – remnants of the avalanche unleashed by the errant Chinese missile.

The man who'd fired that missile was gone as well, but Daiyu and Jian had escaped by driving back into the shelter of the tunnel and staying put until the rumbling ceased. They sat in darkness until the choking dust began to settle and a small gap of light appeared near the top of the tunnel.

'We should go back,' Jian suggested. 'We have a helicopter waiting in Cajamarca. We should make contact with command, secure reinforcements and fly to the ruins. Take them from the sky.'

Daiyu shook her head. 'We go forward,' she insisted. 'Not back. If we keep up a good pace, we can reach La Jalca by midnight. Take them in their sleep.'

'We're at a disadvantage now,' he argued. 'The kill team is gone. The Americans know we're following them.'

'If anything, they think we're dead,' she replied. 'That gives us the advantage. And remember, our mission is to prevent the Americans from finding the

Nighthawk at all costs. Driving all the way back to Cajamarca, reaching out to General Zhang and waiting for more support, will take far too long. We must go forward. You start clearing a way through and I'll gather the weapons and supplies.'

Jian stared at her for a moment and then did as ordered. He stepped from the car, climbed onto the rubble pile and began digging with his bare hands. The loose gravel was easy to move and the small boulders and rocks were no match for his great strength. He tossed them aside with ease and before long he'd dug enough of a channel for them to squirm through.

He emerged into the fresh air, covered from head to toe in dust. Daiyu came out behind him, handed him a backpack and pulled on one of her own. As she scanned the slope for a safe route to take, Jian picked his way to the edge of the cliff, looking for the other car.

'Don't bother,' she called out. 'They're gone.'

He knew that. He looked anyway. It was a long drop. There was no sign of the car at the bottom, just a sloping pile of rock that had buried it.

As Jian stared into the abyss, Daiyu looked upward. A trick of the inner ear, caused by tilting the head backward, exaggerated the grade of the hill. Even knowing that, she was impressed that the Americans had managed to climb it without flipping their vehicle or rolling back down the hill. She'd underestimated them, something she would not do again.

She turned to Jian. 'Ready?'

He nodded.

She pointed to a trail on the right. 'This way looks to have better traction. Follow me.'

The climb was more perilous on foot than in a vehicle. Thorny bushes and high-mountain cacti clawed at them mercilessly. Loose rocks shifted with each step, threatening to turn their ankles and send them sliding back toward the road below, while the air at nearly ten thousand feet was thin enough to leave them lightheaded. By the time they reached the roadway above, they were scratched, bleeding and breathing hard.

Daiyu stood with her hands on her hips. Though the temperature was cool, she was sweating in the sun.

'Rest here for a minute,' she said, taking a drink of the water and handing the bottle to Jian. 'I'm going to scout ahead.'

While Jian drank, Daiyu walked along the road. It continued upward and curved to the left. Beyond that, it flattened out. They were near the top. The plateau lay ahead of them.

As she waited for Jian to catch up, she caught the sound of an engine in the distance. Squinting against the glare of the afternoon sun, she spied a small box truck coming toward them. It was old and worn, a workhorse that showed the wear and tear of too many runs in the mountains. Dented in places, it listed to one side, trailing oil smoke from its exhaust pipe. Still, it would be far better than walking the rest of the way.

She waved it down.

With her long hair set in a ponytail and a backpack over her shoulders, she looked like any other hiker on a trail.

The truck stopped beside her and the passenger window rolled down. A man with rough black hair and a dark face looked out at her. He had small, dark eyes. A similar man was at the wheel. Both were more native than European.

'Are you all right?' the passenger asked in Spanish.

'I need some help,' she replied, also in Spanish. 'The bridge is out. It collapsed. There must have been an earthquake because there was a rockslide as well.'

The men looked over the dashboard. Down the slope, they saw the rubble covering the road and the empty span where the bridge should have been. What they didn't see was Daiyu pulling a Chinese-made pistol from her jacket.

She fired three shots before either of them reacted. All three hit the passenger.

She yanked the door open and pulled him out. He landed dead at her feet as the driver threw his hands up.

'Get out,' she ordered.

He fumbled for the door handle and unlatched it, falling from the truck in his haste. It wasn't fast enough. Daiyu shot him, a single bullet to the head that killed him instantly.

By the time Jian reached her, she'd dragged both dead men to the edge of the bank and shoved them over. They tumbled a short distance and then slid limply down the slope until catching on separate bushes halfway to the bottom.

'You didn't have to kill them,' Jian said. 'They could have been useful. They might have had information.'

She put the pistol away. 'Bringing them along would be a distraction. And by leaving them here, we'd risk the chance of someone spotting them and setting them free.'

She climbed behind the wheel as Jian took the passenger's seat. After a precarious three-point turn, she got the truck moving back toward La Jalca.

The poor truck never topped twenty miles an hour going uphill, but once they were out on the flat top of the plateau, it picked up speed until they were traveling close to forty.

Daiyu checked the time. Instead of reaching La Jalca at midnight, they'd be there by dusk. They might just catch the Americans after all.

29

Cajamarca, Peru

The streets of Cajamarca were cold and wet. A brief spell of rain had left mud in the gutters and puddles everywhere. Rain in the mountains was always a cold rain. The damp got into the bones. Paul and Gamay would have preferred snow.

Walking along the sidewalk, Paul pulled his coat around him and flipped up his collar. 'I think someone is following us,' he whispered.

'The guy in the colorful poncho,' Gamay said. 'I've seen him three times since leaving the airport.'

It might have been a good way to blend, as many of the natives of Cajamarca wore similar ponchos in the cold months, but the pattern was unique and Paul and Gamay both had an eye for fashion.

Catching sight of the man in the reflection of a store window, Paul nodded. The pattern was the same; the fur-lined boots were the same. The man was the same.

'What do you say we get off the main street,' he suggested.

'If it means somewhere warm . . .'

'How about this place,' Paul said, pointing to a brightly painted Internet café.

Gamay read the sign. 'Strong java, stronger Internet, 4K video. Let's go.'

They stepped inside, watched through the glass as the man passed by and saw him return a moment later. Instead of coming in, he sat at the bus stop across the road, apparently content to watch.

Paul was fine with that. He and Gamay moved deeper into the narrow building. Thankful for the warmth, as much as anything.

The café was busy, the coffee, computers and young people creating a perpetual buzz. They found a spot with access to both the front and back doors, logged on to a computer and spent a few minutes browsing.

'Do you think our friend is going to sneak in anytime soon?' Paul asked.

'Doubt it,' Gamay said, 'but we'll see him if he does.'

'In that case, I'm going to make a phone call.'

He stepped away from the desk, found a ladder to the roof and climbed it. Popping out through a trapdoor, Paul climbed onto the roof and lowered the door gently behind him. He wasn't looking to escape; he just needed a clear view of the sky.

After linking up to the NUMA communications system, Paul was patched through to Hiram Yaeger. He got right to the point. 'Kurt needs you and Priya to hack into the NSA's database.'

Of all the staff at NUMA, Hiram Yaeger was the least afraid to flout authority – it was half the reason he kept his hair long and wore decidedly non-corporate clothes to work. But he was surprised to hear this request from one of NUMA's most buttoned-down officers. 'Who are you?' he asked. 'And what have you done with Paul?'

'Very funny,' Paul replied. 'I'm serious. Kurt has reason to believe they're hiding something regarding the *Nighthawk* and its mission. Good reason. And since he's the one out there risking his life – '

He must have been on speakerphone because Priya chimed in. 'I'm not an expert in such matters, but isn't that frowned upon . . . or perhaps illegal?'

'It's not exactly encouraged,' Hiram admitted. 'But we've done it before and never really gotten more than a slap on the wrist.'

'Apparently, the NSA is more forgiving than their reputation suggests,' she replied.

'Preventing a worldwide catastrophe with the information we borrowed might have had something to do with that,' Paul said.

'I have no problem with this,' Hiram said. 'You know that. But we have been warned. Maybe I should run it by Rudi or Dirk.'

'And ruin their plausible deniability?'

'Good point,' Hiram said. 'Okay. We'll give it a shot.'

Paul knew that meant it would get done. 'Kurt wants the information as soon as you can get it. Preferably, before his romantic Sunday drive gets the best of him.'

Hiram promised to do his best and the call ended. Paul looked around to find a large crow staring back at him from another section of the roof.

'Thank God, you're not a parrot,' he said.

The crow cawed and spread its wings. It flew off to the south, and Paul climbed back down into the warmth of the café.

'Get through?' Gamay said.

He nodded and checked the clock on the wall. 'Joe is still several hours away.'

Gamay had already purchased a steaming cup of soup and an alpaca hat. 'Yep,' she said, settling in and tapping away on a keyboard. 'Looks like this café is our temporary home.'

Back in Washington, Hiram and Priya were left to figure out the details of their latest hacking scheme.

'Whether we should do this or not is one thing,' Priya said. 'But how we do it is the more important question.'

'You're not worried?' Hiram asked.

'Worst thing they can do is deport me back to Merrie Olde England. And while I can't stand all the rain, you and Rudi will be the ones who go to jail.'

'Not likely,' Hiram said. 'But it isn't going to be easy to break their code. Each time Max and I have hacked the NSA, they've responded by raising their game. Their security is quite good.'

'*We could overwhelm them with a brute force attack,*' Max suggested over the speakers.

Hiram looked up – as he often did when speaking to Max. 'Let's try something less reminiscent of Genghis Khan.'

Priya was already tapping away at her computer. 'The

NSA may have built the *Nighthawk* in secret, but they didn't design it from scratch. Design cues were taken from the space shuttle and the X-37. Ms Townsend even said something about the *Nighthawk* using common parts from the X-37. If that's the case, NASA probably shared data on the construction process. And that means we might be able to hack into NASA instead of the NSA.'

'Great idea,' Hiram said.

'I prefer the word *brilliant*.'

'Then *brilliant* it is,' Hiram replied. 'To collaborate with NASA, our friends at the NSA would have set up a secure and authenticated connection. If we do as you say and break into NASA first, we can get into the NSA computers through the back door and they might think they're just sharing data with the Johnson Space Center.'

Max chimed in. *'I assign a seventy-three percent chance of success to the plan. And if they do discover the hack, they'll investigate NASA first, giving us more time to make a run for it.'*

'Without legs, you'll be going nowhere,' Hiram said. 'I'm afraid they'll melt you down for scrap.'

'I could get wheels,' Max suggested. *'Like Dr Kashmir.'*

For an instant, Hiram felt awkward, but Priya laughed. 'Trust me, Max, having wheels isn't all it's cracked up to be.'

Hiram laughed as well. 'We'll talk about your mobility issues some other time, Max. Let's break into the space center's network and see if their computers are still on speaking terms with the National Security Agency.'

It was the better part of the day before Priya and Max were able to gain access. Eventually, they had to go through the systems at Cape Canaveral and the Jet Propulsion Laboratory before discovering a link to the NSA database. Shortly, they were receiving copious amounts of information on the *Nighthawk*'s design, test flights and mission parameters.

Priya and Hiram looked at what they could but relied on Max to determine what was important or not, as they soon had over a thousand pages of information.

As Max continued to sort things out, Priya found herself studying the technical papers related to the *Nighthawk*'s construction. 'Look at this,' she said, waving Hiram over to her desk.

He peered down at the image on her computer.

'These are the blueprints and design specs for the X-37.' She pointed. 'And these are the plans for the *Nighthawk*. See anything interesting?'

Hiram pulled his glasses off, cleaned them with a soft cloth and put them back on. 'They're very similar. Almost identical.'

'The only real difference is size,' she said. 'If we scale an original set of plans up, they match. Same engine, same navigation system, same wing design, same heat shield. In fact, aside from a coating of stealth material that burns off on reentry, the heat shield is not much different than the tile system used on the space shuttle since the eighties.'

'So much for the technological leap forward they keep claiming,' Hiram said. 'It's little more than an updated version of an older vehicle.'

He stood up and addressed Max. 'Are you sure we're looking at the correct plans?'

'*Affirmative,*' Max replied.

'How certain are you?'

'*There's a 99.98 percent probability that the plans you're looking at match the vehicle that was launched and is now being sought in South America.*'

'That's pretty certain,' Priya said.

Hiram agreed. 'It doesn't make sense. The Russians took an immense risk to grab it. They exposed their secret Typhoon submarine in an attempt to retrieve the wreckage from where they thought it had crashed, and both they and the Chinese seem willing to risk a war to find it.'

'With the attempts on Kurt and Ms Townsend so far, I'd say a skirmish has already begun,' Priya added.

Hiram nodded. He looked over the plans once again, double-checking the propulsion specifications and the structural blueprints. 'If it isn't the machine that matters, then it has to be something else. Something related to the mission.'

'Perhaps it collected one of our spy satellites. Or one of theirs.'

'Maybe one of each,' Hiram said. 'That would get them hot under the collar.'

'If we knew where it went, we might learn more,' she suggested.

'Max, what can you tell me about the *Nighthawk*'s mission profile?'

The computer voice responded instantly. '*The NSA*

launches the Nighthawk *out of Vandenberg on a modified Titan booster. The vehicle inserts into a polar orbit and stays aloft for extensive periods of time. Seventy-five days on the first launch, eight hundred and fifty-one days on this latest mission.'*

'And yet,' Hiram said, scanning through the page count, 'we seem to have far more data from the first mission than the second. Are you holding something back on us?'

'Mission 1 was a test mission,' Max said. *'Data from all phases of the mission was freely shared with NASA. Mission 2 was an operational event. Fully classified. Only prelaunch data and orbital track information was provided.'*

'Can you match up the *Nighthawk*'s orbital track with known satellites?'

There was a slight pause – unusual for Max, considering how fast her processing speeds were. *'The* Nighthawk *made 14,625 complete orbits and one partial orbit before reentry. At no time did its path intersect with the position of any known satellite. Available data suggests the* Nighthawk *maneuvered* specifically *to avoid any orbital convergence.'*

'Anything else unusual about the path?'

'For ninety-one percent of its time in space, the Nighthawk *remained in the Earth's shadow.'*

'So the *Nighthawk* was staying out of sight,' Hiram said. 'Can't hijack another satellite when you're hiding in the dark and avoiding them like the plague.'

'I'm not sure it could retrieve something if it wanted to,' Priya said. 'Look at this. On the initial blueprints, the cargo bay is an empty space, just like the cargo bay on the shuttle. But on the last set of prelaunch schematics, the entire bay has been filled with equipment.'

Hiram's curiosity grew, he pulled up a chair and settled in beside her. 'What kind of equipment?'

'Cryogenic storage containers, advanced lithium batteries and a bank of devices called *Penning traps* – which must use powerful magnets because the control center and the propulsion bay have been electromagnetically shielded to prevent magnetic interference.'

'Penning traps,' Hiram said, trying to remember where he'd heard that term before.

'According to the schematic, they take up the whole bay.'

. Hiram nodded. He was suddenly very grim. The truth was coming to him and he didn't like it one bit. 'Max, can you correlate the *Nighthawk*'s orbit with evidence of the northern lights?'

'*Affirmative,*' Max said. '*The* Nighthawk *was present in a northern polar orbit during all major flares of the aurora borealis. It was also present over the South Pole during the major and minor flares of the aurora australis, otherwise known as the southern lights. Its positioning indicates direct immersion within the vortex point of the Earth's magnetic field.*'

'*Vortex point?*' Priya asked.

'Where the lines of the Earth's magnetic field converge above the North and South Poles, before they dive down into the Earth.'

By now, Priya had picked up on his tone. 'Do you know what they're doing?'

'Testing a theory,' he said. 'A very dangerous theory.'

She looked at the schematics again, running her finger across the imaginary Penning traps. The term itself gave her the answer. 'They brought something back. Didn't they?'

Hiram nodded. 'I'm afraid so,' he said. 'And it's something far more deadly than any satellite could hope to be.'

30

La Jalca Canyon, Chachapoya ruins

By dusk, the cooking fires had been stoked and several long wooden tables set for a communal meal. Urco introduced Kurt and Emma to the rest of the volunteers and insisted that their arrival was cause for celebration.

Before the food was served, Urco led the group in a traditional invocation. 'It's a Chachapoya prayer,' he explained. 'It cautions us not to begin the feast until all the guests are present and accounted for.'

'Another way to remember the people whose world you're excavating?' Emma asked.

'Precisely,' Urco said. 'We even live like them. In ancient times there was far less trade than today. Each society, each village, had to be self-sufficient. And so are we. We catch rainwater in barrels, grow manioc in the southern section of the clearing. We have the llamas in the corral.'

'Adorable animals,' Emma said.

'I wouldn't get too attached to them,' Kurt whispered.

'Why?'

'I think you're about to eat one.'

She looked ill for a second.

'You can't be self-sufficient in everything,' Kurt said.

Urco disagreed. 'I assure you, we are. As are all the villages our volunteers come from. I tell you, the rest of civilization could cease to exist and we would never know it.'

'I can understand the desire to live that way,' Emma said. 'But wouldn't all the effort put into growing crops and raising animals be better used here, at the dig site? If the food was shipped in, it would leave you more workers to handle the other chores.'

'The road to civilization is both long and treacherous,' he said. 'Both in the real and metaphorical sense. Being self-sufficient keeps us from being dependent on that road in any form. And since I've recently heard that it was closed . . .'

Kurt laughed and took a drink of water.

A moment later, the food was served: bread made from manioc flour, some type of diced vegetable and what looked like venison. The aroma was heavenly.

'Enjoy it, my friends,' Urco said. 'As soon as we're done, I'll show you what you came to see.'

Kurt nodded, buried the impatience he felt and enjoyed a hearty and unusual dinner. As things were cleared away, Kurt and Emma went back to the Range Rover to collect a few items they would need and then rejoined Urco near the bank of solar panels. 'We use these to power our modern equipment.'

'So you're not dependent on civilization,' Emma said, 'but you are beholden to the sun.'

'True,' Urco replied. 'But the sun is far more reliable. Five billion years and counting. Something tells me modern civilization will never match that.'

'So this is where you were when you saw the light in the sky?' Kurt asked.

'Yes,' Urco said. 'I came up the trail from our tents and checked the flashlights. We were going to look into a newly discovered cave that day, so we needed as much light as possible. Satisfied that everything was fully powered, I came over to this stand where our video cameras were connected to their chargers.'

He led them to a cradle where two cameras were supported and attached to the power station via cables.

'I picked up this one,' he said, grabbing it. 'Turned it on and waited. As it powered up, I happened to see a flicker of light in the sky. Once I realized it wasn't a star, I brought the camera up and filmed it.'

He held the camera up to his face, showing them how he'd done it and pretending to track the fiery target across the sky. 'It went from north to south,' he said, tracing the arc with his fingers. 'It vanished behind those peaks.'

'Did you hear anything?' Emma asked.

'Like what? An explosion?'

'Anything at all,' Emma said. 'Explosion, popping, the sound of jet engines.'

'Nothing,' Urco said. 'You can hear the audio on the recording. Just me huffing and puffing.'

Kurt studied the sky, black and punctured with stars. A slight glow from the new moon gave them just enough light to see the outline of the mountains. 'Let's do it.'

She placed her laptop computer on a nearby table and began tapping away. 'Can you set up the tripod for me?'

Kurt unfolded the legs of the aluminum tripod. 'Where *exactly* were you standing?' he asked Urco.

'Right about here,' Urco said, moving several feet to his right.

Kurt extended the legs of the tripod, attached the camera to the central mount and raised it up until it was resting at the same level as Urco's eyes. That done, he connected an HDMI cable from Emma's computer to the camera and switched it on. 'All yours.'

Emma nodded and continued to tap away at the keyboard. Kurt slid behind her and watched as she replayed the original video, pausing it several times. When it finished, she ran it all the way through once again.

'We need an exact distance from here to the peak.' She handed Kurt a laser range finder.

Kurt turned it on and pointed it at the jagged ridge until he got a reading. 'Seven hundred and forty-two feet.'

She typed it in and two outlines appeared on the screen, one displaying the peaks as they appeared through the NUMA camera and the second displaying the peaks from the video Urco had taken.

At Emma's command, the camera moved left and right and then back to the left. She tapped the up arrow and the camera tilted just a bit. The computer took it from there and fine-tuned the image until the two outlines merged exactly. 'That's it.'

At the touch of a button, Emma received the heading of what they assumed to be the *Nighthawk*.

'What about speed and altitude?' Kurt asked.

'For that, we'll need to match this with the new descent profile your friend Hiram is working up.'

Emma tried to initiate a satellite linkup, but it failed.

'It's the mountains,' Urco said. 'You'll have to go up top.'

'You mean, on those ropes?'

'It's the only way to get a signal,' Urco explained. 'How do you feel about a night ascent?'

She sighed. 'Worse than I did about a daytime's.'

Hidden in the dark among the same type of scrub trees that had scratched their exposed skin, Daiyu watched Kurt through a spotting scope. He was talking with the woman and the bearded man. She focused on his lips, trying to make out what he was saying.

'What are they doing?' Jian asked.

'They're calculating something,' she said. 'They're using the video we were told about to get a bearing on the *Nighthawk*.'

'We should be doing that,' Jian suggested.

She and Jian had arrived just after sunset, ditching the truck near one of the fields and hiking the last few miles on foot. They'd made a study of the camp and were trying to decide how best to get at the Americans without having to fight their way through the forty Peruvian men and women of the archaeology group.

'They're trying to connect to their satellite,' she said, reading Emma's lips, 'but they can't get a signal. They're going to higher ground.'

She put the scope away and looked to Jian. 'This is our chance. We have to get that computer.'

31

Urco led Kurt and Emma to the base of the second peak and, with a wolf whistle, called several of his people over. 'I'll go first,' he said, stepping into the harness for the ride to the top.

As he disappeared upward into the night, Kurt glanced at Emma. 'You don't have to go,' he said. 'I can send the data.'

She shook her head. 'I'd never live it down.'

'In that case, think about it this way: it's so dark, you won't be able to tell how high you are.'

'That doesn't help,' she replied.

A double flash from high above told them Urco was safely on the mountaintop. When the harness dropped out of the dark, Kurt grabbed it. 'Ready?'

Emma exhaled and nodded. 'Here,' she said, handing him the computer. 'My hands are shaking already. Won't do us any good if I drop it.'

Kurt took the laptop as she strapped herself in and gave the thumbs-up signal. 'Top floor, please.'

Emma was pulled upward into the dark. Because she was lighter, she rose faster. From Kurt's angle, she almost seemed to be flying.

His turn came moments later. With the harness around him, he held the rope with one hand and gripped the computer with the other. After the initial liftoff, he turned to look out over the camp. Only the fires near the center of camp and a few lights dotted here and there.

He glanced upward. A soft glow surrounded the rigging at the top. It came from the flashlights that Emma and Urco carried, but it was dim and very far away, like a boat on the surface waiting for him to return from a night dive.

As he neared the crest, the lights converged on him. On this particular peak, there was no need for a ladder to make the final ascent; instead, Kurt continued up until the top of the harness tapped against the pulley above him and his feet were level with a broad wooden platform. He stepped onto it with ease, disconnected the harness and handed Emma the computer.

'You should have had that reporter meet you up here,' he mentioned to Urco.

'Then he might never have left,' Urco replied.

'That was quite enjoyable,' Emma said to Kurt. 'I don't know what you were worried about.'

Kurt laughed at that and took a look around. There was a marked difference between this peak and the one he'd met Urco on earlier. For one thing, it was smaller – a dance floor instead of a football field. It had also been improved. Wooden planks had been nailed together and anchored in the stone. They covered most of the surface. Though some ground remained visible at the edges, the decking sloped away so sharply it would have been treacherous to stand on.

On Kurt's right, two plastic storage bins had been nailed to the deck. On his left, a well-braced rig held the zip lines coming to and leading off of the platform. Beyond was nothing but pitiless black.

'Love what you've done with the place,' Kurt joked.

'The terrain made it necessary,' Urco said. 'The ground here is too uneven, and terribly weathered. It made for poor footing, so we built this platform.'

Kurt moved across the creaky boards to a spot beside Emma. She'd taken a seat near the very center and had already flipped the laptop open and was booting up.

As she worked, a brief schematic appeared, depicting the horizon line, the constellations and the track of several NUMA satellites. The computer chose the satellite with the strongest signal.

'Locked in,' Emma said. 'Beginning transmission.'

'I saw your vehicle,' Urco said out of the blue. 'You seem to have gone through a great deal just to get here. You must want this airplane back very badly.'

'We do,' Emma admitted.

'It makes sense,' Urco replied. 'We all want back what we once had.'

A message popped up on the screen. *Download complete. Processing data.*

As the computer began combining the data, it displayed a series of calculations. Emma stared as the numbers danced, but Urco acted blithely uninterested, and Kurt had a sudden impression of danger.

He caught a sound in the wind and then heard a

squeak from the rigging beside him. He turned to see the zip line from the higher peak tensing and moving. He glanced out into the night and spotted a dark shape rushing toward them.

'Look out!'

A stocky man with square shoulders came flying in on the line. He let go of the T-bar as he crossed the threshold and barreled into Urco.

Another figure appeared out of the dark right behind him. This one, a lithe woman, landed with cat-like grace. She whipped out a pistol, targeted Emma and pulled the trigger all at once.

The shot went wide only because Kurt lunged forward and knocked her arm to the side. With one hand on her wrist, Kurt took her to the ground. Several shots fired, but they drilled harmlessly into the wooden deck.

She counterattacked by slamming a knee into his midsection. The bony impact struck with surprising power, but all Kurt cared about was the pistol. He kept her wrist locked in his grasp and banged her arm on the flooring until the weapon came free.

She stretched for it with her other hand, but he punched it away. It slid off the deck and out into the dark.

In the meantime, Urco struggled with the second attacker. They rolled toward the edge, oblivious to how close they were to falling, as they grasped each other and traded punches.

Emma sprang toward them, wrapping her arm around the assailant's thick neck, pulling him back. He reared up, arching his back and reaching for her in vain.

Kurt kept his focus on the woman. She'd gotten loose, hopped to her feet and pulled out a knife with almost inhuman speed. He dropped to the ground as she slashed at him. The blade cut the air above, and he spun on his side, sweeping her feet out from underneath. She landed hard on her back, her head whiplashing into the deck. She made an odd noise and went limp, dropping the knife and rolling over onto her side.

Since the woman appeared to be unconscious, Kurt turned his attention to the melee at the edge of the platform.

By now, the big man had thrown Emma off his back, gotten to his feet and doubled Urco over with a shot to the solar plexus. A brutal shove sent Urco tumbling off the platform and onto the weathered slope of the mountain. He slid, grabbing for anything he could reach, but his hands found only loose rock.

Emma dove for him, stretching out her arm. 'No,' she shouted.

She missed by several feet and Urco continued downward, his fingers scraping across the ground, until he vanished over the edge.

Kurt knew he had to take this wrecking ball of a man out or they would all follow Urco to their deaths. He jumped toward the man and hit him with a leaping kick. Both feet connected with the small of the man's back and he stumbled off the deck, vanishing into the dark. A soft thud marked his end seconds later.

'Help me,' a voice cried from down below. 'Please.'

'It's Urco,' Emma shouted.

They rushed to the edge. Kurt noticed one of the excavation's scaffolding ropes twisting back and forth. 'Hold tight,' he shouted, 'we'll pull you up.'

Kurt found a spot to anchor his feet, gripped the rope with both hands and leaned back. Emma joined him, and Urco rose, one foot at a time.

When he cleared the edge and could assist them using his feet on the slope, the archaeologist all but charged back onto the platform. 'Thank you,' he said, falling at their feet. 'Thank the gods.'

He rolled onto his back, breathing heavily. 'Ms Townsend, your fear of heights is well founded. I'm thinking of taking a similar position – '

He stopped midsentence, interrupted by movement and the sound of steel wheels spinning, as one of the T-bars zoomed away down the zip line.

They turned in unison. The woman was gone.

'She took the computer,' Emma pointed out.

Kurt didn't hesitate. He grabbed the other T-bar, connected it to the rope and launched himself after her.

32

Kurt leapt into the dark and was instantly flying. He gripped the T-bar, brought his knees up and felt the acceleration as the rollers spun ever faster.

This line led from the middle peak down to the first, a distance of three hundred yards and a drop of two hundred feet. It wasn't overly steep, which played to his advantage. Being heavier, and having taken a running start, Kurt closed the gap with the fleeing computer thief.

He crashed into her and wrapped his legs around her waist. She squirmed and twisted loose, then spun and managed to kick him in the shin.

With his momentum used up, they were now traveling at similar speeds. Considering that neither one of them wore a safety harness, her next move was wildly dangerous. She took one hand off of the T-bar and slashed at Kurt with the knife.

The first hack made a small cut on his arm, drawing blood. A second try missed and Kurt kicked the knife out of her hand before she could try again.

She was traveling backward now, fending him off with her feet. She didn't see the end of the line coming and crashed onto the next platform with an ugly tumble.

Kurt hit as hard. The impact sent him sprawling, but he was on top of her before she could move. Holding her to the ground, he bent her arm up behind her back. 'I don't like to hurt women,' he said, 'but I'll break your arm if you don't stop fighting.'

'Damn you,' she said. 'I'll kill you.'

'You had your chance,' he replied, upping the pressure.

She must have been incredibly limber because, even lying facedown, she managed to kick him in the back with her heel.

At that point, Kurt had had enough. He grabbed her by the hair and slammed her head forward, banging her face on the ground. She went limp, out cold.

Not trusting her to stay that way, he tied her up. By the time he was finished, Urco and Emma were sliding down the zip line toward him.

'You got her,' Emma said, undoing her harness.

'And the computer,' Kurt replied, opening the laptop to see if it had been damaged.

As the flashlights illuminated the woman, Kurt saw that she was Asian. Most likely from mainland China.

'Looks like all three powers are now accounted for,' Emma said.

The computer screen lit up, the soft glow illuminating Kurt's face, as the program resumed its calculations. He stared, watching as the lines on the map slowly converged to mark the *Nighthawk*'s final resting spot.

'No way!'

'What is it?' Emma asked.

He turned the computer around, displaying the map to Emma and Urco. A blinking pin marked the crash site.

'Lake of the Condors,' Emma said.

Urco's eyes grew wide in the dark.

Kurt grinned at the irony. 'Looks like you're going to see what's at the bottom of that lake sooner than we thought.'

33

It was too dangerous to move at night. The road to the lake was every bit as treacherous as the drive up from Cajamarca. The woman they'd captured insisted that others would come for her.

'She's probably bluffing,' Kurt said. 'But we're far more vulnerable on an open road in the dark than here.'

Both Urco and Emma agreed. Instead of driving out, they stoked the fires around the camp and borrowed a page from the Chachapoya, taking to the high ground and pulling up all the ropes. If there were Chinese agents or assassins out there, they'd have to scale the mountains by hand to stage an assault.

'We're not supposed to use these caves,' Urco told his volunteers, 'but they belonged to your forefathers, so they should be yours, not the government's.'

Kurt went higher, heading up to the tallest peak. Alone, he made a satellite call to Rudi Gunn, who had returned to Washington. He got the good news first: Joe and the Trouts had arrived in Cajamarca. Then came the bad.

'You were right,' Rudi said. 'The NSA has been hiding something. And it's big, even though it's actually very small.'

Kurt listened as Rudi explained what Hiram and

Priya had found. The explanation was detailed, highly technical and riddled with physics, but Kurt got the basics. 'That's worse than I thought.'

'Worse than any of us thought,' Rudi said. 'Want us to send you more resources?'

'No,' Kurt said. 'It would take too long to get everything in place. Speed and stealth are our best friends, at the moment. If we're right about the *Nighthawk*'s location, we can salvage it tomorrow and get the cargo out and off to wherever the NSA intended to store it. In the meantime, I'm starting to feel like Humphrey Bogart in *Treasure of the Sierra Madre* – suspicious of everyone and everything.'

'Can't say I blame you. We haven't heard from the Russians since you and Joe got back on dry land, but I doubt they're going to give up. And I'm certain we haven't seen the last of our Chinese friends. According to Central Intelligence, they have an army of agents in Peru and Ecuador. Don't be surprised if reinforcements show up when you least expect it.'

'Which is why I need to change the plan.'

'What did you have in mind?'

Kurt was thinking back to the service records of the Special Projects team. Considering who to choose for a difficult task. 'I'm going to send you a set of specs,' he said to Rudi, 'Relay them to Joe and the Trouts, and tell Gamay I'm sorry but she's going to miss the raising of the *Nighthawk*.'

'Understood,' Rudi said. 'I'll look for your message.'

Kurt said good-bye, cut the link and slid the phone

into his pocket. He was ready to head back down when the pulley squeaked as someone came up on the rope. A moment later, hands appeared at the top of the ladder.

He was expecting Urco, but the determined face of Emma Townsend popped up over the edge instead.

Kurt helped her off the ladder. 'This is a surprise.'

She moved toward the center of the peak. 'Turns out sitting in a creepy cave with mummified bodies is worse than scaling heights in the dark.'

Kurt laughed. He found the caves claustrophobic himself. 'I think it's time we leveled with each other,' he said. 'I know how it works. I know you're not at liberty to say much, so I don't blame you, but at this point I need the truth.'

'You *have* the truth,' she said.

'I have part of it,' Kurt said. He sat down, picked up a stone and ran his finger over the smooth surface; the color was faded on one side but deep and rich on the other – two sides to every story. 'When we first met, I wondered why they sent you with us,' he explained. 'It really made no sense. You have a reputation as a trouble-maker in the NSA – a trait I happen to admire – but one that makes you an odd choice to go with the group most likely to find the missing plane.'

'Don't flatter yourself,' she said. 'Or build me up to be something I'm not. They sent everyone they could find. Everyone they could get their hands on.'

'Sure,' Kurt said. 'But we were on the scene three days before anyone else, which gave us a big lead. That, along with our well-earned reputation for finding missing things in the ocean, is why they put you with us. Because if we did find it, they needed someone along for the ride who knew exactly what we were recovering. And even among the shadowed halls of the NSA, very few know what's really going on here. But between that Doctorate in Physics and your ties to NASA, you have to be one of the few.'

She didn't deny it. Nor did she admit anything. 'Time is of the essence,' she said. 'The Russians and the Chinese – '

'Aren't interested in the *Nighthawk*,' he said. 'They want the cargo that it's carrying. They want what it brought back.'

She went as silent as a stone.

'I know about the Penning traps,' Kurt said, 'along with containment units, the cryogenic equipment and the entire system you built to harvest and store antimatter. That's why the *Nighthawk* had a polar orbit. That's why it stayed in the dark, where the temperatures in space are closer to absolute zero. That's why it was up there for three years, because it's a very slow process.'

He let that linger and wondered if he would have to press her further. Finally, she came around.

'Not *anti*matter,' she said. 'A different form of matter. A few scientists call it by the rather awkward name: *un-matter*. We prefer to call it *mixed-state matter*: long-chain molecules made of equal parts of regular matter and antimatter.'

That was news. 'I thought matter and antimatter annihilated each other the instant they touched.'

'Normally, they do,' she said. 'But at temperatures close to absolute zero, molecular structures break down. Matter no longer holds a physical shape and, instead, acts more like a wave than a solid particle. In that condition, matter and antimatter can mix without destructive results, the way two waves of different frequencies can exist superimposed on each other. Using magnetic force and cryogenics to confine and control this mixed-state matter, we realized it could be stored indefinitely. It wasn't long before a member of our research team suggested there might be naturally occurring pools of mixed-state matter floating high above the poles, held stable within the magnetic field.'

'So you built the *Nighthawk* to go test that idea.'

'And we discovered a relative abundance of it.'

'A relative abundance?'

'Far more than we expected,' she said. 'Filaments of the material, spinning in what are essentially magnetic bubbles. Fractions of an ounce, in most cases, but enough to be worth retrieving. So we spent a year modifying the *Nighthawk*, and we filled the cargo bay with a more advanced type of Penning trap, which we call a *containment unit*, and we sent it up again to collect what we could find.'

'And now it's sitting at the bottom of a lake,' Kurt noted. 'And those containment units are running on battery power. What happens when the batteries run out?'

'You know what happens,' she snapped. 'A very large explosion.'

He did know that. He just wanted to hear her say it. 'How large?'

She spoke without emotion. Clinical and cold. It was the dry tone of a distant scientist, not someone who might be vaporized at any instant. 'Eight ounces of antimatter exposed to an equal amount of matter will cause an explosion the equivalent of a ten-mega-ton bomb detonating. Our best estimate puts the load on board the *Nighthawk* somewhere in the range of two hundred kilograms. Almost four hundred pounds.'

'Four hundred pounds!?'

'Approximately,' she said. 'If it all reacted simultaneously – and once some of it reacts, it will all react – the explosive force will be nearly eight thousand mega-tons, or eight giga-tons. The blast will be five times larger than the combined effect of detonating every nuclear weapon in the world's combined arsenal in the same place at the same exact time.'

Kurt just stared at her. He didn't know whether to laugh at the stupidity of what they'd done or curse them for their arrogance. 'And you brought this material to Earth willingly? Compiled it all in the same place? Are you people insane?'

'What would you have us do?' she asked. 'Once we figured out this material was up there, it wasn't going to be long before the Russians and the Chinese made the same discovery. Would you rather they had it? Do you want the designers of Chernobyl playing around with this stuff? The builders of the already crumbling Three Gorges Dam?'

'Of course not,' Kurt said. 'But what's to stop them from retrieving their own supply?'

'The fact that we took it all,' she said. 'It accumulates very slowly. It'll be a thousand years before there's a harvestable amount floating around up there again.'

'Great,' Kurt said. 'Maybe civilization will have dragged itself back from the Stone Age by then.'

'You think I don't know the danger?' she said. 'Do you think it doesn't weigh on me?'

He looked up at the dark night sky. The stars were bright out here, so far away from the nearest city. Tiny balls of fusion, which the Earth would become for a brief instant if they didn't find the *Nighthawk* and keep the containment units functioning.

He turned back toward her. 'At least I finally understand why you were all so certain the *Nighthawk* came down in one piece.'

'We knew the core had to be intact or we'd have all seen the results already.'

'How much time do we have?'

'Seventy-two hours,' she said. 'Maybe less. It depends how much light is reaching the solar panels on the wings.'

'And if the containment units or the cryogenic system fail early?'

'A Nebraska-sized hole in the Andes,' she said. 'A hundred trillion tons of rock instantly vaporized and blasted into the atmosphere. A ninety percent reduction in photosynthesis and biological activity. No one will have to worry about global warming anymore because the Earth will be in frigid darkness for at least five years.'

Not a pleasant scenario, he thought. 'And if we get it back to the United States?'

'The material will be split up into thousands of tiny samples, each no more than half an ounce. They'll be stored in a labyrinth of underground facilities that the NSA has been building for the last three years. A failure at one site will be no worse than a small bomb going off in an underground test location because there will be no other material for it to react with.'

All emotion had left Kurt. There was only one thing that counted now. 'Then we'd damn well better find it and get it locked down.'

'My thoughts exactly,' she replied.

34

A staccato thumping echoed through the high mountain pass. Ground-dwelling animals looked up nervously and then darted away as a thundering orange machine flew between peaks and its great whirling shadow passed over them.

Joe Zavala was at the controls of the Air-Crane once again. The big helicopter was slow and stable, but it wasn't the easiest bird to control in a crosswind. As a result, he was more focused on the flying than the scenery. At least his passengers were enjoying the view.

'Now, this is a view fit for the gods,' Urco's voice called out over the intercom.

Joe glanced back for an instant. The cockpit of the Air-Crane was packed. Kurt sat in the copilot's seat while Emma, Urco and Paul Trout sat on the jump seats behind them.

'It's too bad we couldn't see it at sunrise,' Urco added.

In fact, Joe had seen plenty of the mountains at sunrise, making another run that only he, Kurt and Paul knew about. It had pushed back their arrival at La Jalca. 'Sorry about that,' Joe said. 'We were slightly delayed.'

'Are we trying to make up time by flying through the mountains instead of over them?' Paul asked.

'Talk to Kurt,' Joe said. 'I just go where I'm told to.'

'The Chinese agent claimed she had more support out here,' Kurt said. 'If so, the Air-Crane slowly crossing the sky in a nice straight line would be like a big orange arrow pointing to the crash site.'

'Not to mention a tempting target,' Emma said.

Joe banked to the right, rounding another peak and taking them out over the plunging valley on the far side. 'Besides,' he added, 'this is a lot more fun.'

The mood in the helicopter was upbeat. They were close to finding the missing craft and averting disaster. That hope had given everyone a burst of adrenaline and a second wind.

'Even if they did spot us, it would take forever to get here,' Urco promised. 'The road to the lake is very poor; it makes a goat path look like the German autobahn. It was built by the Inca seven hundred years ago and hasn't been resurfaced since.'

They could see the path from where they were. A long, thin pencil line scraped into the side of the highlands. It curved in and out of the various hills and then began to drop, leading from the high plateau down to the valley and eventually to the lake.

Lake of the Condors sat at the foot of a plateau. It was fed by a river that snaked down from the mountains, entered a gap in the bluff and then shot forward over a ledge and down into the lake.

The drop was two hundred feet, not particularly high for a waterfall, but it poured out of the overhanging rock with substantial force, filling the narrow upper end of the pear-shaped lake.

From the air, it appeared static, a standing wave covered by a veil of spray that sparkled in the sun. Cliffs surrounding it stood like battlements, and the hills sloped downward from there.

'Get your cameras out,' Joe said. 'I'm going to buzz the falls while I look for the best spot to set us down.'

They crossed the lake at an angle, giving everyone a great view of the waterfall. Down below, the mirror surface of the lake reflected the blue sky, the green of the hills and white of the clouds, but the water itself was a dark, inky black.

'The water level is fairly low,' Paul said. 'There's a lot of empty beach around the lower half of the lake.'

Joe saw what Paul was describing: dried silt and stones fifty feet wide encircled that section of the lake. Beyond, a rushing stream took the outflow of the lake on its continuing journey toward lower ground and the Pacific Ocean.

Urco pointed out several features, having been to the lake before. 'You cannot land over there,' he said, pointing to a flat area. 'Too soft. Sometimes a swamp. Best to land up high on the rocks.'

Joe nodded and turned back toward the hills. He found a raised section that looked solid and flat, circled once and put the Air-Crane down on top of it.

Thirty minutes later, they were on the water, cruising across the lake on an inflatable Zodiac. A compact sonar emitter trailed out behind them while a receiver designed to pick up the *Nighthawk*'s beacon – if it was still transmitting – dangled over the side.

While Joe drove the boat, Kurt kept his eyes on the sonar display. The scan showed a flat-bottomed lake filled with sediment and averaging about sixty feet deep. Here and there, small outcroppings of rock appeared, though nothing to indicate a city had ever existed at this location.

'I'm not seeing any skyscrapers,' he said to Urco.

'The ruins lie beneath the silt,' Urco explained. 'As we get closer to the waterfall, you'll see some of them jutting out where the current has scoured the sediment away.'

'Have you been down there?' Kurt asked.

'I don't dive,' he said. 'But some of my people do. I should learn, though. Up on the surface, grave robbers and the elements have taken away so much of what we could discover. But down there, preserved beneath the mud, lie untouched treasures from the past.'

Kurt nodded. He was more interested in an untouched aircraft from the present, but he understood Urco's excitement.

While Kurt and Urco kept their eyes on the sonar scanner, Emma and Paul were working with the under-water receiver. She wore a headset and was listening for a signal. Paul was directing the receiver by hand.

'Anything?' he asked, operating with the skills of a man who'd grown up adjusting the rabbit ears on his TV.

Even with the headphones on, Emma was straining to hear a tiny electronic beep over the wind and the outboard motor. 'Not yet.'

Paul held the unit steady, twisting a lever that turned

the submerged receiver five degrees at a time. 'How about now?'

She shook her head.

Kurt stole a glance her way. Tension lined her face. If the *Nighthawk* wasn't here, they were in major trouble and all but out of time.

He looked back at the sonar display. For the first time, the underwater profile of the lake had begun to change. Small mounds became noticeable and then block-like structures protruding through the silt. The depth was increasing as well.

Kurt looked up; they were nearing the waterfall. The force of the drop and the outflow of water had carved a deeper pool at this end as the current scoured away the sediment and deposited it farther out in the lake.

'You see?' Urco said, pointing to squared-off sections of the screen. 'Streets, avenues, buildings – it's a city. A drowned city.'

Kurt wasn't so sure. He'd seen rock formations that looked man-made before. The Bimini Road off the Bahamas came to mind, as did the Yonaguni ruins near Japan, a place that many thought was a submerged temple complex even though geologists insisted it was nothing more than a formation of stratified granite.

He chose not to burst Urco's bubble, at the moment. 'We'll have to dive on it to get a better look,' Kurt said. 'But I won't deny it's plenty interesting.'

Urco grabbed him by the shoulders and shook him with appreciation. 'You won't be disappointed.'

By now, they'd come close enough to the waterfall

that the overspray was drifting across them. Kurt wiped the screen of the laptop and covered the keyboard.

He glanced at Joe. 'Nothing on this pass. Take us back around.'

Joe nodded and turned the wheel. But instead of turning in front of the falls, he guided them in behind it. Because of the overhang of rock high above and the speed with which the water was traveling when it flew off the edge, there was a thirty-foot gap at the bottom.

The Zodiac cruised into that gap and sped between the curtain of water and the cliffside. The rock wall was dark and wet and pockmarked with caves.

'More burial chambers,' Urco said, pointing. 'I would like it if they remain undisturbed.'

Kurt studied the dark caverns as they sped past. 'Understood,' he said.

The next leg took them down the middle of the lake. They hadn't gone far when Emma held up a hand. 'Slow down,' she said. 'I'm picking up something.'

Joe cut the throttle back, the boat settled and all eyes fell upon Emma.

'Ten degrees to the right,' she requested.

Paul turned the lever and stopped.

'Ten more?' she asked, and then, when he'd done that, added, 'Back five.'

Emma held both hands against the headphones, pressing them to her ears. She looked out over the water and pointed. 'That way. Slowly.'

Joe nudged the throttle and the Zodiac moved forward at a speed just above idle. At Emma's direction, they made a wide circle and then a narrower one, homing in on the signal.

Finally, Emma held up her hand once more and Joe brought the Zodiac to a stop.

As the boat settled, Emma pulled the headphone jack out of the receiver so everyone could hear the signal . . . *Beep* . . . *Beep* . . . *Beep* . . . Steady and low.

'It's here,' she said, a wave of relief washing over her face. 'The *Nighthawk* is here.'

35

With their dive gear on, Emma slipped into the water with Kurt and Joe. They would make the first dive together, though once the *Nighthawk* was physically located, Joe would dry off and prep the Air-Crane for the big lift.

As she descended into the water, Emma noticed the chill in her bones. The water came mostly from snow-melt and the temperature was a frigid fifty degrees. Even wearing heavy, 3:5 wet suits with attached hoods, full-face helmets, boots and gloves, it could be felt.

While the cold was something planned for, dealt with and otherwise ignored, the visibility was a different problem. The water was full of floating sediment stirred up by the waterfall and decomposing plant matter washed down from higher elevations. There was perhaps ten feet of visibility and, at thirty feet, even powerful lights looked as if they were nothing more than glowing candles.

Emma used a light meter to check the incoming energy from the sun. *'This isn't good,'* she announced over the helmet-to-helmet communications system. *'With the water so murky, the system will be charging at fifteen percent efficiency. That won't do much for the batteries. The sooner we raise it, the better.'*

'We have to find it first,' Joe said. 'Which wouldn't be too difficult, except we're looking for a black aircraft, sitting at the bottom of a black lake.'

They were kicking lazily and descending slowly.

'The upper surface of the wing has a reflective strip built into it,' Emma said. 'Hit that with your light and you'll have no problem spotting it.'

The lake was eighty feet deep in the center and at least seventy feet beneath the Zodiac. Emma was two-thirds of the way down before the beam of her diving light reached out and found the bottom.

The silt was dark, the color of coal, but flecked here and there with just enough quartz to sparkle like a black gemstone. Tiny rills in the sediment looked like the ridges of a huge fingerprint.

'Spread out a little and drift with the current,' Kurt suggested. Most of the lake would be free of any appreciable current, but they were still getting a little push from the waterfall and for that reason had gone into the lake upstream of the target area.

Emma did as Kurt suggested, feeling a surprising pang of isolation as Kurt's and Joe's lights dimmed with the distance.

She concentrated on the task at hand, scanning back and forth, looking for any sign of the *Nighthawk*'s tail or the reflective strips glued to the upper surface of her wings. But the first item of consequence was a blur of color, orange and white, billowing gently along the bottom.

Emma felt her heart rate quicken. 'Contact,' she said. 'Parachute.'

She moved toward it and found both of the *Nighthawk*'s parachutes lying on the bottom, half buried in the silt. The free sections were wafting like sea grass as the water flowed over them.

As Kurt and Joe converged on her, she grabbed ahold of the settled nylon and hauled on it. The line was taut.

'*Still attached,*' she said. She pulled herself forward, making her way down the line arm over arm, until a bulky shape came into view. Kurt and Joe swam in behind her. Their lights played across a midnight black curve. Stamped on the side in low-resolution gray were the letters *USAF*.

With all three of their lights pointed down on it, the craft came into view. It was resting solidly on the bottom, its belly and the lower half of its wing touching the silt. Though she'd seen it plenty of times before, it still appeared surprisingly small.

'*Finally,*' she said.

'*How's it look?*' Kurt asked.

Emma drifted over the top of it, checking for damage. '*The fuselage and payload bay are still sealed,*' she said. '*The wings seem to have some gouges where the Russian clamps locked onto it, but nothing catastrophic.*'

She swam forward, arriving at the nose. With her gloved hand, she brushed a layer of silt from a panel on the side of the aircraft. It revealed an electronic touch screen display protected by a scorched plate of transparent Kevlar.

Tapping the panel, she brought it to life. It offered a

bright glow in the dark water. Three bars indicated the condition of the cryogenic system: all were solidly in the green. Another section of the screen indicated that containment units were operating as planned while the final part of the display indicated the power supply in a yellow condition.

'One battery pack has already failed, but the others are compensating,' she said.

'Is this a problem?' Kurt asked.

'Only if another pack goes down. Even as is, we should have at least twenty-four hours to get this thing topside, get the containment units out of it and plug them into the portable fuel cells.'

'No reason to wait,' Kurt said.

Joe floated over beside them. 'What about opening the cargo bay and removing the containment units without ever lifting the aircraft? It would save time and eliminate the danger of something going wrong with the lift. Not to mention prevent any satellite from spotting the Nighthawk once we get it up on the surface.'

Emma shook her head. 'It's too risky in the aquatic environment. All the electronics are sealed and self-contained, but we can't be certain of their condition. Between the vibration of the launch, three years in space, the heat of reentry and the Russian attempt to capture the aircraft, there may be internal damage on a small scale. Loose connections. Gaps in the insulation. If we get everything wet and end up with a short –'

'The lake goes up along with a big chunk of northern Peru,' Kurt said.

'Exactly,' she replied. 'No shortcuts. We have to raise it and get it onto dry land before we do anything else.'

36

The rattle of the gas-powered air compressor carried across the lake from the stern of the Zodiac, a jarring disturbance in an otherwise peaceful setting.

Paul Trout sat beside it, keeping an eye on the compressor and the line that ran over the edge and disappeared into the water. Fifty feet away, a circle of bubbles boiled and churned as the excess air rose up to the surface.

For now, Paul was alone in the boat. Kurt, Joe and Emma had gone back down to prepare the *Nighthawk* for lifting, while Urco had volunteered to go ashore, where he was scouting around for a solid place to set the aircraft down.

Squinting across the lake, Paul could just see the Peruvian. He was higher up on the slope, moving behind a section of tall grasses, thrusting a staff down into the ground in an effort to determine if the soil would hold the *Nighthawk*'s weight.

Using a handheld radio, Paul reached out to him. 'Urco, this is Paul.'

'Go ahead, Mr Paul,' Urco replied.

'Wondering if you're having any luck out there?'

He saw Urco turn his way and wave. *'The shoreline is too soft and muddy to hold much weight. And even back here, away from the edge, it's marshland. I'm going to make my way to higher ground.'*

'Roger that,' Paul said. 'Keep us posted.'

Urco waved and moved off, carrying his staff. Paul watched until Urco was out of sight. Perhaps other eyes were watching him, too, Paul thought. And then he turned his attention back to the compressor and the pressure gauge.

Down below, Kurt was holding the business end of the air hose and feeding it underneath the *Nighthawk*. The compressed air blasting out through the front acted like a drill bit, scouring out the dark silt. The power of Kurt's arms acted like a hydraulic press, forcing it forward.

With each shove, another burst of bubbles and sediment came flowing backward and out toward Kurt, billowing forth in a dark, swirling cloud. As the sediment churned around him, Kurt kept feeding more line into the opening. *'Anything yet?'*

Joe's voice came back slightly distorted as if he were standing in a deep tunnel. Joe was on the other side waiting for the line to pop out. *'Not yet. Keep pushing.'*

Kurt worked the line back and forth and gave it another shove.

'I'm seeing bubbles,' Joe announced. *'You're almost there.'*

Kurt gave the line one more push and felt it move freely. The billowing cloud of silt that had been streaming back toward him relented.

'*Got it,*' Joe said.

'*Phase one complete,*' Kurt said. '*Time for you to do some work, amigo.*'

On the far side of the *Nighthawk*, Joe grabbed the tip of the air hose and pulled it toward him. Using a length of wire, he hooked one of the lifting straps to the valve and tugged hard to make sure it was secure.

'*Strap one attached,*' he said. '*My job is done.*'

'*That was quick,*' Kurt said. '*Maybe I should rethink the division of labor on this project.*'

Joe laughed, watching as the hose and the attached strap were pulled back beneath the *Nighthawk*, moving one arm's length at a time.

While Kurt and Joe placed what would eventually be four braided nylon straps beneath the aircraft, Emma inspected the wings, examining every blemish she found. Many of the outer tiles were damaged. She found hairline cracks and plenty of chips and scrapes, even several spots where the tiles had been torn off completely, presumably when the *Nighthawk* broke the grasp of its Russian captors. But the high-strength alloy beneath was untouched.

'*The wing doesn't appear to be compromised,*' she announced. '*It won't have taken on any water.*'

'*Good to hear,*' Joe replied. '*We're fairly close to the max lifting capacity of the Air-Crane already. We don't need a few tons of lake water to make it worse.*'

'*Agreed,*' Emma said. '*I'm going to check the hardpoints for corrosion and pitting. Would hate for something to break loose just as we claimed victory.'*

As she swam across the top of the aircraft, the air hose broke through the silt once again, releasing a swarm of fine bubbles that swirled up around her. For an instant, it was like swimming in a glass of champagne. She didn't want to get ahead of herself but imagined they'd soon be raising glasses to celebrate the victory.

37

La Jalca Canyon, a half mile away

A half mile away, in the dark throat of a barren cave, there was no sense of victory or even hope for the men imprisoned in it. Only cloying darkness, cold, bone-aching dampness and noise. Constant, unending noise.

The bulk of the waterfall dropped downward just beyond the mouth of the cave. Its tumbling white water hid everything beyond, causing vertigo to anyone who stared into it for too long and blocking out all semblance of detail.

What it hid from the eyes it hid also from the ears as its endless roar echoed off the stone walls, drowning out soft speech, clear thought and even the din of modern men out on the lake.

The two men sitting in the cave hadn't heard the approach of the helicopter this morning nor the outboard motor of the Zodiac nor the excited shouts of discovery that came shortly afterward. Not even the endless rattle of the air compressor could penetrate the wall of sound that shielded them. It was isolation of the body, soul and mind and it had taken its toll already.

After days in this condition, they were numb to it. They sat with their backs to the wall, their knees up and their heads down; an upright version of the foetal position. Their hands were chained in front of them while their ankles were bound together and hooked to heavy iron weights that made walking a difficult task.

Days of growth covered their faces while a layer of grime covered their uniforms. Beneath the dirt, oil and dust could be seen the double-headed eagle of the Russian Air Force and the squadron patch depicting the great claw of a flying raptor grasping another bird from the sky. A star on one man's shoulder indicated his rank as Major. A set of wings on his chest overlaid with measuring tongs indicated he was a test pilot.

He stared into the darkness, weakened by the cold and a lack of food, but in his mind churned thoughts of revenge. So dark was his mood that it took him a moment to notice a shaft of light appearing in the back part of the cave.

The light came down from the surface, through a narrow vertical chute that the two Russians had been forced to descend at gunpoint days before. After reaching the bottom, they'd been chained up and then abandoned by their captors, who had climbed up the shaft, pulled up the rope and blocked out the light by sliding a trapdoor across the top.

The appearance of the light meant the door had been moved aside. It meant something would change. Good or bad, Major Yuri Timonovski welcomed that.

'Someone's coming,' he said.

The second man looked up, his eyes bloodshot and jittery. 'Maybe they're going to feed us.'

'Or kill us,' Timonovski replied. 'I'd take either at this point.'

The end of a rope dropped down the shaft, hitting the ground and curling up like a snake. The hanging part writhed back and forth as someone descended it.

Timonovski stood, ready to face whatever was about to come his way. His legs ached, his back hurt, and he waddled awkwardly in the direction of the intruder, dragging the weights with him.

The weights didn't keep him from moving but were enough to prevent him from climbing. And they made jumping into the lake a suicidal notion. Something he might consider if circumstances did not improve.

Boots appeared at the bottom of the shaft and a rangy man with a heavy beard dropped the last few feet into the cave. Timonovski recognized him instantly: the Falconer, the man they'd been working with since day one. The man who'd promised to deliver the *Nighthawk* to them by hacking its guidance program and overriding the American directives coming from Vandenberg.

Timonovski also knew him as a betrayer. He was certain the Falconer had done something at the last minute that caused the *Nighthawk* to break loose from *Blackjack 1*. And when he'd attempted to break off pursuit and head for the refueling rendezvous, the Falconer had slit the throat of Timonovski's copilot, pulled a snub-nosed pistol and threatened the Major and his flight engineer with death if they didn't do as he ordered.

After following the *Nighthawk* down and watching it parachute into the lake, the Falconer had directed them to a narrow landing strip seven miles from the lake. A group of armed men waited for them and, after being taken hostage, any hopes of escape vanished.

'You're awake,' the Falconer said as he came closer. 'Excellent.'

They spoke English to each other, the only common language between them.

'It's impossible to sleep in here,' Timonovski said.

'Some people find waterfalls soothing.'

'Not when they're right on top of your head.'

The Falconer shrugged.

'I see you're alone,' Timonovski said. 'Have you run out of friends?'

'On the contrary,' the Falconer insisted, 'I am collecting them by the handful as I once collected you.'

Major Timonovski could barely stand the arrogance, but he could do nothing about it. 'What do you want from us now, Birdcaller?'

'I've come to feed you,' the bearded man replied. He shrugged off a backpack, unzipped the top and placed it in front of his captives.

The Major kept his eyes from it, but he couldn't keep the aroma from his nostrils. Perhaps starvation heightened the senses.

Still sitting, the flight engineer scrambled toward the backpack and began plucking items out of it. A plastic container filled with soup came first, bottles of water with added electrolytes were next, followed by a couple of wrapped items.

'Sandwiches,' the engineer said, unwrapping one.

Timonovski found his mouth was watering. 'Is this some kind of trick?'

'Not at all,' the Falconer said. 'You'll need your strength if you're to fly out of here.'

'Fly?'

'You can pilot a helicopter, can't you?'

'Of course,' the Major said. He'd flown everything in the Russian inventory. 'Do you have one?'

'My new friends do,' the Falconer said.

He nodded toward the lake, invisible beyond the mouth of the cave. 'What you can't see – one of the many things you can't see – are American agents submerged in the water and securing the *Nighthawk* as we speak. They're preparing to remove it from the depths. Once they do, I shall take it from them and you will deliver it to the runway where *Blackjack 2* now waits. You will finish your mission, refuel over Venezuela as planned and cross the Atlantic, returning to Russia as great heroes.'

Timonovski was stunned. 'I don't understand. Now you want us to take it back to Moscow? But we already had it. You're the one who set it free. If you hadn't woken it up after *Blackjack 1* captured it – '

'Had I let you proceed, I wouldn't have been able to extract the full payment I desire. But now the price to be paid will be equal to the pain. Indeed, it's much higher than you can possibly imagine.'

'Blood money,' the Major said.

'All wealth is blood money,' the Falconer said. 'In one form or another.'

Major Timonovski just stared.

'If you prefer, I can leave it to the Americans and leave you both here to rot away while going mad from the noise.'

'If this is a trick –'

'Then you will endure it because you have no choice in the matter.'

Timonovski fumed. The Birdcaller was in complete control. But even that had its limits. Even this master manipulator had to deal with gravity. 'We'll never get off the ground,' he said. 'The runway is too short, the *Nighthawk* too heavy. We'll never clear the trees with that thing on our backs.'

The bearded man cocked his head. 'Leave that to me.'

He turned, walked back to the rope and wrapped his hands around it and began to pull himself up. The rope vanished moments later and the column of light was cut off.

Gray darkness and white noise engulfed them once again.

'You should eat,' the flight engineer said. 'Whatever happens, we will need our strength.'

Timonovski ignored him for a moment, pondering the situation, before giving in to the lure of the food. He didn't believe a word of what the Birdcaller promised; somehow, it would be another lie, he was certain of it. But it seemed far better to die on a full stomach than to starve.

38

Off the coast of Ecuador

The Russian salvage fleet was now within a hundred miles of the Ecuadorian coast, though they had yet to discover any sign of either *Blackjack 2* or the American space plane.

It seemed to Constantin Davidov that the race had been lost. The sudden drawdown in American naval activity suggested they'd found it.

Alone in his cabin, Davidov considered returning to Russia and facing the consequences of failure. A knock at the door startled him.

'Come in.'

It was one of the Admiral's staff. 'A message has come in,' he said. 'The Admiral wishes you to meet him in the communications room.'

Davidov hurried to the communications center.

'It's from the Falconer,' Borozdin said.

'He's alive?'

'It would appear,' Borozdin said. 'And since we've found no sign of *Blackjack 2*'s wreckage, we must assume the crew and the aircraft are fine as well.'

'Then where have they been?' Davidov snapped.

'Maybe this will tell you.'

Borozdin handed him a note. It was all code. The Falconer's code. Davidov translated from memory and stared at the curious message. It was cryptic even after it had been deciphered. 'Is this it? Is this the entire communiqué?'

'That's all we received,' Borozdin replied. 'It came in with the Falconer's identification marks. The message is from him.'

'That, I do not doubt,' Davidov replied. 'The man is nothing if not obtuse.'

He stared at the page again. 'The numbers are obviously map coordinates,' he said. 'But the message . . .'

It read:

> *Full delivery.*
> *Bring gold. Coins only.*
> *The price has doubled.*
> *Beware, Americans are watching.*
>
> *RATO.*
> *You have eight hours*

'*Full delivery,*' Borozdin said. 'Does he mean the *Nighthawk* itself?'

'I suspect he does,' Davidov replied.

'That seems doubtful,' Borozdin said. 'You yourself said the Americans must have it by now. Their fleet actions confirm it. It's a money grab, pure and simple. He'll ambush you and take payment for what he could not deliver.'

Davidov rubbed his chin thoughtfully. 'I'm not so sure,' he said.

'Why is that?'

'*RATO,*' Davidov said almost to himself. '*Rocket-assisted takeoff.* It's a plan we discussed if one of the bombers captured the *Nighthawk* but was forced to land. A contingency to get it, and the *Nighthawk*, back in the air together. If he's requesting RATO, maybe he has the *Nighthawk* after all.'

Borozdin shook his head. 'Only you still believe in him, my friend.'

'I believe nothing,' Davidov said. 'But I must not fail, not now, not after all this. Is the satellite sweep of Ecuador and Peru complete?'

'Nearly.'

'And these coordinates?'

Borozdin looked the numbers over and then moved to a computer terminal and typed them in. 'Rudimentary airfield on a high plateau,' he said. 'Completed by a Chinese mining company three years ago. Abandoned.'

'Do we have a recent pass?'

Borozdin accessed the satellite scan. 'Yes,' he said.

'Bring it up and zoom in.'

Borozdin used the cursor to draw a box around the airfield and tapped ENTER. The resolution changed and the photograph resolved. 'No sign of the *Nighthawk*,' he said.

'What's that?' Davidov said, pointing to a distorted shape at one end of the airfield.

Borozdin zoomed in once more and shrugged. 'Hard to tell.'

Davidov disagreed. 'It's an aircraft. A large delta-wing aircraft, hidden beneath a tarp. That's *Blackjack 2*. I have no doubt.'

'If it is, then where are the crew? Why haven't they contacted us?'

'Who knows? It's a very remote area,' Davidov said. 'A miracle they even found that airfield to set down upon.' He stood. 'I need to speak with the quartermaster. And, God protect me, I need a helicopter to get me to Peru.'

'You're not seriously going to fly out there with a suitcase full of gold?'

'I'm going to do exactly that,' Davidov said. 'I'll take four of your commandos with me.'

Borozdin clearly thought the idea was dubious, if not suicidal. But he was a sailor, a man trained to act when circumstances were in his favor and to flee when they weren't. The intelligence service worked differently – they took chances, enormous and sometimes near-suicidal chances. It was their character and their nature and the whole reason behind the attempt to capture the American spacecraft in the first place.

Borozdin offered a more plodding solution. 'We have an Antonov 124 cargo plane waiting in Havana,' Borozdin said. 'Why not dispatch it with a hundred men on board? It's designed for heavy lifting and short fields. It will easily be able to land there, pluck the *Nighthawk* up and carry it away. And you won't have to expose yourself to this treachery.'

The Antonov 124 was a four-engine, heavy-lift transport. It would be perfect for the job. But getting that large aircraft into Peru unnoticed would be near impossible.

'You forget the balance of the message,' Davidov said. 'The Americans are watching. I have no choice. I will ride in one of your infernal helicopters to the coast. We can charter a small turboprop aircraft to take me from there.'

'And if the Falconer double-crosses you?'

'Others will hunt him down,' Davidov said. 'A fact I will remind him of when I see him.'

39

Kurt and Emma were back in the water. They'd positioned four straps beneath the *Nighthawk*, two at the front, two at the back. The straps were spaced so that the aircraft's center of gravity was directly between them.

While Emma attached lifting bags to the ends of each strap, Kurt filled them with air. Known as parachute-style bags because the bottom end remained open even after they were filled, they arrived in a compact folded state but expanded into teardrop shapes the size of a small car.

To keep the strain balanced and prevent the straps from slipping toward one side or the other, Kurt moved from spot to spot, partially inflating one and then swimming to the other side and inflating its counterpart to equalize the buoyancy.

When he was finished, eight inflated yellow bags floated around the sunken craft, jostling against one another in the current. Still, the *Nighthawk* hadn't budged.

'Air bags filled,' Kurt said. *'Straps are tight.'*

'And it hasn't moved an inch,' Emma's voice announced.

Kurt hadn't expected it to. *'The lifting bags aren't enough to pull it from the bottom,'* he said. *'But they'll help the Air-Crane overcome the suction effect created by the layer of silt.'*

Salvage teams called this additional effort the *break-out force*. Depending on the texture of the sediment, it could be a small or large problem. Kurt expected the latter.

At first, it looked as if the *Nighthawk* had touched down without lowering its landing gear and had come to rest on its wide, flat underside. A quick investigation proved otherwise. Burrowing beneath the nose, Emma had found the landing gear not only down and locked but sunk directly into the sediment like the spikes on the bottom of an athletic shoe. Because of this, and the large surface area now in contact with the silt, the break-out force would be huge. Almost as much as the weight of the *Nighthawk* itself.

'I was hoping it might break loose just a little,' Emma said.

She was floating above him. The light strapped to her shoulder illuminating the side of the *Nighthawk* and the hardpoints near the nose. Kicking steadily, she guided a steel cable with gloved hands, connecting it to an attachment point and testing the assembly with several solid pulls. That done, she moved to the other side of the aircraft to connect the second hook.

Kurt looked toward the surface. The Air-Crane hovered somewhere above them, hidden by the silt in the water. Kurt could just make out the dull thumping of its rotors as the sound reverberated off the surface of the lake.

'Lifting cables secured,' Emma announced as she swam out through the forest of yellow bags.

'Looks like we're ready to go,' Kurt said.

'I'll inform Joe,' Emma said.

She swam toward the surface, navigating what was now a maze of cables and straps above and around the downed aircraft.

When she disappeared behind the inflated yellow bags, Kurt was left alone on the lake bottom. 'Moment of truth,' he whispered to himself.

It would only be the first of many. But, if they didn't get that craft off the bottom, nothing else mattered.

Hovering above the lake in the Air-Crane, Joe kept one eye on the gauges and one on the surface of the lake below.

He could just see the circular tops of the yellow air bags through the dark water. They were bunched together and stationary. They looked fully inflated.

'It won't be long now,' he said. 'Are you ready?'

The question was meant for Paul, who sat behind him in the crane operator's seat. 'Yes,' Paul said. 'I've become an expert at operating cranes over the last week. I even know how to throw a submersible like I was casting for a fish.'

Joe could hear the mischievous tone in Paul's words. 'I heard how you launched the *Angler* from the deck of the *Catalina*,' Joe said. 'A neat trick. At this point, it's all about reeling in a big fish and not letting it get away.'

'I'll try to restrain myself.'

Joe made another scan of the gauges. The engine temperature was running high, not in the red zone yet but getting there.

Hovering wasn't easy on the turbines, it meant less airflow to cool the blades. It meant the engine had to work harder and hotter. And even though he was only fifty feet off the lake's surface, the altimeter read ninety-four hundred and change. That meant the air was thin, the rotors getting less bite of air with each circular sweep.

Joe had studied plenty of crashes during his flight training. It was a way to learn from the mistakes of others. As he recalled with a certain morbidity, a great many of those crashes came when operating *hot*, *high* and *heavy*.

The old-timer who'd taught him to fly had insisted that was not a place any pilot ever wanted to find himself, but Joe had no choice. The Air-Crane was already hot and high; as soon as they pulled the *Nighthawk* free of the water, it would be very, very heavy.

He tapped the temperature gauge, thankful for the breeze that was helping cool the turbine. 'Come on,' he whispered. 'Let's get this show on the road.'

'Do you see any dye?' Paul asked.

Kurt and Emma had dye capsules with them. Red to indicate a problem; green to give the all clear and show Paul and Joe the exact flow of the current, so they could align themselves with it as they lifted.

'No,' Joe said. 'But someone's coming up.'

A diver appeared on the surface. In the full suit and helmet, it was impossible to tell which one. The diver flashed a light on and off three times, offered a thumbs-up, and then broke open the green dye capsule.

Joe responded by toggling the landing light on and

off. The diver acknowledged and went back down. 'Cables are in place,' he said. 'Ready to lift.'

'Finally,' Paul replied. 'Hauling in the slack.'

As Paul manipulated the controls, the cables began rising out of the dark lake. One led to the nose of the *Nighthawk* and one to a spot near the tail.

Joe felt weight on the helicopter as soon as the slack was taken up. 'Lock it there,' he said. 'I'll do the rest.'

As Paul locked the winch, Joe added power slowly. This was the most dangerous point: the lift itself. Manipulating the controls with a light touch, he pulled up, allowed the Air-Crane to settle and then pulled up again.

The cables strained and stretched tight, shedding water each time, but after several attempts, the *Nighthawk* remained stuck in the silt down below.

'Come on, baby,' Joe whispered. 'Don't play hard to get.'

He pulled harder and longer on the next try. The rotors thundered above him. The turbines howled. The swirling pattern on the water below swept around and around, but despite continued attempts, the *Nighthawk* would not break free.

A yellow warning light came on indicating high temperature in turbine number one.

'It's no good,' Paul shouted from behind him.

'It's got to come loose soon,' Joe said.

Joe relaxed the power and watched the temperature stabilize just below the red line. 'One more try,' he said. 'I'm going to full power.'

*

314

Down below, Kurt and Emma could tell the Air-Crane was struggling. The cables had groaned and creaked with each successive pull while the drumming of the rotors rose to a crescendo, but the black spacecraft never moved.

'Is it caught on something?' Emma asked.

'It's the suction,' Kurt said. *'Get under the wing. Dig out as much silt as you can.'*

Emma swam for the tip of the right wing and began digging with her gloved hands, scooping at the muck and pushing it out behind her.

Kurt swam to the tail, shoved the air hose beneath the fuselage and opened the valve to full. He fed it in, trying to build up an air bubble that would spread across the underside of the plane and break the effect of the suction.

When he'd pushed the hose in as far as possible, he left it there and swam to the left wing.

Diving beneath it, he began digging out the black silt with his arms and shoveling it away. Reaching deeper and deeper, he was soon beneath the craft – where he'd be trapped and crushed if it rose and then settled.

The sound of the rotors torquing up to full power came again. The cables strained. Kurt stretched deeper and deeper beneath the plane, pulling at the muck with his long arms.

Suddenly, a wave of bubbles surged across the underside of the aircraft. It rose with surprising abruptness and Kurt heard a sucking sound, like the last of the water going down a drain.

He and Emma were pulled in beneath the *Nighthawk* along with the tons of water that were rushing into the space the aircraft had suddenly vacated.

In the swirl of bubbles and sediment, it was impossible to make out anything aside from the light on Emma's shoulder.

Kurt grabbed her arm and pulled.

They kicked hard, swimming together through a storm of swirling black water. After the initial surge, the *Nighthawk* was settling back. Kurt felt his flippers hitting against the underside of the plane as he kicked out from under it. By the time he turned around, the aircraft was rising again, traveling upward through the water, moving slowly but surely. A fountain of bubbles pouring from the air hose chased it toward the surface.

'*Let's get topside,*' Emma said. '*I want to be there when it lands.*'

Kurt nodded and the two of them swam toward the Zodiac's anchor line and then began moving slowly upward.

By the time they emerged into the bright sunshine, the black tail of the *Nighthawk* had broken the surface. It looked like the dorsal fin of an oversized shark or killer whale.

The yellow air bags appeared next, breaching and flopping over on their sides, deflating slowly as the trapped air came out through the open collars.

Above it all, the Air-Crane howled as it began the next stage of the epic lift, hauling the space plane from the grasp of the water and up into the air.

The nose came up first, and then the rest of the craft. Sheets of water poured off the *Nighthawk*'s wings and mud sloughed from the extended landing gear in heavy, dripping globs.

Floating beside the Zodiac, Kurt and Emma watched in awe as the Air-Crane began a slow pivot and moved off toward the firm section of higher ground that Urco had picked to land it on.

Emma pointed to the center of the lake. Silt and foam swirled in an effervescent circle where the *Nighthawk* had been lifted free. The air bags were left behind, sagging on the surface as they slowly deflated.

'We'll clean up later,' Kurt said. 'Let's get to shore and see this thing land.'

Emma removed her fins, tossed them into the boat and grabbed the cargo net they'd set out as a makeshift ladder. She pulled herself upward and flipped up over the edge with surprising speed.

Kurt heard a shout of surprise as she entered the boat and the distinct sound of a struggle. He pulled himself up and spotted a man in the boat wrestling with Emma.

Lunging forward, half in the boat, Kurt got a hand on the assailant, but before he could do any more, a powerful set of arms wrapped around his legs and pulled him back down into the water.

40

Joe felt a strange oscillation through his hands. The Air-Crane was swaying one way and then the other as they headed for the landing area.

'Is that thing moving?' he called out.

'It's trying to,' Paul said. 'It's torquing to the right and then swinging back to the left. Each time, it moves a little more.'

Joe understood instantly. The downwash created by the six-bladed rotor overhead was a minor tornado. That airflow was catching the *Nighthawk*'s vertical stabilizer. It pushed the tail to the left and that swung the nose of the aircraft to the right. When it could twist no more due to the tension on the lines, it swung back in the other direction. A movement that was slowly becoming circular.

The *Nighthawk* continued to sway as they crossed the shallows and then the muddy, barren shoreline. A hundred yards ahead, on higher, firmer ground, Joe saw Urco waving a makeshift flag.

Outlined by tall grasses, the spot Urco had found was flat, rocky and almost circular. It looked like a natural landing pad.

Joe continued toward it, ignoring the yellow temperature light that had come on once again and working the rudder pedals to keep the Air-Crane stable.

Finally over the clearing, he turned the nose into the wind and hovered.

'Come to the right,' Paul said.

'How far?'

'Ten feet.'

Joe eased the Air-Crane over to the right, staring through the clear Plexiglas foot well at the ground below.

'That's it,' Paul said. 'Let her down slowly.'

'No time for that.'

Joe relaxed the pressure on the controls and allowed them to descend, trying to lower the *Nighthawk* gracefully and quickly. It was a partial success. The craft hit with a minor crunch, landing harder than Joe had hoped. The lines went slack and the strain on the engine was reduced.

'*Nighthawk* on solid ground,' Paul said.

'Cut it loose.'

Paul disconnected the line and the metal cable fell to the ground.

The Air-Crane rose upward in response. Freed of all the weight, it felt nimble. Joe powered back as soon as he could, but the yellow warning lights continued to glow. 'We need to get on the ground or we're going to void our warranty.'

Easing away from the *Nighthawk*, Joe aimed for the far edge of the clearing and brought the Air-Crane down for a landing.

The wheels hit with a trio of thumps. Joe powered down to idle but kept the engine running until it had cooled enough to bring the temperature down.

'Hot damn,' Paul said. 'Let's go take a look.'

Joe checked the temperature gauge one last time. It was settling nicely. A second light that would warn of metal shavings in the oil system had never come on. The engines were undamaged. One break in their favor.

He shut everything down, unbuckled his harness and followed Paul out the door. Cutting across the clearing, they found Urco, crouched beneath the aircraft's nose, clearing mud from the landing gear. He looked up as they approached.

'How'd we do?' Paul asked.

'Excellent,' Urco said. 'Exactly as I hoped you would.'

There was something odd about the response. Before Joe could put his finger on it, he saw movement in the tall grass. His first thought was that it was Kurt and Emma coming up from the beach, but, instead, a handful of men pushed through the high grass and out into the clearing. They held weapons in their hands, rifles and shotguns.

Joe turned to make a break for it. But it was too late. A second group of men had come in from behind them.

'Don't fight,' Urco said, standing up and leveling a pistol in Joe's direction. 'There's no need for you to die.'

41

Kurt had been pulled back into the water, a surprising sensation. He'd recovered by kicking hard and pulling his legs clear. No sooner was he free than he felt something heavy wrap around his neck and pull tight. At first he thought it was a metal chain, but he came to realize it was a diver's weight belt.

He grabbed at the belt and pulled, but it was being twisted tight by whoever had swum in behind him. As he struggled with the first attacker, a second diver moved out of the shadow beneath the Zodiac. This one wore a gray wet suit and a squared-off mask. He carried an eight-inch knife, which he thrust toward Kurt.

Using the man behind him as leverage, Kurt twisted to the side. Instead of puncturing his rib cage, the knife only skewered his buoyancy control device, or BCD, sending a flood of bubbles into the water. Before the man could strike again, Kurt kicked him in the face, shattering his square mask and knocking his regulator free. A second kick caught him in the teeth and sent the man fleeing toward the surface.

One down, Kurt thought, *one to go.*

The weight belt was choking him.

As he struggled, both Kurt and his assailant were sinking fast. They grappled all the way to the bottom, where they crashed into the sediment with surprising force.

With somewhere to plant his feet, Kurt gained back some control. He fired an elbow backward into his attacker. The grip loosened but the man grabbed Kurt's main air line and ripped it free.

Kurt felt the helmet pulled to the side, saw a second explosion of silvery air bubbles and was tackled and forced down into the silt before he could do anything about it.

Kurt was on his back. His attacker – whom Kurt recognized as Urco's associate Vargas – was holding him down, pressing him into the sediment as if to bury him. It was a simple strategy. Kurt would black out before long.

Holding his breath, Kurt reached for his own knife, but Vargas kicked his wrist and knocked it free.

In desperation, Kurt fired a punch upward, hoping to catch Vargas in the neck, but the blow was deflected by one of the man's large forearms. A second punch hit Vargas in the solar plexus but did nothing to make him back off.

As Kurt fought, the struggle took on a surreal appearance: sediment swirled around them; the light strapped to Kurt's wrist flicked this way and that. Kurt sensed his muscles growing weary from lack of oxygen. He saw Vargas pull out his own knife and raise it for a lethal blow. It came plunging down hard. At the very same moment, Kurt thrust his knee upward, slamming it into the man's groin.

Both impacts occurred simultaneously.

Vargas spit out his regulator and doubled over in agony. Kurt felt the impact of the blade and watched the water around them churn red in the light.

With a last desperate grab, Kurt reached upward and grabbed Vargas's mouthpiece and snapped it off with a twist.

Vargas reacted with instinctive panic. He pushed off the bottom with both feet, launching himself toward the surface and leaving Kurt behind in a swirling haze of crimson water.

42

Urco stood in the clearing in complete control. Everything was proceeding as he'd designed it.

The *Nighthawk* had been freed from its watery pen and laid at his feet, while agents from each of the competing nations had become his prisoners: the American men and women; the surviving Chinese agent at La Jalca, where she remained in chains until he chose to summon her; and the Russian bomber pilots, in a high cave behind the waterfall.

They were captives now but would soon become his servants – though they didn't know that just yet.

Glancing across the water, he could see his divers in the Zodiac. 'Give me the radio,' he said to one of his men.

A walkie-talkie was handed to him. 'Vargas,' he said, pressing the talk switch down. 'Do you read?'

It didn't take long for a voice to answer. *'I'm here,'* Vargas grunted.

He sounded like he was in pain.

'What happened?'

'We have the woman,' Vargas said. *'But I had to kill Austin. He fought too hard. I gutted him and left him on the bottom. I had no choice.'*

Urco received that news with a trace of disappointment. He'd come to respect Austin in the brief time they'd known each other. The man had offered him the truth about the *Nighthawk* instead of insulting his intelligence with a lie; he'd reacted with introspection instead of arrogance when Urco pointed out the devastation caused by the European viruses to the indigenous population.

'Very well,' Urco said. 'Bring Ms Townsend to me. I require her services.'

'*On our way,*' Vargas replied.

Urco clipped the radio to his belt and turned his attention to the survivors. They were on their knees with their hands behind their heads. Urco's men stood behind them with various weapons drawn.

'Kurt is dead,' he announced.

Neither of the men batted an eye.

'He didn't have to die, but he chose to fight. I hope you take it as a lesson.'

He walked back and forth, listening to the sound of the Zodiac approach. When he noticed that Zavala was eyeing him every step of the way, he approached the helicopter pilot, crouching down in front of him for a better look.

Zavala had a quiet intensity about him. From his features, hair and skin color, Urco could tell he had a large amount of Central American DNA in him.

'Where are you from?' Urco asked.

'New Mexico,' Zavala replied.

'And your parents?'

Zavala was not the hostile sort; his confidence came from within and he appeared less than threatened even in this situation. 'Why would you want to know?'

'Call it *hereditary curiosity*,' Urco said. 'I find many people in this world don't know who they really are. Just by looking at you, I can tell you have European blood in your veins – like I do – and while you're at ease here, your soul is of the Americas. We are cousins. I would suspect to find that much of your blood is from the Olmec and the Maya.'

Zavala did not look away or argue. He was a master of his own emotions. 'My blood is red,' he replied. 'Like everyone else's.'

Urco pursed his lips and stood. 'We shall see.'

By now, the Zodiac had reached the shore. Emma was marched up through the weeds and out into the clearing. She still wore her wet suit. Her mouth was taped.

'Remove that,' Urco said.

'She spits,' Vargas said angrily.

Urco expected she would be trouble. He knew how fiery she could be. He looked her up and down. She was . . . *different*. Age and time had changed her, of course, but there was something more. The weight of knowledge; the invisible burden? He bore it, too. Perhaps he could use that to his advantage, but first he needed her to understand how truly powerless she was.

He turned to Vargas. 'Go get the other boat and begin phase two.'

As Vargas left, Urco reached out and gently removed the tape from her mouth. 'My apologies for such harsh treatment.'

She stood, defiant, casting a challenge at him with her eyes, not seeing but posturing. He accepted that. It was to his benefit that she be blind with rage. At least a little while longer.

'What's the meaning of this?' Emma demanded. 'Who are you working for? The Russians? The Chinese?'

'Of course you're confused,' Urco told her. 'Why wouldn't you be? Right now you're wondering which of your great enemies has corrupted the little servant you found at La Jalca? It must be one of them, mustn't it? Since the rest of the world is filled only with pawns to be moved by the players of the great game. Isn't that what your time at the NSA has taught you?'

She pulled back, no doubt because none of them had ever mentioned the National Security Agency.

'To answer your question,' he continued, 'I work for neither the Russians nor the Chinese but for all of humanity.'

Her gaze tightened and the fine lines around her eyes deepened, enough to suggest he had her thinking. That was good.

'And at this juncture,' he added, 'humanity requires your help.'

'I won't help you do anything.'

'Yes, of course,' he said, waving an indifferent hand. 'You're required to say that. Duly noted, but I assure you, *you will help me*. In fact, you'll literally spring to your feet to do it.'

Without waiting for a reply, he walked over to the *Nighthawk*. The craft was still dripping muddy water from the landing gear. It appeared larger in the clearing but low to the ground, thanks to those stubby legs.

Arriving beside the nose, Urco found the touch

screen panel he was looking for. He tapped it until it came to life and then entered an alphanumeric code. A green indicator flickered and a small door opened just aft of the touch screen panel.

Reaching in, he grasped a recessed handle.

'Don't,' Emma said.

He ignored her and pulled the handle, first to the side and then down. As he released it, the sound of hydraulic actuators powering up became audible. A pressure seal between the cargo bay doors released with a hiss and they slowly began to open.

As the doors locked in place, Urco stepped up on the wing and gazed into the interior. In contrast to the black outer hull, the cargo bay was done in a gleaming, sterile white.

'You don't know what you're doing,' Emma insisted. 'If you're not careful, you'll kill us all.'

'Perhaps you'd like to show me, then? Prevent me from tinkering?'

Emma was led up beside him. They stood together gazing down into the interior of the payload bay. A maze of power packs, wires and cylindrical tubes were lined up front to back. The arrangement was perfectly symmetrical.

'Two by two,' Urco said, pointing out matching components with the words *Cryogenic Containment Unit* stenciled on top.

'You don't understand,' she said.

'Don't fool yourself more than you already have,' he replied. 'We both *understand* exactly what we're looking at.

Mixed-state matter. The most powerful reactant known to exist, gathered for the first time in vast quantities.'

Emma turned toward him. 'And I suggest you leave it alone.'

'I suggested the same thing a decade ago,' he shot back. 'But it's too late for that now, isn't it?'

She stared at him looking confused. He hoped the little riddles were getting to her. He needed her to be off balance.

'Disconnect the first containment unit and hook it up to one of the fuel cells you've brought along,' he said. 'That *was* the next step, wasn't it? Search for the plane, but take the cargo and blow the rest to scrap metal.'

'We never intended to blow anything up, just to –'

'Come now,' he said. 'You were *never* going to carry an eight-ton load over the mountains and all the way back to Cajamarca. The strain that would place on the helicopter would have been dangerously high, not to mention the strain on credibility when the Peruvian officials got wind of it. They'd want to know what it was, why it was here and why they hadn't been informed in the first place.'

He turned and whistled to another group of his men. They went into the Air-Crane and came out carrying a suitcase-sized device; it was one of the fuel cells Joe and Paul had been given in Cajamarca.

Emma looked crestfallen. The exact look he was hoping for. 'We would have come back for the rest of the craft,' she said.

'You may still get that chance,' he replied. 'In the meantime, you will detach the first containment unit, hook it to that fuel cell and make certain it's safe enough to be transported.'

'Transported where?'

'Stop asking questions,' he said. 'You can easily guess where.'

She shook her head. 'I won't do that. It's too dangerous. All of this is too dangerous.'

He could have chosen to threaten her friends at that moment, but he had no intention of wasting time. Most likely, they would all be willing to die rather than co-operate. How dreadfully boring, he thought. No, there was a much easier way.

He turned back to the cargo bay, looking for a piece of equipment with a shape he knew by heart. 'Power converter,' he said. 'Connects the battery pack to the containment unit. Steps up and intensifies the current in order to run the cryogenic pump. Each of the units has one of its own. Thankfully, they're still operating.'

'Yes, but – '

Ignoring her, he pulled out a pistol, extended his arm and fired a single shot. The power converter connected to Containment Unit 1 was punctured instantly.

'No!' she shouted.

It was too late. The damage was done. Warning lights started to flash in the cargo bay and on the exterior panel.

'Release me,' she shouted.

He cut the tape from her wrists and she climbed over the low sill and into the cargo bay. She crouched beside Unit 1, scraping frost from the outer edge of the panel.

Despite a layer of thick insulation, the surface temperature was still forty degrees below zero. The lights showed a complete power disconnect. They had sixty seconds to get the unit hooked up to the replacement pack.

'Bring me one of the fuel cells!' she called out.

'No,' he said. 'Disconnect the unit and remove it. We'll hook up the power cell out here.'

She looked at him, terror in her eyes. There was no arguing. She turned back to the unit and went right to work. He could see her running through a mental checklist. One he knew well.

Switch to internal power.

Remove the voltage regulator.

Disconnect power delivery cord.

Shut off cryogenic exchanger and wait five seconds for the fluid to cycle.

He could see her counting. When she got to 5, she reached beneath the unit. Four latches held it in place. Three of which were easy to access. The fourth, Urco knew, lay in an awkward spot.

He cocked his head to watch as she stretched and winced, trying to pull the latch free with her fingers. With a snap, it came loose. When she brought her hand out, it was bleeding.

She ignored the blood, stood quickly and moved to one side of the unit.

'Help me,' she called out. Each unit weighed a hundred and forty pounds. Powerful magnets and cryogenic tubes filled with slush helium accounted for most of the weight. But inside the tubes and magnetic bottles lay the supply of exotic and deadly matter. Twenty-five pounds of it in each of the eight units.

At her request, Urco climbed into the cargo bay himself. He donned a pair of gloves and grabbed the frame of Unit 1. They lifted together, heaving it upward and carrying it over the lip. Two of his men took it from there and set it down on the wing.

'Please reconnect the device,' Urco asked calmly.

Emma climbed out of the cargo bay, hopped off the edge of the wing and rushed to the fuel cell that had been brought out to them.

Urco imagined a clock was ticking in her head: *But there was plenty of time.*

She flicked through a series of switches on the side of the fuel cell and watched as it came to life, making energy instantly.

She grabbed the power cord and rushed to the containment unit but ran out of cord a foot shy of the connecter.

Urco stood absolutely still; neither did any of his people move. But Joe Zavala did. He jumped to his feet, dashing past the man who was guarding him, grabbing the fuel cell and carrying it closer. Urco grinned at the cooperation.

Emma connected the cord. In quick succession the amber lights blinked out and the entire panel went green. The power was back on. The frozen slush began to circulate again. The antimatter would remain suspended in the magnetic bottles, held safely at a temperature near absolute zero.

Urco smiled and clapped loudly at their efforts. 'Excellent work. I trust we won't have to go through this again.'

Emma's chest heaved as the effort and the adrenaline had sent her heart pounding. She looked up at him and shook her head. 'No,' she said. 'I'd rather not.'

He grinned. Another battle won. The pretense that they could resist him was gone. Wiped from their thoughts. It no longer mattered what he intended to do with the antimatter. Whether he planned to sell it to the Russians or to the Chinese or to auction it off to the highest bidder in a worldwide contest.

It didn't matter whether he promised to free them, kill them, or keep them prisoners until the end of time. None of that mattered. Any and all outcomes were preferable to a world of darkness brought on by the mixed-state matter escaping its magnetic prison and exploding all at once.

He owned them now. He owned them all.

43

Daiyu sat in darkness. She'd been placed in the back of the same truck that she'd hijacked on the mountain road. Her hands and feet were bound with cord, cinched tight by men used to tying off knots that climbers' lives depended on. Despite hours of trying, she could neither loosen the bond nor pull free.

She'd chafed her wrists bloody from the effort before switching tactics. Sliding herself across the wooden floor of the trailer, she'd gone back and forth until she found a rough spot where a nailhead had worked loose from the planks.

Flipping over, she'd positioned her hands near it, writhing in the dark and rubbing the cord across the nail until her muscles cramped from the effort. Collapsing onto her side, she felt for the edge of the rope. It was damaged and fraying, but she couldn't tell if it was enough.

She relaxed, waiting for the painful spasms in her back to pass, so she could begin again.

She would get out. They would not stop her. She would complete her mission. And if she got the chance, she'd kill every one of the Americans and their new Peruvian friends in the process.

Breathing deeply but otherwise still, she caught the sound of voices approaching outside. Heavy boots were scuffing against the dry soil of the mountain road.

She instantly redoubled her efforts, grinding the rope across the exposed nail with maniacal intensity.

It had to snap. It had to.

She heard the key hit the padlock and then the handle being thrown over. An instant later, the door slid upward and the white light of day poured in, blinding her.

As she shut her eyes against it, two men climbed into the vehicle, grabbed her by the feet and pulled.

'No,' she grunted, kicking at them. She was so close to freedom.

The men hauled her out and set her on the ground. With a pull and twist, the knot on her legs came undone. Thoughts of running vanished when she tried to stand and fell to the ground on numb legs that couldn't even support her weight.

She looked upward at the men, squinting in the light. They were only silhouettes. Two standing above her, a third off to the side. A fourth shadow just beyond.

The fourth man spoke English to them. 'What happened to her? Where did the bruises come from?'

To her surprise, there was a familiar tone to the voice.

'She fought with the American,' one of the Peruvians replied.

'Pick her up.'

They grabbed her arms, lifted her and allowed her to lean against the bumper of the truck. The man who sounded familiar came into view. It was Lieutenant Wu, General Zhang's aide.

'Black Jade,' he said quietly. 'The General is astounded to hear that you have been . . . subdued so easily.'

Embarrassment flooded through her, the sense of failure peaking so strongly that she could not look at him.

'Untie her,' Wu ordered.

Why these men were taking orders from the lieutenant, she couldn't guess. But with a nod from the third member of their group, they did as he asked.

The sudden release of her hands brought both great relief and a new wave of pain as she brought her arms in front of her for the first time in hours.

Her hands were caked with dried blood, her wrists rubbed raw from the effort. The cord that had held her captive was frayed within a few strands of breaking. The Peruvian men looked at it suspiciously.

Wu laughed. 'You're lucky I arrived,' he said to the Peruvians. 'She would have killed you all.'

They scoffed at the statement, but that didn't make it any less true.

'Can you walk?' Wu asked.

Daiyu tested her legs. They were tingling with pins and needles, but she would show no more weakness. She nodded and stood.

'Come with me,' Wu said, turning and strolling down the path.

She followed awkwardly, listening as the Peruvian men closed up the truck behind her. The door slid down with a rattle before slamming against the stops. Angry words were exchanged among them.

Daiyu focused on Lieutenant Wu. 'Did General Zhang buy my freedom?'

'Yes and no.'

'I failed you,' she whispered. 'I'm not worthy of being ransomed.'

Wu laughed lightly. 'The General said you would react this way. He also said to tell you he can find diamonds and gold in the ground; that he can either buy or steal them, if he must. But a good operative, one such as yourself, is far harder to come by.'

She felt a wave of pride at the compliment. But it did not change what had happened.

'At any rate,' Wu added, 'it's not you alone that we've paid for but the *Nighthawk*'s cargo.'

Her eyes grew wide.

'There is much you don't know,' he said, leading her around a bend.

A sleek helicopter sat in the road up ahead. It was guarded by two men with assault rifles. Men from home. Allies.

'How did you find me?'

'You recall the name Falconer?'

'The Russian asset.'

'*Our asset,*' Wu insisted, 'though the Russians think he belongs to them. Falconer was on the second Russian bomber, in charge of overriding the American commands from the Vandenberg. He was supposed to abort the capture of the *Nighthawk* and direct it back toward our fleet. Where we would grab it once it hit the water.'

'Obviously, he failed,' she said.

'Partially,' Wu replied. 'Whether that was by design or happenstance, we cannot say. But as it turns out, the man lives. He contacted us, told us where to find you and where to find the *Nighthawk*.'

'But the Americans are already there,' she said. 'With the man from this camp.'

'Yes,' Wu said. 'The Falconer. They are one and the same.'

As she put it all together, she began to laugh. 'And to think I almost killed him.'

'You couldn't know,' Wu said. 'The man has been operating as a triple agent. But the final act is now upon us. General Zhang secured your release with gold. And now, for a pittance in rough-cut diamonds, we will take possession of the cargo.'

A pittance might be fifty million dollars, in Zhang's terms. But it was truly nothing compared to what they were receiving.

They arrived at the helicopter. The side door was pulled back. A body covered in plastic lay on the floor.

'Jian,' she said. *Her brother among the children who had never been born.*

'A casualty of the operation.'

She and Wu climbed in, the armed commandos followed and the pilot began the start procedure. A heavy pack was tossed out to one of the Peruvian men who followed them. It clinked like a bag of loose change.

'Krugerrands,' Wu said.

The Peruvians opened it. One was satisfied, but another was frustrated. An argument broke out, in their native language. It was hard to follow with all of them speaking at once, but she understood enough.

She killed them. We should not be letting her go.

It's been arranged.

I don't like it . . . deserves to die . . .

The sound of the helicopter starting drowned out the rest. But Daiyu could read lips. She focused on the leader of the Peruvian men.

Of course they deserve to die.

Don't worry. They will.

44

Kurt's face was bathed in yellow light. The strange hue and intensity was all he could see no matter where he looked, but it wasn't the afterlife.

After being dragged to the bottom of the lake, Kurt had been on the verge of blacking out when his furious counterattack coincided with the assailant's attempt to plunge the diving knife into his ribs.

The sudden cloud of the red that erupted seemed to leave no doubt who'd gotten the worse end of the deal. As Vargas had pushed off the bottom with both legs and soared up toward the surface, both he and Kurt had every reason to believe that the blade had plunged home.

Kurt's initial thought was that his blood was surprisingly bright. Still, with his main airline ripped out, getting the secondary line attached to the valve on his helmet took precedence over finding a wound and stopping the bleeding.

He'd grabbed his backup line, brought it up to the quick connect port on the side of the helmet and snapped it into place.

A slight hiss told him gas was flowing and he immediately started breathing rapidly, trying to expel the carbon dioxide that had built up in his lungs.

With air flowing, he searched for his wound. By the

time he found it, the swirl of red color around him had begun to thin. The water turned pink and then went clear once again.

Either he was out of blood or . . .

It turned out that he hadn't been impaled. The blade had only sliced a thin crease in his skin. He was bleeding, but the outpouring of crimson came from the red dye capsule, which had taken the brunt of the impact. The knife had split it in two and flooded the water with enough coloring to make it seem like an artery had been gashed open.

Kurt had found the dye capsule, tossed it away and looked upward. He could just make out the bottom of the Zodiac and two figures clinging to it.

Adrenaline urged him to surface and make an immediate attempt to rescue Emma, but the odds were against surviving another battle with the two divers. Not without much oxygen in his tank. And even if he could overcome them, there was still the man in the boat with Emma as a hostage.

If a frontal assault wouldn't work, he thought it might be time to try the stealth approach. *They think I'm dead. Let them keep thinking it, until we make our counterattack.*

He detached the dive light he'd carried, placed it down in the mud and swam from the scene.

If anyone was looking down from the Zodiac, they would see only the stationary light. The diver in the black wet suit, moving in the depths of the black lake, would be as hard to spot as the *Nighthawk* had been.

He moved calmly across the bottom, found the spot

where the *Nighthawk* had been resting and pushed off the bottom. Rising upward and exhaling slowly as he went, Kurt emerged from the dark lake into one of the yellow lifting bags. The voluminous air bag lay on its side, like an oversized Portuguese man-of-war that had washed up on the beach.

Hidden within, Kurt removed his helmet to breathe, unzipped a waterproof pouch on the sleeve of his wet suit and pulled a small transmitter free.

Keeping the compact radio clear of the water, Kurt turned it on and switched to a prearranged frequency. He pressed the transmit button and spoke calmly into the microphone.

'Gamay, this is Kurt,' he said.

A hushed voice came over the radio, imbued with a slight, scolding tone. *'Kurt, I thought they'd killed you. I was about to move in on my own.'*

Tired of being ambushed, Kurt had decided the NUMA team could use a guardian angel to watch over them. With Joe needed to fly the helicopter and only Paul and Gamay to choose from, Kurt had picked Gamay for several reasons.

Most importantly, she was a crack shot. Good with a pistol, but an expert with a rifle. She was also smaller, more agile and more athletic than Paul. Attributes that would help her hide and move from spot to spot without being noticed.

Joe had flown her in early this morning, dropping her off on a high ridge, before heading to La Jalca to pick up Emma, Urco and himself.

Dressed in camouflage and carrying a rifle, Gamay was out there now. 'What's your position?'

'*I'm on the second ridge east of the landing zone,*' she said. '*I can see the clearing, most of the lake and the waterfall.*'

'What about Joe and Paul?'

'*They're in the clearing. They were surrounded as soon as they landed. The* Nighthawk *is down safely. So is the Air-Crane. Paul and Joe are being held just across from it.*'

'And Emma?'

'*They have her working on something,*' Gamay said. '*I can't tell exactly what it is. But they've opened the* Nighthawk *and begun unloading it. Other than that, all seems fairly calm at the moment.*'

'Was it Urco?' Kurt asked, fairly certain that he knew.

'*It was,*' Gamay said. '*How'd you know he couldn't be trusted?*'

'I didn't know,' Kurt admitted. 'But a few odd moments were enough to cause concern. For one thing, he had his satellite antenna aimed low and to the north-west. There's no reason for an archaeologist working in a deep canyon in the Southern Hemisphere to be using a satellite so low on the horizon to bounce his communications. Based on the angle, it had to be a Northern Hemisphere bird out over the Pacific. He'd also claimed to be the cameraman who shot the video of the *Nighthawk* crossing La Jalca, but I noticed that he was a lefty. He writes left, eats left, and yet the footage was filmed by someone holding a camera in their right hand. I couldn't see any reason to lie about something like that, but it was definitely suspicious.'

'*Your intuition is spot-on, as usual,*' Gamay said.

'Not quite,' Kurt said. 'I truly thought we'd be safe until we pulled the containment units out of the *Nighthawk*. I also thought you'd spot anyone coming down the Inca road or up through the valley. What happened?'

'*That part of the plan didn't work,*' she said. '*I haven't blinked in hours. The road in from La Jalca has been empty. The road out to the south has been empty. Nothing has arrived or departed this valley on foot or by wheel or wing since you guys landed.*'

He understood the implication. 'Which means Urco's men were already here, waiting for their moment to attack. I thought their numbers looked a little light this morning. Must have driven over last night.'

'*I counted six down in the clearing, plus the three on the water,*' she said.

'Ten, including Urco,' he noted.

'*Do you think that's it?*'

'No reason it shouldn't be,' he said. 'They've shown their hand. Now it's our turn.'

'*If I circle to the south, I'll have a clear shot at everyone and everything in the clearing,*' she said. '*If you can move in at the same moment, we can catch them in a cross fire.*'

It was a good plan. The problem was the beach. With so much open land running from the edge of the lake to where the tall grass began, Kurt would be seen and shot long before he got into the fight.

'I'll have to circle around as well,' Kurt said.

'*Circle around where?*'

'To the only place I can get out of this lake without

344

being spotted,' Kurt said. 'Unfortunately, that means a trip through the washing machine. I'm just glad the *Nighthawk* didn't land in Niagara.'

'I've always assumed you were crazy,' she said. *'This proves it.'*

'It's the only way to get behind them,' he said. 'Should be okay, if I skirt the edge.'

'You might want to hurry,' Gamay said. *'If you are where I think you are, you have a boat headed straight for you.'*

'Roger that,' Kurt said. 'If the situation changes and the others seem to be in imminent danger, take action without waiting for me. I'll contact you as soon as I'm back on dry land.'

Kurt shut the radio off, slipped it back in the waterproof pouch and zipped the pocket shut. With the growl of the approaching boat to spur him on, he pulled his helmet back on and dove straight down, beginning the most dangerous swim of his life.

45

Kurt descended twenty feet before moving horizontally and passing under the approaching boat.

Rolling over on his back, Kurt watched the wake of the small boat flare out around the air bags and slow. The yellow bags began to move. The occupants of the boat were gathering them in.

Putting space between himself and the cleanup crew, Kurt continued toward the rolling thunder of the waterfall.

As he approached it, the current around him became more turbulent and confused. The falling water dropped into the lake with so much force that it continued downward in a column until it hit the bottom, spreading out in all directions. It scoured away all sediment and loose debris, forming a deep well known as a *plunge pool*, often filled with heavy boulders resting on hardened rock.

Others called this pool the *washing machine* because the downward force of the water caused swirling vortices all around it. They led outward, up and then back down. Horizontal drums of churning liquid.

Water surged away from the falls in general, but get too close and Kurt would be sucked right into the washing machine and shoved downward into the plunge pool.

Unfortunately, to many daredevils who'd gone over Niagara Falls in various barrels, capsules and other vehicles, getting caught in the washing machine at the bottom of the falls had proved more deadly than going over them in the first place. Once they got trapped inside the vortex, it was incredibly difficult to get out. Several attempts ended in disaster when the homemade conveyances survived the drop only to be pinned at the bottom and held there until the occupants ran out of oxygen.

Kurt had no intention of getting into the washing machine. His plan was to swim around the edge of the falls, stay far enough out to avoid trouble and surface behind it. It was a good plan in theory, but the upper end of the lake narrowed so tightly around the falls that it proved difficult.

Pushed outward at first by the churning water, Kurt found himself forced upward as well. Swimming harder, he made a little progress but was still being pushed back nearly as fast as he went forward.

Tired of being caught on a liquid conveyer belt, and well aware that he might be seen at any moment, Kurt angled more directly toward the falls, charging into the semicircle of water that boiled upward from below.

Straining every muscle in his body, he began to make progress. All at once, the outward pressure of the water waned and he was moving forward.

Too far, too fast.

He changed direction and fought the pull of the eddy, trying to use the momentum he'd gained to slingshot around it. Despite his powerful stroke, the vortex had him. He was dragged toward the thundering wall of falling liquid and pulled downward in the grasp of an underwater storm.

There was no fighting it now; he had to go with the flow. Surrounded in the swirling white foam, Kurt was forced deeper and deeper. Even after slowing through seventy feet of water, the column hit bottom with surprising strength.

Kurt was slammed downward and shoved sideways into the rocks. His shoulder took one hit, the aluminum cylinder on his back took another.

He was pushed into a large boulder and then swung around back in the other direction, where he crashed into a pile of rocks worn smooth by the constant tumbling action beneath the falls.

He could feel the water hammering him, pressing him into the stones. His fins were ripped off; water forced itself into a gap where the helmet sealed around his neck, filling the helmet with frigid liquid, cutting off his air supply and chilling his face in the process.

Kurt had ahold of one large boulder – he clung to it and pulled himself along. The water pressed him downward; there was no swimming, only crawling.

He scraped across the two boulders, then pushed up against the wall of stone behind the waterfall and caught under a ledge for a moment. Bracing himself, he refused to be held in the trap. He found a foothold and pushed himself outward and up.

Suddenly, he was on the far side of the vortex.

Instead of crushing him downward, it carried him up on a rapidly ascending elevator.

He breached the surface in a swirl of foam on the back side of the falls.

Kurt lunged forward and pulled himself onto the rocks. He was battered, bruised and exhausted, but the risk had paid off. He was now hidden behind enemy lines.

46

Joe Zavala had been taken down to the rock-strewn beach. His hands were bound with a zip tie, and while his feet were free, his boots and socks had been taken away to make it more difficult and painful should he try to escape or fight.

Paul sat on Joe's left, tied and bound in a similar fashion. Emma was on his right, also restrained. Though many thoughts were competing for Joe's attention, Kurt's death was not at the top of the list. Joe had heard the words, felt the pain they carried and then locked the thought away in some distant corner of his mind. After so many risky adventures together, both of them knew a day like this might arrive. In Joe's position, Kurt would have done the same.

'We're going to get out of here,' Joe said. 'I'm not sure how, but we're going to break free.'

'And then what?' Emma asked.

'Depends on the manner of our escape,' Joe said. 'If we can get to the Air-Crane, we'll fly. If not, we go on foot or by boat on the river. There are rapids downstream, but we could navigate them in the Zodiac.'

'They have to slip up at some point,' Paul said.

'They will,' Joe assured him. 'Until then save your

strength and do everything you can to lull them into thinking they've won.'

'It's not about us,' Emma said. 'I know you want to escape, but there's a far bigger danger here.'

'One we can't prevent without first getting free. You can't give up,' Joe urged.

'Getting free will require fighting,' she explained. 'Most likely, shooting. All within a stone's throw of the frozen supply of mixed-state matter. One stray bullet could set off the disaster. If it means preventing that, I'm fine giving up.'

One of Urco's men came out of the tall grass, where he'd probably been listening. His approach killed off any further conversation. He moved in behind Emma, cut her loose and stood back. 'Come with me,' he said. 'Urco wants your help.'

Emma stood and was led away. Joe sensed she was close to despondency, but then she didn't know there was still hope. She hadn't been privy to Kurt's backup plan. He had wanted it that way. And now, seeing how much power Urco had over her, and how deeply the fear of a disaster had clutched at her heart, Joe was glad he'd kept the secret. He could imagine Emma telling Urco what she knew all in the interest of preventing a catastrophe.

As Emma and the guard left, Joe glanced at Paul.

Paul nodded. He was ready. Joe was ready, too; he'd already been working the zip tie back and forth, twisting his wrists this way and that, in order to weaken the plastic. Before long, it would be weak enough to snap.

Then Joe would rest, waiting for the sound of a rifle firing from somewhere high in the rocks.

Gamay would take out several of their captors before the men knew what hit them. Joe and Paul would spring into action at the same moment and, with a little luck, the tide would be turned.

47

As soon as Kurt's strength returned, he began moving across the rocks behind the waterfall. Not planning to get back in the water, he shed his cumbersome air tank, damaged helmet and deflated BCD. Hooking them together, he tossed them in the water. Empty, the aluminum cylinder would float, but the deflated BCD, with its integrated weights, would drag them down.

They vanished and Kurt continued on foot, looking for a place to start his climb. He would have to climb upward and then over, where the ridge was thick with foliage thanks to the constant overspray from the waterfall.

Climbing it would be easy; getting there was more difficult. The footing behind the waterfall was treacherous. Kurt watched every step. Halfway in, he noticed something that didn't belong in a pristine mountain lake. A sheen of discoloration lay across the wet rocks. Even in the flat light, he could see all the colors of the rainbow.

Oil and water, he thought. Or, more likely, gasoline.

It vanished where the churning water mixed it into the depths but clung to the stones, leading like an arrow into the mouth of a large cave.

That second boat had to come from somewhere.

Kurt picked his way to the mouth of the cave, gazed around the edge and into the darkness. He saw nothing and heard only the echo of the thundering waterfall, but the slick of petrochemical color beckoned him to enter.

He eased back into the water and swam into the cave. The farther in he went, the darker it became, but his eyes adjusted and he began to make out the details. Eighty feet back, the cave jagged to the right and widened; around the bend lay outlines of a camp.

Gas cans, propane canisters and a cookstove sat beside a group of plastic crates that looked exactly like the ones he'd seen at La Jalca. Bedrolls and wool blankets were laid out on a higher section. Spare oxygen tanks for the divers leaned against the cave wall. Beside them sat a stack of boxy items covered with plastic liners.

The camp was empty. Not exactly a surprise, considering the activity out on the lake and in the clearing where the *Nighthawk* had been placed.

'*More burial chambers*,' Kurt whispered, thinking of Urco's statement when they'd cruised near the waterfall. '*I would like it if they remain undisturbed.* Of course you would. Your men were hiding back here.'

Kurt swam to the edge, climbed out of the water and began to pick through the offerings. He found a pair of binoculars and a flashlight but left them where they were since they would obviously be missed.

He dug into one of the plastic boxes and found a

container filled with strips of dried beef. Realizing how hungry he was, he took a sample and chewed on it as he searched the rest of the cavern.

He found no guns or knives, but one of the bins had several boxes of ammunition in it. Another was empty except for cut lengths of color-coded wire. A third held bricks of orange clay that were wrapped in clear plastic. The alphanumeric code *S-10* had been written on the outside of each.

'Semtex,' Kurt muttered, using the brand name of the compound. 'What would you be doing with Semtex?'

The orange clay was a plastic explosive. Manufactured in the Czech Republic, S-10 was the latest version. It was similar to American-made C-4. Each of the bricks would be powerful enough to obliterate a car.

Kurt counted the supply. Assuming the crate had been full, at least half the explosives were already missing.

Finding no other weapons, Kurt pulled one of the bricks free and tucked it into a pocket. Without a blasting cap or an electrical charge, it would be difficult to set off, but it still might come in handy.

Closing the lid on the explosives crate, he moved to the back of the cave, rifled through another box and then moved over to the plastic tarp and the stack of equipment it covered.

Moving a rock that held the tarp down, Kurt peeled the material back and found himself staring at a rectangular piece of equipment that looked incredibly familiar.

Fuel cell.

Not only was it a fuel cell, it was identical in size, shape, design and color to the ones Joe had flown in on the Air-Crane. It was even marked the same; stenciled writing on the outer case read *Type 3 Hydrogen Fuel Cell, Property of the United States Government.*

Kurt touched the control panel, his fingers gliding across a bank of switches until he found the power button. He switched it on and received an immediate indication that it was working and producing power. A display lit up, indicating fully pressurized reservoirs of hydrogen and oxygen. Enough for twenty-six hours of continuous operation.

Under the next tarp was an identical unit. Behind them lay two more. Marks on the ground suggested two other units had been there and were now missing. Looped power cords, neatly banded together sat in a crate beside the units.

Why were they here?

'Explosives without detonators,' Kurt said to himself. 'Replicas or stolen fuel cells, what are you up to Urco?'

The sound of an outboard motor approaching echoed down from the mouth of the cave. Kurt switched off the fuel cell, covered it up and placed the flat rock back on top.

The buzzing motor grew louder and then cut out as a light played across the water. Kurt retreated quietly into the recesses of the cave and took cover.

Peering out over a rock formation, he watched a gray

inflatable with three men in it pull around the bend and drift to the shore. It bumped against the rocks, stopping beside the cookstove.

Two of the three men got out. They carried the deflated yellow air bags and stuffed them one on top of another into a gap in the rocks. That done, they went directly for the fuel cells.

'Cuántos?' the first one said.

'Llevar todos,' the second one replied, pulling up the tarps. *'Una para los americanos, una para el chino, los otros son para los rusos, y para los amigos de Rio.'*

He laughed as he finished.

'Y los explosivos?'

'Están dentro,' the man replied. *'Boom!'* he said, chuckling further.

The other men laughed as well. They selected one of the fuel cells, tested it, as Kurt had, and then switched it off.

The man in the boat grew impatient. *'Vamanos.'*

The men onshore got moving. They carried all four of the fuel cells to the small boat, loaded them inside and then climbed aboard and pushed off.

As soon as they were clear of the rocks, the outboard was lowered back into the water and started with a hard pull. It coughed out a fog of blue smoke as it came to life and the men eased out of sight, heading toward the mouth of the cave.

Kurt waited until he'd heard them speed away and then cautiously stepped from his hiding place. He didn't speak much Spanish, but some of the words were obvious to him.

His mind went to the Semtex he'd found and the joke that had brought out a round of laughter.

'Los explosivos,' Kurt whispered. *'Boom!'*

48

Emma followed her guard as he walked across the beach, cut through the grass and traveled up into the clearing where the *Nighthawk* sat. On the far side, Urco stood among the containment units.

Two of the eight units had been removed. They now rested on the stony ground, each of them connected to a fuel cell.

'Check these over, please,' Urco said.

'What am I looking for?' she asked.

'I want to be sure everything is functioning properly and that they're safe to move.'

It was a simple task. She crouched beside the units and did a quick diagnostic review, all the time wondering why he'd bothered to say *please*.

'The magnetic bottles are stable,' she said. 'The cryogenic systems are operating within accepted parameters. The fuel cells are generating clean power.'

'Good,' Urco said.

She stood. 'I assume you want me to remove the other units?'

'In time,' he said. 'For now, we should discuss your role in things.'

'My role?'

He only smiled and said, 'Walk with me.'

With little choice in the matter, she nodded. 'Lead on.'

They left the guard behind, entering a path cut through the foliage that twisted toward higher ground. Machetes had done the work; freshly cut stalks and fallen blades of the long grass lay across the ground. They'd been trampled down by a fair amount of foot traffic already.

'Are we entering some kind of maze?' she asked.

'We're already deep inside one,' he insisted. 'Working together is the only way out.'

'We *were* working together,' she replied, 'right up until the point where your men attacked us, killed Kurt and took the rest of us hostage.'

'Not *hostages*,' he said, *'captives. Captured thieves,* actually.'

'Excuse me?'

'You're a thief,' he said. 'A well-dressed, Stanford-educated thief. Your entire organization has larceny in its heart and, by extension, the nation you serve. But you've been caught – red-handed, as they say – in the middle of the greatest robbery the world has ever known.'

'You're the one who took the – '

'No,' he said, turning on her and cutting her off. 'I only relieved you of the stolen goods. It was you and your government that engaged in this theft. *You* chose to fly this craft up into the heavens and gather the mixed-state matter from the magnetic field. *You* chose to bring it home to your hidden bunkers at Vandenberg, where you and your people would hoard it for your own purposes.'

'We only did that because – '

He wouldn't let her speak. 'There are five separate treaties governing activities in outer space,' he snapped. 'The United States is a signatory on each and every one. Three of them were drafted by American states- men. Collectively, they forbid every activity you've so recently engaged in, from the militarization of space to the national appropriation of any part of space or any celestial body, such as the Moon.'

As he railed at her, she recalled the ethical arguments internally discussed at the NSA prior to the mission. Arguments put forward and then so easily swatted aside. 'We claimed nothing,' she said. 'We merely retrieved free-floating particles.'

'Are you really going to play the lawyer with me?'

She fell silent and he turned and led her out of the grass and onto a plateau. From here, they looked over the lake seventy feet below. In the distance, the water- fall fell, with its hushed and ceaseless voice.

He turned back her way and bore down. 'Like every- thing else in space, these *free-floating particles* are reserved as part of the *common heritage of all mankind*. They belong to everyone on Earth and to no one person or govern- ment in particular.'

The fury in his voice surprised her. *Why*, she thought, *should he care about such things? How would he even know about them? Or about the wording of some obscure treaties?*

'Who are you?' she asked.

'You still don't recognize me?' he said, sounding almost disappointed. 'Fortunately for me, I suppose. I

361

feared you might spot me when we dined together beneath the cliffs of La Jalca.'

He reached to the side of his face as if to scratch at his ear but instead of scratching began to pull at his beard, slowly removing the portion on the right side of his face. His skin was burned beneath it, not terribly disfigured but scarred and hairless.

'The other side of my beard is real,' he replied, 'but I can grow nothing over here.'

An indentation in his jawline told her the bone had been broken and never healed correctly; a portion of it might have been removed.

'It was the crash and the fire,' he explained.

Suddenly, the pieces came together for her. *This* man was involved in hacking the *Nighthawk*'s control system. He knew about the NSA mission and the antimatter. He was well versed in the international treaties regulating the use of space. And he knew her.

'Beric?' she said.

'So you *do* remember.'

She barely recognized him even now. Years had passed. Age and scars had changed his face. His eyes held no kindness, only bitterness and twisted anger. 'I don't understand? How? Why? Your plane exploded. They told us it was a terror group. They told us we were all in danger.'

'*I was in danger,*' he insisted, as he raised his voice. 'And the terror group was based in Washington DC. Ironically enough, you now work for them.'

'The NSA?' she said. 'Why would they want to harm you? Surely you can't believe what you're saying.'

'I have proof,' his voice accusatory as he moved closer to her. 'And what's more, *they had a motive*. If you recall, I was involved in the initial studies that determined the possibility of antimatter getting trapped in the magnetic field. I was the one who suggested it might be a more stable form of *mixed-state matter* – if it remained cold enough. The head of the program came to me shortly after I submitted my findings. He said they'd been discussing a plan, not just to search for the antimatter *but to actually harvest it*. I objected strenuously. They insisted the purpose was peaceful, but when the funding is coming from the military and the National Security Agency, that stretches credibility just a bit.'

Her head was spinning, but she took in every word.

'*We shall use this for propulsion to push rockets to Mars in eight weeks,*' he said in a false voice. '*To the outer planets in less than a year.* Even to deep space. But it wasn't long before *someone* mentioned the possibility of a weapon.'

His voice growing louder, he shook his head in disgust. 'I threatened to go to the press. To put the information out on the Internet. To tell the whole world, no matter what they did to me. I knew what you're probably discovering right now: it is a mistake, a Pandora's Box we've brought into our homes and managed to hold shut only by the thinnest of margins.'

She saw it now. It *was* a mistake. A disaster in the making. She wished she'd never been a part of it.

'I was threatened with deportation, should I speak a word – thirty years in solitary confinement. I agreed to keep quiet, but they watched me constantly. It seems my word wasn't enough. On that short flight to New Orleans they made their move. My plane exploded over the Gulf of Mexico. It left me like this. I ended up clinging to an abandoned oil rig, my face a cake of blood. I found a life raft the next day and waited for the tide. I made it to shore under cover of darkness. And I chose to remain hidden. I knew if they found me, I would be dead.'

She stared at the scarred complexion, wondering how he'd survived and who had stitched him back together so badly. *A doctor with a gun to his head, perhaps. Or maybe he'd done it himself.* His affect was hideous; he sounded paranoid. She wondered if he'd blown up his own plane to fake his death. Was he so deranged that the difference between good and evil was lost on him? 'So you came here and began plotting revenge?'

'At first, I only wanted to survive and disappear,' he insisted. 'I created Urco. As I learned more and more about the destruction of man by man, it became clear to me.'

He hesitated; taking a step back, he changed the subject. 'Why did you leave NASA and join the clandestine world of the NSA?'

'Because of what happened to you,' she whispered. 'After your death, and the endless news of terrorism and war in other parts of the world, I realized that most of the planet was filled with evil. And that evil must be fought at every turn.'

'You were a pacifist,' he said.

'So were you.'

He nodded slowly and reapplied his beard. 'It seems we've both realized the truth. *Pacifism* in a violent world is another term for *suicide*. Only the evil and violence I see resides in government buildings and ivory towers.'

'There's a difference between governments and terrorists.'

'Only in the scale of their atrocities,' he insisted. 'Learning that was the key to everything. Despite my desire to simply leave it all behind, I soon learned that the *Nighthawk* project had been transferred to the NSA and that the unthinkable was going to be attempted. I began to obsess over ways to expose it without exposing myself. Ways to prevent what you might do. Eight long years has led to this.'

'And what exactly is *this*?' she asked. 'How is it better? The whole world put at risk so you could take the mixed-state matter away from us and give it to the Russians? That's your solution? Hand the most powerful substance ever known to a nation that invades its neighbours, crushes any form of freedom or human rights and poisons its detractors with radioactive isotopes?'

As he stepped toward Emma he said, 'You're so focused on winning. You fail to see the forest for the trees. You fail to understand my position even as I shout it at you. *All governments are evil. All power corrupts.* Of course I'm not working for the Russians. Or for the Chinese. Or for the Americans.' His voice grew tighter and louder. '*They, and you, are all working for me.*'

The statement rang with such megalomania, she could

hardly believe it had come from his mouth. 'What are you talking about?'

She tried to step back but was frozen by the depth of hate in the eyes that bore deeply into hers. 'I needed allies,' he said smugly. '*I* made them a deal. I would hack into the NSA's system and divert the *Nighthawk* into their clutches *if* they would provide the means to collect it.'

'You're the Falconer,' she said.

'I see you've heard the name.'

It made perfect sense now. She realized they'd played right into his hands. 'You designed the automated computer system that operated the X-37 and we used it virtually unchanged in the *Nighthawk*. No wonder you were able to hack into it and redirect the aircraft. No wonder we never found a mole. You were operating remotely the whole time and we weren't looking for a dead man.'

'Your mistake,' he said arrogantly. 'One of many.'

'How'd you do it? How did you get past the encryption?'

He stepped so close to Emma, she could feel his hot breath. 'NASA left a huge back door open to your project,' he said. 'It was so easy to hack, I thought it might be a trap. I received data from every division like clockwork. I probably had more information about the program than any single person actually working on it. And when you decided to bring it back a week early because of the storm, I was literally the first to know.'

Their betrayal was complete. 'But why? To what end?' She hesitated. 'What's the point of all this?'

He stared back at her, his eyes never blinking. She saw him now. The same man but changed, deranged by some mad desire. 'Balance,' he said. 'I gave the Russians a choice, I gave the Chinese a choice and now offer you the same one.'

'Which is?'

'To fight me,' he taunted. 'Or to work for me. And, by extension, to work for the *common heritage of mankind*.'

She wasn't sure where this was going, but it was not something to refuse out of hand. It might give her a chance to seek help. 'I have no idea what you're getting at.'

'It's very simple,' he said, his voice teeming with vengeance. 'I intend to undo what you and your nation have done. Obviously, I can't give the mixed-state matter equally to all the world's citizens or even to each nation or a large group of them. Few have the technological capability to handle it. One part to the Russians, one part to the Chinese, one part to your government and the rest to another group of my choosing.'

She could hardly believe what she was hearing. Was he serious? Her mind drifted back to the Beric she had known and some of his causes. Not only was he a pacifist like her but also an *antinationalist*, of sorts. He'd written an article he'd titled *Duty of the Commons* that argued ownership of anything by a nation-state was the cause of wars and strife. It tied in with what he was suggesting now. 'You want us to share this?'

'Far better that than one country hoarding all of it,' he said.

'Who are you to make such a decision?'

Urco stepped back and smiled. 'The only one who can,' he said smugly, 'since I now control the entire stock.'

She struggled to process the situation. It was all too new. He was unstable, delusional and perhaps even certifiably insane, but he was also brilliant, devious and determined. And, at the moment, in an unquestionable position of control.

'Cooperating with you would be considered treason,' she explained.

'Better to live in prison than to die in a cataclysm.'

She looked away. She didn't want this. Didn't want to help him in any way. But no matter from what angle she approached it at, the answer was always the same: *What choice did she have?*

His plan sounded like madness, but even that was preferable to Armageddon. 'How will I take *our* portion back to America? Will you let us fly it to Cajamarca?'

'No,' he said. 'You will explain what is occurring to your friends and then you'll drive in a vehicle that I possess.'

'How can I drive when the bridge is out?'

'There's another route,' he said. 'A shorter route that goes to the south and then through the pass. It avoids the highest of the mountains. It has its own steep cliffs, yes . . . but I trust you'll drive with the requisite caution.'

She glanced to the north as the sound of a helicopter approaching became audible.

'That will be the Chinese agents,' he said. 'I require your answer.'

She looked him in the eye once more. 'Fine,' she said. 'I'll do as you ask. I have no other choice.'

49

The sound of the helicopter drifted across the open beach.

'Airborne tow truck to haul away our *Nighthawk*?' Paul suggested.

Joe scanned the horizon for the source of the clatter; he spied a black speck in the distance. 'Not a heavy-lifter, by the sound of it. Something faster and more maneuverable.'

'Help maybe?'

'Even less likely,' Joe said. He could hear Urco's men running around and making preparations. 'But if it preoccupies our captors, I'll take it.'

Joe considered whether this might be the moment to break free, but Emma's return with two guards at her side quashed the idea.

'On your feet,' one of the guards said, waving a pistol.

Joe stood wearily. Paul did likewise.

The black speck continued to grow larger, and descend, as it came closer. It crossed the lake at two hundred feet and passed over the beach, whipping the tall grasses behind them into a swirling frenzy. It continued on, landing higher up on the plateau, several hundred feet away.

'Are we done standing at attention,' Paul asked, 'or are we going to do something?'

Surprisingly, Emma replied, 'Urco wants you and Joe to carry the containment units up to the plateau.'

'And if we go on strike?' Joe said.

'Please,' Emma said. 'Just do as he asks.'

Joe could see the strain on her face. He also noticed that she stood *behind* the two guards, not in front of them. As if *they* were taking orders from *her.*

Reluctantly, Joe held out his hands. The man pulled a knife, slid it between Joe's wrists and pulled upward. The zip tie broke with a sharp snap. So much for all his work weakening the plastic. No doubt, he'd have to start again.

Paul's restraints were cut free as well and the two men followed Emma into the grass and up toward the *Nighthawk*. Urco's men followed a few steps behind.

'You've earned their trust pretty quickly,' Joe whispered. 'Tell me there's a reason for that.'

'There is,' she said. 'I'm doing whatever I can to avoid disaster.'

She went on to explain the situation as quickly as possible.

'You know it's going to end badly,' Joe said.

'There are degrees of *badly*,' she said. 'But it's the lesser of two evils at this point.'

Joe understood her reasoning, but he wasn't buying in. The lesser of all evils would be if they could escape, subdue or kill this madman *and* secure the mixed-state matter. A long shot, but he still intended to pull it off.

They entered the clearing, rounded the nose of the *Nighthawk* and found Urco standing in front of the containment units.

He pointed to the first unit. 'You two will carry that one up to the helicopter on the plateau. Ms Townsend will carry the fuel cell. I trust you understand what happens if you drop it.'

'Don't worry,' Joe said. 'Though it might help us to keep our footing if you gave us our boots back.'

'Help you to escape, maybe?'

Joe shrugged. It was worth a try.

He and Paul were handed gloves. They set themselves on either end of the first containment unit and grabbed the handles. Joe could feel chilled air coming off the frosted pipes as soon as he got close to them.

'Ready,' Paul said.

'Up,' Joe replied.

They lifted simultaneously. The unit was hefty, but the weight was distributed evenly and the lifting bars were well positioned. They picked it off the ground with ease and were directed toward the freshly cut pathway.

Joe was at the front of the unit, walking backward and looking over his shoulder to see where he was going. Paul was at the back. Emma walked beside them, lugging the portable fuel cell and keeping the cords from getting tangled.

They arrived at the top of the path a minute later. Four of Urco's men stood there waiting, surrounding the helicopter at various distances. Three held assault rifles, one held a shotgun.

Urco walked past them and began conversing with a petite woman. Even from a distance, Joe could see her physique was well muscled.

'That's the woman who attacked us at La Jalca,' Emma whispered. 'She said her name was Daiyu.'

Joe could see why she'd turned out to be such a handful.

After a nod from Urco, Daiyu walked over to inspect the containment unit. Like him, she had armed men at her disposal. One stood in the helicopter and two others were on the ground with her. They carried short-barreled submachine guns, held at the ready to spray everyone and anyone with a hail of lead.

'A hard bargain is being struck here,' Paul noted.

'So much for honor among thieves.'

'And this is what we've been after all this time?' Daiyu said, running a finger across the frost on the outer casing. 'How am I to be sure there's anything in this metal box?'

'You could open it up and look inside,' Urco suggested. 'Though your brain cells will be vaporized before they process anything you might see.'

Daiyu cut her eyes at him. 'My country does not play games.'

'I know more about your country than you might think,' he said. 'I know your orders from Zhang are to take possession of the containment units and leave the diamonds without confrontation. I receive fifty ounces of them now, and another fifty upon your scientists confirming that the antimatter is stored inside. If you want to haggle, we can do that, but every minute on the ground here increases all of our risks. So if you have an issue, state it; otherwise, take possession and close the deal or turn it down and leave.'

She glared back at him, the fury barely suppressed in her eyes. 'If you're lying, I will hunt you down personally.'

'You would never find me,' he said. 'But have no fear. You're getting what you asked for. To make sure I get what I want, Vargas will travel with you.'

'Acceptable,' she said. 'Have them load it up and bring the second unit. The sooner we get out of here, the better.'

Joe and Paul were urged forward. The pilot helped them lift the unit into the helicopter and then secured it to the floor. Emma made sure the fuel cell and the power cords were strapped down tightly.

That done, they moved off to collect the second unit and they carried it back at double speed.

Joe's initial reaction to Emma's cooperation hadn't changed, but the sooner the Chinese agent and her gunmen left, the quicker he could get back to planning an escape. And by taking one of Urco's most intimidating henchmen with them, the Chinese had unknowingly helped out.

With the second unit loaded aboard, the black helicopter powered up and took off. Even as it left, he and Paul were given a new order: loading another of the containment units into the back of an old Toyota Land Cruiser that Emma was slated to drive.

Emma strapped the unit and the fuel cell down tightly. 'I'll contact Urco as soon as the unit is safely airborne,' she said. 'He's promised to release you at that point.'

Joe knew that wouldn't happen. And from the sound of her voice, Emma knew it, too.

'I'd say wear your seat belt,' Joe replied. 'But I'm assuming you'll be driving carefully.'

She offered a sad look, closed the door and waited as another of Urco's men climbed in the passenger side to make sure she did as she was told.

Joe stepped back as the engine came to life. Still under guard, he and Paul watched as the old Land Cruiser moved off down the dirt road that led south.

Three of the eight containment units were gone, four remained in the *Nighthawk* and one sat in the clearing, awaiting another purchaser.

Perhaps more importantly, two of Urco's men were gone. Two of the biggest and strongest.

As he and Paul were led back to the beach under guard, Joe glanced at the sun. It was falling toward the horizon now. The time to act was soon.

50

From her spot on the ridge, Gamay watched. Wearing high-desert camouflage, she had wrapped a tawny scarf around her head and neck to complete the disguise. She carried a modified Heckler & Koch G36 assault rifle. It had an extended barrel, a high-powered scope and two fold-out legs to steady it for long-range shooting.

This particular weapon had come from a target-shooting enthusiast they'd found in Cajamarca. It wasn't a sniper's rifle, but it was lightweight, accurate and the best they could procure on short notice.

Staring through the high-powered scope, she'd watched the helicopter's arrival and departure; sighted the old Toyota, as it drove off to the south; and followed Paul and Joe, as they were marched back to the beach and placed under guard again.

Not long after that, a white Jeep Cherokee came rumbling down the path. It pulled off the road and several men climbed out of it. They wore blue flight suits. They spoke with Urco and were led over to the Air-Crane.

With each passing minute, Gamay felt the danger grow. Whatever Urco was up to, he would soon have no need for hostages.

She pulled back the sleeve of her camouflage jacket. Kurt had been silent a long time. Had he been anyone else, she'd have assumed he was drowned by now. Still, she couldn't wait much longer.

'Come on, Kurt,' she whispered. 'This is no time to be late.'

Having moved to a firing position, Gamay was more exposed, but she hadn't seen the slightest sign of anyone looking for her.

Finally, the tiny speaker in the earbud came to life. *'Gamay, this is Kurt.'*

'Who else would it be,' she said. 'Glad you didn't drown. A lot has happened since you went on radio silence. By the look of it, Urco's dispersing the mixed-state matter. Selling it off piece by piece. The Chinese landed and took off with two units. Emma drove out of here with another unit in the back of a Land Cruiser.'

'If this was about money, he could have named his price and any one of the three countries involved would have paid it. But instead he wants us all to pay – in blood.'

'What do you mean?'

'I found replicas of the fuel cells in a cave where Urco's people were hiding. I also found a crate of Semtex that was several bricks short, but I couldn't find a single detonator. That tells me the rest are already in place – most likely, in the fuel cells.'

'In the fuel cells,' she said. 'But if he blows them up – '

'He gets a catastrophe,' Kurt said. *'Which is exactly what he wants. A catastrophe for the Americans, the Russians and the Chinese. Or, more likely, for the entire industrialized world.'*

'What purpose could that possibly serve him?'

'Payback,' Kurt said. *'For what the industrial powers did to the indigenous tribes of South America five hundred years ago.*

For what he feels they're still doing today. By dispersing the mixed-state matter the way he is and then detonating it, he can strike a crushing blow against China, Europe, America and whoever else he blames for the fate of the native people. He can set industrialization back a thousand years in most of the world while his people are safe in their mountain pastures, living a technology-free life.'

Gamay listened as Kurt explained his theory. 'The Chinese are already gone,' she said. 'Emma's out of sight as well.'

'We stop Urco first and get to them after.'

A flash of light caught Gamay's eye. A dull whine reaching her on the wind.

She looked back through the scope. The two men in the blue flight suits were still in the Air-Crane. The rotors had begun to turn, moving slowly, reflecting the sunlight.

She could see that the cables leading to the *Nighthawk* had been reattached. The cargo bay had been sealed shut.

'You'd better hurry,' she said. 'I think the Russians are about to take the rest in the Air-Crane.'

'I thought I heard it starting up,' Kurt said. *'I'm on the move now. Wait for my signal and then drop the hammer. Get the men guarding Paul and Joe first. Once they're down, fire at will. Take out everyone you can, but don't risk hitting the* Nighthawk. *And, remember — I'm the guy in the black wet suit.'*

51

Having finished his climb, Kurt moved across the upper part of the landing area of the plateau, darting from one patch of scrub foliage to another in quick, crouching movements.

He was halfway across when the Air-Crane lifted off, rising on a whirlwind of dust, blinding anyone who was foolish enough to open his eyes and look into it.

As it gained altitude, it drew up the same steel cables that had been attached to the *Nighthawk* in the water. They snaked across the ground, rising slowly, until they were taut with tension and the black spacecraft came up slowly off the ground.

The two linked aircraft rotated until they were pointing to the southeast. Finally, they began to move, traveling so cautiously at first that they barely appeared to be making any progress.

With all eyes on the departing craft and no chance that he would be heard, Kurt rushed in. He charged the nearest of Urco's men, tackled the man in a flying leap and slammed him to the ground. A short scuffle ended when Kurt landed a knockout punch.

He grabbed his radio. 'I'm in the clearing and armed. Open fire.'

*

Gamay had been waiting for a call, tracking the men who were guarding Paul and Joe. Taught to shoot by her father at a young age, she'd been around guns all her life. And though she preferred to avoid violence, she'd shot at attackers and been shot at more than a few times during her years with NUMA. It was the nature of the job. Still, as she steadied the barrel and aimed at the men in the clearing she realized this was something she had never done before.

The discomfort vanished as one of the men pulled out his pistol and moved in behind Joe.

Gamay exhaled and pulled the trigger.

The rifle cracked. The man with the pistol dropped to his knees and fell over on his side. Before he hit the ground, Gamay adjusted her aim and fired again, this time hitting the guard that was standing over by Paul.

She saw him tumble, pulled the trigger again for good measure and then switched her sights to a third target. By now, the men were racing in all directions. Her fourth shot winged one of them; her fifth may or may not have struck home as another of Urco's crew dove back into the tall grass.

Down on the rocky beach, Joe heard the rifle shot and thought it sounded like deliverance. He pulled and twisted the new zip tie that had been wrapped around his wrists. It hadn't been weakened as much as the prior one, but he'd been working on it.

Another shot rang out and then another. The men

around them were falling dead or running for safety when Joe finally snapped the restraint.

He immediately grabbed a sharp-edged rock he'd been eyeing and rushed over to Paul.

With a quick pull, Paul was cut free. Joe tossed the rock aside, exchanging it for the pistol in the dead man's hand.

Joe pointed to the ridge that he assumed Gamay to be firing from. 'Get to the bottom of the bluff.'

'Where are you going?'

'To find Urco.'

Paul turned over another of the men Gamay had shot and retrieved a weapon of his own. 'Let's go.'

As Gamay fired from the high ridge, Kurt came in low and fast. He'd taken out two of Urco's men, commandeered a shotgun and rushed forward with it. He wanted to capture Urco, but his surviving men were making things difficult.

Kurt shot one of them as the man sprayed a clip of bullets up at the hills, hoping to hit the sniper.

Rushing past the dead man, he pumped the shotgun and fired at a man who'd taken cover in some bushes. The blast ripped the bush to shreds and left the man lying on the ground, bleeding.

Kurt rushed over to him and kicked the rifle from his hand. 'Urco?'

The man pointed, his finger extending unsteadily toward the path that had been hacked in the grass.

Kurt glanced in that direction and noticed something

being thrown toward them from up above. He sprinted and then dove away, launching himself into the grass just as the brick of Semtex detonated.

The explosion rang in Kurt's ears, momentarily flattened the field of green stalks and rained dirt on him for several long seconds. He was far enough away to avoid serious injury.

The man who'd pointed to Urco was not so lucky.

Kurt was about to move forward when someone tapped him on the leg.

He spun around with his weapon. But instead of enemies, he saw the smiling face of Joe Zavala. Paul Trout was just behind him.

'For a ghost, you're made of surprisingly solid material,' Joe said.

Kurt grinned. 'And easy to sneak up on,' he said. 'Glad to see you both. Believe it or not, I think we're winning, primarily thanks to Gamay's shooting.'

'She'll be hard to live with after saving us,' Paul said. 'But well worth it.'

'How many of them are down?'

'Four down below,' Joe said.

'And I took out three,' Kurt said.

'That leaves only Urco,' Joe said. 'Trust me, I've been counting them obsessively.'

Kurt pointed to the high ground. 'He's up there. But I have a feeling he'll be lobbing bombs at us if we move his way.'

'Maybe Gamay can hit him from her position,' Paul suggested.

Kurt pulled out the radio, gave Gamay a status report and made the request.

'*He's up there, all right,*' Gamay insisted. '*And he's alone. But he's not defenseless.*'

'We got a taste of the explosives,' Kurt said. 'I'm not interested in a second course. Can you hit him?'

'*Maybe,*' she replied. '*But there's a problem with that plan.*'

'Which is . . . ?'

'*He seems to have anticipated this,*' she said. '*He's crouched behind the last of the containment units. And he's got his pistol up against the housing as if it was a living human hostage.*'

Just then, Urco's booming voice called out to them. 'This violence has gone on long enough,' he shouted. 'Throw down your weapons. Or I'll destroy us all.'

52

The battlefield went silent in the wake of Urco's words. Kurt glanced at Joe. 'Apparently, we're not winning . . . yet.'

'We could rush him from three sides,' Joe offered.

'The last thing I want is for him to panic.'

The radio came alive with Gamay's voice. *'I might be able to get a head shot if he moves,'* she said. *'But if I miss . . .'*

'Even if you hit him square, he might squeeze that trigger,' Kurt replied. They had to try something else. He handed Joe the radio. 'I'm going to walk up there.'

'He'll shoot you down.'

'Hopefully,' Kurt said. 'And when he does, you guys drop him.'

Joe looked at Kurt quizzically.

'Clue Gamay in,' Kurt said. 'Once I get moving up the path, you two move through the grass. I'll try to keep him talking as long as possible.'

Kurt stood slowly. He raised the shotgun over his head with both hands like a surrendering soldier. Carrying it high, he walked out of the grass, across the clearing and up the snaking path to the higher ground.

He arrived at the upper clearing and found Urco crouching behind the last containment unit with the pistol up against one of the cryogenic tubes.

Kurt tossed the shotgun away as soon as they made eye contact.

Urco stared. 'Austin,' he said quietly. 'And in far better condition than I was led to believe.'

'Disappointed?' Kurt asked.

'Surprised. Vargas does not often fail at his tasks. Nor does he lie. Not to me. He said you were bleeding out at the bottom of the lake.'

'Don't be too angry with him,' Kurt replied. 'He cut the red dye packet in my vest. Must have thought he'd sliced me deep. An accidental deception. Unlike the one you've created for the world. I have to hand it to you, not many people have the guts to manipulate the three most powerful nations on Earth.'

'I took advantage of an opportunity,' Urco said. 'Nothing more.'

Kurt shook his head. 'It's a little late for false modesty, don't you think? You pulled the strings. We danced. You wanted the *Nighthawk* raised and you got us to raise it for you. You needed someone to pluck it out of the air for you and you convinced the Russians to build a pair of hypersonic bombers to catch it for you. When they needed money – cash-strapped as they are – you manipulated the Chinese into partnering up with them. And you did it with nothing but words. Unless I'm mistaken, you have no money, no political power, no weapons, nothing but that brilliant mind of yours.'

Urco was too smart not to see Kurt's flattery for what it was, but he was also too full of himself not to hang on every word.

'I've fought with terrorists, foreign governments and even billionaires with private armies at their beck and call,' Kurt added. 'And I honestly doubt that I've ever met a more dangerous man. Congratulations, Urco. Or should I call you the Falconer?'

Urco's chin rose at the sound of the name. Intrigued, his gaze hardened on Kurt. 'So you know a thing or two as well. Tell me, where did you hear that name?'

'From the cockpit voice recorder we found in the wreckage of *Blackjack 1*,' Kurt said. 'It survived, even if the pilots didn't. You were on *Blackjack 2*; you were the reason the *Nighthawk* suddenly came back to life again when the Russians thought it had been shut down. And you ignored their pleas to reboot the system with the alpha code. That's why the camera footage from La Jalca was filmed by someone using their right hand. Because you weren't there to film it yourself.'

Urco stared at Kurt and then nodded.

'A brilliant scheme,' Kurt continued. 'You parceled out just enough information to lead us all along by the nose. The part I couldn't understand until recently was, why?'

'Avarice affects even the purest of hearts,' Urco responded.

Kurt had him talking. It was now a conversation. That was Kurt's advantage. He began to walk slowly as he spoke. 'Greed is not your game. If it was, you could have contacted any one of the three nations and demanded a huge sum be transferred to a numbered account in return for the *Nighthawk*'s location. After all, you were the only one who knew where it was. But you didn't. You teased us all along, brought us all in close. As you said at our dinner the other night, the feast cannot begin until *all the guests are present and accounted for.* You didn't sell the mixed-state matter. You gave it away, a portion to each nation that sought it.'

Urco became agitated at Kurt's accusations. 'I was paid in gems.'

'All part of the act,' Kurt said. 'A nice touch in your little drama of revenge. But wealth will do nothing for you when the world comes crashing down. I know what you have in mind. I saw the replica fuel cells in the cave. I found your explosives.'

Urco seemed unnerved by the fact that Kurt had uncovered so much. He held the pistol against the containment unit, but his eyes were focused on Kurt.

'What's the point in hiding the truth?' Kurt said, pressing harder. 'This is the end. Either the end of your world or the end of ours. Do you really want to go out pretending you did this for money? That's the motivation of an industrialist, of a conquistador, of Pizarro and Columbus and every other European who came to the New World. Do you want to throw your lot in with the people who decimated the Inca and Chachapoya?'

'Decimated,' Urco repeated angrily, his voice rose sharply. 'The term means *to kill one in ten.* The Europeans and their filth didn't leave one in ten alive. Their plagues wiped out ninety-five percent of those who lived here. They raped and enslaved the rest. Polluted our blood with theirs. For three-quarters of a century,

we've labeled the evil actions of the Nazis and the purges of Stalin with terms like *Holocaust* and *genocide*, but they were nothing compared to what happened here!'

Urco's sudden fury unbalanced him as Kurt had hoped it would.

'No one alive today had anything to do with that,' Kurt said, moving closer.

'It's still occurring today,' he shouted. 'You point to the past as if the murder and dislocation of the innocent happened once and then ended, but it continues even now. Every hour of every day. Not just here or in the Amazon but in Africa, Asia, the outback of Australia and the cold expanses of the Arctic. The last vestiges of the original peoples are threatened by the *children of the machine*. There is no hope of accommodation. The way industrial people spread like a virus, there will soon be no room left for any other way of life. It has to be stopped. I am the one to stop it. And this is the only way.'

'One bomb for America, one bomb for China, one for someone else and the rest – the vast majority – to make Europe into an inferno as the Russian bomber passes over it. Is that your idea of revenge?'

'Justice.' Urco seethed. 'Long delayed. An eye for an eye. One genocide for another.'

'You can't think you won't be affected here.'

'We live off the land, as do all the children of the soil. You live off the energy of automation and mechanical power. That reliance on industrialization will be your undoing. Without equipment to do their bidding, the children of the machine will starve; they will die of thirst and of heat and of cold. They will destroy one another fighting over what's left. The children of the soil will simply return to what they've always known.'

Urco went cold and the conversation ended.

Kurt edged closer.

'That's far enough,' he said. 'One more step and I'll kill us all.' Urco pulled the hammer back and cocked it. The fate of the world now hung on a hair-trigger response of a man who was literally shaking with anger.

'No,' Kurt said. 'I don't think you will.'

'Don't test me,' Urco said. 'I am more than willing to die.'

'Oh, I'm sure you are,' Kurt said. 'But your plan . . . You're not thinking this through. You can't pull that trigger now. Your other bombs are too close. This one is too powerful. It's a thousand Hiroshimas, maybe five thousand. If you set it off, the shock wave and fireball will engulf the Russians in our stolen helicopter. That will set off a second reaction. The combined effects of which will obliterate Emma Townsend on the road to Cajamarca, triggering a third explosion.

'Even if the Chinese have somehow transferred their containment units to a long-range transport headed for Asia, they can't have gone far. Certainly not far enough to escape the effect of three small suns igniting a hundred miles away. The same shock wave you intend to use on the industrial civilizations of the world will swat that plane out of midair. The gamma rays and EMP burst will fry the circuitry and melt the containment unit. One way or another, that fourth ticking bomb of yours will go off. It *will* be a cataclysm, but it'll be South America that bears the brunt of the disaster and the *children of the machine* who come to render assistance.'

Urco's jaw clenched as Kurt spoke. It was possible he'd already thought it through. Was it even possible that he'd never considered it? But he saw it now, saw it exactly how Kurt had laid it out for him.

Kurt took another step. The only thing he needed to do was prevent Urco from firing by accident.

'Stay where you are!'

'It's over, Urco!'

'I will pull this trigger,' Urco shouted. 'It will still be a cataclysm. And it will affect your society far more than it affects those who live in the jungles, the tundra or the distant plains.'

Kurt was close enough now that he could see the flaring of Urco's nostrils and the wildness in his eyes. He watched a bead of sweat run down his temple and his knuckles turn white on the pistol grip.

'You've got one move left,' Kurt said. 'One shot. It's either the bomb . . . Or me.'

Urco was shaking with fury. A second drop of perspiration trickled down his face. It ran down his beard and stopped for the slightest instant before dropping onto the containment unit. It hit and froze instantly on the supercooled pipe. 'Damn you!' he shouted.

With a shift of his shoulders, Urco snapped the pistol upward, swinging it toward Kurt.

Kurt dove away as two shots rang out almost simultaneously. One near and one sounding off in the distance.

Urco was thrown to the side by the rifle shot, which hit him in the ribs beneath his outstretched arm. He crashed to the ground, still grasping the pistol. Joe rushed forward, leapt on top of him and punched the gun away before he could attempt to fire again.

Kurt looked up from where he'd landed. Urco's shot had missed. The barrel had stuck momentarily to the frost-covered cylinder of the containment unit. He rushed over to assist Joe.

'He's bleeding out fast,' Joe said.

They tried to stanch the bleeding, but the bullet had gone through his body. Too many organs had been hit and damaged. Too much tissue had been torn up.

Kurt gave up trying to save Urco and attempted to force one last answer out of him.

'You're going to die,' he said. 'Don't take half the world with you. Tell me how to stop what you've set in motion.'

Urco gazed at Kurt blankly.

'We'll come back here. We'll help your people and the other people. You're not wrong about what's been and is being done, but you have to help us first.'

Urco looked at him. 'I almost . . . believe you,' he said in a whisper. His eyes were unfocused. 'It's too late,' he said. 'What goes up . . . will never . . . come down.'

53

Urco died without saying anything more. Joe and Paul gathered up the dead and the two survivors. Gamay came running from her hiding place and embraced Paul.

'My compliments to your shooting instructor,' Joe said.

'I'll tell my father,' she said, then turned to Kurt. 'That was some game of brinksmanship.'

'I figured he'd put so much into his plan that he'd do anything but short-circuit it now.'

'What if you'd been wrong?'

'Simple math,' he said. 'One obliterated continent is better than four.'

'Marginally,' she said.

'You'll get no argument from me,' Kurt replied.

'Any idea where this last unit was supposed to go?' Paul asked.

'I heard Urco's men mentioning something about Rio,' Kurt said.

'Considering how much deforestation is occurring in the Amazon, it would make sense to wipe out the largest city on the continent in hopes of putting a stop to it,' Joe said. 'But now what?'

Kurt was grim. 'We've won the battle, but we're

losing the war. We need to warn the Chinese and the Russians and get in touch with the NSA.'

They searched both the camp and Urco's men for any form of long-distance communication. All they found were short-range walkie-talkies, their own satellite phones, which had been destroyed, and Urco's computer with its bulky satellite antenna.

After twenty minutes of trying, Paul said, 'I've seen this before. It's a multistep security program. Even if we could get past the first level, there's probably a second layer of encryption to get through before we can access the satellite communications suite.'

They pressed the two survivors for information, but they could get nothing out of them.

'We don't have time for this,' Kurt said. 'We'll have to do this the old-fashioned way. Up close and personal.'

'We've only got one vehicle and three mega-bombs to chase down,' Joe noted.

'We'll have to split up,' Kurt said. 'You and I will go after the Russians. Paul, you and Gamay take that Jeep Cherokee and see if you can catch Emma.'

'She has an armed escort,' Paul noted.

'Then deal with him.'

'What about the Chinese?' Gamay mentioned. 'They've got to be airborne by now.'

Kurt glanced at his watch. There was nothing they could do about the Chinese at the moment. 'It's a long flight to Beijing; maybe we can figure out how to defuse the bombs and talk to them before they land.'

Without wasting any time, they carried the last

containment unit down the path and out to the narrow dirt road where the Cherokee waited. After loading and securing it, Paul and Gamay got moving. There were no good-byes. Time was too short.

As Paul and Gamay drove off, Kurt and Joe set about chasing down the Russians. The first problem was, knowing where to find them.

'They flew directly over that notch in the ridge and kept on going,' Joe said. 'I can't see any reason they wouldn't be flying in a straight line to whatever destination they had in mind. And considering the weight and control problems I encountered carrying the *Nighthawk*, they can't seriously hope to get too far.'

'I think I know where they're going,' Kurt said. 'Remember the audio from the first bomber's crash? The pilot of *Blackjack 1* was in a panic when the *Nighthawk* began to break free. He was shouting for the Falconer to use the reset codes on the *Nighthawk*. He was calling to *Blackjack 2*.'

'And Urco was the Falconer.'

Kurt nodded. 'Which means *Blackjack 2* did not crash. It landed safely, and probably in the near vicinity. All we have to do is find the closest airfield.'

'There is one,' Joe said. 'About seven miles from here. When I was planning our route, I saw it on the map.'

'That's a long hike,' Kurt said. 'We'd better get to it.'

'We don't need to hike it,' Joe said. 'At least not all the way. The river passes within a mile of the runway. We can take the Zodiac. It'll save us hours.'

54

The seven-mile flight of the Air-Crane would be its last, thought Major Timonovski of the Russian Air Force. The big helicopter was struggling to carry the load in the thin mountain air. The engine temperatures were in the yellow before they'd made it halfway. But with the *Nighthawk*'s nine tons of mass slung beneath them, Timonovski did not dare speed up.

'Red light on engine number two,' the flight engineer said.

'What is it?' Timonovski asked.

'Metal shavings in the oil pan. The main rotor – its transmission is coming apart. We need to put this bird down.'

Timonovski heard the strain in the engineer's voice but shook it off. 'We're almost there,' he said.

He could see the outline of the runway up ahead. *Blackjack 2* was there, no longer covered in the shroud of netting and tarps that the Birdcaller had wrapped around it. Another aircraft was there on the runway as well. A small turboprop.

Ignoring the warning lights, Timonovski brought the orange helicopter and the stolen American spacecraft over the last line of trees and down toward the hard-packed airstrip. A man on the ground flashed a light at them in Morse code.

'So the Birdcaller tells the truth, for once,' he said. After so many lies and tricks, Timonovski half expected to be met by American agents or perhaps the Chinese. 'Contact them on the low-frequency channel.'

The flight engineer dialed up the correct frequency and engaged in a rapid-fire conversation. 'They want us to land the *Nighthawk* on top of the bomber,' he told Timonovski. 'Can we stay airborne that long?'

'I would rather put it down on the side of the runway, but once we land this helicopter, it will never take off again.'

'That's what I thought,' the flight engineer said. 'What should I tell them?'

Timonovski didn't hesitate. 'We chance it.'

He angled toward the sitting bomber, pulled up next to it and put the helicopter into a sideways slip. With a deft touch, he eased them over the resting bomber until they were centered and began to lower the American craft toward it.

The first attempt ended in failure as the swirling downwash of the rotors continued to twist the suspended craft. The second attempt was no better.

'I can't keep it lined up,' Timonovski said.

'We need to put it down,' the flight engineer said. 'We're going to lose the gearbox any minute.'

'One more try,' Timonovski said.

This time, as he moved in, the men from the ground crew appeared on the back of the bomber. They grabbed the *Nighthawk* with their bare hands, hooked ropes around the nose and tail and used their combined weight to arrest the twisting motion. With their help, Timonovski steered the *Nighthawk* into position and felt it bump softly against the armored spine of the bomber.

'Down and locked,' the flight engineer said. 'I'm releasing the cable.'

With an audible snap, the cables were disconnected. The Air-Crane rose quickly in response – and did so with dark smoke pouring from the transmission housing.

A horrible grinding noise soon drowned out the roar of the engines and Timonovski knew they'd lost the gearbox.

'Hold on,' he shouted, angling away from the bomber, the *Nighthawk* and the ground crew.

The smoking helicopter peeled off with what little power remained and then began to fall. Timonovski did what he could to counter the loss of control, but the craft had become unstable. They hit near the shoulder of the runway.

The impact bent the right landing strut and the Air-Crane went over. The rotors struck the ground and shattered into deadly fragments, most of which flew mercifully into the trees.

As the helicopter came to rest on its side, Timonovski shut down the engines and cut the fuel. He turned to see the flight engineer bailing out through the door.

By the time Timonovski pulled off his seat belt and

397

caught up with the engineer, half a dozen members of the ground crew had closed in around them. One was spraying foam from a fire extinguisher toward the engine compartment. Black smoke belched from the vents, but there was no flame.

'Evil things,' said a voice among the crowd.

The Major spied Constantin Davidov. To have the head of the directorate out in the field was a rare sight indeed. The old war-horse was beaming as he rushed forward.

'Evil things?' Major Timonovski asked. 'What things would those be?'

'Helicopters,' Davidov explained. 'Unnatural, noisy and ugly. Little more than torture devices, in my opinion.'

The Major didn't know about Davidov's long ride from Kamchatka to the cruiser *Varyag* in the *Carrier Pigeon*. But he knew better than to question the boss. 'If you say so.'

'I do,' Davidov replied, 'But they have their uses.'

'And their limits,' Timonovski replied. 'As do we all.' He pointed to *Blackjack 2*, with the *Nighthawk* sitting proudly on its back. 'We'll never get off the runway. The field is too short. The trees too high. I told the Birdcaller as much.'

'And he listened,' Davidov said. 'I've brought the RATO boosters. With the rockets to assist us, and a few of those trees chainsawed to the ground, we'll make it without a problem. The ground crew are attaching the boosters as we speak.'

Timonovski squinted. He could see the ground crew hooking up the stubby missile-like canisters to the hard-points beneath the bomber's wings. It was a complex process. 'It seems the Falconer thought of everything.'

'Yes,' Davidov agreed. 'It seems he did.'

55

Emma's route to Cajamarca took her through a wide valley and then up through a narrow pass. At first the road was flat and hemmed in by the mountains, but as they came out of the pass the road began to look like the one she and Kurt had dealt with on the way up. Only now it was dusk and growing darker by the moment.

She had the high beams on, along with the small fog lamps under the bumper and two auxiliary lights mounted on the roof rack. They lit the road well enough, but the drop beyond the narrow shoulder was nothing more than a dark void.

'When this is over, I'm moving to Kansas,' she said.

'What's Kansas?'

The question came from Reyes, the escort Urco had sent with her. He sat in the passenger seat, cocked to the side and holding a 9mm pistol in his hand.

If she drove too fast or too slow, he gave her a dirty look and then complained. Right now she must have been doing fine since he was leaning back and the Beretta was resting on his lap, aimed roughly at her thigh.

'Kansas,' she said, 'is a very flat part of America. None of these mountains to climb or cliffs to fall off.'

His brow furrowed.

'Never mind,' she said. 'I can imagine how that sounds to someone who lives here.'

He said nothing, leaned forward to glance at the speedometer and then leaned back again.

'Are we on a schedule?' she asked.

He didn't reply. Maybe they were.

'Urco didn't need to send you along, you know.'

'I'm here to make sure you do as you promised.'

'Why wouldn't I?' she asked, rounding a curve. 'It's, literally, the only sane thing to do.'

He shrugged.

'And, anyway, what would you do if I refused? Or changed my mind?'

She was just talking, just making conversation on the long drive and perhaps hoping to make him see her as a human being instead of a target. But she'd hit a nerve.

'I shoot you and drive there by myself.'

'Really?' she said, surprised and not surprised all at the same time. 'And then what? Just going to hand over the containment unit and tell my colleagues you're a Good Samaritan who picked it up on the side of the road? For that matter, how would you even find them without me?'

The answer came to her even before she'd finished asking the question. 'Oh, you have a phone,' she said. 'You have *my* phone.'

At almost the same moment, both of them realized that he'd given something away.

A phone could deliver help. It could summon a

rescue team to the lake and military units to swarm over Urco and his followers. *Her* phone could turn the entire situation on its head.

'Pull over,' he said.

'No,' she said. 'It's okay. Let's just drive to Cajamarca.'

'Pull the car over!'

From there, everything happened in a flash. Reyes shouted again and leveled the pistol at her head. She realized this might be her only chance to act and slammed hard on the brakes. The sudden deceleration caused his extended arm to swing forward. His hand smacked against the dashboard and the pistol discharged into the windshield.

As the glass shattered, Emma swung her right arm toward him. Her hand was stiff, her fingers outstretched. The edge of her palm caught him in the throat, a perfect backhand to his Adam's apple.

The blow crushed his windpipe and Reyes dropped the pistol.

Her foot went to the accelerator, slamming it to the floor. He fell back now, thrown off balance again.

As he reeled in the seat, she reached down for the pistol, trying to pluck it off the floor. Her fingers brushed it, but before she could pick it up, he did the unthinkable, lunging for the steering wheel and pushing it hard to the right.

The wheels turned sharply. The Toyota skidded and then went over on its side. The windshield blew out and the old SUV slid toward the far edge of the road and the cliff beyond. It went halfway over the edge and crashed headlong into a gnarled tree that grew from the side of a steep slope and stopped.

The impact knocked Emma unconscious. Whether it was seconds or a minute or more, she didn't know. When she woke up, she was lying on her side and pinned by the steering wheel. A hissing sound could be heard, and she was surrounded by a cloud of steam that was venting from the Toyota's shattered radiator.

Reyes was nowhere to be seen. And with the damaged windshield completely missing, she assumed he'd been ejected.

'That was foolish,' she grunted, angry at herself. Angry at him as well, wherever he was.

She twisted around, felt a spike of pain shoot through her ribs and laid eyes on the containment unit. It remained in place, strapped down as it had been.

Emma stretched far enough to reach the control panel. As her fingers touched the screen, it lit up. The indicators were all green. Power was still flowing through the unit. The magnetic bottles were intact and the cryogenic system was still operating.

'Thank God they didn't give this contract to the lowest bidder,' she whispered.

For obvious reasons, the units were incredibly durable and well made. They'd been designed to survive years in space, cosmic radiation, extremes of heat, cold and pressure, not to mention the turbulence and vibration of reentry and landing or even a minor crash.

Fortunately, the one car accident was not more severe than those conditions.

All Emma had to do was get out of the Land Cruiser, find her former guard and hope that the phone in his pocket had survived his ejection and landing in the road.

She pushed against the steering column that had been loosened by the blow against the tree until she was able to shove it far enough to slide her legs free. Then she pulled them up toward her and eased into a sitting position.

With the Toyota over on its side and the front windshield gone, the easiest way out was forward. Sitting where the driver's window had been, she swung her legs forward. They stretched through the empty space where the windshield had been and touched . . . nothing.

Emma froze. Her legs were dangling as if she was sitting on a swing . . . or a ledge. She looked beneath her. There was ground against the cabin where her side window had been, but it fell away near the front edge.

She leaned forward, grabbing the seat belt for stability. As the steam from the radiator began to dissipate, the rooftop lights played out into the darkness, touching the ground three hundred feet below.

The Land Cruiser was already pointed downward at an angle. The only thing keeping it from dropping was the gnarled tree it had run into.

Emma pulled her legs back in and shifted her weight to climb out the top. A barely audible crack from the tree trunk and a subtle shift in the Toyota's position told her that moving was a bad idea. She went still, wondering how long the tree would hold.

56

Kurt and Joe made excellent time in the Zodiac. They ran with the engine wide open and the current at their backs. A few sets of minor rapids caused little problem and they'd soon traversed twelve miles on the looping river, enabling them to move nearly seven miles as the crow flies – or the *Nighthawk* flew.

'This is as close as we're going to get,' Joe said, navigating based on his memory of the chart and the time.

'I'm ready,' Kurt said. 'Let's go on foot.'

Kurt had changed into regular clothes, and both men were wearing their boots. As soon as Joe beached the Zodiac, they leapt off and began a hike that would be more of a sprint than a walk.

Darkness had fallen, the night air had cooled dramatically and the stars had come out. They shone up above like diamonds on black velvet. Using the stars to navigate, Kurt and Joe continued to cross the rocky ground, moving toward the airfield.

A few yards behind Joe, Kurt felt his knees begin to ache from old football injuries.

'You're getting slow in your old age,' Joe needled.

'While some of us were sitting around all day, I was working,' Kurt said.

'Floating on the lake in an inner tube doesn't count as work where I come from,' Joe said.

'I've basically created my own kind of extreme triathlon,' Kurt insisted. 'Swim under a waterfall, climb up a sheer cliff and now a 2K uphill run in the rarefied air at ten thousand feet of altitude.'

'Under a waterfall?' Joe said. 'Why didn't you swim around it?'

'I tried,' Kurt admitted. 'Not as easy as it sounds.'

Joe laughed. 'I just hope all this running is worth it and we haven't missed our flight.'

Kurt was hoping that, too. There was no way to know until they got there, but having lived near several air bases during his time in the Air Force, Kurt knew how far the roar of military jet engines carried. 'Unless they launched while we were in those rapids, I think we'd have heard a supersonic bomber taking off; I'm sure they'll need full afterburners to do it.'

A droning sound rolling across the plateau stopped the conversation. Both Kurt and Joe slowed down to listen.

'Turboprop,' Joe said, turning until he was facing the sound. The droning grew louder and picked up an odd resonance as a second engine came online.

'They may have switched planes,' Kurt said.

The hike turned into a dead sprint, and with the sound of the turboprop to hone in on, they never wavered. They were still rushing toward the edge of the airstrip when the small plane clawed its way into the night sky, banked to the northeast and flew off into the dark.

'If we get to the Air-Crane,' Joe said, 'we can use the radios. And get them back before they get too high.'

Both men kept running. They arrived at the outskirts of the airstrip, breathing hard and dropping down beside a pine tree for cover.

The Air-Crane was visible across the field, lying on its side and smoking. 'The radios probably still work,' Joe said. 'But the antennas might be sheared off.'

Kurt pointed to a second outline in the gloom, darker than dark, sinister in shape. *Blackjack 2* was still there, with the *Nighthawk* perched on top.

'They wouldn't have bothered placing it so carefully if they were going to leave it behind.'

57

Paul drove as fast as he dared in the Jeep Cherokee. Considering the cargo he was hauling, the type of road and the utter darkness of the moonless night, he was being positively reckless at forty miles per hour.

Sitting beside him, dividing her attention between the portable apocalypse machine they were carrying and the map, Gamay seemed to want him to go faster. 'I can only hope Emma is being as careful as we are,' she said. 'For a variety of reasons.'

Paul had seen the map earlier. He knew it was a race they couldn't win. 'We'll never catch her. The last forty miles into Cajamarca are paved and relatively flat. Once she hits that section, we'll be left in the dust.'

'Maybe we can flag down another car or truck,' Gamay suggested. 'If we're lucky, they might have a radio or a phone.'

'It would have to be a satellite phone up here,' Paul said. 'But maybe as we get closer to town.' He glanced over at the map. 'Coming in from the south, she still has to drive through most of the city before she gets to the airport. That might give us some – '

A shout from Gamay cut him off. 'Paul, look out!'

Paul looked up. A man's body lay in the road, crumpled and broken. Paul hit the brakes, veered around it and brought the vehicle safely to a halt. The body was behind them now, but what loomed ahead was even more surprising. A vehicle tipped over on its side, its front end dangling over the edge of the cliff and held up by the Y-shaped trunk of a tree.

Paul put the transmission in park and grabbed the door handle. As he swung it open, he felt Gamay's hand on his.

'We're not on some backcountry road, Paul,' she said. 'We don't have time for this.'

There was cold reason in her voice, but only because she hadn't realized what Paul had already ascertained. 'It's Emma.'

Gamay's eyes lit up. She looked at the stricken vehicle and nodded.

Paul and Gamay jumped out of the Cherokee, rushing toward the overturned Toyota. The front end was out over the cliff, jammed into the gnarled trunk of the tree. The back end was up in the air, and the entire vehicle was pointing downward as if it were ready to slide off the edge.

The engine was ticking and pinging, while fluids dripped everywhere. The entire balancing act looked so precarious that Paul's first instinct was not to touch anything.

'Emma!' he called out. 'Are you in there?'

'Hello?!' a female voice replied from inside the vehicle.

'Emma, this is Paul,' he shouted, easing around the side. The angle of the vehicle and the condition of the ledge made it impossible to get at the front end. 'Gamay and I are here. We're going to get you out of there.'

'Forget about me,' Emma said, her voice suddenly firm. 'Just get the containment unit out. Pull it out through the back. It's a miracle it hasn't gone off-line already. But trust me, I'm staring into the abyss, and if we fall into this canyon, it's all over.'

Paul moved around to the back end of the SUV and pulled the hatchback open. The door moved slowly and awkwardly, and even that small shift had consequences. The vehicle rocked forward and then back before settling.

'There's a small problem with that plan,' Paul said, studying the situation. 'If we remove the containment unit, the center of gravity will move forward, and unless that tree is a lot stronger than it looks, the whole thing will go over with you inside.'

'I know that,' Emma said. 'I've been sitting here for a long time thinking about it. But there's no other choice. There's no other way. Every time I've tried to move, we've slid farther down. Please, just get that thing out of here before we go.'

Emma might have been willing to throw away her life, but Paul wasn't so quick to give up. 'All we need is more weight on the back end,' he said. 'I weigh at least as much as the containment unit and twice as much as you. If I climb on the back bumper . . .'

'The problem is the tree,' Emma said. 'It's already splitting down the middle; the extra weight might snap it and send us down. Just get that damned thing out of there and let me go.'

'We can pull it back,' Gamay said. 'We could use the bungee cords that are holding down our containment unit and the jumper cables we found in the back of the Cherokee.'

'It's not going to be enough to pull a five-thousand-pound vehicle uphill,' Paul said. 'But it could be enough to keep it from sliding down.'

'Someone will still have to get in there to disconnect the ropes they used to tie their unit down,' Gamay replied.

'*Someone*'s already in there,' Paul said. 'She can loosen everything on her way out.'

Inside the Toyota, Emma listened as Paul explained the plan. It required her to climb over the seats, unhook the nylon rope she'd used to secure the dangerous cargo and wrap the rope around the containment unit several times. Then crawl out the back hatch with the ends of the rope in her hands.

It sounded plausible. And it saved her a trip she didn't want to take. 'I can do that,' she said.

The light around her changed as Gamay moved the Cherokee into position. She held still while Paul laced the jumper cables and the bungee cords through parts of the overturned vehicle and then did the same on the front bumper of the Jeep.

She felt the Land Cruiser rock back to a flatter angle as the Jeep inched backward and pulled everything taut.

She looked back through the vehicle. Paul was standing there, shrouded in the light.

'You're up,' he said.

Despite a primal urge to get out of the doomed vehicle, Emma simultaneously found herself afraid to move a single muscle. For half an hour, she'd been sitting there listening to creaks and groans coming from both the tree and the Land Cruiser. Sitting still had been her only defense; a part of her didn't want to give that up.

She took a deep breath, steeled herself to do what she had to do and nodded to Paul. 'Here goes.'

She twisted around to face backward. The vehicle rocked ever so slightly.

She found a spot for her feet, pushed off and shinned into the back.

The Toyota shifted again, not rocking but sliding.

Emma heard the sound of wood splitting and felt her heart pounding. Through the back hatch she saw Paul grasping onto the bumper and pulling as if it were a tug-of-war.

The movement slowed and then stopped and the only sound was the trickle of pebbles and sand sliding out from underneath the SUV and falling down the slope.

'It's okay,' Paul said. 'We've got it. Keep moving.'

She inched forward and eased around the side of the containment unit. 'Now for the ropes.'

Disconnecting the ropes was fairly easy. And once they were untied, Emma was able to loop them around the containment unit and the attached fuel cell. One loop, two and then a third. That was all the excess length they had.

She pulled it tight, tested the weight and looked up toward Gamay and Paul. 'Ready?'

'Whenever you are,' Paul replied.

Emma took a deep breath. To get to the back hatch, she had to use her legs. She edged around the unit, put her feet on the back of the passenger seat and pushed.

The force caused the seat back to fold forward.

Emma slid. The containment unit slid. The Land Cruiser tilted downward at a steeper angle and she heard the tree splitting down the middle. She grabbed the seat belt to keep from falling out through the gap and crawled upward once again.

'Hurry!' Gamay shouted.

Emma moved as fast as she could.

The Toyota began to slide forward. Two of the bungee cords snapped.

Emma was climbing at a fifty-degree angle now, each move worsened the slide. As she neared the top, Paul let go of the bumper and reached in with his long arms. She tried to hand him the ropes, but instead of grabbing them, he clamped his hands around her wrists and pulled her out.

She hit the ground just as the tree split in half.

She turned to see the Toyota sliding off the edge and into the dark. She set her feet and pulled on the ropes with all her might.

As the back end of the Toyota vanished, the containment unit popped free and landed on the edge of the dirt road. With Paul and Gamay's help, she pulled it safely onto level ground.

A resounding crunch followed far below as the Land Cruiser hit a small ledge and tumbled farther down.

The three of them sat there with the ropes clutched tight in their hands like the exhausted winners of an epic tug-of-war.

Only now did it dawn on Emma that Gamay hadn't been with them earlier. 'What are you doing here?'

'I came to rescue the boys,' Gamay said.

No less confused, Emma crawled to the side of the containment unit to check the readings one more time. Even after the latest bump, everything remained in the green. 'Let's just get this thing on a plane and get it back to the States.'

'Not,' Paul said, 'until after we remove the bomb.'

58

Kurt stared at the runway from the edge of the tree line. He could barely believe their luck. *Blackjack 2* was still on the ground, though a pinprick of light moving back and forth suggested it wouldn't remain for long.

'Flashlight,' Joe said. 'Probably the copilot doing a last-minute inspection before takeoff.'

Without warning, one of the bomber's turbines came to life with an electric whine. The sound blossomed into a throaty roar, and a wave of blue fire appeared behind the bomber.

Then twin sets of landing and taxi lights came on. The four blindingly bright beams lit a wide swath of ground up ahead and directly in front of the plane.

'We need to stop that plane from taking off,' Kurt said.

'We can get to the plane easy enough,' Joe replied. 'But then what?'

'We reason with them,' Kurt said. 'Explain Urco's plan and point out the danger they face.'

'And if they ignore us?'

Kurt pulled out the brick of Semtex. 'Then we re-inforce our argument Teddy Roosevelt style. Let's go.'

They stepped out of the tree line, moving cautiously at first and then picking up the pace as the second of the bomber's four engines came to life. The pilot on the ground could be seen hastening his final inspection and then rushing toward the nose gear and the ladder that led up into the plane.

'We're about to miss our flight,' Joe said. He rushed ahead as the copilot vanished up into the aircraft's belly.

Kurt sprinted to keep up, but he'd exhausted so much energy, his muscles would not respond.

The ladder began to retract. Joe jumped onto it and the ladder groaned with the weight.

Kurt rushed up seconds later, leapt and caught the bottom rung.

'Add ladder climbing to your Ironman,' Joe shouted over the roar of the engines.

Arm over arm, Kurt pulled himself upward until finally he could get a knee on the bottom rung. As soon as he did, the plane lurched forward and began to move.

The movement caused Kurt's knee to slip and he was back to dangling by his arms. Behind him, two of the four engines were screaming in full voice. Their square intakes loomed like mouths ready to devour him, should he fall.

'Come on,' Joe said. 'Stop playing around.'

Kurt pulled himself up, got his knee on the bottom rung and moved higher. As soon as Joe could reach him, he leaned out and grabbed Kurt by the shoulders, yanked him upward and into the plane.

With their weight off of the ladder, it finished retracting and the hatch shut and sealed behind it.

They were in the dark as the bomber turned back into the wind, then the remaining engines came to life and the plane began to roll.

Finally, the floor shifted beneath them, the nose came up and the monstrous bomber, with its wings swept wide, soared up into the air.

'We really have to work on your foot speed,' Joe shouted.

'My speed?' Kurt yelled back. 'I was counting on you holding the door for me.'

The ladder well was dark except for a dim light coming from the inner hatch up above. It was glowing an ominous red.

Joe tested the hatch and shook his head. 'It's locked from the other side.'

59

The rest of the trip to Cajamarca was uneventful. Along the way, Paul and Gamay explained to Emma what she'd missed. It was a roller coaster of emotion. Hearing that Kurt was alive sent her spirits soaring.

In the end, all that mattered was finding a way to stop the bombs from detonating. Meeting up with NSA agents Hurns and Rodriguez at the airport was the first step.

'We have additional fuel cells on the aircraft,' Hurns said. 'Is there any chance the containment units themselves have been tampered with?'

Emma shook her head. 'The entire unit is sealed. Any tampering or attempt to hide something inside would have caused the mixed-state matter to react. That's why Urco chose to rig up the replica fuel cells.'

'Then all we have to do is switch them out and dispose of the bombs.'

'Except that we need the bombs,' Emma replied. 'The Chinese have been airborne for hours. And barring some incredible stroke of luck, the Russians are flying by now as well. Based on what Urco told Kurt, the bombs are rigged to detonate when the planes descend. The only chance they have is if we figure out what type of detonator they've been connected to, how and why it will go off and, more importantly, how to disarm them.'

'Not likely to find a bomb disposal expert in Cajamarca,' Hurns noted.

'I know,' Emma said. 'But we can pipe one in. All we need is a 4K video feed and a high-speed Internet connection. And someone can guide us through step by step.'

'Where are you going to find that at this hour?'

Paul spoke up. 'We know a place,' he said, 'where the caffeine never stops and the Internet is strong.'

After switching the fuel cells at the airport and watching the NSA Gulfstream take off, Paul, Gamay and Emma drove into town. Calls had been made, cooperation arranged and the buildings around the Internet café evacuated.

They'd set up shop in the back of the café, under the lights where they could stream the 4K video feed back to Washington DC and the NUMA Headquarters building. Their only safety devices were a twelve-gauge shotgun and a cast-iron pot the café used to cook soup.

In front of a camera, Emma took the fuel cell apart. Her audience watched from the NUMA conference room, where Rudi, Hiram, Priya and a bomb disposal expert named Collin Kane, who stared at one of the high-definition displays and told them what to do next.

'Connect that gray wire to the metal leg of the table,' Kane said. 'Make sure the unit is grounded. You don't want a static spark.'

Emma moved cautiously, doing as she was told.

Paul and Gamay were outside, a hundred yards away, watching on a video feed. If Emma blew herself up, they would use what they'd seen and take the next bomb apart – hopefully, learning from her mistake.

'Where do I start?'

'You're going to have to reach in and see if you can free the explosives from the case or if they're attached.'

She grounded herself by touching the leg of the table and then reached in and put her hand on the Semtex. She pulled it slowly from the inside of the unit, stopping halfway out. 'It's hooked to a pair of wires.'

'Do not remove them,' Kane warned. 'Most likely, they're instant arm-and-detonate wires designed to prevent what we're trying to do.'

She found there was enough length to pull the explosives out and set them on the table without disconnecting the trailing wires.

'What next?'

'Using a sharp knife, cut away as much of the Semtex as possible without touching the wires. Take each section you remove and separate it from the rest. When you've cut it down as far as possible, we'll test the detonator.'

Emma took a sharp knife and did as instructed. It felt like she was cutting into an apple.

She took the sections to the far side of the room.

'Now you'll have to test the detonator,' Kane told her.

'How?'

'It appears to be a touch screen; tap the front.'

She tapped the detonator and the screen lit up. The

scrolling numbers disappeared and a password screen appeared.

Kane suggested a few ways to get around the password screen, but each was blocked. On the third attempt, the screen went dark. Two numbers appeared. A green number read 50000; the second number it flashed was a steady 26000.

Suddenly, the first number began to decrease, rolling down like a clock.

'What's happening?'

'A second precaution on their part,' Kane said. *A fail deadly.*'

Emma stared, tapping the screen, trying to stop whatever she'd done to trigger the countdown.

'Get rid of it,' Kane said.

Emma tried to stop the countdown.

'You've got to secure it now.'

'It's still attached to the case.'

'Use the shotgun,' he said.

Emma grabbed the shotgun, aimed at the detonator and its scrolling numbers and pulled the trigger.

The twelve-gauge blast obliterated the fragile electronic device and scattered the remnants of the Semtex and the fuel cell across the room. There was no explosion, but the room filled with acrid smoke.

Emma lowered the shotgun and sighed.

'Ready to try again?' Kane said.

Emma nodded. 'Let's get the second unit in here.'

60

Constantin Davidov sat in the copilot's chair watching the pilot and flight engineer run through their tasks. *Blackjack 2* was performing flawlessly. 'How's our payload doing?' he asked.

The flight engineer looked over his board and cycled through the video cameras that were pointed at the *Nighthawk*. 'Payload secure. No sign of any flutter.'

All of them were concerned about a repeat of what happened to *Blackjack 1*.

'Change course to three-five-zero,' Davidov said.

Major Timonovski glanced back at him from the captain's seat. 'Three-five-zero? That will take us to Cuba. I thought we were refueling over Venezuela and heading home.'

'That was the original flight plan, but this aircraft has been through a great deal since then. There is too much risk. We are to land at Manzanillo. An Antonov 124 transport will meet us there. It's large enough to carry the *Nighthawk* internally. It will be safer that way. And it will allow us to move unseen by American eyes.'

The pilot nodded and set in the new course.

'Have you ever been to Cuba?' Davidov asked. 'Either of you?'

'Not I,' Timonovski said.

The flight engineer shook his head. 'Nor have I. Have you been there, comrade?'

'Many times,' Davidov said. 'The first when I was a young man. A thousand years ago, it seems.'

They smiled at that. And Davidov was glad to see their spirits perking up. Both men had appeared so gaunt when they'd arrived at the airfield that Davidov had wondered if they were fit to fly. The Falconer had badly mistreated them. Once they got back to Moscow, Davidov would have to decide what to do about that. In the meantime, he wanted to reward the men for a job well done.

'You'll stay in Havana for two weeks, recuperating. Then you'll bring *Blackjack 2* home and we'll put it in a museum. It is my hope you will find the women and weather as comforting as I once did.'

'Will you be staying with us?' the pilot asked.

'No,' Davidov said. 'I'll be transferring to the Antonov to accompany our prize safely home. It's high time we put this operation to –'

Davidov swallowed the last word. Perhaps it was the change in his posture, but he thought he'd felt a subtle thud reverberate through the metal floor. As he waited, the vibration came again and then once more.

Now that he'd clued in to it, Davidov could feel it continuously: . . . *Thud* . . . *Thud* . . . *Thud* . . . A few seconds between each impact.

He pulled off the noise-cancelling headset he wore. The whistle of air over the skin of the bomber became instantly louder, but so did the dull, repetitive impact. 'Is the *Nighthawk* secure?'

The flight engineer ran all his checks once more. 'No strain on the lockdown bolts. No sign of flutter. It's secure and behaving perfectly.'

Davidov continued to detect the vibration. 'Do you feel that?'

'Feel what?'

'Something's broken loose,' Davidov said. He reached over and pulled the engineer's headset off. 'Listen.'

The weary flight engineer cocked his head, straining to hear the sound. A life around jet aircraft had dulled his hearing, but he picked it up just the same. He put his hand on the control panel and then slid it downward until it touched the floor. 'It's inside.'

Davidov felt so, too. 'We can't afford a system failure. Not now.'

The flight engineer checked his board. 'Everything's operating perfectly. It has to be something we don't have a sensor on. I'll go look around.'

The engineer slipped out of the shoulder straps, grabbed a flashlight and stepped to the cockpit door. Opening it, he stepped through and into the aft section of the airplane.

Davidov followed, grabbing a flashlight of his own.

The aircraft was huge, larger than the American B-1, which it was based on. It had a cavernous bomb bay and other empty crawl spaces.

He watched as the flight engineer checked one inspection panel after another and then lingered near a small crane that was used to hoist material up through the bomb bay doors. 'Anything?'

The engineer was a long way back. He turned around and shook his head.

The banging was closer now, Davidov could feel it through his feet. 'What about the landing gear?'

He turned, looking for an inspection port, and heard another bang, far louder than the rest. He swung back around to see the egress hatch in the floor burst open.

He pointed his flashlight toward it and saw a man with silver hair pop up through the open hatchway. He had a large pistol in his hand. An American HK45.

'In the name of Saint Peter!' Davidov exclaimed.

'Actually, my name is Austin,' the man said, climbing out onto the deck. Another man popped up after him. 'And this is Zavala.'

Davidov was familiar with the names. 'NUMA.'

Austin nodded and stood while Zavala tossed out a metal bar he'd used to bash open the sealed hatch and then climbed free.

'You guys really should have a handle on the inside,' Austin said in a droll American attempt at humor. 'Or at least a doorbell.'

'What are you doing on my plane?' Davidov blurted.

'We're here to prevent you from making a very big mistake,' Austin said.

Davidov felt a wave of anger growing in him, but he realized the opportunity at hand. The Americans had been focused on him this entire time. They hadn't seen the flight engineer sneaking up on them from the other direction.

'The mistake is yours,' Davidov shouted.

The flight engineer lunged at them, swinging the flashlight. Zavala saw him at the last moment and dodged the blow. He threw a quick counterpunch and knocked the weary engineer to the ground.

The distraction lasted just long enough. Davidov sprinted forward, rushed into the cockpit and then turned and slammed the door shut. It pressure-sealed tightly.

'What happened?' Timonovski shouted.

Davidov pressed against the door, looking through the small round peephole in the center. 'We have boarders,' he said.

61

Kurt ran forward and banged against the bomber's cockpit door while Joe prevented the flight engineer from interfering. 'Listen to me,' he shouted. 'We're not here to fight you. We're all in danger.'

From its thickness and the small size of its circular peephole in the middle, Kurt could tell he was leaning against a pressure door. He hoped the men on the other side could hear him through it and over the sound of the engines.

'*You* are most certainly in danger,' a voice shouted back.

'I know what you think. You've won,' Kurt said. 'You've got the *Nighthawk* and the mixed-state matter, but trust me, you're getting more than you bargained for. It's a sucker's prize. A Trojan horse. The Falconer lied to you. He lied to all of us.'

The next words came over an intercom. '*What do you know about the Falconer?*'

Kurt turned, located the intercom and pressed the white button next to it. 'That he's a liar and a master manipulator. That he played you, us and the Chinese against one another.'

'*Of course he is,*' the voice replied nonchalantly. '*That's the business. In the end, he gave us what we wanted.*'

'No, he gave you what *he* wanted,' Kurt replied. 'Enough rope to hang yourself and a billion others. The *Nighthawk* is nothing more than a giant bomb now. A mixed-state matter bomb powerful enough to obliterate half of Europe and set the rest of it back to the Stone Age. It's rigged to blow once you exceed a certain altitude and then descend back below it.'

'How would you know this?'

'He told me as he was dying.'

'A deathbed confession? Do you really expect me to believe that?'

'Not a *confession*,' Kurt said. 'A *boast*. He said we couldn't stop it. That what went up would never come down.'

Silence followed. Kurt glanced back at Joe and the flight engineer.

Joe shook his head softly. 'We're still not winning.'

Kurt turned back to the intercom. 'Who am I speaking with?'

'My name is Constantin Davidov,' the voice replied. *'I'm head of the Directorate for Technical Resources Acquisition.'*

A spy, Kurt thought. A thief. 'Listen to me, *Comrade Davidov*,' Kurt said. 'If the Falconer wanted you to have the *Nighthawk*, why not just call you when he found out where it went down. He knew the location from day one.'

'Because he needed you to raise it for him,' Davidov replied.

'Why would he need that? Is raising a small aircraft from the bottom of a shallow lake beyond the capabilities of the Russian salvage fleet?'

'The difficulty came with the location,' Davidov replied. 'Our ships are not equipped to scale mountains.'

'We did it with four people and one helicopter.'

'Congratulations,' Davidov replied. 'That proves nothing.'

'He imprisoned your pilot and flight engineer. What possible reason could he have had for that?'

Silence.

Kurt turned to look at Joe. He had the flight engineer subdued and the man wasn't fighting. If anything, he looked like he might be on their side.

'Tell him,' Kurt urged.

'It's true,' the engineer shouted. 'The Falconer lied about everything. Every step of the way.'

'I will not take advice from a hostage,' Davidov said.

'At least stop climbing while we talk,' Kurt urged.

'I'm sorry,' Davidov said, 'but your reputation for perseverance and deception precedes you. Save your breath. There is nothing you can possibly say that will cause me to release the Nighthawk into your custody.'

'Looks like the reasoning portion of the evening has ended,' Joe said.

Kurt agreed. He reached into a pocket and brought out the brick of Semtex he'd taken from Urco's cave. He held it up in front of the peephole for Davidov to see.

'You know what this is,' Kurt said. 'Either you open that door or I'll blow it off its hinges.'

'You'll blow the plane apart.'

'That's going to happen anyway.'

Inside the cockpit, Davidov stared at the explosives in the American's hand. The fish-eye effect made it seem larger than it was, but the amount would be more than enough. There was only one alternative.

'Prepare for rapid decompression,' he said to Timonovski. 'And then open the bomb bay doors.'

'They'll be sucked out of the aircraft,' Major Timonovski said. 'The engineer will go with them.'

'Yes,' Davidov replied. 'That's the idea.'

'What if the American is right?' the pilot said. 'Falconer murdered my copilot, he did nothing when the *Nighthawk* was breaking *Blackjack 1*'s spine. Nothing.'

'Do as I order!' Davidov commanded.

Timonovski stared back at him and then shook his head.

'Then I'll do it myself.' He stepped away from the pressure door and lunged for the bomb bay controls.

62

Rudi Gunn sat in NUMA's communications room with Hiram Yaeger, Priya Kashmir and Collin Kane. They were now part of a globe-spanning web of satellite links.

One screen showed the White House Situation Room where the President had convened his Security Council. A second screen displayed Paul, Gamay and Emma at the Internet café in Cajamarca. The Vandenberg control room appeared on the third, where Colonel Hansen and Steve Gowdy were standing by. The fourth connection went all the way to China, where General Zhang of the People's Republic sat and scowled.

As the conversation progressed, with all its requisite arguments, denials and disagreements, Rudi had the sense of a runaway train with five different engineers in the cab, none of whom had their hand on the tiller.

Finally, the group managed to get down to business. Zhang admitted that the Chinese had two of the *Nighthawk*'s containment units on board one of their long-range aircraft and gave away its transponder code.

The path was instantly picked up. Much farther along than anyone had expected.

'Are you sure this is the right aircraft?' someone asked.

'The HL-190 has super cruise ability,' Zhang said. 'It can travel long distances at supersonic speeds.'

The aircraft was five hundred miles northwest of Hawaii. Its altitude was listed at fifty-one thousand feet. Its speed at more than a thousand knots.

'We know all about the HL-190,' Gowdy said. 'Ever since you stole our engine designs.'

'And improved on them,' Zhang said.

The President's chief of staff broke in with a calming tone. 'Gentlemen, we need to work together now or there won't be anything left to argue over. Ms Townsend, please explain what you've discovered.'

'We've taken both bombs apart,' Emma said. She stood calmly on-screen but looked exhausted. 'The first attempted a self-destruct when we made a mistake. The second detonator was neutralized. Once it was removed from the explosives, we discovered a USB access port used to program it. Hiram and Priya took it from there.'

Hiram cleared his throat. 'The device is a combination GPS receiver and altimeter. It becomes active once the aircraft exceeds a certain threshold speed and climbs above a specific altitude. It will detonate when they descend below the threshold altitude again or arrive at their destination.'

'What speed?' General Zhang said. 'What altitude?'

'One hundred and twenty knots,' Hiram said. 'Twenty-six thousand feet.'

'Unfortunately,' Priya added, 'your aircraft has already exceeded both parameters.'

On-screen, Zhang nodded. *'I can see that. How do we stop it?'*

'Your people will have to disarm the bomb before they begin their descent.'

'Why not just dump the fuel cell out the door and be done with it?' Zhang suggested.

'Because of the power requirements of the cryogenic system and the magnetic bottles holding the mixed-state matter,' Emma said. *'It requires an extremely pure flow of power. Tiny surges or fluctuations could be disastrous. You can't just plug the unit into a cigarette lighter.'*

'Don't patronize me,' Zhang snapped. *'It wasn't my people who brought this curse down on us.'*

'But it was your people who tried to steal it,' Emma shot back. *'If they hadn't interrupted the flight, the material would already be safely stored in underground facilities.'*

'Yes,' Zhang said. *'Yours and yours alone.'*

Again the President's chief of staff cut in. *'Please!'* he urged. *'None of that matters at this point. We're all damned lucky that the containment units didn't explode in Peru. And we're fortunate, General Zhang, that your aircraft is still out over the Pacific and not coming in for a landing. That gives us time. We can argue over who the mixed-state matter belongs to later. But first the bomb must be disarmed without damaging the fuel cell.'*

'How is that to be done?'

'It's a fairly simple process. We're prepared to transmit the schematics of the fuel cell, along with everything we know about the detonator, the power demands of the cryogenic unit and the design of the Penning traps. All we ask in return is that your aircraft change course to a more northerly route.'

'Why?'

'Should your agent fail, it's important that the detonation take place as far from civilization as possible.'

'Perhaps I'll order the pilot to turn for California or Hawaii,' Zhang replied testily.

'I promise you,' Colonel Hansen said, jumping in. 'If that aircraft deviates toward any landmass, American or otherwise, it will be shot down.'

Zhang shook his head. 'You are too easily baited, Colonel. Of course I have no intention of doing any such thing. Transmit the information. I have no wish to argue about this again.'

'Turn the aircraft first,' the chief of staff said.

A brief stare-down ensued.

'Very well.'

With that, Zhang's screen went dark. And the four remaining links in the network lapsed into silence.

It fell to Emma to break it. 'What about the Russians?' she asked from the screen. 'What about Kurt and Joe? Have we heard from them?'

'All we know is that the Blackjack and the Nighthawk are airborne,' Colonel Hansen said. 'A satellite pass forty minutes ago showed the rural airfield to be empty. We've launched AWACS from Pensacola and Corpus Christi to look for the bomber's radar signature. Several squadrons of F-22s are being readied to intercept.'

'Intercept?' Emma asked. 'Why would we need to intercept it?'

'To protect ourselves,' Hansen said. 'If the Russian government doesn't believe our claim and they or the pilot act rashly — the way Zhang threatened to a minute ago . . . well, we're dealing with a hypersonic aircraft, covered in stealth materials, that could make it from the coast of South America to Atlanta in twenty minutes. We can't allow that. So we have to find it first and be ready to act when we talk to Moscow.'

'But why would they act rashly?' she asked.

Rudi knew why. Everyone in the room and at the White House and out at Vandenberg knew why. He suspected Emma would have easily guessed the reason if she weren't exhausted.

He jumped in and explained. 'Because they've almost certainly exceeded the speed and altitude thresholds that will prime the detonators. And unlike the Chinese plane, there is no physical way for the occupants of the bomber to get at the *Nighthawk* and disarm them.'

Understanding washed over Emma's face in high-definition. Understanding and grief. *'There's no way to stop it,'* she whispered to herself. *'The pilots are dead men. And if Kurt and Joe are on board, they're dead men, too.'*

63

The HL-190 transport represented the state of the art Chinese aerospace industry. Intended first as an aircraft to fly dignitaries around the world, its interior was trimmed in high style. Active noise cancellation created a superquiet cabin. The air kept at a perfect seventy-two degrees and fifty-one percent humidity by a high-tech system that had twenty sensors spaced throughout the plane. The soft leather seating and lushly carpeted floor were designed specifically to caress the bodies and feet of those used to sitting down and giving orders.

Daiyu had no use for any of it. If not for the remarkable speed with which the aircraft flew, she'd have rather flown back to Shanghai in a sparse military transport.

To her surprise, the burly man who'd accompanied her from the lake seemed to be of a similar mood. Urco had called the man Vargas. He was as rough-spun as any of the group. If he'd been Chinese, he would have lived in a rural village, pushed a plow and carried heavy loads to and from ox-drawn carts, tossing them in and out as if they weighed nothing.

He'd remained awake for the entire flight, and she wondered if this was the first time he'd ever flown. His eyes appeared to be pricked open and slightly blood-shot as if he'd taken a powerful stimulant. After five hours in the air, he'd said no more than a dozen words.

Only when the plane banked to the right did he speak up. 'Why are we changing course?'

'Probably to avoid some weather,' she said. *It wasn't likely. At fifty-one thousand feet, the HL-190 flew above almost all the world's weather.* 'Would you like a drink?' she asked. 'It might help you to relax.'

She stood up and walked to the bar. 'Rice wine? Or maybe you'd prefer *gouqi jiu;* it's made from wolf-berries.'

He shook his head. 'Water.'

She gave him a bottle of Voss.

'Urco must trust you a great deal to send you alone for millions of dollars in diamonds. What will you do with them? And by that I mean what will he do with them since, obviously, you'll deliver the package to him without keeping any for yourself?'

The questions flowed from a combination of bore-dom and training. It was part of her instinct to divide slaves from their masters.

He stood and glared at her.

She stared back, unflinching, and he decided to take a walk down the carpeted aisle. He stopped and looked out through one window, then went to the other side of the plane and looked out another.

Daiyu didn't need to look; he would see nothing but darkness out there.

'How far have we gone?' he asked.

'More than halfway. You should sleep. It will pass the time faster.'

'No,' he grunted.

'Suit yourself.'

The intercom buzzed. *'Daiyu, please come to the cockpit. General Zhang wishes to speak with you.'*

She walked forward, passing Vargas and ignoring his stare.

She entered the cockpit and noticed they were continuing to turn, veering to a more northerly course still. She took a headset from Lieutenant Wu.

'Daiyu,' General Zhang said. *'I must congratulate you for the progress of your mission. You've made me proud.'*

He sounded very dour for a man offering congratulations. 'Thank you, General, but as you know it is not necessary,' she said. 'I do as I'm ordered for the nation. It is my mother and father, as you taught me.'

'Yes,' Zhang said. *'And through no fault of yours, it is now in danger.'*

He went on to explain what he had learned from the Americans. Twice she asked him if he was certain. Twice he admitted he could not be sure the Americans were telling the truth, but he saw no reason for them to lie.

'Our engineers have studied the problem,' he added. *'They've found no way to use the aircraft's electrical system to keep the containment unit safely powered. The voltage and current do not match. You'll have to remove the explosives from the fuel cell without damaging it.'*

'And then?'

'Eject them from the aircraft.'

That was easier said than done, but if they depressurized the cabin, it could be accomplished.

'There may be a problem,' she admitted. 'Urco's courier. It's possible he knows of the plan. He seems very grim. Perhaps contemplating what lies ahead.'

'Martyrs usually are,' Zhang said. *'Dispose of him first. We cannot risk any interference.'*

'It will be taken care of,' she said.

Zhang signed off. Lieutenant Wu took the headset back and offered her his sidearm.

She shook her head. 'Give me your knife.'

With the knife hidden in her sleeve, Daiyu opened the door. Vargas was standing right there.

He lunged first, grabbing her with both hands, lifting her off the floor and throwing her down the aisle.

She landed, sprang back to her feet and rushed back to the cockpit.

Vargas had already plowed forward into the cramped space. He was throwing punches and slamming heads against the wall. With a downward swing of his huge right arm, he clubbed Lieutenant Wu to the ground and then broke his back with a stomp of an oversized foot.

He grabbed the copilot's neck and snapped it with a lethal twist.

Daiyu launched herself at him, aiming the knife for his spine. Even at his size, a severed spine would render him useless. She missed to the right, hitting his fleshy back and plunging the blade as deep as it would go. She twisted it quickly and pulled it out.

Hot blood poured from the wound, but the mountain of a man barely responded.

He turned, backhanded her across the face and went for a choke hold. She threw one arm up beside her neck as a bar. It prevented him from crushing her windpipe or choking the life out of her, but he now had control.

With the power of a hydraulic press, he squeezed her neck and arm until she felt her elbow crack and separate. Excruciating pain shot through her body. She ignored it and brought a knee into his midsection. She might as well have been thumping a rock wall.

He barely reacted, held her tight and reached for her fallen knife. She twisted around in a desperate attempt to break free, came face-to-face with Lieutenant Wu's lifeless eyes and remembered his offer of the sidearm. She thrust her free hand into his jacket, wrapped her fingers around the weapon's carbon fiber grip and –

The knife went into her back.

Daiyu went stiff from the impact, felt the blade being pulled free and then being plunged into her a second time. The second puncture was far less painful than the first. A third was barely felt, as she shuddered and slumped to the floor.

Vargas stood awkwardly; he was bleeding badly from a wound he could not reach. It didn't matter. He knew his own end was near – he'd known it since the moment he'd left the lake. *It was well accepted,* he thought. *At least he would die in the clouds that his ancestors had always aspired to reach.*

He pulled the knife from Daiyu's back, went to the wounded pilot and pressed the bloody blade to his face.

'Call them,' Vargas said. 'Tell them she did as she was told and then resume course to Shanghai.'

'But?'

'Do as I say!'

With Vargas holding the knife to his eye, the pilot got on the radio and made the call. He said everything Vargas had ordered him to say. The Chinese General said some brisk words and then ordered them back on course without emotion.

Vargas watched the pilot turn the aircraft. Urco had shown him on the computer what to look for on the computer screens.

When the plane leveled off again, Vargas smiled and then he cut the pilot's throat.

Lying in a pool of blood, Daiyu understood completely. Vargas was on a suicide mission. And now he'd overcome the only two obstacles he faced: her and Zhang. She was as good as dead, and with Zhang believing the explosives and the detonator had been removed, the Chinese authorities would welcome the aircraft to Shanghai with open arms.

The bomb would detonate as they descended and the matter and antimatter would mix instantly.

Deadly opposites, she thought. *Yin and yang destroying each other, as she'd always believed they would.*

She was the barrier, the only thing preventing the destructive mix. But she would be dead in minutes from the loss of blood. Even if she could somehow kill

Vargas, she couldn't crawl ten feet, let alone take the fuel cell apart and disarm the explosives.

Her eyes started to dim, but her other senses remained for the moment and she realized there was something in her hand. *It was Wu's pistol.*

She knew what she had to do. She couldn't stop the explosion, but she could choose where it happened. And out over the sea was preferable to the destruction happening above her homeland.

Vargas was standing there, his hands on the back of the pilot's chair. She aimed at his head and pulled the trigger.

The shot hit home, splattering blood across the windshield.

Killed instantly, Vargas fell forward. His heavy body landed on the control column. The impact disconnected the autopilot as the computer wrongly assumed that the captain was reasserting human control.

The HL-190 nosed down and began to descend.

Daiyu could just make out the altimeter. They quickly passed below fifty thousand feet. The dials continued to unwind. Forty-nine thousand . . . Forty-eight . . . Forty-seven . . .

64

Kurt saw through the peephole as Davidov made a sudden move toward the control panel. He'd overheard every word and knew what Davidov was planning.

There was no time to shout a warning, no time to do anything but act. With quick precision, Kurt raised the HK45, aimed at Davidov through the door and pulled the trigger twice.

The HK45 boomed and the armor-piercing shells punched through two layers of steel and struck Davidov in the ribs and the thigh. The statesman crumpled to the floor in pain.

'I'm begging you,' Kurt shouted to the pilot. 'Level the plane off and open the door.'

Pushing Davidov aside, the pilot stretched from his seat and released the door. It swung open and Kurt stepped inside. 'What altitude are we at?'

'Thirty-five thousand feet,' the pilot said.

'Too high,' Kurt said. 'Almost certainly too high.'

As if to prove the point, a sudden flash lit up the coal black sky outside the cockpit windows. It came in a staggered flicker, white-purple and then white-blue. It blinded like a nearby lightning strike would, but it was distant and soundless and so far off that the entire western horizon slowly came to life.

As the glowing color spread higher and farther, it gave way to a darker blue and then a greenish color reminiscent of the aurora borealis. It took on a texture, churning in long filaments, twisting and curling back in on itself in a mesmerizing, hypnotic display.

There was no sound, no shock wave, but the radios soon squealed and the computer screens skewed oddly to the right. On the panel above, whole rows of circuit breakers tripped, one after the other.

By now, Joe and the flight engineer had joined Kurt in the bomber's cockpit. As the flight engineer began resetting the tripped breakers, Joe stared out the window.

'What is that?' Davidov said from his position on the floor. He was in pain but not lethally hit. The double-layered steel door had taken much of the force out of Kurt's shots.

'The Chinese plane,' Kurt said quietly.

'The Chinese . . .' Davidov grunted from his position on the floor.

'I told you,' Kurt said. 'He gave a deadly present to all of us.'

Far beyond the horizon, out over the Pacific, a ball of fire, the likes of which no human had ever seen, expanded in spherical shells that stretched fifty and then a hundred and then two hundred miles across before finally fading.

Lightning shot out of the inferno in all directions, along with an electromagnetic storm of X-rays, gamma rays and other forms of ionized radiation. The upper atmosphere was ionized instantly, while down below enough seawater to fill Lake Erie was instantly vaporized. The fire and the shock wave left a circular depression that dented the Pacific to a depth of two hundred feet.

As the shock wave subsided and the ocean sought to level itself, a ring of enormous waves surged into the depression from all sides, eventually colliding and being thrust back outward again.

Several thousand miles away, Kurt, Joe and the Russians were seeing only the reflection of the events. An effect known as a *light echo* filtered through thousands of miles of atmosphere and was distorted by the curvature of the Earth. Yet not one of the five men on board the Russian bomber could take their eyes off of it.

'Something must have gone wrong,' Joe said. 'They can't have reached China yet.'

Kurt helped Davidov up and into a jump seat. The wound to his ribs was broad but not deep; the wound to his leg hadn't hit any vital arteries.

'How far . . . how far away?' Davidov asked.

'Five thousand miles,' Joe estimated, 'give or take.'

'To reach us from five thousand miles away . . .' Davidov said without finishing his thought.

'The Chinese had two units on board,' Kurt said. 'Fifty pounds of mixed-state matter. We're carrying twice that.'

Davidov nodded and gripped the edge of the seat. 'Why? Why would anyone want this? What has Russia done to him?'

'It's not going to explode over Russia,' Kurt said, 'but as you cross Europe.'

Kurt explained the rest of what they knew. Davidov seemed more shocked with each revelation.

'We need to use your communications system,' Kurt said. 'We need to reach our people and find out if there's any possible way to prevent what we just saw from happening again.'

65

Reaching anyone from the bomber proved to be difficult. Every satellite over the Pacific had been rendered inoperative, and though they were over the Caribbean, there was a spillover effect. Communication networks were crashing. And most of the Western world's active resources were busy trying to ascertain the extent of the damage.

Finally, after making contact with a Russian communications satellite over the Atlantic and being relayed through a commercial phone exchange in Poland, they were linked into the NUMA communications room.

'What altitude are you at?' Rudi Gunn asked immediately.

'Thirty-five thousand,' Kurt replied.

The signal was poor because of the ionization in the atmosphere and the mismatch between the Russian equipment and NUMA's, but Kurt could hear the silence plainly. 'We're too high,' he said, not waiting for Rudi to tell him that. 'We know that. What are our options?'

'There aren't any,' Rudi said.

Kurt had expected this. He exchanged glances with the other men in the cockpit. 'We figured that, too. We'll turn out to sea,' he said. 'Do you have a preferred course for us?'

'We do,' Rudi said. *'We've picked a spot in the mid-Atlantic as far from any landmass as possible. All aircraft have been*

ordered out of the area and to land as soon as possible. All ships have been ordered to move away from the location at their best possible speed, though for many of them it won't matter.'

'We can't make the mid-Atlantic,' Major Timonovski said. 'We don't have the fuel.'

'This is an intercontinental bomber,' Joe said.

'We had to reduce the weight in order to clear the trees. We dumped ten thousand gallons back there.'

'How far can we fly on what we have?' Kurt asked.

'Five hundred miles,' Timonovski calculated. 'Not much more.'

'What about aerial refueling?' Joe asked. 'We heard on the cockpit voice recorder from *Blackjack 1* that you were going to refuel near Caracas.'

'Yes,' Davidov said, 'that was the original plan. But when the intercept failed, the tanker was ordered back to Russia. Our plan was to land in Cuba. We would be starting our descent in twenty minutes.'

'Could we link up with an American tanker?'

'We use a different type of fuel,' Major Timonovski said. 'Modified to work with the scramjets.'

Kurt looked at the map. They were halfway between Colombia and Cuba. Five hundred miles in any direction wouldn't be enough.

'We can't put sufficient distance between ourselves and civilization to do much good,' he said. 'We've got to come up with another plan.'

Joe offered a desperate thought. 'There's a windbreak in front of the *Nighthawk*. If we slowed to the very minimum controllable speed –'

Major Timonovski shook his head. 'There is no hatch leading to the top of the fuselage.'

'What if we depressurized the plane and cut a hole in the skin?'

'The skin is titanium,' Davidov replied. 'Double-thick. Even if we could, there's no hope in what you're considering. No matter how we try to secure you, it's not possible to keep you from being swept off the upper surfaces once you're out in the airstream. You'll never be able to get in the cargo bay.'

'If we can cut our way out of the *Blackjack*, maybe we can cut our way into the *Nighthawk* from below,' Joe said. 'Tunnel our way through.'

Unknown to the men on the bomber, the communications were being shared with the White House, Vandenberg and the café in Cajamarca. Emma's voice chiming in alerted them to that fact.

'You won't be able to cut into the Nighthawk *from below,'* she said. *'The entire structure is designed to resist the heat and shock of reentry. Even if you had a high-intensity acetylene torch, you'd never get through.'*

Kurt found himself smiling. Strange, he thought, considering the situation. But he was glad to know at least she and the Trouts were safe. 'What if we use the scramjets?' he suggested. 'Instead of conserving fuel, we get this thing up to maximum speed and altitude. How high can this bomber go?'

'One hundred and twenty thousand feet,' Timonovski replied.

'The problem is, the gamma ray burst,' Rudi told them.

'The higher you go, the farther the devastation spreads. At that height, there will be less physical destruction, but the radiation, the shock front and the electromagnetic pulse will cover sixteen times as much surface area. The simulation we've run suggests that you nose-down at maximum velocity. It will concentrate the damage in one area, but it's still going to be bad.'

'How bad?' Kurt said.

'The other burst was seven hundred miles from Hawaii. It set off seismometers all over the globe. Hawaii's gone dark. The Aleutians have gone dark. The entire Pacific Rim has gone dark. There are likely to be tsunamis and a hot shock front. If we had any satellites working out there, we'd expect to see fires and damage on most shores, effects the equivalent of a large earthquake, but we were lucky that it was so far away. The majority of the radiation and destructive energy dissipated prior to making landfall.'

Kurt looked at the faces around him. Russian and American alike were calm and resigned. 'You know how far we can go,' Kurt said. 'Give us a location when you have one. Until then, we'll conserve as much fuel as possible.'

As Kurt spoke, Major Timonovski adjusted the flight setting to its most efficient mode. The wings came forward and the engines powered back. The *Blackjack 2* rose up and slowed down like a ship meeting a large, lazy swell.

It was peaceful, Kurt thought to himself, quiet. Truly, the calm before the storm.

66

Emma stood in the empty Internet café and felt her knees go weak. Not only would Kurt and Joe be killed but the detonation would inflict lethal damage across a large swath of the Americas and the Caribbean.

'This can't be happening,' she whispered.

She sat down on the floor, tried to breathe and found her lungs would not draw in any air. 'This can't be happening,' she said again.

Gamay approached. 'Breathe slowly,' she urged. 'You're hyperventilating.'

'I killed them all,' Emma said, tears streaming down her face. 'Kurt and Joe, and a hundred million more.'

'It's not your fault.'

'I was part of it!' she snapped, going instantly from despair to anger.

She knew what Gamay was trying to do, but she didn't want to be told how it was going to be all right. It most certainly was *not* going to be all right.

'They're carrying twice the mixed-state matter that was on the Chinese plane. Even from the middle of the Caribbean Sea, the shock wave will cover half the South. Every living soul from Houston to Tampa will be incinerated, irradiated or drowned in a hundred-foot wave. Along with half of Mexico, Central America and every living being on every island in the Caribbean.'

Gamay just stared at her. There was nothing to say.

Emma stood and turned away. In her darkest moment, when she would have rather died than be witness to what was about to happen, the defiance of Hurricane Emma flared the brightest. 'I will not accept this,' she said. 'I will not!'

She pulled free of Gamay's attempt at kindness and willed her tired mind back into action. There had to be a way. There had to be!

She went over the properties of the mixed-state matter, the design of the containment units, tried to calculate the minuscule odds that they would survive if the Semtex detonated. But there was no way to stop the reaction; no known way, aside from the frigid cold of absolute zero, to stop matter and antimatter from annihilating each other.

She paced around the room searching for an answer. The frustration boiled over as she bumped a small table. In a fit of rage, she pushed it across the room. It slid with surprising ease, toppled and gouged a line in the painted concrete floor.

Emma stopped in her tracks, staring at a lengthy scratch. It was white on blue, like a vapor trail in the dusky sky.

Paul took a step toward her.

'Stop,' she said without looking his way. Something had come to mind.

Vapor trail . . . Contrail . . . The thought lingered in

her consciousness. *Streams of tiny ice crystals released by passing aircraft, high in the frigid sky.*

The thought hit with so much force, she almost fell over. 'There is a way,' she whispered. 'There is a way!'

She turned with a snap. 'Get Rudi back on the line. I need to talk to Kurt. I need to talk to him now. Before time runs out.'

67

The scene in the NUMA communications room had become chaotic. With the impending disaster all but certain, all government assets had been turned toward coordinating the efforts to minimize the damage.

Orders were being sent out, troops mobilized. People directed to shelter underground. Anything and everything that could be thought of and acted upon in two hours was being done.

Highways were closed to southbound traffic. Aircraft were ordered to proceed as far north as possible and land within the two-hour window. Information was relayed to Central and South American countries, though there was no assistance to lend and by morning it would be every man, nation and group for themselves.

Into this maelstrom, Emma's attempt to communicate foundered. No line was free, no satellite communication available. No ear open to listening. Everyone too busy sending out orders and making requests.

Everyone except Priya, who'd moved quietly into the background. She thought she'd be safe, but figured by morning she would have no way to contact her family in London. She decided to send them an e-mail now before the worst happened.

As she sat down at the computer, a blinking icon told

her she'd gotten an urgent message. It was from Paul Trout.

Emma thinks there might be another option to prevent disaster. We need to speak with Rudi and NASA Flight Dynamics. CANNOT get thru.

'Rudi,' she said, waving him over.

Rudi was in the midst of five different things and had two other staffers talking in his ear.

'Rudi!' she shouted.

He turned.

'Emma needs to talk with you. She says there may be a way to avert the disaster!'

In the cold, dark cockpit of the bomber, Kurt focused on every static-skewed word.

'The Daedalus Project,' Emma said. *'Remember I told you about it? We planned to use small nuclear explosions for deep-space propulsion. We thought we might be able to accelerate a spacecraft to nearly a tenth the speed of light. The explosions occur behind the craft, the shock wave hits what is known as a* pusher plate *and sends the craft surging forward without destroying it. I believe we can do something similar with the* Nighthawk *using the mixed-state matter. It won't be one big explosion but a long trail of smaller ones. If we vent the right amount of mixed-state matter through the original intake port, it will create a burst of energy and a continuous wave, accelerating the* Nighthawk *back into space before the subsequent explosion.'*

'Won't the mixed-state matter explode the second it hits air?' Kurt asked.

'As long as it remains cold enough, it lives in harmony. In its

455

current condition, it will exit the collection port at 2.7 degrees Kelvin. The air temperature at one hundred and twenty thousand feet is somewhere in the neighborhood of negative eighty degrees. That's still a boiling two hundred and ten degrees Kelvin, and the mixed-state matter will react in less than half a second, but since the Nighthawk *will be moving at four thousand miles an hour, that half-a-second delay will create enough space to build a wave rather than blow the craft apart.'*

Kurt listened intently, visualizing the attempt. 'A wave?'

'A fast and powerful one,' Emma replied.

'Max and the NASA Flight Dynamics team have done the calculations,' Hiram said. 'It could work.'

Kurt grinned. Major Timonovski and the copilot nodded as well.

'We're not dead yet,' Joe said. 'You can't imagine how happy that makes me.'

Even Davidov was smiling through the pain. 'If we survive, a bottle of twenty-year-old scotch for each of you.'

'What do we have to do?' Kurt asked over the radio.

'You have to take the bomber up to its maximum speed and altitude and then release the Nighthawk,' Emma said. *'Reboot the control system with the alpha code and then download a series of commands that we will transmit to you momentarily.'*

'That doesn't sound too hard,' Kurt said. 'What's the catch?'

'The Nighthawk's *antennas are on the top. They have to be or they would burn off on reentry. That means you'll have to be above and in front of the* Nighthawk.'

'Which means we get hit with the wave as well.'

'We could try to use an Air Force satellite,' she said. 'But there's so much ionization in the atmosphere that – '

'No,' Kurt said, cutting off the discussion. 'We get one shot at this. Let's do it right.'

Joe gave the thumbs-up. Davidov nodded enthusiastically. 'Da,' Major Timonovski said.

The flight engineer nodded as well and switched on the antenna dish they'd used to override the *Nighthawk*'s program seven days ago. After a few checks, he turned to Kurt. 'Tell them we are ready.'

It took several minutes for the bomber to get up to supersonic speed and climb above eighty thousand feet. There, it switched over to the scramjets.

The burst of power pushed Kurt back into the seat and he listened as Timonovski called out the Mach number and altitude. Because Joe knew how to fly, he'd been given the copilot's seat. Kurt and Davidov sat behind them in the jump seats, and the flight engineer was at the command station where the Falconer had been days before.

'One hundred and nineteen thousand,' Major Timonovski said. 'Maximum altitude and velocity in five . . . four . . . three . . .'

'Releasing *Nighthawk*,' the flight engineer said.

To avoid *Blackjack 1*'s fate, they flew in a parabolic arc, ejecting the *Nighthawk* as they went over the top.

'*Nighthawk* clear,' the flight engineer said. 'Stabilizer intact.'

Once the *Nighthawk* drifted back far enough, Timonovski brought the bomber up above and in front of the unmanned space plane.

'Separation, two miles,' the flight engineer said. 'Initiating alpha code.'

At the press of a button, the information was sent. Now they waited. Finally, a response came in.

'*Nighthawk* up and functioning,' the flight engineer said. 'Transmitting new orders.'

As Kurt watched the others perform their duties, he triple-checked his shoulder harness and gripped the handhold beside the jump seat. There was nothing else for him to do.

'*Nighthawk* confirms orders received and processed,' the flight engineer said excitedly. 'Initiation in thirty seconds. All systems green.' He turned to Timonovski. 'Let's get the hell out of here.'

Timonovski put the bomber into a turn, banking away from the *Nighthawk*'s course. The turn had to be gradual because of the incredible velocity, but the farther the two courses diverged, the better chance they had of surviving the wave that was about to hit.

The *Blackjack* was pulling hard. Kurt felt the g-forces pressing him down into the seat. He strained to look at his watch. The second hand ticked along the orange face. Each click seemed a lifetime. And then they were all used up.

A flash of blue light filled the sky. Kurt shut his eyes and still saw the glare.

'Hang on!' Joe shouted.

The shock front hit the bomber like a crashing wave. Despite their speed and course away from the *Nighthawk*, the impact was intense as the surge picked the bomber up and shoved it forward.

'Don't fight it,' Kurt grunted.

Timonovski did as Kurt suggested, going with the wave instead of turning against it. Still, the ride was violent, the systems inside the cockpit fried out in seconds, the fuselage buckled and, after ten seconds of buffeting, the left wing folded and the plane rolled over into a dive.

Unseen from inside the bomber, the *Nighthawk* had done precisely as ordered, ejecting a tiny stream of the antimatter out behind it. The reaction was nearly instant, but instead of one giant flash, it left a trail of hundreds and then thousands of flashes in a series that lit up the night sky. At the head of this expanding flare of blue light, the tiny black craft was propelled toward space, accelerating at a rate that would have killed a human occupant.

Seen from the ground, the burst of light looked like glowing ripples in a pond, with each circle of light expanding into the others until the interference pattern formed a maddening kaleidoscope of luminescence, streaking upward and outward to the east.

Perspective was hard to come by from down there. And no one who viewed it with the naked eye could really follow the band of swirling light as it lengthened and stretched before terminating in a blinding flash high above the planet.

The experiment had worked. In three minutes, the *Nighthawk* covered just under five thousand miles, accelerating to a maximum velocity of nearly one hundred and seventy thousand miles per hour, the fastest man-made object of all time.

It was still accelerating when the heat and vibration caused a catastrophic failure in one of the containment units, but by then it was far enough from the Earth's surface to be nothing more than a mind-blowing fireworks display in the night sky.

The men in the falling bomber never saw it; they were knocked about mercilessly and traveling in the opposite direction.

Inside the cockpit, Kurt felt himself whiplashed one way, then the other. He was certain the plane would come apart at any second. Miraculously, it held together, despite the fact that one wing had been ripped off and most of the tail was gone.

It didn't take long to realize that they were in a nose-dive. Light from the artificial sun had temporarily illuminated the Earth and its sea far below.

They were corkscrewing down like *Blackjack 1* had, falling from the sky like a gull with a broken wing.

The spinning motion was disorienting. The loss of pressure threatened to cause him to black out. He remembered the other crew's long descent with only the computer talking.

'We need to eject!' Kurt shouted to Major Timonovski.

The pilot didn't answer. He was still strapped in his seat, but with every move of the plane he was being thrown back and forth like a rag doll.

'Joe, we have to punch out!'

Joe seemed no better than Timonovski. Davidov looked to be awake but too weak to move, and the flight engineer was hanging in the straps, a huge gash to his forehead.

Kurt had no idea how high they were, no idea what would happen if they ejected, but he'd seen the wreckage of the other bomber on the bottom of the sea. That impact he knew they would not survive.

He looked around for an ejection handle. Everything was labeled in Russian. Finally, he spied a red bar with two orange stripes.

He reached for it.

Grasped it.

And with one hard pull, yanked it up and back.

An explosion shook the plane, fire surrounded the cockpit and everything went black.

68

Emma arrived in Washington five days after what they were calling *the event*. It took that long because so much of the world was in chaos. Half the world's satellites were down, most of the communication systems were down, aircraft were being routed by hand and most of those were being used to fly relief supplies to the Pacific.

When she finally arrived in DC, she discovered that land lines were temporarily back in fashion as a line of two hundred people was waiting to use three working pay phones.

She skipped the line. Found a cab and rode into the city. After a long debriefing with the NSA, she walked across town to NUMA. There she found Rudi, Hiram and Priya.

They had old-fashioned paper maps in front of them. Various areas were outlined in green, yellow and red.

'How bad is it?' she asked.

'Nowhere near as bad as it could have been,' Rudi said. 'Hawaii and the Aleutians fared the worst, but physical damage was minimal. A sixteen-foot tsunami hit Waikiki, but the larger wave went to the west. Ironically, Japan shielded the Chinese coast, but since they've been preparing for this since the Tohoku tsunami a few years back, they were ready.'

She'd been hearing the reports for days. She was thankful.

'Surprised the NSA let you come up for air,' Hiram said. 'Figured they'd have you working round the clock on the mixed-state matter you brought home.'

'It's a huge controversy,' she said. 'I think they plan to send it all back into space.'

'The irony,' Rudi said.

'Anyway, they have no more claim over my time,' she said. 'I've resigned. As of an hour ago, I'm officially unemployed.'

'Really?' Rudi said. 'Want to help us?'

He pointed to an open spot at the desk.

'What are you doing?'

'Searching for Kurt, Joe and the Russians,' Priya said.

She looked at the map: it was the eastern Caribbean.

'The Navy and the Coast Guard are a little busy running emergency supplies to the Pacific Rim, so we figured we'd jumpstart the effort on our own,' Rudi explained. 'We've got NUMA assets, private aircraft and chartered boats on the search. These are areas we've checked. And these are other possible search zones.'

'But nothing yet,' she said.

Rudi shook his head.

Emma sat down. 'I'll help any way I can,' she said. 'I hate to think of them out there – suffering, fighting off sharks and dying of thirst.'

'They're tough and well trained,' Rudi said. 'I'm sure none of that will be a problem.'

69

Kurt narrowed his gaze against the blinding glare of the high-noon sun. 'Sharks,' he said grimly. 'The whole lot of you.'

He threw down a hand of cards in disgust, tossing them onto a flat section of wood that was serving as a makeshift poker table.

Across from him, Davidov grinned as he collected a literal pot of gold from the center. 'I assure you, I played honestly,' he said.

'A spymaster who played fairly,' Joe said from the other side of the table. 'I doubt it.'

'Scrupulously,' Davidov insisted. 'Is it my fault you have squandered all your chips?'

Kurt leaned back. They were sitting on a pristine white sand beach with the turquoise Caribbean waters lapping at the shore just beyond. Among their few possessions were a rubber raft, a deck of cards, a bottle of twenty-year-old scotch that was nearly empty and a million dollars in Russian gold coins that Davidov had brought along in case the Falconer tried to gouge him further on the price.

They'd survived ejecting from the bomber because, unlike a fighter aircraft, the *Blackjack* ejected the entire cockpit in an enclosed ballistic capsule. They'd landed in the sea, floating down on three large parachutes and then transferred to the rubber life raft. After a day at sea, they'd rowed ashore on the island and set up a small camp.

Two fires burned. The first, a signal fire; the second, to heat water as part of a jury-rigged desalinization system that Joe had designed. It provided several cups of water each hour. Plenty to keep them going. Though none of them wanted a drop until the scotch was used up.

Using a long, jagged stick as a spear, Kurt had caught several fish, which they'd deboned, cooked and eaten with gusto.

Since then, there had been nothing to do but drink and play cards and wait for someone to rescue them. The gold coins were their chips, but after starting with even amounts, Kurt was down to his last ten chips.

'Deal again,' Kurt said. 'And, this time, from the top of the deck.'

Davidov laughed and shuffled.

As Kurt waited for the cards to be dealt, he grabbed the bottle of scotch, brought it up toward his mouth and then put it back down again. 'I think I hear a boat,' he said.

'Nonsense,' Timonovski said. 'You're just trying to get out of the game.'

Despite the Russian's doubts, the sound grew louder until a twenty-foot fiberglass powerboat rounded the point and cruised into the empty cove. It came straight toward them and the signal fire, beaching on the sand a few yards from the poker table.

A young man in a red polo shirt and white shorts was at the wheel. He jumped down onto the shore. 'What are you people doing here?' His official tone clashed with the outfit and the soft lilt of his Caribbean accent.

'Losing at poker,' Kurt said.

The others laughed. The young man seemed baffled.

'You can't be here,' he said. 'This is private property.'

'We didn't have much of a choice,' Joe said. 'Our plane crashed. We bailed out. This is where we ended up.'

'But why did you stay on this side of the island?' the man asked.

Kurt, Joe and the Russians looked at one another, confused by the strange conversation.

'Is the other side of the island more hospitable?' Davidov asked.

'I should hope so,' the man said. 'They have a Ritz-Carlton over there.'

Kurt looked at Joe and burst into laughter. The island was several miles across; the center was all hills and sand dunes; it had appeared completely deserted. It was pitch black at night, without the slightest hint of civilization.

'Don't they have lights at the Ritz-Carlton?' Kurt asked.

'All lights are out since the big flash in the sky.'

'Ahh,' Kurt said. 'That's kind of our fault.'

Joe and the Russians laughed at that, but the man in the red polo shirt did not seem amused.

Kurt held out the last of his gold coins. 'I offer ten thousand dollars for a ride to the Ritz.'

Joe held up a hand as if he were bidding at an auction. 'And another ten thousand if you tell everyone you found us at sea.'

'Good thinking,' Kurt said. 'Well worth it.'

The man looked at them as if they were crazy. Sunburned, scruffy, ripped clothing and a near-empty bottle of scotch confirmed it for him, but he couldn't leave them there.

He ignored what he must have believed was fake gold and walked back to his boat. 'Come on,' he said. 'I'll take you. But rooms are expensive. They may want you to pay up front.'

As they climbed into the boat, Kurt offered a sly grin. He had the scotch. Joe, Davidov, Timonovski and the flight engineer carried the gold. 'I'm sure something can be arranged.'